ROMY HAUSMANN

Anatomy of a Killer

Translated from the German by

Jamie Bulloch

QUERCUS

First published in the German language as *Perfect Day* by
dtv Verlagsgesellschaft mbH & Co. KG. München, in 2022
First published in Great Britain in 2023 by

QUERCUS

Quercus Editions Ltd
Carmelite House
50 Victoria Embankment
London EC4Y 0DZ

An Hachette UK company

Perfect Day by Romy Hausmann
© 2022 dtv Verlagsgesellschaft mbH & Co. KG. München
English translation copyright © 2022 by Jamie Bulloch

A CIP catalogue record for this book is available
from the British Library

HB ISBN 978 1 52942 238 2
TPB ISBN 978 1 52942 239 9
EBOOK ISBN 978 1 52942 241 2

10 9 8 7 6 5 4 3 2 1

Typeset by CC Book Production
Printed and bound in Great Britain by Clays Ltd, Elcograf S.p.A.

Papers used by Quercus are from well-managed forests and other responsible sources.

For you, Papa.
For your humour and your strength.
You are Iron Man.

The power of fantasy can be comforting.
Or deadly.

It's a Thursday when Ann dies – the most miserable of deaths. She lies on her back, her legs stiffly outstretched, pressing her trembling hands to the gaping wound in her chest. The men have removed her heart; they just cut it from her body and took it with them. She wants to scream but can't, as other sounds are coming from her throat: gurgling, wheezing. Lights explode on her retina – it's a strain, such a terrible strain, and she just wishes it were over; she can't cope anymore. And so she lets go, she falls, closes her eyes, ready . . . Behind her closed eyes, it's a better place. There the sun glistens, the sky is blue and she sits on her father's shoulders, waving her arms around as if she could fly. It's long in the past – she's seven and Dad calls her his 'Beetle'. He holds her tightly and securely by the legs; she doesn't have to worry, not anymore.

So this is what it's like, she tells herself. This is death.

And it can happen so quickly.

A moment ago this Thursday was just a Thursday. They were waiting for their dinner, a pizza delivery from Casa Mamma. Dad had put some music on, a Lou Reed record from the 1970s, before Ann was born. A time when her father was young, reckless and foolish. She would grin when he said such things. Dad, foolish? Never! How preposterous was that? But all the same she liked the record, which he must have played more often than any other; it was a backdrop to Ann's childhood. Wood was crackling in the fire and it smelled as if Dad had lit it with paper. Ann hated this smoky tang with its hint of acute danger. As if the entire house could go up in flames at any moment.

'Where's our dinner?' came the typical whinge from Ann, which Dad poked fun at.

'While we're waiting, why don't you make yourself useful and fetch some more logs?' he said, handing her the wood basket. Ann pulled a face. When she was hungry, she wasn't in the mood for banter.

In the garden, November had created shapes that looked even stranger in the shadowy glow of the terrace lamps. The bushes, bent under the weight of the snow like hunched old ladies, seemed to be heading for the mountain beneath which her old trampoline was hiding. Ann trudged over to the woodshed, tossed a few logs into the basket and returned to the house.

That was when the dying began.

First the light shooting through the window from the other side of the house, the front. Blue circles suddenly dancing in the room. Ann, standing there in bewilderment with the basket, and her father, joking about their pizzas now being delivered express by the emergency services – the restaurant must have sensed how distraught his Beetle got when she was hungry.

But then . . .

The front door bursting open and the men storming in. Throwing themselves on Dad and wrestling him to the ground.

There must have been a whole lot of shouting because Ann saw wide-open mouths. But she heard nothing; all of them were bellowing silently under the high-pitched tone that filled her head like tinnitus. The men yanked her father, yanked him to his feet, yanked him towards the door. Ann clutched her wood basket. She saw Dad flounder backwards and turn to her. His utterly empty face. Then they took him away, out into the night. Two of the men stayed inside the house, trying to explain to her what had just happened. Their words sliced into Ann's chest, gouging deeper and deeper until they finally reached her heart. She fainted. The basket fell to the floor. The thudding of logs was followed by the clunk of her skull. Ann's body began to convulse, to twitch; she wheezed, whimpered, and it felt really bad until she got here: the world behind her closed eyelids, where her heart is still intact, where it's summer and with Dad's help she can fly. She's seven years old, his 'Beetle', and Lou Reed is singing about a perfect day.

'We need a paramedic!' An unfamiliar voice cuts in from somewhere, getting louder. It orders Ann to breathe: breathe in on one, out on two, and to stay calm, as calm as possible.

'Here, the asthma spray!'

She feels her head being moved. Rough fingers force open her mouth and push something hard inside. Her throat turns cold, her chest relaxes. Sluggishly she opens her eyes. Someone is bending over her.

'It's good to have you back,' the happy fool says. He has no idea of hell.

3

NEW LEAD IN BERLIN RIBBON MURDERS CASE:
55-year-old arrested after thirteen-year manhunt

Berlin (JW) – On Thursday evening a 55-year-old man was arrested in relation to the series of dramatic murders dating back to 2004. The man is suspected of having abducted the victims, whose ages range from 6 to 10, taking them to various remote locations in the vicinity of Berlin and then killing them. The suspect left red ribbons to ensure the bodies were found. Most recently, the body of schoolgirl Sophie K. (7) was discovered in a cabin in Königswald. The week before, the girl had been kidnapped from a playground in Berlin-Schmargendorf. The police revealed that a witness statement led them to the 55-year-old.

ANN

BERLIN, 24 DECEMBER 2017
(Six weeks later)

It's as if the city has been cleared out; I can't see a single car or person, not even a stray dog. The shop windows are black, the entrances obstructed by roller shutters. Berlin is dead, everything is. Except for me. The last survivor, the only person left after the end of the world. Only me and Berlin and the festive lighting hanging everywhere, which flashes deceptively in rhythm, as if the city did have a heartbeat, after all, a last hint of life.

I'm in a hurry; my steps are rapid and ungainly. Slush splashes up to my knees. So what? My trousers ought to have been washed a while ago. I used to be vain, but that's in the past now. Zoe changed the locks to our flat and just left a small travel bag for me on the landing. From time to time I imagine her sitting at uni in my dark red velvet jeans or wearing my golden sequin top on a date. It's okay, or, as Saskia E.'s father recently said in an interview: *The pain threshold shifts.* At some point, things that used to hurt like a flesh wound only feel like a scratch. Saskia E. was victim number seven, murdered three years ago at Christmas 2014.

I quicken my pace, chasing away shadows and footsteps that aren't there. Sometimes there's a splash of blood instead of snow. Saskia's father was right about this too: *Inevitably you go a bit mad.* He does the rounds of the media as a distraction. I have a distraction too, but it's work. Although I've no idea who's going to drift into a grubby fast-food joint like Big Murphy's today of all days – they would have to be very, very lonely. The truth is, the city isn't dead. It's still alive, of course, and how. It has merely withdrawn into its warm, lovingly decorated sitting rooms. It's sitting at tables laden with food, folded napkins and the best cutlery. It's giving each other presents and revelling in eyes that light up. It's happy, this city, and the only ones left out today are those at the very bottom. It's Sunday. And Christmas Eve.

'There you are! Finally!' Behind the till Antony flails his arms about. He's Cuban, just turned twenty-one, and he's been in Berlin for two years all on his own, without his parents or four siblings who still live in Moa, an industrial city on the north-east coast of Cuba. He needs the money he earns at Big Murphy's to finance his studies and his room, but most of all for the transfers he sends home every month via Western Union.

I close the glass door behind me and look around. A single table is occupied, by an old man whose face appears to be nothing but eyes and a beard. He's wearing a dirty brown coat, and as he bites into a floppy burger, I can see fingerless gloves full of holes. Ketchup drips out of the bun like thick, red tears.

'Yes, thank God, given the rush on here,' I mutter as I wander past him and into the changing room.

My uniform consists of a short-sleeved, green polyester shirt and brown trousers that open at the sides: ventilation slits. You come to appreciate them when, in the cramped kitchen, oil at 180 degrees is bubbling in five deep fat fryers at once.

It's not the best job in the world, but it was almost criminally easy to get. No written application, no references, no CV. Just a phone call and the next day a job interview using my dead mother's maiden name. The manageress liked me at once; I came across as uncomplicated. Working hours, overtime, even the salary: I didn't care. All that interested me was having my wages paid in cash. And that was fine so long as I signed for it. After some rudimentary training in hygiene, infection control and accident prevention, I was shown the ropes.

Today there are only three of us here: Antony, who's looking after the till and the drinks; Michelle, who's preparing the burgers in the kitchen; and me, who right now is helping her, because nobody's coming to the drive-in that I'm responsible for. Of course not: it's Christmas Eve.

'You all right, Ann? You're so quiet today.' Dear, sweet, simple Michelle. How concerned she sounds. She's in her mid-forties, her hair dyed a yellowish colour, and she's always plastered with make-up, which at the start of her shift makes her look at least five years younger, but later, when it has gathered in the wrinkles around her eyes, has the opposite effect.

'Sure, everything's fine,' I say, for no reason poking my finger into the container with the tomatoes.

Michelle nudges me in the side to cheer me up. 'I find Christmas depressing too, if that's what's bothering you. For three whole days, everyone behaving as if all was right with the world. Peace, love and light a candle. Yeah, right.' Michelle is a single mother

7

of two teenage boys and a grown-up daughter. Her eldest hasn't celebrated Christmas with her for years, and the boys are with their father this year. 'What about yours?'

She means my daughter. I'd called her Diana, because I couldn't think of anything better when I was put on the spot. Diana, after the Roman goddess of hunting – not, as Michelle thinks, after the dead princess. But basically it doesn't matter what my daughter's called. She happened when I was eighteen, happy-go-lucky and naïve, one of those silly young girls who's just careless. Now I'm twenty-four and I have to earn money for her, just as everyone here at Big Murphy's has to earn money for someone. All I say is, 'With her father too,' and fiddle with the tomatoes again. I don't want to look at Michelle.

'What are you giving her?' is the next question, and the first thing that comes to mind is: 'A trampoline.'

Just like the trampoline I got for Christmas when I was Diana's age. The box the frame came in was brown, and so huge that it would have needed several rolls of paper to wrap it up. So my father simply tied a large red ribbon around it. As soon as it was spring and the sun had sucked up the last of the dampness the snow had left in the soil, he would construct it in the garden with his fingers that were all thumbs, the touching clumsiness of an academic. He would position it so that when he sat at the desk in his study he only had to peer out of the window to see me jumping. I liked my present, I really did. But then, in the depths of winter, I couldn't do anything with it. So I asked him to take the metal rods out of the box, then I climbed in and put the lid on. My father found this interesting, astonishing, strange. With that look of his which reflects his need to ana-lyse everything, he asked me what was going through my head when I lay in my box, as quiet as a mouse, perfectly still and with my eyes closed. He thought it might have something to do with my mother. And that I was trying to find out what it was like to lie in a coffin.

'But Dad,' I countered, 'this isn't a coffin. It's just a box and I'm lying in it.'

'Great!' Michelle looks really excited, then a second later her face assumes a touch of sadness. I know she's worried her sons might take after their father, who's already twice served time for assault. 'Enjoy it while Diana's still young.' Sighing, she wipes her sweaty brow with the back of her hand. 'The moment they get to twelve, they don't want to know you anymore and start stealing from your purse to buy weed.' When she takes her hand away from her face I see brown streaks and her left eyebrow is slightly paler than before. Now she's laughing again, like she always does when she realises that frying oil is the best make-up remover. But maybe she's also laughing to hold back the tears. I know the feeling, but I'm ashamed nonetheless. So many lies. Perhaps Michelle would understand if I explained. Perhaps she wouldn't judge me; she is a good person, after all. On the other hand, that's what I thought of Zoe too.

'Earth to Ann. Ann, come in, please!' Putting on a voice, Michelle speaks into her fist as if it were a radio. I suppose that's what mums are like. When their children are young they get used to doing silly things they never grow out of.

'Sorry, I was lost in thought.'

'I noticed.' Grinning, she points to the monitor showing the pictures from the drive-in. A car has just pulled up. 'Customers.'

I hurriedly slip on the headset and take a deep breath before pressing the button that connects the microphone to the intercom outside.

'Happy Christmas and a warm welcome to Big Murphy's Burgers and Fries.' I can't believe how friendly I sound, how unfazed. It seems that, like my headset, I've also got a button, an inner button, that switches me into a different mode if I press it hard enough. *You just function*, Saskia E.'s father said in the newspaper, and he's right.

'May I have your order, please?'

I can only hear static at first.

'Hello?'

Puzzled, I stick my head out of the window. The intercom is five or six metres away. Only when customers have given their order do they move up to the serving window. From this distance, however, all I see is the silhouette of a car, its headlights stamping two bright circles in the late afternoon darkness.

The static goes silent and a man's voice crackles, 'You didn't really think you'd get away from me that easily, did you?'

Frite. (Ann, 7 years old)
a frite is like when you get an electric shock. your hart jumps up and when it goes back down again its still beating faster than before and sometimes it hurts. theres buzzing in your ears and you feel so cold that you shiver, then the frite nose its worked and maybe it stops. but sometimes a frite is just a joke and you get scared for no reason, then you have to larf because you were silly and fell for the frite.

'You muppet!'

I laugh hysterically. Jakob, it's only Jakob, sitting outside in his car, having given me one hell of a fright via the intercom. Jakob, who's laughing too now.

'That's no way to greet your customers. I think I'm going to have to complain to the management.'

'To get me sacked at Christmas? Charming.' Seeing the look on Michelle's face, I whisper, 'Jakob.' She grins and raises her left, unpainted eyebrow. I'm embarrassed that she knows about us, even though there's actually nothing to know. I adjust the microphone in front of my mouth and stick my head out of the serving window again. I still can't see anything but the car in the darkness and two circles of light.

'What are you doing here, Jakob?'

'You said you hate Christmas and don't want to celebrate. And I said I couldn't allow that.'

'I guess you're right.'

That was yesterday. I was on the till when Jakob appeared at the counter and ordered a 'Big Murphy's Mega Meal'. He comes in often, almost every day. I even arrange my breaks to coincide with him. We sweep the snow from the bench in the Big Murphy's car park and sit there, a coy distance apart like two people who'd really like to arrange a proper date. But they don't; the woman has her reasons and the man clearly has sufficient tact to realise that she'd give him the brush-off. He thinks she's studying German and working at Big Murphy's to cover her rent. And he probably finds her a bit prim too. So he tries to lighten the mood by telling her funny anecdotes about his work at a recycling centre in Kreuzberg. She likes the idea of him helping people get rid of their relics. Their bulky rubbish, worn-out clothes, empty paint tins, cardboard boxes, batteries, garden waste. Most of all she likes the idea of him climbing on to the overflowing paper skips and jumping up and down until the mountains of paper sink beneath his weight, making room for more. His gangly arms whirling in the air, his short, dark hair dancing up and down and his blue eyes gleaming with boyish exuberance. She finds him so carefree, so unencumbered.

'Well, and that's why I thought we might . . .'

I sigh. Today, of all days, Jakob seems to have decided to narrow the distance between us.

'I can't, I'm afraid.'

'But you don't even know what—'

'I've got to work.'

'That's not a problem. I'll wait for you.'

'My shift doesn't finish till nine.'

'Doesn't matter.'

'No, that's too late. Anyway, I'll be exhausted and stinking of frying oil.' Tugging at a greasy black hair in front of my eyes, I look at it and wonder if I had a shower before going to bed last night. I can't recollect taking one. All I remember is an insipid microwave dinner, collapsing on to the sofa like a sack of flour and watching *E.T. the Extra-Terrestrial* because I wanted to cry as a release, out of emotion for once, rather than pain. 'Another time, okay?' On the monitor, I see, to my relief, another car turn into the drive-in lane behind Jakob. 'Now you have to place an order or move on.'

I hear him mutter something unintelligible, then he drives past the serving window – speedily and without glancing in my direction. I close my eyes briefly and take a deep breath. Pressing the button on the headset as well as my inner one, I smile and say, 'Happy Christmas and welcome to Big Murphy's Burgers and Fries. How can I help you?'

Do you remember . . . ?
– 22 December 2014, Christmas three years ago.
– What's wrong with our tree?
– It's plastic, Ann.
– It's a tradition, Dad. We've had this tree ever since I can remember.
– That's even worse.
– What now?
– I know a place in Blumenthal woods . . .
– Are you going to chop one down? You're joking, Dad. With an axe?
– No, I'm going to gnaw at the trunk until I've bitten it all the way through. Of course with an axe!
– Do you remember when you tried to put my trampoline up? You drilled into your finger.
– Did I end up sorting out the trampoline?
– Did we end up in A&E?
– Come on, my Beetle. Where I'm going to take you is a wonderful place. And we'll have a proper Christmas tree like normal people do.
– When have we ever wanted to be like other people? Quite apart from the fact that you can't just go marching into the woods and take down any tree you like. Imagine if everyone did that!
– We'll just be careful not to get caught.

13

   – You're crazy.

   – And you're my daughter, so welcome to the club!

And that's precisely what we were, wasn't it, Dad? A really exclusive club, just the two of us, ready to confront the rest of the world if necessary. You comforted me whenever I cried about Mum. Left me to it when I hated her and wished she were in hell. You plaited my hair and told me goodnight stories. You told me about womanhood, gave me tea for my cramps and chocolate when I was ravenous. You covered for me when, heartbroken for the first time, I scratched Nico's 125cc because he'd been fooling around with my best friend Eva.

His mother came knocking at our door.

'Are you trying to tell me my daughter did that?' you said to her. 'Never!'

'But I saw her with my own eyes yesterday evening. Hanging around in our street. And the damage was there this morning. Do you know how long Nico saved up for it?'

'Look, I'm really very sorry, but you must be mistaken. My daughter was at home all evening. We were playing chess.'

And you always let me win at chess, because you didn't want me to feel like a loser. You know me so well, Dad. And I know you.

That's why it's a shock every time.

Pixellating the face doesn't make it any easier.

They write about you and seem to be so sure of what they're saying.

I'm halfway home, standing by a newspaper dispenser, staring at tomorrow's edition of one of the largest Berlin newspapers, lit up by a streetlamp. The front page carries a report about how the E. family is planning to spend the Christmas holidays, now that the suspected killer, the man who is presumed to have done all those terrible things – *you!* – is finally in prison, or at least in custody. They will be putting up a Christmas tree for the first time in three years, Jörg E. (43) says. He is crying and smiling simultaneously, the editor adds. At the bottom it says: 'Continue reading on page 3.' I don't know if I want to. Recalling this episode from 2014 is enough. The first time you wanted to have a real tree and were planning to go to Blumenthal woods to cut one down. That same year was the first Christmas the E. family spent without their 'darling little Saskia (8)'. She'd been abducted a few days earlier by an unknown person. She was found dead in a hut in the first week of January. In Blumenthal woods.

A coincidence, I know, Dad.

You're not a killer.

They're so dreadfully mistaken, but they refuse to see this. They'd rather keep spreading their lies, their godawful lies.

Anger. (Ann, 7 years old)

anger is invissible like air and creeps into you when you get very angry. you start with a lump in your throat and you breath like a bull. your hart starts beating very fast and you grind your teeth so you calm down, but it doesn't work because anger is stronger than you and it explodes in your body and because you cant cope you start moving your arms and legs and hitting and kiking. thats the only way to get the anger out of your body and to be left in piece. I was angry once at my MUMMY but I didnt hit her because she was sik. you mustnt hit someone if there sik. shes dead now sadly.

Someone shouts, 'Ann!' and puts their arms around my waist. I'm swept off my feet and I kick at thin air, where before there was the newspaper dispenser. All the same I keep kicking. I'm not going to stop; I can't stop. I'm determined to destroy the lies, even if all I can do at the moment is target a newspaper dispenser.

'Ann!' the voice calls out again and the grip tightens around my waist. 'For Christ's sake, what are you doing?' I'm spun around. 'Stop it!'

I'm going to do nothing of the sort; I mean to fight, destroy. Metal crunches, plastic shatters and paper tatters. Until I gradually lose my strength.

'It's okay, it's all right,' the voice says. Jakob's voice – Jakob again. He gently releases me from his grasp, now that I've finally calmed down. In silence we first look at each other, then at what used to be a newspaper dispenser. The frame is bent, the box is battered and there's a crack in the acrylic viewing window. The newspapers lie shredded in the slush.

Exhausted, I shuffle off to the nearest porch; I need to sit down. The steps are cold and wet, but I don't care; I'm sweating and panting as if I'd just completed a marathon. In the cycle lane in front of me is Jakob's red jeep, the driver's door open. He sits beside me. Judging by his expression he wants to know what just happened, but doesn't have the right words on his lips. I've no idea what to say either. How can I explain this outburst, this other Ann he's never seen before, who attacks newspaper dispensers like a madwoman? Apart from telling him the truth, of course. Have you ever wondered whether the man in the paper, the one they call the 'monster', has any family? Yes, he does, Jakob. Me. I'm the daughter of the supposed ribbon murderer, who is alleged to have abducted and killed nine little girls over the past thirteen years. I was there when they arrested him. I was visiting him that Thursday evening, six weeks ago. We'd ordered pizza and opened a bottle of red wine. When the doorbell went we thought it was the deliveryman. But it was a SWAT team, a dozen men at least. They pounced on my father, handcuffed him and took him away. They were going to take me too and have me give a statement, but I had an asthma attack. And what was I meant to tell them anyway? He's innocent, you fools! He's been in custody ever since and they're linking up their ludicrous chain of evidence, which is supposed to end in a noose around his neck. That's why I'm so furious, Jakob. I'm furious and I'm absolutely terrified.

I don't say any of this; I say nothing. Because it's pointless. Zoe didn't understand either, even though we've known each other for three years and even lived together. It's not that she thinks my father's guilty, she says, absolutely not. And she's really sorry, but she's just got this bad feeling about it. It won't be long before the journalists pitch up and lay siege to our flat, she says. All the whispers at university and the fact that she's got two younger siblings around the age of those girls who were killed. *Please, Ann, don't be cross with me.* No, Zoe, not at all, it's fine.

'Are you all right now?' Jakob asks.

I mumble something.

'Okay, good.' He puts out his hands and straightens the collar of my old, thickly padded denim jacket. It's Dad's jacket and I can sink in it, not only physically. Sometimes, when I take it off the hook, I imagine he's just removed it and hung it up there. And when I put it on, I fancy I can still feel a residue of his bodily warmth.

Instinctively I knock Jakob's hands away.

'Sorry,' he says, startled. 'I was just trying—'

'No, no, it's okay. *I'm* sorry. I'm just a bit sensitive today. What are you doing here, anyway?'

He shrugs.

'I drove past Big Murphy's again, hoping you might've changed your mind. But I saw your colleague, who said you'd already left. So I headed back home, and then . . .' He nods at the road – presumably to indicate he'd driven past by chance – and then at the wreck of the newspaper dispenser.

'I don't know what came over me. Maybe a bout of Christmas depression that got slightly out of hand.'

I try to distract him with a smile, but Jakob remains uncomfortably serious.

'You lied to me, Ann,' he says. His words are like a bucket of cold water in my face.

I blink frantically. 'What?'

'Your daughter.'

'My . . . ?'

'It's what your colleague just told me. She sent you home a little earlier so you could set up the trampoline before your daughter gets home from her father's tomorrow.' As if in slow motion, his gaze wanders to the pile of shredded newspapers with their headline about the murders.

It suddenly hits me.

My aloof manner. My neglected appearance – unwashed, dyed black hair, and clothes full of stains. My pale face, the bags under my eyes from the sleepless nights. This angry outburst. And, most of all, a daughter I never told him about. As if she didn't exist – *anymore*.

US

You're like a song that's planted itself in my head, a stubborn melody. You're expertly arranged, a perfect harmony of beauty and innocence. Every one of your notes goes to the centre of my heart. I purse my lips and hum to myself, softly, very softly, because nobody must hear you. I don't want to share you. Ever again.

I arrived silently, like a ghost, like a shadow in the night. A screwdriver and thirty seconds was all it took the shadow to force open the window on the ground floor. On a standard window you only need to use a screwdriver in two places, as the shadow learned from an information film the police – the police! – had put online to warn people of the tricks burglars use, and to encourage the use of security windows. Idiots. I climbed in, crept my way through the building and found you sleeping like an angel. The moonlight on your face – how beautiful you were, so lovely, lovely.

'Wake up, princess,' I whispered softly, and you opened your eyes. You looked at me as if you'd long been expecting me to come. And you had, hadn't you? I could read it in your face. You didn't have to say anything; I could hear your thoughts, as loudly and clearly as words.

'Take me with you,' you begged. I carefully lifted you in my arms. Your head lay peacefully on my shoulder; you let yourself be carried away just like that. We disappeared via the window I'd come in through and hurried to the car I'd rented. I wrapped you in the warm, cuddly blanket that was lying ready on the back seat. It was winter after all, and I didn't want you to freeze.

'Go back to sleep, my sweetheart,' I said. 'And don't worry. When the sun comes up, we'll be somewhere different, far away where nobody will find us.'

I kept my word, didn't I?

Nobody's found us, nobody has a clue.

You and I, or death. It's as simple as that.

ANN

BERLIN, 25 DECEMBER 2017

At first there's just the hissing in my ears, then comes the stabbing pain in my skull. I try to open my eyes, but in vain. My eyelids are heavy, my lashes stuck together. I'm lying softly, but uncomfortably. I move gingerly, first stretching my legs out, then placing a hand on my head where the pain is raging.

What happened?

Yesterday evening . . .

Jakob was asking about my daughter. I realised there was a dreadful misunderstanding. He thought I was the mother of one of the victims, who'd flipped out when the newspaper reminded her that she'd never again celebrate Christmas with her child. I felt like leaping to my feet and making myself scarce. But I suspected that would only make it worse. And that Jakob was the sort of guy who'd come running after me in a situation like that. So I had no option but to admit that I'd merely invented my daughter.

'I thought a bit of sympathy couldn't hurt, seeing as I had no other qualifications to bring to the job. Everyone at Big Murphy's is working to look after children or family, you know, and it creates a sort of bond between them. They're different from me.'

'What are you like, then?'

I shrugged. 'Complicated, I reckon.'

'Really?'

'Well, what I told you about my German studies is roughly true. I mean, I was studying until recently, at least. I just need a break at the moment, you understand? So I can think about my life and that.'

'A minor crisis, then?'

'That sort of thing.'

'What about the newspaper dispenser?'

'Okay,' I conceded. 'Maybe it's a slightly bigger crisis. Christmas really grates.'

Jakob sighed. 'Come on, I'll take you home.' He got up and offered me his hand. 'Don't worry, this isn't a date, just a lift. I mean, all manner of nutters could be roaming the streets at this time of night.'

My eyes automatically darted to the left and right across the deserted Christmas streets. There was nobody here. Nobody apart from him and me. But I got into his car and, instead of letting him drop me off a few streets further down and disappearing into the entrance of any old building, I unthinkingly directed him to our house.

This is where I grew up and this is where I moved after Zoe booted me out of our flat. My home, although since the police were here, it's no longer what it once was. For three whole days, officers turned the whole place upside down in search of potential evidence, and their approach was anything but gentle. They even broke one of the photos from the mantelpiece; now there's a big crack in the glass, behind which my father and I are grinning in front of the Eiffel Tower. Every time I catch sight of the picture now, it breaks my heart.

Jakob didn't have a clue about any of this when he parked his car in our drive last night. 'Wow, what a lovely house!' he said, but that wasn't true. Without Dad there, it was just empty and dark, like an ugly black hole in the middle of the neighbouring houses, all lit cosily. All of a sudden I didn't fancy getting out anymore.

'Tell me about your idea,' I said.

'What idea?'

'You know, the one you were going to surprise me with at Big Murphy's this afternoon.'

He grinned. His idea was two six-packs waiting behind the passenger seat . . .

I blink. In a blur I can make out our coffee table, on it a dozen beer bottles, some of which have toppled over. The crystal bowl, which still had chocolates in it on the evening Dad was arrested, is overflowing with cigarette butts. The absurd idea of getting up and sorting out the chaos before Dad comes home shoots through my mind. He'd be especially upset by the cigarette butts. Although my asthma isn't that bad, I still have it. I sit up, prop my elbows on my thighs and bury my head in my hands. Construction work is going on inside my head: hammering, drilling, sawing and planing, all at once. I can also hear the clatter of crockery coming from the kitchen, and soon afterwards the hum of the coffee machine.

I can't believe it. Not only that Jakob now knows where I live, but that I actually invited him in, him and his beer. We spent the evening and the night together. And he's still here.

'Good morning!' as if on cue, somewhere amongst the din of the building site in my head. I hear the clinking of glass on glass, Jakob clearing the coffee table. Several times he goes from the sitting room to the kitchen and back again. I stay where I am until the table is clear and there's a cup of coffee on it.

'How are you feeling?'

'Hungover.'

'Surprise, surprise,' he says, laughing. 'I stopped counting when you got to your sixth bottle.'

I reach for the cup, not so much because I need a slug of coffee, but more to distract from my embarrassment. Jakob sits opposite me on the coffee table, so close that our knees are almost touching.

'What's the time?' I ask, after a while spent blowing on my coffee and trying to get my head right. I need to be in Moabit at eleven. I'm allowed to see my father, but only according to the strict rules of custody visits: 1. Discussing the crime is forbidden. 2. A prison guard will be present throughout the visit. 3. Everything will be recorded on video.

'Just gone nine,' Jakob replies, pointing at the clothes I had on yesterday and slept in too. 'So you've got plenty of time for a shower beforehand.'

Beforehand – it takes a moment for the word and its meaning to settle. But then they do and I put my cup back on the table in horror. Coffee sloshes over the rim.

'Don't worry, Ann. Nothing happened last night. You slept here and I slept over there,' he says, nodding to the second sofa opposite mine, separated by the table. But I know at once that this isn't true. Something did happen last night. The worst. And Jakob knows it too. A sense of unease spreads, as if the entire living room were being flooded by a viscous liquid, the level rising and rising continually until it comes up to our chins.

'I'm sorry. I didn't mean to embarrass you. I can imagine how dreadful the situation must be for you. Actually, no . . .' he says, shaking his head. 'Actually, I can't even begin to imagine. It's just . . . if you need a friend, I'll be there for you.' He raises his hands and adds, 'No ulterior motive, I give you my word.' I don't feel reassured.

Yesterday evening.

The images in my head are hazy and shaky, as if they'd been taken by an ancient camera. The sound is like it's canned. Lou Reed is playing on the record player. Bottle tops are popping. I'm being silly and want to dance. I want to be normal again, totally naïve. Let go of everything for a moment. I'm circling like an aeroplane in a blue sky; the sun is shining. Here it's much nicer than outside in the cold, black orbit. Here it's warm and I'm not on my own. I want to break free, rid myself of all my baggage. Slurring my words, I confess to him that the story of the German student with an existential crisis is only half the truth. That the real reason I'm working at Big Murphy's is because I'm terrified of going mad if I surrender to my misery. That I invented a child out of cowardice and pure egotism because I want there to be at least one place – even if it's just a grubby fast-food outlet – where I can be someone else apart from my father's daughter.

Who they say is a murderer.

Who they say has a scheme. Little girls and red ribbons that lead to their bodies.

They make a half-hearted attempt to disguise his face then

print it in their rags and write about deep cuts and huge pools of blood. I don't believe a word of it, not one of their despicable lies, and yet . . . it's so painful, so unbelievably painful. It's a pain that tears at all my limbs, trying to dismember me alive. A pain that puts my heart out of sync and drives my head mad, and I don't want this anymore, I can't go on like this, I really need a break. So, Lou Reed, sing, sing for me, sing louder, just let me dance and forget it all. And you, Jakob – my only friend, even though we haven't known each other that long – I'm so glad you're here, for everyone else has gone. I don't have Zoe or anyone else anymore. Thanks for dancing with me and giving me strength. Because tomorrow's going to be a difficult day. I have to be in Moabit at eleven, where he's being held on remand, but soon, after the trial, he'll be transferred to Tegel where he'll remain, like the proper criminals, the real monsters, permanently, for life, unless a miracle occurs and they realise their mistake. Come on, Jakob, let's dance some more. Give me a moment elsewhere. Just you and me and the beer and Lou Reed . . . and then the film snaps – it all goes black. My memory of the rest is hazy: Jakob carrying me to the sofa, covering me with a blanket and maybe whispering some nice words in my ear: 'Goodnight, Ann. Don't worry, everything will be fine.'

That was yesterday evening.

I sniff – a really pathetic sound. It suits me. 'I didn't mean to tell you everything, you know.'

'I realise that.'

'You have to promise me to keep it to yourself. Enough people know already. The university, the neighbours, friends – or should I say, those who used to be friends.'

'What? How? Your father's name has never been published.'

'But the police questioned everyone who knows us. And these people aren't exactly stupid. Of course our friends recognise his photo in the paper, whether or not he's got that ridiculous black bar over his eyes, which is supposed to preserve the last remnants of his supposed human rights. I'm just waiting for the moment when one of them decides to talk to the press, thereby unleashing the entire mob on me.' The sensation-seeking, the vindictive. The press pack camping outside our house and following my every move. Parents like Jörg E., the father of little Saskia, who will try to track me down and make me pay for the alleged crimes of my father. Merely thinking about it makes me shudder.

His gaze sweeps our living room. The dark green velvet sofa I'm sitting on, the other one he spent the night on, and between them the small mahogany table. The fireplace and all those framed pictures on the mantelpiece: pictures of us, Dad. It's a little journey through time in photo format, with changing shades and styles of hair – you turn greyer and I more colourful; you seem to shrink as my body stretches; fashions change, everything changes, apart from one thing: in each of these pictures we're laughing and very close.

The floor-to-ceiling bookshelves, three metres wide: Schopenhauer, Seneca, Nietzsche and Camus; Munch and Macke prints on walls painted dark red with distemper. So that's how he lives, the alleged killer. This is where he brought up his daughter, who claims she wasn't aware of any of the dreadful crimes he's accused of.

'Maybe you should consider living somewhere else for a while,' Jakob says when his eyes finally come to rest on me. 'I mean, you're right. At some point you'll become the focus of press interest, seeing as you're his daughter.'

'No, that would be like making a statement. If I moved away, everyone would think I'm trying to distance myself from him. And I don't want to do that, not at all. I mean, I know he's innocent.'

Jakob looks pensive. 'There's another option.'

'What?'

'Instead of waiting for the press to come at you, you could make the first move yourself. Seek out a trustworthy journalist and give them an exclusive interview with your version of what happened. You'd be the one pulling the strings and you'd set the parameters.'

'Trustworthy? Yeah, right.'

'Ann.' Jakob sighs. 'You can't hold it against people for wanting to know what happened. Let's face it, nine girls have died and somebody is responsible.'

'But not my father, that's for sure.'

'He's the one who's come to the police's attention, though.'

'Because he was unlucky! Really bloody unlucky, Jakob!'

'Look, with these investigations, I mean . . . it's not like they just pick out some name at random from the phone book when looking for a suspect.' It takes both of us a moment to grasp what he's just said. 'Oh God, I'm sorry. That was silly of me. I wasn't trying to—'

'Imply that my father's guilty? Hurt me? Forget it, your opinion doesn't bother me. You're just some guy from the recycling centre. What do you know?' I've no desire to continue this discussion, and my watch says I don't have to either. 'I should take a shower now, otherwise I'll be late.' I get up from the sofa. 'Thanks for the beer. I'll see you out.'

'It's all right, Ann. You don't need to.' The tone of his voice. And the expression on his face. I can still feel his disappointment long after the door has closed behind him.

Sadness. (Ann, 7 years old)
its not true that when your sad you always have to cry and your nose is runny. Sometimes sadness is much deeper inside and blocks the tears from coming. It feels very cold and dark like sitting in a tower, like the old tower Rapunzel sits in in my book of fairy tales, but without windows. And also theres no door. your really frezing and the cold makes you very tired. You want to get out of the tower becaus you know that the sun is shining outside. But you cant go out becaus youve forgotten where the exit is.

As he sets out the latest findings, my father's lawyer, who was waiting for me in the meeting room, speaks softly, staring at his hands clasped on the table rather than looking at me. Larissa Meller is the latest finding, an unsolved case from fourteen years ago. Soon after my father's arrest, they were already speculating that her death might be linked to the series of killings of young girls, but now the police are certain. Larissa was ten when, one June afternoon in 2003, she set off on her red bike from her home in Hellersdorf with a friend and never came back. A few days later, someone out walking found the bike near the ponds in Hönow; three months later a body was discovered in a wooden hut. Although the hut was only a few hundred metres from where the bike had been found, it was so overgrown that the police had missed it in the course of their large-scale search of the area. They immediately suspected the body might be Larissa's, but it took weeks for a definitive identification. That June had been hot but very rainy too, and so the body was in a terrible state. They also found size 42 footprints, which were made in the rain then dried and preserved by the subsequent heat. At the time, the investigation stalled through a lack of further evidence, so of course it's handy my father also happens to have size 42 shoes. Now Larissa is said to have been the first victim in the series of killings. Only in her case there were no ribbons leading to her body.

'The police are speculating whether Larissa was the reason why the killer used red ribbons later. Maybe he felt bad that the mother had to see her child in such a state.' He's still avoiding looking me in the eye; instead he's kneading his hands so firmly that the skin is turning red in places. 'At any rate, neither her nor any of the other victims show signs of sexual abuse, which means the killer must have been driven by a different motive.'

Having listened silently in disbelief to the term 'the killer' being used as a synonym for 'your father', all I can think of saying is, 'You're his friend, Ludwig.' It sounds like a question.

Ludwig Abramczyk used to be one of Berlin's top lawyers. He's sixty-two and has actually been in retirement for three months, which he's spending at his hunter's cabin in the Polish forest. He's returned in his smart, tailor-made suit specifically for my father's sake, and thus slipped back into his old role. To *help*.

'That's precisely why I'm here, Anni. But he's being very difficult. If you ask him what he was doing at any of the times in question, he either says nothing at all or just comes out with his philosophical stuff.'

'Come off it. As if you could remember what you were doing some afternoon in June fourteen years ago.'

'But he's not even getting worked up about the charges, let alone making an effort to rebut them! He's confronted with nine murders – ten, now, assuming that Larissa's death is part of the series – and all he does is sit there in silence.'

'Because he's distraught! Clearly not even his best friend seems to think he's innocent.' I can see my accusation explode in Ludwig's face. His friend Walter, with whom he spent endless summer nights on the terrace, or by our fire in winter, brandishing their whisky glasses, cracking jokes and having discussions. There was always a topic. Ludwig, who in his work as a defence lawyer had come face to face with so much human wickedness, and my father, who as a philosopher and anthropologist was fascinated by this wickedness, its motives and mechanisms. Barbecues in our garden. My father, often in his own world mentally, letting the sausages burn, and Ludwig, grabbing the tongs to take over just in time. And me, Walter's daughter, little Anni who he's known ever since she took her first wobbly steps on her chubby baby legs. Who he watched grow up, raised by the most loving father you could imagine. His goddaughter, now sitting opposite and who's utterly disappointed in him.

'Please don't be unfair,' he says, after I've said my angry piece. 'You know full well that I'll do everything in my power. But the longer he keeps quiet, the trickier it gets.'

I look up at the ceiling and see cracks in the concrete. Like the cracks in the photograph on our mantelpiece after the police search. Cracks that have marred our entire life. *Because he was unlucky*, is what I said to Jakob this morning. Unlucky that he happened to bump into an acquaintance in the Königswald just before the last body was found. Soon afterwards this very same acquaintance came across one of the notorious red rib-bons, which the media had talked about so often in relation to a number of murders, and then the hut where the lifeless body of a seven-year-old girl lay in a huge pool of blood. Of course the man immediately called the police and, when asked if he'd met anyone in the woods, gave my father's name. This in itself probably wouldn't have been enough to arrest him. But there was also that fricking lecture he'd given a few years ago at the university, and especially the newspaper articles he'd used as a basis for discussion. Then the sighting of a dark Audi A6 near an earlier crime scene, and a black Audi A6 parked in our garage which is registered to my father . . .

'Why?' I ask Ludwig. 'Why should he have committed those murders? I mean, he has a daughter himself, and you know I'm his whole life. He always loved and protected me, and would have been beside himself if anything bad had happened to me. As he would be now. So why should he, of all people, inflict such pain on other parents?'

'I don't know.'

'But isn't that precisely the point? Isn't it always about a motive? Evidence can be misinterpreted. It's even possible to cobble evidence together maliciously if you're out to harm someone, isn't it?'

Ludwig nods, slightly reluctantly, it seems. Whereas I shake my head. 'It wasn't him. There was nothing in the world that could have made him do something like that.'

'Oh, Anni.' Over the table, Ludwig reaches for my left hand and turns it so the palm is facing upwards. Then he pushes my watch strap so he can stroke the little scar on my wrist with his thumb. I was very little when I hurt myself there. 'All of us get the odd scratch and scrape over the course of our life. And not every one is visible on the outside.'

I yank back my hand, speechless.

'You can never see into someone's mind, my child. Not even the mind of those you think you know best. All I want is for you to be prepared for everything. The clues—'

'The clues! Are you listening to anything I'm saying?'

'Anni—'

'You're all so fixated on him that you've become blind to another possibility.'

'What's that?'

'You know, another killer! Are the police investigating every angle? No. It was Dad and that's that, case solved. And if I say that this can't be right, I'm treated like an idiot who can't handle the truth.' I begin chewing my bottom lip. 'Maybe I ought to give an interview after all.'

'What? For God's sake, get that out of your head at once.'

'But if the public understood what kind of a person he really is, it might put pressure on the police to be more thorough in their investigation and so find the real guilty party.'

'No, no, no!' Ludwig says, emphasising each word. Then comes a long speech. The press are an unruly mob. Very few journalists these days feel like they're on a mission, still keen to uncover the truth and look for facts. On the contrary, most just go for the entertainment value; they're out for blood and drama, circulation figures and ratings. This – and only this – is what drives them. If I were to speak to them, Ludwig warns, I might only make things worse. 'You'd be the most help to your father trying to keep your own life under control. That way you'd take a lot of worry off his mind.'

I roll my eyes and utter a drawn-out, 'Blah, blaaaah ...' but this time Ludwig is unfazed.

'And you would help me by appealing to his conscience and getting him to cooperate.'

'I thought it was forbidden to discuss the charge.'

'And you shouldn't do it directly. You should only say what's necessary to make him aware how serious the situation is. The department of public prosecution knows the reason for your visit, so don't worry, okay?'

I nod, even though I don't have a good feeling about this. Something doesn't seem right.

US

I know you're used to better. The big beautiful house. The lovingly decorated children's room in the attic extension. The big garden with the pool . . . You're a real water baby, aren't you, princess? In summer I watched you wearing your plump armbands, splashing around in the pool and squealing with pleasure. Your lips had turned slightly blue; perhaps one ought to have been stricter, made you get out of the water and wrapped you in a thick towel. But seeing your enthusiasm, that innocent, genuine liveliness which only a child can display, made me forget my misgivings and plunged me into the moment. No, I didn't have to worry about you; you weren't stupid. You would get yourself out of the pool when you began to freeze and no longer felt comfortable. I secretly hoped that wouldn't happen for ages; I wanted this moment to last for ever. The sun laying itself over all the colours like a filter, making them rich and vibrant. Your unrestrained joy. Drops of water flying through the air as if in slow motion. I felt as if I were watching a film; I was desperate to press 'pause' and for ever freeze the image of you looking so happy.

Now we're here and I know you don't particularly like it. You're the princess from the big beautiful castle; you don't belong in this dump. But sometimes you simply don't have the choice, and surely the most important thing is that we're together. Just as you are everything for me, I am everything for you. Only through me can you stay alive; if I abandon you, you're dead.

ANN

BERLIN, 25 DECEMBER 2017

Meeting my father – in this concrete room with the neon ceiling light that flickers nervously and the sparse furnishings, a table and two chairs; in this bloody cold, bleak place where he doesn't belong – feels like being crushed under foot. Mentally it wrestles me to the ground, this feeling; it assaults me with blows to the stomach so overpowering I can barely stop myself from retching. Opposite me, slouched, is a man who used to sit upright, his back always straight. He was tall and dignified, his short grey hair neatly parted and combed.

'I'm so pleased to see you, my Beetle,' a stranger says with sunken, narrow shoulders, hollow cheeks, messy hair and vacant eyes. It doesn't sound as if he's pleased; there's no trace of emotion in his voice, monotone like a machine's.

I say, 'Dad,' and start to howl because I'm so horrified at what's left of him. Only then does his dead face stir.

'How are you?' he asks. 'Tell me. No need to be brave.'

I shake my head because this isn't about me. *I'm* not the one who's been framed and locked up. *I'm* not the one being accused of ten counts of murder. 'Ludwig told me you're refusing to cooperate. You're not saying where you were when the crimes were committed, nor are you making any effort to explain the evidence. But you've got to, Dad. Listen to me!'

I look around uncertainly. This isn't the first time I've seen my father since his arrest. But we've never met without a prison warder in the room. Today, though, I'd be grateful for a reprimand or at least a clearing of the throat when I step on to forbidden territory. I'm not allowed to talk about the charge, but I've got to try to make my father break his silence. I don't want to do anything wrong, especially as all conversations between prisoners and visitors are recorded on video. 'I know it all seems so stupid. You must think it's ridiculous to have to clear yourself of something so absurd. But please believe me, your pride isn't going to get you anywhere here. On the contrary, you *must* tell the police you're not the killer, you just *have* to.'

'Oh . . .' He gives a feeble shrug. 'They're not interested in protestations of innocence here. They've made up their minds, they've got a clear picture. Like the prisoners in Plato's cave.' Again something darts across his face, maybe the memory of how only six weeks ago he was still giving lectures, trying to make the great philosophers accessible to his students. He taught at the university for thirty years, was invited to all the big conferences, and received countless international accolades. He's a luminary in the field of philosophical anthropology, a branch of the philosophy of human nature. Professor Dr Walter Lesniak, the former renowned anthropologist, who since his arrest has seemingly been paralysed with shock, and has forgotten one of the basic human skills: speech. The ability to explain yourself. To protest.

'Dad, for God's sake,' I say, grabbing his hands, which feel limp and cold. He lets me take them without squeezing mine back. 'Don't you understand what your silence is doing? They see it as an admission of guilt! You've got to help Ludwig refute the evidence! He can't do anything for you if you won't cooperate. For Christ's sake, make a bit of an effort, however hard it is for you.'

He stares at me through narrow slits, as if on drugs, an understandable feeling. I've often felt like I was on a bad trip recently. But his eyes are unnerving. They're both dreamy and somehow piercing.

'What about you, Ann? Are you making an effort? Or are you still frying burgers instead of going to university?'

'I've already told you, Dad. We've got other problems to deal with right now.'

Ten other problems, to be exact. Ten girls that the killer kidnapped and took to a variety of secluded spots in the Greater Berlin area. He brought them to woods, industrial sites or abandoned construction sites, where there was always a hut, a shed, a cellar or some deserted room that was ideal for his purposes. Ludwig said the girls died of blood loss from deep cuts, according to forensics. I don't know any more than that; Ludwig's keeping the details from me and there's no more to be got from the papers. They say only that the police are withholding certain details for reasons related to the investigation.

'Dad, there's a killer running around freely out there. All he has to do is change his methods or hunting ground and he'll be able to continue committing his crimes unchecked, because you're in prison for him, and for the rest of your life too. If you don't cooperate, the truth won't come to light and—'

'*Truth*. Most of us experience the world only in the way that their own perspective allows. "Man is . . ."'

'". . . the measure of all things." Protagoras, I know.' Now I understand Ludwig's despair. Time for another attempt; I'll try him with a mind game. More girls are going to die because he's obstructing the investigation with his silence. 'They're wasting their time on you when they ought to be hunting the real killer. Do you realise what that means?' My father doesn't react; his drugged expression drives me crazy. 'It means you'll be complicit if another girl dies.'

Nothing.

'Please, Dad! I know it's hard. But if you don't want to talk to the police or Ludwig, then at least talk to me. I'm still your Beetle, aren't I?'

He gives no more than a faint smile. A smile that's unfamiliar, as if he'd copied it from someone else because he's forgetting how to do it himself. He must be dreadfully exhausted by all this. Where are you, Dad? I want to ask the stranger. And: don't you remember us?

Walter and his Beetle.

That's not just the plaits and goodnight stories, tea and chocolate to help with tummy aches, or an alibi when a moped has been scratched. It's Walter explaining to his Beetle why she hasn't got a mummy anymore like the other children do. Treating Beetle's wounds and not allowing her to lie torpidly in her cardboard coffin. Teaching her how to be happy again. Walter, who has always been there for his Beetle, and Beetle, who now realises it's time to return the favour. Because they're a team, an exclusive club – lined up against the rest of the world if necessary.

'I'm sorry,' a prison officer interrupts us as he enters the room. 'Your time is up.'

My father has to go back behind bars. Hugging him as tightly as I can, I whisper, 'I love you, Dad.'

'In that case, stop frying burgers, Ann,' he replies with that crooked, unfamiliar smile. 'You've got the rest of your life ahead of you. Don't throw it away on my account.'

I nod and I mean it. Don't worry, Dad. I've got another job now. I'm going to get you out of prison.

Ditermination. (Ann, 7 years old)

Ditermination means you really want something bad. You feel it tingling in your body like if you had ants under your skin. And your hart beats fast and exsitedly. But its not bad and it doesnt hurt. Your hart is just exsited about what will happen if your ditermination works. Becaus then you get what you want and your happy.

I don't know what to do with myself, only that I need to move, bring my body into line with the activity of my brain. So I stomp around in circles in the prison car park, waiting for Ludwig who's having another conversation inside. He's offered to drive me home after meeting Dad, which I'll happily take him up on as it'll save me having to take the underground. I never used to notice how many people use the time on public transport to read the newspaper. But I do now, as my father's on every other front page.

The fact that the suspect in custody is a university professor has leaked out and the press are using it to make sensational comparisons. They've already made reference to the Russian Oleg Sokolov, a highly respected historian who specialised in the Napoleonic era. Sokolov taught at St Petersburg University before he chopped up his young lover and disposed of the pieces in the Moyka. Or Hannibal Lecter, who isn't even a real person, quite apart from the fact that he's a psychiatrist rather than a professor. And he ate his victims, for heaven's sake. Nonetheless, in every case, it's the same killer profile, one which merely makes the crimes even more sinister. It's a man of intellect and prestige. Not a degenerate killer who acts on impulse, who doesn't know what he's doing, but a highly intelligent monster with a sophisticated plan. 'Professor Death!' one newspaper proclaimed only a few days ago, its article speculating about barbaric experiments and not shying away from making the most vulgar parallels to concentration camp doctors.

All this is absurd, of course, but ubiquitous too. The craving for sensationalism is eating its way through the city like acid. It's corroding people's eyes and reason, and with every day, the calls get louder to publicly unmask the man disguised in the photo and finally bring him to court.

'I hope you didn't have to wait long!' Ludwig hurries over to me. His left hand is swinging his briefcase; his right is already feeling for the car keys in his coat pocket.

'Only a few minutes.'

'That's good,' he says, opening the car and putting the briefcase on the back seat. 'Get in.'

'There's something I wanted to ask you,' I say as we drive out of the car park.

'Go ahead.'

'Are you doing any deals with the department of public prosecution in the background?'

'What? What makes you think that?'

'Well, you said the DPP already knows that I've discussed the case with Dad. That sounds to me a bit like you're in cahoots.'

'They would have found out from the video footage anyway, so, yes, I thought it better to straighten things out in advance. And before you ask, it was also agreed that you should be able to meet your father without supervision today.'

'Why?'

'Call it my Christmas present to you both. Before I retired, the public prosecutor and I used to play tennis together on Tuesdays. This brings the odd benefit from time to time.' Ludwig shoots me a brief glance. 'But, to return to your question, no, I'm not making any deals.' He indicates to turn on to the Strasse des 17. Juni. The metronomic clicking synchronises my heartbeat.

'Ludwig?'

'Yes?'

'I'd like to see the police files. Or at least your documents.'

'What?'

'I feel I could help if I had a more detailed understanding of things, especially because Dad . . .' I break off when his face flashes before me. Those empty eyes and the strangely unfamiliar smile, which he forced himself to make for my sake. 'I think he's given up.'

Ludwig doesn't respond.

'I have to know what happened to the girls,' I add. 'And I mean everything! I need the details.'

'Believe me, my child. There are good reasons why the police are keeping certain pieces of information under wraps. People are going crazy enough as it is. Ribbons are being auctioned on the internet, supposedly from the original crime scenes. And did you read about the desecration of that grave?'

I shake my head.

'One of the girl's graves, not long ago,' he says. 'Those responsible stole all the decorations – candles, flowers, everything that was there – leaving it as empty as an abandoned field.' He puts his indicator on again, this time to enter a petrol station.

'Who'd do a thing like that?'

'Souvenir hunters, Anni! The same sickos who auction the ribbons. It's hard for the police to go after these people too. They can barely keep up.' He stops behind a red jeep. *Jakob*, I immediately think, but it's a young woman who's just come back from paying and is getting into her car. Ludwig waits for her to drive off, takes her place by the pump and switches off the engine. 'Do you want anything? You used to love those caramel bars.'

'No, thanks.'

'All right. I promise to be as quick as I can.'

In the wing mirror I watch him put the nozzle into the tank and look around innocently. I wait tensely until I hear a plop. Ludwig returns the nozzle to its holder, closes the fuel cap and pats the sides of his coat in search of his wallet. Then he goes into the kiosk, and I'm betting he'll buy me a caramel bar anyway. He wants to cheer me up like you do a child – with sweets and some affection. He ought to know that I was never that easy – a bit of sugar and a pat on the head: risible! I was a difficult child, with a few difficult phases. The first was after my mother's death, the second in puberty. At fourteen I was really bad, always getting caught when I was up to no good. Smoking weed with the older boys behind the dining hall instead of going to lessons. Slitting open the mats in the gym. Locking my friend Eva in the girls' loos because I wanted to stop her getting to the drama club auditions on time . . .

'Right, then,' Ludwig says a few minutes later. He flops on to the driver's seat and closes the door. 'You can eat it later if you're not hungry now,' he says, smiling, as he hands me the caramel bar. I smile too – I knew it – and tear open the colourful wrapping at once. I'm really not hungry, but I don't want to open the rucksack on my lap and put it in there.

Yes, at fourteen I was permanently getting into trouble. But sometimes not. My maths teacher, for example, never worked out who stole the answers to a forthcoming test from his briefcase.

Unlike yesterday, when the city looked extinct, there's an extraordinary amount of traffic today. I wonder where everyone's going. My guess is that they're paying festive visits to relatives, or taking minibreaks, which is reassuring, but at the same time feels horribly unfair. There are some little lives the world is indifferent to; it keeps turning as if nothing were happening.

Only when we're close to home do the roads get quiet again, dead in that typical Christmas way, and I realise that this upsets me just as much. Ludwig stops outside our house. The usual phrases. If I need anything. If there's anything he can do. I say no to everything; I'll manage. Big Murphy's is closed today and tomorrow, and I just fancy having a rest, a sleep, watching films and eating pasta with ketchup and cheese.

'But don't forget,' he says, putting his thumb to his right ear and little finger to his mouth. 'You just have to call, anytime.'

I thank him and get out of his car as fast as I can.

Walking to the house, I realise how dirty the ground-floor windows are; the rain and snow of the past few weeks have left crazy artworks of speckles and smears. We used to have a cleaning lady but she doesn't come anymore. Soon after Dad was arrested, she called to say she'd have to stop until further notice for health reasons – her back, her hips, etc. I guessed at once that the police must have gone round to question her. But I didn't probe; I didn't want to know. Instead I thanked her for all the years she'd worked for us, for having tidied up my squeaky baby toys and picture books, and for always bringing me a cake for my birthday because Mum's illness meant she couldn't bake me one. I asked her to put the house key in the letter box whenever it suited her; she did it less than two hours later.

'Happy Christmas, Ann!' I hear at my back, just as I'm about to unlock the front door. I don't bother turning around; I know the voice is that of our neighbour, Elke Harbert. Elke also uses the same cleaning lady, the only difference being that she's still working for the Harberts despite her supposed aches and pains. Sometimes, when I'm making my morning coffee, I can see her through our kitchen window, ducking as she scurries past our hedge to get next door.

'You too, Elke,' I rattle off flatly. I know full well what's about to come. Since the arrest, Elke and her husband, Caspian, have been turning up at least once a week, trying to get me to come to dinner. But I don't have to accept their invitation to know how the evening would unfold: uncertain looks and awkward silences over an aperitif, then by the time we're on to the main course and the third glass of wine, the first questions would be fired at me. *Is it really true . . . ?* Of course not! Have you gone mad? *But the papers* . . . Lies. *And on the telly they said* . . . No, thanks. The mere thought of it is quite enough for me.

'I was going to ask whether you'd like to come and have goose with us tonight.'

'Thanks, that's very sweet of you, but I've got something else on.'

A brief pause, then: 'You're making a big mistake, Ann.'

Now I do turn round. The way she stands there, in the middle of our snowy drive, in her light jeans and pink blouse, which immediately repulses me because it's ironed so perfectly. Not even the faintest crease has the courage to rebel against the immaculate appearance. 'I'm sorry. What mistake?'

'Shutting yourself away like this. I'm really worried about you.' She kneads her hands; it's cold today and she isn't wearing a coat over her thin blouse. I wonder if she thinks I'm embarrassed about my father. That this is the reason why I'm avoiding going over there. The anger is back, welling up inside me; I feel like grabbing Elke by her starched, pink collar and yelling, 'How dare you, you stupid cow! If I'm ashamed of anyone at all, it's people like you who've been our neighbours for over twenty years and bloody well ought to know better!'

But I keep my cool. After all, Elke isn't a newspaper dispenser, she's a human being who could be seriously hurt. I assure her that everything's okay and thank her politely – for whatever. Then I unlock the front door.

'Eva's coming too.'

I flinch, as if she'd just given me a slap. Eva, probably the only – albeit major – crease in the otherwise impeccably ironed life of Elke and Caspian Harbert. Their daughter, who took flight

47

the moment she'd finished school. Away from the strict mother and her lapdog of a husband, away from a house full of scatter cushions and the stench of Dettol, away from the pressure to achieve and the feeling of never being good enough. I can't recall her ever visiting her parents since, not at Christmas nor on any other occasion. Dream on, Elke.

'All I'm saying is . . . the two of you used to be inseparable.'

We were. Until Eva abandoned me as well as her parents, absconding with Nico, the boy whose motorbike I'd scratched the previous year out of jealousy. There were rumours that she might be pregnant by him, and even more rumours when Nico returned to Berlin alone only a few months later.

'Send her my regards,' I mutter, before dashing into the house and locking the door behind me. I close my eyes and take calm breaths until I start hearing noises coming from upstairs. A chair scraping across the old floorboards, then footsteps creaking. Finally I hear the door to the study and my father's voice. 'Beetle? Is that you?'

Who else could it be, Dad?

'How was uni?' The footsteps come closer.

Boring as usual. German isn't exactly the thing for adrenaline junkies.

'I could have told you that straight off.' The stairs creak beneath his lively tread. Now he's beside me, saying, 'Shall we have a coffee first? You look like you could do with one.'

I smile and open my eyes. But there's nobody there – of course not; it's just my imagination. A few moments that are lovely to begin with, then painful as they fade. I slip the rucksack off my back, take off his jacket and then the boots, which have left a brownish puddle on the light-coloured floorboards. It doesn't bother me. I want to go into the kitchen to make some coffee and also to fetch the cup from the living room that's been on the table since this morning – save resources, the dishwasher is full. Although I go straight past the windows that lead on to the terrace, I don't see it at first, not until I'm grabbing the cup and look up by chance.

Just my imagination again, is my first thought.

I blink a few times, to be certain. But no matter how often I open and close my eyes, it's still there: the red ribbon tied around a branch of the dead oleander on our terrace.

RECORDING 01

Berlin, 7 May 2021

– To be honest, I'd imagined you to be quite different.

– Really? How?

– Well, I mean, I've seen photos of you, of course, but . . . I thought you'd have some evil aura about you. I thought it would be tangible somehow. Do you understand?

– Oh dear!

– Yes, silly, isn't it?

– Oh well, I suspect you're rather nervous. You have been after me for years, I suppose. So am I right in my assumption that this is going to be the grand finale? You and me and all our cards on the table, hmm? The end of the hunt, the hunter trapped.

– Is that how you see yourself? As a hunter?

– No, as a matter of fact, but I get the impression you like a bit of drama. People like me are supposed to have difficulty reading others. But do you know what? I always had a good inkling of my opponent's needs. You learn what people want, their longings, fears, desires – basically all of these are mere templates you can interpret according to a fixed pattern.

– So you're more of an actor, then?

– Yes, and I think a rather good one at that. By the way, does your mother know what you're doing here? Isn't she worried about you?

– My mother? I don't know what my mother's got—

– Calm down. You want me to share my secrets with you. It's not something one does with any old person, is it? I'd like to get to know you first.

– I . . . All right, I don't have a mother anymore. She's dead. But if she were still alive, I'd tell her she needn't worry.

– *(grins)* But I'm a killer. And I've got nothing to lose.

– Are you threatening me?

– Is that how you feel? Threatened by me? Intimidated? Inferior?

– *(audibly swallows)* I didn't come here to play games, but because I wanted to know who you are.

– 'Wanted'? Are you saying you do know now? Well, that was quick, I take my hat off to you.

– No, I . . . I mean . . .

– Good God, why don't you relax, and let's get this done with a modicum of dignity. It is the grand finale, after all! It would be a real shame if, after all the effort you've put in, you failed now, wouldn't it?

ANN

BERLIN, 25 DECEMBER 2017

It's like a scavenger hunt, only there's no treasure at the end, only the discovery of a dead child. Red ribbons pointing the way to the bodies, and now a red ribbon tied to a branch of the old oleander on our terrace. For a few seconds I just stand there, rigid, staring and unable to comprehend. It's like a tsunami: all my thoughts and feelings retreat into the distance, where they gather and tower up to come surging forth and crush me.

Then I suddenly realise: the killer.

He's free and he was here.

He's left me a sign.

Slipping from my hand, the coffee cup crashes to the floor and breaks. I stagger, check my balance on the armrest of the sofa, then teeter backwards until I feel the wall behind me – a cold, hard wall that offers support, its firmness reassuring.

Nonsense, it's all nonsense. Now I've thought it through, of course the ribbon murderer wasn't here, that's absurd. What would he want from me? Why would he provoke me, given that he must be thrilled my father's in prison in his place? No, what must have happened is what I've been fearing for a while: my father's identity has been revealed. He's no longer a disguised face in a photo by the name of 'university professor (55)'; now he's Dr Walter Lesniak, a verifiable individual with an address and a daughter who's being tracked down. Maybe by Jörg E., the man who's always doing the media rounds, father of little Saskia, victim number seven. It was him, or another father, mother, grandfather. Someone who's lost a child to the serial killer. Who's now found me and wants to torture me just as their own child was tortured. Because I'm someone's daughter too. *His* daughter. An eye for an eye.

I tense my jaw; fear and helplessness give way to blazing anger. Marching to the terrace door, I yank it open and inspect the red ribbon. It looks new, barely touched by the weather, as if it's only just been tied there. My eyes flit around. Footprints, definitely a man's. I follow them through the snow; they lead from the rear garden door to our terrace and back. Suddenly I find myself standing on the little path that runs behind our garden. The footprints are mingled with countless others; lots of neighbours go walking here or take their dogs out. It's impossible to work out where the intruder came from or in which direction he fled. I turn around a few times, wheezing alarmingly. I ran out without any shoes on and now my socks are soaking up the wet. The cold, the distress. If I don't calm down, this is going to end in another attack. Breathe, no matter how. Cautious movements, back inside the house. I don't know if I've shut the terrace door properly; I can only think about my asthma spray. A reverberation of the cold pulses in my feet, niggling me. But it's no good, I lurch into the hallway, over to my rucksack. Only in emergencies, the doctor said. Shake the cartridge, put the mouthpiece between your lips, lean your head back, breathe in slowly and deeply while pressing the spray button, then hold your breath for five seconds. 5 – 4 – 3 – 2 – 1. I breathe a sigh of relief. I'm all right again; I don't suffer as badly as others. My asthma is more like a rubber band that can be stretched and stretched and stretched until it finally breaks. I drop to the floor; I want to sit down, just for a moment, until the rubber-band sensation has eased a little. Then I put the spray back into the rucksack and take my mobile out. My first attempt goes straight to voicemail; the second time Ludwig answers immediately. From the background noises I can tell that he's still in the car. I try to sound as composed as possible: the red ribbon on the oleander, the footsteps in the garden, someone was here.

'What? What are you talking about, Anni?'

Once again. The red ribbon, the footsteps.

'They've found me, Ludwig!'

'Who's found you?'

'Some relatives, I imagine! Don't you get it? We need to inform the police!'

'I fear there's very little they'll be able to do. Nothing has been damaged, nor has anyone physically assaulted you. Trespassing on private property – no more than that.'

'Are you being serious?'

'Listen. I understand you're shaken up, but the situation is like this: someone was in your garden and tied a red ribbon to the oleander—'

'The message is: we have found you.'

'Anni—'

'Are you saying I just ought to accept it?'

'Once again: someone was in your garden and tied a red ribbon to the oleander. Nothing else actually happened. At most, the police will tell you to be circumspect and get in touch if anything worse happens, if the person comes back or if you feel threatened . . .'

I hang up in consternation. But Ludwig's probably right; calling the police won't help. They'll only think I'm being hysterical and deal with me exactly as he said: monitor the situation, get in touch if something *really* happens. A *really* that's based on more than just a state of mind, the oppressive feeling that, in crossing the boundary to their property, someone has also violated a personal boundary. My home, the place where – at moments in my imagination, at least – everything can be as it used to be. My old home, it's all I've got left. I slip my mobile into my trouser pocket and take the grey cardboard file from the rucksack.

I've got to be quick. It won't be long before Ludwig realises that something important is missing. He'll run back over the day and soon remember that he left me alone in the car at the petrol station, alone with his briefcase on the back seat. He'll also recall that only a few minutes earlier I'd asked if I could see these papers.

This isn't the only reason why there's no time to lose. Somebody was here, if only in our garden this time. All the same, this person is one of those I have to convince of my father's innocence as soon as possible, before they go further next time and I find myself in serious danger. Who knows what desperate people are capable of when they believe they're in the right and become impatient? Who knows if the red ribbon isn't just a means to pressurise the man that they believe to be the killer to finally break his silence, having refused to make a confession till now?

*

Dad's study. Where he prepared his lectures and wrote his papers. Where he was inspired and we weren't allowed to disturb him. A room the real world had no access to, a place that seemed to be from another dimension. Maybe I'm secretly hoping that something of the particular intellect enveloping this room will rub off on me as I climb the stairs with Ludwig's file and another cup of coffee. The room is at the end of the landing, beyond the bedrooms and the two bathrooms. Its windows look out on to the garden, offering the perfect view of me as a child, whooping and roaring as I leaped around on the trampoline down there. The perfect view if the intruder were to return.

I always find it painful to think of the police storming into this room during the course of their search. At first they only wanted to because the door was locked. I tried to explain the rationale behind it, tell them that this room was especially private, as intimate as an organ or a thought you don't share, which belongs to you alone. They didn't understand this, of course, and threatened to break down the door if I didn't get them the key immediately. In the desk they then found the fricking newspaper articles; I bet the public prosecutor jumped for joy. An entire folder of reports on the ribbon murderer – of course this must be some sort of trophy collection. But that wasn't the case. I know the file and also know that my father kept the articles for a lecture on 'The Dark Side of Human Beings'. These cases were clearly a perfect way to underpin the often very theoretical discussion with true-life events. His students – most, at least – loved their professor for not torturing them with pure theory. At home we discussed the cases a few times too, most recently on the evening he was arrested.

On the kitchen counter was that day's edition of a newspaper in which Jörg E., Saskia's father, commented on the death of another girl.

'Do you think the children realised that they'd die?' Dad asked me. 'Do you reckon their immature brains could comprehend this fact?'

'No,' I replied. 'I think they hoped for a miracle right up to the last moment. Everyone would do that, wouldn't they? No matter what age. Just think of Mum. Until the very end, she said, *I'll be all right.*' I shook my head. 'But it's good to have hope, if only to counter the fear. Something you can cling to before you enter oblivion.'

'Oblivion? I thought you believed in God?'

'I do. Well, God or something else – a higher power, yes. I just don't believe we get a second round in the hereafter, so to speak. I believe in this one life, and when the lights go out here . . . well, they stay out.'

'Or maybe they don't. Euripides said, "Who knoweth if to die be but to live, and that called life by mortals be but death?"'

'To establish this beyond doubt I'd have to sacrifice my own life, so no, thanks. I'm far more interested in finding out where the hell our pizzas are. I'm about to die of hunger here . . .'

The pizzas didn't come, but the blue lights did. The police. They took my father away and searched the house, including this room. I don't want to think how their mere presence defiled it. I want to think that there's enough of my father here still to hold and guide me. Just as I sometimes can feel his residual warmth in his jacket when I put it on.

Having fished the key from the large vase that stands on a

console table at the end of the landing, I unlock the door almost devoutly. And it is really true. Apart from the fact that documents and books torn from the shelves still lie scattered on the floor, and the drawers are wide open – I haven't yet felt able to tidy the chaos left behind by the search team – I only have to take a deep breath. The smell of old paper. The wood of the desk. The leather of the sofa. Something comfortingly stale, and dust dancing in the sunlight – a huge amount of dust, because even our cleaning lady, who kept the rest of the house clinically clean, didn't have access to this room. I breathe and sense his presence. Hang in there, Dad, just a while longer. I'll find something to exonerate you. I'll get you out of prison, I promise.

Confidens. (Ann, 7 years old)
Confidens is a bit like hope but that you know for sure that something is going to be good and your looking forward to it but with hope theres also the possibility that something wont be good. Like when I hoped MUMMY wood get better but she died. This means that confidens is better than hope and if you have the choice you shud always chose confidens.

I begin by tidying up – superficially, at least. The books go back on the shelves and all the paper into the drawers of the desk. I find a folder with short essays in which Beetle recorded her feelings in spidery handwriting, and a tatty wooden box. Inside is my old school ID card, a rosary with broken links, the torn ticket to my leavers' ball, a sewing kit from a hotel on the Baltic, a few mussel shells and a flat, triangular stone that Dad gave me many years ago to remind me I'm strong enough to overcome the worst. My old talisman. I place it in my palm, feel its cool, smooth surface and trace its pattern. I'm confused as to how it could have ended up in this mishmash of meaningless things. Was I not going to keep it on me at all times? I ought to, especially in this situation, which has completely redefined 'the worst' as a term. I finish by sorting out the pen holder, and put the chair back in its place, not too far under the desk, but so that Dad could immediately sit on it if he came into this room right now to work. I've done it; I've created some order, both around me and inside me. My head is clear, my mind alert, my heart beating a nervy staccato. I sit cross-legged on the floor and spread out the contents of Ludwig's folder in front of me. First there are the copies of all the documents – witness statements, résumés, forensic reports, summaries of the presumed circumstances of the crimes and the current state of investigation, including all the evidence – merely words, technical-speak lacking all feeling. But then come the photographs, beginning with those that the parents must have given to the police when their daughters were still classified as missing. Photos of animated girls in a variety of everyday situations, all of them with one thing in common: in every image they're laughing. I start hearing it, only very softly at first, as if from a memory. But it doesn't stop at that. I can see them as if they were real: a little blonde girl, dancing through the study in her tutu. Another, with brown plaits, holding up her huge cone of sweets as she gives me a proud smile, revealing the gaps between her teeth. A third, suddenly sitting on the leather sofa, with a puppy on her lap. That's Saskia. I recognise her at once because her picture is always printed alongside that of her ubiquitous father. The room fills, the laughter growing louder and more real. I realise how badly mistaken I've been. These aren't just ten 'problems' as I still thought this morning, but real people with names, families, interests and a future that's been stolen from them. No first kisses, no first heartbreak, no finishing school, no becoming adults. Just a big black nothingness. Tears flow. Such injustice. Who's responsible? Who played God and what gave him the right? Why should someone like that be allowed to live, to experience what he's maliciously stolen from others?

I thought you believed in God?

Not in moments like this, I'm sorry.

Leaping to my feet, I run into the bathroom to throw up, retching so loudly that the noises echo off the tiles. Noises that capture and drown out everything. Even the footsteps on the stairs. The footsteps along the landing. The footsteps that stop outside the open bathroom door. I simply didn't hear them, and only realise when a shadow looms in the corner of my eye.

US

Now don't look so sad, my sweetheart! We talked about that yesterday, didn't we? I realise you'd rather have had a proper Christmas, with a tree and lots of presents like you're used to. Last year, for example, you got a pink bicycle with a Princess Lillifee pennant that stuck up from the pannier rack like an antenna. You were so thrilled, riding up and down the snowy drive. I almost cried watching your unsteady legs on that bike, and every time you pedalled, the pennant would move above you like a dodgy windscreen wiper. But we have to be grateful for what we've got, and we are, aren't we? Yes, we are. We've got us – and Cosmo. Look, Cosmo's here! Your favourite teddy with a button in place of his left eye. Listen to what he has to say: 'Hello, little princess, it's me, your Cosmo. I don't think our new home's bad at all.' And Milly, I even thought of your little Milly. Can you hear her purring? She feels happy here too . . . No? You don't want to smile? Not even a teensy-weensy little bit? But you've got such an enchanting smile . . . Oh, I know! I know what'll cheer you up! Let's give you a bath, my angel. We'll give you a bath and make you pretty! Brush your sweet locks and put on an especially beautiful dress in honour of the day. I'll make us something delicious and we'll eat together, by candlelight. How about ravioli with tomato sauce? It's unhealthy and gooey, but what the hell. We make our own rules here, don't we? Aren't we happy? Yes, we are, my sweetheart, we're unbelievably happy.

ANN

BERLIN, 25 DECEMBER 2017

Her.

The shock is like a blast, a violent inner explosion. I try to jump up but my body is sheer chaos; my legs just twitch and my hands can't get a hold. By contrast, she stands there in the door, tall and superior, a faint smile on her lips. She's not saying anything, which is the worst thing. I want to ask her how she got in. What the hell she thinks she's doing here, in our house and in general, after all these years. Maybe I'd ask too whether she's real or just a hallucination like the girls in the study. Only my mouth feels blocked and my throat constricted. And she, she's making no move to help me and resolve the situation herself. She seems to be enjoying the fact that I'm squatting beside the loo, looking surprised and incapacitated. I manage no more than an 'Eva', but even that's too much. It feels as if I were opening the door to a storeroom that's been piled high with rubbish for years, eventually getting so full that I had to press against the door with all my body weight to close it. Now I've opened it again and its entire contents come spilling out, battering me. Years, images, memories.

'You still remember me, then,' she says, her grin getting wider.

Of course I do, even though she's changed a lot. Her hair, once long and strawberry-blonde, has now been dyed dark brown and only comes down to her chin. She looks pale, as if made from porcelain. She's also lost weight – too much, in my opinion. She's thin like one of the lines on her wide pullover and her narrow jeans. But she's genuine, real, I can't blink her away. Eva, the ugliest, meanest person on earth. She broke my heart when she went off with Nico back then.

I try to restore some order to myself, starting with my body. Bracing my feet on the floor, I reach for the rim of the sink and pull myself up. I hope she doesn't notice that every fibre of me is trembling. I don't want her to think of herself as my wound; I've been taken by surprise, that's all, and she's not even a scab anymore.

'What are you doing here? How did you even get in?'

She shrugs. 'Your bell seems to be broken, I tried a few times . . .'

I nod. I switched the bell off a while ago now. Nobody ever came who I wanted to let in anyway. Usually it was Eva's mother inviting me to dinner yet again.

'. . . so I wandered around the house, like in the old days, and saw that the terrace door was open.' The terrace door – I must have forgotten to close it properly after being completely thrown by the red ribbon on the oleander. 'You should really be more careful now that you're here on your own.' The amused look, the supercilious tone; she's trying to provoke me, and she's succeeding too.

'What about you, Eva? Do you think it's normal to march into a strange house?'

'In case you don't remember, this house was never strange to me. Quite the opposite – for a long time I felt more at home here than with my own parents.'

'How touching.'

She gives a slightly forced laugh. 'I see you still bear a grudge for what happened with Nico.'

'Rubbish! I'd just like to know what you think you're doing in my house.'

'My mother sent me in the hope that I'd be able to swing it and get you to come to dinner after all. She doesn't want you spending Christmas on your own.'

'Tell her you tried everything.'

'As you wish,' she says, turning to go. I put my hands up and massage the sides of my head. Listening to Eva's footsteps, I'm relieved to hear them get further away. Until I realise they're heading in the wrong direction. I rush after Eva, but don't catch up with her until she's already in the study, in the middle of all the papers and photographs of happy little girls.

'Holy shit!'

'Yes, exactly: holy shit. What do you think you're doing, Eva? Just get out!'

'What's this?' she says, bending down to one of the pictures. 'Where did you get all of this?'

'Doesn't matter, leave it!' I try snatching the photo, but she turns away with it.

'Do you know I never actually came into this room? I spent half my childhood in your house, but this door was always closed. We knew we weren't allowed to disturb your father when he was working, even though he never actually said that to us.'

'Are you deaf? I want you to leave. Now!'

She looks at me – the face she presents today is swimming once more with childish features. Eva, my Eva, part of me for so many years. My fury writhes, flattened by the feelings from the storeroom jammed with rubbish.

'You just left,' I hiss between clenched jaws. It sounds pitiful and feeble.

The photograph in her hand begins to tremble faintly; it's as if her smug smile has been wiped away. Has Eva got a storeroom like mine? Things she's locked away for her own protection?

'I know,' she says softly.

'You didn't think I was worth a goodbye, an explanation.' I purse my lips; I don't want to sound like an injured bird, make myself small and vulnerable before someone who's shattered my ribcage and squashed my heart.

She nods uneasily. 'It was an emergency, wasn't it? You were my second family, my better family.'

'Is this something that's only occurred to you now? After more than seven bloody years ?'

'I buy every newspaper that reports on the case.'

I shake my head. 'I don't. It only makes me angry.'

'At your father or the journalists?'

'What? The journalists, of course! Come on, Eva, you know my dad! Surely you can't believe he's got anything to do with it.' I point at the carpet of documents at our feet. 'Somewhere in all of this there's a mistake and I'm determined to find it.'

'Ann . . .' Now she's the one sounding feeble. 'Maybe—'

'No, not *maybe*. Go, get out of here. You're no longer welcome in this house. When you packed your bags to bugger off with Nico, you discarded us and your past life like a redundant tool.'

Eva doesn't budge an inch. Her gaze penetrates me effortlessly; my skin is made of cellophane and I'm transparent. Because the fact is, I don't really want her to go. I've never stopped missing her. And I'm longing for support.

'Who's that?' she asks warily, meaning the girl in the photo she's holding. I crane my neck. It's a portrait; the little girl has red hair and freckles.

'I don't know,' I reply, moving my index finger in a circle. 'Turn it around; the names are written on the back.'

'Larissa Meller,' Eva reads out.

I nod discreetly. Larissa was the girl Ludwig told me about, the most recent development in the case. 'She was ten when she disappeared in June 2003 on a bike ride,' I say, repeating what I remember. 'Her body was found three months later in a hut by the Weihenpfuhl. The police reckon she was the ribbon murderer's first victim.'

'How exactly did he . . .' Eva falters, but it's obvious what she wants to know. It's the question whose answer is still hiding in Ludwig's folder, deliberately sealed in a large brown envelope. An answer whose details are known by very few. Not even Jörg E., Sakia's father, who doesn't usually omit a single detail, has ever spoken about it; presumably the police have made him swear to keep quiet on this matter, because, according to Ludwig, they've got their reasons for withholding certain details. When questions are asked as to exactly how the girls died, the vague line is that they bled to death from their cut wounds.

'There are photographs of that too,' I say quietly.

Eva's eyes grow large. 'Do you really want to see them?'

'I have to. So . . . thank your mum for the invitation. Or tell her she knows where she can stick her sympathy. Whichever you consider more appropriate.' I essay a smile, but Eva shakes her head.

'Forget it. I'll tell her to make us up two plates. We'll eat here.'

She's out of the study in a flash, so quickly that she forgets to give me back the photo of Larissa. I can only hope she realises before she gets home and Elke catches a glimpse.

It's a good half hour before she comes back. I'd almost given up on her and felt angry at myself for being taken in by her again.

'Sorry,' Eva says when she's at the front door, carrying two plates covered in tinfoil. After she went, I carefully locked the door to the terrace and switched the bell on again. 'I had to have a bit of a discussion with Mum. She couldn't understand why we wanted to eat here instead.' She hands me the plates and takes off her boots.

'Did you tell her?'

'Are you crazy? You know my mum.'

'True.' With my head, I indicate that she should follow me upstairs. One half of me has already put cutlery, napkins, two glasses and a bottle of wine on the desk, whereas the other half is just shaking its head. How can I get involved with Eva again so quickly after everything that happened? Maybe because, amongst all the emotions in my inner storeroom of rubbish, there was always the secret hope I'd see her again one day. Surely I still mean something to her; it must be true or she'd never have come back.

When Eva lifts the foil from one of the plates, the goose leg with its red cabbage gives off a Christmas aroma, an illusion that immediately feels wrong to both of us.

'We could eat later,' I say, ashamed of the wine and glasses, which seem just as inappropriate, as if I were trying to exploit a dreadful occasion for my own benefit. Two former friends, toasting with Chardonnay their reunion in the shadow of ten dead children. I pour the wine anyway, and I'm happy to see Eva empty her glass in one go.

'While you were at your parents', I started looking at some of these documents, especially the evidence that's been gathered.'

Eva holds her glass out to me, a silent prompt.

'And the photos of . . .' she begins, but can't say more than, 'you know.'

'No, not yet.' We drink in sync, both eagerly and quickly in the hope it will give us the necessary courage for what's in store. 'Did you bring the photo of Larissa back? I have to return the folder in its entirety when we're done or I'll be in even more trouble than I'm already in.'

Eva puts her empty glass on the desk then reaches behind and pulls the photo from her waistband like a gun. 'Here.' She gives it another close inspection before handing it back to me. 'She'd be our age now.'

'True.'

'Where do you think she was going when she disappeared that June afternoon?'

I shrug. 'Maybe nowhere in particular, maybe she was just exploring the area. Would that be so odd?'

At Larissa's age, Eva and I often went out on our bikes. Our trips sometimes took us far, down farm tracks, through woods and marshes, and to an old gravel pit which we fantasised was a sea. The best fun we had was when Eva could stay the night at ours and we didn't have to keep an eye on the time to ensure she'd be back home punctually for dinner. Elke was reluctant to allow sleepovers; she was worried my father wouldn't much care whether we ate healthily or went to bed on time. In one respect she was right: my father did give us a lot of leeway. Not because he was ignorant, but because he wanted to see us happy. He pumped our tyres up – clumsily, but he did it – before we set off, gave us money so we could buy ice creams on the way, and told us to have fun.

Fourteen years later Eva and I are on a journey again together. Ten stories take us through the entire Greater Berlin area, each ending at the moment the crime scene photographer pressed the button on his camera. The girls were called Jana, Kati, Olivia, Laetitia, Hayet, Jenny, Saskia, Alina and Sophie. We find them in woodland huts, cellars and warehouses, where they lie before us, their faces pointing upwards or tilted limply to the side. Some have their eyes closed and look as if they're sleeping. Others stare horrified into the void. And then there's Larissa – all that's left of her is an unrecognisable black something with matted red hair.

Eva cries bitterly; she can barely speak. But I don't want her to either. I'm the one with a clear head; I have the overview, the plan.

'It's essential we find out the significance of the gaps between murders. He kills in 2003, 2004, 2005, 2007, 2008, 2011, 2013, 2014, 2016, 2017. What sort of a cycle is that? And what's with the years 2006, 2009, 2010, 2012 and 2015? Nothing happens in those years. What's the killer doing during this time? Is he ill? Is he in prison for other crimes? Or is he abroad seeking victims there?'

When Eva swallows, I ignore it. My mind is in overdrive.

'Whoever killed those girls must have a few gaps in his CV that relate to these very years. My father doesn't. He was never ill for a long period, let alone ever in prison. He's never even run a red light in his life, but nobody's interested in that.'

Eva makes a noise again; the sight of the dead girls must have really unsettled her. But it's what she wanted. She wanted to help with the research and the photos are part of that.

'They just come up with their arbitrary evidence, and, in all honesty – I want to hear you say it, Eva – it really is arbitrary, isn't it? Size 42 shoes and a dark Audi? I mean, how many other men in Berlin fit the bill? Must be tens of thousands at least.' I point at the papers, including the document listing the evidence. 'Otherwise all they've got is a partial fingerprint – smudged so it's useless – and a few textile fibres, probably from a shirt. What they don't have is any DNA or mobile phone data to prove my father was in the vicinity of the crime scenes. Nothing certain.'

Eva shakes her head as if I'd asked her a question. Her face is so contorted with pain that her tear-stained mascara is running in oddly crooked lines.

'And okay, then there's the acquaintance who ran into my father on a walk near the last crime scene,' I continue breathlessly. 'But that could have been a coincidence, couldn't it? Turn it round and you could also say my father ran into this acquaintance. So why isn't he under suspicion? I admit, the newspaper articles in his desk give the wrong impression, but he'd kept them for his lecture series, for God's sake! He was analysing these articles as part of his research, because that was his specialism: "Evil in humans as an anthropological, cultural and historical constant, and philosophical views of death". I was always really impressed by the weightiness of the topic. And very proud of him because his lectures and seminars were in great demand. Most students found his approach cool, apart from this one girl, a prissy nerd . . .' My thoughts are racing at such speed that my speech can hardly keep up. 'She complained to the dean because she thought what my father was doing was disrespectful, verging on abuse of the dead children for' – here I make air quotes – '"study purposes". Discussions with the university management ensued and the complaint was officially recorded. But that dozy woman – I expect she'd watched too many serial killer documentaries – she only had to go to the police too, didn't she? My father was questioned, and of course he was able to point out to the officers that science *has* to use material from real life to produce findings that can be taken seriously. It was relatively easy to convey this to the police. Back then, at least. And finally, there's the photofit image that was put together from details provided by a woman who claimed to have seen Saskia with a strange man.' I thrust the picture above my head. 'This is a joke, isn't it?' I say, waving it around so it rustles noisily in the air. 'Look at the nose: far too small and broad. Then this bloated chin and the close-together eyes. It looks more like your dad than—'

'Please stop!'

'Or Ludwig, that would be a great Ludwig, wouldn't it? Do you remember Ludwig? He used to come here often—'

'Ann! That's enough!'

I recoil and blink as if I'd been dreaming. Eva wipes her eyes with the back of her hand, smearing the lines from the mascara that's run. Her face now looks sooty, as if she'd just escaped a major fire in the nick of time.

'I'm really sorry,' she whispers.

'So am I, Eva . . . We can't change the fate of these poor girls. But we can—'

'I'm sorry for you.' Without taking her eyes off me, she pulls up the left sleeve of her jumper as if in slow motion. 'You saw it too, Ann. The same thing ten times, each girl.' She puts her right index finger on her wrist and traces an invisible line to her elbow. My heart is vibrating; I no longer feel individual beats, just a pervasive tension.

'But . . . but that's crazy.'

'Really?' She grabs my left hand and turns it so my wrist is facing upwards. We both look at my scar. Now we know how the girls were killed. It wasn't the photographs from the crime scenes that showed us – it was difficult to make out anything in them due to all the blood – but the other pictures in the brown envelope. Small, stiff bodies, their wounds cleaned, lying on cold metal tables in forensics labs.

The killer slit the girls' wrists.

I was six when my mum died of leukaemia. My mind doesn't have more than a few flickering images of a bald woman lying in a bed. I remember she was always weak, jittery, and had to take a mountain of medicines. Sometimes she let me tip out the contents of her pill box and then rearrange them again. We'd pretend that I was Cinderella sorting through the peas. I nonetheless loved her very much – not for what we did together, for that wasn't much; our world played out in a hospital room – but for the feeling she gave me. Because she was so sick that each new day seemed to her like a miracle, she treated me as if I were one too. It was very different with my father back then. Not that he was cold or unapproachable. But there was something mechanical about him, which is probably quite normal if you've got to function all the time. And he did. He bore the responsibility for a terminally ill wife and a little child.

But then it was just the two of us. He told me stories from the other place Mum was now – happy and healthy – a wonderful garden beneath a permanently blue sky. I tried to imagine her going for walks there amongst knee-high flowers with blooms the size of cabbages, and her having long hair again, long blonde hair that glistened in the sun. I'd never seen her like that in real life; for me she was only ever ill and bedridden. All the same, I didn't cry for my mum. I didn't admit to myself that I missed her, or was angry because I felt betrayed by a version of her I'd never had the chance to meet. In fact, I showed no emotion at all, until the point came when I didn't feel anything either. Noticing that something wasn't right with me, my father got very worried. He took me off to child psychologists and bereavement experts, and kept asking me how I felt. He wanted to know everything in great detail, wanted me to describe at length what was happening inside me, every tiny nuance. But there wasn't anything. One day – it was summer and very hot – I fell off my bike on the gravel path behind our house. A large, sharp stone dug into my left wrist. Eva, who was there, immediately started screaming and ran off to get my dad. I just sat there, watching the blood run down my arm, marvelling at the pain I felt. After all those months I'd spent as if numbed, this was like a release. I didn't want it to subside, the pain. I wanted to scream and cry and explode with this feeling. I twisted the stone deeper into the wound. At that moment Eva came back with Dad . . .

'Are you out of your mind?' I jerk my hand away. 'My father almost lost it because he was worried his six-year-old was a suicide risk. It took him years to finally realise that it was just a stupid, one-off thing. Do you imagine he'd do something that reminded him of this? Of one of the most traumatic episodes in his life?'

'Those are your words,' Eva says, making a dismissive gesture. 'All I did was point out that your wrist was cut too, once.'

'But it wasn't my father who did that, it was me!'

Eva doesn't respond. Her mascara-smeared face makes me aggressive.

'Just say something!'

'Okay.'

'Okay?'

'I can see we're not going to get anywhere like this. So let's leave your dad out of it for the time being and take a neutral approach.'

'Meaning?'

'We'll start at the beginning. With serial killers, the first victim often plays a crucial role. Later, the choice of victim may be random, but the killer often has a close connection or even personal relationship to the first one.'

'You mean Larissa?'

Eva nods. 'What do we have on her?'

Together, we sift through the documents that are explicitly about Larissa. I want to divvy them up and get cracking, but Eva begs me to make her a coffee. The wine and all the emotion have made her quite woozy. When I come back from the kitchen, she's sitting on the floor, deep in piles of paper.

'Right, Larissa lived with her pregnant mother, one-year-old half-brother and her stepfather in a block of flats in Hellersdorf. As you know, she'd been missing for three months when her body was found by the Weihenpfuhl. Apart from size 42 footprints, there were no leads, so the official investigation was soon called off. But the stepfather believed he had a lead. He suspected a friend of the family . . .' She puts out her hand and wiggles her fingers. I don't understand what she's getting at to begin with, but then realise that I'm still holding her cup of coffee.

'Oh, sorry,' I say, giving it to her. 'What sort of friend?'

Eva takes a sip. And another. I'm getting nervous. I grab the top sheet of paper from the pile in her lap and skim the statement made by Larissa's stepfather. At a party a few months before Larissa disappeared, he caught the said friend sitting with Larissa on her bed and brushing her hair.

'A site manager by the name of Marcus Steinhausen,' I read out loud.

'Not so fast,' Eva says, putting her cup down and picking up another piece of paper. 'Although the stepfather voiced his suspicion to the police right after Larissa went missing, Steinhausen had a watertight alibi. When Larissa's body was found, the stepfather, who'd never stopped suspecting Steinhausen, went through the roof. He went to see Steinhausen and badly beat him up, which earned him his first spell inside. Two years later, he had another go at Steinhausen, fracturing his skull. When he recovered, Steinhausen moved away, but it's unclear where he went. At least there's no new address in the documentation.' She puts the piece of paper down and looks at me sympathetically – why, I don't understand.

'What we've got is a lead, Eva!'

'What? No! What we've got is a stepfather who became so obsessed by his hunch that he ended up in prison. Not to mention an innocent man who almost lost his life as a result.'

'You think this Steinhausen is innocent just because he was able to come up with an alibi? That sort of thing can be organised. We should talk to them.'

'To who?'

'Larissa Müller's family. There must be a reason why the stepfather is so—'

'Meller.'

'What?'

'You made a mistake. It's Meller, not Müller. But I don't think—'

'Meller,' I repeat. A name that sparks something in me. Just a hazy feeling, like a mist. When I check it in the documents, the mist is no more. It doesn't thin out, it doesn't lift gradually – it's gone in a flash, as if at the flick of a switch.

'My God!' I pant. 'I know her!'

US

You really must have liked that, my angel. Just look at your dress, it's got all dirty. You sweet, clumsy little thing! We're going to have to get you changed right away, but it doesn't matter. It's late anyway and time you were in your pyjamas. Come on, I'll carry you to the bathroom . . . You know, I've been thinking. It's Christmas, after all, and, well . . . you've every reason to be a bit disappointed. But something has occurred to me, the ultimate present for you, princess: a friend! How about that? Shall I get you a friend, a real, flesh-and-blood friend, just for you? I've even got an idea who it would be. Her name's Sarah. She's a bit older than you, but I think you'd get on famously. I've been watching her for quite a while, watching her very closely. Her expressions, my angel. I can read her face: she's longing for it too. Life isn't that great for her at home; her mother's a dragon who doesn't deserve such a charming, lovely daughter. And it's not fair on Sarah that she's not appreciated. Do you want her to visit us? Should I go and fetch her? Yes, I think I should. But not until tomorrow. It's too late today, we have to go to bed. Come on, my angel, off to bed. We'll snuggle up really close, just as you like it. I'll hold you as tightly as I can and cover your head with a thousand kisses until you've fallen asleep.

ANN

BERLIN, 26 DECEMBER 2017

'You knew Larissa?' Eva's eyes are wide open.

For now all I can manage is a vague movement of my head. The surname – I can't believe it. Ludwig mentioned it during our conversation in the prison and I remember being overcome by a feeling of unease. I thought this was because I was worried he might be in cahoots with the DPP. But maybe it was the name gnawing away at me. And then Eva read it from Larissa's photograph. So far I must have heard Meller at least twice without really registering it. Even though for the past few weeks I've seen the name on an almost daily basis, stitched on the chest pocket of a green polyester shirt. And Larissa's file confirms it.

'No,' I say. 'But I know her mother.'

'You know . . . ?'

I skim once more the information I find on Larissa's family. Her mother's first name: Michelle.

'It must be her, it all fits.'

My colleague Michelle, who told me on Christmas Eve that her grown-up daughter hasn't spent Christmas with her in ages. Michelle with an ex-husband who's twice been in prison for

GBH, and two sons who are now teenagers. Michelle who, as I may have suspected, sometimes laughs only to stop herself from crying. But I've always believed those tears were a result of the stress of being a single mother and the additional burden of the job. Now it dawns on me why she always wears so much make-up. Every morning she stands at the bathroom mirror, and paints on a mask, from behind which she feels able to face the world.

Eva's getting impatient; I fill her in.

'Wow!' she says, unable to say any more either.

I think out loud. I need to speak to Michelle if I want to find out what significance her daughter could have had for the killer. But there's a problem: she knows me by my dead mother's maiden name, as Ann de Groot, and thinks I'm a single mother too.

'Are you saying the woman doesn't have a clue who you really are?' The expression on Eva's face speaks volumes. As if she supects I might have deliberately applied to Big Murphy's to work side by side with the mother of one of the victims. She's wrong, but I don't want to waste any time explaining myself, having to justify myself over a coincidence.

'I have to call her and ask for a meeting!' I pick up my mobile and scroll through my phone book.

'You've got her number?'

'Of course. We're work colleagues, we need to be in touch about shifts.'

'You must be crazy!' Eva snatches my mobile away. 'The poor woman has no idea what's coming to her. You can't wake her up at one in the morning and out of the blue confront her with the worst nightmare of her life.'

Bloody hell, of course I can't. 'Okay, but tomorrow morning then.'

'There's no guarantee she'll want to talk to you, you'd better bear that in mind. Some people would rather block out things like that. Quite apart from the fact that you're the daughter of the main suspect.'

She's right. To make Michelle realise the urgency of my concern I'd have to take off my mask, regardless of the consequences. I don't care that it might lose me my job at Big Murphy's. But what if Michelle flips out, goes to the press and I end up being accused of harassing one of the victims' mothers? A headline like that definitely wouldn't help my father. My thoughts are interrupted by a gentle snapping: Eva deep in contemplation, nibbling at her thumbnail.

'I have to risk it, Eva. You'd understand if you'd seen him in prison. He's completely changed, so empty, so strange. As if part of him had died and been replaced by mechanical components.'

Eva slides over and embraces me for a long moment. Then she offers to come with me if Michelle does agree to a meeting.

'I'll think about it,' I say.

The rest of my night is sleepless. Eva's gone home and I can't think of anything else but my forthcoming conversation with Michelle. I fetch a knife from the kitchen, switch on the terrace light, put a chair beside the pot with the oleander and sit there, wrapped in a thick blanket, with all my thoughts and the miserable hours until morning before me. How do you speak to a grieving mother about the murder of her child? How do you ask her for help when you're the daughter of the main suspect?

I work out phrases, rework them, pondering individual words, searching for those that seem most sensitive: suitable packaging. Yet with each new attempt, I merely arrive at the same conclusion: in a situation like this, there's simply no way of approaching it delicately. I'm going to shock, horrify and agitate Michelle, no matter how carefully I try to formulate my sentences. The content always remains the same.

I begin to cry. The things I've got to deal with now. How dramatically my life has changed. On this very day last year there was a party in this house, an over-the-top cheesy Christmas party where everybody had to wear ugly festive jumpers and flashing plastic antlers on their heads. Everyone was there: Dad, Zoe and many, many others I'd regarded as friends or at least good acquaintances. I've often wondered why none of them has yet spoken to the press in return for a nice little remuneration. Now I think I know. It's the fear of what the whole affair might say about themselves. They've happily spent a lot of time with an alleged killer. They've enjoyed his company and drunk his wine, and if the accusations turned out to be true, they'd be complicit for having been so stupid and blind. This risk isn't worth a little remuneration. They're cowardly and fake, the lot of them. I ought to be grateful that this thing with my father has enabled me to see their true faces. I wipe away the pointless tears; everything can spur you on, even hatred.

Picking up my mobile, I open the browser and type the name 'Marcus Steinhausen' into the search engine. Nothing. How is that possible? If, as the files say, Steinhausen worked as a site manager, it must be possible to find a few of the projects he worked on. I try 'Steinhausen', 'Berlin' and 'construction' in all possible variations – still nothing. I'm frustrated. And tired. And maybe a bit paranoid, seeing as beside my chair a kitchen knife is close to hand, with a blade that must be twenty centimetres long. I almost wish that the man who tied the ribbon to the oleander would come back. Now, right now, on this night that feels as if it's never going to end. I'd have every right to defend myself and no scruples about doing so, the realisation of which horrifies me. But it's the truth. I shake my head. One year ago. It may have been phony, but it was fun. We laughed and danced and kept coming up with new excuses to gather under the mistletoe hanging from the chandelier in the hallway.

I close the search for Marcus Steinhausen and open my address book instead. Three hundred and sixteen contacts. The last number I saved is Jakob's. He gave it to me when we were sitting on the bench outside Big Murphy's and said I should ring it when I got the chance so he'd have my number too. He still doesn't have it. I go to my messages. The most recent is from Zoe, five weeks ago. *Please don't be angry with me.* I haven't replied, until now.

I miss you, despite everything, I write.

I miss you all.

Loneliness. (Ann, 8 years old)

Loneliness is not a nice feeling. I imagine it has a sharp knife and can cut you off from the rest of the world with just one cut. Then you float away out into the universe. Eva thinks its nice in the universe because of all the stars. But thats not true. Its just cold and black and you dont have any air to breath. Without air you will die so loneliness is a very dangerous feeling too.

'Hello?'

Michelle sounds sleepy, which isn't surprising as it's only just gone half past seven – and it's Boxing Day. I ask if I can come over; I really need to talk to her. She wants to know what it's about, but of course I can't tell her, or she might hang up. So I just stammer something about a supposed emergency and resort to saying 'please' as often as I can.

'To be honest, you're beginning to frighten me.' In her voice I can hear an anxious smile.

'No, no, that's the last thing . . . it's just . . . please, Michelle . . .'

'It's all right, calm down. I'm at home all day, you can come round whenever you like.'

I'm out of the house less than ten minutes later. Last night I wasn't sure whether I would actually take up Eva's offer to accompany me. Out of concern for my father, we'd patched things up for a few hours – a provisional stitch job. I've no idea how long it will last until it bursts open, nor what's beneath it. And yet now I'm at her door, ringing the bell. Maybe because loneliness is more painful than anything else.

It's Elke who opens the door, in a pink fleece dressing gown and with a pale, puffy face. She looks as if she's had little sleep, or even none like me. Eva appears briefly behind her mum's shoulder before I hear her clattering up the stairs, presumably to get dressed.

'Come in,' Elke says. 'We can have a nice leisurely breakfast together.'

Gratefully I decline, as ever. 'Eva and I have something planned.'

I evade her obtrusive attempt to find out more by stepping a few paces back and pretending to stretch my legs. But Elke stays in the doorway and watches me. It's very uncomfortable.

'Ready!' Eva calls, pushing past her mother.

'Would it be okay if we took your car?' Without waiting for an answer, I head straight for the passenger side of the Mini with its Frankfurt number plate. I haven't got behind the wheel of a car since I hit a deer two years ago. Sometimes I still dream of the huge, terrified eyes of the roe staring into my headlights, not to mention the plates and screws in my jaw. Eva knows nothing about this, but she doesn't ask any questions either, just takes the keys from her coat pocket to unlock the car.

'If I were her I would've moved away,' she says, putting the address Michelle gave me into her satnav. She still lives in Hellersdorf, in the small flat she shared with Larissa. 'I mean, I can understand it if your daughter's missing and you remain tied to a certain place by hope. But when you know for sure she's dead, and there'll never be a *one day*, when she's suddenly standing outside your front door . . . No, I couldn't hack that.'

'Because of all the memories, you mean?'

Eva concentrates as she reverses the Mini out of her parents' drive.

'Memories are only lovely when there's hope,' she says. 'After that they destroy you.'

We say nothing for a while until I find the silence uncomfortable.

'So, you're living in Frankfurt now?'

'How do you know that?'

'Your number plate.' I smile. She doesn't need to know that I often looked for her online, especially in the first few years after she left. Without success. No Eva Harbert on social media or on any company or college websites. She seemed to have vanished like a ghost and I couldn't even find out from her mother where she was. Although, till yesterday, I'd thought Elke didn't know herself and had only not said so because she was ashamed. What would people have thought of her? Similarly, I keep it to myself that I even tried talking to Nico. He took off with Eva and came back on his own a few months later, albeit only for a while. He told me to forget it. Eva didn't want any contact, and I felt as if I'd hit a sore spot. Maybe the rumours were indeed true that he'd got her pregnant and they'd eloped in a flight of romance, but soon realised that they weren't right for each other.

Eva nods. 'Of course. For a long time now – in fact, since the beginning. Nico's got relations in Frankfurt. We stayed with them for a few weeks after leaving Berlin.'

I flinch. Although I'd just been thinking about Nico myself, hearing Eva utter his name feels like a sting.

'Go ahead and ask me,' she says, after a quick glance in my direction. 'Ask me whatever you want.'

'None of my business.'

'But you're interested.' She laughs. 'We were together a long time, even if Nico popped back to Berlin for a spell. His father was undergoing chemotherapy and Nico had to help his mother with everything for a while. Then he returned to me in Frankfurt.'

'I see.' I swallow a stone. It's only small, like a pebble from the shore that the tide has smoothed down over the years, and yet I can feel it. I clear my throat. 'People were speculating you'd become pregnant.'

'So typical.' She laughs again. 'No, in truth I wasn't pregnant. Nico and I were very much in love and wanted to put all the crap here behind us. It lasted until a few months ago.'

'That *is* a long time.'

'Eight years.' For a while we fall silent again, then she asks, 'What about you? Anyone in your life?'

'Yes, but . . . this isn't probably the right time.'

'To be happy with another person, you first have to learn to come to terms with yourself.'

'Amen.'

'What else? When you told me yesterday about Michelle and the burger joint, you mentioned you were studying again.'

'Yes: German. Fourth semester. We'll see if and when I continue. Maybe I'll change uni or abandon it altogether. I don't know yet.'

'Fourth semester?'

I shrug. 'I took a break after the first two years to travel around France and then I changed subjects. It happens, doesn't it? Not every CV is without its gaps.'

'Yes.' Eva sounds pensive.

'What?'

'Talking of CVs without gaps, yesterday you worked out that there were years without any murders. What if that isn't the case? If the killer was active but the victims escaped before he could murder them?'

I shake my head. 'Well, they would have gone to the police, don't you think?'

'Adults, the parents might have gone to the police. But we're talking about children here, Ann! What if they didn't tell their parents anything because they didn't understand what had happened to them? If they thought it was something else or they were ashamed because they thought they themselves were to blame?'

'I don't know, Eva.'

'Why not? Do you think a child can't feel shame? Do you think a child wouldn't wonder what they might have done to deserve it, or whether they'd provoked someone?'

'Sure, it's possible, but ... I think it's more likely that the killer didn't keep going merely because he couldn't. If we get too complicated in our reasoning, we'll end up overlooking the simplest solution.'

Eva mutters. Neither of us say anything else until we park outside Michelle's house. 'Should I come in or wait out here for you?'

'Wait,' I decide. 'I don't know how Michelle will react if I turn up with someone else unannounced.' I get out. 'But thanks for your support, I'm really grateful,' I add before closing the passenger door.

I wander along the path to the door as if to the scaffold: with heavy steps, tense shoulders and bowed head. To my right is a playground covered in snow. Maybe Larissa used to play here. Scarcely has that thought crossed my mind than my imagination effaces the snow and a green meadow sprouts in its place. Larissa is dangling her legs from the swing and squinting into the sun, when, against the light, the dark silhouette of a man looms menacingly before her. I shake my head and the image dissolves. The playground is as it was: in the grey snow of the early morning and without Larissa.

When I get to the front door, I look for a bell beside the name Meller. There are twenty flats in this ugly, bright yellow block. I have to ring several times before I hear a buzz and push open the thick, streaky glass door. When I get to the seventh floor, Michelle is already standing in the doorway. She's made up as ever, but her dyed blonde hair hasn't been styled. She's wearing grey tracksuit bottoms and a light top with dots on it, which seems to be part of a pyjama set. I get the impression her tentative smile is wavering between uncertainty and a hunch.

'Come in,' she says, stepping aside. I thank her and take my boots off on the mat.

Even the hallway gets to me. The walls are hung with photographs, almost all of them showing Larissa in every stage of her life, from infancy to her school induction.

'I hardly took any photos of her in the last few years,' Michelle says, shutting the door to her flat. I turn around to her in shock.

'That's why you've come, isn't it? Because of Larissa?'

'I . . .'

'Only a couple of days ago there was this newspaper article, an interview with Saskia's dad. It said the alleged killer also has a daughter.'

Two days ago – now it flashes through my mind: *Continue reading on page 3*. An article I was so keen to avoid I demolished the newspaper dispenser instead. I give an indecisive shrug. There are lots of daughters in Berlin, hundreds of thousands of them.

'What's more, two days ago you signed your cash receipt at the end of your shift with "Lesniak" instead of "de Groot" like usual. You were so all over the place that day you didn't even notice, did you?'

I purse my lips and my heart begins to gallop. How could I have made such a stupid mistake? At least I've been saved the trouble of having to gently let Michelle know who I really am. But I'm even more ashamed. How must she have felt when she realised her work colleague had been deceiving her all these weeks?

'Do you know what comes up first when you search for "Lesniak" and "Berlin" on the internet?'

I nod apprehensively. My father – that's what you find. Walter Lesniak, a university professor, just like the alleged killer who's in custody. 'So you put two and two together.'

'I wasn't completely sure. But when you called this morning, so upset and so early, I knew, yes.'

'And even so, you're prepared to help me?'

'Looks like it. Come on.'

She takes me into her sitting room. It's small and untidy, and here too there are lots of photos on the walls. Only some of them show Michelle's sons: two boys, redheads like Larissa, looking grumpy. Michelle removes an overflowing washing basket from the sofa and invites me to sit down. She remains standing and looks down at me, her jaw muscles twitching.

'About four weeks ago I was told that Larissa's death was probably linked to the series of killings, and a few days ago this was confirmed as definite. I should be shocked, no? But I'm not. It's as if I suspected this long ago. Only I can't make out where you come into it. How's it possible that the daughter of my child's alleged killer gets a job in the very place where I work? I mean, it can hardly be a coincidence.'

Although I'm still wearing Dad's thick jacket, I suddenly feel cold. I can understand Michelle's mistrust and yet I don't have another explanation except for the fact that it's just that: a coincidence. A totally crazy, unbelievable coincidence of the sort that only fate can cook up when hatching plans for people. When two paths have to cross.

Set on being honest with her, I tell Michelle about the weeks since the arrest. That I didn't want to go to uni anymore because I was worried about the looks I'd get and the gossip. But that I couldn't sit around doing nothing at home, where my despair and memories were on the verge of driving me crazy. This was why I looked for an undertaking, something to attach me to the real world, to give me a reason to get up in the morning. An undertaking that I found in the job at Big Murphy's. I don't know if she believes me, but at least she doesn't immediately ask me to leave.

'I dream about it almost every night,' she says instead, wandering over to the window and peering out. 'I see my little girl running through the woods, desperately trying to escape her pursuer. She stumbles, trips and keeps hitting her shoulder because she can barely see anything in the dark. In her thoughts she's calling for her mummy, but I'm not there. She's all on her own. Eventually she gets so tired that she slumps to the ground behind a thick tree trunk. She makes herself as small as a mouse, just like when she used to play hide-and-seek here at home, always squeezing herself into the gap between the back of the sofa and the wall. She knows she has to be very quiet to not give herself away. Maybe he'll give up if he doesn't find her, or at least he'll go off in another direction. And in fact she *is* lucky: from somewhere in the distance comes a loud crack that catches his attention. He follows the noise and moves away from her. She gets to her feet and keeps running; she's so brave – Mummy's big brave girl. Then the miracle occurs: the woods end in a road. She's made it, she's escaped from him! And there's something else, two shining circles, getting bigger and bigger: a car. She sets off on a final sprint, flailing her arms about, her whole body screaming for attention. Sitting in that car is someone who can help her. Someone who'll take her back to her mummy. The driver stops the car right beside her. The door opens – but it's too late. It's him: the man who chased her through the woods. He drags her to the car and locks her in the boot, where it's cramped and stuffy, and just as black as it was in the woods. She feels they're driving on a bumpy road. She knows it leads back to the hut, where terrifying tools hang on the wall. Old screwdrivers, an axe with a rusty blade and a saw with sharp teeth. The car stops. When the man lifts her from the boot, her body is completely limp, abandoned by all hope, no fighting spirit left. She allows herself to be carried back to the hut. In her head she sings herself a lullaby. *Goodnight, Mummy. I love you anyway . . .'*

Michelle, who was standing at the window with her back to me, turns around so abruptly that I jump. Black trickles of mascara are running down her face; it's hard to look at. Feeling uneasy, I shift my position on the sofa Larissa used to love playing hide-and-seek behind, and try to find the right words. There was nothing in the forensics report to suggest that she did try to flee before her death and almost managed to escape the killer. But I can understand that it's painful for Michelle not to know how the abduction took place and what really happened while Larissa was at the mercy of her killer. All she's got is the outcome: her dead child, murdered by a stranger and left for months in a remote woodland hut until there was scarcely anything left of her apart from a rotting black body and her dishevelled red hair. I assume that Michelle's subconscious is trying to fill the gaps in knowledge in its own way, and making her suffer from the never-changing reality that, as a mother, she wasn't there when her daughter needed her most.

'I'm so dreadfully sorry, Michelle,' I say softly. It's stupid, banal and worthless – I realise that. But I can't think of anything better to say.

'It's not your fault,' she says, sounding composed again, and sits on the arm of the sofa at some distance from me. 'No child can be held responsible for what their parents do.'

'But that's precisely why I'm here, Michelle! It wasn't my dad! There's no proof, just a few tenuous leads, most of which are based on coincidence.'

'Nobody gets thrown in custody just because of a few coincidences. What kind of state would we be living in if that happened?'

'The problem is, he simply won't say anything, which the investigation team take as an admission of guilt.' Craving understanding, I look at her, but her eyes return to the window.

'After Larissa's death, everything fell apart. I was pregnant with Ben at the time and Toby had just turned one. I was good for nothing, I spent all day crying in bed. I couldn't even cook for Toby. Rainer, my ex, couldn't watch this happen. He was almost manic in his attempt to find out what had happened to Larissa, especially who did it to her.' She gives me a sympathetic smile. 'You remind me a bit of him.'

I ignore her comment, but it's good that she's the one to bring up the subject of her ex-husband. 'At the time he suspected a friend of yours: Marcus Steinhausen.'

Michelle nods. 'Marcus was an odd guy, highly educated, very polite and obliging, but . . . hmm.' She thinks for a moment, as if she doesn't know exactly where to begin. 'So, he was a site manager, in a completely different league from my ex, who was just a simple labourer. Despite this, he was crazy about Rainer, desperate to be friends with him. Rainer used to be very sociable and was always a happy soul. Marcus must have liked this and Rainer loved the attention. It wasn't long before he brought

Marcus home, and he was . . .' – she appears to be searching for the right words – 'so eerily perfect.' She nods in satisfaction. 'Yes, there's no other way to describe it. For each of us, he seemed to be exactly what we needed at any moment, able to switch roles at the press of a button. With Rainer, he drank beer and told dirty jokes, only to appear in the kitchen a few minutes later and lend a hand with the cooking. He helped Larissa with her homework or rocked Toby in his baby bouncer. In time, he started paying for stuff. To begin with, it was just bits of shopping, like when he'd noticed we were running out of milk or beer. Later he paid for Rainer's car to be repaired – actually Rainer borrowed the money from him, but Marcus refused to be paid back and got really angry when Rainer tried to do so.'

'Didn't you think it weird that a stranger suddenly muscled his way into your life?'

Michelle sighs. 'In retrospect, yes. But at the time . . . somehow we just got used to it; it became totally normal. Especially as we never had much money and were for ever having to budget. Marcus's contributions were very welcome indeed.' She looks at me. 'That sounds like he had to pay for our friendship. But it wasn't like that. We never made any demands or asked him for anything. He just did it as a matter of course, as if he really was a member of our family.'

'Didn't he have any family himself?'

Michelle bursts out laughing. 'Now we're getting to the nub of it. Marcus came round to ours almost every day after work, but he rarely stayed later than eight o'clock. You could set your watch by it, for at that time the calls would begin. We would hear him try to placate his wife, who clearly wanted him to come home.

He told us he was married and had a daughter too. But Rainer and I felt that things weren't great at home, at least as far as his marriage was concerned. Once when I talked to Marcus about the situation, he showed me a photograph of him with his family, looking very happy, which was at odds with the phone calls, and especially with the fact that he was always at ours rather than at home. But I didn't say anything, and Rainer thought it was just a male thing. Then came the evening when Marcus left punctually but forgot his mobile in our flat. Rainer decided to drive it over to his. He knew where Marcus lived because he'd dropped him off there once. A nice little house in Lichtenberg, a bit old-fashioned, with a garden complete with gnomes, that sort of thing. So Rainer went there, but rather than Marcus opening the door, it was a grumpy old woman. Marcus still lived with his mum, you see, and she kept him on a short leash. There was no wife and daughter. It was the mother who always rang when he was late. At that moment, Rainer lost all respect for Marcus, but I sort of felt sorry for him. He must have spent his whole life in his brother's shadow – at least that was the impression Rainer got from chatting to the mother. Every sentence she began with Marcus ended in a comparison with his brother, and Marcus never came off well. Sure, his brother had an even better job, his own house and a real family. But ultimately it was Marcus who gave up so much to look after their mother. I understood why he liked talking to people about a life he wasn't leading. I mean, imagine it. He'd even shown me a photo of what he claimed to be him and his family! As it turned out, the photo was actually of his brother with wife and child.' Michelle shakes her head. 'But I don't need to spell all of this out, do I? You ought to know what it's like when reality is so hard to bear that you begin inventing a different life for yourself.' Touché – I look at the floor. Luckily Michelle doesn't prolong this uncomfortable moment any longer, and continues, 'I felt sorry for him, yes, I felt really sorry for him. So I invited him to my birthday party, but that day something happened. Rainer caught Marcus brushing Larissa's hair on her bed. That was weird enough in itself! She was also telling him she was upset because yet another baby was on the way and she already got so little attention because of Toby. Marcus told her she didn't need to worry, he would look after her if necessary. Rainer blew his top. He threw Marcus out of the flat and forbade him from ever turning up here again.'

'And after that you didn't have any more contact with him?'

'Well . . . in the first couple of weeks after my party, we saw him a few times through the kitchen window,' Michelle says, pointing over her shoulder. 'He was hanging around outside and occasionally he'd leave chocolates or flowers at the door.' She shakes her head. 'That stopped a good while before Larissa went missing. But Rainer was obsessed by the idea that Marcus could have something to do with her death. When, in 2005, the body of another small girl was found – as it happened, on a construction site where Rainer and Marcus had worked together a few years earlier – that was that, as far as my husband was concerned. It couldn't be a coincidence.'

'But you thought it could?' I ask doubtfully, and the only answer I get is a scornful look. I suppose only ten minutes ago I was the one trying to convince Michelle of another crazy coincidence. 'I'm only saying because—'

'It's all right,' she interrupts me. 'Of course I thought it was strange to begin with. But Marcus had a watertight alibi for this too. Rainer's refusal to believe it saw him end up in prison for GBH. Which left me sitting there with two small children – and without my Larissa.' An awkward smile darts across her face. 'You know, I wasn't a particularly good mum to her. And not just because I let her get abducted and killed.' Again she points over her shoulder, towards the hallway. 'The last photo I took of her was on her first day at school, more than three years before her death. But I just took it for granted that she was there, and then I met Rainer and, well, you know. It was wonderful to be newly in love again, after Larissa's father had dumped me soon after she was born. With Rainer I had the chance to start from scratch again. We got married quickly.' Another brief smile, then she looks bitter. 'I had to get the photo the police used for their search from my parents. Can you believe that? What sort of a mother am I who has to phone around when she's asked for an up-to-date picture of her daughter? But you wouldn't know about that.'

'No,' I say quietly.

'No,' Michelle echoes. 'You know nothing about motherhood, nothing at all. He slit her wrist. But because she was the first and there were so few clues pointing towards a violent crime, for a long time the police entertained the theory that she might have done it herself. How bad must a ten-year-old's home life be if she commits suicide? That's the sort of question they ask you, and they treat you like a monster. They even look into whether the other two children are okay and whether they might not be better off in a foster family.'

'I can understand you're angry, Michelle.'

'No, after fourteen years, I'm not angry anymore. I'm just tired, in every respect. I always thought I'd want to look the killer in the eye and ask him why he took my girl. Now that I know Larissa was only one of many, just a child who happened to be in the wrong place at the wrong time, I realise I wouldn't get a satisfactory answer. They should put him away for the rest of his life so that more children don't die, nor their families in a different way.' She gives me a searching look. 'But it makes no difference if I tell you this or not. You can't understand it because you're not a mother. You only said you were one to get a job at Big Murphy's and wangle sympathy from your colleagues.'

I nod, embarrassed. Michelle's probably had enough of me being here so I've got to get more information out of her as quickly as possible. 'Do you think I could have a word with your ex-husband?'

'Rainer?' The noise she makes is something in between amusement and resignation. 'He's been drinking himself stupid these last few years. Every time the boys come back from him unscathed, I'm delighted. I'd happily give you his address. But I doubt you'll hear more from him than his absurd conspiracy theories about how sloppy the police were.' Getting up from the arm of the sofa, she goes over to a chest of drawers and takes out a notepad and pen.

'What about Marcus Steinhausen? The police file says he moved away, but doesn't give his new address.'

'No idea.' Michelle laughs. 'But I bet Rainer's got a few theories about that too.' She turns around and holds out a piece of paper with her ex-husband's address. But when I try to take it she doesn't let go. 'I don't want to condemn your father before he's found guilty, Ann. But if it was him who did it, he can only hope he's locked away for the rest of his life.'

Is that supposed to be a threat? I open my mouth, but don't have the courage to ask.

Then Michelle does let go and immediately gives me a hug.

'Be careful, girl,' she whispers in my ear. 'It's a dangerous world out there.'

US

Good morning, princess! Did you sleep well? I've been up a long time – I was tormented by a bad dream. I was running through the woods, looking for you everywhere. I was calling your name, so distraught that my voice cracked and tears were streaming down my face. I knew you just wanted to play hide-and-seek, but I couldn't find you until I came to a clearing. People were there, walkers and a hunter with a shotgun. They stood, heads bowed, in a circle around something. Around *somebody*. I knew at once that something bad must have happened, something to do with me. I pushed my way through the people and saw you there, lying on your back, arms outstretched like wings, your palms facing upwards. Your body was untouched and as beautiful as ever, but your eyes, princess. Your eyes were two black holes with worms crawling out of them. I sank to my knees. My tears ran and I touched my face. But they weren't tears, they were worms, like the ones on your face. I opened my mouth to scream, but no sound came out, only black butterflies. At this point I woke up. What was that, princess? A dark premonition? A warning? I realise more clearly now that we have to safeguard our happiness. I'm not going to let anything bad happen to you, do you hear me? Nobody's ever going to separate us again. Here, my sweetheart, take Cosmo and your fairy-tale book with the pretty pictures. That'll keep you occupied till I'm back. We'll do what we usually do when I leave the house: we'll lock you securely in your room and I'll take the key with me. It's better that way, sweetheart, you know that. We'll lock you away like valuable treasure in the safe. And you've got to be a very good girl, okay? I can't say how long I'll be. Or even if it'll work tonight. It's still Christmas, after all, when people stay at home playing families. Even those that aren't really proper families. Oh, they make me sick, I hate them so much! I'd rather not think about it as it only makes me furious. Can I have a cuddle? Yes, that's good – you see, I'm calming down already, I'm already feeling better. And maybe we'll be lucky, maybe it *will* work today. If it does, that's your Christmas present from me: your new best friend Sarah. Isn't it exciting? I just hope she's as well behaved as you when I get her. Just imagine if she started screaming and kicking because she wasn't so quick to understand how lucky she was. Yes, that would be a real shame, especially for her.

ANN

BERLIN, 26 DECEMBER 2017

We're on our way to Rainer Meller's place in Marzahn. Outside, the Landsberger Chaussee flies past, almost entirely swallowed up this morning by the grey fumes from laundry extractors. It's hard to identify the street signs, tower blocks and trees on either side of the road, and it's only possible at all if you're familiar with the area. It seems almost symbolic. Like my father's innocence, shrouded by a thick fog of prejudice, police ignorance and his own silence. But I know these streets and, more importantly, I know you, Dad. I know that the truth lies behind the fog.

'Marcus Steinhausen told Larissa he'd look after her.'

Eva sighs. 'My God, sounds like a total loser with an excessive longing for family.'

'Or a deranged paedophile!'

'The children weren't sexually abused.'

'That doesn't mean he didn't intend to when he kidnapped them!'

'Are you saying he then backs down because he thinks sexual abuse is a step too far? But murder isn't?'

I shake my head. 'Oh, I don't know. Let's just have a chat with Rainer Meller. Maybe we'll be wiser after that.'

'In three hundred metres you will have reached your destination,' the satnav announces, at which Eva slows down and searches for a parking space. I examine her profile. She looks like her mother, a slimmer, almost bony Elke Harbert, without pink blouse and pearl necklace, but with a paler complexion, hair dyed dark, and chewed fingernails. I wonder what it must be like to take after someone you despise. When every morning you see that person in your own reflection. And I think this is the case. If Eva wasn't pregnant and so didn't leave home for fear of her parents' reaction, it must have been Elke who drove her away. Elke and her obsession with cleanliness, her high demands, her plumped-up sofa cushions, her entire being which is nothing but a façade. I recall Eva once being grounded when we were in the sixth class because Elke thought she hadn't revised enough for an English test. Grounded for a whole week because she got a C. I rarely came home with better marks than this at the time, and my father would merely shrug.

'All school does is teach you to learn things by heart,' he said. 'What really counts is that you learn to think independently, to feel, to question things. Only then can you understand the world.'

I miss him so much.

'Can I ask you something, Eva?'

'Sure.'

'Why did you come back? Now, after so much time, to your . . .' I break off, out of politeness.

'. . . parents, who you basically can't stand?' Eva finishes my sentence, laughs, then at once turns serious again. 'Apart from the fact that I'd read about your father's arrest in the paper, it would've been the first Christmas I'd have spent alone, after splitting up with Nico. The idea of it sort of gave me the creeps. It's . . . you know, I haven't been feeling great these past few weeks. I have bad dreams, I'm permanently tense and nervous, I just can't relax anymore. I keep wondering whether it was right to have run off like that. Whether the path that seemed easier at the time turned out to be the harder one in the end.' She turns to me and looks sad. 'As for my parents, well, parents always try to do their best, but the best isn't always good.'

I nod; I feel sorry for Eva.

'How about you come along this time and we talk to Michelle's ex-husband together? It'll be like the old days. You and me . . .'

'The best team,' she says, finishing my sentence and smiling. 'Why not?'

Apart from the colour – a dirty green – Rainer Meller's block is scarcely different from the building in Hellersdorf where he used to live with Michelle. An ugly box offering no more than functional living space. Here there's no playground, but a larger car park with tyre tracks snaking through the slush. For a public holiday it looks shockingly empty. This confirms my theory that people might live here, but they're never really at home. After ringing several times without any luck, we're about to turn back when a window opens on the third floor.

'What?' a man bleats down at us. It must be Rainer Meller, who even at a distance seems quite a bit older than Michelle. Either he *is* older, or he looks worn out from the worry of the past few years.

'Hello,' I reply, waving. 'Herr Meller? We've come from your ex-wife and we urgently need to talk to you. About' – I lower my voice because I think it's inappropriate to shout her name out here – 'Larissa.' For a second or two his expression freezes, then he slams the window. Defeated, I look at Eva, who raises her eyebrows and turns around when we hear a buzz: Rainer Meller has opened the door.

'Are you from the youth welfare office?' he asks as soon as we've got to the third floor.

'No,' I say, surprised.

'Police? Press?' Clamped between his fingers is a cigarette he must have just lit.

I shake my head and am about to explain, but Eva gets there first: 'We're private investigators and we've got a few questions.' I don't know what to make of this lie at first, especially as it seems so ridiculous and blatant. But then I see the enthusiasm in Meller's eyes and suspect that Eva has hit the right nerve to stir his readiness to talk.

'I knew it! Come in, come in,' he says excitedly, stepping aside for us.

Apart from the fact that the flat is very smoky, it's almost excessively tidy. The shoes form a guard of honour in the hallway, the coats hang from hooks at absurdly regular intervals and the lino, although it squeaks with every step, is shiny and neutralises the stale smoke with a strong smell of beeswax. Meller has a grey crew cut and an olive-green shirt with a stiff collar, which makes him look more like an army general reject than a construction worker. As we go down the hallway, we pass an open door giving on to a children's room. Michelle and Rainer Meller's two sons are sitting at a computer with their backs to us; I hear shooting and swearing. Their father shuts the door and shows us into the sitting room.

I'm dumbstruck. The furniture – sofa, coffee table and sideboard with a television on it – has all been pushed into a tiny corner, while the rest of the room is set out like a private detective's office from a cheap TV series. A computer monitor sits on a huge desk, beside it an opened bottle of schnapps. Stuck to the wall behind are countless newspaper articles and printouts of photos, some already slightly faded, as well as a spider's web of connections made from woollen threads, which at first glance look unfathomable.

'Shit,' Eva mutters quietly.

I nod.

The photos are blurry, but they all seem to be of the same man from a distance in a variety of situations: getting out of a car, entering a house, mowing the lawn, pushing an old lady's wheelchair, standing by a grave with his head bowed.

Meller doesn't bother with any preamble. 'Marcus Steinhausen, born 16 August 1971 in Beelitz.' He smiles, revealing teeth yellowed from nicotine. 'I knew one day someone would come help me convict him. I've tons of material about this wanker,' he says, making an extravagant gesture at the wall. 'And I also realised you wouldn't come until most of the donkey work was done. That's just what you cops are like, isn't it? You keep your arses stuck to your office chairs for as long as you can, but the moment things start moving, you can't wait to get in on the act. Just like the fucking papers. How often have I called up editors to tell them my latest discoveries? Either I'm told they'll only work with reliable information from the police, or they keep me hanging on until the line eventually goes dead.' He takes a nervous drag on his cigarette, then emits the smoke with a hoarse laugh. '*Reliable information!* All they care about is interviewing Saskia's dad! These days that bloke can turn on the waterworks at will!' Meller shakes his head in resignation, then his face at once brightens. 'But I knew it!'

Eva and I exchange uncertain glances. We're still flabbergasted by the set-up of this ludicrous detective agency and Meller's chutzpa. Eva's the first to snap out of it.

'What did you know?' she asks Meller, who's looking at us expectantly.

'Well, that poor bloke you've been dragging though the media these last few weeks is nothing but a fall guy, because you had to come up with someone to keep the public happy! But it wasn't him. No, it wasn't him and I knew that at once. One of those university eggheads! I've worked for blokes like that plenty of times. They can't even tie their own fucking shoelaces without looking at a book to see how it's done! And he's supposed to be a killer? Bollocks!' Now Meller shakes his head so vigorously that his whole body starts moving and the ash from his cigarette crumbles to the floor. He leaves the room as if slightly drunk, only to return immediately with a dustpan and brush.

Eva looks away when he bends down to clear up the ash, as if it's something very intimate she doesn't want to intrude on. 'But, as I'm sure you also discovered, there *are* leads that point to this man.'

'You call a few little coincidences leads?' Meller stands back up and with his foot clatters the dustpan and brush to one side, a noise that makes Eva spin around and grab my arm. The broad-chested

Meller towers before us, menacingly pointing his index finger. 'Look, what I showed you about Marcus Steinhausen – now *those* are leads! For fuck's sake, do you win your police badges in a lottery? How come your shitty outfit only seems to employ useless fuckers?'

'Once again, we're not from the police, we're private investigators,' Eva says firmly.

Meller looks at us as if this is the first time he's heard it.

'Who are you working for?' he asks, with narrowed eyes.

'I'm afraid we can't tell you that,' I chime in circumspectly. 'But you can be sure we're keen to find out the truth. Just like you.'

Meller holds up his thumb and forefinger, barely half a centimetre apart. 'I'm that close,' he growls, nodding to reinforce his claim. Then he goes over to the desk, unscrews the top from the schnapps bottle and takes a sip.

I look at Eva, who suggestively raises an eyebrow and nods at the sitting-room door. But I don't want to go. As strange as Meller is, I'm thrilled to have finally come across someone who shares my belief that Dad is innocent.

'That would mean that Marcus Steinhausen has given the police a number of false alibis,' I tell him.

'Couldn't be more false!' Meller says, wiping his mouth and putting the bottle back on the desk. 'Those so-called friends who've given him alibis – he's bribed them! I'm one hundred per cent certain of it! You see, one of the boys worked with us on the site. He was never friends with Marcus, he just kept borrowing money off him. Marcus had no friends apart from me!' He pounds his fist on his chest. 'I was his only friend! And how did he thank me?'

'Did you tell the police that he might have bribed the witnesses?'

'Of course! They questioned the guys on site too, but the wanker denied it all.'

Eva opens her mouth, but I get in first. 'Do you have an idea where we could find Marcus Steinhausen?'

Meller comes over to us. His face is contorted into a peculiar grin that makes me shudder. 'I told you I've already done most of the donkey work.'

RECORDING 02

Berlin, 7 May 2021

– I'd like to talk about Larissa Meller.

– Why her in particular?

– For two reasons. First, I met her mother, and so it feels – how should I put it? – personal. And then Larissa was the first. It's said that the first victim plays a special role for the killer.

– Is that so?

– It's proven, yes.

– *(grins)* What other clichés have you got up your sleeve? The killer who had a difficult childhood, a strict father or no father at all, an indifferent mother or a controlling one, and who started torturing small animals at primary school? A loner, always a bit odd, who later had problems with women. None would let him near them, but little girls couldn't defend themselves, he was able to dominate them.

– But that's often the case.

– *(laughs)* Tell me about your childhood.

– My . . . ?

– Why not? It doesn't look like we need to bother with my story. You seem to know it all already.

– No, I've just . . . I've looked into the topic and read up on it.

– I'm not a topic, I'm a human being, just like you.

– With respect, you can't compare us. It's never crossed my mind to abduct little girls, slit their wrists and watch them bleed to death.

– Have you read up on this too? What do you say to a bit of biology? The human body contains between three and seven litres of blood. If a person loses more than one and a half litres, they become weak, thirsty and start to freeze. At this point the loss of blood must be stopped or the brain won't get enough oxygen and the person will lose consciousness. Death occurs shortly afterwards. When exactly depends on how big the injured vessel is . . .

– I don't think I want to hear this.

– If the aorta is damaged, for example, it's often only a matter of seconds. It's more interesting when veins or smaller arteries are damaged. Then it can take hours.

– (clears the throat) Back to Larissa.

– Two hours and thirteen minutes.

– Jesus, I didn't mean that.

– I got used to timing it, you see? Some girls, even though they were younger, smaller or more delicate, took longer to die. This must have partly been down to the fact that the cuts I made were always slightly different. I mean, I'm no surgeon and I didn't have a scalpel either. All the same, an artery's an artery, you'd think. Anyway, I came to the conclusion that dying isn't just a physical process. Of course, when the body's started

109

dying, you can't stop it. But I often got the impression that internal resistance was definitely able to prolong the whole thing.

– And the sight of this – a defenceless girl struggling against death, all that blood – excited you?

– Excited? Good God, I beg you. I don't like the term, it always has a sexual connotation. And it's empty too, so empty that it doesn't even begin to express what I felt.

– What did you feel?

– Everything.

ANN

BERLIN, 26 DECEMBER 2017

That he's already done the donkey work.

What does that mean?

He couldn't tell us, he had to show us.

Okay.

We left the flat in Marzahn together with Rainer Meller. Beforehand, he told his two sons he had to go out for a while, and promised them pizza for lunch.

On the way to the stairs we don't speak. Meller's in front; behind him Eva and I go down side by side. I try to catch her eye a few times, but in vain. She looks withdrawn; perhaps like me she's pondering what Meller has said. That he's already done the donkey work. Surely all it means is that he's tracked down Steinhausen – address unknown – off his own bat. I know this, it's obvious. And yet I have to be careful not to form a picture in my mind showing Meller at night with a shovel, at his feet a hand sticking out of the dug earth begging for help and mercy. I know it's absurd and that I ought to be happy to have an important lead thanks to Meller. Marcus Steinhausen, the oddball who pretended to his closest friends that he had a wife and daughter, even though he still lived at home with his mother. Who bought himself alibis for good reason. Assuming, of course, what Meller told us is correct. Well, we're about to find out, and the mere thought of that makes me feel what could almost be described as elated. I still can't quite comprehend what lies ahead of us, but I sense we're on the right track. We follow Meller across the car park to his grey Volvo, a classic family car.

'In you get,' he says after unlocking the vehicle, and I'm just about to pull the handle of the passenger door when I feel Eva's hand on my arm.

'We'll follow you in our car, Herr Meller,' she asserts, pulling me along with her.

'Have you gone mad?' is the first thing I hear her say when we're in her Mini and she starts the engine. 'Were you seriously going to ride with that nutter?' The car sounds disgruntled when she brusquely puts it into reverse.

'It doesn't matter how we get to Steinhausen. The main thing is that we get there at all.'

'You're wrong, it does matter! Meller is a very sick man.' She guides the Mini to the car park exit behind Meller's Volvo and indicates. Right, although I only notice this when she turns the steering wheel to the right too.

'What are you doing?' I thrust my hands to the side, ready to steer the other way. Meller's Volvo turned left. Eva brakes so abruptly that the seat belt cuts through my thick jacket and into my chest. Deeply shocked, I let go of the wheel and point at the Volvo that stops by the side of the road a fair distance away. Meller must have seen in his mirror that we'd stopped. 'Drive! He's waiting!'

Eva shakes her head. 'No way are we wasting any more of our time with this guy. I could smell the booze on his breath when we arrived.'

I roll my eyes. 'For God's sake . . .'

'Come off it, how can you not see what his problem is? It's so obvious.'

'He wants to find out the truth, just like us! Honestly, Eva, what's wrong with you? We've finally got a lead and you want to pull out?'

'No, Ann, what the hell is wrong with *you*? What was it you told me about those photos at Michelle's? That she didn't take another one of her daughter after her school induction and had to ask her parents so she could give an up-to-date picture to the police? Do you want to know how I interpret that? I'll tell you. The moment Meller entered Michelle's life, Larissa was completely ignored. It's irrelevant that he adopted her after the wedding – she never got anything out of him except for his surname. Michelle and he had their fresh start as a couple, had their own child, the next was already on its way, and Larissa was merely a millstone around their necks. But then she was murdered and the two developed their own mechanisms for coping with their feelings of guilt. Michelle tries to function while Meller gets bogged down in completely fanciful theories . . . I mean, you were in that sitting room too! You saw the pinboard with the newspaper cuttings and that crazy web of woollen threads! And all the photos of Steinhausen! He's persecuted him!'

'And yet with all of this, he's got further than the police. He found out that Steinhausen had no alibi, but he did have a motive. Think about—'

'No, that's precisely it!' she interrupts me. 'He *thinks* he's found out that Steinhausen didn't have an alibi. Do you really believe the police wouldn't have checked it out in such a serious case? Meller's a serious alcoholic who suffers from delusions!'

'For a man who's so disturbed, it's astonishing how well he keeps on top of his flat, don't you think? Everything is clean and tidy, suggesting someone who's still got a hold on reality.'

'This outward obsession with order can also be an unconscious counter-mechanism.'

I burst out laughing. 'What are you now, a fricking psychologist?'

'Yes, Ann, that's exactly what I am!' Incensed, she slams the palm of her hand on the wheel, catching the horn. 'I spent eleven fricking semesters studying psychology! I did my fricking master's, and for the past few months, I've been working in the fricking psychological counselling centre for victims of crime and their relatives at Frankfurt University Hospital! I know people like Rainer Meller! I work with them on a daily basis! They look for their own ways to deal with the pain and feelings of guilt, and do you know what? Sometimes these ways lead them straight into the psychiatric clinic.'

I'm silenced. I stare at her, stunned. And somehow time stands still. It's as if Eva had punched me in the face without warning. This pale, thin girl with the chewed fingernails is apparently an expert, way ahead of me, still floundering in my fourth semester. In her analysis of the situation, in her knowledge – which with a CV like hers must be well-grounded – in everything, in fact. I feel small and betrayed once more. Time is moving again, trickling away in an embarrassing silence.

'Let's not argue,' Eva says eventually, her tone gentle. Then she gives a start and a curt scream. I flinch too. Rainer Meller is standing by the passenger door, peering in at us.

'Everything all right?' he asks, his voice muffled by the closed window.

We nod in sync.

'Let's be off, then!' he says impatiently. 'What are we still waiting for?'

Marcus Steinhausen is a gaunt type. Very different from the photos in Meller's sitting room, in which he looks healthy and well groomed. He has greasy, ash-blond hair that hangs in thin strands down to his chin. Hollow cheeks, pimply skin. Most striking of all are those dark, almost black, penetrating eyes. He's living back in the house in Lichtenberg he used to share with his mother. She's not there; she must be in a care home or dead. He doesn't seem happy to see us or Meller at his door, but he lets us in all the same. Eva and me, at least. He tells our escort, who's almost beaten him to death twice, to get lost. Meller's about to make a fuss, but Eva manages to calm him down. Of course she does, she's a psychologist, after all, and knows how to deal with relatives who are practically mad with rage and pain.

Now the two of us are in the sitting room, on armchairs upholstered in reddish-brown velvet, with crocheted cushions as headrests. More cushions on the tiled coffee table. The air is dusty and stale; it smells of an inability to shake off the past in the wake of a serious problem. Although his mother is no longer around, it seems as if Steinhausen doesn't dare change even the smallest thing here. We hear him clattering crockery in the kitchen. After inviting us to take a seat, he said he was going to make coffee.

Heavy, ruched curtains with a flowery pattern hang in front of the windows. They could be grey, beige or merely yellowed; it's impossible to tell because they're drawn and make the room so dark that, without the light from an ornate brass lamp on a small table, we wouldn't be able to see anything at all. After my eyes have become accustomed to the dimness, I allow my gaze to wander. It alights on a piano. I imagine Steinhausen taking lessons as a child, and his mother rapping him on the knuckles whenever he played a wrong note while practising. On top of the piano are photographs.

'Ann,' Eva hisses when I get up to take a closer look. 'Don't! He'll be back in a sec and think we're snooping around!' But that's exactly what we're doing, that's why we're here – so I ignore her warning.

The photos.

Two toddlers, on either side of their mother, holding her hand. One is Marcus Steinhausen, the other must be his brother. Michelle was right: they really do look similar. It's winter; they're wearing thick clothes and staring into the camera with serious, deadpan faces. The next photo is of the mother sitting stiffly in one of the armchairs, the headrest framing her head like a halo. Marcus and his brother, now teenagers, are on the armrests, again wearing those serious, careworn expressions that look as if they'd never experienced the slightest moment of joy or happiness. Another portrait of Frau Steinhausen on her own, sepia-toned and as if from a different time. And then another family photo, this time of the Mellers. Michelle and Larissa as I know them, but Rainer Meller's face has Steinhausen's stuck over it.

'Oh Jesus!' I splutter, and that's all I say because the pattern repeats itself: the next photo is of Larissa in the arms of a man whose face has also been replaced by Marcus Steinhausen's.

'Get away from there!' Eva sounds anxious. Without saying a word or turning around, I wave behind my back to get her to come over to the piano.

Now a photo of Larissa on her own. It looks like she's on holiday; she's wearing a bathing costume and holding an ice cream.

'Eva, you've really got to—'

A cough. A cough and someone's breath on the back of my neck. I recoil and spin around.

Right beside me is a grinning Steinhausen. 'Well, Ann. Find what you were looking for?'

I instinctively throw my hands up in defence.

Resounding laughter rains down on me, big hailstones of cold, biting sounds. 'You must know that old proverb? Curiosity killed the cat?'

I recoil again. 'What?'

'I asked if you knew the proverb.' Eva glances to the side. 'Curiosity killed the cat. It's what my grandma always used to say.' Feeling palpitations, I put a hand to my chest. No, we're not in Marcus Steinhausen's sitting room, we're still following Rainer Meller's Volvo. Although the journey did go via Lichtenberg, where Steinhausen used to live with his mother, we're now more than twenty kilometres away, and with every kilometre, I realise the horrific vision I've just fallen into is only getting crazier.

'All I'm saying,' Eva continues – she hasn't realised my imagination's been playing games with me – 'is that I've experienced this myself. Sometimes it's not a good idea to dig too deeply. It can change your entire life.'

I can't help laughing. 'I thought you were a psychologist? Isn't your entire profession all about digging as deep as you can?'

'Yes, but afterwards it's also our job to teach people how to deal with what they've found.'

'Really, Eva, I don't understand you. You stay up half the night with me, supposedly because you're as keen as I am on finding out the truth. But the moment things get serious and we actually have a lead, you suddenly start getting obstructive. What's that all about? What was yesterday for you? Just a game, like when we were kids and used to play detectives, following some mysterious animal tracks on the edge of the woods? Just a game to escape the boredom of your family dinner?'

Eva shakes her head and briefly takes a hand off the wheel to point at Meller's Volvo, which right now is taking the turn to Henningsdorf. 'We're going too far here. God knows where he's taking us.'

'You can offer to give him therapy when you get the chance. But before that let's see what he wants to show us.'

'A building site?' Stupidly, Eva blinks a few times, as if there were a chance her eyes were playing tricks on her. 'What on earth are we doing here?'

'That's what we're about to find out,' I say, annoyed. I unclick my belt before she parks the Mini beside Meller's Volvo at a construction fence, which separates the huge site on the southern fringes of Henningsdorf from the access road.

'Ann, please . . .' It sounds like she's imploring me, but I'm already out of the car. Behind the fence is a space, covered in snow, that ends in a huge crater. Around it are a handful of weather-beaten construction trailers, and behind them, the half-built shell of a tower block. I can't see a crane or any other construction machinery, but the walls of the shell are already covered in plenty of graffiti, some of which has already faded. Work seems to have stopped on this building site some time ago. Kati comes to mind. The nine-year-old girl whose body was found in a place just like this back in 2005. What was it Michelle said? *When, in 2005, the body of another small girl was found – as it happened, on a construction site where Rainer and Marcus had worked together a few years earlier – that was that, as far my husband was concerned. It couldn't be a coincidence.*

It couldn't be a coincidence echoes around my head.

Meller has come up to me. He's holding a torch. 'In 2000 they built a trading estate in the north of the city, but soon after the construction work began, it proved to be too small.' He nods at the huge area of wasteland, even more desolate beneath its covering of snow. 'Everything here was supposed to be bigger, more modern, but scarcely had we got going than we ran into problems with environmental protection. Apparently it's a nesting area for red kites, which was never on anyone's radar before . . . What's happened to your colleague?'

I follow his eyes to Eva's Mini. She's still sitting in the driver's seat. 'Hang on a sec.'

A moment later I'm knocking on the side window, while silently mouthing, 'Come on!' Eventually she gets out.

'I think this is the building site where Kati's body was found,' I whisper to her as we follow Meller, a few metres behind him. 'He hasn't said as such, but it would fit.'

'And what are we actually doing here?' Eva whispers back. 'Did he give you any idea when you were chatting just now?'

119

'No, but think about it. If this really is the building site in question, then perhaps Meller has belatedly discovered something else here to link Steinhausen to Kati's murder.' Although I'd been assuming that Meller would take us to Steinhausen, I'm happy to go along with this scenario if it helps exonerate my father.

'Mind how you go!' Meller calls out over his shoulder. 'There's all sorts of building rubble and metal bars lying around here that you can't always see because of the snow.'

I raise my hand to signal we understand.

'Where the hell is he taking us?' Eva whispers, but I can't answer that either.

Until we get to the shell.

Until, under Meller's supervision, we've squeezed through a makeshift entrance hung with a stubborn tarpaulin and made our way down what seems like endless corridors into the underground part of the building. Until we've arrived at a basement room sectioned off by another tarpaulin and also blocked by an upright old mattress. Until we enter the room and Meller waves around the torch he switched on to make it easier for us to find our way in the darkness down here.

Now we're hit by the realisation of where Meller has brought us: to the place he's keeping captive the man he believes killed his stepdaughter. To Marcus Steinhausen, who's sitting on a chair in the middle of the room. His hands are behind his back, probably tied to the chair, and his ankles secured to the legs. Marcus Steinhausen with a bloody gag in his mouth. The left-hand side of his face bruised and swollen around the eye. A scabbed-over cut on his forehead and brown stains on the inner thighs of his jeans. All of this makes it obvious that he must have been down here at Meller's mercy for a fair while. He lifts his head feebly and blinks lethargically with his sunken eye into the torch beam.

Eva clutches my arm. I look at her, she looks back, her eyes wide in horror and her mouth agape, speechless. I freeze – my heart has stopped beating and I'm no longer breathing. This can't be true, it's fake. Reality has been ruptured and I'm just having a bad dream, like I did in the car earlier.

Light!

We jump when the room is abruptly flooded with brightness. Meller has switched on a construction lamp that hangs by a long cable from one of the metal ceiling girders. As it swings it makes a freaky interplay between light and shadows. Rumbling and buzzing at the back of the room, a box has come to life. It looks like an outsized chainsaw, only without the blade – a generator, I assume. To our left another chair is against the wall, an empty half-litre bottle of cola on the seat and a pizza box on the floor beside it. I try to picture Meller sitting on this chair opposite Steinhausen, enjoying his pizza in front of a man who's been going mad with hunger and thirst down here for God knows how long. But I can't. Not even my imagination, which effortlessly concocted the horror story of the doctored family photos for our meeting with Steinhausen, is capable of that.

'Right then, ladies.' Meller's voice drones over the hum of the generator. 'Let's get this fucker to talk.' He checks the pockets of his anorak in turn, but evidently doesn't find what he's looking for. 'Shit. I'll be right back.' Before we can react, he's left the room.

Steinhausen is writhing in his chair. Although the sounds he's making are muffled by the gag, he's clearly panicking. It seems as if he knows the fate that's awaiting him. Eva comes to her senses first. Letting go of my arm, she hurries over to Steinhausen. It's only when I realise she's trying to untie his hands that I shudder and follow her to have a go at the cable ties binding his ankles to the legs of the chair. My fingers are sweaty and shaky, and the acrid smell of all the excretions that have collected in his trousers makes me turn away briefly every few moments. The teeth of the cable ties are still not budging.

'I can't do it, Eva! I can't get him free!'

'You have to, for fuck's sake.' I don't know whether that's aimed at me or her, now that she's likewise realised we need some scissors or a knife to set Steinhausen free. The fact that neither of these are to hand has an even more unthinkable implication: any minute Meller will be back and then we'll have to watch him . . .

I pause in my thoughts.

Steinhausen, who may be the reason why my father's in prison, being presented to all the world as the ribbon murderer.

'Ann!' Eve must have noticed my hesitation. As has Steinhausen, who also realises that time's running out, and now that my hands have stopped fiddling with the cable ties has started waggling in his chair and shouting louder into the gag.

'No chance without scissors,' I say, slowly getting up again to remove the gag, which is sodden with blood, snot and spit.

'I'm calling the police!' Eva says, whipping the phone out of her coat pocket.

Steinhausen gasps for air like a fish out of water. His top lip is swollen and sore, his bottom one seems to be one big scab. 'Thanks,' he mutters, barely intelligibly.

'No reception down here!' Eva.

'Is it true?' Me.

Steinhausen blinks with one eye; I look at him as if he were a work of abstract art. He's no longer the gaunt man from my vision with straggly longish hair and penetrating black eyes. He looks like he does on Meller's photos: shockingly normal. A perfectly normal, nondescript man with short blond hair and freckles beneath the swollen eyes that almost make him appear friendly.

'I'll try upstairs!' Eva says, running past us. Now we're alone, Steinhausen and I.

'Is it true?' I repeat, more insistently this time.

He cries, he begs. 'Please . . . home . . . my wife . . . daughter . . .'

Before I've formulated my next thought, my hand shoots forwards and catches him flat on his left ear.

Steinhausen howls.

'You're lying even now?' I hate the way my voice is quavering. How it betrays my uncertainty and my horror that I've just slapped a man that someone else has already beaten half to death. My left ear begins burning too, like a phantom pain; it's probably the shame. I've crossed a boundary – I'm no better. Eva is better than me, Eva's doing the right thing. She's calling the police, who'll come and arrest Meller and rescue Steinhausen. The police, who'll no doubt allow him to roam free while they keep sinking their teeth into my father instead.

Steinhausen mumbles something, but I don't hear him. I hear my father, who can sense my dilemma and is trying to reassure me.

'You're a good person, Beetle.'

Am I, Dad? Am I still a good person if I want a little more time alone with Steinhausen before the police arrive?

'You can forget that!' I'm rattled by the thunder of Meller's voice. When I turn around he's pushing Eva back into the cellar room. He's confiscated her mobile and an iron bar is wedged in the crook of his arm. Eva stumbles over to me. 'Your colleague felt it was her duty to call the cops to – how did she put it? – *protect a badly injured, innocent man from rash behaviour on my part.*' He spits out a beastly laugh. 'And of course to protect me from myself!' Taking hold of the iron bar, he brandishes it in our direction like a dagger. 'No effing way!' His eyes move from me to Eva, they fix on her as he flings the mobile phone to the floor, where it shatters noisily. 'Did you hear me? It's neither your duty nor your fucking right! This here is my mission, mine and mine alone!'

Eva raises and lowers her hands gently, as if trying to tame a crazed animal. 'Herr Meller, the police will be here soon . . .'

'No,' the animal growls. 'I'm not going to let you fuck everything up when I'm so close.' With the iron bar he forces us into the far corner of the room, while Steinhausen starts yelling for help. Meller drops the bar and lands a punch on his chin. Everything inside me winces – since my car accident a couple of years ago I know what a jaw breaking sounds like. Tiny drops of blood fly as if in slow motion, a fine spray that looks black in the makeshift light of the construction lamp. Steinhausen's head flops limply on to his left shoulder. An overpowering silence grips the room, the unspoken question being if Steinhausen is unconscious.

He is – in the best-case scenario.

And maybe he is. Meller makes sure by grabbing Steinhausen's hair, yanking his head back and putting his hand under his nose to check for breathing.

He definitely is, thank God; Meller nods at us.

'I've put this fucker in hospital twice already,' he says. 'And

I went down for it. Six months the first time – utter nonsense. The judge realised my head was a fucking mess and so accepted there were extenuating circumstances. But when I got out I saw Steinhausen was behaving as if nothing had happened. He was still living in Lichtenberg, going to work, cutting the hedge, pushing his mother around in a wheelchair.' I think of the photos on Meller's pinboard, showing Steinhausen in different everyday situations; they might date from this time. 'Then little Kati was killed – here!' Meller opens out his arms. 'I tried to beat the truth out of him, but the problem was, I was just a touch too keen. A few kicks and the tosser had a fractured fucking skull. Which meant he was back in hospital and I was back in the nick. Five years this time, no more mercy from the judge. So I was inside when Steinhausen came out of rehabilitation. He made use of his chance and did a runner. But not only that!' I see blobs of spittle fly from his mouth. 'Or don't you think it's strange that no children were kidnapped while this wanker was in hospital, licking his wounds? I read the paper every day when I was banged up – nothing! No children murdered when he was out of action! Am I meant to believe that's a coincidence?' He shakes his head and I copy him, as if hypnotised. 'At any rate, for years after I came out, I couldn't for the life of me find out where he was. But then, a few weeks ago, his mum died and I knew that now, now he'd come back like the dutiful son he is . . .' Meller is a wild beast, prowling around this basement room as if he were cooped up in a cage. He moves from left to right and from right to left, menacingly entranced, describing how Steinhausen lurked at the funeral. He photographed that too, I realise. Steinhausen standing beside his mother's grave. But this time he intended to be smarter, Meller continues. Instead of nabbing Steinhausen at the cemetery, he followed him to his new home. 'He was awarded compensation for his injuries – a tidy sum. His lawyer was a real crafty bugger. Together with the money he had already put aside, the fucker was now able to afford a fancy bungalow in the leafy suburbs! And there's me in my shitty little room in Marzahn, agonising over what had happened to Larissa.' He spent days watching Steinhausen, driven by a vague hunch that something was about to happen, something fateful, something incontrovertible. 'And it did happen.' Meller breaks off abruptly and gives us a triumphant look. 'One morning I followed him to a primary school. It was 22 December, the last day before the Christmas holidays. He was hanging around the playground, ogling a group of little girls while they were having a snowball fight. They were laughing, giggling. Alive.' His face darkens. 'For now.'

He doesn't have to say any more. Both Eva and I know this was the moment when Meller pounced, overwhelmed Steinhausen and dragged him to this basement.

'Originally I was going to take him to the hut by the Weihenpfuhl, but the terrain there's so rough that I couldn't have driven with Steinhausen in the boot. And nobody ever strays out here.' His gaze sweeps the room, coming to rest on Steinhausen, who's still unconscious. 'I would have already finished the job, but it's Christmas and I've got my boys to think of.'

I look to the floor in embarrassment when I grasp another piece of the puzzle that is the Meller family tragedy. A father who, by all appearances, is devoted to solving the death of his stepdaughter, and yet interrupts this – his most important mission – to offer some normality to his sons, at least at Christmastime.

'What? Why are you gawping like that?' Meller's voice

thunders like a sudden storm. I frantically wipe my eyes. 'I've treated the tosser far better than he deserves!' In a flash he's hurried over to a canister beside the entrance, which I hadn't noticed before. He's jittery as he turns the red screw top, and then he empties the contents in Steinhausen's face. As if on cue, Steinhausen comes to, flouncing and gasping in panic, like a drowning man.

'It's true, isn't it, Marcus?' Meller says, bending down to Steinhausen. 'I've treated you far better than you deserve during your little stay down here. But now's the time to put an end to the Christmas charity.' Dropping the canister, which clunks on the floor, he stands up and takes a mobile out of his jacket coat pocket. This must be why he left the basement earlier: he'd forgotten his mobile. Which he now needs – 'Showtime, arse-hole!' – to record Steinhausen's confession. 'And you're going to tell all, every little detail. About what you did to Larissa and all those other girls. And why . . .' All of a sudden he starts shaking; first just his shoulders, then his entire body is quivering with pain. 'Why?' he repeats. A *why* which this time seems to be refer-ring only to his stepdaughter and perhaps is questioning more than just the murder itself. Why did it get to that stage? Why didn't he look after Larissa more when she was still alive?

'. . . It . . . it . . . wasn't . . . wasn't . . . me . . .' Steinhausen mum-bles with his badly swollen lip, then howls. This only gets Meller more worked up. Slipping the mobile back into his coat pocket, he bends down to pick up the metal rod.

Eva takes a pace forwards; I hold her back. Meller isn't going to kill Steinhausen. He only wants answers. Just like us.

He takes a swing.

No, he's not going to kill him, absolutely not, no way. Not even here, in this strange space where reality has sprung a leak.

The rod swishes through the air.

Meller's bluffing. Just before the metal comes into contact with Steinhausen's skull and shatters it, he'll stop – I'm sure about that.

And I'm right.

Meller doesn't kill Steinhausen.

He kills Eva.

RECORDING 03

Berlin, 7 May 2021

— You must have wondered about killing at some time or other.

— Of course. That's why I'm asking you about your emotions. I can imagine that you sort of – how can I put it? – get into a different state of mind. A kind of intoxication, ecstasy. And fury, fury must be in the mix too, because you need strength to kill like you did. Either fury or a profound conviction. Something, at any rate, that gives you this strength.

— Hmm. I think it's more likely the latter. I'm not an angry person. How about you? Do you have angry outbursts?

— I can get angry, sure. I mean, everyone does, don't they?

— Not me.

— Maybe you just don't realise it.

— That's possible. *(grins)* But, to be honest, it didn't require that much strength, at least not to overpower the girls. They were in a state of total shock. My attacks came as such surprises that very few of them put up anything like resistance. I threw them to the ground and sat on them, clamping their arms with

128

my knees. That's not hard when their bodies are so small and delicate. Only the cuts required a bit of strength, that's true. Human skin is very elastic. It's like pigs' skin, did you know that?

- Yes, I think I've heard that before.
- Indicative, isn't it? Humans, pigs. Continue.
- Continue?
- What do you imagine it's like to kill? Come on, make a bit of an effort!
- Well, I assume it might have something to do with power too? That . . . oh, I don't know, you feel like God when deciding about another person's life?
- Careful, you're slipping into cliché now.
- Isn't it right what I'm saying?
- Is that how it would be for you? Would you like to play God for a time?
- Not in this way, no. (clears throat) Can we talk about Larissa now?
- In a minute. There's one thing I'd like to know first. Who would you kill if you knew there would be no consequences . . . ?
- I don't think—
- Come on, be bold. You've got a free pass.
- Do you want to hear me say I'd kill you? Make me realise that everyone's capable of murder? That's ridiculous.
- It is. Particularly as I wouldn't have to make you realise it, you know it yourself. And you feel caught out. I can see it in your face and in the way you're clenching your fists. Are you here because of the murders? You want to know how and why it all happened? You've had so much time to prepare for me – and what do you do? You get distracted and ruffled like a little girl. Like *those* little girls. How did the killer manage to keep abducting

children without anyone noticing? I'll tell you: just like that! I didn't have to go hunting children, I could pluck them like apples from a tree. Be friendly, tell them a story or promise to buy them an ice cream or show them a special place. You distract people by giving them your undivided attention, making them feel that everything is about them. Some people are flattered, others unsettled, but either way it always leads to the goal.

– How did you lure Larissa?

– Larissa? With an excursion. I told her I was going to the Weiher but couldn't remember the way. She agreed to show me and asked if we could take her bike. You see, she didn't dare ring the bell at home to put it in the hall, as her mother was just having a siesta. But she didn't want to leave it outside, either, because her old one had recently been stolen, which got her into big trouble with her stepfather. Poor girl.

– A poor girl you took advantage of.

– I see it differently.

– How?

– Give and take. We helped each other.

– Are you trying to suggest that you did the girl a favour by killing her?

– For heaven's sake, what a silly thing to say. I'm sure she would have liked to go on living if she'd had the choice. But . . . are you all right? You look a bit pale and we haven't even started talking properly yet.

– It's fine, no problem.

– Are you sure? Okay. Then give me your left hand.

– My . . . ? What for?

– You wanted to know everything in detail, didn't you?

ANN

I'm acquainted with death. I've seen its workings a few times. It launched a ruthless attack on my mother's face, twisting her eyeballs upwards and wrenching open her mouth into an eternal, silent scream. It came for my grandfather while he was asleep; he was still smiling as if he'd just had a lovely dream. My uncle, who died of a brain aneurysm, looked surprised, as if he couldn't believe it. Nine girls, mercifully from photographs only, who the killer left behind as if they were dolls fallen from a shelf; and Larissa, who was no longer recognisable. Now death has taken possession of Eva's body. She's lying on the cold concrete floor of this basement, her limbs contorted, her head in a pool of blood. Her eyes are closed as if in a slumber; they won't open no matter how firmly I grip her shoulders, no matter how loud I scream. Death is limp, heavy and ungainly. It's a whooshing in my head, like the roar of a waterfall. It's a room that starts turning, slowly at first, then faster and faster; it's a carousel and I can't see where to get off. It's a siren wailing in the distance, which against the roaring waterfall only creeps into my numbed consciousness as a muffled sound. It's a sudden commotion in the basement: people, voices, someone pulling me away from Eva. She was the one who made the emergency call before Meller caught her with the mobile and forced her back down here. Now she's dead. Dead. Slain by Meller when she tried to stop him attacking Steinhausen with the metal rod. Someone grabs my arm and asks if I'm all right, if I'm injured too. I can't reply, I'm breathing as if through a straw, I stare and pant until everything blurs. Death lays two delicate little butterflies on my eyelashes, which flutter until I finally give in and shut my lids. Then I'm away, swallowed by a kind, empty blackness, and I thank death for this at least.

Shock. (Ann, 8 years old)

When you have a shock its like when something is switched off for a bit like a mixer or some other machine. Nothing works anymore, you cant move and you cant think either. Maybe your trembling but you dont notice it. A shock is normally bad but sometimes it isnt. Because there are moments when you woud rather not feel anything. You just have to watch out the shock doesnt last too long or too many feelings get stuck inside you and you get blocked up or explode.

I'm sitting in a row of hard chairs with brown, washable vinyl covers, my head leaning against a white wall, gazing up at the cold light of the neon tubes. My nostrils are irritated by the acrid smell of disinfectant; I try my best to breathe deeply and calmly. Even though I'd rather scream. Grab one of these fricking washable chairs and smash it against the fricking white wall until it shatters and splinters, until paint and concrete crumble, raging until I collapse with exhaustion, back into another restorative blackness. And when I wake up again, none of this will have happened, everything will have merely been a bad dream. Breathe, breathe, breathe. Drawing my knees up on to the seat, I close my eyes. Bad idea; behind my closed lids is Eva's lifeless body, her head in a pool of blood. Stop it! I chide myself. She's alive, she is alive! Her heart is beating as it ought to and the doctors have said that this sort of coma is perfectly normal with a serious traumatic brain injury. She might wake up in the next few hours. They told me I should call someone and get them to pick me up. But I don't want to leave. I want Eva to sense I'm here. She can, can't she? I'm sure she can.

Steinhausen's being treated somewhere in this building too. I know nothing about his condition and whether he might have more injures than the ones I could superficially see in the basement. Nor do I know if the police have already questioned him about what happened, the circumstances surrounding events and, if so, how fruitful this was. I'm not under any illusion that the police will get more out of him than Meller, whose interrogation technique consisted of fists and a metal rod. No, Steinhausen will keep his mouth shut – especially now that he's safe. And there's nothing I can do about it. Even if I found out which ward and room he's in, he'd only have to press the patient bell and I'd be carted away before I'd uttered a word. And what should I say to him anyway? What could I threaten him with to make him talk? I've got nothing. My only chance is to beg the police to check Steinhausen out again without appearing like a demented Rainer Meller.

My mobile buzzes. In a better reality my father would have sent me a message now: *Just stay where you are. I'm on my way, my Beetle.* I've no idea why I check, even though I know it can't be from him. It's only the notification that my battery is almost empty. And something else that I missed earlier: an unread message from this morning. From Zoe of all people: *Nice of you to get in touch. I often wonder how you are. I'm fine. Do you remember . . .* Zoe, who was desperate to do a term abroad in Cornwall. A few days ago she was accepted. *It worked! PS, I miss you too.*

My fingers twitch over the keyboard. Zoe is going away – that's a painful thought. Although as far as I'm concerned, Zoe's already been far away for much longer.

'Ann!' The voice cuts cleanly down the length of the corridor. I leap up from my chair. Elke and Caspian Herbert come rushing towards me. What the hell happened? How the hell could it have happened? Elke, whose forceful grip on my arm I can feel all the way to my bones even through Dad's thick jacket. Her face, which has dropped in shock, her skin like a balloon emptied of air, and white, so white, almost as white as the walls here in the corridor of the neurological intensive care unit. In contrast to her eyes, which are huge, piercing and streaked with entire networks of red veins. Beside her stands the empty shell of Eva's father, Caspian. He doesn't blink, just stares at me with equally red eyes and a half-opened, speechless mouth.

'What did you drag our daughter into?' Elke says, shaking me; I don't resist. It doesn't matter that it was Rainer Meller wielding the metal rod, hitting Eva by accident. All that counts is that she was only in that basement because of me. 'Look me in the eye!' I can't. My gaze sticks to the lapel of her purple woollen coat, and the fact that she hasn't buttoned it up correctly is a further reminder of the enormity of the situation. Elke, who's always so perfect and who would never, ever step out of the house so sloppily. Unless she got a phone call from the hospital urging her to come at once because something bad had happened to her daughter.

Unable to bear it any longer, I wriggle free and run down the corridor to the lift. I hammer the button, wait impatiently for the ding and squeeze myself into the cabin before the door has fully opened, obstructing those who are trying to get out. They grumble and curse but I don't care; I simply have to get away from Eva's parents, I need to get out of here, I want to go home. But not even this will be granted to me, it seems; the taxi stand outside the hospital entrance is empty. Just like my phone battery. I wait a while for a cab to arrive, but the driver won't take me, saying someone else has booked him. 'Public holiday,' he explains curtly with a shrug. I've got no option but to go back into the hospital and ask if they can call me a taxi.

I join the queue of those waiting at reception. I'm nervous; I have to get back home before I completely lose it and break down howling.

'Stop fidgeting!' the woman in front of me hisses. It takes me a second or two to realise that she's not talking to me, but the little girl beside her who keeps tugging at the sleeves of her coat.

'Why can't we go to the playground, Mummy?'

'Oh, Amelie, it's all wet because of the snow. Anyway, we have to ask about Daddy first,' the woman explains, breathing a sigh of relief when the receptionist becomes free. My nose begins to run; everything is coming at once, liquefying. I never had a mother I could annoy. I only ever had my dad. I'm the girl with more than three hundred meaningless telephone numbers on my mobile. The girl who had her best friend back for a brief moment. Eva, who from the outset didn't want us to follow Meller on to the construction site. Eva, who even tried to dissuade me.

Putting my hand over my mouth, I start panting. I need a taxi as soon as possible. I'm pushing forwards, ignoring the blue tape stuck to the floor to safeguard confidentiality. Soon I'm so close to the mother–daughter team that the woman would be able to feel my breath on the back of her neck if she wasn't wearing a thick scarf. And then I hear it. 'My name is Steinhausen. I'd like to know which ward my husband's on.'

The ground opens up, the hole is deep and black. I plummet for a while, then the impact makes me realise what a Frau Steinhausen asking after her husband means. It means that Marcus Steinhausen was telling the truth in the basement earlier. *Please . . . home . . . my wife . . . daughter*, I hear him in my mind, before I slapped him for these very words. *You're lying even now?*

I can't believe how readily I let Meller's delusions influence me. It didn't occur to me for even a second that Steinhausen, who'd always wanted his own family, might have actually acquired one in the meantime. And yet the assaults by Meller, both of them life-threatening, could easily have provided him with the long-awaited reason to finally cut ties with his mother and embark on a new life. Eva was right: I'm no better than the people who homed in on my father. Steinhausen is innocent. The lead I thought I had never actually existed.

Electricity shoots through my body and my legs blunder in the direction of the exit. I don't want a taxi anymore, I just want to get out of here, fast. I don't even mind walking, running until my body collapses.

'Amelie, wait!'

Steinhausen's daughter steps into the revolving door along-side me, then leaps out and makes for the playground that is to the left. The girl's mother comes storming out behind her a few seconds later. 'Not on the slide, Amelie! It's full of snow! If you're wet, they won't let us see Daddy!'

I stop and watch the two of them. And then, without knowing why, I follow them. Perhaps it's my bad conscience. Perhaps I do after all want to be slightly different from those I despise for their prejudice. Maybe I want to do something right, at least one thing on this day that feels so totally wrong. 'Excuse me?'

The woman turns around. I put her in her mid-forties, about as old as Michelle. A few grey strands stick out from her lush, dark-brown hair, as if they'd gone astray. She looks friendly, but very tired too. 'Yes?'

'I couldn't help overhearing that you're the wife of Herr Steinhausen.'

'I'm Susanne Steinhausen, yes,' she says warily. I don't look like a hospital employee coming to tell her she can see her husband now.

I point to the hospital behind me. 'My name is Ann. I was there when it happened to your husband. At the construction site, I mean . . .'

'What?' The woman's eyes grow large.

'It's thanks to my friend Eva that your husband . . .' I break off when I see Frau Steinhausen's eyes well with tears. Like Elke and Caspian, she is another of those people who've had to take a call today that they'd rather not have received. 'Is he in a very critical condition?'

'He's out of danger, but . . .' She shakes her head. 'Andreas and

I were going to get a divorce. Ever since I moved out in summer we've done nothing but argue. About money, about the house and especially about our youngest daughter.' She nods towards the little girl, who's sweeping snow from the swing. 'Had he died today, it would have meant that I'd had a really bad go at him the last time I ever saw him. And yet we used to love each other so much.'

I awkwardly put out my hand and pat her arm. 'Maybe this is a good day to make peace.' I smile – and then it hits me. 'Andreas?'

The wife looks confused.

'Your husband?'

'Andreas is my husband, yes.'

'Not Marcus? Marcus Steinhausen?'

'No, my husband is Andreas.' Now she's sounding impatient. 'Marcus is his brother.'

'His . . .' The machinery inside my head is finding it hard to get into gear; small, rusty wheels turn slowly, clattering like an old clock. Brothers who look so similar that Marcus could even show Michelle, who knew him well, a photo of Andreas with his family without her noticing the difference. Brothers so similar that Meller didn't doubt for a second he'd grabbed the right man from the school playground. Andreas Steinhausen, who was probably only there to pick up his little daughter Amelie. I imagine him not having a clue what's going on to begin with, then trying to persuade Meller he's made a big mistake. But Meller's so delirious that he's not listening. He keeps pummelling his fists into the face of the man he believes to be his stepdaughter's killer, until Andreas Steinhausen is barely able to speak anymore.

Once again I reach out for his wife's arm, not to comfort

her this time, but in my own self-interest, to keep me on my feet when the cogs inside my head finally creak into place. If Andreas Steinhausen is the patient in this hospital, then Marcus Steinhausen is still out there somewhere. Unscathed, at liberty and possibly guilty of ten murders.

Am I all right?

Am I feeling sick?

Do I need to sit down?

I'm not saying anything, I'm just swaying, reeling, gaping. Frau Steinhausen takes the initiative. She summons her daughter from the swing, links arms with me and takes me back inside, to the café, where she finds us a table by the window. Maybe she thinks the view of the snowy park will soothe me, or at least it can't do any harm.

'I'll be right back,' she says to both me and her daughter, who sits opposite me and is allowed to play with her mum's mobile until she comes back. I don't realise how overtly I'm staring at the child until she looks up and waves the screen in front of me with a smile. A masked cartoon girl in a ladybird outfit is swinging across the roofs in Paris.

'Do you want to watch? That's Marinette. She's a superhero, but nobody knows that because she's still at school.' I shake my head. As if offended by my ignorance, Amelie sticks out her tongue, gets up from her chair and immediately sits down again at the neighbouring table, her back turned. I gaze out of the window and think of Eva. Of how everything can change in a matter of seconds. And how absurd it is that the life you know and utter chaos are often separated by a mere breath.

'Here we are,' Frau Steinhausen says, placing a tray on the

table. Hot chocolate for her daughter, tea for her and a cola for me, to get my circulation going again. I'm so overwhelmed by her kindness that I almost start to cry. But I can't; I have to pull myself together. She's Marcus Steinhausen's sister-in-law and might be able to help me. I say the first thing that comes into my head: 'I think my father's in prison because of Marcus.' That's unfortunate and ill-considered of me, because of course now she's going to start asking questions. What's my father in prison for? What exactly is he accused of? What do I think Marcus did?

But there's nothing. No curiosity, no eyes wide in astonishment. Only: 'I'm not surprised.' She asks the girl to give her the mobile – 'Just for a bit,' as she assures the protesting child – and shows me photographs from their last family holiday on the Baltic. Andreas, her and two of their three daughters, the younger two. 'Look, Amelie, do you remember?' she asks the girl, but Amelie's sulking.

I can understand Frau Steinhausen. She can't wait to be let in to see her husband so she can tell him that the last six months aren't important. I'm envious of her for this, the chance to simply wipe the past half year from the table like a careless mess.

'Frau Steinhausen,' I say, to get her attention.

'Hmm?' She looks up. 'Oh yes, I'm sorry. Here, Amelie,' she says, giving her the mobile back.

'But that's not all,' I continue, earning a frown from her. 'I mean that my father's in prison because of Marcus. All that stuff only happened to your husband because somebody mistook him for Marcus.' Leaning into her, I lower my voice. 'You must've heard of the ribbon murders?'

She nods, perplexed.

'The stepfather of one of the victims is convinced that Marcus is the ribbon murderer.'

'And that's why he . . . Andreas . . . ?' Shocked, she slaps a hand over her mouth. 'Oh my God.'

'Could you tell me something about him? Please, Frau Steinhausen. Just like your husband, my father is the victim of a mix-up, and all of this is only because—'

'Of him?' Frau Steinhausen says, narrowing her eyes – a look of incredulity and why not? First the thing with her husband and now me, a complete stranger who's appeared out of the blue, accusing her brother-in-law of multiple murders. I can see her mind working away, wondering if all this is really happening. It's a feeling I know only too well.

'Frau Steinhausen, I know this might sound totally absurd and—'

She interrupts me with a heavy sigh. 'Or maybe not. You know . . .' She rubs her brow. 'When I think about it . . . oh God. Basically this man only ever caused trouble.' I give her a moment to collect herself. 'Andreas is just a year older than Marcus,' she says eventually. 'But as their father died when they were young, he was everything to Marcus: brother, father, a role model in every respect. People often think they're twins, although—'

'Look!' Amelie squeals. Her chair scrapes noisily across the tiled floor of the café when she leaps up. In a flash she's standing beside me, holding the mobile so close to my face that my vision goes blurry. 'That's Adrien. He's a superhero too, just like Marinette, but she doesn't realise even though they're best friends. Silly, isn't it?' She grins at me. 'Surely you'd notice that!'

'Amelie!' her mother says sternly. 'Leave the woman alone and sit back down in your chair.' We wait until Amelie obeys.

'Twins,' I say, reminding Susanne Steinhausen of what she was saying before we were interrupted.

She shakes her head. 'Utter nonsense. Yes, they do look similar, but that's mainly because Marcus always copied Andreas. Whatever haircut Andreas had, Marcus had his done the same way. Clothes, even some gestures and his laugh – Marcus seemed to imitate everything.'

'Wow, that's—'

'Creepy? Sure is. In the early days of my relationship with Andreas, I didn't take it so seriously, but increasingly it became a problem. It was like Marcus was studying him. Marcus was always there! Wherever we went, he wanted to be with us. If he knew we were going out to dinner, he'd suddenly appear at the restaurant and join us as if we'd arranged to meet there. Or at the cinema. It got especially bad after the birth of our first daughter. By then we had our own house, but he came to visit all the time and meddled in our life. Once I found him carrying the screaming baby on his arm, patting her back and saying something like, "It's okay, Daddy's here." *Daddy!* Can you imagine?' Yes, I can, because I've heard a similar story from Michelle, albeit not so extreme.

'It got to the point where enough was enough, as far as I was concerned. I realised that my husband, as the big brother, felt responsible for him. And that he had a bad conscience because Marcus looked after their mother on his own. But it couldn't go on like that. Eventually Andreas agreed to move, to Potsdam at least. That was far enough away to stop Marcus from turning up on the doorstep every day. As time went on, he did in fact come less often, but I expect that was because he'd found a girlfriend.'

'A girlfriend?' I almost knock my cola over in excitement.

'Yes. What was her name again?' Frau Steinhausen hesitates. 'Oh, it doesn't matter. I don't suppose they're still together anyway – I mean, it was ages ago.'

'Are you saying you haven't had any contact with Marcus for a long time?'

'Not for years, no. I do know he spent some time in rehabilitation. Then he put my mother-in-law in a care home and vanished. We couldn't even get in touch with him about the funeral because we didn't have an up-to-date phone number for him.' She clasps her cup with both hands and stares at her tea in silence for a few seconds. 'To be honest, it never occurred to us to look for him. We were glad to be rid of him.'

'But do you have an idea of where he might be? Even an inkling?'

When she looks up, her cold eyes pierce me. 'He's a rat. And rats always find holes to crawl into.'

I nod. Marcus Steinhausen, the rat. The monster. I thank his sister-in-law and say goodbye, but not without first giving her my telephone number, which she punches straight into her mobile. In case she thinks of anything else that might be of use to me. This happens far more quickly than expected – as I'm walking out of the café.

'Ann!' she calls out behind me. I turn around and wander back. 'It began with M. Melanie, Manuela . . .'

I shrug; I've no idea what she's getting at.

'The name of his girlfriend!' she explains. 'I remember now. It began with M.'

'M?' I gasp. No way. That can't be true. I ask to borrow Susanne Steinhausen's mobile, which forces her to engage in another little battle with Amelie, who's still watching her video. The child only relents with the promise of an ice cream. I start by going on the internet. Because my battery's empty I can't access my phone book, and I don't know Ludwig's number off by heart. The landline at his home address is unknown; he must have disconnected it seeing as he spends most of his time as a gentleman of independent means in Poland. But there is an entry under the name of his housekeeper, who still works sporadically for him when he's staying at his old place in Berlin, like now. Her husband answers, then passes me to her, who's known me for years – little Anni, how lovely to get a Christmas call from you. She asks how I am, but I don't have time for small talk, especially as I don't want to spend too long using someone else's phone. I ask her for Ludwig's mobile number which, somewhat surprised, she gives me. Finally I get through to Ludwig. Sounding puzzled, he asks me what number I'm calling from. I promise to explain it all later, but for now: 'I have to see you, right away. Outside police headquarters.'

'What?'

'I can't go on my own, I need your support. It's essential we speak to the inspector responsible for Dad's case.' When he doesn't respond, I add, 'There was an incident today at a construction site in Henningsdorf, Ludwig. Something bad.'

'What? What sort of incident? Are you all right?'

'Marcus Steinhausen's brother was seriously injured and my friend Eva . . .' My voice cracks; I clear my throat. 'I was there, Ludwig. I'm a witness and I have to make a statement. We'll meet at police HQ, okay?' I hang up. I finish by ordering a taxi, then I thank the patient Frau Steinhausen and hurry out of the building.

US

Sarah, Sarah, sweet little Sarah. So alone, so sad. You're shivering, you poor thing. Come with me, don't be afraid. We'll go and play in the woods. It's a fairy-tale game. You like fairy tales, don't you? Of course you do, all children love fairy tales. And, do you know what? You're the main character! Do you want to hear your story? Then listen carefully. Once upon a time, there was a little girl who was born with a heart of pure gold. Or at least that's what people said in the village where she lived. One day an evil dragon heard about this and decided he would steal the girl's heart. He wanted to destroy it because everything that was good and beautiful stirred his hatred. It reminded him that he himself was just a nasty old dragon. The girl had to flee. She ran as fast as she could to escape from the dragon . . . Go on, sweetheart, run! Run faster and don't turn around! Did you hear that? The cracking in the bushes? That's him! He's close on your heels! Come here, let's hide, right here behind this thick tree trunk. Shall I tell you a secret? Dragons don't always look like dragons. Not all of them are huge and black or dark green, with spines and scales and spouting fire from their huge mouths. Some are masters of disguise. They look like perfectly normal people, like men or women. They lead you astray and then to ruin. Some of them, with a bit of magic, can transform themselves so they don't just look human, they actually become human. Others can't do that as the evil inside them is too strong. They are lost souls. Are you afraid? No, no, don't be afraid. You're safe with me. I'll take you to a secret place, a magical place. It's a castle, and in the castle lives another girl with a golden heart, a princess. Would you like to meet her? Yes? I thought so. She wants to meet you too, she's been looking forward to it. We'll go and see her now, okay? But beforehand we have put out a few of the red ribbons I brought with me, look. What are they for? Oh, it wouldn't interest you, sweetheart. Let's just say it's a surprise for the dragon.

ANN

BERLIN, 26 DECEMBER 2017

'For God's sake, what kept you?' Ludwig's grey hair looks totally dishevelled; he must have been running his fingers through it while he was waiting outside police HQ in the drizzle, getting ever more nervous.

'I'm sorry, I'm really sorry! The taxi didn't come for ages.'

Now comes the roasting. I'm lucky; if it wasn't for his enormous heart, he'd be long gone by now. Especially after everything I've done. I know at once he's talking about the folder.

'I can explain.'

'What's there to explain, Anni? You asked me if you could have my documents and I said no. But instead of respecting that, you stole them from me. I realised yesterday evening that the folder was missing. You were lucky I resisted the urge to jump in my car and drive over to read you the riot act.'

'You could have called me.'

'Would you have answered if you'd seen it was my number?'

'No.'

'No,' he repeats, shaking his head in resignation.

'I'm sorry.'

'We're not done with this, my girl.' He points to the building in front of us. 'So, what are we doing here?'

I'm well aware that my statement is long and muddled. I'm likewise aware that duty inspectors prefer listening to long, muddled statements on regular workdays rather than at the fag end of Boxing Day, where such things just mean overtime – time they'd rather be spending with their families. I don't hold it against Inspector Brandner that he makes me sense all of this as he looks at me across his desk. He's about the same age as Ludwig, with thinning hair, large bags under his eyes and frown lines that suggest he's often narrowed his eyes at all the things he's seen and heard during his many years in this job. Even when he doesn't, he still looks sceptical. If he didn't know Ludwig personally and have huge respect for him, I bet the inspector would have fobbed me off with a 'pop in another time' rather than allow me to sit here now. On the other hand, two officers were supposed to have questioned me at the hospital about the events at the construction site, but I was in too much shock to be of any use. So they asked me to go to police HQ the moment I felt better.

Now I am feeling better and I'm here with the complete chronology of the day, ending with my conversation with Marcus Steinhausen's sister-in-law.

'Okay, Frau Lesniak, duly noted. Thanks.' That's all.

I look to Ludwig for help, who's sitting beside me like an embarrassed father before his badly behaved daughter's headmaster. And the worst thing is that he's saying nothing.

'Marcus Steinhausen was obsessed first with his brother's family and then with the Mellers. He told his sister-in-law he'd got himself a girlfriend. She recalls that the name began with M. M for Michelle. Don't you understand? Marcus Steinhausen lied! Just as he lied to Michelle when he passed off his brother's family as his own.'

No reaction, neither from Ludwig nor Brandner.

'Okay,' I say, acknowledging defeat. 'I admit I've no idea how all of this fits together. But it's clear that it *does* fit together. And that Steinhausen is someone it's worth taking a closer look into. With his history and his obvious psychological issues, he fits the profile of the ribbon murderer far better than my father.'

The inspector raises his eyebrows in amazement. 'The profile?'

I nod keenly. 'Whatever Meller did and however wrong it was – I think he was correct. Marcus Steinhausen—'

Brandner turns to Ludwig. 'Did she just say something about "the profile"?'

And that was it. Brandner laughs as if he's just heard a brilliant joke. And I'm the punchline. A civilian who feels the calling to investigate. Hilarious. Then comes a lecture, delivered in a serious tone. My father is not in custody on some whim, and certainly not without reason. And Steinhausen was eliminated as a potential suspect years ago because he had alibis. Perhaps – an artificially sympathetic look – I should consider getting professional help to deal with my personal circumstances, which must be difficult. Not a police professional, but somebody familiar with the human psyche. A professional like Eva.

I don't say anything else; I just listen until Brandner has finished and says goodbye, not without the words, 'Get better soon' – of course not.

Shame. (Ann, 9 years old)

When your ashamed it feels like you shrink until your very small. But you wish you could be even smaller and even invisible for a bit. But unfortunately your not invisible, you can see this because everyone stares at you. And the staring burns you so badly that your face goes red and your ears get very hot. That's very embarassing.

We drive in Ludwig's car. He offers me his spare room for the night. We could go out to a restaurant first or order a takeaway if I don't feel like being out in public. I just want to go home. 'It's been a difficult day, Anni,' he tries. 'It's a difficult time for you overall at the—'

'Please, Ludwig, leave it.'

He shakes his head. 'I can't, my girl. Your father isn't here to look after you. But I am.'

'And that's why you left me high and dry in front of Inspector Brandner? I could have done with your support.'

'Anni, you've got to stop getting obsessed by all of this. You saw today what happened to your friend Eva. Isn't that enough? What more has to happen?'

'I don't want to talk about Eva.'

'But we have to.'

'No, what we really have to talk about is why, as our lawyer, you're wasting the opportunity to put the police on to a very promising lead! Surely you want the real killer to be caught, don't you?'

'Anni,' and this weary sigh – I can't listen to it anymore. Leaning my head against the window, I switch off. Now Ludwig's words are nothing but indistinct sounds, while the lights from the streetlamps and houses racing past are a blur in the darkness. It's like a slipstream dragging me with it, into a different setting where there are also lights, lights on a Christmas tree. It's only plastic but it's tradition. A fire is crackling; I hear soft music and a little girl's laughter. Christmas, Dad, like we used to celebrate it. As we might never be able to celebrate it again. Just as nothing might ever be the same as it once was. I don't know if I can cope with this possibility, Dad. I'm so terribly scared.

'Oh, my Beetle,' you would say now. 'Do you remember the story I once told you when you were a girl? The story about fear?'

Yes, but please tell me again. I'd love to have something I can believe in.

'All right, listen carefully . . . Once upon a time, there was a farmer who set off in his donkey cart for Constantinople. On the way he was stopped by a hunchbacked old woman who begged him to take her along. He let her climb aboard, but when she was sitting next to him on the box and he was able to see her face, he almost jumped in horror. "Who are you?" he asked. "I am cholera," the old woman replied. At once the farmer ordered her to get off his cart and make her own way. He was very frightened. But the old woman promised to spare him and only kill five people in Constantinople if he let her travel with him. As security she gave him a special dagger, the only weapon that could kill her. "We'll see each other again in two days," she said. "If I've broken my promise, you can kill me."

'Over the next couple of days, however, a total of 125 people died in Constantinople. And the farmer, who himself was fine, did indeed see the old woman again, and was going to thrust the dagger into her. "Don't do that," she said. "I kept my promise and only killed five people. It was fear that accounted for the other hundred and twenty."'

Have you ever been afraid, Daddy?

'Yes, my Beetle. That time you injured yourself with the sharp stone. I'll never forget how I felt—'

'Ann?' Ludwig says, interrupting my thoughts. 'Have you been listening to me?'

I say yes, to whatever.

'All right then, would you prefer Thai or Chinese?'

'What?'

'What food should I order? You can't have been listening to me.'

'Yes, yes, I was. It's just . . . I'm not really hungry.'

'Your appetite will come when the food does. And no more buts now, or I'll tell your father you nicked my folder.'

I shrug. Ludwig ought to know that it's hard to faze my father; he's had to put up with a lot from me. Ann and the cut wrist when she was six. Ann and her complicated puberty. Ann who does stupid things because she's unhappy in love. Ann who turns the car over. When did he ever lose it, Ludwig? When did he ever scream at me? My father, who was always controlled, his analytical gaze. He would ask me why I did what I'd done and what I was feeling when I did it. I'd describe my despair, my anger, my fear and he would understand me.

'Don't forget he's in prison now,' Ludwig says, as if he'd read my thoughts. 'You saw for yourself when you visited how much the circumstances have changed him. He's got enough problems at the moment, don't add to that list by becoming another one.'

I could object that I seem to be the only person making a serious attempt to solve his problems, but I hold my tongue. The last thing I want now is an argument; I don't have the energy for it, not after the day I've had.

When Ludwig parks the car, I see that the Harberts' house is as dark as ours; Elke and Caspian must still be at the hospital. Maybe I oughtn't be on my own tonight. I think of my father, of Eva, of Zoe and Jakob and everyone whose company I would far prefer to Ludwig's. But none of them are around. I sniff and persuade myself that an evening with Ludwig will at least give me the opportunity to convince him of my theory about Marcus Steinhausen.

'Thai,' I say, before reaching for the door handle to get out. 'Some kind of curry with coconut milk, but not too hot.'

'There we go,' Ludwig says, smiling. 'I'll hurry.'

I close the passenger door and watch the car until the darkness has swallowed its taillights. Then I turn to face our house and my eye catches one of the upstairs windows: my bedroom. I can't work it out at first, not in its entirety – only that something is different. The black shape doesn't belong there and my curtains shouldn't be moving.

I blink, confused. There's nothing up there anymore. No black figure, no movement of the curtains. Just another figment of my imagination, I reassure myself. Just my overloaded brain short-circuiting again. All the same I should take a look, make sure. There's no way I can let Ludwig come back to find the problem child still standing on the drive because she doesn't dare enter her own house.

I approach the house tentatively nonetheless.

'Do you remember the story of fear, my Beetle?' I hear my father say inside my head. 'The fear of fear gives rise to more suffering than the actual cause.'

Yes, Dad.

The silence is loud. It's the metallic scraping of the key in the lock. It's the sigh of the hinges as the door's pushed open, and the whimper of the handle. It's every single step that the heavy soles of my boots make on the tiled floor. It's the sliding sound of the carving knife I take out of the wooden block on the work surface. It's the clicking of my left knee when I climb the first step of the stairs and the groan of the wood on the second. It's another step and yet another, getting louder with each successive one taking me up the stairs, until they end on the landing.

I stop. Listen. My room is the second on the right. I can't hear anything. I'd just have to touch the wall next to me; that's where the light switch is. I don't do it; I don't turn the light on. Something is stopping me, a feeling. I edge forwards to my room. The door is open. That was me, I think, I left it open.

And yet . . . this feeling. It has bitten into my neck with sharp teeth.

My room is my room is my room. I can't make out any disruption to the system of forms and outlines accentuated in the dark by the streetlamps outside. I go over to the window.

There's nobody here. Nobody was here.

Get better soon, Inspector Brandner says in my mind. I shake my head in resignation about myself.

Outside a car is approaching. That can't be Ludwig already; it'll take him at least half an hour to return with our dinner. Pushing the curtains apart, I crane my neck. It's the Harberts' car turning into the drive next door. The outdoor lights come on; Elke and Caspian get out. I watch them go up to the house; it looks as if they're shuffling, weak and tired after the worst of all possible days. There's a clunk when Elke turns the key in the lock, and another clunk when she shuts the front door behind them.

The view from my bedroom window is ideal if you want to keep an eye on what's going on outside. If a car arrives. If someone comes home who could interrupt you. But my bedroom window is closed. So it couldn't have been Elke and Caspian who made the clunking noises.

I know exactly where they came from.

I heard them everyday when my father, lost in thought, would pace up and down on the old floorboards in his study. Carefully I slip my boots off. Then I creep back on to the landing, holding the knife in front of my stomach, tightly clutching the handle.

First my gaze falls on the console table at the end of the landing, the vase that has its fixed place in the middle of it. There's something comforting about symmetry, something dependable. I squint to make sure, though it's hard in the darkness, punctuated only dimly by the light from the streetlamp. But I'm sure of it: the vase is no longer exactly in the middle; it's a few centimetres off-centre to the right. I creep further down the landing. The study is still a few paces away on the left, but I can already see it: the door.

The only door in this house that – normally – is never open. Which I keep locked to preserve a sense of importance, hiding the key in the vase on the console.

My heartbeat goes wild, blood roars in my ears. I tense every muscle, an animal ready to pounce into the study in a single bound.

Then everything happens very fast. In the dark, crashing into a wall and being dragged off my feet. The room tipping and me losing my knife. The clank as it hits the floor. A moment later I slam into the wooden boards, a stifled cry. My opponent teeters and falls too, a hoarse panting. In panic, I feel the floor for my knife. My opponent hobbles out the door. Finding my weapon, I try to get up, but a pain in my right shoulder pushes me down. I fight against it, struggle to my feet, go after my foe. Their footsteps are already clattering on the stairs. I'm quicker; I know this staircase, having often taken it in the dark. My left hand shoots forwards, comes into contact with material and tugs at it; my opponent stumbles. I let go just in time, grabbing on to the banister before they can drag me with them down the last few stairs. A dull thud then suddenly it's silent again. Only two people breathing jerkily in the darkness, both numb with shock. Then, groaning. My knees trembling, I make my way down, my knife aimed at the noise. At the bottom of the stairs, I press the light switch and the groaning briefly stops. Standing as tall as I can, I look down at my foe, lying at my feet, doubled up with pain. A man. He's wearing dark clothes and a black balaclava that disguises his entire face apart from the wide-open blue eyes staring up at me, prompting something I can't put a finger on. I turn the knife in my hand to signal that he ought to stay precisely where he is and not try anything stupid. He blinks a few times rapidly in succession. Either he's understood my warning or he's merely adjusting his eyes to the surprising brightness of the hall light. My mind comes to life like a spluttering engine. Laid out in front of me is none other than Marcus Steinhausen. The man I've been trying to find. But who found me first. Slowly, very slowly, I kneel before him, still firmly clutching the knife with my right hand, while the left one reaches for the balaclava. I pull it off his head.

And freeze.

Now I know what it was about those blue eyes. I know them. I've seen them glisten when the man they belong to tells me in my lunch breaks how he crushes the old cardboard boxes at the recycling centre.

RECORDING 04
Berlin, 7 May 2021

- *(laughs)* Oh, you're afraid.
- No, I'm not.
- All right then, give me your hand. I want to show you exactly where I made the cut.
- No, I think you just want to test my reaction and unnerve me.
- Your mind seems to be elsewhere at the moment. Otherwise you'd make more of an effort. I'd have already explained your mistake to you.
- What mistake?
- No, you first. You're questioning my motivation, and I'm just as keen to know about your decision. You say you want to understand.
- Yes.
- Why? Do you feel affected personally?
- Look, like I already told you, I've met Larissa Meller's mother.
- Oh, but that's not all, is it? On the contrary, that's just a tiny bit

of it, maybe even just an excuse. I did some research into you before agreeing to our meeting.

– So what? I don't have any skeletons in my cupboard.

– We all have those.

– In your case there are ten of them, and not just proverbial ones. Talking of which, let's get back to Larissa. What did she trigger in you? Did she remind you of somebody? Why was she your first victim?

– Ah, yes, your mistake. You believe Larissa must have had a particular significance because she was the first one.

– Yes.

– No.

– No? She had no particular significance?

– Of course she did! They all did! I can remember every single name and every face. I know their family backgrounds, whether they had siblings or pets, and what their favourite subjects at school were. They were happy to tell me all of this quite openly because they sensed I was really interested. For the brief moment when our lives overlapped, there was nothing more important to me than each of those girls. The trust they felt outweighed the fear, the unease, their parents' warnings. I mean, that's what we drum into our children from an early age, isn't it? Never go with strangers. But are we adults any better? We go out, have one glass too many and all of a sudden end up in bed with someone who just happened to be in the same place at the same time.

– Is this part of your motivation? Is it about people's gullibility? Or were you trying to punish parents you didn't think had looked after their children well enough?

- No, those are merely findings. By the way, I've just remembered you had a few problems when you were younger.
- What are you getting at?
- So much for not having any skeletons in the cupboard. You were charged with criminal damage because you slashed your teacher's tyres. Twenty hours of community service and a counselling session with the juvenile court service, am I right?
- So? That was just a moment of stupidity. I was naïve and I was in with the wrong crowd.
- I think it might be quite similar.
- What are you talking about?
- Well, you mentioned needing strength to cut through skin. It might be similar to slashing a tyre. Although it has to be said that I've never slashed anyone's tyres. *(clicks his tongue several times)* That really is pointless and unnecessary.

ANN

BERLIN, 26 DECEMBER 2017

It's shortly after half past nine in the evening and I'm back in Brandner's office at police HQ. This time I seem to be arousing a different sort of pity in him, for in addition to the coffee I've been given, the inspector has also placed a tin in front of me. The writing on the lid spitefully wishes me a 'Happy Christmas'. I open the tin if only to be able to put the lid upside down.

'My wife baked them,' Brandner says, giving me a strained smile over his desk. Although I feel queasy, I poke around inside the tin and plump for a lebkuchen with chocolate icing. Ludwig's here too. Not long after I tore the balaclava from the intruder's face, he returned with our dinner. He was the one who called the police. Now he's sitting beside me, his arm across the back of my chair, which I take to be a sign of his protectiveness. He's got a bad conscience, just like Brandner, who's not sharing his wife's baked masterpieces without good reason. *Get better soon*, my arse. In addition to the red ribbon on our oleander and all my research, now I've been attacked too, and injured in the process. My right shoulder is bruised and there's a cut on my right brow. It's a really impressive-looking wound;

each time the men catch a glimpse of it, they're reminded to go easy on me.

'The thing with the files might be a problem,' Brandner says, waiting until I've finished eating. As if I hadn't picked out a lebkuchen but a sedative that takes a while to work. 'Who knew you had the folder?'

'Only my friend Eva, no one else.'

The inspector holds back his displeasure as best he can; the only thing he doesn't have under control is his twitching jaw.

'What are you thinking, Martin?' Ludwig asks him.

'Well, there are a number of possibilities as to who could benefit from such information. From that bunch of souvenir hunters who auction supposed crime scene material online, to relatives who think the investigation is proceeding too slowly. Then the press, of course, eager to boost sales figures with hitherto unpublished details. Or even—'

'The real murderer, trying to find out if you're on to him and how close you are,' I say, finishing his sentence.

Brandner just gives a curt, sullen nod, before turning to Ludwig once more. 'I don't have to tell you what I think of your having let her get hold of these documents.'

'No,' Ludwig replies. He neglects to mention how exactly the folder came to be in my possession.

'And are you sure that nothing else was stolen, Frau Lesniak? Neither from the study nor from the rest of the house? Just the files?'

I shrug, giving myself a sharp pain on my right side. *That's going to be a nice bruise*, said the doctor who had to make a note of my physical condition for the records.

'Not that I'm aware.'

Brandner mutters. 'The fact that the folder was the only thing stolen suggests the intruder had deliberately targeted it. But this doesn't fit your claim that nobody could have known about it.'

'Nobody apart from Eva Harbert,' Ludwig corrects him, looking at me.

'Absolutely no way! Who would Eva have told? And when? We were together the whole time until . . .' I blink wildly as the image of her lifeless body tries to form in my head again, her head in the pool of blood, her stiff, half-opened eyes. 'Absolutely no way,' I repeat shakily.

'It's all right,' Ludwig says, moving his hand from the chair to my back.

'I'm sorry, Frau Lesniak,' Brandner says, pointedly pushing the biscuit tin towards me. He must think I need another dose. 'I don't mean to upset you; I'm trying to protect you.'

Even though I don't fancy it, I take another one, this time a shortbread heart with a jam filling. Once again, Brandner waits until I've finished before asking the question that I must have already answered several times this evening. 'And are you really sure you didn't recognise the intruder?'

'Absolutely sure,' I say, nodding. 'I hadn't turned any lights on, so it was pitch-black in the house when I tore the balaclava off his face. Then he knocked me over and disappeared through the terrace door.'

You would approve, Dad.

Maybe you'd even be a bit proud of me. I'm following the great philosophers: Machiavelli, Bentham, Kant. I've checked the end and the means. The end is not exclusively selfish, but morally right and important for the common good as well: the longer you're in prison, the longer the real killer remains free, able to claim the lives of more innocent victims. The end is to expand the police's narrow view, the means is the break-in. They have to investigate and thus explore every possibility, including that Steinhausen might be behind it. I know it wasn't him, but the police have no option but to take a closer look at Steinhausen. They have to check out everyone who might have had a reason for breaking into our house now that I've started asking questions. I'm still sure they'll hit on Steinhausen one way or another, but until I've got clear, definitive proof of his guilt, outwardly I need to be careful. They mustn't think that, like Meller, I've developed an obsession about this man. They need to take me seriously when the time comes.

The end justifies the means.

It's okay that I lied, slightly twisting the circumstances of the attack in my favour. It's okay, that doesn't make me a bad person, does it, Dad?

'Don't worry, Anni,' Ludwig says in your place. I'm beside him in the passenger seat, sitting slightly crooked from the pain in my shoulder. I'm nervous to boot, but not because – as he probably thinks – I'm traumatised by the attack. 'I'm going to take better care of you from now on.'

'I'm fine, Ludwig,' I protest for the umpteenth time, starting to sound annoyed. Which is counterproductive because he mustn't become suspicious. I'm Anni, who was standing in the doorway when he came back with dinner. Anni, as if paralysed, and holding a black balaclava. Anni, who could only stammer when she told him about the intruder she'd surprised in the study. It had been a man, that much was certain. But she couldn't see him properly in the dark. He'd wrestled her to the floor then escaped via the terrace. Ludwig immediately sat her in his car where she could feel safe while he went into the house, switched on the lights and inspected everything before calling the police.

'Really I am,' Anni insists, giving him a conciliatory smile. 'After all, nothing bad happened. I just want to go home and get into my bed.'

'You want to do what?' Ludwig looks aghast. 'No way. You're going to stay at my place tonight.'

'Honestly, there's no need. I—'

'Really? What happens if the intruder comes back?'

'After that turnout? The police spent two hours searching the house, garden and garage, securing evidence. If I were the intruder, I'd get out of the city as quick as I could.'

'There's still the question of how he got into the house in the first place.'

I lower my eyes guiltily, just like earlier when giving my statement to Inspector Brandner. 'The terrace door. I must have left it open again, there's no other explanation I can think of.'

Ludwig sighs. 'I realise you've been out of sorts recently, Anni. And I can understand it too, but—'

'I really should be more careful, especially now I'm living in the house on my own,' I say, finishing his sentence with the words Eva said to me yesterday. A yesterday that seems an eternity ago. 'I know, Ludwig.'

'Apart from that, the meaning of the red ribbon on your oleander needs looking into again. That might have been him too.'

'Do you think he's been watching me for a while?'

Ludwig just growls quietly, the reaction of the man who only yesterday was still downplaying this and stopping me from notifying the police. *Someone was in your garden and tied a red ribbon to the oleander. Nothing else actually happened*, a shrug of the shoulders. All the same, I don't protest anymore when he takes the wrong turn. I'm desperate to go back home, but Ludwig's arguments are better and he has a more credible scenario. We say nothing more until he turns into his drive.

'Here we are,' he says, reaching behind for the bag with the two styrofoam boxes from the Thai restaurant.

We get out. Before us is his swanky villa, a house whose art nouveau opulence spits a big fat 'ner, ner, ner, ner, ner' in the face of every guest. This is home to someone who's made it, who doesn't know what to do with his money. Ludwig could have sold the place after entering retirement – which he's spending in the forests of his Polish homeland – and simply stayed in a hotel on his sporadic visits to Berlin. But he doesn't do this because he doesn't have to. He can afford to keep a house he no longer lives in, like an outsized trophy, a memorial to his life's work.

'The world will look a very different place after you've had a good night's sleep,' he says, punching a code into the number pad beside the front door. People like Ludwig aren't surprised by intruders in their studies because nobody can get past the alarm system. In the hallway I put my rucksack down and take my boots off. I'd really love to go straight to bed, but I know Ludwig. He will want to be sure that I really am all right. Moreover, he won't be able to sleep himself until he's soothed his conscience with a little paternal care towards me. But he must – he must fall asleep if he's not going to notice me stealing out of his house in the middle of the night. I've thought it over very carefully. I'll ruffle the bedclothes a bit in the spare room, then wait for a while before doing a runner. And tomorrow, when he realises I'm not there and calls me, I'll simply tell him I got up early and didn't want to wake him. I've got everything under control, Dad. I'm not going to let myself be helplessly churned up by the chaos any longer; that's enough now.

I go into the kitchen, fetch two cups from the cupboard and then tap my way through the functions of the coffee machine, which is complicated if you've never used it before. But I have, on numerous occasions. I know which drawer I'll find a packet of cigarettes in. Ludwig, who hasn't smoked in ages apart from the odd cigar on special occasions, keeps one there for emergencies. For emergencies like me. I also know that there's an ashtray hidden next to the cleaning things in the cupboard under the sink, and where to find the matches. I know I have to open the window, not because of Ludwig but Frau Cluth, the housekeeper, who gave me his mobile number earlier. She'll moan – she always has – if you're careless enough to fill the room with smoke. I know all this because I've been a regular visitor here. As a little girl I used to sit at this kitchen table with a cup of hot chocolate and a roll that Frau Cluth had buttered for me. I climbed on the leather armchairs in the library or built a camp in the loft while Ludwig and my father were deep in conversation.

'Are you smoking again?' Ludwig asks, entering the kitchen and putting the bag with our dinner on the work surface. He's got changed and is now wearing a cardigan with a shawl collar rather than his jacket. I sit at the table puffing smoke rings into the air. Zoe showed me how to do it after we'd been out dancing one night, which ended on the balcony of the student halls of residence where she was living. Slightly puff your cheeks, keep the smoke in, form an 'O' with your lips, then carefully push your tongue forwards. As simple as that and yet for the life of me I couldn't do it. Now that I can, Zoe is living alone in our flat and getting ready for her term abroad – Cornwall, without me.

'Off and on,' I say to Ludwig. 'But please don't tell Dad. You know, my asthma and all that.'

He mutters something and fetches a cigar. We drink our coffee and smoke. The food remains untouched in its bag.

'I know you're as unconvinced by my Steinhausen theory as Brandner and the rest of the force. But I also know I'm right. I can't say for sure where this feeling comes from, only that it's uncannily strong.'

'You're unmistakably your father's daughter.' Ludwig laughs. 'For him, feelings have always been more important than facts too. It's a miracle he turned into such a successful academic.'

I shake my head. 'That's not completely right. Feelings lead to deeds and deeds lead to facts, he always says. He regards them as the basis of everything. And he's right about that, isn't he? I don't think there's any question he's asked me more often in my life than: *What were you feeling?* He would never be fobbed off, he always wanted to know precisely. When I was a little girl, I even had to write short compositions about my feelings and give them to him so he could see I really had engaged with them.' I laugh too, but only briefly. 'As far as I'm concerned, it makes it even worse that someone like him – someone who's always been so genuinely interested in others – is now locked away in a tiny, cold cell. And nobody's asking what *he* is feeling.'

'He could save himself a lot of bother if he started talking, Anni. You're behaving as if nobody wants to listen to him. But that's not the case. On the contrary.'

'You don't understand him.' I stub out my cigarette with brisk, ungainly movements. 'None of you understand him. He's a highly sensitive man. These charges have broken him.'

Leaning back, Ludwig crosses his arms.

Whereas I lean forwards over the table. 'Marcus Steinhausen, Ludwig. The police are going to investigate him over the break-in. And you have to make sure their enquiry is thorough.'

'You need sleep, my child.'

'It's not a question of whether he's got an alibi for this evening. It's whether he's the ribbon murderer.'

Ludwig gets up and leaves the kitchen without a word of explanation. I check my watch – just before midnight. Barely four hours since I caught the intruder in our house. Ludwig's right: I really need to go to bed.

No sooner am I on my feet than he comes back with two glasses containing a brown liquid. A single malt, I bet. From the globe bar in his library. As a child I was fascinated watching Ludwig flip back the northern half of the globe to take out one of the valuable bottles inside. He sets the glasses on the table, swapping them for the coffee cups. I sit down again without protest. A sip can't hurt, not today – today warrants a huge gulp.

'There's something not right about the case as set out by the investigation team,' I say, putting my glass on the table. I must have taken a larger sip than I'd thought – it doesn't matter; I can hold my drink. 'They're missing something.'

'Something that you're going to find.' His words surprise me as much as the smile that accompanies them. Until now, Ludwig has given me the impression that although he's taking the break-in seriously, he's not so convinced by my theories about Marcus Steinhausen. I nod all the same. Which feels strange. As if the weight of my head had increased; it's as heavy as a stone I'm trying to balance on the thin, feeble spindle that used to be my neck.

'The motive,' I say, attempting to sound unfazed. 'I've asked you about this before, but you didn't give me an answer and I couldn't find anything in the documents either. What reason would my father have had to kill ten little girls?'

Ludwig raises his glass to me once more and I join him in a sip, in the hope the alcohol will loosen his tongue.

'Well?'

'You've read the files. Which means you know the girls' wrists were slit. The left one, as in your case.' He leans towards me. 'Although they can't say for sure, the forensics team believe the killer used a knife with a very blunt blade. Do you have any idea how much strength is needed to slit the wrist of someone with a blunt knife?'

'But that's exactly my point, Ludwig! Nobody did it to me! There was no madman with a knife. It was me, myself!'

'The left wrist, Anni,' he insists. 'Do you seriously believe in such coincidences?'

'A few weeks after I started working at Big Murphy's, I found out that my colleague was the mother of the first victim. So, yes, Ludwig! I do believe in coincidences! Unbelievable coincidences!'

'Oh, my child,' Ludwig says, his outline faintly blurring.

I blink a few times until my vision is sharp again. 'And that's still no reason,' I say, sticking to my guns. This time I'm not going to give in.

Ludwig points his chin at my glass. I drink up – why not? 'As an anthropologist, your father's a scientist, Anni. And as a philosopher, he's a thinker striving for answers to the fundamental questions in life.'

I want to object but my tongue is stuck to the roof of my mouth. Ludwig puts his hand on mine. 'Death is also part of life.'

His face dissolves, everything dissolves. It's as if everything before me is a painting which someone has poured water over. Colours run, flowing into one another, everything fluid. There's something wrong with me; my weighty head slumps on to my chest. Once again I try to say something, but it feels as if my lips have been stitched together.

'Anni,' I hear Ludwig's muffled voice. 'You've got into something that isn't good for you.'

Summoning all my strength, I manage to lift my head, which rolls around on my neck uncontrollably.

'But trust me.' All of a sudden his voice is by my ear, very close; it's a whisper and a warm breath. When did he get up from his chair and wander around the table? 'Everything's going to be all right.'

Do you remember?

Six years ago, when Eva disappeared from the city overnight.

I'd already been suffering heartache for a long time. Eva and Nico felt like my asthma – a chronic illness that was unpleasant but which I'd learned to live with. I'd realised, at least, that I couldn't lock Eva away, not like when we were fourteen and I wanted her to miss her drama club audition. I'd simply shoved her into a toilet cubicle and barricaded the door from the outside with the caretaker's broom. I didn't want her to get the part of Luise in Schiller's *Kabale und Liebe*. We'd read the play in our German lessons and I knew that there would be a Ferdinand she would have to fall in love with. Three years later this Ferdinand was called Nico and I was powerless. I had to tolerate their relationship if I wanted to avoid losing Eva completely. But that was precisely what happened just a year later, right after our school-leaving party. Eva and Nico went away together and didn't come back. With every day that passed, my heart broke anew and I began to wonder why I hadn't already collapsed and died of a cardiac arrest. I was so exhausted by grief and yet couldn't find rest. All I wanted to do was to sleep – not die, for God's sake! – just enjoy a long, restorative sleep. And when I woke up, my body and mind would be refreshed, my appetite would have returned and I'd see that although a world without Eva was different, it was still nice and worth living.

They were your pills, Dad. You kept having phases where you were so consumed by work that you couldn't switch your mind off at night. I took too many, a silly accident. It felt as if I were lying outstretched in a swamp. With every breath, my body grew heavier and I sank slightly deeper. My heartbeat slackened, getting slower and slower, which seemed wrong in view of the gathering panic I felt. I sensed I was going under and was absolutely terrified. I just managed to call out to you and point sluggishly to the tube on my bedside table.

'Am I going to die now, Dad?' I also managed to say.

'Don't worry, my silly Beetle,' you said, putting a hand on my head. 'You'd have to swallow a kilo of these pills to be in danger. You're just going to have a deep, long sleep.'

Then I sank into the swamp.

I'm getting a similar feeling now in Ludwig's kitchen. My body unbelievably heavy, my heartbeat like deep, lengthy sighs. I slump on my chair into a thick, grey fog. I'm just about aware of Ludwig grabbing me under the arms and also feel the pain in my right shoulder. Am I going to die now, Ludwig? I want to ask, but that's too many words, too much effort. All I manage is a pitiful, meek, 'Why?'

US

Drink, Sarah, drink up. This is a magic drink. It will help you have a wonderful dream. And when you wake up, I'll take you to see the princess. She has to rest too, just like you, because it's late and it's been an exciting day. I'm going to go out again, I have to. They've started looking for you. The police are here already with their men and dogs, their searchlights and even a helicopter. They're playing blind man's bluff – cold, cold, very cold, I want to shout out. But I don't, of course, because their ignorance is handy for us. We don't want to take any risks, we mustn't. That's why I'm going to join them, the police and the people from the village. I'm going to be part of the search; that way I'll be up to date and find out when it's getting dicey for us. It's an old trick – be there, but invisible, like a ghost or a shadow in the night. Now, sleep well, my sweetheart, settle down. When I'm back, I'll lie down beside you. I'll be very close, hold you tightly and stroke your lovely soft hair. You'll feel it, even in your sleep; you'll feel safe and protected, just like you deserve. The princess is always asking me to lie beside her too, just her and me, with the rest of the world far away. And of course I'm happy to do it, I do everything for her. That's what you really want too, isn't it, sweetheart? Someone who does everything for you. You'd like to be a princess too, wouldn't you?

ANN

I wake with a start in panic, my heartbeat and breathing at maximum speed. I'm in bed in Ludwig's spare room. The digital alarm clock on the bedside table says that I've slept for a good ten hours; it's almost noon. My thoughts are black, even briefly entertaining the possibility that Ludwig might have interfered with me. I push the duvet back. He's only taken off the jumper over my T-shirt; other than that I'm fully clothed. Despite this, I feel naked because I was at his mercy. He decided to sedate me with sleeping pills or something similar; he had power over me. And even if he only did it out of concern for me, it makes no difference. I swing my legs over the edge of the mattress. My body combats these snappy movements with a dizziness, but I won't give in. It's been more than sixteen hours since I apprehended the intruder. I have to get home. Putting on my jumper, which is on the chair beside the bed, I grab my rucksack and make for the door. For a moment it occurs to me that Ludwig might have locked me in, but I'm wrong, thank God. I hurry down the stairs, almost stumbling.

'Morning, sleepy head!' Ludwig calls out as I pass the kitchen. He gets up from a lavishly laid breakfast table. Without responding, I hasten down the corridor to the coatrack to fetch my jacket and boots.

'Anni? Is everything okay?' Now he's standing there, looking at me in astonishment, as I yank my jacket off the hook and make heavy weather putting it on with my injured shoulder.

'Nothing's okay. You should be ashamed of yourself!'

'What are you talking about?' He takes another step towards me and tries to help me with the jacket. I turn away. 'Anni, I really don't know what—'

'Really? Are you going to try to deny it? You gave me a sleeping pill!'

'I . . . what?'

I don't reply. He knows exactly what he did. But I don't want to discuss it anymore; I don't have the time or the inclination. I've got to get home, right now. Ludwig thwarted my plan of slipping back home during the night. Now half a day has gone and the worst-case scenario is nagging at my mind.

'Anni . . .' His tone changes: a sanctimonious purr. 'I'm worried about you.'

'Oh really? Just like you're worried about Dad?'

'What's that supposed to mean?'

'It means you're being astonishingly passive seeing as Marcus Steinhausen is a serious lead. A lead that might help exonerate your client.' I flop down on to the floor inelegantly to put on my boots. 'Shouldn't you already be in Inspector Brandner's office, making sure he interrogates Steinhausen again?'

'I'm just trying to protect you, child.'

'From Steinhausen? You've got a funny way of—'

'From yourself, Ann.'

Those words are like a slap to the face. I look at him as if numbed. 'Fuck you!' That's the last thing he hears me say before I leave his house.

I run as if my life depended on it.

My shoulder hurts from the jarring as I pound the streets, and my eyebrow throbs. I don't find a taxi until I get to Richard-Wagner-Platz. Judging by the driver's glances in his rear-view mirror, he's suspicious of me. I could have been boozing all night; at the very least I look like trouble with my scruffy black hair and the plaster on my face. And I don't stop panting.

'Let me know if you want me to stop for a bit, won't you?' He must be worrying about me vomiting all over his upholstery.

'It's okay, I'm fine. I'm just in a real hurry.' It is winter, after all; even during the day the temperature is below freezing, to say nothing of the nights. A feeling tightens around my chest. What if I've made a huge mistake?

'Are you really okay?' The driver again.

'Couldn't you drive faster?'

'I'm doing fifty as it is.'

And I'm doing my head in. I slide my hands beneath my thighs; my whole body is shaking. Behind my closed eyelids is Eva, and alongside her, the realisation of how everything can change in a few seconds. A conclusion I'd reached a while ago. I can't help burp – a mouthful of sour fermented whisky from last night. My plan was different. I just wanted to drink a tiny sip with Ludwig, to soothe his conscience, then steal away secretly. I'd have got home in time. What now?

Where we live is a 30 kph zone; I'm going up the wall. I beg the driver to let me out here, two streets away from our house. I don't even hear the price he mentions; I just shove a twenty in his hand, leap out of the cab and start running again.

Please, I didn't mean . . .

I'm throbbing with pain and tension, exploding with speculation. What if . . . ?

I run faster, already feeling for the unfamiliar key. The jeep is on the corner of a street, around two hundred metres from our house. Now, in the snow and sunshine, its redness is crying out for attention, whereas I didn't notice it yesterday evening, when Ludwig and I drove past it after our visit to Brandner.

Please . . .

I'm still running when I point the key at the vehicle to open the central locking.

I yank open the hatch to the boot.

He flinches, blinks. He's still alive.

I smile and say, 'Hello, Jakob. Now we can chat in peace.'

Recap:

On Thursday, 9 November 2017, around 9 p.m., an unnamed suspect was arrested at home in the connection with the ribbon murders, a series of killings stretching back a number of years. This message arrived at exactly 21.24 in the editorial office, where the journalist Jakob Wesseling was doing overtime writing another article. Like an animal advancing on its prey before the rest of the pack, he immediately seized on the topic, not without sensing the possibility of being promoted to deputy chief editor. Although the police were still keeping the identity of the suspect under wraps, Jakob knew exactly who he had to call at HQ to get hold of the name. A name he couldn't publish immediately – in part to protect his source – but which gave him a huge research advantage over his rivals. And Jakob did his research. This was going to be massive. A reportage, a glimpse behind the scenes, shedding light on the depths of the souls of those involved, a special spread or even an entire special issue, and he, as a much sought-after expert, would be invited on to TV talk shows and podcasts as soon as the anonymity of the suspect was lifted. Who was Professor Walter Lesniak? How could a killer raise a child? Why hadn't his daughter been aware of anything? Or did she know about it, maybe? What secrets was she hiding?

Jakob, for whom it was a doddle to find out Lesniak's address. Whose daughter now lived a very secluded life there. Jakob began watching her. Whenever anyone rang the doorbell, she would send them away, and she herself only rarely left the house, at most to go shopping. Moreover, in the first couple of weeks after her father's arrest she was still blonde. He felt it would be pointless to intercept her and solicit an interview. And there was no use him ringing her doorbell if friends and acquaintances were being turned away on the spot. But then one morning she left the house with black hair. The new colour seemed to have changed her; whereas she'd been stooped before, now he fancied she was walking more upright. He followed her to a fast-food outlet called Big Murphy's, where she was having a job interview that day, and got the idea of making friends with her.

From all the interviews he conducted as a journalist, he'd developed a keen sense for people. She was someone you had to be patient with. Someone who was lonely. So he made up a role for himself: the uncomplicated, carefree and cheerful Jakob from the recycling centre. A guy who didn't look as if he'd saddle her with any additional burdens. Who you could just go for a beer with and listen to music. A friend who made it easy to open up, a confidant.

On Christmas Eve he managed it.

They drank, they danced, she talked.

Jakob, who at the end of that evening laid a plastered Ann on the sofa. Covered her and sat beside her for a moment, sweeping strands of her hair from her face. To make sure she really had fallen asleep. Jakob, who made use of an opportunity his rivals could only dream of: snooping around Professor Walter Lesniak's house undisturbed. He switched off the light and, using the torch on his mobile, roamed every room. He inspected the contents of the cutlery drawer in the kitchen as well as the book spines on the sitting-room shelves. When he was finished on the ground floor he went upstairs. Now he knew which aftershave Lesniak used ('Fahrenheit' by Dior) and that Ann didn't wear tangas (but briefs, with a preference for pink and light grey). But he was most interested in the room at the end of the landing, which surely couldn't be locked for no reason. Jakob felt the door frame, but didn't find a key on top. Looking around, he saw the console table in front of the window and opened the drawers. In the left-hand one the Lesniaks kept their candles; in the right, a random selection of small things that didn't appear to have found a place elsewhere: spare buttons, sellotape, a roll of parcel string, a few CDs. On the shelf beneath the desk were books – shamelessly commercial literature, too unworthy for the shelves in the sitting room. But no key. Jakob had no idea why he now reached for the vase. Coincidence, instinct, or just one final, not particularly serious attempt to convince himself that he had really searched everything in this house? And so he got hold of the key. But at that very moment, he heard noises coming from downstairs. A sigh, a few words babbled in sleep – or was she merely dozing? His eyes darted to the window above the console table. It hadn't occurred to him that he hadn't used his mobile-phone torch for a while; it was already light outside. He'd have to come back another time to find out what was behind the locked door. He briefly toyed with the idea of hanging on to the key, but felt it was too risky. What if Ann noticed it was missing? Someone who had good reason to lock a room would also be minded to keep an eye on the key. So he returned it to the vase and went back downstairs. He checked on Ann, who was no longer breathing so deeply and slowly. By the time she woke up – which couldn't be long now – he had to work out how to get into the house unnoticed next time. When Ann stirred, Jakob darted into the hallway. He thought of those films in which door locks were opened with credit cards. But Jakob wasn't a cunning Hollywood burglar; he wasn't capable of that sort of thing. He was, however, a cunning journalist, and as such he had a professional eye for details. Hanging beside the coat hooks was a bunch of keys, including the one for the Audi. Because the car belonged to Walter Lesniak, Jakob could assume the bunch of keys was his too. Each of the five keys had a plastic tag. The red one said 'Uni office', the blue one 'Uni Library', the green one 'Garage' and the yellow one what he'd been looking for: 'Home'. Jakob fiddled the key off the small metal ring and slipped it into his trouser pocket. Then he made some coffee. For Ann who was going to wake up soon . . .

*

'. . . For Ann who he fucked over big time.' I'm leaning against the work surface, my hands crossed, shaking my head in disbelief. Jakob is sitting at the table. He looks pale, wrecked by what must have been the longest night of his life. The woollen blanket I've fetched him from the sitting room is over his shoulders like a coat. He's warming his hands on a mug of tea. In spite of everything, he doesn't appear in the least ashamed; while he was talking, he even managed to look me overtly in the eye.

'As if what you did was any different.'

'What?'

'The way you tricked your colleagues at Big Murphy's.'

'Oh, I see, and for that you think I deserved this charade.'

'I'd be very happy to discuss whether I deserved to be locked in my boot for half a day,' he says, slamming the palms of his hands on the table and getting up. 'I could have died, Ann!'

'Sit. Down.' On the work surface are a knife and my mobile, both within reach. One glance at them is enough, along with the fact that, after last night, he's no longer able to size me up. I could be Ann who acted on impulse, or Ann who doesn't care about anything anymore. I might call the police and report him as the intruder from last night, or thrust my knife into his chest. I could even do both, and justify the one thing as self-defence against the other. So he does what I ask and drops back on to his chair.

'Fine. What now?'

I clench my jaws. I don't want him to know how I feel. That I can hardly believe how we got into this situation. Him lying there, yesterday evening, at the bottom of our stairs. Me kneeling over him, expecting to discover Marcus Steinhausen's face beneath the balaclava. Instead it was Jakob, my friend. We'd danced together to Lou Reed. We'd circled like aeroplanes in a blue summer sky. Jakob the traitor. He scratched the record and broke my wings.

Disappointment. (Ann, 9 years old)

Disappointment feels like having water poured in your face. First your sad and you want to cry because you never thought someone could be so mean. And then your angry at yourself because you were so stupid to trust that person. That's why your to blame for your disappointment too and next time you should be more clever.

Yesterday evening.

I waved the knife about as I frisked Jakob's body. 'Who are you?' I said, shouting and howling. He just lay there, dazed after falling down the stairs, dazed after the shock of having been unmasked. In the inside pocket of his coat, I found a wallet as well as his car keys, and inside that his press ID. Fury paralysed my wits, leaving nothing but bitter hatred and the thought that Ludwig might be back with our food soon and so I didn't have much time. I tugged at Jakob's body until I'd forced him to his feet. He made an attempt to resist, but I was the one with the knife. I wasn't going to let him go. The garage, I thought. Or – even better – our car, to stop him drawing attention to himself by shouting and banging. Then I had another idea: I could use the break-in to steer the investigation back towards Steinhausen. Although then the police would go searching our house for clues and would definitely examine the garage as well.

'Where did you park?' I asked. Jakob, who in his state probably thought I just wanted to get rid of him as quickly as possible, told me. We took a detour via the garage, where I knew there was a roll of thick masking tape left over from when I helped Dad redecorate the sitting room a few months ago . . .

'You must realise you can't keep me detained here for ever,' Jakob says now, in the kitchen, rubbing his mouth. The masking tape I used to gag him has left visible red marks. 'Yesterday evening, after I'd fallen down the stairs, I was easy prey. I was completely out of it and you had a knife.'

'That hasn't changed,' I say, nodding to the knife beside me.

He shakes his head. 'You're not like that, Ann. I simply don't believe it.'

'By all means stand up and go to the door if you want to find out.'

'Let's both agree that this whole thing has got out of hand. We've both made mistakes.'

'Nice try.'

'I need to see a doctor, Ann!' Now he wrings his hands and forces a pained expression on to his face. 'I fell down the stairs and lay in a car boot for twelve hours in freezing temperatures. I've got hypothermia and I might have damaged a vertebra. For fuck's sake, Ann, honestly, why are you doing this?'

Without answering, I take hold of the knife and move towards him. Jakob leaps up from his chair and lurches backwards. Smiling, I withdraw to my initial position and put the knife back down beside me. 'You seem fine to me.'

Jakob growls; his reflexes have given him away. 'All right, what do you want?'

'Like I said, I want to talk.' With my chin I motion for him to sit down again. 'What were you looking for in my father's study? For proof the police have overlooked?'

'I dunno, perhaps. It seemed strange, at least, that the room was locked. And then I found the documents.'

The documents. Ludwig's folder, which I claimed the burglar had stolen. In fact, I'd actually hidden it in my rucksack before Ludwig returned and now it's lying on the kitchen table in front of Jakob, its cover closed.

'You're on thin ice, you know that, Ann?'

I nod feebly. He's right. This isn't me. The crack running through my life since my father's death seems to end in a crater that's getting wider and wider, swallowing up ever larger pieces of my old world. And maybe me as well. I hid the folder because I thought it would be good if the burglar had taken something linked to the case. Besides, it can't hurt to keep hold of the information about the case. Merely the thoughts my mind has been entertaining – they're so callous, so calculating. I had no problem forcing Jakob into his car boot, switching off all the lights in the house and then waiting as the distraught victim for Ludwig.

The end justifies the means, I tell myself. I'm not a bad person, just determined.

'You're not a hostage, Jakob. You can leave whenever you like.' I pointedly take the knife and return it to the block on the work surface. 'Go back to your paper, sit in front of your computer and write an article about your miserable night in the boot of your car. Or . . .' I smile.

'Or what?'

'You help me and end up writing the article of your life about one of the greatest miscarriages of justice this country has ever seen.'

*

It's the *or*, of course. Someone who's gone as far as Jakob has doesn't shuffle off without reaching the end. I remember what he said to me on Christmas Day: *Seek out a trustworthy journalist and give them an exclusive interview with your version of what happened.* From day one, *he* wanted to be that journalist. And when he broached the subject of my supposed daughter after my attack on the newspaper dispenser, this was just an attempt to break my shell. He already knew I didn't have children; he'd been watching me, studying me for weeks by then.

I don't trust him one bit, Dad. But I trust his ego. He'll do anything and everything for his story. And I've got support again.

Jakob's now in one of your jumpers. He's used your shower gel and shampoo. I don't like it, but I didn't want him to go home just for a hot shower. We can't waste any more time. He's read through all the documents in Ludwig's folder and he listened attentively as I told him about the past couple of days. He believes me, or at least he doesn't think it out of the question that Steinhausen, given his backstory, could be the real ribbon murderer.

'The guy's got to be somewhere,' was the last thing he said before unlocking my laptop to comb the internet. Sitting opposite him, I've drawn up a timeline of the murders in the hope of stumbling across a pattern.

> June 2003 – Larissa, 10
> January 2004 – Jana, 8
> June 2005 – Kati, 9
> 2006 – Nothing
> September 2007 – Olivia, 7

March 2008 – Laetitia, 10
2009 – Nothing
2010 – Nothing
April 2011 – Hayet, 9
2012 – Nothing
October 2013 – Jenny, 6
December 2014 – Saskia, 8
2015 – Nothing
July 2016 – Alina, 9
November 2017 – Sophie, 7

'One killing per year, albeit at different times, and then there are the years of inactivity: 2006, 2009, 2010, 2012 and 2015,' I summarise, sighing. 'That isn't a pattern. It could—' I'm interrupted by the ringing of my mobile, which is charging beside the empty fruit bowl on the work surface. I get up to check: it's Ludwig. Either he wants to appeal to my conscience or apologise. I reject the call.

'If you ask me, one murder per year is enough of a pattern,' Jakob says, when he sees I'm not going to take the call. 'As for those years when he takes a break, you're right. Either he didn't kill anyone because he couldn't, or he was abroad. Or there's a third possibility: the bodies simply haven't been found. When exactly was Steinhausen in rehab?'

I check the papers. 'September to October 2003, and then again from June to October 2005.'

'So he could . . .'

'Yes, he could. What have you found?'

'I've got . . .' Jakob starts to turn the laptop to face me, then stops. 'I've got a confession to make.'

'Okay?'

'Maybe it wasn't Steinhausen who tied the red ribbon to your olive tree.'

'Who, then?'

'Maybe there's a journalist out there who thought a little psychological pressure might help you open up.' He lowers his eyes, probably in expectation of my next outburst – screaming, scolding, swishing the knife. But I don't even shrug; I'm not surprised.

'Say something, Ann.'

'It's an oleander, you idiot.'

'That's not what I mean.'

'I realise that,' I say, shaking my head. 'It doesn't change anything.'

'With regards to Steinhausen or between us?'

'Steinhausen. I didn't get why he would threaten me and risk blowing his cover.'

'And between us?'

'*Maybe*,' I say harshly, 'you know by now that I'm able to defend myself, and so in the future you'll spare yourself the bother of trying to provoke me.' I nod at the laptop. 'Show me what you've found.'

A website. From Spain. *Servicio de artesano*, a tradesman working near Málaga. My heart leaps when Jakob points to a M. Steinhausen on the homepage. I'm already breathing with excitement, but Jakob beats me to it: 'Not so fast. This site hasn't been updated in over three years and it's impossible to say for certain that this is our Steinhausen.'

'But Steinhausen used to work as a site manager . . .'

'Which doesn't automatically make him a tradesman.'

'Surely we can find that out?'

My mobile rings once more. Again it's Ludwig and again I'm about to reject the call. But . . . if I do, he might decide to jump into his car and drive over here.

'Excuse me for a sec,' I say to Jakob, then answer the phone. 'Hello, Ludwig.'

'Anni.' As so often, it sounds like a sigh, only less resigned and more exhausted. Our row seems to have really affected him.

'Let's talk about it another time, Ludwig, okay? It doesn't suit—'

'No, listen to me,' he interrupts assertively. 'I've spent at least half an hour wondering whether ringing you is the right thing to do. But I thought I had to, to prove you have no reason to doubt me. Anni, it's like this . . .'

Ludwig waffles on and on – I can't take any more, not a single word.

It's only when he asks me if I've understood that I manage a 'yes', a lie. I've heard his words, but when it comes to their meaning my mind has abandoned me.

Six minutes, fourteen seconds, I see on the screen when we hang up. That's how long the call lasted. Jakob is standing beside me, stroking my arm. I didn't notice him get up from the table.

'Ann? What's wrong?' Now I can feel his hand on my cheek.

I shake my head. Sometimes it only takes a second to change an entire life. That's how it was with Dad's arrest and also with Eva in the basement of the building site. But sometimes it takes a moment longer. Six minutes and fourteen seconds, to be precise.

I look at Jakob. 'Steinhausen isn't in Spain. But I know where we can find him.'

'What?'

I nod. What Ludwig just told me is both horrific and a miracle: *Anni, it's like this. There seems to be a new case. In Schergel, in the Bavarian Forest.*

US

Sarah, sweetheart, wake up, wake up. I know you feel a bit woozy, but that's not bad. It's the magic working, you see? We're now going to eat together: you, me and the princess. Yes, that's right, the princess. Finally, it's time for you to meet her. But first we need to take you to the loo. You have to do a wee, Sarah, be a good girl and do a wee so we don't have another accident. That wouldn't be very nice, would it? I often wet myself when I was your age, you know. I was so scared when my mummy shouted at me that I lost control over my body. I'm not saying she was a bad person, she just had weak nerves and wasn't able to come to terms with her own anger. But all that's in the past and unimportant now. Oh, look at your hair! It's all dishevelled. Let me comb it for you, sweetie, okay? And then we'll go into the kitchen. Your legs are still too feeble, I'd better carry you, come here. By the way, I've made a sausage casserole. Do you like that? I hope so. I want you to be very happy here. This is your place, sit down, Sarah, go on, sit down. Oh no, don't topple off the chair, sweetheart! Lean back. It might be best if I fed you. Open your mouth like a good girl – yes, that's right, that's good. The way you're looking at her . . . I can understand. She's gorgeous, isn't she? What about you, princess? Are you still angry that I slept beside

Sarah last night? I just wanted her to feel comfortable, seeing as how everything here is still unfamiliar to her. Surely you understand that? Of course you do. Isn't this marvellous, the three of us? I could get used to this. The two of you are such lovely girls, such lovely, beautiful, well-behaved girls . . . Now, now, Sarah, careful! Chew slowly and swallow – it's no wonder you're sick if you bolt it down. We'll have to clean you up and then I think you should have another lie-down. I can read both of you a story if you like. What's your favourite story, Sarah? *Sleeping Beauty*? That's perfect.

ANN

BERLIN – SCHERGEL, 27 DECEMBER 2017

'A seven-year-old girl, Sarah, from Schergel, a village in the Bavarian Forest with just under a thousand inhabitants. Yesterday she and her mum went for a festive lunch with friends who also live in the village. Her mum sent her home early. It wasn't far, just a few streets in a place where it's impossible to disappear unnoticed. But when the mother got home in the afternoon to find Sarah not there, that's exactly what seemed to have happened: Sarah had gone and nobody had seen her. By the evening, friends and neighbours had gathered to search the village and surrounding area. There was no sign of Sarah, but they did find red ribbons in a wood.'

'Red ribbons, but no body?' Jakob narrows his eye in puzzlement. 'Where did the ribbons lead to?'

'Nowhere, according to my father's lawyer. They were just put at random in the wood.'

'That doesn't make sense.'

'No, maybe it does,' I say, then relay the rest of what Ludwig said, about the two possibilities the police in Schergel are considering. 'Either the abductor still has Sarah in his power – but for some reason he thought it important to let the police know he's active again and that they've arrested the wrong man – or the alternative is that it's a copycat crime, or just a bad joke in poor taste. If so, the question still remains: where is Sarah? She's not going to have run away and put out the red ribbons herself.'

'What are you going to do now?'

'I think you can guess that, can't you?'

'Good,' Jakob says, nodding decisively. 'I'm in.'

His jeep is parked in our drive, the boot facing the garage. I moved it myself this lunchtime from around the corner. I didn't want a neighbour to see Jakob climb out of the boot, let alone risk a scene in the street. My concerns about that were greater than my inherent anxiety about getting behind the wheel of a car, and it was only a few metres down the road. Now Jakob suggests we take turns driving to Schergel and that I go first, giving him the opportunity to do some more research, but also to establish contact with the police and try to find out more details.

'I haven't driven since I had a car accident two years ago,' I say, smiling helplessly.

'It's high time you did then.' He takes from me the bag I packed in a hurry, puts it in the boot, and then goes around to the passenger side as if the matter were decided. Not wanting to show any weakness, I get in and start the engine, while Jakob programmes the satnav. Schergel seems to be so small that only its main street is listed.

'Five hours, twenty minutes,' he says, doing the calculations. 'We won't be there before eight, half eight.' Particularly as we have to go past his flat first so he can pack a few things and pick up his laptop.

I shrug my shoulders, and the pain immediately flares up in the right one again.

'Everything all right?'

'It's okay,' I say, then ask him to find a news station on the radio. 'We have to take the gamble that we're going to get there too late. But until we hear that Sarah's been found, there's still the possibility the killer is keeping her captive. And so long as that's the case, it's also likely that he's in the vicinity of Schergel. He wouldn't have any reason to take her elsewhere. With the Berlin killings, he always stayed in the surrounding area.'

'That's not certain. He might change his pattern. I mean, hasn't he done that already? There's already been a victim this year: the little girl found in the Königswald. This would be the first time he's killed twice in a calendar year. And he's chosen a different region.'

'But it's also the first time that someone else is in prison, robbing him of the dubious fame of being the ribbon murderer.'

Jakob sighs.

'What?'

'Or is this really a copycat crime?'

I shake my head. 'Call me crazy, but I know we're on the right track. I can just sense it.'

'Red light!'

I brake just in time. We're jerked forwards abruptly, before being thrown back into our seats. My heart misses a beat – the memory. That appalling Saturday night two years ago: Zoe and I at a party in Spreenhagen. We had an argument and I drove home without her, furious and exhausted – but most of all, I shouldn't have been behind the wheel because I'd drunk too much. A shortcut I thought was a good idea at the time. A road through the woods that was so narrow and bendy it required a degree of concentration that a few bottles of beer had sluiced from my head. And then, as if in a bad film, the deer suddenly there in the middle of the road. Wrenching the wheel to the side, I found myself racing down a slope. Time lost its dimension, stretching, extending, then I heard the deafening crack. The crack of branches, of metal and finally of my jaw. The airbag activated too late. The driver's door had jammed into a tree, but I managed to crawl over to the passenger side and call my father on my mobile. I remember blood running from my mouth down my wrist as I spoke, trying to convey where I was. He came. The ambulance came too. I lay on a stretcher, my father holding my trembling hand. 'How do you feel?' he said, and I gave a pained smile with my bloody mouth. He could see how I was; he could imagine it too. In hospital they put splints and screws in my jaw and for the next few weeks all I could eat was soup and yoghurt.

'Ann?'

'Yes?'

'It's green.'

'Sorry.'

Jakob mumbles something.

'What?'

'I'm just thinking . . . You said the red ribbons were placed at random in the wood. Which means there's no way of working out the beginning and end of the trail?'

'So far as I know, yes. Why?'

He says nothing. It's only when I tap his thigh that he reacts. 'Just because Sarah's body isn't lying there for all to see doesn't mean she isn't there at all.' He pauses. 'Maybe they should try digging.'

'Maybe,' I repeat, snorting in frustration. 'This is exactly what gets me so down, you know? Everything is just *maybe, perhaps, possibly, conceivably* – all fricking speculation. My entire life is uncertain. There's nothing genuine, nothing real left, nothing I can rely on.'

'You can rely on me.'

I snort again, in amusement this time. 'Two liars heading off to find out the truth. Sounds like the beginning of a rather stupid joke.'

'Or the beginning of a first-rate reportage.' He puts out his hand. 'I live over there on the left. You can park right outside. I won't be long.'

The beginning of a first-rate reportage. I'm glad he's reminded me who I'm dealing with. We're not friends, we never were. We're of use to each other, no more, no less. And it's like a game, an exchange. I tell him about my childhood, which feels like a summer's day, about a little girl sitting on her father's shoulders with her arms outstretched. In return I make Jakob call the hospital and claim to be a journalist reporting on the incident at the construction site, so they'll give him information about Eva's condition. They certainly wouldn't say anything to me; I'm not related to Eva and those who are – Elke and Caspian – want me to go to hell.

'Unchanged but stable' is what Jakob eventually finds out. 'The doctor treating her says there haven't been any complications so far, which is a good sign.'

I thank him by talking about my puberty. Me as a difficult teenager always getting into trouble, and my wonderful father, a human instruction manual on how to bring up children. Someone who was always controlled and dependable. Never, not once, did he scream at me, shout, or even use harsh language, let alone slap my cheeky teen face – or any other part of my body, for that matter. And they reckon someone like that could have slit the wrists of ten little girls? Jakob records with the dictation app on his mobile, while scribbling in a notebook on his lap.

Then it's his turn again. This time he calls his contact at the police – Inspector Brandner's secretary, as he reveals to me. A young woman he sometimes meets for a drink out of work – nothing serious, but incredibly useful. I refrain from passing comment. I don't care about Jakob's private life and his morality; I just want to know what she said. It's sobering but unsurprising. 'Finding Sarah is the top priority. The local police are being assisted by search teams from nearby towns. So far, however, there are no new leads and . . .' He breaks off.

'Go on, I can pretty much guess already.'

'Although they're not ruling anything out, they're moving further towards the idea that this is a copycat crime. I'm sorry, Ann.' He does actually manage to sound concerned. 'They're saying it's the most probable—'

'"Everything that is merely probable is probably false,"' I interrupt him, smiling when he looks baffled. 'A quote by René Descartes. He wasn't just a philosopher, but a mathematician and scientist too. For him, doubting everything was the basis of all knowledge.'

'You mean I know that I know nothing?'

I shake my head. 'Wrong guy. That was Socrates. Who, by the way, actually said: "I know that I don't know." Your version comes from a mistake in translation. Socrates never claimed he knew nothing. Instead he questioned what it meant to know.'

'Jesus!' Jakob laughs. 'Maybe you ought to have studied philosophy rather than German.'

'I did to begin with, for four semesters. But the world becomes unpleasant when you only ask questions rather than simply living life. It's enough to have one person in the family doing it.'

'What about your mother?'

'Didn't you find out in your research? She died of cancer when I was six.'

'I'm sorry.'

'That's okay.'

'My mother's dead too. She died last year, following a stroke. I really miss her.'

I sigh. 'I miss mine too, even though I hardly have any memories of her. But I think that's quite normal. I mean, our parents determine a large chunk of our identity, don't they?'

'So if – and this is purely hypothetical, so don't flip out and lock me in the boot again – your father was convicted beyond all doubt of being the ribbon murderer—'

'I wouldn't only lose my father, but my identity too.'

Jakob scribbles something; I appear to have given him a quotation for his article. 'I understand,' he says, but he doesn't, he can't. For him these are just words, whereas for me my entire existence depends on it. Who would I be – what would remain of me? – if everything I've been up till now turned out to be a lie?

Security. (Ann, 9 years old)
Security means you don't have to worry even if something bad happens. Like when you lie awake in bed at night and there is thunder and lightening outside, but you know nothing is going to happen because Daddy has made sure that we have a lightening conducter. Without this the lightening could hit our house and then my room might burn down and I might die. But I don't believe that is going to happen. Because of the lightening conducter and because Mummy is already dead. People can't keep dying in the same family otherwise there would be nobody left.

Although Jakob took over the driving when it started getting dark, we haven't sped up. We keep having to stop so he can take a pee. He suspects he got a touch of hypothermia during the night but he's refraining from any reproachful looks. We get to Schergel just after half past nine. The village sits between the mountains, as if encircled, a deep hole that's very difficult to climb out of once you've fallen in. We follow the only road that snakes past houses set far apart from each other. Barely any streetlamps, an oppressive darkness that baffles me. I'd expected light, all sorts of light. Light in the houses, light from the search-lights, flashing blue lights. But there's not the slightest indication that a child has disappeared from here, presumably kidnapped by a dangerous serial killer.

'Are we really in the right place?'

Jakob just grins. Of course this is the right place – it's what the sign said, and what the satnav says too.

We keep driving down the road until we come to more houses, arranged around a circle, the centre of which is marked by a

long, scrawny maypole without a crown. The heart of the village.
Parked here are half a dozen patrol cars and police minibuses.
But where the hell is the activity? People swinging their torches
in all directions, search dogs excitedly tugging on their leads,
desperate calls for Sarah?

Nothing of the sort. Only a village that looks as if the night-
time bell had already been rung.

'What now?' I ask. Jakob points at the large building on the
other side of the circle: an inn. At least there appears to be some
sort of life, bathed in a yellow light, behind its leaded windows.
Shapes of people moving through the room.

'I come from a village like this originally,' he says, parking the
jeep outside a small grocery opposite. 'Life is very different from
in the city. Usually there's great cohesion amongst the people,
which has its advantages. On the other hand, it gives rise to a
sort of hostility to anything that comes from outside.'

'You mean they might not welcome the police here?'

'No, not that. It's just they might not help with the search to
the extent that you would expect, because they see the disappearance of a child here as a stain on the village. It doesn't fit
with the way they perceive themselves, it dents their pride. After
all, it's precisely what differentiates them from a big city like
Berlin: being sheltered, safe, people looking out for each other.'
Switching off the ignition, he turns to me. 'Somewhere there's
always an Auntie Erna leaning out of the kitchen window, playing
village sheriff.'

'Wow, it's great to know you don't have any prejudices.' I take
my mobile from the rucksack and see I've missed several calls en
route. Two from Big Murphy's, another from Michelle, who's also

sent me a message. I ought to have been back at work today, on the late shift starting at four. *None of the others know anything. I've told them you're sick. Take a few days off and have a think about whether you want to continue doing the job. Michelle.* Then Ludwig, who tried calling about an hour ago, no doubt to find out my whereabouts. He's no idea we've come to Schergel; he'd give me hell if he knew.

'Is everything okay, Ann?'

'Yes.' I quickly slip the mobile back in my bag. 'I'm just amazed at you, I really am. I mean, as a journalist you should always be neutral and impartial, shouldn't you?'

'As I said: I grew up in a village like this.'

We get out. Jakob locks the car and we make for the inn. 'And I also want you to be mentally prepared for this. The moment we go in, it's going to be like one of those old cowboy films. Two strangers enter the saloon, conversation stops and everyone eyes us up and down suspiciously . . .'

We're only a few steps from the door when it opens suddenly. Police officers come pouring out and head for their vehicles.

'You see? They're not keen on interlopers here. We'd better watch our step or we won't get any information out of them.'

I roll my eyes and go ahead. 'That doesn't mean they've been shown the door. Maybe they just went in for something to eat and now they're finished.'

The inn is called 'Zum alten Brock'. It's furnished in rustic oak, the air is thick and the tiles sticky. It smells of spilled beer, sweat and gravy. My attention is drawn at once to the silver serving platters, at least five on each table. Some still have a few sandwiches, others are empty save for the odd crumb and the parsley garnish. A fat old man with a shiny bald head peels away from a group of people in civilian clothes, some of whom are holding beer tankards.

'Welcome, welcome!' he says, his arms wide open, and all eyes now focus on us. 'Police, psychological support, press?'

'No, no,' Jakob stammers beside me. 'Just, er . . . passing through.'

The man looks visibly disappointed. 'You can have a room but the kitchen's closed,' he says, turning away. I think of Eva, who immediately sensed who we had to pretend to be so that Rainer Meller would talk to us.

'Press! From Berlin!' I call out, then say more quietly to Jakob, 'Come on, show him your press pass.'

The man's name is Brock. Together with his wife, who he introduces to us, he's the owner of this place, which has been in his family for three generations. One of the Schergel old guard, a village elder, chairman of the local council and treasurer of the heritage association – he comes up with all sorts of labels to make us aware just whose serving platters are on those tables. We also get two tankards of beer on the house and a promise of the best accommodation. Because we're journalists – finally, some journalists! – and what's more, we're from Berlin. Although the regional paper was here today too, all the guy did was take a few photographs of the police search. Which makes Brock's face turn red with indignation.

'They're only interested when there's a dead body,' he complains, and he's probably right. So long as Sarah's still missing, there's hope, and hope doesn't sell papers. 'They don't even think it *was* the ribbon murderer who took the little girl, because he's meant to be in prison in Berlin. But who put all those red ribbons in the woods, then?'

To signal my agreement, I lift my tankard and take a sip of beer. The group that was standing in the middle of the room when we came in has now gathered around the table where Brock has placed us. It's the best table, normally reserved for the council. Jakob sits next to me, on the corner bench covered in coarse woven fabric, looking stiff and bewildered. *Things happen differently here*, he just whispered to me. And he wasn't talking about canapés.

'What are the police up to?' I ask Brock, in reference to the men we just saw leaving the pub. 'Have they clocked off for the day?'

'No, no, they just needed a little break for refreshment. In fact, they're expanding the search area tonight. The village community was out there too, all day long, looking for the little one. The police wanted to discourage us, worried that we might destroy potential evidence. But they were banging their heads against a brick wall there.' He turns to the group around us. 'Sarah will come back home!' General agreement, clinking of tankards. 'She's Kerstin's daughter, you know. Kerstin Seiler, who runs the butcher's here, a good woman. She's all on her own with the child and does her work too.' He shakes his head. 'She doesn't deserve this, does Kerstin.'

'Who does?' I say quietly, thinking of Michelle, whose entire family died along with Larissa.

'I'm sure the police have questioned all of you already,' Jakob chimes in. He finally seems to have stirred from his numbness. 'But did you notice anything in the days before Sarah's abduction? Any unfamiliar faces in the village?'

'Well,' Brock says, rubbing his chin. 'Helping with the search yesterday and today there was all manner of outsiders. But in the days beforehand . . .' He shrugs. 'I mean, it was Christmas, wasn't it? Not much happening here. Even though it's a wonderful place to spend your Christmas holiday. The woods, the mountains, the old fortress ruins. We've spent years trying to raise our tourist profile. I've got a few holiday houses of my own on the upper common, if you fancy taking a look.' Again the clinking of tankards, no doubt toasting the magnificent local landscape.

'It's really shit that there's no photo of Steinhausen on the internet,' I whisper to Jakob, but no sooner have I said this than something occurs to me: brothers whose resemblance has deceived many people. I take out my mobile with trembling fingers and do an image search for Andreas Steinhausen. Apart from the blond hair and freckles, he has scarcely anything in common with the man on the chair with a swollen eye and fat lip who I saw in the basement of the construction site. Nonetheless I recognise him at once. The architecture practice he owns has a website with photographs of all the members of staff. I hold out my screen to Brock and the others. 'Recognise this man?'

'Hard to say; maybe, maybe not. Is that him? Is that the guy who's taken our Sarah?'

'Yes,' I say.

'No,' Jakob says. 'But he is someone we'd like to speak to. Talking of which, do you think it would be possible to have a word with Sarah's mother?'

Brock gets up at once. 'Come with me.'

In a second. First Jakob and I have to get something clear, just between us two. We do it outside in a whisper. Am I out of my mind, setting the village mob on to Steinhausen? 'Just imagine if he really did turn up here and they recognised him from the photo you showed them. He'd be lynched, Ann! And if later people are asking, *How could that have happened?*, the spotlight will fall on those two journalists from Berlin, who were so reckless with their information.'

'Are you worried about your reputation, or do you really sympathise with that bloke? Steinhausen is a murderer, Jakob!'

Jakob grabs my arm and I immediately feel a stabbing pain in my injured shoulder. 'No, right at the moment your father is the murderer and Steinhausen is just a lead. Can you get that into your head?'

I jerk my arm to free myself from his grip, which causes more pain, but most of all I feel anger. At Jakob, who's right. I mustn't make any mistakes now. Steinhausen could be close by. What if he got wind of the fact that he's no longer a phantom? That the village mob is openly looking for a blond man with freckles? He would disappear, perhaps for good. And he'd take Sarah with him or dispose of her.

'I understand,' I growl.

'Good. Then let's talk to the mother.'

A mother like Michelle. I picture her lying on the rug in her sitting room, writhing with anxiety, her chest open; and us, the supposed journalists, lusting after sensation, leaning over her, rummaging in her pain, disembowelling her. The worst thing is that Jakob seems to think nothing of it. He strides buoyantly as we follow Brock to the butcher's, which is opposite the inn, with only the round marketplace in between. Jakob, who's concerned about the safety of a killer, but who has no scruples when it comes to the victims. I feel sick.

A few minutes later we're sitting in the large, cold kitchen of

Seiler, the butcher's. It's inhospitable here, the floor and walls all covered in tiles. Like a repurposed slaughter room, I think, all the more so when I spot a drain the size of a beer mat beside my foot. Only the units along with the cooker and fridge, and the chunky wooden dining table suggest that this is a kitchen. Sarah's mother, Kerstin Seiler, is a petite woman, more like an overgrown little girl. It's strange to think that she slaughters animals and processes them into the joints and cuts that will later be on display in her shop. Her face is young and pale; her dark ponytail looks as if it had been tied a few days ago and not touched since. She's sitting limply on a chair, the focal point of a tragedy, slightly apart from the table where Jakob and I have sat. A man with gelled hair and a severe side parting is standing just to the right of her, his hand protectively on her shoulder. He's barely taller than me, in stark contrast to his beefy upper body with its pumped biceps that he puts on show in his stained, white sleeveless T-shirt, despite the temperature. This is Schmitti, from Schmitti's Garage, Brock told us. Kerstin Seiler's fiancé, a good bloke – he can fix everything that goes wrong in Schergel, from a car to a toaster. To Kerstin's left is a friend, an attractive blonde woman who strokes her knee and passes her fresh tissues at irregular intervals. Everything about her face is so delicate, perfect and symmetrical – it reminds me of Zoe. I would often stare at Zoe, simply fascinated by the interplay of her features. When the woman catches me gazing at her, I look away. Brock is leaning against the edge of the table. He's really selling us to Kerstin Seiler: Jakob and me, two important journalists who are going to bring the search for Sarah to the attention of the media nationwide. Frau Seiler doesn't seem to hear a word he's saying;

she just sobs. Schmitti, on the other hand, gives us suspicious looks vicariously. Me with my baggy turquoise knitted hat over my unwashed, jet-black dyed hair, and the plaster above my eyebrow as if I'd just been in a street fight; and Jakob, who's still wearing my father's jumper, its old-fashioned diamond pattern making him look like a penniless student.

'What good's it going to do Sarah being in the national newspapers?' he snarls at Brock. 'What's important is that the police are here looking for her. And that's exactly what's happening. So how would it help us?'

'Come on, Schmitti, it means Schergel will be on everyone's radar! We'd get more people volunteering to join the search. And if the kidnapper tries to flee with her, he won't get very far, because everyone will recognise Sarah as the missing girl.'

Schmitti growls again. '*Schergel will be on everyone's radar* . . . Is that your new ploy to attract tourists, Peter? Or nutters who get a kick out of visiting crime scenes? I mean, those people have to stay somewhere and eat too, don't they?'

Brock takes a step forwards, as does Schmitti, who plants himself in front of Kerstin like a barricade.

'How dare you accuse me of trying to profit from the disappearance of an innocent little girl!'

'No, Peter, how dare you—'

'Wait!' I say, getting to my feet. 'We won't publish anything you're not happy with. We only want to help.' I look at Jakob, who ought to be backing me up, but he's just sitting there, arms crossed like a passive spectator.

'We had a row,' a voice says softly from behind Schmitti's back. Kerstin Seiler, who's now commanding everyone's attention.

'Kerstin, you don't have to—' her fiancé says, but she shakes her head.

'We were invited for lunch with friends. I sent Sarah home early because she was playing up. She was so loud and hyper, she kept interrupting every conversation – she was being impossible. I grabbed her by the arm, dragged her into the hall and told her she was being a right nuisance.' Kerstin sobs loudly. 'It was all my fault that she was out there on her own. If I'd been with her . . .'

'You mustn't write any of that!' Schmitti hisses. 'Nobody must find that out, least of all the police.'

I look at him, puzzled.

'That there was an argument!' he explains. 'The police won't take the thing seriously anymore because they'll think Sarah simply ran away. They might even stop their search.'

'I don't think there's any danger of that. I mean, they found the red ribbons, just . . .' I break off, ashamed.

'Just like the ribbon murderer always left,' Kerstin Seiler's friend says, finishing my sentence, dabbing her eyes with a tissue.

'I'm sorry,' I say softly, but it's too late. The air is thick and heavy with unspoken speculation and fears. It's Schmitti who brings an end to the unpleasant situation.

'Right then. Here's the plan. You're going to leave now, all of you. It's late and Kerstin really needs some peace and quiet. You' – he points at Brock – 'are going to keep your nose out of it from now on. The two of you' – Jakob and me – 'can make yourselves useful by joining the search tomorrow. We're going to the upper common. The more we are, the better. And Nathalie' – that's the friend's name – 'I'm going to take you home now. Your little one will be wondering where her mummy's got to.'

'But Kerstin can't be on her—' the woman tries to protest.

'I'll stay the night with her,' Schmitti says. 'And then we'll all meet back here tomorrow morning, seven o'clock.' He gives Jakob and me a look of defiance. 'Woe betide anyone who's not punctual.'

US

Can you hear that, my girl? The shouting. It's echoing up from the valley. It's the red ribbons in the woods making them sound shriller, louder, more panicky. Was it too early to put out the ribbons? Maybe. But they're all part of it, just like the missing shoe in the *Cinderella* story or the poisoned apple in *Snow White*. Look, Sarah! Come here, I'll lift you up so you can look out of the window. The men from the search unit have been having a break, but they're getting going again now. It's said that the first twenty-four hours after someone goes missing are the most important – you've been missing considerably longer than that. What's more, it's supposed to get down to minus ten or more tonight again; they must be really worried. The dancing lights of the torches in the woods, the shouts, all the commotion – and just for you, my sweetie, just for you. What would they give to get you back unharmed, hmm? What do you think? Their lives, they'd answer if they were asked. That's what they've all said, in the paper, on telly, all the parents who've ever spoken publicly about it. *I'd swap my life for my daughter's.* That sort of thing's easy to say when it's not an option. I mean, they've never been offered a deal like that: *You've got the choice. Your child's going to die unless you sacrifice yourself.* That's not what this is about. That was never part of this story. Still, saying something like that sounds good. Words society expects to hear in such a situation. But what I want to know is, how many of these people really meant it? If they were given the offer to swap places with their children, how many would take it up? Let me tell you, sweetie: none of them. But your mummy, she might be very close right now. She's at rock bottom, broken, chastened. You know what that means, don't you? It means it's time, Sarah. The last act, then the end.

ANN

A restless night, a peculiar dream. Me, sitting motionless on the bed in room 113. It's a simple room: a bed, above it Christ on his cross as a reminder, a wardrobe with a double door and a narrow desk. The only slight nods to luxury are a small television set, a kettle, a basket with a selection of teas, sugar sachets and capsules of condensed milk, and a cup. I'm still fully dressed in my coat, hat and boots. Beside the bed is my bag, with tracksuit bottoms and the fresh sweatshirt I could wear to sleep in after a nice shower. Jakob has the room next door. I'm grateful for the wall between us, for some distance. I'm exhausted and confused. As if I were trapped in one of those psychedelic spirals that open and close again and seem to be permanently rearranging themselves, while I desperately look for a fixed point to focus on. But the spiral twists and turns, overloading my brain. Why Schergel, this tiny, anonymous village in the Bavarian Forest? What has driven Steinhausen here?

I dream that I get up from the bed, in a trance, being controlled remotely. I leave my room, cross the landing to the stairs, and then creep downstairs. I turn the key in the back door and step out into the night. I dream I'm running. There's no particular goal; I tell myself to be guided by my instinct. Down the main street, past houses where only the odd light is on. A few insomniacs who likewise feel it's wrong to happily go to bed while Sarah's outside somewhere, in the cold, in danger, terrified for her life. Maybe she's no longer alive. Maybe she's lying undiscovered in the woods, her face blue and the blood from the deep wound on her wrist already frozen. Something is driving me, I dream, driving me on. The distance between houses increases, the broad road becomes narrow and uneven beneath the blanket of snow. There's no longer any light to help guide me; it's a darkness I've never experienced in the city. I take my mobile out of my coat pocket and turn on the torch, but it has a tiny radius. I spin around, first in one direction, then the other. I'm wheezing as I breathe, hemmed in by the blackness closing in on me. *The fear of fear gives rise to more suffering than the actual cause* . . . I don't believe myself. I try to shout for help but the cold constricts my throat. My chest contracts. My spray, is all I can think. My asthma spray, which is in my rucksack, which in turn is on the desk of room 113. I dream I fall to my knees; now I'm on all fours in the snow, not knowing what to do next. They say you don't die in your dreams; you always wake up in time. So I roll on to my side, curl up and wait. Soon I'll wake up, I must wake up soon . . .

My mobile rings. A sound that bores into my head like a nasty little hand drill. I sit bolt upright in bed. Orientation. Room 113 and sunshine slanting dazzlingly through the window. My heart racing, my mouth gasping in panic for oxygen, as if I'd just been holding my breath for minutes. Jakob sitting on the edge of the bed. His outstretched hand stroking my cheek.

'Hey, nice and calm now,' he says gently, then turns away and remarks, 'She's really hot.'

I recoil in sheer panic. What's Jakob doing in my room? How did he get in here? What's happened?

'We should at least take her temperature,' a woman says, and a moment later Frau Brock, the landlady, comes into view. She sits on the other side of the bed and hands me a thermometer. 'Here, put this under your armpit. And then drink your tea.'

A cup is thrust into my hand and sympathetic smiles come from both sides of the bed.

'You gave us quite a fright.'

I can barely get a sound out, but Jakob seems to understand me. 'Just after three o'clock this morning, Kerstin Seiler's fiancé, Schmitti, found you on the lane from the village to the woods. You were completely frozen and torpid.'

'He called my husband and tried to keep you warm until Peter arrived with the car to bring you back here,' Frau Brock adds.

I shake my head in bewilderment. I recall my dream, ending with me curled up in the snow, and nothing else. There's no Schmitti finding me, and no Brock heaving me into his car. There's nobody carrying me up the stairs to room 113, taking off my wet clothes and putting me to bed in my underwear.

'What were you doing?' Jakob asks, but I just shake my head again. Looking for Sarah? For Steinhausen? I don't know; I wasn't even aware I'd left the inn.

The thermometer beeps.

'Your temperature's just a bit high, no cause for concern,' Frau

Brock says, smiling again. I still feel totally spaced out, and the sun is so blinding that tears come to my eyes. Seven o'clock sharp, I remember. That's when we were going to meet at the butcher's. To search for Sarah on the upper common. It would have still been dark then.

'What's the time?'

'Just after nine,' Jakob says.

'What about the search?'

'A few have set off already,' Frau Brock says, getting up off the bed. 'Your colleague and I wanted to make sure you were okay before heading out ourselves.'

'What? No!' Flinging the duvet aside, I leap up on to my wobbly legs. 'I'm coming too! You've got to wait for me! I'll get dressed in a jiffy.'

'Oh, Ann . . .' Jakob thinks I'm stubborn.

Yes, yes, I am, I always have been.

He also thinks I ought to take it easy.

Thanks, but no need. That was strange, last night, I realise. But let's not get it out of proportion. It must have been my nerves, a little blackout; this sort of thing can happen after all I've been through recently. End of discussion, I hop into the bathroom, Jakob stays in my room.

Meanwhile Frau Brock has gone downstairs to make a breakfast I can take with me. I don't want anything to eat and I've told her that, but she says I've got to get something in my tummy, even if it's just a dry roll.

'You haven't told anyone about my dad, have you?' I ask Jakob through the closed bathroom door. It's horrible, this bathroom. Cramped and windowless, with ventilation that sounds like a broken hair dryer. There's a yellowish light and it smells mouldy. I try to breathe through my mouth as much as possible.

'As an explanation for your crazy little nocturnal outing, you mean? Of course not. I told them that we've spent the past few weeks researching a complicated story and you haven't had much sleep. Talking of which . . . are you getting enough at the moment? Studies suggest that even after twenty-four hours without sleep, the human brain finds it more difficult to process information. Occasionally people develop symptoms similar to those displayed by schizophrenia patients, who are bad at distinguishing important things from unimportant ones, or unable to do so altogether.'

My reflection rolls its eyes and mutters, 'He knows that, but he can't distinguish an oleander from an olive.'

'Ready,' I call as I step out of the bathroom shortly afterwards. Jakob's standing beside the desk where my mobile is. I see him pull his hand away – caught in the act.

'You've had three or four calls this morning. Maybe you ought to see who's been trying to ring.'

I do. It's Ludwig who's called and who also sent me a message: *Where are you?*

Very soon, I promise him in my head. Then I put the mobile in my rucksack and grab my coat.

'How come Schmitti found me? Have you got any idea?'

Jakob looks at me. 'Hmm?'

'Well, you were all wondering what I was doing on the lane in the middle of the night. What about Schmitti? Why was he there?'

'He said Kerstin Seiler had remembered something. Apparently there's an old haystack where Sarah plays sometimes. When Schmitti went to take a look, he practically stumbled across you.

'He was on his own?'

'Just like you.'

'Yes, but I . . . I wasn't quite myself.'

Jakob grins. 'Who is?'

When we enter the dining room, we interrupt Brock and his wife in conversation. In the middle of the table they're sitting at is a thermos. Beside it a camera and two fist-sized objects wrapped in foil. I guess they're my rolls.

'Okay, let's go,' Brock says, standing up.

'Just a moment,' I say, because I hear my phone ringing again in the rucksack. I know it's Ludwig before I take the mobile out and glance at the screen. I nip outside because I don't want the others to hear my conversation. It's absolutely freezing out here. The sun has gone in again, leaving an ugly winter greyness. A few people are out in groups and Sarah's name echoes from somewhere in the distance.

I take the call. 'Hello, Ludwig.'

He says he's tried to reach me half a dozen times already. Now he's standing outside our house but nobody's answering the door. Where the hell am I?

'I've come to Schergel.'

You've got to be joking, he says. Have I lost my mind completely? And an astonishing array of expletives for an educated man in his prime.

'I had to do it, Ludwig. I know he's here.'

'Who? Steinhausen? For Christ's sake, Anni, stop meddling and let the police get on with their work!' He screams so loudly that it grates in the earpiece of my mobile. It's so unpleasant that my patience is wearing thin. I don't want to be patronised anymore.

'Oh, so I should copy you, should I? Just sit around doing bugger all?'

'I can't believe the—'

'You're right. I am being impertinent. I mean, you do everything for your clients, don't you? Your commitment even stretches to slipping me sleeping pills.'

'How can you think that of me? I didn't give you anything, do you hear? I'd never . . .'

Whatever he's saying goes in one ear and out the other when my attention fixes on what's happening on the other side of the marketplace. A crowd is gathering outside the butcher's. People are streaming as if in rays towards a centre, a single point. I almost drop my mobile when I realise what this point actually is: it's Sarah.

Throwing open the door to the pub, I scream, 'Sarah! Sarah's back!' I see Jakob and the others leap up from the table, hear the clatter of the chairs. We dash across the marketplace to the butcher's, right into a wall of people. There could be thirty, or even fifty. Brock's massive frame clears a way through for us to the front, where it's almost reverentially quiet compared to the back. Schmitti is lifting Sarah into his arms. He's taken his coat off and wrapped her in it like a cocoon. She's got a face like a doll, with large round eyes and a heart-shaped mouth. But she looks blank, just staring into nothingness. Beside her is Kerstin Seiler, pale and stiff, her face as expressionless as her daughter's. A puzzling sight, but I expect she's still in shock. Her friend, the petite blonde, is there too, offering Kerstin a tissue she clearly doesn't need. I wince when Brock's elbow digs into my side as he thrusts his hands up to take a photo of the miracle. My eyes meet Jakob's. He appears to find it as hard to believe as I do. As everyone does. Sarah is back, she's alive. She got away from Steinhausen.

US

You found the way back – respect, little Sarah. It's a long way, and in this cold weather too. That shows willpower and remarkable determination. Your reappearance caused a huge commotion; of course it did. They're practically pouncing on you, they're all gawping. You're a sensation. The girl who escaped from the ribbon murderer. That Schmitti is showing you off like a trophy; your mother is so vulgar.

It went wrong, all so wrong.

The wrong ending.

If I could do what I want to do, I'd push them aside and grab you, here and now. I'd snatch you from Schmitti's arms and run away with you. But then it would be over for good; I realise that. They'd arrest me. So I've got no choice but to observe the situation from my cover.

You won't tell them anything, will you, Sarah? Surely you're not going to expose me? No, you won't; you're well aware of the consequences, you know what's at stake.

Calm, calm, stay calm, I tell myself. It's just gone wrong. But that doesn't mean it's over. And isn't that the lovely thing about a story? It's flexible, it can change with every new word. And who else has the power over the characters and the narrative, if it isn't the person who created them?

ANN

SCHERGEL, 28 DECEMBER 2017

Another hospital corridor, again the typical sterile smell. I think of Eva and how she was admitted to hospital only two days ago. Two days that have felt like an eternity, as have the past few weeks – a yawning gap between me and my earlier life. The time before Dad's arrest, I think. A time I can scarcely comprehend now, and only remember as if it were a film where the main character looked like me. In my new reality, for the past two and a half hours Jakob and I have been hanging around the coffee machine in the waiting area of the children's ward. From here we can see the closed door of the room where Sarah is. Her mother is with her, as well as two police officers and a psychologist, who are carrying out a preliminary interview. We know this from Brock, Schmitti and Kerstin Seiler's blonde friend, who were also in Sarah's room, but have been sent out for the questioning. Schmitti's standing with us, the blonde woman has excused herself to ring her mother, and Brock has one ear pinned to the door, which I find both appalling and practical. For we can be confident that everything he overhears will be relayed to us without delay.

'Physically she's fine, apart from a few bruises,' Schmitti says, giving us the essence of the doctor's diagnosis. He's a changed man, so much friendlier and more open than yesterday evening at the butcher's. 'But they've found traces of an unknown substance in her urine and so now they're giving her a blood test too. And she's not speaking. Not a word. Must be the shock.'

I nod. If she's lucky, it's only shock, I think, recalling the conversation I had with Eva a couple of days ago. About the gaps in the chronology of the killings. Eva thought there might be victims who'd escaped Steinhausen's clutches, but felt too ashamed to tell anyone. They'd kept it to themselves to this day, years of silence which might last for ever. Disgruntled, I take a sip from the paper cup Jakob got me from the machine. This is my third coffee and I'm only drinking it to have something to do.

'Doesn't the girl have a father?' Jakob asks, nodding in the direction of Sarah's room.

'Pff,' Schmitti responds. He's also holding a cup of coffee. 'A total loser. He's the one who originally comes from Schergel, not Kerstin. The butcher's belonged to his uncle, who died ages ago. Kerstin only moved here because of Sarah's dad; they had the child and ran the butcher's together. Although basically she did all the work. He spent most of his time popping over the border to the Czech Republic to have his way with whores. Then one day he never came back. Since then, Kerstin's had nobody apart from us – a blessing and a curse.' Pointing at Brock, he laughs. 'No, seriously, it's what makes our village so special. We'll take in anyone who's willing to integrate into the community. And Kerstin isn't the only single mum in the village. There's Nathalie too.' He points over his shoulder. Nathalie – that's right, that's her name. Kerstin's blonde friend who reminds me so wonderfully and yet painfully of Zoe. I spent the whole morning racking my brains, but her name eluded me. 'She moved here from Wuppertal, literally fled from her violent ex, poor thing. Up until a few weeks ago, she kept herself totally shut off from everyone, but in the meantime she's been working in the butcher's with Kerstin. And at the kindergarten, two of the teachers are a gay couple. They're from Munich and they wanted to escape the consumer society with their own little house and a few chickens.'

Two more things that remind me of Zoe: Wuppertal, where she comes from, and the dream of making a fresh start, somewhere completely different. Where the sky is blue and there are no vapour trails. A little cottage with colourful shutters and a garden she would allow to become elegantly overgrown, preferably in Cornwall. A feeling washes over me, a scene from the past: Zoe's head in my lap, my finger tracing the contours of her face. 'What will become of me when you're dancing barefoot in your magical English garden?' I ask.

She laughs. 'Either you can stay here in Berlin, devoured by longing, or you can come with me . . .'

I hastily take a sip of my coffee, as if it were a medicine for forgetting. Eva was right: *Memories are only lovely when there's hope.*

'Goodness gracious!' comes the exclamation of surprise from Brock, attracting all of our attention. The door to Sarah's room has opened right by his nose, and no sooner have the two officers and the psychologist come out than he slips in. Schmitti too hands me his half-drunk coffee and hurries into Sarah's room.

Jakob clears his throat. 'Now you can watch a professional at work,' he announces, intercepting the officers and psychologist. He tells them he's from the press and asks for information. But they give him the brush-off. Ongoing investigation. 'Be patient until we make an official statement, Mr Newshound,' one of the officers says before the group head for the lifts. Pointing his index finger in my direction, Jakob says, 'You dare,' but I don't feel like passing comment. Because although I'm relieved that Sarah has come back home unharmed, I find it unsettling too. What does it mean that Steinhausen's victim slipped from his clutches? Is he going to disappear? Will he simply snatch another girl or will he try to approach Sarah again? She is, after all, a witness who could describe and identify him. I look around: the corridor is empty, nobody here apart from us. All the same, I'd feel more comfortable if the police posted someone outside Sarah's room, like you see sometimes in films. 'She must be safe here?' I ask Jakob. He sighs.

'We don't even know what really happened, Ann. But I don't think you need worry about—'

'Where is everybody?' Nathalie interrupts him, having come back from her phone call.

Jakob points at Sarah's room. 'Maybe we ought to go in too,' he says as we watch her head for the door. 'It doesn't seem to bother Sarah's mother that people are piling in. The poor child.'

'Maybe she's just glad not to have to go through this on her own.'

He laughs. 'You'd make a terrible journalist. Far too sentimental.'

'It's what my father taught me,' I say. It's a fleeting pain, like pulling off a plaster, but there's no denying it's there. 'Everything that happens in the world, every single action and every consequence, is based on an emotion.'

'I always thought scientists were only interested in facts.' Jakob reaches for Schmitti's coffee, which I'm still holding, takes a sip and pulls a face.

'Folks!' So abruptly that both of us jump. Brock comes out of Sarah's room and hastens excitedly towards us. 'I've got something for you!'

'New information?'

He waves the camera in his hand. 'Schmitti and Nathalie didn't think I should, but – well!'

'Go on, tell us!'

'It'll cost you fifty euros,' he says, and after Jakob and I nod in unison, he shows us a photo on the screen. Sarah in her hospital bed. He made her close her eyes specially for the photo. All he says is, 'I thought this would be good for your article,' and winks. But what he means is: the girl – white face, pale lips, but most of all the way she's lying there, eyes closed and hands crossed above the covers – looks dead.

I have a brain fade: 'How can you be so fricking callous?'

'Ann!' Jakob says, trying to keep me in check.

And Brock, in indignation: 'Look, I'll happily go and sell my information to another paper!'

'No, no, Herr Brock,' Jakob insists. 'She didn't mean it like that.'

Oh yes, she did. But she realises that new information is more important than her personal opinion. So she apologises, gritting her teeth. Brock accepts the apology, along with the fifty euros from her purse. For that we make him delete the photograph under our supervision and get him to promise he won't take any more of Sarah in her hospital bed.

'She told the police officers she was with a princess in a castle,' he now starts up, theatrically planting his bloated body on one of the chairs in the waiting area. 'Hiding from the evil dragon.'

'Which princess?' Jakob asks.

'What sort of castle?' I ask.

Brock can't answer either question; apparently Sarah didn't say any more. Fifty euros for a smattering of words, and even these don't make any sense. I sigh. 'Is there a castle nearby she might have meant?'

Brock says no, not a castle, but there are some old fortress ruins. 'Maybe we should take a look around there,' Jakob says.

'Or,' I ponder, 'she's talking about something completely different. When we were children, my friend Eva and I had other names for the places where we used to play. There was a raised hide we used to call the tower, and an old gravel pit was our sea.'

Jakob looks at me as if I'm not all there; he must have been a very unimaginative child.

'I mean, she's hardly likely to have been with a real princess either,' I add. 'And so far as I know, dragons don't exist.' My gaze catches Kerstin Seiler, who right now is coming out of her daughter's room with Schmitti and Nathalie. I stride purposefully towards them. 'Excuse me, Frau Seiler, just a quick question. Can you think of where Sarah was talking about when she spoke of a castle? Or who the princess and dragon might be?'

'Piss off!' she snarls, scurrying away, followed by Schmitti. I turn to Nathalie, helplessly.

'You do know the doctors found bruises on Sarah?' she says sotto voce.

I try to square this with Kerstin's angry reaction. *A deranged paedophile*, comes to mind. These were the words Eva used when we were wondering what motive might be driving the ribbon murderer.

'But her abductor didn't . . .' I slap my hand over my mouth.

226

Nathalie shakes her head. 'No, no, it's not that. It's the fact that the bruises are older,' she says, giving me an emphatic look. 'Sarah didn't get them from the kidnapper.'

RECORDING 05
Berlin, 7 May 2021

- Are you saying that criminal damage is a pointless act, whereas murder isn't?
- If you put it that way, yes. Why else did you slash your teacher's tyres?
- Like I said, I was in with the wrong crowd. I think I just wanted to be cool. There were no higher motives.
- You see?
- *(sighs)* Okay, I took the bait. Well?
- Well, what?
- Your *higher motives*.
- Oh God, that tone.
- What were you expecting?
- Expecting? Nothing. More like wishing. I wish for impartiality, more for your sake than mine. Because you say you want to understand, and I actually believe you do. But how can you understand when your preformed opinion is in the way? You regard me as a psychopath, don't you?
- I, er . . . I don't know . . .
- Go ahead and say it, don't be shy. You wouldn't be the only one. In your eyes, what makes someone a psychopath?
- Well, to the best of my knowledge, psychopaths are people who

have no feelings about their crimes, neither empathy, nor regret, nor guilt.

– There is an official checklist for diagnosing psychopathy, did you know that? It's called PCL-R, and it contains twenty points, a lack of empathy or guilt being just two of these. Others include a low threshold of boredom, a tendency to infidelity, criminal activity when young, impulsiveness, or a parasitic lifestyle where they exploit other people for money or favours. It's hard to believe that such a weighty diagnosis should be based on these commonplace attributes, isn't it?

– To be honest, I'm not really sure what you're getting at.

– I'm trying to point out that I'm probably just as much or as little a psychopath as you are, and that understanding psychopathy becomes difficult once you start specifying such rigid patterns of thought.

– With respect, the fact that you committed the worst crime a person is capable of – and did it over and over again, ten times – isn't a pattern of thought, but a fact. And this is something you know yourself, everybody does, there's no need for discussion. According to the Bible, murder is a sin and according to the law, it's a serious crime. But precisely because of this, I'm even keener to understand what made you cross that line. What did Larissa trigger in you to turn you into a killer?

– Oh yes, that's right. You wanted to know why she was the first, and my response was that you were mistaken.

– Really?

– Think back. It'll come to you.

– Once again, that's not how this works. I'm not here to play games with you, but to talk about the murders. About Larissa and all the other girls.

– Laura, Miriam, Jana, Kati, Olivia, Laetitia, Hayet, Jenny, Saskia, Alina, Sophie. You see, I wasn't lying. I still remember all their names, and for each of these there's a face in my head. Take little Laura. Blonde, big blue eyes, pink T-shirt with a horse on it. She was sitting on the kerb, in roller skates and with a fresh cut to her knee, but she wasn't crying. It was in Hellersdorf, very close to where Larissa lived too, and I just happened to be passing in the car. I stopped and asked if I could help her. She thanked me, but refused.

– Clearly you didn't accept that.

– No, I persuaded her to get into my car by telling her I knew a place where all the little girls learned to roller skate. Did you roller skate as a child too?

– In-liners, yes. In-liners, roller skates, bike, skateboard, I pretty much tried them all, and I expect I fell over endlessly.

– You can't remember exactly?

– No, I . . . I mean you forget a lot from your childhood.

– Or you distort it afterwards.

– Yes, that's possible. The more time that passes, the further your childhood recedes into the background, apart from the really formative experiences.

– Oh, I think you're wrong there. Those formative experiences are like stories – you keep telling them over and over again until one day their content is completely different. What's yours?

– My what?

– The most formative experience of your childhood?

ANN

SCHERGEL, 28 DECEMBER 2017

We're back at the inn from the hospital, having a briefing at the table that's normally reserved for the council. In front of us are two huge plates with dumplings, beans, roast pork and a sea of dark brown gravy, on the top of which a thin brown skin has formed. I eat even though I'm not hungry; it's pure common sense. All I've had in the past few days are the two biscuits baked by Inspector Brandner's wife and half a ham roll, left over from the police officers' supper at the pub last night. I remember the two plates that are still in my father's study. The dinner that Elke made for Eva and me: goose leg with red cabbage. When I get home again, the smell of that rotten food will have stunk out the entire room.

Jakob takes huge mouthfuls, like he did in the lunch breaks at Big Murphy's where he managed to devour the largest burgers in what felt like seconds. 'Dustbin,' I teased him, and we laughed. I really liked him, my friend Jakob from the recycling centre, with his bobbing dark locks of hair and the childish exuberance in his eyes.

'What's up?' he asks, chewing. I shake my head.

Brock offered to take us up to the ruins after lunch. Apparently they're beyond one of the adjacent areas of woodland, near a gorge. About half an hour by car, then a few minutes' walk. I don't want to go, because I don't think Sarah meant the ruins when she talked about a castle. Nor do I believe we'll find Steinhausen huddled there amongst the derelict walls.

'Think about it, Jakob. You only spent one night in these temperatures in the boot of your car and now you always need the loo. But Sarah doesn't have the slightest sign of hypothermia, even though she's supposed to have spent two whole days and nights out in the woods. That's practically impossible, do you see? She must have been kept inside, somewhere protected and warmish, at least.'

'It's all a question of having the right gear. There are thermal sleeping bags, thermal mats, and he could have made a fire too.' Jakob quickly shovels a mouthful of beans down him. 'And the ruins of an old fortress are similar to a castle, aren't they? I really don't understand why you want to pass up on this opportunity.'

'The opportunity to see the ruins? We're not fricking tourists, for God's sake!' I slam my cutlery down on to the side of my plate; it clatters unpleasantly. Leaning over to Jakob, I lower my voice. Brock, who's drying beer glasses behind the bar, doesn't have to hear everything. I'm surprised he didn't stay at the hospital with Kerstin and Sarah, like Schmitti and Nathalie. He seems to find it more important to keep an eye on the work of the journalists who've come from Berlin. Or to spread a new rumour. Sarah with her bruises, and particularly whether her own mother might have had something to do with them. 'You heard Brock. It takes half an hour to get to the ruins by car, and then there's a walk on top of that. Do you seriously believe a seven-year-old girl could have managed that on her own? She'd never have found her way back to the village. No way.' I shake my head energetically. Once, when we were ten, Eva got lost in a section of the Grunewald, not far from where we lived. We'd often played there; it was where our tower was – the old raised hide. And although we knew the way off by heart, she spent hours wandering about until my father eventually found her.

'She must have been really close to here. In the village.'

'You mean the village that the police spent two days turning upside down? Is this where her abductor is supposed to be hiding, undetected by Sherlock Brock and all the others?' His laughter turns into a sigh. 'Ann, if you're being honest with yourself, you'll have realised by now that it must have been a copycat crime. Maybe just some stupid teenager playing a sick joke with the red ribbons to put the wind up the community here. And when the police turned up with this huge posse, he got cold feet and let Sarah go.' Unfazed, he cuts a piece of meat. 'Could this be the very reason why Sarah's not talking? She knows her abductor and doesn't want him to get into trouble.'

I'm flummoxed. And aghast. Jakob's theory makes sense. But I know it's wrong, I know, I just do. I begin to tremble for a different reason. Jakob's sitting here, happily eating his fill of the daily special. I realise he doesn't care what story he gets in the end. The key thing is that it's different from what his rivals write about the ribbon murders. And whatever happens, it will be because nobody else has exclusive access to the daughter of the chief suspect. As far as he's concerned, I'm a job; he's never left any doubt about that. And yet it hurts again.

'Ann? Is everything all right?' Something in my expression makes Jakob put his cutlery down now too. Maybe I've turned pale or done the opposite: come out in nervous red blotches.

'I need some fresh air.'

Jakob makes to get up.

'No, you continue eating.' I stop him. 'I just need a few minutes to myself.'

'What about the ruins?'

'I'll think about it,' I say, grabbing my rucksack, leaving the table and, a few seconds later, the dining area.

I really want a cigarette now. And maybe something sweet too. The small grocer's, which Jakob's jeep is still parked in front of, is open. The cashier adjusts the slightly wonky name badge on her apron and greets me effusively. I am, after all, an important journalist, as she will already have learned. Wandering down the aisles I spy a familiar face: Nathalie. She's filling a shopping trolley with tins of food, and at her feet is a basket filled with sliced bread, cat food, margarine and all manner of other stuff.

'You're back from the hospital,' I say stupidly, pointing at her shopping. 'Looks like you're feeding an entire company.'

'Yes,' she says, sweeping a hair behind her ear, almost looking embarrassed. 'I don't like shopping so I always get as many supplies as I can in one go.' She pushes the trolley, which under the weight of its load is as obstinate as an old dog. I bend down to pick up her basket to take it to the cash desk. She lets me go first as I'm only getting a packet of cigarettes and a bar of chocolate.

When the cashier has scanned all her items, I help Nathalie pack away the tins, and in my thoughts I'm briefly back with Zoe on our weekly Saturday shop. We're only buying trash food to put in small bowls for our film night. It will go straight on our hips. So what? We'll make up for it tomorrow with smoothies for breakfast. I sniff. Berlin is Schergel and Nathalie is Zoe, and the cashier asks if there's any news about Sarah.

'She's doing well in the circumstances,' Nathalie says.

The cashier looks slightly disappointed – no new gossip.

'Is it true, then?' she probes. She means the thing about the bruises, the vague suspicion that now hangs over Kerstin.

I can see Nathalie struggling to keep her cool, but then it all comes out. 'Everyone makes mistakes. Big ones too sometimes. But everyone also deserves a second chance. It's only if they don't . . .' She breaks off. Whether she wanted to or not, she's confirmed the rumour. When it appears she realises this too, she gasps in horror. The cashier gives a mortified smile.

'Come on, we ought to go,' I say softly, and so we leave the shop, Nathalie pulling her trolley, and me with the laden basket.

'Where's your car?' I ask, but she doesn't have one. 'Okay,' I say in astonishment. 'Is it far to where you live?'

'It's fine,' she replies evasively, reaching for the basket. The sliced bread and a tin of cat food topple into the snow.

'Oh dear! How about I go with you for a bit? I wanted a walk anyway to clear my head.' Without waiting for an answer, I slip my rucksack off my shoulders and stuff the bread and cat food in it.

'A bit, all right then.' Nathalie's smile reminds me of Dad's when I last saw him in prison. It looks slightly fake, as if her face had almost forgotten how to do it. And that's the impression she gives overall: shy, and strangely lost when not with Schmitti and Kerstin. She says she's living in one of Brock's holiday houses on the upper common with her mother and daughter. 'It's quite far. You really don't have to come the whole way.'

'That's all right.' I try not to let show how much of an effort it is to heave her basket. I can only carry it in my left hand as otherwise my right shoulder whinges. 'Schmitti told me you're working with Kerstin at the butcher's.'

'Oh, I just help out here and there in the background. Vacuum-packing meat, cleaning. Can you imagine what the place looks like after an animal has been slaughtered? The blood sprays all over the room, right up to the ceiling. You have to hose the tiles down.'

I glance at Nathalie. Her boots look high quality and her coat is from an expensive brand. They must be from a time when she couldn't have even dreamed she'd one day be cleaning in a butcher's for pocket money.

'It's just everywhere. Look here!' She stops abruptly and points at a stain on her jeans. It's only small but clearly visible.

'Does it come out?'

'With bleach, yes.' She sighs. 'I tell myself every day that I'm doing it for my daughter.'

I nod. Nathalie is my chance. She's a friend of Kerstin's and through her job spends a lot of time with the family. 'Sarah talked of a castle. Have you got any idea what place she might have meant?'

She shakes her head then starts walking again. I follow her. For a while we don't talk; she looks lost in thought. Maybe she's still thinking about her outburst in front of the cashier, or wondering what people are now thinking of her. For if Kerstin Seiler really did beat her daughter, she and Schmitti ought to have noticed something and acted correspondingly. I'd love to tell her I know how something like this feels. Only then I wouldn't be a respectable journalist anymore, but Ann, the daughter of the alleged ribbon murderer. I bet I'd scare them off, her and the entire village, and my hunt for Marcus Steinhausen would be over.

The path climbs; it's difficult but beautiful. A winter panorama that could be from the front of a postcard. Before us is nothing but a white expanse that pushes its way into the woods in the distance like a tongue. In the middle of all this, surrounded by a few solitary trees, a small house.

'That's where you live?'

'Yes,' Nathalie says with a smile. 'Idyllic, isn't it?'

'Absolutely, but . . .' I turn around to estimate the distance from the village, 'a little bit isolated too, no?'

'I don't have a choice,' she says, letting go of the trolley and resting her hands on her knees as if taking a short break. 'You must have heard of the circumstances in which we ended up in Schergel?' Still bent over, she gives me a searching look. 'Don't be shy. I've been living here almost two months and I know only too well about how the village gossip works.'

'Well, I've heard you had problems with your ex-husband.' I put the basket down to relieve my aching arm.

Nathalie stands up straight again; her face looks sad and serious. 'That's not the extent of it. It's more . . . we're hiding from him.' She points to the little house in the distance. 'My daughter would love to go to kindergarten, but she's not ready yet. She jumps with fright at the slightest noise and is still having nightmares.'

'I didn't know that. I'm sorry.'

She nods. 'Yes. We cut ourselves off completely in the first few weeks, but people in the village are curious. They're only trying to help, but, well . . . At any rate, I realised you're never really alone anywhere in the world, and I had to put my cards on the table. After all, if everyone knows the score, it helps keep us safe.' She laughs. 'Brock rolled up his sleeves and said, "If your ex turns up here, we'll give him a good hiding."' She takes the handle of the trolley and gets going again. I follow her, deep in thought. Nathalie is like me, only she works in a butcher's rather than a burger joint, an attempt to preserve at least a vestige of normality and avoid going crazy under the burden of one's life history.

We approach the house. Half of it is cladded with horizontal planks and there's a balcony beneath the pointed roof that must have a breathtaking view over the valley.

'Where do you come from originally?'

'Wiesbaden. And you're from Berlin, aren't you?' By way of explanation, she adds, 'Village radio.'

'Oh, I see. Berlin, exactly.'

'Do you know the weekly market in Nestorstrasse?' As if at the push of a button, the hint of a smile gives way to a serious expression. 'And I suppose that's also the reason why you're here, isn't it? Because the other ten girls all came from Berlin?'

'That's right, yes. My colleague and I are writing about the case.'

We stop outside the house. It's small, but on three floors and divided into two apartments. The bottom one is empty, according to Nathalie. To keep it that way, she's renting it as well, she tells me. Because the house is on a slope, the front door to the upper, larger apartment, where Nathalie lives with her family, is accessed via steps on the left-hand side. Plenty of steps that are going to require plenty of effort again. 'Just put the basket down here, I'll take it inside in a minute,' Nathalie says, as if she's read my thoughts, heaving the trolley up the first few steps.

'I'm not going to abandon you with just a few metres to go,' I reply with a laugh. Only now do I notice that all the shutters are closed. 'When you're working at the butcher's or go shopping, does your mum look after your daughter?'

'Yes, she's almost eighty and physically not very fit anymore. So she doesn't venture outside on her own these days. But she gets on brilliantly with Lenia. I don't know what I'd do without her.' Nathalie opens the front door and calls out, 'I'm back!' I don't catch the response because I'm still a few steps behind. She manoeuvres the trolley into the entrance, then comes back to me to take the basket. 'Thanks so much. Will you find your way back to the village, or should we have dropped a few crumbs on the way?'

'Keep going straight, I know.'

'Thanks again.'

'No problem, my pleasure . . .' I stop short when out of the blue Nathalie hugs me. Maybe she's sensed how similar we are. For a few seconds I'm worried my eyes will fill with tears, but the moment passes, as does the impulse to tell her who I really am. She lets go of me and says, 'Right, then' – my cue to leave. She waves at me from the top of the steps; I keep turning back to see if she's still standing there. So gorgeous to look at in spite of all her pain. Then she suddenly goes into the house and I shake my head, amused by myself. Oh, Ann . . .

Bond. (Ann, 10 years old)
A bond is a magical feeling and that's why it's a bit unbelievable too.
You never have to think too hard about what your saying because you
know the other person will understand you anyway. Your like twins
even if your not related and nobody can separate us even though Eva
sometimes says girls should love boys. But it's not what you should
do, it's about finding someone you feel like a twin with.

My head is empty, yet at the same time swimming with a thousand thoughts, none of which can be fished out in isolation. With every metre, every step I get closer to the centre of the village, I become more ponderous, angry, disillusioned, until I finally reach the inn and am utterly livid. We don't have a new lead, just a child who won't say anything, and otherwise, no idea. Jakob is still sitting at the same table, although now he's got his laptop in front of him rather than a plate. When he sees me he leaps to his feet.

'Where've you been? I've been looking for you.'

'Why?' I gesture to him to sit back down and plump myself on the chair opposite, the same one I sat on for lunch – a shitty metaphor: everything's the same, nothing has changed, and no doubt we'll be sitting here like this tomorrow, and the day after that, because we're stuck, bloody well stuck again unless a miracle occurs and Sarah opens her mouth. 'Were you worried the copycat might have got me?'

'What copycat?' Frau Brock asks, coming over to our table with a cup of coffee for Jakob. 'Would you like one too?'

I shake my head. *The village radio* comes to mind, the expression Nathalie used. But it's a chance. 'Tell me, Frau Brock: Sarah's disappearance and the red ribbons in the woods . . .'

'Yes?' In a flash she's sitting beside us. Jakob nudges his laptop to one side to make way for Frau Brock's crossed arms on the table.

'You're all very observant here in Schergel. What are people saying? Who could have done something like that and why?'

She leans across the table conspiratorially. 'My husband says it's the real ribbon murderer. It's definitely him.'

I look around. Brock's nowhere to be seen, not a good sign considering that he's been shadowing us ever since we arrived in Schergel.

'That's why a meeting's been called for this evening,' his wife continues excitedly. 'We want to discuss the precautions we should take, and make a plan of how we can help the police clear this up.'

'The invitation to this meeting has even gone out nationally,' Jakob remarks sarcastically. 'That's why I was looking for you.' He turns his laptop so I can see the screen. It's the online edition of one of Germany's best-known dailies, even bigger than the one he works for. A photograph. Sarah, her face pixellated, in Schmitti's arms, beside Kerstin and Nathalie. None of the adults' faces are pixellated and they're easily recognisable. That was this morning in front of the butcher's. Sarah, who'd suddenly reappeared, the miracle; and Brock capturing the moment with his camera.

My hands shoot across the table and pull the laptop closer. The headline of the article accompanying the photograph reads: *Have they got the wrong man?* Beside it, a small photo of my father, doctored to make him unrecognisable. The screen turns blurry, I can't make out whole sentences, only scraps of text. A little girl, abducted in the style of the notorious ribbon murderer. An idyllic village in great danger. The police, who undertook a large-scale search but did little else, either to help the terrified inhabitants or to solve the case. But, most strikingly, a quote from the village publican and chairman of the local council, Peter Brock: 'We're looking specifically for a man with short blond hair and freckles.'

I look Jakob square in the eye. 'This is a disaster,' I say, unable to manage any more. A few days ago I'd have been happy if the reporting had been in my father's favour, but now the timing couldn't be less helpful. My head throws up images, the worst-case scenario: people from everywhere flooding to Schergel because they're inquisitive, and eager to take part in the murder hunt as if it were some kind of tourist event. Other journalists, now that the first major article on Schergel has appeared, wanting to get a piece of the story as quickly as possible and arriving in their droves too. But, most importantly, Steinhausen, who, if he's still in the area after Sarah's escape, is now going to do a runner.

'Hopefully Kerstin will have had a good rest by this evening,' Frau Brock says, her voice mingling with my thoughts. 'As the mother of the victim, her presence would help people realise how serious the situation is.'

Jakob and I first look at each other, then at Frau Brock.

'God knows we'd all be deeply shocked if the rumours turn out to be true,' she adds. 'But she should have the chance to explain herself, shouldn't she? I mean, Sarah might have got those bruises while playing.'

Jakob is the first to twig. 'Are you saying Kerstin Seiler's back home?'

'Yes, why?'

'She's not with Sarah in the hospital anymore?'

'No, she left early this afternoon. She wanted a hot bath and a nap.'

Jakob flips shut his laptop and both of us spring to our feet in sync. We don't need to discuss our plan; both of us realise we have to see Kerstin at once. Maybe we can make her understand how important it is to decipher Sarah's words without her feeling under attack again. It's worth a try – maybe we'll get lucky and find Steinhausen in his hideaway before he disappears.

We leave the inn at a canter; I stop when we're halfway across the marketplace.

'What's up?'

'Sarah,' I say, grabbing Jakob's sleeve. 'Right now she's alone in the hospital.'

'No chance, I bet Schmitti or Nathalie are there while her mum—'

'Takes a nice hot bath?' What an absurd thought; I shake my head. 'No, Nathalie definitely isn't there. I just met her out shopping.'

Jakob gestures to me to go on. 'Somebody will be there for sure. And the police will have posted someone outside her room.'

'Hopefully.'

'For sure.'

As the butcher's is a residential house too, we start by ringing at the front door – in vain. So we decide to try through the shop. The lights are off even though it's already getting dark outside, and we can't detect any movement inside. On a whim, Jakob tries the handle; the shop is indeed open. A bell above the door announces our entry.

'Hello?' Jakob calls out. 'Frau Seiler?'

Our footsteps squeak on the tiles and the drinks fridge buzzes monotonously. A blueish light illuminates the empty counter, the only, inadequate source of light in the room.

'Can you smell that?' I whisper. A strange, unpleasantly sweet aroma.

'That's what freshly slaughtered meat smells like,' Jakob whispers back. 'It hangs around. I know it because my grandad was a butcher too. His house smelled like this even years after he'd retired and closed the shop.'

We come to the corridor behind the counter, separated off by a plastic curtain.

'Frau Seiler!' Jakob calls out again. When there's still no answer, he raises his eyebrows at me. I point my chin at the curtain, but he's hesitant.

'What if she's in the bath?'

'If she is, she's hardly likely to have left the shop open, is she?' Jakob shrugs.

'Let's call it investigative journalism,' I say, pushing ahead.

A cold, dark corridor, tiled like everything here. I think of Nathalie, who told me how she had to hose down the tiles after an animal had been slaughtered.

'Frau Seiler? Are you here?' There are two rooms on either side of the corridor; straight ahead are the stairs to the living quarters. 'It's us: Ann and Jakob from the newspaper!'

Who – cowed by the darkness, the smell and the fact that everything in this house is washable – advance very slowly until they finally come to an open door on the right-hand side. It's a cold store with a flickering light, dim but satisfactory enough to see. I thrust my hand blindly behind me, for Jakob, for support.

Someone makes a sound, probably me too. Someone shouts, 'Shit!' probably Jakob, who now pushes me to the side and rushes into the room. Towards the body lying on the floor. In all that blood on the washable tiles.

RECORDING 06
Berlin, 7 May 2021

- I'm assuming your silence means you don't want to share your childhood experiences with me. Ah well, listen in and I'll begin. My childhood. With your love of cliché, you'll feel vindicated now, but in truth I did have a strict upbringing. I wasn't beaten and nor were there any other unjust punishments. But it was all about discipline, obeying the rules and being able to show what we'd achieved. My brother, in particular, always felt he had to prove himself. We competed with each other from an early age and soon we went beyond the usual benchmarks, such as school grades or good behaviour, which your parents would praise you for. I vividly remember the time I was sitting in a tree in our garden, boasting how high I'd climbed. In response, my brother climbed over the rose trellis and on to our garage roof. Then he took a run up and jumped down. But he landed badly, breaking his left ankle. I won't forget the noise, nor his screams. I'd never heard him make such a sound before, never heard anyone do it, in fact.
- Did you like the sound? The girls must have screamed too.
- Some did, yes. Most, however, were shocked into silence. Do you have siblings?
- No, I'm an only child.
- Would you have liked some?

- No, basically . . . It was okay as it was. I always had lots of friends.
- So did I, believe it or not. And yet I never felt as if I belonged.
- Because you felt different?
- Sort of, yes. There were things I began thinking of at an early age. Things that kept me awake some nights.
- Certain . . . fantasies?
- No. No, not fantasies, that sounds so . . . no, that sounds all wrong. Just like the word 'excited' you used earlier. Surely you know I never touched any of the girls inappropriately.
- You just killed them.
- But I didn't deprive them of their dignity. On the contrary, I gave them meaning. And they gave meaning to me.
- A meaning that was otherwise missing from your life.
- Yes, that's exactly right. Tell me, have you read the files on the murder cases?
- Of course, several times. Why do you ask?
- I'll let you mull this over until the next time we meet.
- What, no, hold on! Are you going to send me home? Now?
- What was your favourite subject at school?
- My er . . . German. German and PE, I'd say.
- I see.
- I see? What now?
- Now go home and have a think.

ANN

SCHERGEL, 28 DECEMBER 2017

It's as if I've been catapulted back in time, back to the basement where Eva is lying like that, on a cold floor, in her own blood. How sure I was she must be dead, but she was alive, thank God, she was alive. It must be exactly the same now. A horrendous sight, a shock that momentarily clamps the blood vessels in my body and brings everything to a standstill. But it looks worse than it is. Kerstin Seiler isn't dead. She's lying there, blood everywhere, as if her body were floating on a lake, blood on her clothes and smeared all over her stiff face. The meat hook in the side of her neck. Jakob kneeling over her, checking for a pulse, while I remain in the doorway, just trying to stay on my feet. There's no reason to collapse now because he's just about to look at me and say she's alive.

But she needs help, of course, she needs immediate help. Frantically I feel for my mobile and call an ambulance. Now Jakob does look at me and just shakes his head. I don't know what that's supposed to mean; I yell down the phone – Schergel, butcher's, a woman with a serious neck wound, 'Please come quick!'

Jakob gets up. From the knees downwards his trousers are red, just like his hands that have been touching the body.

Me: 'They're on their way.' Him: 'It's too late.' I refuse to believe it; I *can't* believe it. Because this is just like it was with Eva. I want to check myself, I want to go over to Kerstin, lay her head in my lap and tell her everything's going to be fine, the ambulance is on its way. Jakob doesn't let me; he holds me firmly with his bloody hands until I calm down. Then he takes me out of the cold store, back to the dark, chilly corridor, back through the shop, back outside. We leave red footprints behind. The tiles will have to be hosed down.

Disbelief. (Ann, 10 years old)

Disbelief feels like when you walk across a frozen lake and then you suddenly break the ice and it's like your paralised with shock and cold, even your brain. You can't understand what's happening and that's why you forget you have to move and hurry away from the crack or you'll end up under the ice and drown. That's why disbelief is a very dangerous feeling, you must'nt stand there in disbelief too long or you'll die.

I open the curtains in room 113. People have gathered outside the butcher's, bringing candles. I strain to see if Nathalie's there. I've been thinking of her a lot over the past few hours. Kerstin's death will hit her hard – a painful blow to the stomach, a cruel fist in her face. I know this as if I knew her, and I sort of do in a funny way. I felt it when she hugged me.

I have to realise it's dark outside; the faces are merely small dots blurred by the candlelight in the blackness. The mortuary van has driven off and there are just two police cars left. The crime scene has been secured, Jakob and I have been questioned and our personal details taken. How did we end up finding Kerstin Seiler, what did we want from her? The truth: Jakob is a journalist writing about the ribbon murderer, and I'm the daughter of the chief suspect. Frowns, incomprehension. A story and a background that defy cursory explanation. So we've got to come back to the police station in Bad Kötzting tomorrow morning to fill in the gaps. I feel like Bill Murray in *Groundhog Day*: police, hospital, bodies covered in blood. I'm stuck in a fricking time loop, a nightmare. And why? My father's still in prison; I haven't achieved anything. On the contrary, all I'm doing is causing chaos.

Jakob's face appears in the reflection of the windowpane. Standing right behind me, he puts his hand on my shoulder. I still see the blood on it, even though he's had a thorough wash. Both of us took a shower, first Jakob, then me. As if what we've just been through could be rinsed down the drain along with the blood. The police have taken our clothes in a plastic bag. Jakob's coat and his blood-smeared trousers for forensic examination. To confirm that all the blood got on him when he was checking Kerstin for a pulse, rather than when he killed her. My – *Dad's* – jacket has gone too because Jakob touched it with his bloody hands. I'm already missing it; I feel as if I've lost more than just an item of clothing.

I turn around, straight into Jakob's embrace. Jakob, who holds me tight, my cheek against his chest, and his heart beating comfortingly. He strokes my hair. There are no words. I think of Sarah. Imagine the police psychologist trying to make her understand what's happened. They told us that her hospital room is being guarded around the clock. For it may have been Sarah's abductor who killed Kerstin. But why? Nothing makes sense anymore; only one thing is clearer than ever: Sarah needs to talk. She has to say what happened from the moment when, on her way home alone on Boxing Day, she met her kidnapper. What he looked like. Where he took her. How she was able to escape from him. A loud sobbing reclaims me from my tangled thoughts. It's me, crying and sobbing so uncontrollably that my whole body is shaking. Jakob continues to hold me, stoically, firmly, solidly.

'I just want to wake up.'

'I know,' he says. Then he lifts my chin and kisses me. It's the situation, the deep despair, two people clutching each other because there's nothing else. It feels good somehow, and yet . . . I pull away, turn away.

'Have I done something wrong?'

I shake my head. Think back. How we used to sit in the Big Murphy's car park during my lunch break, separated by the coy distance of two people who'd really like to arrange a proper date. But they don't; the woman has her reasons.

'There is someone,' I tell him, then sniff and wipe the tears from my eyes. 'That's to say, there was someone until recently. I'm not quite over it yet.'

'Okay, I understand. Sorry.'

'Me too.'

'Did it fall apart because of the thing with your dad?'

'Yes.'

I drop on to the bed; Jakob sits beside me.

'Then he's a fool, Ann, he really is. Whatever your father might or might not have done, it's got nothing to do with you. You're a good person. Most of the time, at least.'

'Locking you in the boot – I imagine you still hold that against me.'

'You've no idea. I've had to pee at least a dozen times today already.'

I lean my head against his shoulder. 'What are we going to do now?'

'What should we do? There's no point going to pay Sarah a visit at the hospital. First, they wouldn't let us in, and second – even if they did – there's no way she'd talk to two strangers. I think we've no choice but to leave it all to the police and hope they can clear the bloody thing up.' He puts an arm around me and kisses me on my head. 'We ought to go home.'

'Home,' I repeat. The mere thought of it makes me tense up. Back to Berlin where my father's in prison, Eva's in hospital and Ludwig's waiting to lecture me. Where there's nothing but ruins, debris and pain. 'Shit, it can't be *that* difficult, Jakob!' I lift my head and look at him. 'Logic! Logic's the way to solve this. Think! Why would Marcus Steinhausen kill Kerstin? What would he gain by it?'

'You still believe it then.'

'What?'

'That Steinhausen's behind all of this.'

'When you said today that Sarah might be keeping her mouth shut because she knows her kidnapper, I had a moment or two of doubt. But now . . .' I get up from the bed and pace up and down the room. 'No copycat who merely wanted to put the wind up the village would commit murder, would they? That must be going too far! That could only be someone who's utterly ruthless. Who's used to killing.' I stop right in front of Jakob. 'Out of all the dreadful things that have happened over the last few days, do you know what the worst one is for me?'

His response is to raise his eyebrows. I pull up my left sleeve and hold out my wrist. 'The moment when Eva and I found out *how* he killed the girls.'

Jakob takes my hand and examines the scar. 'What happened?'

'About nine months after Mum died I had an accident on my bike. A stone dug into my wrist and cut it.' As I gently turn my wrist in Jakob's grip, the scar shimmers in the light. 'It's a piece of information the police don't know about. It would fit far too neatly with the clues they've already got.'

'So you did have doubts about your father.'

'I don't know if I'd call it doubts. But it's the only thing I still can't explain. Why does he kill the girls in this way? On the other hand, maybe you start drawing parallels like mad if you're searching for meaning. Maybe you come across connections that don't really exist. Things your mind bolts together by itself because it's desperate to understand. But now,' I say, carefully taking my hand out of his, 'I'm more certain than ever. Kerstin's murder is the proof.'

'Of your father's innocence?' Jakob rubs his brow. 'I mean, you're right. Someone who just wanted to give the village a fright, then got such cold feet when the police turned up that he let Sarah go, wouldn't be capable of committing such a gruesome murder the very next day. I mean, he really . . .' He shakes his head as he breaks off. I crouch down and put my hands on his knees.

'We can't go home, Jakob, please! Think about it. He could have done a runner when Sarah escaped. Or at least hidden and kept quiet. But he didn't. On the contrary, by killing her mother, he's literally shouting in our faces: *I'm still here, you fools!* He's making fun of us.'

'I don't know,' Jakob says, sighing. 'What are you suggesting?'

'We mustn't let ourselves get led astray! You could call Brandner's secretary and find out if Sarah's said anything yet. And then I think we ought to talk to Schmitti and Nathalie again. Even if they don't know what Sarah meant by the castle, dragon and princess, they can tell us whose Sarah's friends are. Children don't share everything with adults, but they might with their best friend.'

'Sure, I don't mind,' Jakob says, fishing his mobile from his trouser pocket. 'Let's see if we strike lucky, it's already gone eight o'clock.'

I stand up and move to the window.

In spite of the cold, the people are bravely keeping up their vigil outside the butcher's. Is it fear? The fear of being next? Curiosity? The feeling of not wanting to be idle, of needing to do something even if it's only hanging around outside?

Behind me I hear Jakob asking about Sarah, before grumbling several times. 'Okay, I understand,' he says, then enquires about the general state of the investigation.

Meanwhile I watch some of the people outside head for the inn. Brock's meeting, I recall. *We want to discuss the precautions we should take, and make a plan of how we can help the police clear this up*, his wife told us this afternoon. And: *As the mother of the victim, her presence would help people realise how serious the situation is.*

Now Kerstin is dead. Did she really leave her traumatised child on her own in the hospital just hours after she'd escaped from her abductor? Could her own state of mind at that moment really have been more important than her daughter, who she thought she'd lost for ever? I don't want to think that Kerstin would still be alive if she'd stayed with Sarah – but that's what runs through my mind. I turn to Jakob, who's just said goodbye and is taking his phone from his ear. He opens his mouth to start speaking but I'm quicker.

'What if the killer wasn't after Kerstin at all? What if he just found out that she was back from the hospital and so assumed that she had Sarah with her? I mean, it wouldn't occur to anybody that a loving mother would abandon her child in a situation like that. He wanted Sarah! He wanted to take her back! And when she wasn't there, he lost it. Think about it: the meat hook. He didn't take it along as a murder weapon, he grabbed it on impulse at the butcher's, a knee-jerk reaction when he realised his original plan wouldn't work.'

'It's possible,' Jakob agrees, pointing to his mobile. 'The girl still hasn't spoken since her mention of the castle. Not even when she was told her mother had died . . .' He shakes his head. 'She's now on sedatives and tomorrow she'll be transferred to the children's psychiatric department. They've also located her father, who's on his way. By the way . . . I suppose you know that a few months after his second period in rehab, Steinhausen spent quite a while as an inpatient in a psychotherapy clinic?'

'What? When?'

He nods. 'From February to November 2006. A specialist clinic in the Allgäu.'

I grab my rucksack, which is on the floor beside the desk, and open it in such haste that the bag of sliced bread and tin of cat food fall by my feet. Nathalie's things I'd packed in there and must have forgotten to give back to her. Leaving them where they are, I pull out Ludwig's folder and the notes we've made about the murders, including the timeline.

'You said 2006?' My eyes dart from the piece of paper in my hand to Jakob.

'Yes. After the second attack by Larissa's stepfather, he suffered post-traumatic stress disorder, nightmares, paranoia, the whole works.'

'In 2006?' I ask again, just to be sure. *Whoever killed those girls must have a few gaps in his CV*, is what I told Eva three days ago. And a gap, a complete year that passed without a girl dying, is precisely what happened in 2006. I put the sheet of paper under Jakob's nose. 'So? Believe me now?'

The air in the dining room is stale: too many bodies crammed together. Sweat and bad breath, the windows already fogged up. Jakob and I are standing at the back, by the door that connects the dining room with the stairs to the guest rooms. I can't make out if people from outside or other journalists have turned up. But I do see Nathalie, standing on the opposite side of the room by the exit. The way her eyes keep darting around like a timid animal makes her seem nervous. Brock looks unusually tall behind his bar. Jakob, who's got a better view, says he's standing on an upturned beer crate. When Brock rings the bell, the angry murmur subsides. First: Kerstin Seiler, one of their own, whose life has been gruesomely cut short. Then: Schmitti, who'll now be choosing a coffin rather than an engagement ring.

'The man responsible for this is known as the "ribbon murderer". For more than a decade, he's terrorised Berlin and now it seems it's our turn. But, ladies and gentlemen, we're not going to accept that. We're not going to lock up our children. We're not going to barricade ourselves away for fear that he might break into our houses as he did into Kerstin's. We're not going to let ourselves be slaughtered like defenceless livestock.' The mob starts baying its agreement; Brock can only bring the meeting under control by ringing his bell again. 'From this evening, a village guard will begin their duty. We will conduct patrols both day and night. To assist the police, we will also set up an office where observations and suspicions relating to Sarah's abduction and Kerstin's murder can be recorded. Totally discreet, of course.'

'If he hasn't already done so, Steinhausen's going to pack his things and clear off now,' Jakob whispers into my ear.

'Or he'll have the time of his life running rings around this pompous crowd,' I reply.

'Pompous?' He shakes his head. 'Highly dangerous, if you ask me. They're going to get completely manic about it now. How long is it going to be, do you think, before they lose control of the whole thing and start tearing each other apart if they can't find the guilty party?'

'You're right. Steinhausen's hardly going to turn himself in.'

'Shhh,' the woman beside us says, pointing to the bar. She's urging us to listen to Brock, who's just begun reading out a list of names for the patrols. I crane my neck towards the exit. Nathalie's still here, but seems on the verge of leaving.

'Be back in a sec,' I say to Jakob, and head for the door behind me. As well as leading to the stairs, the corridor also goes to the rear exit that I took last night during my blackout. I have to hurry because although I've avoided the scrum in the dining area, I still have to make my way around the building.

'Nathalie!'

Walking quickly, she's already halfway across the marketplace.

'Please wait!'

She has no intention of that and instead keeps going, even faster now, it seems. I speed up too, breaking into a run until I finally catch up with her behind the butcher's.

'What do you want?' The hostility in her voice takes me by surprise.

'I just wanted . . . er . . . I'm really sorry about Kerstin.'

Leaning her head back, Nathalie gazes up at the black sky. I gently put my hand on her sleeve.

'A couple of days ago, I almost lost a friend too. Her name's Eva. I've known her since we were children. She was seriously injured and is now in a coma. The doctors say she's stable and making a textbook recovery. But I still don't dare ring the hospital because I'm terrified they'll tell me her condition has got worse.'

Nathalie looks at me, her eyes astonishingly alert and large in an otherwise very weary face. 'Is it true?' Although her tone is different now, milder, the question is still puzzling. I shrug, at a loss. 'I mean, I know it's not true you're a journalist,' she clarifies. 'Someone found out what you told the police officers who questioned you after . . . er . . .' She tails off. I nod as a sign that she doesn't have to spell it out. 'Anyway, they say you're the daughter of the man they arrested in Berlin.'

My heart stops momentarily; I'm mystified. Nobody has spoken to me about this, not even Brock. And yet, in whatever way, it must surely come like a bombshell that I'm the daughter of the chief suspect.

'Don't lose sleep over it, everybody has their own lies. And Brock's bound to talk to you about it,' Nathalie says, as if she's read my mind. 'He thinks your father's innocent and he's wondering how he can use you to get the media's attention for his campaign here. I've got to go now.' Her last words are harsher again, just like the way she shakes my hand from her arm and moves away. Stomping off purposefully. I don't want to let her go.

'I'm sorry about that too!' I hurry to keep pace with her. 'I didn't want to lie to anyone. But you can't imagine what it's like. I'm trying to prove my father's innocence, but till now I've been completely on my own. Apart from my friend Eva, and Jakob – who really is a journalist, by the way – nobody's been prepared to listen to me.'

Nathalie stops. Something's weird. As if from nowhere, the night has descended on to her face, souring her features and paralysing her expression.

'Nathalie?'

'It's not your fault, Ann. But what he did is unforgivable.'

'What do you mean?'

'Ann!' Jakob's voice cuts across the marketplace. I whip around, first to him, then back to Nathalie, who's running away.

'Nathalie!' I cry, setting off after her.

'Ann!' Jakob again. 'Stop! It's important! They know who he is!'

Marcus Steinhausen – it strikes me like lightning. I stop so abruptly that I almost slip, and Nathalie vanishes into the darkness.

US

Nathalie, Nathalie, Nathalie.

Keep running, you won't get away.

Run like Sarah ran away from the dragon. Defend yourself like her mother tried to defend herself. Throwing her hands up, ducking desperately – still the heavy metal hook sank into her neck. The blood spurting everywhere and her gurgling like a blocked drain. She collapsed to her knees, forced into humiliation at least for the final moments. Too late, you miserable, worthless creature.

Run, Nathalie. Save yourself.

It won't be long before everyone knows.

What then? A final battle? Fine by me. I will protect my little princess by all means necessary. We've become good at hiding, expert. And nobody will destroy what we have created.

Spring, my angel, think of spring.

When the meadows turn green and are dotted with daisies, ground elder and red clover. We'll dance in the sunshine, squint at the light. You are my courage, my comfort, my life. I'm ready for anything.

ANN

SCHERGEL, 28 DECEMBER 2017

I'm sitting huddled by the shower in room 113. Although there are two doors between me and the insistent knocking, it still sounds deafening, like menacing fists striking wood which is about to succumb. I feel like howling. And anyhow, Brock doesn't have to break down the door; he could simply use his master key.

Please, stop! Stop knocking, leave me in peace!

'It seems like he's not going to go away,' Jakob says from the other side of the bathroom door, his voice muffled. It sounds like a question, as if he's asking my permission to sort the matter out.

'I don't care what you do,' I call out. 'I just want him to stop!' I need peace and quiet, for God's sake. I have to concentrate. In my head there's something I can't get at, as if it's covered, buried under this fricking racket. All I know is that it's got something to do with Nathalie.

It was already too late to turn around and follow her after Jakob had pointed out my misapprehension. *They know who he is.*

I thought he meant Marcus Steinhausen.

No, Ann, your father! They know he's in custody in Berlin as the chief suspect. Brock just announced the fact: an innocent man is in prison for the crimes of the real ribbon murderer, who's now wreaking terror here. The most heinous crime in German history, a huge scandal.

We slipped back into the pub via the rear entrance to avoid the crush in the dining room. *They want to know everything and they see you as the greatest support in their hunt for the ribbon murderer.*

The knocking has stopped and a murmur has taken its place. Jakob trying to get rid of Brock. I only catch snippets of their conversation. Brock is insisting on talking to me, especially as we wormed our way into his village under false pretences.

'Please, Herr Brock, let it wait till tomorrow, okay? It's all very unsettling for her.' And I need a good sleep first, he adds. Just like Kerstin Seiler, I think. Kerstin, who also wanted some sleep and is now dead. I start shaking. I'm a total mess and I need to sort myself out.

Nathalie. It's all to do with Nathalie. My encounter with her, the things she said. *It's not your fault, Ann. But what he did is unforgivable.*

Did that sound like she knows my father? Like she thinks he's the killer? That's impossible; she lives here in Schergel with a mother who's verging on eighty and a daughter of kindergarten age. Although they only moved here a few weeks ago . . .

'Ann?' Jakob through the closed bathroom door. 'He's gone but he wants to talk to you in the morning. He's in a bit of a huff that we kept the truth from him.'

'Okay, thanks.'

'Are you going to come out now?'

'Just give me a moment.'

'I'll make us some tea if you—'

'Jakob, please!' I yell at the door, which I'm immediately sorry for. But I do need my peace, not only from Brock and his knocking, but from everyone, including Jakob. Peace to order my thoughts. To understand. 'Just give me a few more minutes, okay?' I say again, this time more softly. Jakob responds with silence. I hear his footsteps moving away, then the mattress springs faintly creaking: Jakob must have settled down on my bed. I breathe a sigh of relief.

Okay, Nathalie.

She originally comes from Wuppertal, Schmitti said. She, on the other hand, told me she moved here to Schergel from Wiesbaden. Two cities beginning with W; Schmitti might have got them mixed up. But how does she know the Nestorstrasse weekly market in Berlin?

And I suppose that's also the reason why you're here, isn't it? she says in my memory of our conversation this afternoon. *Because the other eleven girls all came from Berlin?*

Eleven!

Leaping to my feet, I tear open the bathroom door. Jakob's slouched on my bed, busy on his phone. It slips from his hand when I hurl his name across the room. 'Just imagine this, all right?'

'All – all right.'

'Your daughter is kidnapped by the ribbon murderer, but, like Sarah, manages to escape . . .'

Eva's theory now hammering inside my head: victims who didn't go to the police.

Jakob sits upright. 'And?'

'What would you do?'

'What do you mean, what would I do? I'd go to the police, of course. And no doubt my child would need therapy too.'

I wave my arms around wildly, an expansive gesture. 'Look at the upheaval! Interrogation by the police, which Sarah finds so intimidating that she's not saying a word! Probing questions from a psychologist! Medicines and child psychiatry!'

Jakob gives me a searching look.

'Do you know the weekly market in Nestorstrasse?' I ask him, but all I get is the same expression. 'It's in Wilmersdorf, Jakob! And it's tiny. Even you don't know it, though you live close by!'

'I really don't understand what you're—'

I throw my hands up and grab my head. I wish Jakob could look inside here, simply penetrate the few millimetres of skull with his gaze and access my mental world. But of course he can't, so I need to explain what's going on inside my mind, and I've got to be patient, focused, organised. I take a deep breath. Compose myself. A new approach, as calm as possible. 'Do you know what you could also do with your traumatised daughter to spare her all this upheaval? You could put her in the car and drive a few hundred kilometres away. You could find a safe place and shut yourself away to finally give your child some peace and quiet. It would have to be secluded, this place, but not too remote in case you need help. You tell the people around you that you've fled from your ex-partner so they don't wonder why you're behaving slightly oddly. That way you stop them being too nosy, while also securing their support. Just like she said: *everybody has their own lies.*'

'What? Who said—'

'Nathalie! That's what she told me earlier: *everybody has their own lies.*'

'Is this about Nathalie?'

I nod wildly. 'And do you know what else she said, albeit this afternoon when I helped her with her shopping?'

'You helped—?'

'She talked of *eleven* girls who'd fallen victim to the ribbon murderer. *Eleven!* Not ten! And before you say anything, no, she can't have included Sarah. Her exact words were: *Because the other eleven girls all came from Berlin.*'

Jakob gets up off the bed, muttering, and wanders over to the window. Although I'm finding it hard to keep quiet, I leave him to ponder his thoughts for a moment. I realise this is quite a lot for him to take in: a brand-new theory, a bizarre scenario. 'It doesn't sound completely off the wall,' he says eventually, turning back to me. 'But I think it's more likely that Nathalie – like everyone else – has simply read the papers and seen the news. And someone not directly involved wouldn't know for sure whether there were ten or eleven victims.'

'All right, then, what about Nestorstrasse? How would she know that if she comes from Wuppertal? Or Wiesbaden? Or from wherever else – maybe even Berlin?'

'Don't tell me you've never visited another city as a tourist. How about relatives living elsewhere?' He comes closer and places his hands on my shoulders. 'You've got to understand—'

'No, you've got to understand, Jakob! We were wondering how Steinhausen hit on Schergel. What he's doing here. It's because of Nathalie! She's the reason! He's playing games with her! He wants her to know he's here and that's why he kidnapped her friend's daughter and killed Kerstin. He wants to torture her, present her with a window on her own future. As if to tell her that she won't even be able to save her child from him.'

Now Jakob bursts out laughing. 'We're talking about the woman who earlier on walked through a dark village all on her own. Would you do that if you felt there was a crazed killer after you and your daughter?'

'She was completely on edge, Jakob! She literally hotfooted it out of the meeting! She knows! She knows her family's in danger! But it seems like she's going to confront the killer on her own!' Within seconds, I've taken a second sweatshirt from my bag, in an attempt to make up for the jacket that the police confiscated. Jakob just gawps. 'For goodness' sake, Ann!'

That sceptical look he's giving me. There's concern in his face; he's become genuinely friendly towards me, or at least has got used to me and my ways. But of course there's the other side to him, the journalist, who in this situation can spot something fantastic to milk. If the protagonist is right, she's a heroine who might end up saving a number of lives. But what would he have to write if she's wrong? That she got carried away and became obsessed with her quest to prove her father's innocence?

'Don't worry, I haven't forgotten why you came with me to Schergel,' I say. 'I just want you to realise that I've begun to properly trust you.' As if to prove it, I hold out my left arm with the scar on my wrist. 'Only five people know about this: my dad, Eva, my friend Zoe, Ludwig – and you.'

'I trust you too,' Jakob says, nodding, although he doesn't look me in the eye.

'Let's go then. You can always decide later whether you came as a friend or journalist. And to be quite honest, Jakob, I'd rather read an article about an overly cautious madwoman who got it wrong than someone who failed to act at the right moment.'

He nods again, decisively this time, and straight at me.

We leave the inn quietly and again by the back entrance. Judging by the noise coming from the dining room, the meeting is still in full flow. Out the front is a group of smokers; we go the long way round like thieves in the night. Taking the car might attract attention so we walk. Jakob asks me what I'm expecting. I say I just want to talk to Nathalie. I want to know what's up. That's all. We're not in some film where we turn up in the nick of time, as the killer is launching the big finale. And yet it's a strange feeling walking along the dark village street – a cold feeling on the back of the neck that we're being watched or followed.

'We haven't even got a weapon,' Jakob comments, making a sound that was probably meant to be a laugh, but which got caught somewhere in his throat. 'I mean, when I think of everything you said . . . the idea that Steinhausen's playing games with Nathalie. If all of that is really true . . .' Another sound, with a slight quiver in its tone. And he's right. How can I be so convinced and yet so careless? What if we really do come across Steinhausen? I shake my head – just at myself. It's true, Ann. You've gone mad, you've totally lost it. The thing with Dad, the thing with Eva and then Nathalie, whose pretty face has got you in all of a fluster. You're distraught, bewildered and lonely.

'Is this the right way?' Jakob does a 360-degree turn as he walks. We've left the village behind and now the path to the upper common rises before us. At least I hope it's that. I think of Nathalie and how she asked if she ought to have dropped a few crumbs of bread for me. *Keep going straight*, I replied.

'Keep going straight,' I now tell Jakob. And I'm right.

A veil of mist has gathered below the house, which in the

moonlight looks like thick, white smoke. The snow reflects it too; it's the only light to guide us. Inside the house itself, all is dark, or at least that's how it looks, for, just like this afternoon, the shutters are closed.

'Looks abandoned,' Jakob whispers as we approach from the side in a wide arc.

'They've got to be there,' I answer. 'Nathalie doesn't have a car. They wouldn't be able to get away from here so quickly.'

'Maybe they're already asleep.'

'Maybe.'

We extend our arc around the front of the house to make for a stand of trees, which means wading laboriously through knee-high snow, as hard as concrete. It breaks and crunches far too loudly in this eerie silence. Here we stay hidden for a while; we call it 'observation', though it's more likely uncertainty as to what to do next.

'Okay, Jakob,' I say, when I notice that his eyes are on me rather than the house. 'This is what we'll do: you wait here and I'll wander over.' I wave my mobile. 'Put your phone on silent. I'll call you and stay on the line while I talk to her. That way you'll hear everything and can intervene if necessary.'

He shakes his head. 'No way. We'll go together. What if Steinhausen really—?'

'Let's assume that everything's fine and I've only come to see Nathalie for a chat. I don't want to frighten the poor woman.'

'You're not so sure anymore, are you?'

'To be honest, I don't feel like I know anything anymore.'

I trudge off towards the house through the crunching snow, metre by metre. My heart seems to be ahead of me, its tempo has left me far behind. I get to the simple black steps, which the cold of the night has covered with a layer of ice, and I move slowly, carefully, but, most of all, quietly. As if I were doing something illicit. As if I shouldn't be here.

Now I'm outside the front door. In the moonlight I can make out the bell. It's still possible for me to turn around and go.

'Decisions, my Beetle,' I hear my father say with a smile. The sound of his voice in my head soothes me at once. '"Our reason can tell us what we should avoid doing. But our heart can tell us what we have to do."'

Who said that? Blaise Pascal?

'Joseph Joubert, my love. And now . . .'

I nod at thin air and press the bell.

Nothing. I try again and listen. Has the bell been disconnected? Perhaps – I mean, that's exactly what I did at home. I knock, tentatively at first, then slightly louder. 'Nathalie?' I try to call out, but it's no more than a hoarse whisper. I look at my mobile; I'm still on the line to Jakob. 'I don't think the bell's working,' I say in a hushed voice.

'Come back, then, forget it,' says Jakob, my voice of reason.

But my heart sends me around the house. Logs for the stove are piled up against the wall. Instinctively I look up. No smoke drifting from the chimney. I continue to tiptoe, passing a corner. To my left is another wall of firewood and on the other side, a strip of land beneath the thick layer of snow which could be a garden. I try peeking through the slats of one of the shutters, but see nothing, only darkness. Then a noise. I freeze. Listen. A faint clatter. It's not coming from inside, but my ears tell me it's very close, behind the next corner of the house. I go on. As quietly and cautiously as I possibly can, always one foot in front of the other. A tawny owl shrieks. And then there's another noise. A clicking, like someone using a lighter. In my ears I now hear the rushing of blood, like a waterfall, that masks everything else. 'Do it!' my heart screams. And I obey. I take the final, decisive step around the corner.

First I see the tiny red light, on the ground to my left. Then the black shape of a person getting up from a sitting position as if in slow motion. I hear the hissing voice asking who's there. My mouth opens, but I merely croak. Then the figure reaches for something. A long handle; something metallic scrapes across the icy ground. I see the flash of the steel blade of an axe. I want to run away but it's too late.

RECORDING 07
Berlin, 10 May 2021

- So, I'm back.
- Of course you are . . . *(coughs)* I'm sorry. Did you make use of the weekend to think about our last meeting?
- Yes, I did. I listened to the recordings as well. We were talking about the girl with the roller skates.
- Do you remember her name?
- Yes, Laura. Her name was Laura. You lured her into your car under the pretence that you were going to show her a good place for skating. What happened then?
- I took her to the Kuhlake in Spandau. Do you know the area? Really pretty. There was a hut there, so overgrown that it looked as if the walls were made of ivy and brambles. As if

nature herself had made the hut sprout there and someone had
recently nailed a few wooden slats to it. I told Laura that the hut
was on the way to the roller-skating place, and she believed me.
She even put her hand in mine as we walked. If we'd bumped
into anyone, they'd have thought it was a father going for a walk
with his little daughter. That did actually happen a few times.
Someone seeing me with one of the girls, I mean.

— And nobody ever got suspicious?

— Well, I don't look like a dangerous person. Even you remarked
on that at the beginning. You said you'd imagined me differently.
And that's why you feel guilty.

— What? Why should I feel guilty?

— Because you're another of those people who failed to notice
anything. But console yourself with the fact that nobody
did, really, nobody at all. You feel guilty most of all, however,
because you can't find me repulsive, no matter how hard you
try. My crimes, maybe. But as a person you find me fascinating,
you like being here, you enjoy our conversations. And you think
that's wrong. After all, I'm a criminal, a serial killer, shattering
your ideal image of the world. Let me remind you that the world
cannot be controlled and it has a number of cracks that can't
be patched up. You're not only wondering how I came to kill the
girls, but more importantly, what it must be like to act outside of
all norms. Am I right?

— I haven't thought about that.

— Yes, you have. You've done nothing else since you first met me
three days ago.

— No, I've been dwelling on something different.

— Such as?

- The nature of our conversations, the constant feeling that you're playing with me, making me dance like a silly monkey.
- Dance, oh, dancing. Maybe I ought to have danced more often in my life. People who dance usually look so relaxed, as if they're in a different sphere. I've always enjoyed watching people dance, and have even tried it myself, just as I've tried out lots of things that I thought might make me happy. But, because I couldn't find my way into this sphere, I soon gave up dancing.
- But killing, did that make you happy?
- Not the killing. The death. The death made me feel alive. Like with an organ transplant, when a heart is removed from a dying person and put into another person's body so they can go on living.
- But nobody kills the heart donors; they die of their own accord.
- Oh, heavens, you're nitpicking again. Now, just imagine that only one of us can survive this meeting. Is it going to be you or me? According to your morality, you'd rather die than kill me. Is that the case? Really? Are you absolutely sure?

ANN

SCHERGEL, 28 DECEMBER 2017

'You?' a reedy voice says.

My rigid body twitches and I open my eyes wide. Still alive, breathing, heart pounding. Only now do I let out a scream; it's a delayed shock. The figure comes towards me, the axe thuds on the frozen ground and I'm blinded by the bright light of a torch.

'Are you out of your mind? What are you doing here? I thought . . .'

'Ann!' cries another voice in the distance. Jakob, who must have been alarmed by my scream. 'What's happening, Ann?'

Bit by bit I come to my senses. Nathalie. It's just Nathalie. In a towelling dressing gown, black, blue or grey – some dark colour I can't make out in this light. And just thick woolly socks on her feet. As if she's unaffected by this biting cold, as if she has no feeling. Her hair is tied in a messy bun. A few stray strands stick to her forehead. 'I . . . I just, er wanted . . . to talk to you,' I stammer, distracted by the effort of trying to take in my surroundings. The place I just saw Nathalie squatting as a black figure. A dark patch on the ground. A square, set with fist-sized stones and, in the middle, also formed of stones: a heart. And finally the red light. A lantern with a cemetery candle in it. A grave . . .

Do you remember . . . ?

Mum, who's now lying under the black earth. White lilies, red candles. I'm six years old. I'm not crying; my feelings are as dead as my mother.

It was me who discovered her like that: her eyeballs rolled upwards and her mouth wide open as if about to scream. I'd just been chattering away on the carpet beside her bed, her little Cinderella who sorted out her pills. She'd just been laughing at something I'd said. Then it suddenly fell silent. I got up to check. Her eyes, her mouth and the way her hand had tensed around the side rail of her bed.

I'm stiff and utterly numb, a person who's still breathing but who is no longer really alive. My father tries to explain death to me, but even he, with his profound understanding of the world, has reached his limits.

– Why are the candles red, Daddy?
– Those aren't normal candles. Those are soul lights, my Beetle. They're showing Mummy's soul the way to the other side.
– Mummy doesn't need to be shown the way anymore, Daddy. She's dead.
– Only her body is dead. Her soul lives on.
– Why can't we see it then?
– That's not possible. A soul is invisible.
– So how do we know there is a soul?
– The world is more than our eyes can see. And even if we think

we see something clearly, sometimes we're wrong because we're interpreting rather than truly understanding.

– Huh? What does that mean?

– It means that understanding is painful, Ann. Maybe the most painful thing of all. Let me tell you a story. It comes from a very wise man called Plato . . .

'Our kitten,' Nathalie says, interrupting my memories and pointing at the grave. 'It had epilepsy and died after an attack. My daughter simply won't stop crying. We loved that little thing so much.'

Now I remember the packet of cat food in my rucksack. Nathalie only bought it this afternoon. Which means she's lost her friend and her pet within a day of each other.

'I'm sorry.'

'I thought there ought to be a definite place for Lenia to come. It's good for the grieving process, as I'm sure you know.' She bends down to the lantern with the grave candle and pushes it more firmly into the ground. 'It's just a little candle and yet it lights up the night. Quite comforting, don't you think?'

I nod. 'Lenia . . . Is that your daughter's name?'

'Ann!' Jakob again. Only now do I notice that my mobile is on the ground. I must have dropped it in shock.

'What's going on?' Nathalie asks, pointing her torch at it.

I pick the phone up, say, 'Everything's okay, Jakob,' then end the call. 'You must think it's weird that I should be creeping around your house at this hour. But I was worried about you.' I look past her at the terrace door, which is open. She could invite me in, where there's light and somewhere to sit. Instead she switches off the torch, clamps it under her arm and bends down for the axe. I instinctively take a step backwards.

'The frozen ground,' she says, nodding at the cat's grave. 'And stubborn tree roots too. You were lucky I recognised you in time.'

'I rang the bell,' I say in my defence. 'Besides, you could have put a light on.'

Leaning the axe against the wall of the house, she pulls the belt on her dressing gown tighter, the torch still clamped under her arm. The cold seems to be getting to her after all. 'No, I couldn't, I'm afraid. Something's up with the electrics. Nothing's been working since this afternoon, no light, no cooker, nothing. I need to let Brock know, though I don't suppose I'm high on his list of priorities at the moment. Come in.'

I follow her through the terrace door into the sitting room. It's bitterly cold, even in here, and it smells a bit musty, like my bathroom at the inn. Maybe there's mould on the walls. To the left, beneath the shuttered windows, I can see the outline of a sofa with a coffee table in front of it and an old-fashioned standard lamp beside it. To the right, some narrow stairs lead up.

'I was going to wait with the grave till tomorrow morning because of the light,' Nathalie says, moving to the table and placing the torch on it. Once again the click of a lighter. This time she lights the candles on the table – half a dozen stumps, burned to different heights, on the bare wood with nothing beneath them. 'But Lenia was crying so much and wouldn't calm down. She got to the point where she almost collapsed with exhaustion.' She bends down, takes off her woolly socks, rolls them up together and thoughtlessly drops them on the floor. At the sight of her bare feet on the cold tiles, I wrap my arms around my chest. The two sweatshirts I'm wearing, one on top of the other, are no substitute for Dad's jacket.

'You get used to some things,' Nathalie says, as if she could read my mind. 'But not others.'

I just nod, still overwhelmed by the situation. Not to mention the cold, the musty smell and the flickering shadows cast by the candlelight.

'Do sit down. Would you like some tea? My mother and the little one are both asleep so we should try to keep the noise down.'

I shake my head. I mustn't forget why I've actually come here. 'Does the name Marcus Steinhausen mean anything to you?'

A brief silence, shadows dancing on her face. 'No, who's he?'

'Are you sure?'

No answer, just the dancing shadows.

'How do you know the weekly market in Nestorstrasse if you lived in Wuppertal before moving to Schergel?'

'The . . . ? Oh yes, that. I've got friends in Berlin. They took me there once when I was on a visit. Is that why you've come all the way up here? To interrogate me? What's this about?'

She's about to turn away but I grab the sleeve of her dressing gown. 'You're afraid, Nathalie. I can sense it. You know who I am. Now tell me who you are!'

'Please, not so loud.'

'I can help you!'

Jerking out of my grip, she looks over at the stairs. 'You'll wake the entire house up.' A diversionary tactic I'm not going to fall for.

'Wiesbaden,' I say.

'What?'

'Schmitti told me you come from Wuppertal. Whereas this afternoon you told me yourself you come from Wiesbaden.'

She shakes her head. 'Wuppertal! I said Wuppertal. You must have misheard. And now I'd like to know what this is all about.'

'I'm just trying to make sense of our conversation earlier. Make sense of *you*. As well as the whole situation here in Schergel. Sarah's disappearance and Kerstin's murder. You talked of eleven girls the ribbon murderer abducted in Berlin. How did you get that number?'

Nathalie thumps her chest as if trying to calm her heartbeat. But she doesn't answer me, she says nothing.

'Please, Nathalie.' My eyes well with tears. 'Does this violent ex-husband of yours really exist? Or is it what I'm thinking? Was your little daughter one of the victims too? Only that, like Sarah, she managed to escape her kidnapper?'

'My ex-husband . . .' she repeats, her voice cracking.

'Did he really hurt you? Or Lenia? Or are we actually talking about someone quite different?'

Nathalie sways; I grab her arm again, to support her this time.

'Are you feeling unwell? Do you want to sit down?'

She shakes her head, very slowly, as if mechanically. 'In November. It happened in November.'

'What happened in November?'

'He . . .' She falters.

'Speak, Nathalie! I want to help you!'

'Nobody can help us.'

'Yes, I can! I'll do everything possible, I promise. Now, please just talk to me.'

Nathalie looks at me for a long moment. I open my mouth to

implore her again – the truth, please, I beg you! – but it doesn't work; I'm silent as if under a strange spell. Her gaze works it way deeper and deeper, first into me, then through me. 'He kidnapped Lenia from a playground and took her to a hut in the Königswald,' she begins, in a voice that sounds monotonous, almost trance-like. 'When he took his eye off her briefly, she saw her chance and ran off. She'd made her way through the woods for more than a kilometre when she came across some walkers. She told them she was lost. Luckily she knew our address by heart.'

My stomach churns and I don't feel steady on my feet. I'm not mad; I've been right the whole time.

Nathalie closes her eyes. 'When the two walkers brought her home, I knew at once that something dreadful must have hap-pened,' she continues as if everything were playing out again behind her closed lids, now, at this very moment. 'Can you see her breaking down in my arms, Ann? Her tiny body shuddering and quaking? Can you hear her crying so terribly? There, there, my darling, it's okay. Your mummy's here. What happened? Tell me, Lenia, speak to me! She is speaking. Oh God . . .' Nathalie, her eyes still closed, is now swaying so badly that I'm finding it hard to keep hold of her. I push her forwards to the sofa; I want her to sit down. 'It must have been the ribbon murderer. That's how he works, that's his pattern. He kidnaps little girls and takes them away to kill them. What has he done to my baby? And what . . .' She sobs intensely. 'What are we going to do now? What if he means to snatch her back? If he looks for her and finds her? Can we trust the police to protect us from him? Those same people who've been trying to catch him for fourteen years but failing time and again? We have to go away, my angel, far, far away. Don't worry, okay? Your mummy will make sure you're safe.'

I flop down wearily beside Nathalie, take her hand and hold it tightly. She opens her eyes and is back here with me now, back in her sitting room.

'So then you left Berlin?'

Nathalie nods. 'I decided to rent a car and leave our one outside our block so nobody would notice we'd gone. That would give us a head start . . .'

'Your mother was the only one you told.'

'Yes. I packed everything that would fit in the boot and we just drove off, heading south. It was pure coincidence that we came to Schergel, but I thought at once that this would be the perfect place. Remote, insignificant, just the tiniest of dots on the map. We would be safe here. At the entrance to the village was a sign about renting rooms and holiday homes – ask at the inn. Right away I thought Brock was a money-grubbing show-off, but that also had its advantages. He likes cash as he can slip it past the tax authorities. When I put a few notes on the counter he didn't even insist on seeing my ID, let alone make me sign any sort of agreement or other form. Two hundred and thirty euros a week for both apartments, which is basically the entire holiday home. That would be tricky once my savings were used up, but what kind of a problem is that compared to . . .'

'It's okay.'

'No, Ann, it's not okay. It's hell.' Now she in turn squeezes my hand so firmly that I can feel my knuckles. 'I had to lie to them all, all those people who were so kind to me, the entire village. But people notice if you shut yourself away altogether, and you end up achieving the exact opposite of what you'd intended. So you integrate a bit, to stop drawing unnecessary attention to yourself. To avoid questions and suspicion.'

'That's why you invented the story about your violent ex-husband.'

She shrugs. 'They all took pity on us and Kerstin even offered me the job at the butcher's. We needed the money, and now I was always able to find out what people were gossiping about in the village. In case—'

'He came back,' I say, finishing her sentence. 'Nathalie . . .' I wonder how to put this and why I'm finding it so difficult, because basically both of us know: it's happened. The man she wanted to protect her family from has tracked her down.

'I'm really sorry,' Nathalie says, beating me to it. Something I can't understand. 'It's not your fault.'

'My . . . ?'

Freeing her hand from my grip, she strokes my cheek instead. 'Since his arrest, they've only shown his picture in the papers and on the telly with a black bar over the eyes. But Lenia is sure. The nose, the mouth, the grey hair. She recognised him. It was him, Ann. It was your father.'

For a moment I'm falling, but the moment is short and I land on my feet. Because I've been doing a lot of falling recently, because it's something you learn. But most of all because I don't believe what she's saying. It's not true. Is it? Dear God, please don't let it be true. 'Let me speak to Lenia!'

'No way! You haven't got the slightest idea what we've been through! Because of your father, Ann!' Nathalie leaps up from the sofa, as do I.

Lenia must be mistaken. Of course she's deeply traumatised. Just like Sarah, who's silent, Nathalie's daughter is processing her trauma by pinning it on my father. As the alleged ribbon murderer, he's been in the press so often, always that same photograph with the black bar over his eyes. It's the perfect projection screen, isn't it? Isn't it?

'Please, Nathalie! You've got to understand that I have to be absolutely certain! This is about someone's life!'

'Yes, my daughter's! I want you to go now, at once!' She hurries into the hallway, wrenches the key and throws open the door. 'Get out of here!'

'Nathalie . . .'

'I've told you to go!' She's got a glass in her hand; I don't know where that's come from. But it doesn't matter, nothing matters now.

It was him, Ann. It was your father.

No. Nonononono. 'So who kidnapped Sarah? And killed Kerstin? Nathalie!'

With a firm shove, she pushes me out of the house and closes the door.

Despair. (Ann, 11 years old)

Despair is a bad feeling. It's like sitting on a small raft without a mast, sail or paddle, and just drifting on the sea in the middle of the night. Everything's dark and you can't see the shore and you don't have any hope, because there's no wind and so there are no waves either. All you can do is wait to see what happens, and maybe pray. But God doesn't always hear you.

I stagger down the outdoor steps as if I'd been badly injured. My mind is wrapped in swathes of apathy. I can see Jakob rushing towards me, but it doesn't feel real, more like a scene from a film.

'What happened?' he asks, though his voice barely reaches me. I want to return to the world behind my closed eyelids, want it to be intact again. I want to be five again, happy and unsuspecting. But most of all I want my asthma spray.

'Ann?!' Jakob again. He manoeuvres my body down the remaining steps as if it were a bulky piece of furniture. I wonder how he could have got here so quickly, but then I reckon he must have made his way to the house when I ended our conversation.

'It's all right,' I croak when we're at the bottom.

But Jakob doesn't believe me; he can hear the whistling in my breathing, the rattling in my chest, and it sounds really horrible, critical. 'Oh God! Sit down!'

Not wanting to, I drag myself onwards, desperate to get away from this house, away from Nathalie and Lenia and the mother and the dead cat, further and further, down the hill. Jakob is frantically prancing about beside me. I wheeze, flounder and eventually my knees give way in the middle of the path, as if someone had kicked me from behind. Jakob kneels beside me, cradling my head in his hands.

'Asthma,' I whimper.

'What? Shit!' Letting go of my head, he reaches in his trouser pocket for his mobile.

'No!' I punch the air: my protest against his intention to call for an ambulance. 'Really, I'll be better again in a sec.'

He hesitantly slips the mobile back in his pocket while I breathe against the constrictive feeling in my chest, in on one, out on two, again and again. And indeed it does get better.

'What happened in there?' Jakob says, pointing back to where Nathalie's house is a mere outline, black against the moonlight.

I shake my head and put out a hand so he can help me up. 'The air. I think the house is full of mould.' Jakob pulls me to my feet. 'It must have been too much for my asthma.'

'That's all? I heard shouting.'

'I got a fright. She was sitting behind the house in the pitch-black, digging a grave for their dead cat.'

'At this time?'

'Parents do that sort of thing,' I say, shedding a tear. 'Once my father drove three hours from Berlin to the Baltic in the middle of the night just after we'd got back from holiday. I'd left my diary at the hotel and almost had a breakdown.'

Jakob wrings his hands impatiently. Right now he's not interested in the diary of my fourteen-year-old self. But what happened inside Nathalie's house.

Decisions, my Beetle . . .

The head. The heart.

I shrug. 'I'm sorry about tonight. It was a total non-starter. The name Marcus Steinhausen seemed to ring no bells at all. And she knows the weekly market in Nestorstrasse from a visit to friends in Berlin.' Sluggishly I get moving again, back towards the village. My jeans are soaked and sticking to my legs. I'm walking as if I were made of wood.

Jakob catches up with me. 'So we're no further than we were before. The only difference being that her mouldy house almost killed you. What now?'

'No idea. I'm just completely shattered.'

*

There are two parts to me. One is numb, the other hurting. I stare at the ceiling, doubling up inside. Jakob's lying next to me, snoring softly. Every time I move, I find myself sticking to him in some way. He's not wearing a T-shirt and he's sweating. I don't want to feel his bare, warm skin, but the bed is too narrow to get away from him. It was his idea to spend the night in the same room. In view of the situation, it's safer, he said, and I expect he also wanted to be there to support me, sensing I was a bit of a mess. Maybe he was hoping for more too. So I told him that the fool I'm still hung up on goes by the name of Zoe. He found that exciting, which is still the best reaction you can expect from many people to a woman loving another woman. Normally this gets me worked up. But *normally* no longer exists; it's an adverb from a forgotten time.

Now everything is just surreal. Supposedly my father is the ribbon murderer; it's actually him, in all seriousness, unquestionably, it really, really, really is him. Nathalie said this to my face without leaving the slightest room for doubt. *Lenia is sure. The nose, the mouth, the grey hair. She recognised him. It was him, Ann. It was your father.*

Oughtn't I to hate him now? Be livid? Feel as if my entire existence had been betrayed? Instead I feel more like I've got a hangover. A state that's unpleasant but only temporary. And yet I know that Nathalie wouldn't have had any reason to lie to me. On the other hand, I still have my doubts as to whether a profoundly traumatised child can be taken seriously as a witness. The only positive side to this is that Nathalie hasn't gone to the police with Lenia. She hasn't made an official statement that might incriminate my father, and, in my estimation, she won't for the time being. She just wants some peace for her daughter. My head is buzzing; I need some peace and quiet too. Finding a position in which I can feel as little as possible of Jakob's body despite the lack of space, I try to get some sleep. In my dream my father is chasing Larissa Meller through the woods. I'm there too, helping him.

RECORDING 08

Berlin, 10 May 2021

– This discussion has nothing to do with your crimes, so I'm not going to get caught up in it. We were talking about Laura, the girl with the roller skates. You took her to the Kuhlake in Spandau. What happened then?
– You appear to be in a hurry.
– No, but you're starting to wear my patience thin. I'm here to discuss the girls, the cases.
– Yes, of course, do forgive me. So, Laura. Oh, she was really charming. And clearly she hadn't got out of Hellersdorf often. Nature fascinated her – the glittering water, the aromatic grass, a carpet of thousands of wood anemones – 'like in a fairy tale,' she said. And her excitement when we got to the hut! How enviable children are! That genuineness, that enthusiasm for little things. I asked her if she would do me a favour – stick out her left hand and close her eyes.
– And then?
– I did it. I grabbed her wrist and made the first cut.
– How did she react?
– Well, she didn't scream at first. She just opened her eyes and

stared at me. But right after that, she tore herself free with a strength and determination you couldn't imagine in a child, and then she ran off.

– Are you saying she escaped? The girl survived?

– (*chuckles*) Last time I asked you what your favourite subjects at school were, do you remember?

– You're doing it again.

– What?

– Dangling a carrot in front of my nose, only to pull it away again.

– Do you want to know what my favourite subjects were?

– No, I want to talk about Laura.

– Art and religious studies.

– (*sighs*) I see. Typical subjects you can bluff your way through.

– More like subjects that allow plenty of scope for discussion.

– Whatever. We were talking about Laura.

– No, we were talking about our favourite subjects. Yours were German and PE, I recall. I'm extremely attentive and observant, which has stood me in good stead throughout my life. For example, I know a great deal about you now.

– What's that supposed to mean?

– Laura, Miriam, Larissa, Jana, Kati, Olivia, Laetitia, Hayet, Jenny, Saskia, Alina and Sophie.

– Laura, Miriam, Larissa . . . (*pants*) There were more! There weren't ten, but . . .

– (*slow handclap*) Twelve.

– So Laura didn't survive.

– No, not her.

– *Not her?* But that means someone else did?

ANN

SCHERGEL, 29 DECEMBER 2017

When I wake up, it's not quite yet light. My right eyelid is stuck and there's a stain on the pillow. Blood? I sit bolt upright and make a sound that wakes Jakob. He reaches past me to the bed-side table and switches on the light. Then he stares at me and leaps out of bed. Soon afterwards I hear the rushing of water in the bathroom, then he comes back with a handful of damp, scrunched-up loo paper. It burns when he puts it on my face. Now I understand; it is actually blood on the pillow. And I also understand what's happened: the stitches have unravelled and my eyebrow has opened up again. My sleep was very restive, which is no surprise given that I was chasing my father through the woods. I've been brought back down to reality with a bump. Yesterday, Kerstin Seiler's murder, my visit to Nathalie, the end of the world. I knock Jakob's hand away from my face; I can't take being touched.

'Going for a shower,' I say, getting out of bed and gathering up my clothes that I put on the radiator to dry. Yesterday Jakob asked me what we were going to do now. All that's certain is that we have to go to the police station in Bad Kötzting this morning to give our statements about finding Kerstin's body. And that Jakob promised Brock a conversation with me.

On the way to the bathroom, my attention is caught by the bedroom door. There's a water glass on the handle. 'Jakob?'

'Oh, that.' He wanders past me into the bathroom, and again I hear the sound of running water, briefly this time. 'Just a security measure. I mean, there's a killer running around in the village.'

Fascinated, I go to inspect the construction close up while Jakob comes back from the bathroom. I hardly notice that he's filled the kettle. 'If someone presses the handle from outside . . .'

'The glass falls off and smashes on the floor.'

'An ingenious alarm system.'

I know someone else with an alarm system like that. Nathalie, who suddenly had a glass in her hand when she threw me out of her house yesterday. I didn't see where it had come from – perhaps because she'd just taken it off the handle? There's a click behind me and then the sound of water heating in the kettle.

I spin around. 'What are you doing?'

'Why not? I mean, breakfast doesn't begin until half past seven. Or have you been rationing them?' Laughing, Jakob dangles a tea bag over his cup. 'If you insist, I'll give you one from my room later.'

Do sit down. Would you like some tea?

'You need electricity to make tea.'

'Yes,' he says, laughing again. 'Or fire. But I reckon we've got enough problems in this village already without setting light to the place. Especially now that everyone knows who you are. Brock is going to fall on you like I will his breakfast buffet. God, I'm absolutely famished . . .'

His words fade beneath Nathalie's voice in my mind. Yesterday evening: *Something's up with the electrics. Nothing's been working since this afternoon, no light, no cooker, nothing.* And yet she offered to make me a cup of tea just a moment later.

'Ann?'

'What?'

'Would you like one too?'

Without responding, I rush into the bathroom with my pile of clothes. No time for tea, no time for explanations.

When I come back out, the television is on. A children's programme. Jakob's back in bed, the remote control on his bare tummy. He's fallen asleep, an empty teacup on the bedside table. For a moment I stand there, looking at him, unsure whether to wake him and ask him to come with me. Then I realise I've already made my decision – yesterday, when I only told him about half of my conversation with Nathalie. Just like I kept to myself what occurred to me about the glass on the door handle, and the kettle.

I don't have a choice.

I silently put on my boots, grab my rucksack and leave the room. It's quiet in the pub – the breakfast preparations don't seem to be underway yet – and it's tranquil outside too, on the marketplace. I imagine Brock and his wife lying in bed, the whole village still asleep, exhausted from the previous day and all the beer that was drunk during the meeting.

I have to be sure, I *have* to be. So I make my way yet again up to Nathalie's house on the upper common. I walk briskly; my shadow, leading its own life beneath the light of the streetlamps, is making me feel uncomfortable. I look back over my shoulder several times, and several times I hear crunching footsteps in the snow that aren't there. But Jakob's right: a killer's still running around this village. He might be lying in wait for me behind the corner of the next house or the next tree, and nobody would see anything happen. So much for the village guard that Brock said would be up and running yesterday evening, doing round-the-clock patrols. I quicken my pace. Something is more important than danger. The minutest of possibilities, the last straw.

The shutters closed even during the day.

No electric light that might draw attention to the fact that this house is being lived in.

The glass over the handle as an improvised alarm system.

Nathalie's lightning reaction as she grabbed the axe. As if she were on permanent alert and prepared for everything.

But most of all, this: why hasn't she gone back to Berlin if she's so sure that the man she believes to be her daughter's abductor has been locked up in prison for almost seven weeks?

And who's she afraid of?

The answer: Kerstin Seiler's killer, of course. But why should she be his next target? Her house is outside the village; nobody unfamiliar in this area would find it. So the killer must know her.

I shake my head; I just don't get it. There's only one thing I know: Nathalie's lying. For some reason she's still lying. And I've got to find out why. Apart from this, they can tell me as often as they like that my dad's the ribbon murderer, but I'll never be well and truly convinced of his guilt while words are still words and, like the evidence, don't constitute clear proof. I stop and rummage in my rucksack amongst Nathalie's things – the bread and now redundant cat food – for the packet of cigarettes I bought at the shop yesterday. Then for my lighter, but fruitlessly. I check my trouser pockets. For a moment I think I've got it, but it must still be in the jacket that the police took away for forensic examination. I take something else out instead: my old talisman that I found in the wooden box in Dad's study. The stone that dug into my wrist almost twenty years ago. Which Dad saved after the bike accident and gave me later as a reminder of the terrible experience I'd survived. On the sharp side, some brown discolouration is still visible. My blood. This stone that seems to be a sign, an encouragement to follow my feelings. A minor miracle just when I need it.

A few minutes later, the incline to the upper common appears before me. The holiday house is already in view, a dead, black outline, as if it had been slotted into an equally black bay of trees. And right there . . . maybe it only occurs to me because I've just been thinking about smoking. A tiny, luminous red dot, the glow of a cigarette. Am I mistaken? I blink. It glows again, the little red dot in the gloom. Then something moves – *someone!* – from the cover of the trees and makes straight for Nathalie's house. I instinctively squat and narrow my eyes, concentrating as hard as possible. Now I see it, I see it perfectly. A tall figure, not Nathalie this time. A man, creeping past the downstairs apartment. He stops, looks around. Gets moving again, approaches the steps. My brain is in overdrive: Steinhausen. He's here.

I start running the rest of the way up the slope. Nathalie, Lenia and the grandmother. Unsuspecting, maybe still asleep in their beds. When the glass slides off the door handle and smashes on the floor, it'll be too late. He'll already be inside the house. I speed up, remember the mobile in my rucksack, and ponder: call the police or Jakob? It would take too much time. Time that Nathalie and her family don't have. I reach the house, the steps. Then I think of the axe that Nathalie used yesterday evening to hack out the tree roots from the hole for the cat's grave. She leaned it next to the terrace door. A weapon. I don't mean to hurt anyone, just keep them at bay. But to get to the axe, I'd have to go past the front door and along three sides of the house.

The front door – relief. It hasn't been touched. He wasn't so far ahead of me that he could have cracked the lock, gone into the house and closed the door again from the inside. Besides, I didn't hear the breaking of glass. I put my ear to the wood and listen. Nothing. Has he got in some other way? Through the terrace door, perhaps? Or has he only come to nose around, have a recce? Did he spot me and bolt?

I creep my way around, one wall after another, until I get to the terrace. The lantern on the cat's grave. *It's just a little candle and yet it lights up the night.* The axe. It's gone. Did Nathalie put it somewhere else after I left? Or is it in the wrong hands? I look around nervously. The terrace door – also shut, with closed shutters. I peek through the slats. There's flickering light in the sitting room, candles like yesterday evening. Have they been burning all night? A shadow flits past; I flinch. It could just be Nathalie. Or the killer. I want to undo the catch that keeps the shutters fastened on the inside. So I try to slide my hand through the gap, but it doesn't fit.

My stone, my talisman! It's flat, triangular, and large enough that I can hold it by the wide end and push the narrow tip under the catch until it flips to the other side with a clack. I open the shutters and get another shock. Through the window I see

Nathalie wander over to the coffee table and pick up one of the candles. She looks like a ghost, she's spaced out. Surely she must have noticed the shutters being opened only a metre and a half away from her? I knock on the window.

Nothing, she doesn't react. Just stands there holding the candle, staring into the flame. I knock again. Now. Now her eyes see me and she tentatively comes closer; in the gloom of dawn she probably doesn't recognise me immediately. I gesticulate wildly and mouth her name. I don't want to be loud; someone apart from me is prowling around out here.

She opens the door, visibly surprised. 'Ann? What are you doing here, after—'

'After our argument yesterday evening? Let's just forget that, okay?' I push my way into the room and immediately lock the door behind me. 'There's someone here, Nathalie! I saw a man creeping around the house. Just now.'

'What? Who would . . . ?' She falters, her face suddenly vacant. 'Are we in danger?'

'I'm afraid we are. You lied to me, didn't you?' I slip the rucksack off my shoulder and drop it to the floor, prompted by the crazy thought that I might be about to get into a fight, and will need to be as agile as possible – no unnecessary encumbrance on my back.

Nathalie looks away.

'It's okay.' I reach for the candle, which has started shaking alarmingly in her hand, put it back on the table and pick up instead the torch that is there too. 'None of that matters now. We'll call the police and barricade ourselves in here till they come. It would be best if we took one of the upstairs rooms. Where's your family?'

Nathalie points behind her. 'We're just having breakfast. Ann . . .' She grabs my arm. Her grip is so desperate, so tight that I feel it in my bones. 'I'm scared.'

'I know. Me too. But we'll get through this, okay?'

Nathalie lets go of my arm. I switch on the torch.

'We should keep the overhead light off. We mustn't serve our-selves up to him on a platter. If he wants to get us, he's going to have to work for it.'

Nathalie looks horrified.

'I'm sorry,' I quickly add. 'That was inappropriate.'

I hurry across the sitting room. It's not hard to find the way to the kitchen; the house is small and the ground floor is probably only half the size of the apartment I shared with Zoe. The beam from the torch jerks haphazardly, staccato impressions, one per heartbeat. The furnishings, like those in the sitting room, aren't much cop in here either – the veneer is already peeling away from the nut-brown kitchen units. A fridge with a children's drawing stuck to it with magnets, together with signature: Lenia. A sink with days' worth of dirty dishes piled in it. A bin, its lid gaping open like a mouth stuffed with food. Empty tins of preserved food like the ones Nathalie bought masses of at the grocer's yesterday. The breakfast table laid with two plates, two cups, two sets of cutlery. A carton of milk, a pot of tea or coffee, crispbread, butter, jam. I've no time to think or embark on lengthy explanations. 'Come on!' I call to the old woman and little girl. 'We've got to . . .'

I falter.

Both of them ought to be staring at me now. Me, a strange woman in their house, a shock this early in the morning. The moment when everything falls apart, weeks of playing hide-and-seek, of uncertainty and permanent tension, but also the slight hope that they might have come through it all, and finally the great misapprehension. They ought to be beside themselves, terrified, confused, shocked. They ought to be *something*. But they're not.

The kitchen's empty.

I wave the torch about in disbelief. Finding a light switch, I push it. It's as I'd suspected: Nathalie lied about the electricity. The kitchen is bright, but remains empty.

'It happened in November,' I hear a voice behind me. Dropping the torch, I whip around and look directly at Nathalie. 'He kidnapped Lenia from a playground and took her to a hut in the Königswald.'

I nod as if on autopilot. That's precisely what she said yesterday, even using the same words. 'But where . . . ?' I ask, my throat constricted. Because there could still be a rational explanation for why there's nobody at this table, no Lenia, no grandmother. A different explanation from the one that's brewing in my head, like a storm suddenly filling a clear sky with darkness.

Nathalie says nothing.

I pant. Now I understand. The storm is raging. 'She . . . she didn't make it, did she? She couldn't escape because the ribbon murderer killed her just like the other girls in Berlin.'

Her face twitches with incomprehension. She staggers past me to one of the chairs, where she places a hand on the backrest. As if someone were sitting there.

'Don't worry, my little princess,' she says with a soft voice, her eyes staring into the void. 'Nobody's ever going to part us again.' Then, directed at me, 'Not even her.'

RECORDING 09
Berlin, 10 May 2021

– Wrong. I'm sorry. They all died. Beginning with Laura and ending with Sophie.

– That means Larissa wasn't the first.

– No, that was Laura, in summer 2001. One year later, in autumn 2002, came Miriam, and only then Larissa.

– That's what you meant when you said I was mistaken. My mistake was to think Larissa was the first victim. Correct?

– Correct.

– But they never connected Laura and Miriam to you.

– No, but they couldn't because those two girls were never found. As far as Laura is concerned . . . that was my first time, even though the idea had been fermenting in me for quite a while. But the impulse to actually do it came spontaneously when I saw her sitting by the road.

– You say it was spontaneous, but you had the weapon on you.

– I'd been carrying it around with me for some time. Like I say, the idea had been fermenting in me, and I'd often imagined doing it. So when I came across Laura, everything just slotted together.

– What did you do with her body?

– What would you have done with it?

– I've never thought about that and nor do I wish to.

– I heard about someone who once sawed up a body and then drove across the country, breaking into various farms and placing the parts in pigsties. Pigs are omnivores, you see, and because dead flesh just smells of carrion rather than humans, they'll happily eat it.

— Why are you telling me this?

— Because I'd like to know your opinion on it.

— What do you expect me to say? It's disgusting!

— I see.

— What do you mean by 'I see'? Please don't tell me you're that man! You didn't feed Laura to pigs, did you?

— What do you take me for? That sort of thing would never have crossed my mind. First, I put Laura in the boot of my car, then I drove home. Although I'd imagined killing, just like you it had never occurred to me what I'd do with a dead body. I had to spend some time thinking it through. That night I drove back to the Kuhlake with Laura in the boot, and a shovel, to bury her. The following year, when I killed Miriam, I had the shovel with me.

— Where did you take Miriam?

— To the Blumenthaler Wald. Very close to where Saskia later died.

— Does this mean that the parents of Laura and Miriam still don't know what happened to their daughters?

— You're right, they don't. I suspect the girls are still officially classified as missing. It was only when it came to the third girl, Larissa, that I decided it would be better not to bury her. I'd allow the parents to do that.

— You got a bad conscience?

— No, it was more theoretical. I knew it was wrong to bury them and deprive the parents of the opportunity. The parents ought to find them and make a grave for them.

— (laughs) With respect, it sounds strange to hear the word

'wrong' coming from your mouth. And this distinction you make: you thought it was right to kill the girls, but wrong to bury them?

— I didn't say I thought it was right. 'Necessary' would be more accurate.

— Was it like a compulsion, then?

— I'd call it an urge.

— Where did this urge come from? What did Laura trigger in you to turn you into a killer, unable to stop murdering?

— Well, clearly, I have stopped.

— Yes, but not voluntarily. It was only your arrest that put an end to your crimes for good.

— My arrest. (*laughs*) In dubio pro reo, don't you think? Absolutely crucial was what happened in Schergel. Even I hadn't expected this turn of events.

ANN

SCHERGEL, 29 DECEMBER 2017

I want to get out of this kitchen, away from Nathalie; I'm finding her creepy. *Don't worry, my little princess,* she reassured the empty chair. *Nobody's ever going to part us again.* Stumbling backwards into something, I squeal in shock. I turn around; it's just the fridge. I stare at the drawing stuck to it. On the left is a small figure wearing a sprawling dress and a crown. A monster is making its way into the picture from the right. It's dark green with spiky-looking scales and fire shooting from its huge, open mouth between sharp teeth. It occupies the entire length of the piece of paper; it must be three or four times as big as the girl with the crown. The princess and the dragon, just like Sarah said.

But there's someone else: a third figure in the middle. A being in a long dress, perhaps an angel or a good fairy. With yellow hair – blonde, like Nathalie's. In her outstretched hand, she's holding a sword or a knife, something with a blade at least, the tip of which she's pressing against the dragon's neck.

Reeling, I turn back to Nathalie, who's still in exactly the same position: standing, her hand on the back of the chair, looking at me.

'Sarah?' is all I say at first, because, no, that can't be true. That's completely crazy. 'Is that the reason she's not making a statement? Because she knows you and doesn't want you to get into trouble?' Nathalie doesn't react. 'By castle, she meant your house, didn't she? Sarah was here the whole time, which was why there were no signs of hypothermia . . .' I look at her in silent supplication. Interrupt me. Tell me I'm wrong. Ask me if I've taken leave of my senses. Say something, anything.

Nothing.

'But why? Why would you kidnap that little girl? I mean, Kerstin was your friend . . .' I pause. Kerstin Seiler, who's now dead, murdered. Lenia's old drawing on the fridge, which suddenly seems like a prophecy. The fairy holding the blade to the dragon's neck. And Kerstin, who later had a meat hook rammed into her neck. No! No, no, no, no!

'What have you done?' I bellow, throwing myself at her. Grabbing her, shaking her. She allows me to do it, as if her body were just a shell and the rest of her somewhere completely different. 'Talk to me!'

She cocks her head. Reaches for my wrists in slow motion, tightening her fingers around them. I shake myself free.

'Children,' she begins quietly, 'are the greatest gift, Ann. Kerstin didn't understand that.'

I gasp. Is this a confession?

She smiles. 'Lenia was desperate for a friend. I knew at once she'd get on well with Sarah. And Kerstin would have the opportunity to rethink her role as a mother. Killing two birds with one stone.'

I cautiously take a step backwards. It *is* a confession. Only now

I'm no longer sure I want to hear it. Nathalie, who I was so taken by because she reminded me of a feeling. Of Zoe, of love. Please don't let her be a bad person.

'Kerstin didn't treat Sarah well,' she says, clutching the left side of her chest; maybe her heart is as painful as mine. 'The little one was for ever in her way; Kerstin always made her feel she was interrupting. The butcher's was important, Schmitti was important. But what about Sarah? It was dreadful, Ann. When I came to work, she wouldn't leave my side. She sucked up the attention I paid to her like a sponge. Although she never said so, I soon suspected that Kerstin was beating her. And?' She raises her eyebrows at me. 'I was right! Or how else do you think she got those bruises they found on her body in hospital?'

I don't reply; I can't.

'I thought Kerstin needed to have her eyes opened,' Nathalie continues, in a voice I'd fall for in other circumstances, so warm and soft. 'To have an experience like the one I'd had. Because, do you know what, Ann? When your child disappears and you fear for their life, it makes you humble, really humble. You pray to God, offering him one deal after another. And if, like me, you're lucky, he listens to you and grants you a miracle.'

I look to the empty chair, but don't dare say anything.

'That's exactly what Kerstin was forced to go through,' Nathalie continues. Her tone has changed; now she sounds cold. 'I wanted her to be devoured by worry, I wanted it to turn her into a new person. And I thought it had worked, I really did! She cried her eyes out when Sarah disappeared, she almost died with worry. But then she got her daughter back and everything went wrong! Think back to the moment outside the butcher's. Kerstin was like a stone – she didn't even pick her little girl up, let alone shed a tear out of relief or gratitude. I suppose you could make allowances for the shock. But what was all that later? In the hospital? She let Brock photograph Sarah like an exhibition piece and exploit the poor girl's misery. She left her child alone and drove home to have a rest. Have a rest, Ann! Is that the sign of a good mother? Is that someone who's reformed and making the most of their second chance?'

I shake my head, but not in response to her question. I'm thinking of yesterday. How I bumped into Nathalie in the grocer's and then accompanied her home. The fleck of blood on her trousers – now I know where that's from. She was wearing a black, knee-length winter coat. Who knows what she looked like under that? How much blood was there on her? I feel terrible. Guilty. Because I wandered beside her like a loving puppy, hauling her shopping up the hill while Kerstin lay dying in the cold store of the butcher's. Why didn't I realise anything? She might be still alive if she'd got help earlier.

'She wasn't a good person, Ann,' Nathalie says insistently.

'So that gave you the right to kill her, did it? Was it up to you to pass judgement on Kerstin for leaving her daughter alone? What is wrong with you? The girl was here while you sat with her mother late into the night, hypocritically comforting her. It was more important to you to delight in the mother's suffering than to look after Sarah.'

'Do you think Sarah was unhappy here? On the contrary, Ann! She didn't want to leave! She enjoyed having a proper mother around, telling her stories, cooking for her, giving her baths and cuddling her! And of course I made sure she'd be fine when I wasn't home. During those periods she'd be out for the count like Sleeping Beauty.'

'You couldn't know that for sure! She could have woken up and got scared in this strange, dark house.'

'She wouldn't've woken up.'

'You . . .' *They've found traces of an unknown substance in her urine*, I think, recalling what Schmitti said in the hospital. 'You drugged her?'

'Who do you think I am? Benzodiazepine isn't a drug! I took it myself for a while.' She gives a twisted smile. 'Besides, *Sleeping Beauty* is Sarah's favourite fairy tale.'

I can't believe it. 'You still think you're a heroine, don't you? You should have contacted the child welfare office. They would have helped Sarah. But no. Instead you traumatised the girl for the rest of her—'

'The child welfare office?' She laughs. 'They wouldn't have done anything because Sarah would never have betrayed her mother. And Kerstin – they'd have been taken in by Kerstin, she was able to wrap everyone around her little finger.'

Just like you, I think wearily. 'You're no heroine, Nathalie. You're no better than the man who took Lenia away from you.'

I see her shoulders tense and hear her strained breathing through gritted teeth – someone trying to get a grip on themselves. My eyes dart around, trying to gauge the distance between Nathalie and the cutlery drawers. In one of those there will be a knife.

'There's someone outside, Nathalie,' I say urgently. 'Someone who clearly has a reason to creep around your house at dawn.' For a moment I think of Schmitti, who could have found out what Nathalie did to his fiancée. Then I remember that Schmitti is barely taller than me, unlike the figure I saw. Steinhausen! is my next thought. But that wouldn't make sense after Nathalie's confession. Would it? 'Whoever he is, he might be really angry with you. Let's call the police. For your protection.'

'The police? Those losers who spent fourteen years standing back and watching the psychopath you call your father kill little girls?'

I'm seized by something bright and gleaming: rage. At a mentally ill killer who takes the liberty of judging others, and at myself because I happily let myself be deluded by her.

'My Lenia was lucky, but what about the others who your father—'

'Lenia didn't identify anyone, Nathalie,' I growl. 'Neither my father nor anyone else. And do you know why?' I take a step towards her, then kick the chair as hard as I can. 'Because nobody's sitting here, you deranged woman!'

The chair crashes to the floor and Nathalie exhales audibly. Taking advantage of her shock, I rush out of the kitchen into the sitting room, where I grab my rucksack. I need to get out of here. I tug the handle of the terrace door but I'm not fast enough.

'You're not going to call the police!' Then comes a blow to my back which momentarily leaves me unable to breathe. Losing my balance, I fall, and am just able to put my hands out before my jaw goes crashing on to the tiles. Now Nathalie's on top of me, her knees clamping my sides, her weight pressing my chest against the floor, and her fists pounding me. I thrust my elbow backwards, hitting her in the stomach, then I hear her clatter into the terrace door. The glass quivers noisily. Crawling forwards, I

seize one of the straps of my rucksack. I then crawl in the opposite direction, to the hallway and front door. All of a sudden, her
hand takes hold of my leg. I kick, once, twice, hard and harder;
a whimpering sound tells me I must have hit her. I'm free. I get
to my feet, my chest wheezing. Nathalie is lying bent double on
the floor. She gives me a beseeching look; I just shake my head.
It's over, and at the same time it's not. I've just solved a murder.
And yet my father's still going to be in prison.

I'm sorry, Dad. I'm so, so sorry.

I stagger to the front door and turn the key in the lock. The
glass slides off the handle and smashes. I can't hear anything; it
all happens silently, or at least the sounds don't reach my ears.
I blink hard. Blood is obstructing my vision. My eyebrow must
have opened up again. I'm not in a good way, and not merely
because of that. My body feels like one big bruise; my circulation
is careening.

I can't do any more. Forgive me, Dad.

I stumble down the steps outside; I need to get away as fast
as possible in case Nathalie comes after me. I need to find a safe
place and notify the police from there. I need to breathe, in on
one, out on two. The stand of trees where I hid with Jakob yesterday. Here I'll be protected but have a good view of the house.
I duck behind a thick trunk, then rummage in my rucksack. The
bread and cat food land in the snow. I wipe my eyes – tears and
blood. My mobile. I press the first two numbers, and am about
to tap the third when from behind a hand rests on my shoulder.
Nathalie, is my first thought, but I'm wrong. It's a man's hand. I
turn to look and just manage to pant 'Steinhausen' before passing
out and toppling into the snow.

US

What are we going to do now, princess? What on earth will we do now? Help me, tell me what to do. Ann is so mistaken, but she doesn't realise it. She thinks she knows what happened – she thinks she knows everything! – and that's exactly what she'll tell the police. A catastrophe. Because once we're on the police's radar, it won't be long before *he* comes. What if Ann's right and he's already here? Is everything we've undertaken to be in vain? That would be my fault, my darling, my own bloody fault, I know. I never should have got myself mixed up in it. I shouldn't have taken Sarah or told Kerstin my opinion. How could I forget myself so badly and ruin everything? What do you think, princess? Should I look at your picture, the picture on the fridge? The way you drew me, so full of confidence in my abilities. Me, your eternal protector, with my sword at the dragon's neck. My oath that nobody will ever succeed in parting us.

One last battle, of course. My word still stands, it stands for ever. You know that, my darling. But you've got to help me. Mummy feels a bit weak, Mummy needs you. Will you do that, yes? Will you help Mummy? Will you help me look for a knife?

ANN

SCHERGEL, 29 DECEMBER 2017

When I come round, I'm sitting in the snow, my back against a tree trunk. My body is stiff from the cold, my head is heavy, and my thoughts are like porridge. Before me, the maltreated face from the basement of the construction site, overlapped a second later by the portrait photo from the architectural practice's website. Steinhausen, Steinhausen, Steinhausen. I start to scream. Two hands grab my head roughly. One holds it tight, the other clamps my mouth. I stare at him, the man kneeling before me. Pale skin, bags under the eyes, deeply etched lines on his forehead, dark stubble, hollow cheeks.

That's not Steinhausen.

It's a total stranger.

'Okay?' the man asks, slightly relaxing his grip. I nod as an understanding that he can take his hand away from my mouth. He does.

'Who are you?'

'That's not important,' he says, shaking his head. He looks nervous; his eyes flick between me and Nathalie's house. 'You were just in there with her. I watched you. What happened?'

I freeze. This isn't Steinhausen, it's the man I saw creeping around the house. I smell stale smoke and think of the tiny glowing dot in the distance. It's him, I'm absolutely certain of it. And there's something menacing about him.

'I don't know what you're talking about.'

Again he grabs my face, his hand squashing my cheeks together. But he's shaking, everything about him is shaking, even his voice. 'I'm talking about her! About Nathalie!'

I shake my head; I'm no traitor. Not even after everything she's done.

The man lets go of me. He gets to his feet and paces up and down while rubbing his brow, then his neck, clearly thinking things through. I tentatively stand up. To his left I can see a branch, a long, thick piece of wood in the middle of the snow. I just have to reach it.

'What do you want from her?' I ask to distract him, while I edge towards the branch.

He stops and looks at me. 'Are you a friend?'

'Sort of.'

In a flash he leaps towards me and grabs my upper arm. 'Then help her by helping me. I'm Steffen Fester, her ex-husband.'

'Steffen Fester,' I repeat, drawing out the words. And yet I couldn't care less about his name. All I'm thinking about is what till now I've believed was an excuse to disguise Nathalie's real reason for fleeing Berlin: that her ex-husband behaved violently towards her.

'I've been looking for her for weeks ...'

'Let me go – now!' I hiss. The fact that he does tells me he's uncertain. Or unpredictable. I take a large step to the side, a step

further towards the thick branch I've nominated to defend me –
but without taking my eye off Fester. He's very tall, with broad,
angular shoulders, and his emaciated face exudes an alarming
harshness.

'Where's my mobile?' I ask. I remember trying to call the police
before passing out.

'Oh yes. You dropped it in the snow.' He reaches nervously into
his coat pocket and holds out the phone and a cloth handkerchief.
'For your face.'

I take both, dab my eyebrow and say, 'I'm going to call the
police now, okay? Because whatever's going on between you and
Nathalie, it would be better for all concerned if it were sorted
out under supervision.'

'No, no, no!' Again he comes at me, but this time I'm quicker.
Two large, quick steps and I'm facing him with the branch.

'You're not going anywhere near me or Nathalie, understood?'

He makes a placatory gesture, as if I had a real weapon in my
hands rather than just an improvised bit of wood. That's fine by
me; I jab the wood in his direction to make him keep his distance.
Fester stumbles but recovers.

'You don't understand. If you call the police, she'll kill herself, definitely. And then I'll never find out where she took our
daughter.'

'Lenia?'

He nods. 'She ran off with her.'

'Don't try to muck me around. I know Lenia's dead.'

Fester grits his teeth. 'I'm talking about her remains.'

'Her . . . ?'

'Not now, please . . .' Later, he says. He'll give me a detailed explanation later. 'We need to go to Nathalie right now before she gets any silly ideas!'

Not with me. I don't trust him and I make a few provisos, or I'll call the police. Fester agrees sulkily, but insists we head for the house without any further delay. I have trouble keeping up with him. He runs, he pants, he tries giving me the story in a nut-shell. The grave had already been dug and Lenia's body laid out for the burial. But then, the night before the funeral, there was a break-in at the funeral director's and the body was stolen. Fester immediately suspected his ex-wife was responsible. He felt justi-fied when he went to the family home he'd left to Nathalie after their separation and found it deserted. He also discovered she'd hired a car, as well as the fact that this car had been returned in Munich a few days later. He assumed that she was either there or somewhere nearby. Only later did it occur to him that Nathalie might have hidden Lenia first, before giving the car back and then simply taking the bus, the train or hitchhiking to her new bolthole, which might not be that close to Munich after all. In the end he was led to Schergel by an online newspaper article about a little girl who had returned home safe and sound after a sus-pected abduction. He'd recognised Nathalie in the accompanying photograph. I nod, realising that he's talking about the picture Brock took outside the butcher's yesterday morning.

'I've read all there is to read about the ribbon murderer,' he says. 'If only because after Lenia's death, Nathalie seemed to be obsessed with the man.'

'Does this mean you've been searching for her for weeks on your own?' I ask, still suspicious. 'Why didn't you put the police on to it?'

He did, of course, he says. But nothing much came of it. Nathalie was a grown woman, they told him, who could go where she liked when she liked. Especially as the substantial sum of money she'd withdrawn from her bank beforehand suggested that Nathalie had *wanted* to go – it was her free decision rather than a case of coercion or even abduction. And as far as Lenia was concerned . . . He stops abruptly. We're at the house. 'No leads so far in your case of the missing body, they said.' He lowers his gaze. 'You might find this hard to believe, but . . . once upon a time I really loved Nathalie.'

'You don't want her to go to prison.'

He nods. 'She doesn't belong there. She needs help.'

He climbs the steps; I follow him. 'Herr Fester?'

'Yes?'

'The girl you read about in the online article. It was Nathalie who kidnapped her.'

He stops again, as if he'd been struck by lightning.

'And there's more. She also—'

'She needs help,' he reiterates, more emphatically this time, and climbs the rest of the steps to the front door.

He wants me to try, to knock, call her name.

'I don't know how she's going to react to seeing me,' is his reasoning.

I shake my head. 'She was landing punches on me only a few minutes ago. I doubt I'll do any better.'

'Please, we've got to give it a try.'

I hesitate. His story sounds convincing, and yet . . . 'What are you planning to do to her?'

Rather than answer me, he now jiggles the handle, gently at

first, then more forcefully. 'Nathalie!' his voice thunders. 'Open the bloody door!'

My stomach tightens; there's a vague hunch rumbling inside. Something bad's about to happen. I feel for the stone in my trouser pocket, for support, for protection. Fester lets go of the door and dashes around the house. 'What the . . . ?' he cries in horror when he discovers the grave behind the terrace.

'That's her cat,' I explain, upon which he puts a hand in front of his mouth.

'Oh no. Our Milly? She took her from Berlin too. And she—'

I just nod.

Fester hammers against the shutters in front of the terrace door, which Nathalie must have closed again after I ran out of the house.

'Wait . . .' I tighten the grip around the stone in my hand, in the knowledge that it's the very tool Fester could use right now. 'She's not going to end up in prison. People will realise she's sick. Please, let's call the police.'

'I want my daughter back,' he says. He picks up a large and – judging by the way he's breathing – heavy piece of wood, which he slams against the shutters until they break open. I jump with fright when he also uses it to smash the glass. But tears come to my eyes too. I don't know why. I've seen the monster inside Nathalie. I've seen it in Kerstin Seiler's lifeless body, in the wound in her neck, in the sea of blood. I've experienced it myself, earlier when she came rushing at me. And yet I fear for her.

'Herr Fester, wouldn't it be better if we called the police?' We climb through the frame of the terrace door, one at a time. The candles are now out. Fester turns around like a spinning top, then rushes to the windows above the sofa to open the shutters.

'Didn't you smell that when you were here?'

'Yes . . . I . . . I did,' I stammer. 'That's the mould—'

'That's Lenia!'

He hastens towards the kitchen, whereas I run up the stairs to the top floor. Straight ahead is the bathroom; its door is open. On either side of it are two other rooms.

'She's not here!' Fester shouts from downstairs.

No, I think. Because she's here. Nathalie. In the room to the left of the stairs. A bedroom. She's sitting in a thin white nightie on the floor beside an unmade bed. Her legs outstretched, a teddy in her lap. The smell . . . I wish I could still believe it was just mould. Half a dozen grave candles are lined up by the closed shutters. The room flickers black and red.

Those are soul lights, my Beetle.

'Ann.' She smiles as if in a trance. 'You're back. You didn't leave us all alone.' How weak she looks, how vulnerable. A gorgeous, broken work of art. A monster. Right beside her is a knife. Not one with a long blade, more like a vegetable knife, and yet it's a knife, an unpredictable weapon.

'Have you found Nathalie?' Footsteps clatter on the stairs. Without thinking about it, I throw myself against the door and lock us in.

'Your ex-husband is here. He says you took Lenia, Lenia's—'

'What the . . . ?' The handle is wrenched several times. Then Fester pounds his fists against the door.

'But you already know this, Ann,' Nathalie replies. 'I had to get Lenia to safety.'

I approach her slowly, focusing on the knife. One slight movement, not much more than a twitch, and it would be in her hand. 'Can I sit down next to you?' I carefully squat down and try to discreetly nudge the knife away with my foot.

'Open up!' followed by a thud against the door that's so hard the frame shakes. I wince, whereas Nathalie looks alarmingly calm.

'Have you taken something?' The Sleeping Beauty pills.

'Nathalie!' That's Fester, now forcing his whole weight against the door.

'He's not going to go away,' I say. 'He wants to know where Lenia is.'

'She's hidden herself away. She hates it when people argue.'

I instinctively tilt my head so I can take a glimpse beneath the bed. But I don't see anything.

Nathalie closes her eyes and smiles. 'Don't worry, my little princess. Ann has come back to help us. Everything's going to be all right.' I swallow with difficulty and understand. Nathalie too has a world behind her closed eyes. Only her world isn't content with a space in her imagination. Did she perhaps use Sarah's abduction to enact her version of how Lenia's story should have turned out? She must have been disappointed by the finale, though, the moment when Sarah returned unscathed and her mother failed to react as Nathalie had envisioned. How she herself would have reacted had Lenia actually managed to escape.

'Do you remember what happened to your daughter, Nathalie?'

She opens her eyes and her smile widens. Then she nods at the knife by the tip of my boot.

'Today could be the day you bring the real ribbon murderer to justice. Do you realise that, Ann?'

'No, no, Nathalie,' I say, pointing to the door. 'The man out there is your ex-husband, not the . . .' I stop. She's just smiling, smiling on and on.

'It's our story, Ann. Our truth.'

'But . . .' I shake my head in confusion. 'You said yourself that you think my father's—'

At that moment the hinges crack and the door gives way. Fester rushes at Nathalie and yanks her up by the arm. 'Where's my daughter?'

'Ann!' Nathalie whimpers. Grabbing the knife, I get up too.

'Where is she?' Fester is livid. His concern for his ex-wife seems to have been obliterated. Instead he's now flinging her around like a playful dog might an old rag doll. 'Tell me where she is!'

'You left us,' Nathalie howls at him. 'You have no right to see your daughter anymore.' This seems to hit Fester as unerringly as a bullet in the stomach. Letting go of her, he teeters backwards.

'Nathalie, please, you've got to—'

'He made his decision, Ann. Since last year he's been in love with a secretary. He packed his things and just upped sticks.'

'My new relationship has got nothing to do with any of this. I still looked after Lenia,' Fester says. Pain flickers in his face. 'I picked her up for the weekend every fortnight.'

'Every fortnight, yes. Then you bought her toys, took her to the zoo or went for an ice cream. You call that looking after?' She moves over to him, swaying. Again I wonder if she's taken anything – sleeping pills, Benzowhatevers, the stuff she gave Sarah – and perhaps too much of it. 'Having a child is so sacred, a gift. You showed you weren't worthy of it.'

Fester's jaw twitches; he seems to be chewing words, unde-cided whether to utter or swallow them.

'Two birds with one stone, Ann,' Nathalie says. 'He never deserved to be a father.' She now looks at me – not my face, but the knife in my hand. 'Not even before the kidnapping, when he was still with us. Two years ago, for example. In 2015, Steffen. Do you remember what happened?'

Fester opens and closes his mouth.

Nathalie laughs idly. 'Lenia fell and knocked out her front teeth. And who looked after her? Who comforted her, fed her? It wasn't you, it was me! You just went to work as usual and left everything to me. Or earlier, in 2012, only a few weeks after she was born. The bad fever fits. Who sat at her bedside day and night? Who cooled her little body and held her hand? Me, Steffen, only ever me!'

I purse my lips, thinking of my father who was so different from Steffen Fester. Like Nathalie, he sat by my bed, held my hand and fed me. And he was always there for me. In 2015, after my car accident. In 2012, during my existential crisis, which ended up with me changing subjects. He even took leave from the univer-sity to travel across France with me, so I could clear my head . . .

'I was always there when Lenia needed me. There was nothing more important in my life. I was her good fairy. The one who fought against the dragon, against sickness, fear and all the bad things.'

'Don't do this, Nathalie,' Fester begs. 'Don't paint me like that, it's unfair. You know I did my best over all the years to make both of you happy.'

I feel giddy; the knife is trembling in my hand. I want them to stop, both of them.

'You made sure we had a certain standard of living, Steffen, that's all. But we never needed a big house or extravagant holidays. We just needed each other and you're not going to take that away from us. Lenia and I—'

I can't take this any longer; I don't want to hear any more. 'Lenia is dead, Nathalie!' I shout. 'You've got to stop lying to yourself!'

'No, Ann! No, she isn't!' she exclaims, making an uncoordinated gesture. 'This is precisely what I've been trying to get through to you the whole time! It's *our* story, we're writing it ourselves! It's dynamic and can change with every word. We alone have the power over the characters and what happens. Look at him—'

'Nathalie, what are you talking about?' Fester comes towards her, but Nathalie is unfazed and remains facing me.

'*He* could be the ribbon murderer! Let's say he's just admitted it to us! He's kidnapped and killed little girls for so many years. Because he's a sick bastard by nature. Just look what he did to me, Ann! When I became suspicious of Steffen and fled Berlin because I was afraid of him, he came looking for me and finally tracked me down here. Look! Just look what he's capable of!'

Then everything happens very fast.

She rushes at me. Grabs my right wrist and thrusts it towards her. The knife is now stuck in Nathalie's stomach. I want to scream, pull the knife out, do something – but no, I'm totally paralysed. Fester steps in, tries to grab the knife. Now Nathalie forces my hand in his direction. He screams and falls to the floor. I hear myself screaming too, I scream and scream; I'm never going to stop. Everything stretches out, I now see it all in slow motion.

Nathalie, bent over, struggling to the bed, collapsing on it. Fester, his hand pressed to the left side of his chest, falling to his knees. 'Tell me where she is!' he beseeches.

But Nathalie closes her eyes and smiles. 'And they all lived . . .'

US

. . . happily ever after.

Right, my angel, that's it, time to go to sleep. That really was a long story tonight . . . What? What are you saying? That it wasn't a proper ending and you want to hear what happened afterwards? What my little angel wants, my little angel gets. So listen carefully. Mummy was lying injured on the bed. The dragon was dead. Our friend Ann called an ambulance and the police. She told the officers what had happened and especially about the confession she'd just heard. Before the dragon died, you see, he admitted that he'd killed lots of little girls, crimes which Ann's father was innocently in prison for. For a long time Mummy had suspected that something wasn't right about the man we'd thought of as your daddy. That in reality he was just a dragon in a clever disguise. That's also why we had to leave Berlin. But then the dragon tracked us down and of course he was really angry. He killed Kerstin because I'd confided in her. He was worried, you see, that Kerstin might get the police involved, and he had to do everything he could to prevent this. He even tried to kill Ann, but I managed to stop him just in time. Now he's dead and we don't have to be frightened ever again. He won't hunt us anymore, and we can look forward to a future we've more than deserved after all the hardships we've suffered. Spring, my angel, spring is on its way. You and I, we'll dance hand in hand across the meadow, amongst daisies, ground elder and red clover. We'll puff up our cheeks and send dandelion clocks on their way. Free, we're free. Don't worry that they're taking us to hospital first. It's quite normal and unfortunately we have to go because I'm hurt. Can you see? There's blood coming out of my tummy and my lovely white nightie is soaked red. It looks worse than it really is, but of course the doctors have to patch it up. Apart from the physical injuries, they're going to want to give us psychological treatment too, my darling. But you don't have to worry about this either, as it's also perfectly normal after what we've been through. They'll say that we're suffering severe trauma brought on by our stressful flight from your father, the dragon, the child-killer who's caused so much misery. But we stopped him, my darling, we put an end to his terrible deeds. You and I and our dear friend Ann. Even the papers are writing about us, you know? They're saying I'm a heroine. It's flattering but no, no, really not. I'm not a heroine. I'm just a mother who would defeat any dragon out of love for her child. We did it, we got through it. Because we will get through everything so long as we're together. You and I, princess, for ever and ever and ever . . .

That really is the end now, okay. We badly need some sleep as it's been an exhausting day. I love you, princess. Goodnight . . .

ANN

SCHERGEL, 29 DECEMBER 2017

Nathalie has lost a lot of blood; the ambulance has already departed. Police cars are parked beneath the property. Although the blue lights are flashing silently, light is still light and it's doing what light does: attracting the moths. The first villagers, the nosy ones, those after a bit of a thrill. Brock is bound to be here soon with his camera, and Jakob, too, I hope. A few police officers ensure the locals are kept at an adequate distance from the house. I'm sitting on the frozen steps by the front door. How long have I been here? I don't know. It's light now; the sky is blue and there's even some sunshine. As if nature didn't know what's appropriate on a day like this. Everything ought to be grey and murky, as if the sky had slipped and were hanging menacingly over my head, about to collapse at any moment. At least I can rely on the iciness. It's eating its way through my jeans, my kidneys are aching, and I bet I'm going to catch the most severe cold of my life after today. I don't care; there are worse things in life. A woman who chooses to get stabbed by a knife and, on top of this, injures her ex-husband. Steffen Fester's lucky he was wearing a thick coat. Although the wound between his ribs is more than a scratch, the treatment he got from the emergency doctor means he can stay here while the police search the house. I take the stone from my trouser pocket. A reminder of what I've come through in my life.

'Here you are.' Steffen Fester comes up from behind and stands next to me. He takes off his coat, puts it around my shoulders and groans as he sits down. There's a huge bloodstain on his beige cardigan.

'You ought to be in hospital,' I say.

Fester glances at the stain. 'What's that compared to the nightmare of these last few weeks?'

I just nod, twiddling the stone in my hand, deep in thought.

'She never was . . .' Fester shakes his head. 'You know, she was a perfectly normal woman, never unstable in any way. She even got through Lenia's illness with such courage and optimism. Although she was aware of the risks, she always said they were just statistics, and they mostly concerned men who died before they reached the age of 56.'

'Lenia was ill? I'm sorry, I didn't know.'

For a few seconds, Fester's face is expressionless, then he makes a noise signalling astonishment.

'But that's what this was all about.'

'What do you mean?'

'Well . . .' Fester looks at me as if I've lost my marbles. 'Lenia had epilepsy. Although she took medication regularly, she still had the occasional seizure. Two years ago, in 2015, she had a serious fit in which she fell, knocking out her front teeth. After that, they adjusted her medication and things went really well. I couldn't imagine that . . .' He shakes his head again. 'I didn't leave Nathalie because of Lenia's illness, you've got to believe me. We just drifted apart. She and Lenia stayed on in our old house. Anyway . . .' He looks down at his hands. 'It was a Saturday morning on one of the weekends I was going to have Lenia. I turned up early and Nathalie was still in her nightie when she opened the door to me. She said Lenia was still asleep and that we'd wake her up together.' I hear him swallow. 'We found her lying on her tummy with her head in the pillow. She'd bitten her tongue, making it bleed, and wet herself. She must have had a serious fit in her sleep, probably leading to breathing problems. But because she didn't wake up, she didn't realise she wasn't getting any air. It was too late.'

I realise my own breathing is fitful, my chest constricting. 'But I thought the ribbon murderer . . .'

'It happened in early November,' Fester says. 'At the time when the latest case in the series of ribbon murders was all over the media. The girl . . . I think her name was Sophie. She was abducted from a playground and dragged off to the Königswald.'

I nod weakly. According to Nathalie, that was exactly what had happened to Lenia. *He kidnapped Lenia from a playground and took her to a hut in the Königswald.*

'Nathalie became completely obsessed with the story,' Fester continues. 'I think she blamed herself for Lenia's death, as if she ought to have noticed there was something wrong with her. But she slept soundly while our daughter died in the next-door room. You must have seen the picture on the fridge?'

'Yes.'

'Lenia saw her illness as a wicked dragon and her mother as her protector. Nathalie believed she'd failed at the crucial moment.

And because she couldn't get over this, she projected the guilt on to someone else. A sort of defence mechanism. She even told the people at the funeral director's that Lenia had been a victim of the ribbon murderer.'

'But at the time she still realised Lenia was dead?'

Fester nods. 'At that point, yes. But when the grave was dug and Lenia was laid out for the burial, her mind finally went to pieces. She snatched the body and then . . .'

'She invented her own story,' I say, finishing Fester's sentence.

'One step after another into madness,' he says, putting his hands in front of his face and beginning to sob.

I stroke his back. 'What about Nathalie's mother? Nathalie said she didn't just come here with Lenia, but with her mother in tow as well.'

'Nathalie's mum is in a care home in Berlin,' Fester sobs into his hands. 'They didn't get on.'

I try putting myself in Nathalie's shoes; I think aloud.

'Nathalie knew that people would have become suspicious if she'd worked at the butcher's and left her little daughter at home alone. So she invented a babysitter as well.' The tears come to my eyes too. 'I'm so sorry about all of this. My suspicions ought to have been raised earlier.'

He looks up and gives a faint shrug. 'How could they have been? We see what people make us believe.'

'No, that's not the problem. It's that we accept it far too easily.' I immediately think of the bloodstain on Nathalie's trousers. I'll always wonder whether Kerstin Seiler's life could have been saved. Whether I could have saved her, but failed at the crucial moment too. I also think of all those weeks that Nathalie lived here amongst people who regard themselves as a community. They were all curious and yet nobody was really interested. And I'm no exception in this regard. I was focused only on Steinhausen and proving my theory that he's the real ribbon murderer. In the end was I just thinking of myself too?

'Look who we've got here,' we hear a female voice say behind us. We turn around. A policewoman has just come out of the front door, holding a black kitten. 'This sweet little thing was hiding under the bed the whole time.'

'Milly!' Fester calls out, getting up in visible pain.

It comes to me in a flash. 'I know where you'll find Lenia!'

Do you remember . . . ?

– Beside Mummy's grave.

– Let me tell you a story. It's by a very wise man called Plato. He was a philosopher—

– Like you?

– Yes, but he was far more important. He did what I try to do: find answers, for himself and other people, to the fundamental questions in life. For, as I've said, nothing in this world is clear and simple. Just because we don't see something, it doesn't mean it doesn't exist, and vice versa. And even if we can agree on the existence of something, we still interpret it in different ways—

– Tell the story now.

– I see the little madam is impatient. Okay then. We humans are sitting in a dark cave. We're tied up so that we can look in one direction only – at a wall where we see shadows. We think the shadows are real; we don't know any different, after all. And yet, in truth, these shadows are the outlines of what's happening behind us, cast by the light from the cave entrance. But we don't know this, because the way we've been tied up means we can't turn around. Only if we're able to free ourselves can we go to the light and see the things as they really are. But here's the crux: quite apart from the fact that our shackles are tight and unbreakable, we've got used to them. Just like our eyes have got used to the darkness inside the cave and would hurt really badly when they were first exposed to the light. Basically we've got used to what we consider to be our reality, and it would be painful for us on so many levels to have to admit that we were wrong. That our reality doesn't – in reality – exist and never has existed . . . Oh dear, look at that face you're making. Maybe you're still a bit too little for this story.

– I understood it, Daddy. You have to be brave about the real things.

– Not bad, my Beetle. But most importantly, we always have to think very carefully about things. Our senses – sight, hearing, smell, taste and touch – can deceive us. With those alone, we'll never fully understand the world. We have to think. And feel . . .

Feel . . . I wish I didn't, Dad. It's too much. Too much pain, grief and despair. I don't know what to do with it all. I'm still sitting on the steps, running the point of my stone along the scar – only very gently, without any pressure. The stone that taught me how to feel in the first place. Something that right now seems like a curse. On the other side of the house, behind the terrace, they're excavating the grave where Nathalie claimed to have buried Milly. I hear the cutting of the spade, which is loud in the frozen ground, and finally Fester howling like a wounded animal. I know he's suffering, suffering immensely, but now that he's found Lenia, he'll be able to find peace too. Unlike me. My story doesn't have an ending; there's only one thing I've managed to establish for sure: the feelings I've allowed to guide me over the last few days, the instinct I've been following blindly, have deceived me. Steinhausen was never here. Although I know I've helped someone achieve certainty, what about me? And you, Dad?

Realisation. (Ann, 24 years old)

Sometimes it hits you like a lightning bolt, suddenly and powerfully, as if at the flick of a switch, a flash of light in the dark night. An awareness, like a revelation, to which even your body immediately reacts, with shock, panic, a racing heart and sickness. But the biggest, the most important realisations sometimes come very quietly, very superficially and softly, like a gas you've been breathing in for quite a while before you suffocate from it. And yet it was all there from the very beginning . . .

Last summer. The evening after a perfect day, our tiny balcony, bare feet, a bottle of wine. The view over the city, the prospect of our future. A little cottage with colourful shutters and a garden she would allow to become elegantly overgrown.

'Either you can stay here in Berlin, devoured by longing, or you can come with me,' Zoe said, having already hatched a plan. She would apply for a semester abroad in Cornwall, a first step towards her dream. 'The only thing is, it's difficult to get one. The selection process can take up to a year.' In the end, it only took half a year . . .

Because I loved her. Because Cornwall was so important to her and she was so excited: 'Here, this is for you.'

'What is it?' she asked, puzzled.

Something so important to me that it would never have ended up in a mishmash of meaningless things.

'That's the stone I cut my wrist on when I was a child. My father kept it and gave it to me later. It's still got my blood on it.'

Zoe, eyeing me critically.

'It's thanks to this stone that I'm able to love you,' I explained.

'It's more than just a stone then.'

'Yes. It'll bring you luck for Cornwall and remind you what you mean to me.'

It fulfilled its purpose. Only three days ago she messaged me, saying she'd been accepted to go to Cornwall. *It worked!* How did I not pick up on that? How could I forget that I'd given her the stone? I ought to have realised when I was tidying up Dad's study and found the wooden box. Or, if not then, when Zoe messaged me. I stare down the steps to the hole that the stone has made in the snow.

Two stones. Blood on both. But only one is mine, the one I gave to Zoe. I feel giddy, like when Nathalie and Steffen Fester were arguing earlier on. *Two years ago, for example. In 2015, Steffen. Do you remember what happened? Lenia fell and knocked out her front teeth. And who looked after her? Who comforted her, fed her?*

In 2015, my car accident, my father nursing me back to health. In 2012, my existential crisis, our trip through France. In 2010,

Eva and Nico disappearing from Berlin, and me in despair every day. In 2009, Eva falling in love with Nico, breaking my heart. In 2006, I'm thirteen and an adolescent nightmare.

I was always there when Lenia needed me. There was nothing more important in my life.

2015. 2012. 2010. 2009. 2006. You were always there when I needed you. Because there was nothing more important in your life.

Shaking, I get to my feet and go down the steps to where the stone landed in the snow. I just stand there, gazing at it.

Although they can't say for sure, the forensics team believe the killer used a knife with a very blunt blade, Ludwig says again inside my head.

Or it wasn't a knife at all, I answer him silently.

Decisions, my Beetle . . .

BERLIN, 21 FEBRUARY 2018

Dear Dad,

As Ludwig is keeping you updated, you'll know I was in Schergel and what happened to me there. All the same, I'd like to explain my decision to you, and find myself – as you're bound to recognise – quoting Kant: 'Act only according to that maxim whereby you can, at the same time, will that it should become a universal law.' I couldn't just make the stone disappear; it had to be examined. Because ten murders are not a scratched moped. And even if I can't undo what's happened, it's still my duty to provide clarity to the victims' families. Michelle, who for years has merely been trying to make it from one day to the next. Rainer Meller, who was effectively driven crazy by his theories about Larissa's death. Saskia E.'s father, who's been appearing in public as an attempt at therapy. And all the other parents and relatives who till now have had to deal with uncertainty as well as their loss. I know myself how bad that is, albeit in a very different way. So, yes, I did it for me too. To give me certainty. I gave the police the stone in Schergel, explaining my theory and requesting they pass it on to the appropriate authority for examination. The results came in the second week of January: they'd found traces of DNA that could clearly be attributed to the dead girls. I can't say it surprised me, after I'd worked out that no murders had taken place in those years when I'd been a demanding, needy daughter. I still harboured hope until the end. So much so that, after my telephone conversation with Inspector Brandner, who told me about the result of the DNA analysis, I immediately called Jakob to ask him to drive me to the hospital. Systems overload, a nervous breakdown. I spent two weeks as an inpatient, and was prescribed medication and counselling. In theory, I realise I'm not responsible for your crimes, but I can't get over the fact that surely I ought to have noticed something. Or that if I'd made even more trouble over the course of my life, fewer girls would probably have died. There's no medication for that, nor the right words.

So you really are the ribbon murderer, Dad.

You killed ten girls and destroyed the lives of their loved ones.

You're 'Professor Death'.

And I'm your daughter. Ludwig says I shouldn't be fixated on my belief that our parents determine the largest part of our identity. According to him, my identity is only who I – me, myself! – decide to be. I'm sure you know that I'm staying with him at the moment. He didn't have to persuade me; I asked him. For one thing, now that the trial has started, our name has leaked out and journalists from all over the place are besieging our house. But also I don't want to be alone. I'm clinging to the illusion of a family, even if Ludwig is only my godfather. But he's there. As is Jakob, who hasn't yet finished his reportage. He says he feels that nothing he puts to paper can even begin to capture the enormity of this story, and I say, 'I know.' 'You're not to blame, Ann,' he adds, as well as a few other cute words that might reach my ears, but not my heart or soul.

And so I beg you, Dad, please talk. Finally make a confession. The trial begins tomorrow and the evidence, particularly the stone, will lead to your conviction. You're guilty, there's no doubt about this, and remaining silent won't do you any favours, not for you. But you'd help the girls' relatives to understand. And not just them, but me too. This is me we're talking about, your little Beetle. Help me, Dad, please. I'm not going to come to the trial, but I promise to visit as soon as you've made your confession.

Ann

BERLIN, 02 MARCH 2018

Dad,

I still think of that moment when, sitting outside Nathalie's house, it dawned on me that Zoe had my stone, whereas I'd been carrying a totally different one around for days. Recalling what Ludwig had said about the weapon. They were so set on their theory of it being a knife that when the house was searched, nobody gave the slightest thought to the brown-grey stone amongst all the other stuff in the wooden box in your desk. Things like this happen; after all, even the most dedicated police officers are human beings, who, like in Plato's allegory, sit in a cave and stare at shadows.

I've done nothing different for twenty-four years either.

And I liked our cave, Dad. The shadows that were my reality. My shackles that I didn't find tight and unbreakable, but more like a support. Our cave was my home and part of me will always miss it. I'll miss you.

You were a good father.

And a great thinker. As an academic, you wanted to find answers to the questions of life and, as Ludwig said, death is also part of life. But there came a point when theories were no longer enough, were they? You wanted to carry out practical studies and, what was worse, you did carry them out, at the expense of the lives of ten little girls, at the expense of entire families.

I can't believe that the world is still turning. That the sun rises and sets, that I'm breathing and am alive. It all seems so strange and wrong.

At least Eva is feeling better. I visit her almost every day. Two weeks ago she woke up after almost two months in a coma, and has been making fantastic progress since. She can already eat on her own again. And talk. And so I now know the real reason why she came back to Berlin after all these years. She speaks of a feeling, something indefinite that's been nagging her for many years and which may have influenced many of her life decisions – for example, the decision to leave Berlin, or to become a psychologist. Back in May 2003, when we were ten and Eva got lost in the Grunewald for no apparent reason. She says she doesn't have a concrete memory of that day; it's like a black hole in her consciousness, as if she'd blocked it out. All she knows is that you were the one who found her. But sometimes she dreams that you took her there in the first place, claiming that I was waiting there for you.

Was Eva to be your first victim?

She came back to Berlin after hearing about your arrest, with the aim of finding this out. She didn't say anything to me when she realised how convinced I was of your innocence – she is, after all, a psychologist, which in itself means she's very circumspect – and anyway, she wasn't sure herself. We don't want to accuse you of anything, but there's no denying she had red hair as a child, just like Larissa Meller, who you abducted shortly afterwards in June 2003.

And there's something else I'm wondering. Did it ever cross your mind *to kill me? Is it possible the girls were merely substitutes? In the darkest moments, I think it might have been better. My life for that of so many others.*

Oh, Dad – for Christ's sake, Dad!

Help me understand it all. It's not going to change anything; the sentence is fixed – life imprisonment. And for my part, I'm sticking to my guns: I won't visit you until you're ready to talk.

Ann

BERLIN, 13 MAY 2018

I was at Ludwig's yesterday evening. You remember I stayed with him for a while. I imagine he would have gone back to Poland a while ago, but he's still here – out of concern for me, I think. We drank whisky, a bit like that evening which ended with me thinking he'd slipped a sleeping pill in my drink. Now I know of course that he'd have never done anything like that. I'd been drinking on an empty stomach; I was tired, run-down and paranoid, which was more than enough for a breakdown that evening. I just didn't want to see it. Like Nathalie, I put together my own puzzle, twisting pieces and simply forcing in corners that didn't fit. I made connections where there weren't any, turned coincidences into evidence and simply rewrote the story. Until the end blew up in my face.

Ludwig knows how to cheer me up, but I can see from his face how much he's suffering too. He's lost his best friend; we share the pain, the self-reproach, the doubts. And yet he represented you as your lawyer to the very end. I asked him why he didn't stop acting for you. He replied that he needed his brain to engage with what had happened so he could process it. He recommends I do the same and says I should visit you. But my condition still holds, Dad: I won't come until you break your silence.

Anyway, yesterday we raised a glass to his birthday as well as to hope. Although, to be honest, having met Nathalie, I'm no longer so certain that hope is exclusively a good thing. I mean, look at me. I got utterly carried away because of a hope. I expect that's why strangely I also felt such a connection to Nathalie. Subconsciously I recognised myself in her. Her stomach wound has healed without complication, by the way, and the treatment she's getting in an excellent psychiatric institution seems to be helping her too. I imagine that's where she'll stay, because there's no way the court will send her to a normal prison for having killed Kerstin Seiler, kidnapped Sarah and injured her ex-husband. An assessor has concluded that she wasn't of sound mind. As it turns out, she'd been living for weeks in the house with Lenia's body. She bathed and dressed her, read to her, played with her; they even had meals together. Sarah must have 'met' Lenia too. Ludwig, who's keeping me in the loop about her case, says the public prosecutor will argue that Nathalie was sufficiently compos mentis to let Sarah go free on the day they were going to search the upper common, i.e., where Nathalie lived. This was when she buried Lenia's body too.

'You can only lose if you try to find sense in madness,' Ludwig said with a shrug. Then we looked at each other in horror, well aware that this isn't just true of Nathalie, but you too.

Please, Dad, don't let me go on begging.

Give me an explanation, finally.

Ann

BERLIN, 17 JUNE 2018

I don't understand why you're torturing me like this. Isn't it bad enough that I've got to spend the rest of my life bearing the stigma of being the ribbon murderer's daughter? Don't you owe me this, for God's sake?

By staying silent, you're ruining everything that ever made you a good father.

BERLIN, 26 JUNE 2018

This is our last chance, Dad. Next week I'm leaving for Cornwall. I'm going to move in with Zoe.

Please!

BERLIN, 2 JULY 2018

If I'm not worth an explanation, then it's no longer worth me thinking of you as my father.

Farewell.

RECORDING 10
Berlin, 10 May 2021

— Do you have children?

— No, I don't. I'm still young and so I've got plenty of time left for that. But also, hmm . . . when I work on certain topics like your case, I sometimes think it would be better not to bring any children into this world. Although I haven't experienced it myself, I think that loving a child must be the most intense emotion there is. But this love can break you too. Saskia E.'s mother committed suicide, did you know that?

— No.

— Yes, she did. A few months after your trial, it was. She just couldn't get any closure, which must be partly down to the fact that you've never spoken about your crimes. The question of why still hangs over everything like a shadow.

— But the public prosecutor came up with a reasonable answer, don't you think?

— That you wanted to study death?

— Precisely.

— But why exactly in that way? Why at the expense of the lives of those innocent children? I've done my homework and found out that there are already plenty of studies on the topic, but those were carried out by interviewing people who'd had near-death experiences. Nobody had to suffer for these interviews.

— That may well be true, but the findings are based on the statements of adults. I'm convinced that the adult mind, through age and life experiences alone, tends to put things in a self-constructed context that is far more subjective. By contrast, what could be more authentic than the mind and soul of a child? Who would give you a more honest answer? Those girls were still young enough to be genuine, and old enough to articulate themselves in an intelligible way. I questioned them as the blood was running out of them. I asked them what they were feeling, what they were seeing, as their circulation gradually became weaker and their eyelids began to flutter. It was fascinating. They were freezing, they were scared, their breathing was panicky. But then, the longer it went on, the calmer and clearer they became. They told me about nice experiences they'd had with their parents, or about their pets. Some of them saw a light. It was uplifting, especially as they took their last breaths.

— What specifically did you find out?

— Love. I think that summarises what I discovered. They thought

335

of lovely things, their families and animals. They made sure their final moments weren't dark and panicky, but full of love and light.

– With respect, that's a pretty sick interpretation. It sounds as if you did good work. But you didn't. You killed twelve innocent children and caused immeasurable pain to their families.

– In the end, that's nothing more than an interpretation too. I wish I could show you my notes, although it has to be pointed out that the number of girls was far too small to constitute a meaningful study.

– Where are they, these notes?

– I burned them, I'm afraid. Rather rash of me.

– When?

– The evening I was arrested, just before the police turned up. I had a hunch that I might be in trouble after I'd bumped into that acquaintance in the Königswald. Particularly as I'd already been questioned about the murders in relation to a lecture I'd given . . . Are you all right? You look so pale again.

– No matter how hard I try, I simply can't understand. Especially as you're a father yourself.

– Yes, that's right, I am a father. That was always the best thing about me. *She* was the best thing about me. And what's more, she was the one who gave me the red ribbon idea.

– She?

– Oh, please, Herr Wesseling! Didn't I tell you last time that I did some research into you beforehand? I know your personal connection to the cases isn't that you met Larissa Meller's mother, but that you're a friend of my daughter's. That's also why, out of all the requests for interviews I've had over the years, yours is the only one I've consented to. Or did you think it was down to your reputation as a journalist? Don't delude yourself, there are plenty in your profession more talented than you.

— *(clears throat)* Anyway, are you saying it was Ann who put you on to the idea of the red ribbons?

— Uh-huh. The first Christmas after my wife's death, I gave her a trampoline. The box was too big for wrapping paper so I just tied a red ribbon around it. Ann put it around her head like a hairband – to make herself pretty, as she said. Then she lay in the box as if it were a coffin. Those images imprinted themselves on my mind. A lost girl who wanted to be found. And, later, other lost girls who also had to be found.

— You do realise the damage you've done to your daughter too?

— 'Pain and suffering are always inevitable for a large intelligence and a deep heart,' Dostoevsky said.

— She wrote you letters!

— I read them.

— You ought to have talked to her.

— To say what? She wasn't at the stage where she could understand.

— Nobody, Herr Lesniak, will ever understand.

— *(chuckles)* It's possible.

— All the same, I'd be interested to know why, after all these years, you're now ready to talk.

— Oh, Jakob . . . May I call you Jakob? The reason is her: Ann. You're friends with her. And I'm ill, as you may have been told.

— Yes.

— Well, I'm ill and she's stubborn. She made it very clear to me that she won't visit until I break my silence. But now she has to.

337

You are going to play her these recordings, aren't you?

— If she wants to hear them.

— She will. And if not, then persuade her to, please.

— But everything you've said to me you could have told her to her
   face.

— Yes, but this way we'll have more time to discuss things that
   only concern us. And she'll be prepared; I won't take her by
   surprise or shock her. It's important she has a clear head when
   she visits me. (*clears throat*) Ann, if you're listening to this,
   come with a clear head and with the memory of everything
   you've overcome in your life so far. And as for you, Jakob, have
   a good think about whether you really do want to write a book
   about experiences you've never had yourself. You won't end up
   with anything better than probabilities, and 'everything that is
   merely probable . . .'

— '. . . is probably false.' René Descartes, I believe.

— Well, well. Not bad, my boy.

ANN

BERLIN, 19 MAY 2021

Life finds a way through. It uses the tiniest cracks to burst forth, even in the most adverse conditions, like a seedling through asphalt. A laugh that pinches at first, because it's been so long since you used those muscles; a laugh that sounds soft, subdued and perhaps faintly artificial. And then one day you laugh properly again, a loud, booming laugh of such intensity that it makes your tummy hurt. Then happiness forces itself on you; it doesn't ask about guilt, or right and wrong – happiness is blind and deaf, and that's a good thing.

Almost three and a half years have passed.

I'm twenty-eight now.

Zoe and I made up because, well, people are people, because they make mistakes; they're overwhelmed or anxious, or just sometimes plain stupid. Maybe because Zoe was lonely in Cornwall too, and the thing about loneliness is it makes you romanticise things, it softens you, it stirs regret and longing, and in the end there's a message written on impulse that determines your future: *I wish you were here*. Six months later we married on the beach in St Ives and, half a year after that, thanks to a sperm donor, Zoe was pregnant with our son Noah. We never spoke about why it was her rather than me who carried the baby. There are unwritten rules when you live with the daughter of a killer, and one of these is avoiding the subject of genetics. I know myself that I'm being silly about this, but a leopard can't change its spots.

Cornwall was lovely, even though we didn't get that cottage with colourful shutters and a wild garden. We did, however, have a nice apartment on the Penryn River. Despite this, we decided to move back to Berlin, given that we would soon have a baby and could do with the support of Zoe's parents. And there was a house too: the one I grew up in. Zoe had her reservations at first, but I was able to convince her that, in the end, a house is just a house – just a few walls and a roof, a man-made construct. It's also got a beautiful garden and is big enough for each of us to have our own retreat. Mine is the study. Sometimes I stand there by the window, gazing out at Noah, who's now one and a half, playing on the trampoline under Zoe's supervision. It's a new trampoline; mine was completely rusty so we got rid of it. Zoe works half-days as a translator in the cultural department of the Berlin senate; I stay at home with Noah. I haven't finished my German studies, but what's ironic is that all my father's academic publications will probably enable me to enjoy a comfortable life for many years.

Life is beautiful.

But it's no fairy tale.

There are good moments, full of blind, deaf happiness. And there are the others. Those that are as dazzling as strobe lights and as loud as piercing screams.

Zoe and I are arguing more often. She calls me difficult and I call her unsympathetic. This happens when two people in love collide like two stars. Either they fuse together or break apart and dissipate in clouds of gas. I don't know how our relationship is going to pan out, only that it's lost a little of its lustre. Zoe's never experienced anything that's rattled the depths of her soul and destroyed her entire world. Her worst memory is her grandmother's funeral a few years ago. The grandmother who was eighty-five and died in her sleep, in peace and after a life of fulfilment. Zoe says she still can't believe that her nana isn't here anymore. I know I can't hold this against her, but I do it unconsciously. I permanently make her feel that she's naïve and doesn't have a clue about real life. She hates me for this; I hate myself for it too.

The truth is, it's never over. No matter what people say – Ludwig, Jakob, any therapist. It gets better but it's never properly all right again. Sometimes I go into the garage, sit in the car and scream, just like that. And each time that 'Perfect Day' plays, I begin to cry. Because this song always brings back the summer when I was seven and sat on my father's shoulders with my arms outstretched. As if, thanks to him, I could fly. And then, towards the end of the song, when Lou Reed sings, with that strange monotony in his voice, about reaping what you sow, my grief is replaced by fear, a paralysing, ice-cold fear. If my father's a monster, then who am I? What am I capable of? Is evil passed down the generations or is it a choice? Coincidence? A devious game of chance in which a higher power deals the cards on a whim? Or more like a cold that some people catch, while others, those with a more robust immune system, are spared? I don't know; I don't even know why I choose to put the song on again and again when basically all it does is torment me.

It's so fricking complicated.

Only in Noah's presence does everything crumble away. For him I don't have a past or any inner demons. For him I'm just his mummy. He's not expecting any explanations, apologies; he's just content with a few biscuits, my time and my love. Jakob is his godfather and one of the few people who doesn't ask questions if I suddenly fall silent. He never finished his article about my father. But he has been working on a book for ages. I've got nothing against it, because there's always someone writing a book about those sorts of crimes and people like my father. I'd rather have Jakob doing it than a stranger. Especially as he was always clear that the book he's writing would also have to look at my father's side of the story. He calls it 'journalistic duty of care', but both of us know it's about money too. My father's never talked about his crimes, not even to me. A testimony would be a sensation. That's why Jakob isn't the only one who's kept requesting interviews over the years. My father turned them all down.

Until the beginning of this month. He's allowed Jakob to talk to him over a number of sessions. I've listened to the recordings of these and tried to form a judgement. Do I hear a psychopath, with his endless provocative digressions, making fun of Jakob by circumventing questions and throwing them back in Jakob's face? Or is this, by contrast, a man desperately stalling for time because he's suffering from having nobody to talk to and play his intellectual games with? I haven't reached a conclusion – the man on the recordings is a stranger to me; all I recognise is his voice. The police have heard the whole thing too and now they have to check if my father committed any other murders. For if what he says in Jakob's interview is true, he didn't start killing in 2003, but back in 2001, two years after my mother's death. Two more dead children, two more destroyed families, more guilt and pain for everyone. For my part, I don't know how much more I can take. Despite this – or maybe because of it – today I'm granting him his wish that I visit him. After more than three years, since my visit at Christmas 2017, before Schergel, before the truth. I would have come long ago if he'd ever made a confession.

On the other hand, he never before asked me for a visit or even answered the letters I wrote to him.

So today's the day.

Ludwig organised the meeting and has come from Poland especially. We often visit him there. Zoe stopped going a while back, but Noah loves the woods and the wild nature. He's over the moon when a deer appears in Ludwig's garden, or he sees a wild boar burrowing. Ludwig says he'll make a hunter out of him when he's old enough.

We're driving in his car, and haven't said a word since we got in. The sun is bright, shining off the buildings that race past, and the sky is blue. Summer's almost here.

We turn into the prison car park.

'Ready?' Ludwig asks.

I give him an honest answer: 'No.'

Once inside, I hand over my bag, Ludwig his mobile, wallet and car keys. We're allowed to keep our watches on and we're only scanned by a detector rather than being searched by hand. Ludwig's name prevents any of those unpleasantries – he's a personal guest of the prison governor. Handy for us, but not without its risks. Nobody would have noticed if either of us had something in our coat pockets that the metal detector didn't pick up.

We're taken to a special visitors' room where we wait outside the door until the governor comes. Handshakes all around and Ludwig jokingly enquiring after the man's handicap. I giggle. It feels like Ludwig's played them all at tennis or golf.

Then the governor explains how this is going to work. 'As we discussed, we'll refrain from posting an officer in the room. But he'll wait right outside the door. Just in—'

'Nothing's going to happen,' I say. 'He is still my father, after all.'

'Of course.' The governor nods keenly. 'You have half an hour. If you wish to leave earlier, just knock. The officer will let you out.'

I thank him. Then I turn to Ludwig. 'For days I've been thinking about what to say. I've even been practising in front of the mirror.'

Ludwig gives me a hug. 'You'll be fine,' he says, adding that he'll wait for me in the governor's office.

The room isn't any different from the one I met my father in three and a half years ago. The same pale walls, the soft buzzing of the neon lights on the ceiling, the sparse furnishings consisting of a table and two chairs. And yet everything is different. Back then, my father was my father, the person I loved most in the world, who I trusted unfailingly, who I believed to be innocent. Today he's a convicted killer. And I'm stigmatised.

When we got married, I took Zoe's surname, which means I'm now Ann Brambach. I'm just a random woman amongst three and a half million people in Berlin. It's been a long time since the media were interested in me; my face was only in the papers a few times in 2018, around the time of the trial. So it's completely absurd for me to sometimes think that people are staring at me.

And even more absurd that, in spite of everything, I should occasionally find myself envying Nathalie. Seen from the outside, she's anything but enviable. She's imprisoned in a psychiatric institution, up to her eyeballs with medication. But internally, it's possible she's doing better than I am. Because she took a clear decision: to inhabit her own story, the world behind her closed eyelids. She's happy there.

I take a seat. My left arm is trembling; I feel sick. Briefly, I fancy I can hear footsteps out in the corridor. Heavy, sluggish footsteps, redolent of evil. I've often imagined what my father might look like now, drained by the last few years, illness and himself. Jakob has already warned me that he must have got very thin.

The door opens; I leap up as if conditioned.

He's dragging his feet, but walking upright.

He must have lost five kilos at least. Ten, maybe.

His hair is almost white. Cut short with a precise parting. He's got a beard, which I've never seen on him before. It suits him, allows him to look respectable, like the captain of a large boat.

However . . . the way he's moving, his emaciated physique, his thin face that looks grey.

'My Beetle,' he says. It's like a death blow, a command for my tears.

'I'll be outside if you need me,' says the prison officer who brought him in.

'Thanks,' my father replies politely. He makes a gesture which I take to be an invitation to sit. He does the same.

I hastily wipe my eyes and clear my throat. 'Here we are then.'

He nods. 'Indeed. How do you feel?'

I swallow with difficulty; the back of my chair is hard and

digging into me. All the same I try to sit up. My pride, my defiance, my disappointment. For three and a half years, my father has refused to give me an explanation; all my life he's been deceiving me. If I'm unable to hate him, at the very least I want to make him feel this. He's still the man who carried me on his shoulders. And he looks so ill. Colon cancer, his death sentence. It might be quick, or he could waste away.

'I haven't come to talk about me.'

A smile twitches on one side of his mouth. 'You must have heard the recordings your friend Jakob Wesseling did. So now you know everything.'

'I know what happened, yes. And yet, I still don't understand. On the contrary, it comes across as so banal, despite the barbarity of it all. You wanted to study death, and to do this, you committed murder. What a cliché.'

'Death is neither banal nor a cliché, Ann. It's humanity's last great unanswered question. Think of your mother. Did you never want to know what she saw or felt at the end, after her face was stuck in a scream?'

I shake my head. 'She was in pain, Dad. That's all. She wanted to scream in pain, but she didn't have the strength to.'

'That's what you're guessing, Ann. But you don't know.'

'What about you? Do you know now? Do you? You've destroyed dozens of lives to find out this answer. What good does it do, Dad? All of us are going to die one way or another. And for this reason alone, it makes no difference if it's heaven, hell or just the big black void waiting for us at the end, because there's nothing we can do to change it. We're born to live and then, at some point, to die. That's nature.'

'No, Ann, that's blind acceptance. And man is definitely not created for that. We search for meaning in our existence, an intended purpose. Look at yourself – you're the best example of this. You listened to Wesseling's recordings and yet you still came today. Because for you, it's not enough to know what happened when, where and how. You can't be done with this until you see some meaning in the whole thing.'

'Once again, Dad. This isn't about me.'

'But of course it is, Ann! It's only ever been about you, my Beetle.'

I breathe as if I'm ragged. How often have I wondered whether he was just looking for a sort of substitute in those girls because he really wanted to kill me?

He still has no trouble reading me. 'It never even crossed my mind to hurt you. I didn't even manage it with Eva. And do you know why?'

I shake my head.

'Because I knew how much she meant to you. You, Ann, were my life. My greatest gift and my greatest insight. Only through you was I able to feel. Because, you know . . .' He looks at his hands. They've become old, just like him. His pale skin is dotted with brown spots; blue veins protrude conspicuously. 'I'm ill.'

'They've told me.'

He looks up. 'I don't mean the cancer. All my life I've suffered from a completely different condition. It's not a recognised illness – at least not for people who merely invent terms for the condition, but never have to live with it – alexithymia. I suffer from alexithymia.'

'Ale . . . what?'

'Alexithymia.'

I shake my head in bewilderment.

'Alexithymia means you feel little or nothing at all. You don't have any idea what it's like to be frustrated. All your life you wonder: is grief painful? What does rage feel like? Or love? I don't know, Ann. I've never really been overcome by an emotion. My heart has never raced, nor has my throat ever felt constricted. What is envy? What is hatred? For other people, emotions are like bulldozers; for me, they're more like . . .' He looks up as if the correct description were stuck to the ceiling. 'A breath of wind,' he says finally, looking me in the eye again. 'A breeze that gently wafts past almost without my noticing.'

'You . . . ?' I pause while my thoughts begin racing, uncontrolled, back in time. Memories like spotlights. Eva getting an earful and being grounded because of a bad grade, whereas my father just shrugged. All the shit I got up to aged fourteen. Joints, beer, skipping school and slitting mats in the gym. Locking Eva in the girls' loo. It's true: he never shouted at me. Never sent me to my room. When I scratched Nico's moped and Dad covered for me. When I had the accident in 2015 through my own fault: too much beer. He didn't just pay the fine, he also got Ludwig to see to it that I didn't lose my licence. No dressing-down, no shouting. Just these words: 'Don't do it again, my Beetle. I still need you.' My dad, the eternal stoic, fazed by nothing. And his arrest – of course. All those things I attributed his clueless behaviour to: shock, tiredness, pride, defiance. Can it really have just been *nothing*? Nothing at all, merely emptiness?

'But . . . what about Mum? You loved her, didn't you? Or me . . .

348

What about me? You did everything for me. You always looked after me.'

'That's my problem, Ann. I know I love you. And that you belong to me. But . . .'

'You don't feel it? How can that be true, Dad?' I shake my head for this very reason: it can't be true. 'I distinctly remember how worried you were about me when I closed up after Mum died . . .' When I didn't feel anything, my head adds. Just like you.

He nods. 'Alexithymia can be hereditary, but it can also be brought on by serious trauma. Which means I could see you had two risk factors.'

'That's why you dragged me off to the child psychologist,' I conclude. 'And that's why I always had to explain my feelings in great detail and even write them down. You didn't want me to become like you, did you?'

'No, I didn't. It may sound paradoxical, but people like me – and by the way, there are far more of us than you could possibly imagine – are not completely cold. They're often very aware of being different from other people. And they suffer from this. They suffer when they come across someone who is wildly happy, and all they can do is imitate this person, simulate a laugh like an actor. They practise interpersonal rituals until they're as comfortable with them as a tailored suit. But they never feel complete.' He cocks his head. His eyes are clear and cutting sharply right into my thoughts. 'How is someone to understand the world if they cannot feel it?'

'"The Allegory of the Cave,"' I say, it having just come into my head. 'I remember exactly what you told me: *Our senses – sight, hearing, smell, taste and touch – can deceive us. With those alone, we'll*

349

never fully understand the world. We have to think. And feel. But that was precisely what—'

'I wasn't capable of, ever.' His laugh ends in a coughing fit. The sounds pain me. 'My immune system isn't the best these days,' he explains with a shrug. 'Well, now you know. Professor Walter Lesniak, the great, internationally renowned philosopher and anthropologist. He wants to answer all the questions about life and the world, but he'll never succeed because he's lacking the vital piece.'

I breathe to calm my heart down and counter the misplaced empathy. 'You say that lots of people suffer from this thing. How many?'

'According to studies, around fourteen per cent.'

'What, and all of these go off and start killing people?'

'No, but not all of them have seen the light either.'

'The light?'

'It's hard to go back into the cave, my Beetle, when you've been outside and seen the light.'

'What bloody light?'

'In my case, you were the light, Ann.'

'Me?'

'Your bicycle accident, do you remember? Your bleeding? The deep hole in your wrist that functioned like an outlet for all the pent-up, suppressed feelings inside you.' He pulls his hands apart. 'And it was like a miracle, for in that moment, I felt something too, Ann! For the first time in my life, it was more than just a breath of wind, an insignificant breeze. I felt your pain, your distress, your fascination. I felt anxiety, the fear of losing you. The determination to protect you from anything bad. For a few seconds, it was all there, so real, so great and overpowering, rather than just dry theory. It was genuine! But also over far too quickly.'

'So you didn't start killing two years after Mum's death, but one year after my bike accident.' I slap a hand over my mouth. I was the trigger. 'The first girl, Laura, who didn't cry despite her cut knee. She reminded you of me and the bike accident.'

'I'd have done anything to experience that again.'

'And you did.'

'Yes, I did.'

'You re-enacted it time and again. You didn't just want to study death, but yourself. And that's what you meant when you told Jakob in the interview that the girls had given you a meaning. They allowed you to feel something. You're sick, Dad! In many respects.'

My comment doesn't affect him; he just smiles. 'Do you remember the conclusion of the allegory, Ann? The person who manages to get out returns to the cave to tell the other prisoners what he's discovered. But they just ridicule him and, worse than that, they're so attached to their view of the world – to their shadows – that they want to seize and kill him. That's what happened to Socrates, Plato's teacher. The Athenians sentenced him to death for what he said. He was to poison himself by drinking hemlock. Socrates didn't resist, he said, "Cheers!" and drank up.' Dad leans across the table. 'What do you feel now? Disgust? Sympathy? What, Ann?'

I shake my head. 'What about the stone? You gave the one from my accident to me and I passed it on to Zoe.'

351

'I happened to find a similar one when I was out walking. Ought that not to have been a sign?'

'You used it to kill.'

'Yes, I did. What are you feeling, Ann? Tell me.'

'Forget it. I'd feel like a dealer giving a junkie a shot.'

'No, no, no, my Beetle.' He reaches for my hand. 'None of this is your fault. You were my emotion. Like a prosthesis for a maimed body. You were my light, my everything.'

'And doesn't that very fact make me complicit?'

'That's a fascinating thought. Is it possible that I was a better father to you because I gave myself an outburst of emotion once a year?'

I pull my hand out from under his. 'You're not being serious?'

'I don't know, my Beetle. But what I do know for certain is that you made me a better person, a more complete person.' I suddenly think of 'Perfect Day', the second verse where Lou Reed tells the person being addressed that because of him – or her – he was able to completely forget himself and persuade himself he was someone different.

'Don't go thinking your crimes haven't had an effect on my life. Zoe and I are on the verge of separating.'

'Really? Why?'

'Why? Because she hasn't been through what I have. And for this reason, she can't understand. She's stuck in her little, cosy world, whereas I . . .' I stop when I see something flash in his face: my worry, a feeling that nourishes him. 'What am I saying? We're going to get a grip on our problems. And whatever happens, I'll have my little Noah. He's—'

'Your light,' my father says, completing my sentence for me. He looks around for the camera that's above the door in the corner. Then he holds out the palm of his hand towards me and says, smiling, 'Cheers, my Beetle!'

Love. (Ann, 28 years old)

Love leaves us with no choice. We don't go searching for it; it's love itself that seeks and finds us. It nestles deep inside us as the essence of our existence. Everything we feel derives from love. Hope, belief, confidence, determination. But hate too, as well as fear, anger and all the negative emotions that sometimes turn us into beasts. In the end, they too come from love that has been disappointed or violated. Love is the most delicate but at the same time strongest thing in us humans. And it's always present. Sometimes large, colourful, loud and shiny like the colours of summer. Sometimes barely perceptible, a mere waft and a whisper. Just a small red light, but one that's still visible, even in the deepest, darkest night. And even when there is nothing remaining of us, love is our last prayer. Our last breath.

My father died on the evening of 19 May 2021, just a few hours after my visit. He was found lifeless in his cell after slitting his left wrist; assistance came too late. How he got hold of the stone that was astonishingly similar to the one he'd killed the girls with years earlier is unknown. It's suspected that he found it during his yard exercise one day and smuggled it back into his cell. In an official statement released to the media, it said his health had rapidly deteriorated because of his bowel cancer, ultimately leading to his death.

I know better, everything.

But most of all, I know he did it for me, so I could draw a line under all that had happened and finally find peace. That alone shows he must have been capable of feeling something. I hope he was aware of this before he died.

I'm avoiding as far as I can the question of whether I've forgiven him. What he did can't be forgiven, but now I've understood it to a certain extent. I'd never say that out loud, for fear that people might confuse what I mean by 'understand' with 'relativise' or 'justify'. It's not like that at all, of course; I know perfectly well what's right and wrong, otherwise I'd never have voluntarily given the stone to the police in Schergel for examination. But at least I can, to some degree, understand what drove him. Just like Nathalie, he kept striving to get to a certain point, and this point simply wouldn't let him go. What for Nathalie was the day when, in her fantasy, Lenia escaped from the ribbon murderer, was for my father the day when he first felt something in his life. The day of my bicycle accident. And just like Nathalie, he wasn't content with imagining it in his mind; he allowed it to become reality. The fact is, there were two sides to Walter Lesniak the man: one of these was a brutal killer; the other, my father, perhaps the best I could have had. And yes, I do now distinguish between the two. But I keep this to myself as well, for fear of being judged by others.

Thanks to the interview with Jakob, two previously unsolved murders from 2001 and 2002 – seven-year-old Laura and nine-year-old Miriam – were later proven to have been committed by him. Their families now have certainty.

Jakob's still working on his book. He says he wants to give it time to make best possible sense of the story. In the course of his research, he recently discovered that Marcus Steinhausen emigrated to Spain in 2010. He met a woman there, started a family and worked as a tradesman. In 2014, Marcus Steinhausen died in a car accident.

Eva has fully recovered from her injuries. She still works as a psychologist at the psychological counselling centre for victims of crime and their relatives at Frankfurt University Hospital. She and Nico are back together and plan to get married this summer.

Michelle Meller has remarried too. In 2018, her ex-husband Rainer Meller stood trial for false imprisonment and two charges of grievous bodily harm. He was found guilty and is currently serving a ten-year sentence.

Sarah Seiler is living with her father in Čachrov in the Czech Republic. She's eleven years old now and at secondary school. Once a week she still sees her therapist, though she's doing really well, which must be in part down to her father who, having been a washout in the early years of her life, is trying extremely hard to finally be the father his daughter needs.

Steffen Fester has a healthy little girl with his second wife. He says he can see lots of Lenia in her.

Lenia is buried in a cemetery in Schöneberg.

Nathalie is still in a secure psychiatric unit near Berlin. Once a month she's allowed visitors under supervision. She looks good and talks enthusiastically about her release, which in her world seems to be just around the corner.

Zoe moved out. Noah and I are still living in the house in Charlottenburg. Every evening we light a candle, place it on the windowsill in the study and look at the flickering shadows on the wall. Noah always sees something different: dinosaurs or monster trucks or a castle in a storm. Whereas I see a man carrying a little girl on his shoulders. Always. And then it's summer, I'm seven years old and Lou Reed is singing about a perfect day.

AFTERWORD AND ACKNOWLEDGEMENTS

Although I've written about a specific phenomenon in this novel, I make no claim to understand the reality of living with such a condition. What must it be like when love is just the breath of a breeze and every tear no more than a meaningless physical reaction? To be honest, I don't know. I can only assume that those affected are burdened by a life in which many things are complicated and, often, just one feeling is clear: the feeling of being different, maybe even 'wrong'. Despite this, those affected do their best to integrate and – unlike in this novel – are, of course, not necessarily a danger to society. I hope I've succeeded in describing a character who is clearly an individual case; it's essential that my readers realise this. Because what's at issue here is respect. Life is a lottery – we can't choose where, when and as whom we're born, nor the conditions in which we begin our lives. We don't even have complete control over what we do with our lives, apart from one thing: every day we can decide afresh how we treat each other.

I'm someone who's incredibly profligate with their emotions, and being so emotional gets me into hot water sometimes, because it makes me vulnerable and leaves me exposed. Nonetheless, I think that all of us ought to be grateful for the power of our feelings, realise that the positive ones are as important for our personal development as the negative ones, and let ourselves get carried away by them more often – no matter what others think, whether we make fools of ourselves or make ourselves vulnerable. For our feelings determine a large chunk of our identity, and each emotion has a right to exist, in a world where not everyone has the ability to feel anything at all, and in a world that is often cold enough. So let's be loud and feisty, let's laugh and love and cry and shout. It's more than okay; it's right and it's important.

As I write these lines, I find myself becoming overwhelmed by emotion once more. By gratitude for this life that I'm able to lead and in which I can invent stories for you. By gratitude for the people standing by me on this adventure that I still find absolutely incredible. Here I'd like to thank three special women: Caterina Schäfer, my agent; my editor Bianca Dombrowa; and you, Mum. You three were my most important supports as *Perfect Day* came to fruition. You put up with me, comforted me, motivated me, nourished me with your clever ideas and kept reminding me why I embarked on becoming a storyteller, and that I can and must continue to go my own way.

Thanks too to all the committed people at dtv who understand what writing means to me, and who frequently (have to) let me take my own path, especially Barbara Laugwitz, Andrea Seiber and Gudrun Marx.

I'm indebted to my foreign publishers and translators, thanks to whom my stories can now be read in so many countries – particularly Stefanie Bierwerth, Jamie Bulloch and Christine Kopprasch, who've helped me overcome another personal hurdle over the past year: establishing direct contact with my foreign readers despite my linguistic shortcomings. What at first was accompanied by a pounding heart and sweaty palms has now become so enriching (as well as great fun) – and that's all down to you.

I'd also like to give special and long overdue thanks to Astrid Eckert, as well as to my family, friends and of course you the readers, bloggers, booksellers and event organisers. Thanks for reading my stories and telling others about them.

Finally to you, Lou Reed, up there in heaven. Thanks for that song. Say hi to "kleine Miep" from me.

From my heart,

Romy

Lily White

SUSAN ISAACS

MICHAEL JOSEPH
LONDON

To my daughter-in-law, Leslie Stern,
with admiration and love

MICHAEL JOSEPH LTD
Published by the Penguin Group
27 Wrights Lane, London W8 5TZ, England
Penguin Viking Inc., 375 Hudson Street, New York, New York 10014, USA
Penguin Books Australia Ltd, Ringwood, Victoria, Australia
Penguin Books Canada Ltd, 10 Alcorn Avenue, Toronto, Ontario, Canada M4V 3B2
Penguin Books (NZ) Ltd, 182–190 Wairau Road, Auckland 10, New Zealand

Penguin Books Ltd, Registered Offices: Harmondsworth, Middlesex, England

First published in Great Britain 1997
1 3 5 7 9 10 8 6 4 2

Copyright © 1996 by Susan Isaacs

Set in 11.5/12.75pt Monotype Sabon and 10.25/12.75pt Monotype Optima
Photoset by Rowland Phototypesetting Ltd, Bury St Edmunds, Suffolk
Printed in England by Clays Ltd, St Ives plc

A CIP catalogue record for this book is available from the British Library

ISBN 0 7181 4199 7

Acknowledgments

In researching *Lily White*, I spent time in the library, in jail and in court. I also sought help and information from the people listed below. Being a novelist and not a reporter, however, I did not hesitate to twist their facts to serve the needs of my fiction. I thank them for their kindness and apologize for my inaccuracies:

Robert Anderson, Frank Argano, Jim Bartell, Brian Bochicchio, Joan Brenner, Thomas DiNapoli, Jonathan Dolger, Janet Franzese, Eric Gould, Cara Nash Iason, Lawrence Iason, Leonard Klein, Edward M. Lane, Judith Lane, Anthony Lepsis, Ellen Markowski, Susie Miller, Henry Putzel III, Ralph Smith, Sheila Riesel, Cynthia Scott, George Stofsky, Andrea Vizcarrando, Paul Vizcarrando, Claire Weinberg, Mina Weiner, John R. Wing, Jay Zises, Justin Zises and Susan Zises.

Additionally, I am especially grateful for the generosity and incredible patience of three fine lawyers: Arnold Abramowitz, Linda Fairstein and Sara Moss. (And thanks for lunch.)

I thank my assistant, AnneMarie Palmer, for her hard work, her good humor and her commendable equanimity.

The interior designer, Susan Lawton, answered every question I had about antiques, furnishings and architecture with her usual authority and awesome wit.

I appreciate the aid of the librarians at the New York and the Port Washington (N.Y.) Public Libraries.

This is the sixth book for me and my editor, Larry Ashmead. For me, it has been a joyous collaboration. I thank him for his guidance, for the mail, the books, the early-morning jokes—and for giving me all the time I needed to finish the novel as I wanted it finished.

My agent, Owen Laster, has been a fount of wisdom, a rock of strength and a wonderful guy.

I thank my wonderful children, Andrew and Elizabeth Abramowitz, and my daughter-in-law, Leslie Stern, for their love, support and fine editorial advice.

Lastly, my eternal love and gratitude to my own in-house counsel, Elkan Abramowitz. He is (and I'm being objective here) the best person in the world.

One

I was never a virgin.

Okay: In the technical sense, of course I was. But even in my dewy days, I never gazed at the world wide-eyed with wonder. If I wasn't born shrewd, at least I grew up too smart to be naive. So how come in the prime of my life, at the height of my powers, I could not foresee what would happen in the Torkelson case? Was I too street smart? Had I been around the block so many times that I finally lost my sense of direction?

A brief digression: Ages ago, soon after I became a criminal defense lawyer, Fat Mikey LoTriglio hailed me across the vast concrete expanse of the courthouse steps. "Hey, girlie!" His tomato of a face wore an expression that seemed (I squinted) amiable, pretty surprising considering he'd just been sprung from Elmira after doing two and a half years on the three counts of aggravated assault I'd prosecuted him for.

"Come over here," he called out. "Hey, I'm not gonna kill you." In Fat Mikey's world, that was not hyperbole but a promise; he got busy straightening his tie to demonstrate he was not concealing a Walther PPK. "I hear you're not working for the D.A. anymore," he boomed. I strolled over, smiling to show I didn't hold any grudges either, and offered my hand, which he shook in the overly vigorous manner of a man trying to show a professional woman that he's comfortable with professional women. Then I handed him my business card. I was not unaware that Fat Mikey was one of three organized crime figures the cops routinely picked

1

up for questioning on matters of Mob-related mayhem. To have Fat Mikey as a client was to have an annuity.

He glanced down at my card to recall my name. "Lee?"

Naturally, I didn't respond "Fat?" And to call him "Mike" after having called him "a vulture feasting on society's entrails" in my summation might seem presumptuous. So I murmured a polite "Mmm?"

"A girl like you from a good family—"

"Are you kidding?" I started to say, but he wouldn't let me.

"I could tell you got class, watching you at the trial," he went on. "You know how? Good posture—and not just in the morning. Plus you say 'whom.' Anyways, you really think you can make a living defending guys like me?" He didn't seem so much sexist as sincerely curious. I nodded encouragingly. "This is what you had in mind when you went to law school?" he inquired.

"No. Back then I was leaning toward Eskimo fishing rights. But this is what I'm good at."

He shook his head at my folly. "When—pardon my French—a guy's ass is in a sling, you think he's gonna hire a girl who says 'whom'?"

"If he's partial to his ass he will."

Fat Mikey's upper lip twitched. For him, that was a smile. Then, almost paternally, he shook a beefy index finger at me. "A girl like you should be more particular about the company she keeps."

Years later, I would learn how wise Fat Mikey was.

Nevertheless, from the beginning I knew there were limits to keeping bad company. I could be sympathetic to my clients without getting emotionally involved: A lot of them had sad childhoods. Many had been victims of grievous social injustice, or of terrible parents (who were themselves victims of terrible parents). Still, I never forgot they were criminals. And while I may have delighted in a bad guy's black humor, or a tough broad's cynicism, I was never one of those attorneys who got naughty thrills socializing with hoods. You'd never catch me inviting a client—let's say Melody

Ann Toth, for argument's sake—to go shopping and out for Caesar salads so we could chitchat about old beaux ... or about what she might expect at her upcoming trial for robbing three branches of the Long Island Savings Bank on what might have been an otherwise boring Thursday.

For their part, most of my clients (including Fat Mikey, who retained me two years after that conversation on the courthouse steps) wouldn't think I was exactly a laugh a minute either. Whatever their personal definition of a good time was, I wasn't it. Unlike me, Fat Mikey simply did not get a bang out of crocheting afghans or listening to National Public Radio. With fists the size of rump roasts, Mikey looked like what he was: a man for whom aggravated assault was not just a profession but a pleasure. As for Melody Ann, with her pink-blonde hair that resembled attic insulation, the only reason she'd go shopping at Saks would be to knock off the Estée Lauder counter when she ran out of lip liner. My clients had no reason or desire to pass for upper middle class.

For that reason alone, Norman Torkelson was different right from the beginning.

Of course, a con man cannot look like a crook and expect to make a living. If Norman Torkelson had resembled the no-good rat he was, he would have been a sawed-off runt with a skinny mustache like a plucked eyebrow. But then the nine hundred or so women he had proposed marriage to would have told him: Get lost, creepo.

However, he was not sawed off; he was six feet five. Lucky for him, since in America everyone knows a man's character increases in excellence in direct proportion to his height. Not that Norman was content with mere tallness; he was clever enough to trip over his own size-thirteen feet every so often, which made him ... Some of the descriptions in the witnesses' statements taken over the years from victims of his scams were: "sensitive," "tragic, like Abraham Lincoln," and (my personal favorite) "caring." So all those women to whom he proposed said yes—Yes, my love! Yes, Norman! (or Yes, whatever alias he was using)—and got their hearts broken.

3

I wonder now: What if we hadn't met in the Nassau County Correctional Center? What if he hadn't been wearing the official uniform—pants and shirt in an orange that inevitably leeched the life out of every inmate's face? Would I have wanted to trace with my fingertips the lines of his Mount Rushmore face? No. I would not have.

Still (before I leave the subject of color), even the vicious glow of that orange could not hide the fact that Norman's eyes were such a startling blue they seemed more a Crayola than an eye color: Viking blue, a shade somewhere between royal and turquoise. If not for those eyes, would the hundreds of women thrilled to empty their bank accounts for him have found themselves destitute, suddenly dependent on disgusted relatives or the public dole?

However, let's not go overboard on the blue eyes business. A con man cannot afford to be suspiciously handsome, and Norman Torkelson was not. First of all, he had a too teeny nose. Instead of the cute upward tilt you'd expect from a nose like that, it hooked; in certain lights, you'd swear Norman was half man, half parakeet. So not gorgeous—an asset to a con man because true beauty evokes curiosity. And not slick. At least, he didn't seem slick. Like any professional swindler, he was just convincing enough to persuade a woman who had never met a man from Yale that he had gone to Yale.

Furthermore, a competent con man never overacts. Norman may have listened avidly when a woman spoke, but he never pretended to drown in the depths of her eyes; he didn't shift around in his seat either, crossing his leg to hide an alleged erection. Oh, one more handy imperfection: He had a slight lisp.

I heard his first words as: "I thwear I didn't do it, Mth. White." He lowered his big head and whispered, "Jethuth!"

"It's not me you have to convince, Mr. Torkelson," I told him. "I'm on your side. It's the D.A. who's a problem."

He clutched the top of the white Formica barrier that separates inmates from their visitors. "Please," he begged me, "call me Norman."

4

Amazing: He threw his entire being behind that request. His forehead furrowed, his shoulders tensed, his Adam's apple bulged, every part of him seemed to yearn: Call me Norman.

A con man's hokey trick? Absolutely. I tried to be cool, glancing around the visitors' room, a huge space filled with rows of Formica-topped tables, which resembled a school cafeteria. However, instead of patrolling teachers there were armed guards carrying semiautomatic rifles, and closed-circuit cameras.

Despite the ugly publicness of the place, I felt a private flush of gratification at my client's request: Please, call me Norman. Almost as if he had willed it, I actually eased my attaché case off my lap and set it by my feet, then pushed my chair back so he could get a fuller view: I carried on as if I were OD'ing on estrogen. I actually crossed my legs, movie starlet style, and began to inscribe a sexy O with my foot.

Naturally, all this took place within a microsecond. Then I realized I was being manipulated—which only proved to me what I'd already suspected. Norman Torkelson was not a great con artist. Just a fairly competent one.

"I was not—and I quote—conning Bobette out of her money!" he announced in that very instant.

"Norman," I said, uncrossing my legs, "let's get our priorities straight. The fraud by false pretenses charge is the least of your problems right now."

"Bobette and I were *friends*," he insisted. "She was *lending* me the money. I told her: 'Have your attorney draw up the proper paperwork, with whatever interest you feel is fair. I'll sign it. I won't have it any other way!' "

"Norman." I tried to cut him off.

"This was a legitimate business transaction!"

"It may have been, but right now you're not in business. You're in the slammer, and Bobette Frisch is on ice over at the medical examiner's." A small shudder vibrated his shoulders, a not unusual reaction new clients display when I talk like a defense lawyer—i.e., straight. But I believe straight is better than cute, especially when a guy is looking

5

at fifteen to life. Let me amend that: Straight is better than cute, period, which is not to say a lawyer can't mitigate the effects of brutal directness with an empathetic smile and a mastery of the New York penal code. I peered right into Norman's eyes. "You're facing a murder charge," I reminded him.

"I didn't touch her!" Norman unclasped his hands and gripped his side of the table. "How can they think I could take a human life?"

I shook my head despondently to show how utterly unthinkable such a notion was to me and then explained in my tranquilizing, consoling, I-know-you-don't-deserve-to-be-in-the-hoosegow voice: "From what I gather, at around two-thirty last Friday, Bobette went into her bank and withdrew forty-eight thousand of the fifty-two thousand dollars she had in her account. After that, no one seems to have seen her—until yesterday."

"Who . . ." He cleared his throat, presumably to show me how choked up he was. "Who found her?" he asked.

"Some local kids. They were selling chocolate bars so their high school band could go to the Hula Bowl. When they knocked on her door, they smelled something. One of their parents called the cops, and the cops found Bobette. There was no sign of the money."

Norman sat back in his molded plastic chair as if amazed: No sign of the money?! The performance over, he leaned forward, his face flushing with outrage. "How did the cops get to me?"

"Fingerprints?" I suggested helpfully.

It is the rare miscreant who comes right out and tells his attorney: I'm a crook. Career criminals are too sophisticated to admit to a specific crime, because they know their lawyer cannot put them on the stand if the lawyer knows they are going to lie through their teeth. Besides, most have an aversion to responsibility (to say nothing of an antipathy to reality). They cry out: "Who, me? I didn't do anything." And it goes double for someone accused of murder. They not only deny guilt; they play victim: Why are you picking on *me*? As their lawyer, my job isn't to get them to confess; it's to give them the best defense possible. To do that, I have to nudge them, gently, until they're facing the facts.

"Fingerprints?" he repeated. I studied him as he mulled that one over, rubbing his big chin with his big-boned hand. For my money, anything over six feet in a man is wasted on height, but a lot of women do delight in leaning against something the size of a Plymouth Voyager. It makes them feel protected, petite—and it probably makes them anticipate a sex organ larger than the average totem pole. Sadly, I thought about the utter joy that would light up some two-hundred-fifty-pound lonelyheart when Norman would beseech her: Lean on me, darling.

"You're wondering how they found you?" I asked. Norman shrugged, which meant he was dying to know. So was I. "You didn't give Bobette your real name?"

"Only because I was afraid her lawyer might want to do a credit check. Need I tell you how long that can take?"

"What name did you give her?"

"Denton Wylie."

"Ever use that name before?" He shook his head, not without a touch of pride. Less industrious con men have a roster of about ten names, or they stick with some variation on their actual initials: Jimmy Dellacroce on one scam, John Doughtery on the next, and so forth. The pros take on a new name each time. It makes life harder for the cops. But my guess is it must make a con man feel clean, as if rising from a pure stream after being baptized by total immersion. "Did you have your phone listed under Denton Wylie?"

"No."

"The place you're living?"

"No."

"What name are you using there?" He hesitated, and before he could make up something new, I added: "I've got to figure out how the cops got to you."

"Robert McNulty," he admitted reluctantly.

"And your address?"

"I gave it to your secretary when I made my call."

"The real one. If I have to send out an investigator, you're going to go broke fast if he winds up checking out the address of a vacant lot." He took one of those shaky deep breaths made up of small, nervous inhalations. "Norman, you've got to give me something to work with."

"Fifty-four Homewood Avenue—in Mineola. It's an apartment." I waited. "Apartment 3-C."

"Do you work alone?"

"Of course," he responded. He sounded so utterly convincing. I figured he was lying through his teeth. He was. "I live with someone," he said after a half minute. (Try sitting in the inmates' visiting room with your lawyer eyeballing you, and you'll see how oppressive thirty seconds of silence can be.) "She's just . . . I love her."

"What's her name?"

"Mary. She's the sweetest, most innocent person in the world."

"Mary what?"

"Mary Dean. We live together. I swear to you, Miss White, by everything I hold holy, I work alone. Mary doesn't even know . . ." He covered his face with his hands and rubbed his forehead with his fingertips, hard, almost brutally, as if applying counter pressure on a terrific headache.

Well, why shouldn't he have a headache? It was too early to know how much evidence the cops really had, but Sam Franklin, the Homicide sergeant in charge of the case, offered me a hint a half hour later, when I suggested it might be possible that the police had acted too fast and that Norman Torkelson, although admittedly having a rap sheet that could circle the globe sixteen times, might not have choked Ms. Frisch to death and a murderer could (at that very moment) be running amok on Long Island. "Whoever did it could kill again!" I said passionately into the phone.

"I don't have time for your act today Lee," Sam said, which suggested he had already been assured by an assistant D.A. in the Homicide Bureau that this was a good case. Then he hung up the phone disdainfully, not bothering (as

8

he usually did) to slam it down. So I had to revise my estimate. Not a good case: a great case.

But I should begin at the beginning. I should—

Two

In truth, Lee White, B.A., Cornell University, J.D., New York University School of Law, did not have a clue as to where the beginning really was. She might have told you it was the moment J. J. O'Shaughnessy (a retired lawyer devoting his golden years to twirling wisps of hair that grew from his ears while watching Court TV in the Dominican Village retirement home in Amityville, Long Island) referred an old client, Norman Torkelson to his poker buddy Chuckie Phalen; Chuckie, busy trying a first-degree arson case, passed Norman over to his law partner, Lee.

Or if Lee was in a rare reflective mood—let's say sitting with her gentleman (a lawyer himself) before a roaring fire—she'd muse: It must have begun the summer after my second year in law school, when I was interning in the Manhattan D.A.'s office. Do you know, that was the first time in my life that I ever had an abstract thought! It sneaked right up and bit me on the ass. The gentleman, amused would chuckle. Lee would go on: All of a sudden—ka-boom!—I comprehended the beauty of the criminal justice system, its balance, and that a person accused of a crime is also entitled to a defense—*must* have one—even if he is utter scum and guilty as hell.

But Lee White, like most people, had no idea where the real beginning really began. So to commence:

Let us start with the White business. Had she been a premature baby, her last name would have been Weiss. Two weeks before her birth day, her father, Leonard, took off from work to go to court and change the family's surname to White so that the son he was anticipating could flash his birth certificate anywhere in America and not be challenged.

10

Although now White, Leonard and his wife, Sylvia, did not abandon the old-world custom of naming a baby for a dead and inevitably boring relative. Leonard and Sylvia called their surprise daughter Lily Rose, after Sylvia's maternal grandmother, Leah Rivka Mutterperl, a woman who became distraught upon realizing, on her second day aboard the S.S. *Polonia*, bound for Ellis Island, that she had left her false teeth on a washstand in a hovel in a shtetl about sixty miles due south of Cracow three weeks earlier and who never again was able to regain her equanimity.

Before Weiss and White, the family's name had actually been Weissberg until 1948—two years before Lee's birth—when Leonard shortened it to Weiss. When asked, "Weiss?" by a customer who acted as if she had heard something unpleasant, he replied (too quickly): "Weiss means 'white.' It's actually a very common German name . . . like White is here." As the fur trade was in those days an industry of men named Glickstern and Steinberg and Rubin, the knowing smile on his customer's face mortified Leonard and determined him to be White, although it took him two years to get up the courage to actually do it.

In any case, until Lee was born, Leonard and Sylvia were so confident in the imminence of a son (whom they planned to name Bartholomew, after Leonard's grandfather Baruch Weissberg) that they barely gave a thought to what to name a daughter, much less to how silly Lily White sounded, especially when, after a few months it became obvious that the girl's coloring was going to be decidedly Mediterranean.

Fortunately, their firstborn's childish pronunciation of Lily was Lee-Lee, so in a sense, Lee christened herself . . . although in the case of the Weissberg-Weiss-Whites, christened is obviously not the right word, while "jewed" would be not only a misnomer but might give offense, however unintended—somewhat the way "lily white" began to in 1954, in those months just after *Brown* v. *Board of Education* was handed down.

That Leonard WWW would be sensitive to the feelings of the Negro is not surprising, since he was the incarnation of that old Nixonian saw that Jews live like Episcopalians and vote like Puerto Ricans. His liberalism, however, was not the usual concern for the underdog. He really didn't care about the underdog unless the underdog had managed to get a few bucks together and was in the market for a fur garment for his wife or lady friend. No, Leonard's liberalism was his inescapable inheritance from his card-carrying-Communist father, Nat, a shop steward for the Fur Workers' Union, and his big-hearted, big-mouthed mother, Bella.

Leonard received one further legacy: While Nat could not help his son gain admission to Harvard or obtain a seat on the stock exchange, he was able to secure him a position as floor boy in the back room at Frosty Furs in Forest Hills. Thus began his career: in 1942, seventeen-year-old Leonard—safe from the Army's clutches because of a quirky kidney—traveled from Borough Park in Brooklyn to Queens. He swept the floors and scoured from workbenches the reeking grease that dripped off untreated raccoon pelts. He stretched lynx skins on a board for the cutter and marked patterns onto garments. He was a hard worker, and an excellent one too. But nothing he did was good enough for his boss. Whenever there were no customers around, his boss, Isadore Frumkin, would growl, "Move yer whatsis, sonny boy!" He would scrutinize Leonard's every move with the tight-clenched face of the congenitally sadistic.

Was revenge on Mr. Frumkin the spark that made Leonard determine that someday *he* would be the boss of Frosty Furs and when he was, he would treat his floor boy like a human being? Who knows what ignites the entrepreneurial fire in a young man? Rebellion against his Trotskyite father? The ignominy of sweeping up scraps of muskrat and cigarette butts as well as the curlicues of oily lettuce that appeared to molt from the wet-breaded sardine sandwich Milton Kuperschmidt, the cutter, devoured every noon? Was it glancing out the window onto Austin Street and seeing Mr. Frumkin's resplendent 1942 Packard illuminating the February dusk? Or could it have been observing Mr. Frumkin, kneeling on the floor to better gauge the hemline of Mrs. Whitcomb Knoll's broadtail, casually run his hand up Mrs. Knoll's pale and silky and Protestant calf?

In those days, Queens was not yet the vigorous ethnic mishmash it is today. Entire neighborhoods—Douglaston Manor, Forest Hills Gardens—were not merely lily white: even the lightest Jews were prohibited, and, indeed, Catholics—including the fairest, without

O's or Mc's or excessive offspring—were encouraged to reside elsewhere. To young Leonard, delivering a lapin muff and bonnet for Mrs. William Warren's little Amanda, or picking up Mrs. Bradley Mercer's nutria jacket (onto which Mr. Bradley had upchucked five Rob Roys and Welsh rarebit on New Year's Eve) for a cleaning, Forest Hills Gardens was paradise. A mere three-block walk from the store put him on a street where flaxen-haired angels tossed balls to airborne blond dogs. Velvet lawns encircled four-bedroom, mullion-windowed houses that Leonard was soon to learn were called (albeit redundantly) English Tudor.

He rarely saw the masters of the house; they were a half world away, fighting Heinies and Japs. Or at least they were in Manhattan, writing advertising copy for stool softeners.

But the women stayed home in those days, and Leonard moved quickly from being merely enamored to falling in love with them all: the debutante daughters, the newlyweds, the young mothers, the matrons, the menopausal. It was, of course, pure prejudice, the viewing of an entire group as the Perfect One: a woman in tennis whites, with shiny hair and a voice as soft and luxe as lynx. (Clearly, this passion for anything female and Episcopalian was an indication that Leonard had a few unresolved odds and ends in the Oedipal department; they would remain problematical even after he undertook psychotherapy a decade later. It should be noted here, however, that his mother, Bella, a good-hearted, effusive woman who claimed a brief career as a character actress in the Yiddish theater, weighed nearly three hundred pounds and had dyed her frizzy hair the color of a rusty steel wool pad. Bella's voice was so lacking in mellifluence that a simple "How are you, *tataleh*?" was, to her son, more agonizing than a thousand pieces of fresh chalk screeching along a blackboard.)

But these women of the Gardens were so removed from Leonard's experience they might as well have belonged to another species. He could only worship them from afar. While he could easily (very easily) picture himself wrapping a golden sable cape around pearly shoulders in the front hall of one of the grander Tudors and hearing a grateful wifely "Thank you, Leonard, my dearest," he could not actually bring himself to smile his wide, engaging smile at one of them, so afraid was he of rejection—or perhaps of acceptance. His only sexual encounters took place in another borough: exchanging chaste kisses with Brooklyn stenographers—and feeling up Flo Feinman, the Slut of Borough Park. Secretly, he was afraid he would never find anyone he would desire enough to marry.

Six years passed. Since this is Lee's story, not Leonard's, suffice it to say that much happened in that time. Although Leonard remained innocent of the wondrous topography of women, in business he was on his way to being a man of the world. He had risen higher than he had ever dreamed—thanks to that louse Isadore Frumkin. Leonard's boss's black market diet of marbled steak and Hershey bars led, inexorably, to a crippling heart attack shortly after V-J Day. Leonard, backed by a loan arranged by an eager-beaver junior vice president of the East New York Savings Bank (a member of Nat's Communist cell), became the owner of Frosty Furs just before Christmas in 1946. A year later, he proved he was a natural capitalist. Business was booming to such an extent that he repaid his bank loan, bought a 1947 Lincoln Continental that made Mr. Frumkin's Packard look like a hunk of junk—and told his father, "Absolutely no contributions to Communist front organizations!" when Nat hit him up for a fifty-dollar contribution to the Soviet-American Folk Dance League.

Leonard was not only putting some distance between himself and his past. He was also hard at work to get the polish he hadn't been born with. He went to the theater and saw Cornelia Otis Skinner in *Lady Windermere's Fan* (which he'd thought might have something to do with the fashion business). He listened to WQXR for culture. He went to the movies for diction lessons (although he did drop his lord-of-the-manor "How teddibly luffly of you" pretty quickly after his mother, Bella, started yukking it up, mistakenly believing that her son was indulging in a rare moment of frivolity and doing an imitation of Ronald Colman in *The Late George Apley*).

But his urbanity wasn't entirely superficial; Leonard went to every Furriers Industry Council meeting and absorbed his tony Manhattan colleagues' wisdom on everything from remodeling Astrakhan coats to what whiskey to drink (Johnnie Walker Black) and precisely how to order it ("on the rocks, splash of soda—no twist, sweetheart"). He overcame his natural shyness by forcing himself to ask his customers leading questions. ("What are your Thanksgiving plans, Mrs. Fiske?" "No, really, I'd love to hear about your Easter centerpiece, Mrs. Guilfoyle.") Thus he gathered an enormous amount of data on the folkways of the preeminent stratum of the upper middle class.

Gradually, the young man gained confidence. His customers began to find him charming: "Mrs. Johnston, that seal would clap his flippers if he could see you in his coat! No, seriously. I mean it. You look"—he'd take a deep breath as if to clear his head so he could find the perfect word—"lovely." At twenty-three, Leonard was almost on top of the world. He had money in his pocket, a firm jaw, a head of lustrous jet-black hair (more than one customer thought of him as a Jewish Robert Taylor), and a developing sense of style. All he needed was a wife.

Early in 1948, Sylvia Bernstein came into Tudor Rose (the fur salon's new name, which Leonard selected after nights in the library poring over everything from Amy Vanderbilt to *Boutell's Heraldry*). Leonard checked out her well-cut gray wool suit with its flared-at-the-hips peplum jacket which only the slimmest women could wear successfully, looked into her blue-gray eyes, took in her prominent cheekbones and her sleek, blond-streaked hair and thought, in essence: Hubba hubba! But he acted all business, assuming she'd been recommended to him by one of his more genteel customers. Wait, she had no wedding ring. So she must be one of his customers' daughters. Ah well, at least she might be good for a red fox chubby. He asked, "May I help you, Miss . . . ?" When she answered, in the most euphonious tones possible: "Sylvia Bernstein," he would have fainted, if he hadn't found himself falling in love.

It wasn't just her looks. Sylvia had class, Leonard was relieved to discover. All right, people hearing her speak would realize she wasn't a Vassar girl. But she never, even on the hottest summer day, left the house without wearing gloves. Her apartment building was classy too (Tudor style, no less), with leaded windows in the lobby and a lion stantant on the pediment over the elevator. Not only that: Her mother, at age forty-five, was still a natural blond.

And her father was a judge!

The first time Leonard met the Bernsteins, he could scarcely breathe. That was how emotional he became, wishing that he could have had such parents. They were perfect.

Take Sylvia's mother. Not only did she cook and clean. If sock-darning were a competitive sport, Eva Bernstein would have had a mantel full of trophies. What a housewife! But there were holes too big for even Eva to repair, and when one of these occurred, she would adopt the sock as her own, wearing it and its non-holey brother over her stocking feet so she could glide through the apartment without running her nylons or disturbing her husband, Judge Bernstein. "Shhh!" she'd warn Sylvia and Sylvia's younger brother, Victor. "The Judge is taking a nap!" "The Judge is reading!" "The Judge is on the phone!"

Judge Arthur Bernstein was more than a pillar of rectitude; he was a five-foot-nine-inch pillar of quietude. In the Queens Domestic Relations Court, where he presided, court stenographers griped that they deserved battle pay, they had to strain so hard to hear his feathery voice. But other than that, there were no complaints. His reputation was neither sterling nor tarnished; he was not unduly harsh with the litigants who appeared before him (although he did seem a little too eager to rule an ex-wife's petition for support out of order if her ex-husband was represented by a lawyer with links to the Ronald Goldberger Kew Gardens Democratic Club). However, to colleagues, neighbors, friends, and certainly to Leonard, Arthur Bernstein was nothing but a gentleman. He removed his hat in the presence of a lady. He wore an alpaca coat, used a small but genuine tortoiseshell holder for his Philip Morrises. When expressing gratitude to anyone, he simply nodded—but in such a gracious and dignified way that he made those who vocalized their "thank you"s seem almost vulgar.

And compared to Leonard's parents! Nat the Commie had an articulated opinion on everything, from dialectical materialism to how to grow string beans on the fire escape: "Hey, Lenny, you don't drown 'em, you schmendrick. You water 'em every other day!" And Bella, with her demands that he loosen up! Each day as he left for work she made a game of blocking the door. "What d'ya got, an ice cube up your *tuchis*, Lenny? Smile! It don't cost nothin'." He'd try to sidestep her and grab for the doorknob, but despite her bulk, she was more agile than he. "Come on, pretend I'm a lady buying a fur. 'Excuse me, my good man,'" she'd twitter, giving what was actually a pretty fair imitation of a Vanderbilt voice. "'I'm looking for something smart in a mouton, finger-tiplength.'" Eventually, Bella would start to guffaw at her own performance, doubling over with laughter; that's when Leonard would make his break for freedom.

In those days, young men did not get their own apartments, so Leonard was doubly grateful to Sylvia: for getting him out of his personal hell in Brooklyn and for giving him a judge and a natural blonde for in-laws. And of course, Sylvia was grateful to him, because at age twenty-two, she had no prospects. The loss of Selwyn Youdelman, a Brooklyn Law School graduate with offices in Kew Gardens, had devastated her parents a year earlier. That the loss was due to his choosing another girl over Sylvia made it more painful to the Bernsteins than if he had merely died. Sylvia knew that they blamed her for his leaving, that she'd shown off her artistic nature too much, that she'd kept pushing him to go to operas and museums, while all a normal fellow wanted to do was go see *The Bells of St. Mary's*, for God's sake, or go for a malted. "I *didn't* push him!" Sylvia explained tearfully.

"Shhh!" her mother responded. "The Judge is in the bathroom." Both women took a moment to compose themselves and whisper more quietly.

"He asked *me* what did I want to do," Sylvia tried to explain, "so I said I read how they had a Turner exhibition at the Metropolitan Museum. He's this English guy. And Selwyn was the one who said how he loves good pictures and never gets enough of them."

"That doesn't mean he actually wants to go into the city on a weekday night! The man is an attorney!" Sour acid rose from Sylvia's gut and burned the back of her throat. She wanted to throw up. But the Judge was in the bathroom, and even if he finished right away, it would have to air out or she'd never stop vomiting for the rest of her life. She rushed away from her mother, into the bedroom she shared with her brother, flung herself facedown on her bed, and wept—silently.

Unfair! Unfair! She'd bring a date into the apartment, and right away he'd hook his finger over his tie to loosen it, as if he were suffocating. Well, why not? The place was gloomy, airless. The windows were never open, the blinds were always drawn tight, and there was barely enough light—just enough to see the dust sparkles dancing in the living room air. Even before her mother could breathe, "Shhh! The Judge," the date would get that Lemme-outta-here look, like he was inside Boris Karloff's tomb.

But Leonard actually liked her parents! She knew part of it was that they had wall-to-wall carpeting and his parents were, as he explained, working-class people. But even guys who'd been all hepped up because her father was a judge—like Selwyn—were somehow repelled by the silence in that apartment, by the radio that hadn't been turned on since FDR died. There was something about the Judge, she realized, that was . . . not right. And her mother, too, was . . . not right.

Not right? Wacko was probably closer to the truth, but that would have been too revolutionary a notion for Sylvia. And while Leonard (had he been cross-examined under oath) might have admitted something was not quite right about the Bernsteins, the cryptlike quiet made him feel they were, at the very least, a classy family.

In fact, the first time Sylvia let him put his hand under her skirt, he was thinking: I'm bringing Sleeping Beauty to life. He was thrilled with her. Sitting on her living room couch, her parents inside, sleeping, he wanted to whisper, "Your thighs are as soft as chinchilla." But he stopped himself because he didn't want her to get the wrong idea and think he was low class, comparing her to a rodent, or worse, that he thought her thighs were furry, although they did feel a little . . . fuzzy. So he kept mum, always a good idea in the Bernstein apartment.

Three months later, when Leonard asked for Sylvia's hand, an idea suddenly popped into his head. He decided that in addition to an engagement ring, he would give his Beauty a silver fox stole that would set off her pale prettiness. Which was too bad, because Beauty *and* her mother had been thinking more in terms of a Breath of Spring mink jacket, if not a full-length coat. Still, a fox stole is better than nothing: Even though he was not a professional man, not even a college graduate, not even a guy with a couple of years at CCNY, Sylvia knew Leonard was the best she could hope for. At least he was nice looking, and he owned a decent business, which was nothing to be ashamed about—even though she was.

Well! Three years later, when Lee was born, things had certainly changed! But more about that when the time comes.

Three

Bobette Frisch stood apart from my client's usual victims. Most of Norman Torkelson's women lay somewhere between vulnerable and defenseless. Not Bobette. Starting out in Brooklyn, a venue not known for fragile females, she moved due east to Queens in the early sixties when she was about twenty. She worked as a waitress at a tavern in Flushing called the Dew Drop Inn. A couple of years later, when the crowd got meaner and the barkeeper took to tucking a hammer behind the Wild Turkey for protection, she moved east again, this time into Nassau County.

Like me, Bobette wanted a career. She took a bartending course and found a job at Murray's Shamrock in Williston Park. It took her another ten years, but she finally moved from labor to management, after convincing Murray's frantic creditors that the joint could actually turn a tidy profit if it were run by someone sober enough to use a cash register. She became half-owner—keeping an eagle eye on the goings-on so no bartender could pour free drinks for his pals. She tossed out the roughnecks and was always on the lookout for known queasers: to get them up and out of the place so they wouldn't (as they say with such delicacy here on Long Island) blow their chunks all over the bar.

Bobette watched over her property from a dimly lit table way in the back. This turned out to be a good idea. First of all, she apparently wasn't the talkative type. She greeted patrons with a friendly enough "Hiya," but that was it in the conversation department. If she had an opinion on the Yankees or school taxes or the novels of Danielle Steel, she kept it to herself. After the murder, bar patrons who had no idea what she was like created their own Bobette Frisch for the media, murmuring into the Channel 12 mike: "You could see sweetness in her face. But it was, uh, um, a quiet sweetness. What's happening, that someone like that gets killed?" And: "She was ultra shy. You know? But a wonderful human being." However, an anonymous *Newsday* source referred to her as a "major cheapo who wouldn't let you owe her two bucks," and someone interviewed in the *Post* referred to her as Blobette. The blob business is a little unfair. According to the charts, Bobette was not terribly overweight. Her body, unfortunately, resembled a beer keg, stout and compact. Her oval face, framed by light brown hair, might have been pretty, or at least not unappealing, except that she had fleshy folds that ran from either side of her mouth down either side of her chin. Thus her jaw appeared to be attached in the manner of a marionette's. Patrons of the bar first took to calling her Mrs. Howdy Doody, then inevitably, behind her back, Mrs. Doody.

Bobette was shrewd about money. By the eighties, she owned three bars and two apartment buildings. Starting at four every morning, she made the rounds in her frost-beige Cadillac Eldorado from Williston Park to Franklin Square to Hicksville and personally picked up each night's receipts. She collected her monthly rents in person.

Neither the cops nor my investigator ever found a scintilla of evidence that she was a pushover when it came to guys, or that she might be susceptible to a sweet talker who would con her out of her life savings. On the contrary: She was all business. When queried about her love life, the people who dealt with her drew a total blank. Huh? Wha'? "Bobette" and "sex" did not seem to belong in a single sentence.

This was her life: She managed her holdings—which included her own modest but pretty two-story colonial on a sixty-by-one-hundred-foot plot in Merrick. Each Tuesday she visited the Mane Event salon and got her hair washed and set in a style Patricia Nixon favored in the 1956 campaign; once a month, she had it cut and colored. Every single Saturday afternoon she went to the movies and, afterward, stopped at Mario's for a salad and an order of linguine and clam sauce, which she took home with her. She attended mass at St. Agnes Cathedral in Rockville Centre every Sunday morning at ten-thirty. The local libraries or video rental stores had no record of her.

Her parents were dead. She had one brother, in Cherry Hill, New Jersey, a mechanic at a Honda dealership. She had no enemies. She had no friends.

I cleared my throat and asked the cop: "What makes you think Bobette's dealings with Norman Torkelson were anything other than business?"

Since he had successfully ignored me for the last five minutes, I knew Sergeant Samuel Franklin would not enjoy a reminder that he and I were standing within two feet of each other. Sam sucked in his already sunken cheeks. A second later, he took in a mouthful of air and blew up the lower half of his face. Ergo, he could then make a revolting noise at me as he exhaled and yet, technically, be not guilty of making fart sounds at a lawyer.

Sam was the archetype for all those smug "Think Thin!" pieces that have plagued me since adolescence, the articles that advise you to mimic the behavior of the congenitally lean. "Do natural-born skinnies just lounge around? No, no and no again. They're *always* in action! So get going!"

Sam never stopped moving. So skinny that you could test your recollection of tenth-grade biology by trying to name each protruding bone on his skeletal frame, Sam burned calories as easily as I stored them. Besides keeping his face in constant motion, he was always tapping his feet, cracking his knuckles, twisting his torso, stretching and flexing his arms. This time he added head swiveling, checking out the acoustical ceiling tile, the floor, the doors along the hallway of the D.A.'s Office. It went beyond his usual hyperkinetics; much of this movement was to avoid looking at me.

"Don't the cops investigate homicides anymore?" I asked, using my courtroom voice so he couldn't pretend not to hear me. Sam, my former friend, drummed his twiglike fingers on the file folder he was clutching; his skin had grown so dry

that pale cracks crisscrossed his knuckles. "Come on, Sam."
He kept trying to ignore me. Unfortunately, he was successful. "What's going on here?" I persisted. "You dust for
prints, run them through the computer, come up with some
guy who happens to have a criminal record. So you say, 'Oh,
goody, let's charge this Norman Torkelson with murder.
That way, we can all take the weekend off.'"

"We're supposed to wait for Ms. Nuñez to discuss this,"
Sam said to the dangling frosted globe of a municipal lighting
fixture, thus managing to respond to my protest without
fully acknowledging my presence. The absent Holly Nuñez
was the newest assistant district attorney in the Homicide
unit.

"We've been waiting for twenty minutes! She made a ten-
thirty appointment."

"The secretary said she was in the ladies room," Sam
explained to the lighting fixture.

"I'll go find her."

"I wouldn't."

"Why not?"

No answer. The fingers on his left hand were pulling at
his pants leg, trying to get it to fall properly over his shoe.
It didn't work. In his baggy navy trousers, he looked like a
Weight Watchers lecturer modeling his old clothes to display
his eighty-pound loss.

"Sam, take a long, hard look at Norman's rap sheet. Do
you see anything resembling violent behavior?" His only
answer was an I-am-being-incredibly-patient inhalation followed by an exhalation between pursed lips. That pissed me
off, which I guess was the point. "Norman Torkelson did
not kill Bobette Frisch," I told him. "Guys like Norman hate
women too much to kill them. They don't want the pain
they cause to come to an end."

He was not moved by this dandy insight. But then, there
was nothing I could say anymore that would move Sam
Franklin. The thing of it was, years before, when I first came
to the Nassau County D.A.'s from the Manhattan D.A.'s, we'd
been buddies. He had recently joined the force after getting
a master's degree in sociology from Adelphi. He'd been hand-

some back then, with the pulled-tight skin and prominent cheekbones of those Calvin Klein underwear models. He looked absolutely stunning in his blue patrolman's uniform. Sam had been the arresting officer on a robbery case assigned to me. What a cutie-pie! was my first thought. But my second was: He's smart. I was impressed—wowed, actually—by his written report. It was so thorough, so cogent, so downright lively (and actually grammatical), I could hardly believe a cop wrote it. Anyway, we hit it off. We both loathed the D.A., loved jazz, enjoyed each other's humor, and respected each other's political convictions—the last not exactly a challenge, as we were both a step and a half to the left of Democratic center.

Also, we discovered we were united in a secret conviction that although we'd both been born and bred on Long Island, we were too big for this burg. Over biweekly melted cheese sandwiches at Bob and Cathie's Coffee Shop, we could tell each other what we couldn't say to our colleagues: I coulda been a contender.

SAM: I coulda been a contender; a social worker evaluating grant applications for the Ford Foundation, but after our fourth kid, my wife was diagnosed manic-depressive and I needed bigger bucks and a better medical plan.

ME: I coulda been a contender, one of the top litigators in New York. NBC and CNN camera crews would have dropped by my office to hear my analysis every time a celebrity got arrested on a criminal charge. Except my husband let me know, without ever saying a word, that he wanted out of Manhattan—and that our marriage depended on my following him to the suburbs.

Two big fish in a small pond: That's how we saw ourselves. Although to be honest, none of the other fish swimming alongside us ever suggested they felt that Sam Franklin and I were in any way exceptional. Still, we offered each other validation: Hey, you could have been great. You have it in you. However, since both of us were busy puffing ourselves up in the other's company to show how smart we were, how uncomplaining about the hand we'd been dealt, any admission of vulnerability was unthinkable. Thus genuine closeness was impossible. But we put away a lot of melted cheese and white bread together. We probably had crushes on each other. It was a blow when I left the D.A.'s to go into private practice and our friendship died. Abruptly.

I'd noticed small changes in Sam, but his good company and better cheekbones had kept me from seeing the truth: Five years on the force had turned him from that rarity—a do-gooder with a tough mind—into a right-wing lunkhead. To him, I was suddenly disgraceful. No, wicked. I had gone over to the other side. He stopped saying "Hi!" and took to giving me a fast, hard nod that said: *criminal* lawyer. He insinuated that the only reason individuals accused of a crime were permitted legal representation was undue pressure from the Pinko-Fruitcake Lobby. One day, I ran into Sam right before lunch. When I suggested we could agree to disagree yet still go to Bob and Cathie's for number 14s, he stared at me amazed that I could even dream of such a possibility. So I went back to my office and Xeroxed the Sixth Amendment on my letterhead and mailed it to him. Naturally, he didn't respond. The next time I saw him, at Mr. Big's, a bar where a lot of cops hang out, I said, "Hey, Sam? That little section of the Constitution of the United States? Did you read it?"

Sam said: "It made me want to puke." The words came out lightly, but that's because there were about twenty people standing around us. What made me want to puke was I knew he meant it.

Just before Holly Nuñez herself came into view, her heels came clacking down the hall. I had ten seconds left: I could not appeal to Sam's sense of guilt, since he no longer had one, so I decided to play to his pride. "Fast work doesn't mean good work," I told him. "Twenty bucks I'm going to learn on discovery that your investigation went beyond indifferent—all the way to sloppy."

"Bullshit," Sam began, but he caught himself after the "Bull." Smiling, knowing I'd gotten to him, I gave Holly a warm greeting, even though I could see she'd just spent nearly thirty minutes setting her hair on hot rollers. Her normally stick-straight hair was pumped up and round, like a beach toy. A peach-colored electrical cord dangled from her tote bag. Dead giveaways. Two seconds later, I understood: the hair exhibition was to show me she could afford to be arrogant because the prosecution was holding all the marbles. I hate it when lawyers pull this sort of cheap trick, and double-hate it when that lawyer is female; it reinforces the stereotype about women being so devoted to playing games that they can't be relied on to act as adults.

"Sorry," Holly said, trying to sound breathless, although it is conceivable that the malodorous cloud of hair spray hovering about her head was causing breathing distress.

"No problem," Sam and I responded in an inadvertent duet.

Holly's tiny office was a cube with the lowest ceiling the building code allowed, and with three people in it, you had to work to avoid a panic attack. Plus the place was just plain ugly. Whichever subanthropoidal Republican bureaucrat had chosen the wall color from a paint chip probably thought he was choosing off-white, but the color turned out corpse-yellow. As there were no funds in the county budget to clean the windows, one wall was a rectangular painting of the gray residue of foul weather and pollution. Holly had done her best to liven up the space in predictable Don't-worry-that-I'll-cut-your-balls-off-with-a-pinking-shears-because-as-you-can-see-I-am-not-threatening female litigator tradition. She'd hung a couple of framed museum posters—a Cassatt mother and child and a Renoir ballerina—and set an oxblood vase filled with silk delphiniums and hydrangeas on her desk. But the truth was, the only place less inviting than an assistant D.A.'s office was a men's cell in Building D of the correctional center.

"What have you got, Holly?" I asked. Sam presented his folder to Holly. Like that of a knight handing over his sword to his liege lady, his action made it clear who was in charge. Since this definitely wasn't Sam's modus operandi—he usually held forth as if he were senior partner to any assistant D.A. he was working with—I figured there had been a power struggle. The amazing thing was that Holly had won a fight against Sam Franklin that all the big, hairy-chested, street-smart, politically connected assistants routinely lost.

She opened the folder as if she couldn't wait to read it. Such damn chipperness: Except for her sparkly dark eyes and her name, however, there was nothing about her to indicate she was Hispanic. Still, I knew the Nuñez was legit because my partner, Chuckie Phalen had gotten into a fight with her for speaking Spanish. She was in the Robbery Unit then and meandered over to the defense table and kept making comments to Chuckie's client in Spanish before court convened. Naturally the client was delighted to have some-one speaking his language in this dread, alien place, began talking a blue streak. "Shut your trap!" Chuckie had boomed at him. Then he turned to Holly and threatened her with everything except death. "I was only saying it was a nice day," Holly chirped. "Yeah," the client agreed. "A nice day." The client wound up with five to seven in Sing Sing.

After five minutes with the folder, it was clear that for all her eagerbeaverness, Holly was either a slow or a very thorough reader. Sam kept busy moving his feet around as if following diagrams for variations of the cha-cha; his seated dance got faster and faster.

One of the blessings of middle age is that while you do need reading glasses, your long-range vision improves. So I had no trouble making out the papers that covered Holly's desk. (Any criminal lawyer worth his/her salt learns how to read upside down.) A couple of subpoena forms, a fax from the United States Attorney in the Eastern District of New York regarding jurisdiction over a bank robbery/homicide—and the first of the Horchow spring issues. It featured a wicker basket overflowing with pastel gloves. I felt that sim-ultaneous rush of yearning and giddiness mail order catalogs induce, and was actually rubbing the suede of a celadon size seven between my mental fingers when I spotted a couple of Polaroids stuck under a corner of the telephone. The first crime scene photos, made so the investigators have something to work with while the lab develops the actual photos which have a much clearer resolution. The Polaroids were face-up, but I had a hunch the body was Bobette's. I reached across

Holly's desk, and since neither Holly nor Sam slapped my hand, I picked up the pictures and checked out the information on the backs: "Bobette Frances Frisch, DOB Oct 26, 1940."

Bobette was wearing one of those lavender peignoir and nightgown sets meant for new brides. At least I've always assumed that's whom they were for, since who else but a honeymooner has the leisure to manipulate seventeen layers of chiffon in order to urinate? She lay on dark carpet, blue or purple, the kind with wavy lines cut in so it looks as if it had been plowed. The nightclothes were bunched up around her waist. Her heavy hips were pinched inward to accommodate the tight space between the dark wood leg of a coffee table and the couch from which she'd probably fallen. Three tan bank envelopes lay nearby on the carpet, near her thigh, ripped open.

In the cruel light of the camera's flash, Bobette's bare legs and hips were, literally, dead white, except for a slight shadow of pubic hair. I'd been a prosecutor and a defense lawyer for too many years to be horrified by any but the most brutal crime scene photos. (Also, I think we women lawyers train ourselves not to flinch, so our more swinish male colleagues won't think we're weak and, therefore, worthy of the contempt in which they would dearly love to hold us. I have no idea why we're perpetually fighting this stereotype and proving how tough we are. It would be a great pretrial ploy to convince opposing counsel that we are prime wusses before going into court and trouncing them.)

Anyway, back to Bobette. Her peignoir set formed a lavender puddle around the upper part of her body, so if you squinted and ignored the blackened bruises on her neck . . .

"Strangled?" I asked.

"Uh-huh," Holly muttered, not looking up from her reading.

"But not raped?" I continued hopefully. They weren't talking. "It looks as if the nightgown worked its way up when she fell off the couch. I don't see any indications of bruises on the lower extremities." Holly read on and Sam remained silent, so I couldn't tell if they were holding back on playing a sexual assault card or if there really hadn't been any sexual attack. Still, with imprints of large fingers on Bobette's neck visible even in the photograph, I couldn't pretend that the injuries which led to her death were self-inflicted.

"I can't cut you any slack on this one, Lee," Holly finally said. She closed the folder. "We've got too much."

"Give me a for instance," I said lightly. She looked dubious, the mark of a novice, because any experienced prosecutor would be glad to show you she's holding all the cards. In order to get you to plead your client guilty, she'll be up front with you about all the damaging information, especially if it's incontestable, like physical evidence. "Are you playing poker with me, Holly?" I asked.

She blinked her big, black and very pretty eyes. "No!" she said. She belonged in Colorado or California, doing something aerobic. She was entirely too cheerful for Long Island. "I wouldn't play poker with an old pro like you," she assured. Instantly, I could see, she regretted saying "old," but it was too late.

"Old," I said, "but not yet senile." Before she could apologize and thus no longer feel she somehow owed me one, I added: "I know you found my client's fingerprints."

"Not just on a door bell or somewhere innocuous. On the tape that was used to tie up all the bank envelopes together. The bank officer did it for her. You can see three of the envelopes in that picture." Then she added, with much fervor, "*Ripped* apart."

"Torn open," I said calmly. "Anyway, my client doesn't deny knowing her. In fact, he was in a business deal with her."

"Lee," Holly said, "he wiped the doorknob and the switch plate of the light near the front door. But he left prints all *over* the house! On the thermostat in the living room! On the toilet flusher in the bathroom off her bedroom!"

"That just puts him there on a day between 1890 and the present."

Holly flashed me a nauseatingly perky smile, as if to say: Aren't you cute! But then she added: "You're forgetting his

29

prints on the Scotch tape. She picked up those envelopes Friday."

"So maybe he was waiting in a car right outside the bank. She handed him the envelope and . . ." Holly's smile turned into that amused prosecutorial smirk that says: Do you really think a jury is going to believe *that*?

"Anything else?" I asked, not allowing myself to show that I would dearly love to wipe that smirk off her face. "Because if this is your case, it's spectacularly unimpressive."

Holly patted her inflated coiffeur. "How about an eyewitness who puts your client at the scene right around the time of the murder?"

I could practice criminal law for the next hundred years and a remark like that would still get me—*whomp!*—right in the gut. But over the years, I'd learned to keep my gut to myself. "Define 'around the time of the murder' for me," I suggested.

Holly leafed through the file, looking for an answer. Sam, I was sure, had the autopsy report memorized. He indicated as much by stopping his cha-cha and leaning forward in his seat. Holly actually glanced up at him, but did not give him permission to speak. Sam and I waited. Finally she announced: "The M.E. says the murder took place between six P.M. Friday and eight A.M. Saturday."

"And your eagle-eyed witness says what?" I asked.

"The witness saw the accused at approximately six-thirty P.M."

I gave her what the man in my life refers to as my Barbara Stanwyck Knowing Smile. "Last *Friday*? Your witness is positive of that?" This is about a third of what I do for a living: smile knowingly as if there is nothing else to do but be amused at the extent of human folly, so the smilee will think: Maybe my case isn't as good as I thought.

"Last Friday," Holly maintained, her eyes bright, her own smile spirited, as if to say, Gee, this litigation stuff is *fun*! For someone with the last name of Nuñez, no matter how assimilated, you'd think she'd have retained a little Spanish *dolor*. But she displayed as much tragic sense of life as a drum majorette.

30

"And where did the eyewitness see my client?"

"In the company of the deceased—at her house."

Oy. "Was the decedent already deceased at that point in time?" I inquired politely.

At this juncture, almost any other new assistant in the Homicide Bureau would have peered over at the cop in charge of the case, or at least hesitated. Not Holly. "No. She and the accused were seen walking together on the street, then going up into the deceased's house." She paused. "Hand in hand."

"First of all, assuming your witness saw Bobette Frisch with a man who is indeed my client—an assumption I, for one, am not about to make. Does that sound like a tête-à-tête that's going to end up in murder—or dinner? I vote for dinner. Second of all—"

"It was your client. His car was parked in the driveway of Bobette Frisch's house. The witness is her tenant. Ms. Frisch rented out a room, bath, and kitchenette in the basement. Torkelson's car was blocking the tenant's, and he'd rung the upstairs bell. Ms. Frisch was out, so the tenant waited by the driveway, pacing, having a fit. He couldn't get his car out and he works nights, something with computers over at Snapple in Valley Stream. He said this was the second time Torkelson—"

"Or someone else," I interrupted.

"Or someone else six foot five with a little beaky nose and blue eyes," Sam burst out. Holly licked her index finger and began lifting off bits of lint from her desk blotter. A meaningless gesture, yet Sam immediately understood he should not have spoken up. "'scuse me, Holly," he said, much too fast. Was his voice actually tremulous? At best, it was an octave higher than usual. How the hell did she do that? Twenty-eight, twenty-nine years old, and she was able to make Sam Franklin squeak like a rookie.

"You know," I said, hating to interrupt such rich psychological interplay, "about the tall guy your witness saw: You see someone tall one time, and the next time someone large looms over you, you don't bother looking up. You assume it's the same tall man. But it could have been *anyone* tall."

"It was Norman Torkelson," said Holly, cutting me off. "Our witness not only saw them together but called the local precinct and reported Torkelson's car—and the license plate." She didn't even give me a second to comfort myself by thinking: Norman is far too gifted a con man to ever drive a car registered in his name. "It was listed under Robert McNulty, at 54 Homewood Avenue. Apartment 3-C," she reported. "In Mineola." I couldn't believe it! What a jerk! "We sent a couple of guys over there Sunday," she went on, "and there was your client, Norman Torkelson, a.k.a. Robert McNulty, a.k.a . . ." She opened the file folder again. I really didn't want to hear the upcoming recitation, but I had no choice. ". . . Henry Reuther, a.k.a. Philip Nugent, a.k.a. William Brightman, a.k.a.—"

"Holly, I'm not telling you he's never used an alias or been arrested or convicted of fraud. I'm only saying he is not a killer. If it was Norman at Bobette's, he wouldn't leave her dead. He'd leave her with a smile on her face and a song in her heart. I'm only saying—"

"*I'm* only saying he can plead to second-degree homicide and I'll recommend twenty-five years."

"You know I can't accept that, Holly," I said, moving forward in my seat as if ready to stomp out of her office, which of course I had no intention of doing. I'd spend another twenty minutes dickering and come out with twenty.

Except Holly stared at her watch and an expression of horror passed over her face. She rose. "Take it or leave it," she said, real fast. Then she added: "Sorry, but I have an urgent appointment and I'm fifteen minutes late." She stood and quickly fluttered all ten fingers at me. "New acrylics," she explained. "Do I have to explain? You *know* how long they take. I mean, forever."

"*Acrylics*?" my partner, Chuckie Phalen, demanded. I'd wandered downstairs and into the courtroom where he was trying his arson case and waiting until the judge—who truly believed the governor was, any second, going to nominate him to run for an opening on the Court of Appeals as a reward for having gone to Harvard Law School—declared a recess. As these recesses happened on the average of every fifteen minutes so the judge could call Albany and demand "Any news yet?" I hadn't had to wait long.

"What the hell are acrylics?" Chuckie demanded.

"Fake nails."

Chuckie Phalen, at sixty-eight years old, was one of those second-generation Irish-American males who prefer a night out with the boys to any other human endeavor, so I elaborated: "Artificial fingernails. So she can have long nails that don't break."

"If a guy A.D.A. pulled something like that . . ."

Already I regretted complaining to Chuckie because by nightfall, the quarter of the Nassau County criminal defense bar that hung out at TJ's Taproom would be snickering over "acrylics" and, to an Old Boy, would recount the story for the ten or twenty years whenever someone brought up the notion that a female performing some role in the courtroom beyond stenography might not be a bad idea. That I and a couple of other women attorneys were somehow absolved of the taint of frivolity in the first degree didn't make me feel any better. It just meant that for some reason, the boys at TJ's had declared us members of some neutral, nonthreatening gender that had nothing to do with other girl lawyers.

Chuckie pushed back his chair from the defense table and stretched out his short legs. Even that minor exertion caused him to breathe hard, and with each breath, I could hear the faint whistle of the emphysema that was killing him. And perched on the edge of the table, I could smell the bitter odor of cigarettes that clung to his dark-gray suit; it commingled with the harsher stench of the cigars he and his pals lit up five nights a week at TJ's.

"I hope Holly Nuñez will be a little more flexible," I mused. "I'd hate to have to go to trial with this guy."

"He's guilty," Chuckie said, not even bothering to put a question mark at the end of his question.

"If he's not, then there's a guy with his size-giant fingers who made some nasty marks on one Bobette Frisch's neck. Oh, and that same guy seems to have left his prints everywhere in her house, including on the Scotch tape that was tying together all the bank envelopes with the forty-eight thousand bucks she'd withdrawn earlier that day." I glanced down. A run had formed near the toe of my black panty hose and was working its way past my shoe, over my instep, so I could add to the pleasure of my day by having to run into Bloomingdale's and buy five more pairs, one of which I'd leave in my glove compartment, one in my attaché case, and three in my office, and yet the next time I had a run, as if by witchcraft, the panty hose would have vanished and once again I'd be back at the Bloomingdale's hosiery counter, where I know the saleslady by name: Dorothy. "If I could put Norman on the stand, he could probably con a jury into thinking he won the Nobel Prize for goodness. But he has a record."

"A long one," Chuckie wheezed, knowing without being told.

"The longest. And he was pulling the marriage con."

"Aw, no." Chuckie shook his small head with great sadness. I tried to imagine Chuckie sitting beside Norman at a defense table. He was short, and slight to the point of being tiny. If there were a class play for sixty-eight-year-olds, Chuckie Phalen would be cast as a leprechaun. "You can't put a fella like that on the stand." He glanced up at me. His eyes were eclipsed by cataracts. "Did he actually marry them?"

"No. Just proposed, as far as I can tell. I haven't read the whole printout, because there aren't enough hours in a day. But he tells them he came from an upper-class family, went to Yale, the family lost its money, but he made it back in 'investments.' Except then his wife took him to the cleaners, got custody of his kids, and now he's down on his luck. Your heart would break from reading some of the witness reports."

"*My* heart? In Phalen and White, Attorneys-at-Law," he said, just as the bailiff shuffled back into the courtroom, "there's only one heart capable of breakage. It ain't mine, Lee."

And on the subject of hearts, the next morning in the visitors' center, I watched Norman Torkelson react to the news about an eyewitness who not only could place him at the crime scene at an hour when the homicide, according to the medical examiner, might have occurred, but also called the local precinct to complain about his car, thereby giving the cops a record of his license plate number. He pressed his hand against his chest. "But the car wasn't registered in my name!" he declared.

"It was registered to Robert McNulty, the same name you used for your apartment."

"It couldn't have been!" he replied, angry that I would accuse him of such rank amateurism. "I sent Mary over to Motor Vehicles with ID for . . ." He thought for a minute. "Daniel Stevenson. I distinctly remember that. I told her, 'Take the Dan ID and—'"

"Maybe she just grabbed the wrong papers."

Norman's face flushed red, then deepened to a fierce purple. Just as I was about to leap up and call a guard over—Hey! Get this guy to the infirmary, fast!—he regained his composure. The dark cast receded, the hands relaxed as he crossed his arms over his chest. "It's not that she's unintelligent," he said quietly. "People think that, but they're wrong. It's just . . . Mary's an innocent. She doesn't get it." He shrugged. "I guess that's why . . ." His face colored. Pink this time. "I love her," he said softly. "You should see her. Then you'd understand . . ."

"And Bobette?" I asked.

"Business," he said crisply. "Nothing going on there. Strictly dollars and cents."

"You know, I've seen your record, read some of the complaints against you. You might want to consider being more direct with me. I need all the help I can get, and the D.A.'s Office is not in a generous mood when it comes to . . ." I paused for effect. Hokey, but I knew it would work. ". . . homicide."

"How can I impress upon you that this was strictly a business deal? We didn't have sexual relations."

Of course, the problem with most professional criminals is that you never know if they're lying. The smarter ones, however, tend to be straight when it is in their best interests to tell the truth. With con men, this generalization does not always apply. The pleasure of the lie might be headier than the joy of freedom. "If you did have sex," I said, "there may be evidence of it. A person can wipe door handles clean and still leave fingerprints. And he can leave body fluids, if not semen then saliva, or a hair or two with roots on them and—"

"No sex," Norman said. His tone was harsh, as if he were a teacher and I an incorrigible, the worst student. "No sex!" He waved the guard over to take him back to his cell. "No sex!"

Four

S-E-X.

It is as good a way as any to return to the marriage of Lee's parents. So let's spell it out. The first letter, S: for svelte. Before Lee's birth, Sylvia had a model's figure—that is, she had a large, finely shaped head that sat atop a long neck, which arose from a body that had as many curves as the average flagpole. Besides being thin, Sylvia was one of those born-chic people who can put on the plainest white shirt, fold back the cuffs, lift the collar, and—voilà—look as though she'd been done by Monsieur Dior. But in the weeks postpartum, it became clear that her outline had softened. Her chemistry had changed, her cell walls losing a bit of their resilience, and even though she'd gained only ten pounds, her pre-pregnancy waist had thickened. Her hips became almost curvy. Not just that: Her bosom swelled from what her mother-in-law, Bella, referred to as "a coupla fried eggs" to two noticeable bumps beneath her cashmere sweater set. Note the cashmere.

Tudor Rose Furs was a gold mine. By the late forties and early fifties, soldiers and sailors, back in civilian jobs, were celebrating the peace and reveling in a booming economy. They wanted to make up for lost time. How better to show the stuff they were made of than to buy a fur coat for the little woman? (Or a fur boa for the little woman's competition?) By 1951, Leonard and Sylvia were able to buy their first house, a luxury, luxury ranch, as the real estate agent solemnly described it.

Just over four miles north and ten miles east of Forest Hills, their house might have inhabited another galaxy. For the son of a Commie and the daughter of a not-dishonest judge, Great Neck was so profoundly luxurious that the Whites kept saying to each other: "I want to pinch myself." Their house, the agent assured them, had all the latest features. Not all: But on its over-half-an-acre plot, it did have a stone fireplace that opened onto both the living room and the den, a finished basement, with built-in cedar storage bins that doubled as seating, and, behind louvered doors right off the kitchen, a laundry center.

"I want to pinch myself," Sylvia admitted to Leonard as she ran her hand over the chilly white porcelain of the dryer. Leonard's hand cupped her buttock and gave it a fast pinch. The male in him loved the feel of her newer, rounder, more ample ass, even as the snob yearned for the prepregnant Sylvia, whose hollow cheeks and fleshless flanks announced: No sloppy lower-middle-class excess here. He couldn't get over his disappointment that she had let herself lose that sucked-in-cheek, snooty look he'd prized. She still looked like Lauren Bacall's twin sister, but a twin who couldn't lay off the halvah.

And another thing. Once they got past the thrill of home owner-ship and finished with the business of the marriage—should the master bathroom have gray or peach tiles? could they afford to go to France on vacation? and if so, should they leave Lily with his parents or her parents?—he had nothing to say to Sylvia. Nor did she seem to think she owed him any talk. He could understand her lack of conversational ability because he was aware of her background: Nobody said anything at the Bernsteins' for fear of disturbing the Judge. But he could not forget that article he'd seen in *Collier's* written by a Ph.D. psychologist. "Are You Married to Your Best Friend?" That title was a slap in the face.

Would a best friend just shrug—she'd shrugged!—when he'd taken her out to a French restaurant and ordered wine and con-fided his dream of opening a store in Manhattan, on the Upper East Side, away from the fur district, and have it so elegant that only the most silk-stocking types would feel comfortable going in? Of course, once they were customers, *everyone* would want to go. Although the rude-crude types would be told they had to make an appointment. Not that he didn't want their business. Frankly, they bought at least double what tightwad rich Christians did, but—see, Sylvia?—he wanted them to feel they were tres-passing. They would have more respect for the store that way. Not store. Salon. And wait till those Christian ladies walked in the front door! They would love it, with skinny Frenchmen for salesmen who would say "May I help you?" in French. He'd even looked it up in the Forest Hills branch of the Queens Borough Public Library: "*Puis-je vous aider?*," although he didn't dare to try to say it himself, being smart enough to realize the first word was probably not pronounced "Poo is-gee." But of course Leonard would insist the salesmen switch to English if he saw the customer getting scared. Fear was bad, he explained. Intimidation, on the other hand, was good, because then the customer and her husband would order an even better garment, just to prove they could afford to buy in such classy surroundings.

So he'd poured all this out to his wife for almost an hour and a half, and she'd *shrugged*. "Is that all you can say?" he'd demanded. Finally, she'd said, "I think it sounds wonderful," but he could tell she didn't. She was probably scared. Selling a booming business in Queens and opening up cold in Manhattan. Such a risk. Didn't she realize he woke up at four in the morning with his intestines tied in knots? Such a huge outlay, what with inventory and a showroom with parquet floors and those antique French chairs with arms that cost about two hundred dollars each.

Still, the way her skirt fit over her backside, like the skin on a knockwurst . . .

"I said pinch *myself*," Sylvia laughed, wriggling out of his grasp, moving into the kitchen to deal with the bags of groceries that filled the room. Stock up, Leonard had commanded her the day before, their first full day as home owners. She had left the baby with her mother, who was helping out till they got settled, and had gone on a shopping spree that had left the assistant manager of the A & P with his jaw hanging open—although he *had* been able to say: Can I have one of the boys put your bags in your car, Mrs. . . . And she'd filled in his blank. White, she'd said. To be perfectly honest, it had been humiliating, going from Weissberg to Weiss to White, but now that they were in a new community, starting out fresh as White, knowing he wouldn't change it again (despite a few days' flirtation with "Whyte"), she was glad Leonard had insisted. Anyway, the A & P assistant manager—he was very broad-shouldered, probably from lifting all those cartons of canned peaches—he said . . .

"How much did you spend?" Leonard inquired.

39

"What you gave me," Sylvia responded, a little edgy because she *had* gone overboard, sweeping roll upon roll of paper towels into her cart, stocking up on Chicken of the Sea chunk white like the tuna was pheasant under glass or something. And she had pulled jar after jar of preserves off the shelf, until she had strawberry, black-currant, cherry, raspberry, gooseberry, plum, apple butter, and orange marmalade.

But to his credit, Leonard wasn't cheap. Nothing but the best. Well, not *the* best, because the best kind of a house was an English Tudor or something called a Georgian, he'd told her. Except then your furniture had to be antiques or at least come from B. Altman, so it was better to have a modern house. Then it could be spare. Spare. That was his new favorite word; it superseded "classic," which came after "luxuriant," which supplanted "discriminating." He always had some snotty new word. To be honest, he had some nerve acting so snotty, what with Lard Lady, his mother, and his old man, Nathan the Red. "Spare." Well, her clothes were spare, but then, she'd always had terrific taste. It was part of her artistic talent. Like, with her Hardy Amies green wool suit: a green felt hat trimmed with green feathers, but black suede pumps. She didn't want to believe it when the salesgirl had suggested green alligator. No! She knew when enough was enough. Black suede gloves, large gold button earrings, and *that was it.* No bracelet, no necklace, no scarf. Spare.

She loved buying. The dark jewel colors of the jams in the A & P. The sleek Danish-modern coffee table with those skinny blond legs that made it look as though it was tiptoeing over the cocoa-colored carpet. And on top of the table, casual, as if someone had just stopped reading them, not in a neat pile, the half-price artbooks she'd found in a store down the block from the obstetrician's: how the dark red on the Utrillo's cover echoed the scarlets and carmines on the Rembrandt's. She wasn't like some women, buy-buy-buy out of boredom. She loved what she bought, took pleasure in an object every time she saw it in her home. Okay, not a box of Lipton's tea bags. But like that petticoat she'd bought in 1949, in a lilac so pale it was almost gray; it had narrow ribbon shoulder straps and scalloped ribbon trim along the hemline. Every time she opened her lingerie drawer, she'd feel good, just seeing it—and the yellow nightgown with the quilted bed jacket too.

40

She thought about her things a lot, and about things she saw when she went to the city, things she couldn't afford but remembered as if they belonged to her. She never forgot something once it caught her eye. Like in an antique store window on East Fifty-eighth, a silver tea set with the most delicate leafy pattern etched into it. The lid of the pot and the sugar bowl cover were topped with roses made out of silver. Incredible work. The last time she passed it, the store owner had waved to her from inside the store. Like I know just how you feel. Wait: more than that. I know you'll be back. He was very good-looking, with white hair and a white mustache, wearing a dark-gray suit that was almost black. Very slim. Neat. Like a well-packed cigarette.

Leonard was clean. There was no man on earth cleaner. He used four Q-Tips every morning on his ears. But he wasn't . . . what was that word he'd liked but not loved? Fastidious. He'd used that for a week or two. But he wasn't fastidious, because he wasn't in complete control over himself, not like the man in the antique store, with his hankie sticking out of his pocket in six perfect points. Nervous, Leonard would run his hand through his hair, and by late afternoon the Brylcreemed ends would no longer lie flat, but would coil like tiny springs at the back of his neck. Or he'd dribble something on his tie, a tiny drop of something, but then a poppy seed would stick to it. And in terms of looks: He wasn't dapper, but he wasn't a man's man either, like the assistant manager at the A & P, with black hair peeking out from under his white undershirt, making little twirlies right below his neck. Or her still-life teacher, Jeffrey, at the Great Neck Center for the Fine Arts, with his black eyes and tight blue jeans. Leonard was just okay-looking. Dark-brown hair, brown eyes. Okay. Skin? Not like he had pockmarks, but you could see pores on his cheeks. Five-feet eight-and-a-half, even though it said five-ten on his driver's license, so not quite tall enough. Not getting fat, but in the last year, in his new, slim English jacket, it looked like he was wearing a fox boa under it instead of a belt.

Let us leave Leonard's love handles and Sylvia's mind and return to S-E-X once again. The E. If the vertical stroke is the institution of marriage, and the two Whites are the horizontal lines on either end, then clearly there is something between them. Remember, this was now 1951. They were neither sophisticates nor libertines,

41

so it was nothing kinky. They seemed like a happy couple. They said "I love you" to each other every night just before they went off to sleep. They had sexual intercourse three times a week. At this point in their lives, the mere thought of taking a lover had never crossed either of their minds, so whatever was between them was certainly not another man or another woman.

They had more disposable income than Great Neck neighbors twice their age. True, Leonard's big plans might put them in the poorhouse, but as the Bankers Trust Company was willing to underwrite his grandiose fantasies of a showroom with Louis XV bergères on Lexington Avenue and East Sixty-fifth Street, its sales force taught from birth to inquire *"Puis-je vous aider?,"* it was not money that had come between them.

Could it have been that having a child had caused some rift? Highly dubious. If not a great child, our heroine was certainly an awfully nice one. In the late spring of 1951, Lily Rose White, thirteen months old, had three teeth and a sweet smile. Well, sweet when it came to friendly people, a smile in response to a smile: up on the right side, a quiver on the left—before spreading across her face and lighting up her big brown eyes. Definitely not one of those Aren't-I-fabulous smiles the born-confident flash. But engaging enough.

And she got better in the ensuing months. Some ordinary children are, for a short period, overcome by a monomania that lights them up like a holy spirit. Who knows why an ordinary little boy becomes incandescent at the sight of a garbage truck? Or how a plain little girl transcends her commonality and becomes a toddler goddess at the sight of an animal? For Lily Rose White, a blue jay evoked delight, a cat rapture, and a dog ... bliss beyond all understanding. Sylvia learned that the fastest way to obtain her daughter's cooperation was to threaten to withhold either the blouse with a Scottish terrier appliquéd on the collar or a cup decorated with an owl and pussycat. Leonard was the more positive parent. He discovered that to take this nice enough (but after ten minutes of peekaboo rather boring) female child to the Bronx Zoo was to turn her into the Best Kid in the World. Show her a tapir and she'd howl with jubilation, a giraffe and she'd fall into silent awe.

So it was not the child who came between Mr. and Mrs. Leonard

White. What was happening that while allowing them to say "I love you" to each other once every twenty-four hours did not allow them to *feel* love? It is easy to tick off items on a list: Narcissism. Lack of trust. Self-loathing, the belief that anyone worth loving could not love them. Emotional immaturity. But the truth is, some questions have no answer. Suffice it to say that although Mr. and Mrs. White looked as if they had it all, they did not. They were wanting.

Having avoided that issue, let us not avoid concluding S-E-X. Note how the two lines of the X intersect at only one point. Well, two years after their move to Great Neck, Sylvia and Leonard came together. She was two months pregnant with their second child. (A son, Leonard prayed to no one in particular. John Bradley White? Radley Wilson White? Did he dare Dalton Kendall White III?) Having successfully lost the ten pounds she had gained with Lee and not yet put it back on, as she would inevitably and irrevocably do, Sylvia had regained some of that high-cheeked, honey-haired elegance one would anticipate from the wife of a polo player, assuming one knew polo players. On those nights when she would stop by the salon to wait for him before they went out for dinner with other furrier couples or to the Museum of Modern Art, where she had made him—he was grateful—become a Donor so they got invitations to all the openings, Leonard could see his customers' heads turn: Who *is* that woman in the Lanvin evening suit, its jacket lined with leopard-print silk, a leopard coat slung casually over her arm? Sylvia was at her peak.

As was Leonard. He was now the proprietor of Le Fourreur, a Manhattan fur salon so exclusive that it was rumored that Mrs. John Foster Dulles was told in no uncertain terms that she'd have to wait two months if she wanted a full-length tawny brown ranch mink. *That* was how great the demand was for exclusive designs by Jean-Louis, Leonard's couturier. The rumor about Mrs. Dulles was not true. It had been made up and spread by Leonard, who also invented "Jean-Louis" for his designer, who until then had been Bobby Anello, hitherto of Westchester Fancy Furs.

Rumor was only one of Leonard's many marketing strategies. He called the twenty percent break he routinely offered all his good customers a "fashion industry deep discount" when he phoned the editors of *Vogue, Harper's Bazaar*, the *New York Times*, and the *Herald Tribune* to tell them about it. When they dropped by Le Fourreur, he charmed them by serving tea in Haviland cups and by throwing in a black or silver fox stole with whatever garment they bought and paid for as a way of saying Thank you for your patronage. After a spectacular December 1952 season, the Whites were no longer comfortable. They were well-to-do.

Sylvia had charge accounts at Saks Fifth Avenue, Tailored Woman, and Henri Bendel. Leonard went from ready-made English suits off the rack at Moe Ginsburg's to perusing a book of swatches in a suite in the Plaza that M. Thierry Boucault, the noted Parisian haberdasher, occupied on his semiannual trips to New York. They hired a live-in maid. They bought a suite of signed Picasso lithographs for the living room. They donated money to the United Way and the Boy Scouts. They bought a Christmas tree. (However, Leonard could not figure out how to get it to stand up on its own. He forbade Sylvia to ask the maid how to do it, so the tree lay dying on the living room floor until the second of January. They waited until the following year for their first real Christmas: Leonard spent a half hour on an early December Saturday at Colonial Nursery and Garden Supplies, pretending to survey their inventory of snow shovels but actually checking out their Christmas tree. Its secret was finally revealed: underneath a ladylike green velveteen skirt lay a clunky metal brace. To decorate their tree, Sylvia spent an entire day at Bergdorf Goodman—without even stopping for lunch—choosing ornaments: blown-glass orbs within orbs, a galaxy of silver stars.) And they sold their house two weeks before the raspberry bushes Sylvia had planted in the fertile soil of Great Neck bore their first fruit. Once again, the Whites moved eastward and upward.

Getting back to the X for a moment. Sylvia had some bad times right after her first child's birth. There she was, drained, pulled at by episiotomy stitches and dragged down by the blues, and Leonard had sauntered into her hospital room with a huge bouquet of white roses and an I-don't-care-that-it's-not-a-boy grin, and she'd thought: Who is this man? Of course, she knew he was her husband, and the father of her baby, but he had looked so strange. Those big lips, the insides displaying themselves, pink and wet, like some insect-eating tropical flower. He'd come over and sat on the edge of the bed, taking her hand in his. She tried to gaze into his eyes, but those giant lips filled her range of vision and they moved, inexorably, toward her, puckering slightly for a kiss. She wanted to shriek the way that woman did in—what was that horror picture?—*I Walked with a Zombie*. Grotesque! Abominable! Please, please don't get any closer! Don't . . .

Well, he'd kissed her and she lived through it. In the next couple of years, however, those horrible moments recurred, and a couple of times the lips seemed to puff up right before her eyes. How could his customers think he was so attractive, the Christian ones with husbands whose lips were never any wider than zippers?

But things had gotten better. And better. They'd had a good anniversary the past June. Leonard had taken her to the best restaurant in the city, Le Pavillon, where he'd shaken the hand of the man in the front, except she realized he was giving a bribe or a tip or whatever. The man had glanced into his hand and gotten very charming and offered them a nice table. Leonard ordered champagne and then let the wine waiter pick out their wines, and by the end of the evening, Sylvia slipped her foot out of her black peau de soie Chanel sling-back and was using it to rub the inside of Leonard's thigh. And that September, he told her to meet him in the store—salon—right after closing. He asked her to try on the Russian sable Mrs. General Motors had ordered. But then he said: "This is too good for Mrs. General Motors. Why don't you keep it?" When she finally comprehended what he was talking about, she almost fainted from joy, and the salesmen, who were still there and Dolly, the model/bookkeeper, who'd peeked out from the office, had applauded.

Thus the intersecting of the X. Sylvia finally understood what his customers saw in her husband. While no one would call Leonard conventionally handsome, with his made-to-order suits and beautifully cut hair he could look ultra smart—in an Italian kind of way, but upperclass Italian, from Italy. She remembered how once she'd loathed his lips, but now realized that if you looked at him as a whole, he was very appealing. Now and then, even stunning.

And Leonard's heart softened too. He realized that while his wife's diction all but shouted "Born in Brooklyn! Bred in Queens!"

throughout her childhood she'd been forced to whisper instead of talk. So who heard the accent? To look at her, she could be an English horsewoman.

But after the legs of the X cross, they again part. So it was with Mr. and Mrs. White. In her third month of pregnancy with her second daughter (who would be named Robin Renée), Sylvia came down with terrible morning sickness. Then it became all-day sickness. Leonard worried about how thin she was getting, how bad it was for the baby because sometimes Sylvia's entire dinner would be a single Ritz cracker. Her face became spotty and her hair lost its shine, but when he got home, he would take her in his arms and say something reassuring, like: "It won't last forever."

But instead of being comforted, she got all weepy and clung to him. Sitting beside him in the movies over the weekend, hugging his arm, stuffing it in the divide between her two swollen breasts. Butting her pillow against his at night, so he could feel her hot breath on the back of his neck. And it wasn't just physical clinging. She called him first thing in the morning: How was the ride in on the Long Island Rail Road? Late morning: Who are you having lunch with? Early afternoon: What did you have for lunch? Was it good? Did you have dessert? Late afternoon: How's it going? Any good customers stop in? Early evening: What train are you taking home? She's pregnant, he told himself. And she loves me.

But that made him realize that she had never before displayed this interest, this passion for him. Did the hormone changes in her make her feel more free? Well, she hadn't been so free when she was pregnant with Lee. In fact, sometimes he knew Sylvia was pretending to get excited, and she was a lousy pretender. Oooo. Oooo. Always Oooo, repeated two times. But now she had a repertoire of noises, and they were for real. She'd become crazy for him. Now that he was well-to-do.

Now she always was ready for him. Not just ready: If he didn't come to her, she'd come to him. Now, no matter what she wore, her nipples always stuck out. He could feel them when she clung to him. Well, he thought, trying hard to be fair, I'm a big shot now. That's very attractive to women. But a voice called up from his subconscious: Hey, Len. Is that the real thing, when the girl has to see sable before she falls in love?

A couple of months after she fell for her husband, Sylvia

46

dropped by the salon on her way to Tailored Woman, to use the bathroom. Leonard introduced her to Mrs. Wriston Brandt, wife of *the* senior partner in *the* biggest Wall Street law firm, a man once referred to as "Mr. Trusts and Estates" by the *Wall Street Journal.* Instead of saying "How do you do," or, if that was too stuffy, "Hello," Sylvia had said "Hi." But the way she said it, all nasally, with that New York intonation. It came out "Hoy." To his credit, Leonard admitted to himself that he was a terrible snob—and that the only decent pedigree in the entire White household belonged to their new collie, Duchess. But still . . . "Hoy."

Mere weeks after the Mrs. Wriston Brandt incident, Leonard was going over accounts payable with Dolly Young (who had come to New York from Bristol, Massachusetts, to be a Conover model but who failed, not for want of oblique facial planes but for lack of length, being only five feet four). The key point here is that in her entire life, Dolly never said "Hi." Always "Hello." She also said "think yew" for "thank you." In both instances, her speech patterns had to do with regional usage rather than social class. As she and Leonard were looking over the Pincus Notions and Trimmings invoice, Dolly said, "They rob us blind and they don't even say think yew," impulsively, Leonard kissed her.

Thus began an affair that lasted for decades.

Five

If I'm right in believing that I'm typical of most American women, then there's got to be millions of bottles of used-but-once hair conditioner abandoned on the floors of showers and the ledges of bathtubs from Maine to Hawaii. Makeup kits must hold so many unfinished mascara wands that each house in the United States could supply a company of Rockettes. And as for the national glut of rejected moisturizers: Better forgotten in medicine cabinets than tossed onto the country's landfills where they could trigger an ecological calamity.

Is this another tirade about how the beauty industry exploits the low self-esteem of American women? Nope, just the opposite. All those social critics: they don't know their ass from a hole in the ground. They carry on about the insecurities of American women and completely ignore the extravagant self-confidence we display. Critics! Listen to the female ego. It's not saying: I loathe myself. No, it's telling you: I am a mere taupe eye shadow away from gorgeousness. Each of us has a breathtaking creature locked inside. And all we need to break through to infinite desirability is a new brand of thigh cream.

Take me, for instance. You'd think, having lived forty-five years, I'd have picked up on God's message: "Lee White, Esq., is not going to be a sex goddess in her lifetime." But no, I don't hear it. Nor do the rest of my sister Americans. Because nothing except death can kill that ravishing dame who walks in beauty inside us. If a normal adult female's just-before-sleep dream is a sweeter, more graceful, poreless version of herself, then what woman does the one-in-a-million true beauty fantasize about? A flatulent, bezitted battle-ax? Right now, you may be tempted to tap me on the shoulder and ask: Hey, what does all this have to do with the Torkelson case? So I'll tell you: All this is a prelude to Mary Dean walking into my office.

It didn't hit me right away that she was the most beautiful creature I'd ever seen in my life. No, keeping pace with my secretary, Sandi, who was ushering her in, she was just a tall young woman, twenty-two or so, with a ton of makeup on, wearing . . . The man in my life once told me there was no one in the world more mean-spirited than a New York clothes snob. So I censored my nasty thoughts about her kelly-green suit with forest-green velveteen lapels. I stood to greet her. "Have a seat, Ms. Dean."

"Thanks," she said, speaking with nervous quickness. Instead of realizing that my right hand was extended in order to shake hers, she thrust a tightly stuffed envelope into it.

"Oh," I said, taken aback by her nervousness. I'd assumed Norman would have himself a cooler cookie. The envelope, no doubt, contained my retainer: fifteen thousand dollars. Cash, and from the heft of it, probably hundreds. A not unusual method of payment, since many of my clients weren't interested in check writing—not if the check was going to diminish their own assets. They liked paying by check only if the assets belonged to somebody else. (Soon after we became partners, Chuckie Phalen told me a precautionary tale: One year out of law school, he'd taken a check from some client. When he went to cash it—after the jury had come back with an acquittal—he happened to glance at the name across the top, the person whose account it was: Charles Michael Phalen, Counselor-at-Law.)

As Mary was still standing, I motioned for her to sit. Then I handed over the envelope to Sandi, who left my office to return to her desk, where she would open it and make sure the retainer was inside—not just a wad of cutup newspaper. You'd think I'd have hated practicing law this way, dealing with such overt sleazeballs. But every time I worked on a nice, clean white-collar criminal matter—sales tax evasion, co-op conversion fraud—a giant yawn arose inside me that the biggest corporate check couldn't stifle.

Mary, still jittery, hadn't taken a seat. She clutched her purse tight against her chest in a pathetically defensive posture, her shoulders and head thrust forward. She stared out the window. It was one of those nasty days in early May, more appropriate to March, rainy, gray, with a low, chill wind that blew down the street and bit at your ankles. I spoke so sweetly I practically cooed: "Please sit down."

"Jeez," she said, alighting on the edge of an armchair in front of my desk. "Sorry. I didn't mean to take up so much of your time." The backs of her hands were red. Her nails were chewed down so low they sliced into the flesh of her fingers. Then she babbled, a long, agitated apology about how the police had impounded Norman's car and how the taxi she'd called hadn't come and how just when she thought she was okay, she discovered the bus she was on was headed to Long Beach. Normally, I would have cut her off as courteously as possible, but suddenly I found myself transfixed by Mary's looks.

First of all, I realized her face was a flawless oval. True, the heavy makeup she was wearing was unflattering, chalky, especially against the peachy glow of her neck. Her cheeks were as bright as geraniums. The lipstick she wore, a neon orange, was applied so thickly that when she formed words beginning with b or p it looked as though her lips would meld. Still, I could see that the makeup was not meant to hide serious imperfections. Her skin appeared flawless.

Mary's too white face was framed by shiny black curls that spilled over her shoulders. The hairdo was neither the elegant three hundred dollar frenzy of a Manhattan cut nor the sculpted perfection of big Texas hair. To me, it looked like a homey attempt to copy the none-of-that-androgyny-shit-for-me style of a Dolly or a Wynonna. Unlike country music stars, however, Mary's hair was not tier upon tier of faultless curlicues. In the sodden weather, the tresses on her shoulders had lost their verve and lay limp, wormlike, on her green suit jacket.

Obviously, she'd chosen the suit color to play up her lumi-

50

nous eyes. Those eyes didn't need any help. On the contrary, the suit was green overkill. In truth, though, nothing could detract from those eyes, not even the opalescent pistachio shadow that covered her lids and orbital rims up to her brows, not the greasy black pencil liner.

Now, as to the rest of Mary Dean: Her nose would have been perfect except it had the tiniest indentation at the tip, as if she'd pressed on it throughout childhood, trying to get it to turn up. And her lips: full, but pretty, not those collagen-injected trout-mouths that had become so trendy. And just before she sat, I finally noticed the figure. High-breasted, tiny-waisted, long-legged. An ambulatory Barbie doll.

Except Mary was human. She was sweating and gave off an odor that was a combination of natural musk, wet wool and cheap perfume—gardenia? jasmine?—that I bet had the word "Jungle" as part of its name. I watched a drop of perspiration slide down her left temple, past her jaw to her chin. It would have dribbled onto her neck, only she wiped it away with the back of her hand. In doing so, she lost control of the black patent-leather envelope-purse she'd been hugging to her chest. It dropped to the floor. Bending to pick it up, she cracked her forehead against the edge of my desk. "Aaah!" she cried, a yelp of pain.

A shudder chattered my teeth and shivered my shoulders, that frisson that comes when you empathize too intensely. For that second, my forehead throbbed in the same spot where she'd hit her head. I buzzed Sandi, requesting a cup of ice, fast. I must have sounded a little desperate because Sandi rushed in with it seconds later. Already a huge red rectangle, like a ledge, was protruding from Mary's brow. I wrapped the ice in a few tissues and pressed it against the bump. Sandi stood by "How are you feeling?" I asked Mary after a minute.

"A little . . ." Her lovely eyes, floating upward, looked slightly dopey. Tiny black pearls of mascara dotted her lashes.

"You'll be fine in a minute," Sandi assured her, too briskly. Sandi's only other job had been with a malpractice firm. She

51

lived in constant terror of lawsuits. Over the years, I tried to reassure her: No one's going to sue me, but if they do, I can handle it. Nothing I could say could bring her peace. Besides the usual secretarial chores, she stood eternally vigilant, protecting the two oversophisticated rubes—me and Chuckie—from certain ruin at the hands of the shyster lawyers our scum-bucket clients would hire to sue us.

"I can manage now," I told Sandi, who clearly did not believe she should leave me alone with a con man's sweetie who had probably arranged her own subdural hematoma just so she could haul me into court and bring me to utter ruin. "I'm okay, Sandi. Thanks for the ice." Reluctantly, casting a knowing and hostile glance at Mary (whose eyes, fortunately, were still swimming in her head), Sandi left.

After a moment, Mary whispered: "Sorry."

I took off the ice. "Are you all right?"

"I'm fine." Except "fine" came out shakily, in two syllables.

"Are you nauseous?" I asked. "Does your head hurt?"

"No, really, I'm fine," Mary reassured me, offering me a lovely smile. "Just, you know, getting bonked like that. Wowie!" She laughed at her own clumsiness. An instant later, she burst into sobs.

"Does it hurt?" I asked.

"It's not . . . my head," she explained, taking a giant hiccup of air. "It's . . . Norman."

"It must be—" I was going to say something objective and mealy-mouthed, like "difficult," but instead I said: "—awful for you."

"He's in jail for *murder*. And it's all my fault." Her fault? I waited, putting on my Totally Neutral face, an expression of absolute indifference I've cultivated so as to do nothing to either encourage or discourage the person sitting across from me. It's important that I hear it all: the craziness, the bizarre confessions, the monstrous lies that pour forth from that armchair by my desk. Mary took a large, loud gulp of air and went on. "If I hadn't been premenstrual . . . I mean, I get food on the brain. All I was thinking about was stuffing myself. How I was going to stop at BK and shove in a

Double Whopper with cheese. And onion rings—they're so salty, I love 'em. I was thinking that I had to remember to buy those teeny Breath Asure things so Norman wouldn't know I'd been to BK, because he gets super PO'd when I eat junk food. And I was thinking about a vanilla shake too. Even french fries. I've never been a big potato person, so you can imagine how bad off I was. So when I left for Motor Vehicle I grabbed the Bob ID instead of the Dan ID. All the names he uses, I get mixed up, even though the last time he tested me I only got one wrong. If I'd've used Dan, they wouldn't have traced the car back to the apartment."

"They would have found him, though. His fingerprints were all over Bobette's place."

"But we could've gotten away once we knew the old lady was dead. The cops would've had to search every house on Long Island. They wouldn't have found us in time. Instead—" She started to cry again. "—they came and knocked on the door. And I opened it! I didn't even say 'Who's there?' If I'd've done that, Norm could've gotten out the back."

"When they're arresting someone on a murder charge, they usually have people staked out in back." But I didn't want to make her feel too comfortable. Since I couldn't get anything much from my client to help in my defense of him, I naturally decided to try Mary. She was feeling horribly guilty. Not for being an accessory before and after the fact to a crime—at best, fraud; at worst, homicide. No, she felt guilty for failing Norman.

"Take it easy," I said, and handed her a couple of tissues. (I keep a box in my top desk drawer so I can easily hand a bunch to a weepy client or, more commonly, a nonweepy, sociopathic client's hysterical family.) "Maybe we'll be able to do something for Norman."

"He told me it was hopeless, that the cops think he did it."

"They do. But that's why we have trial by jury. And that's why you've retained me. Maybe among all of us we can figure something out that will convince the jury that Norman is not guilty."

"He is *innocent,*" Mary corrected me, and blew her nose. A too ladylike puff, not the HONK! a good-sized, healthy young woman would naturally produce. "He didn't do it!"

"Then help me find something so I can prove it."

"He left that house *one second* after that witness saw him with Bobette, and he came right home to me and we were together from then on. *Every minute* until the cops came."

"What was his relationship with Bobette?" I asked.

She drew up into a prim position, feet and knees together, hands in lap. "He said not to talk about anything."

"Why not?"

"Because . . . you know." I could think of several reasons, the main one being that he did indeed kill Bobette and was worried Mary would unintentionally give it away. If I were Norman, I'd be worried too. I couldn't tell if Mary was simpleminded or merely so new at grown-up life that she hadn't learned to lie without chewing the inside of her cheek and turning red. "Norman said: 'No matter who, keep your lip zipped, and I mean zipped *all the way* up.'"

"Look, I've been a lawyer too long to expect him to break down and confess to me—"

"He didn't do it!"

"Fine. But if I'm going to help him prove that, I need all the information I can get, good or bad. I'd rather learn it from him than get a big surprise from the prosecutor." Then I added ominously: "She is one scary dame."

"Oh, God," Mary whimpered. She began to nibble her thumbnail. Instead of trying to allay her fear, I narrowed my eyes and flared my nostrils. Suddenly I became one scary dame too, which is what I wanted. I didn't relish going into court with Mary testifying to Norman's alibi. She'd turn to mush after thirty seconds on cross. Plus I sensed that Holly had one of those solid circumstantial cases that make defense lawyers like me pine for the good old days of being prosecutors—when the world was young and the facts were on our side. So I had to scare Mary into opening up. I also figured talking to her would be better than talking to Norman; with Mary, at least, I had a chance of hearing something resembling the truth. But she remained mum.

"Too bad you can't help him," I said, and pushed back my chair, as if I were about to stand to see her out. But she remained where she was, on the edge of her seat. She reached out and grabbed onto the desk, a huge old thing made from a farmhouse table. It looked as though she was trying to drag it toward her.

"If I talk to you," she asked me, "would you have to tell Norman?"

"Well . . ." I stalled. It was one of those questions only a chairman of a bar association ethics committee could love: Is an attorney's ethical obligation of full and complete disclosure of information to a client paramount? Or is counsel duty-bound to cork it if silence is what it costs to buy information that will save said client? "How about this, Mary? Unless it's a matter of life and death, I won't say a word to him. Okay?"

"Okay."

"Tell me about Norman and Bobette's relationship."

"Strictly business," she declared, with finality.

"Then how come she was found dead in a nightgown and negligee?"

"Maybe the murderer changed her clothes after he killed her!" she suggested, pleased with herself. For the first time, she allowed herself to wriggle back into the big armchair, lean back, and cross her legs. Her shoes were designed not for an unseasonably cold May morning but for a gala midsummer bash: Two narrow straps of gold just beyond her toes and another around her ankle were all that held them on. The heels were high gold daggers.

"The murderer didn't change her clothes," I said. "The autopsy would have indicated that Bobette had been moved postmortem. How come she was in her nightgown?" Mary chewed the inside of her cheek a little more, a buying-time mannerism I knew I would never grow to love. She could have said: Norman left before she changed out of her regular stuff. Or: She got into a sexy nightgown because her boyfriend—*the guy who killed her*—was coming over. I explained: "Norman was seen at her place at six-thirty in the evening. You said he left immediately after the man who

55

is the witness saw him. So say that was at six forty-five."
Mary inched forward. "From Merrick to your apartment
. . . Fifteen, twenty minutes? Sometime around seven—day-
light-saving time—so it was still light outside, this lifelong
spinster puts on a sexy negligee?"

"But he was with me the whole . . ." She sputtered to a
halt. She didn't know what to say. Even if I spent weeks
preparing her testimony, she'd be a lousy witness. Forget
street smarts: She lacked the confidence to utter a simple
declarative sentence and leave it alone. "I should say he was
with me the whole time, shouldn't I?"

"If that's the truth," I said. "But I'd like to keep you off
the stand. You seem to get a little nervous when you're under
the gun."

"You said it!" she agreed.

"So you can see why I need to know more about what was
going on. I need something I can use to trip up the D.A."

"Right."

"So let's talk about Norman and Bobette—honestly."

Mary uncrossed her legs, blinked her lashes and opened
her eyes wide. "Okay."

"You're telling me what went on between Norman and
Bobette was strictly a business deal. If I know that's nonsense, can you imagine what Holly Nuñez, the assistant D.A.,
knows? She's had a whole squad of homicide cops investigating Norman Torkelson. Now, was he conning Bobette
Frisch?" A little-girl shrug, head to the side. Her mannerisms
were overly cutesy for such a tall woman. For such a beauty.
Either she'd bloomed quite late in adolescence or her mother
had been petite and revoltingly winsome. "That's a yes, he
was conning her?"

"Uh . . . yes. But he wasn't having sex with her."

Right. "Really?"

"Really. I mean, he told me he *never* had sex with them,
even before he met me. He said lonely women . . ." She
wasn't so naive that she didn't know what Norman did
was reprehensible. But it didn't seem to appall her; at that
moment, she was just slightly unsure of how to present it.
"Lonely women . . ."

"Say it straight."

"Lonely women . . . I *can't* say it. I can't think of the word. It means 'can't get enough.'"

"Insatiable?"

"That's it!" she squealed. "Hey, you and Norman should play Scrabble!"

"'Lonely women are insatiable . . .'" I prompted her.

"So if you start having sex, they'll milk you dry. I mean, if he was doing them, do you think he'd have time for me?"

"So he never goes near them?" I asked.

"He *cuddles* them," she explained serenely, the way Norman must have explained it to her: I know this sounds incredible, Mary, my angel, but it is the truth, and (he'd offer her a sad little shrug here) that's what I'm stuck with. "He holds them and gives them back rubs. Sometimes he'll kiss them, but a cheek kiss or a forehead kiss. Not a kiss kiss."

The drizzle turned to downpour. Raindrops smacked against the windowpane and were driven down diagonal paths by a sharp wind. At the same moment, Mary and I peered down at her feet, naked except for the flimsy gold shoes. They were not just big feet, but spread out, like a hod carrier's—if the hod carrier had given himself a pedicure with coral polish.

"How did Norman meet Bobette?" I asked.

"The usual way."

"You agreed to help me help Norman, Ms. Dean."

"Mary."

"Mary, I want to know everything you know."

"Okay. But I forgot what you just asked me."

"Where did he and Bobette meet?"

"Right! Um, through the personals. In *Newsday*."

"His ad or hers?"

"Oh, his. We use the same ad in every city, except with a different beginning. Like, we used 'Heart of my Heart' in Louisville and 'True Love is Precious Gift' in Scranton."

"On Long Island?"

"'Looking for Love.' Norm says if any cops or private

detectives are tracking him, they're not going to read the whole ad, but . . . You know what his motto is?"

"What?"

"You can't be too careful!" She proclaimed it with pride, throwing back her shoulders, holding her head high, the way a titan of industry's wife would reveal the slogan for a multi-million dollar advertising campaign for her husband's corporation.

"What else did the ad say? The part that was always the same."

"'DWM'—that's divorced white man . . . Maybe the M is for male. Anyhow, 'DWM, thirty-five, handsome, tall Yale graduate, business executive, wants the real thing.'" Mary burst into a rich laugh. "Norman says: 'They don't know *my* real thing is their money.' Let's see . . . the real thing. Oh, 'You must enjoy Shakespeare's sonnets, beautiful music, travel, and long, romantic walks. Don't want dates. Want a relationship. Please respond with long letter and picture. Help me. I have a hole in my heart.'"

She waited expectantly, so I said: "I bet it worked like a charm."

My acknowledgment of Norman's literary gift seemed to please her. She smiled benevolently. "So then we, like, hang out and wait for the mail."

"Do you get a lot of it?"

"A ton! You wouldn't believe it. Then he makes a pitcher of martinis and I cut up teensy little cheese cubes and we read them and put them into piles."

"Such as."

"Garbage: Too young, living with family, student, low-pay job like waitressing. Or if she has kids or any family she has to take care of—unless it's a total vegetable relative. Then there's Too Pretty. We don't want someone who's using the personals just because she's bored with the guys she already has; she wouldn't be desperate enough. Too Smart: like doctors, lawyers. We watch out for real good vocabulary. Norm says: 'If *I* have to look up the words she uses in a dictionary, she's too smart for me.' Or a couple of times: women cops! We put the letters from Yale grads on

58

the Too Smart pile too, because Norm could slip up and they'd know it. But you wouldn't believe their letters! They really oughta give a course there: How to Get a Guy. Then there are the Iffys: medium-paying jobs, but there's maybe a pension, or she might have put a lot in the bank. You know, like nurses, teachers. And then"—she paused to run the tip of her tongue across her upper lip; her voice grew husky—"there's Pay Dirt."

I wanted to take a hot bath, scrub off what I was hearing with a loofah and anti-bacterial soap. It wasn't so much the sordidness of what Mary was saying but the sheer pleasure with which she rolled around in the dirt. The mockery, the cruelty, the exultation. I buzzed Sandi and asked for a ginger tea to allay what I knew was incipient nausea. (Sandi and I had a beverage pact. Each time I buzzed her for something to drink, she got a day where she could leave fifteen minutes early. What else could a feminist, knee-jerk-liberal employer do? Naturally, I made the deal knowing that she is an obsessive-compulsive worker; in the six years she'd been with me, she'd left early twice.) "Who gets on the Pay Dirt pile?" I asked.

"Anyone with a fancy address. Norman does his home-work and really knows where the rich neighborhoods are in each city we go to. Anyone who has a business. Like Bobette. Anyone who's been to Europe or on one of those cross-country tours. That's why he puts in about loving travel; if they've actually done it, it can spell m-o-n-e-y."

Mary told me that while there was no variation in the ads, Norman's responses to the letters he received were tailored to each woman. A little flattery here ("Fifty-one isn't old!"), a little bridled lust there ("I could not keep my eyes from that exquisite curve where your hand meets your wrist. Excuse me. I don't mean to be overstepping the bounds. But I hope you'll forgive it if I say you look like you combine elegance and emotion, which is a *very* interesting combination, I must say"). From her wallet, she drew out copies of the photos he sent to them when he wrote them back. There were two. One in a suit and tie, sitting on the edge of a mahogany desk, his arms crossed across his chest, a Mona Lisa smile on his lips—what a *Business Week* centerfold might look like. The other in corduroys and a plaid shirt, a lock of his hair tumbling over his brow, his sleeves rolled up above his elbow, leaning against a tree in the middle of an autumn forest. Norman would decide from the tone of a woman's letter which photo to send.

"And then?" I asked.

Mary clapped her hands together, gleeful. "Well, a half hour before the first date, I go to the cocktail lounge or restaurant—Norman says, if they sound like they don't want to drink, meet them for lunch. It's what's called an expense of doing business. But some of these fatsos, they can order three courses, so no dinners. One of them once—"

"You work with Norman?" I asked, amazed that she had any active role in a confidence game. She struck me as someone who could get flustered inserting her card into an automatic teller machine.

"Sure."

"I didn't realize he had a business partner. You were saying that you show up about a half hour before he gets there. To make sure it isn't a setup?"

"Yes!" she said, delighted with my powers of deduction. "Norman says: 'You've got to cover your *a-s-s* in this business.'" Especially with a rap sheet like his, I thought. Where did he find this girl? Yes, I know: woman. But Mary was barely into her twenties. True, she didn't have it all, but she had a lot. Movie star beautiful—if she'd invest in a chisel and chip away those layers of makeup. A sweetie-pie manner. Well, until she spoke about Norman's crimes. Then something sexual, a throaty intensity I didn't want to hear, crept into her tone.

"On the first date, Norm lets the woman do the talking. I mean, you'd think they'd know they should draw the man out, but he said their talking is the key. They're desperate to talk, and he's such a great listener. You know why?"

She waited, so I asked, "Why?"

"Because he really *does* listen. Never forgets a thing. Never mixes up one with the other, even if he's working two at the same time, which he hardly ever does now. He says he

60

used to do it when he was in his twenties but it knocked him out, the traveling back and forth and having to write double love letters and make double good-night-I-love-you and good-morning-I-love-you phone calls." She paused and cocked her head to the side. "Is this helping you?"

"It may." If I'd been a male lawyer, I probably would have delighted in her sitting across from me in that green suit, with coral toenails shining up at me. My partner, Chuckie, would have told her: You're a bright spot on such a dreary day, dear. But Mary was a blight on my landscape. I love my country lawyer's office, with its blue-and-white toile couch, and framed photos of the Long Island coast— real beauties—that my guy took; they hang on the wall next to my diplomas. True, I'm stuck in one of those awful modern suburban office buildings, white brick and tinted glass, its upper floors occupied by doctors and lawyers, its lower by upscale podiatrists and marginal software companies. But inside I'd made it comforting. With her garish kelly-green suit, Mary was jarring.

Why, you might ask, having comfortably chatted up multiple murderers and wife-batterers sitting in that very same blue-and-white-checked arm chair, did I so object to Mary Dean? I don't know—except to say that her girlish pride in Norman's cruelty to women had a rough sexual side that she didn't bother to hide. Forget hide: she flaunted it. What was with this dame that she was putting on this kind of show? "Tell me about the con," I said.

"Well, nothing on the first date," she said, sitting back in her chair, getting comfortable. "That's just to capture them. That's not the word, is it?"

"Captivate."

"Right!" She massaged the calf of her right leg in a way that, to a man, would be a come-on, but to a premenopausal woman was merely discomforting. Her mind wasn't on me, though. It was on Norman and the titillation of the con, and that made her every move self-aware, sensual. "So the next time, if things go okay, they're giving him dinner at their place. That's 'cause he talked about how down in the dumps he's gotten with TV dinners or eating out, and ninety-nine percent of the time they pick up on that. So he brings French wine and they talk and he tells about his divorce a little."

"Is this a real divorce?" I asked, wishing she'd stop feeling up her leg.

"Of course not!" Mary chuckled, amused, as if I'd made a dreadful faux pas. "He's never been married." Then her amusement faded. "We're supposed to be married, though. June first. A June wedding."

I didn't want to hear a about how she was the first woman he had ever loved and how she was banking on me to get him off. "What does he tell his marks about a divorce?" I asked.

"That he'd built up a great little business. An investment advisory newsletter. See, that way they start asking him advice about their stocks and money stuff and he gets a fast idea of what they have and how much they know. But that he'd put his business in his wife's name and she won't give it back to him. The business is useless without him, but his wife let it go bust. He tells them she was from a rich family, so it didn't matter to her. She just wanted to hurt him." She lifted a limp lock of hair from her shoulder and began spooling it between her index fingers, as if rolling a pin curl.

"And he did this with Bobette? She made him dinner?"

"Yes. Yankee pot roast. Norm said it was really yucky pot roast."

Then he told her about the business and showed her pictures of his kids. Boy pictures from a wallet he lifted in a mall in Chicago. He's not a pickpocket or anything, but if someone's buying stuff and leaves a wallet on the counter, he'll take it, 'cause he sometimes finds good family pictures. This last one was excellent. It had a few pictures of the same two boys, so he kept one for his wallet and had the others blown up and put in picture frames. They look *so* real."

"He doesn't use the credit cards he takes?"

"No. He says it's too risky. But he uses the ID, just not in the state he lifted it."

"So he showed her the boy pictures." She nodded too hard. I realized that it was a gimmick, to show off her bobbing curls. "Any reason why not girl pictures?" I, mother of a daughter, asked.

"Name one woman in the world who'd want a stepdaughter! A stepson isn't so bad, and these are two cute boys. One's in a Little League uniform. Norman named one Joey and the other Whatever-name-Norman's-using, junior."

"What does he do after that?" I pressed on.

"Nothing till the third date. That's at the Love Nest."

"What's the Love Nest?"

"A little furnished place we take. Not for us. We have our own place. The Love Nest's for him and the mark. See, Norman always used to use one place with his girlfriends and the marks, but then the girlfriends used to have to get out whenever the marks were coming over. And they'd have to hide a big suitcase or a Hefty bag filled with all their stuff in the car trunk, so the mark wouldn't get wise. When I started working with Norm, that's what I had to do." She smiled and blushed like a happy bride. "But then he said he couldn't take me having to live like that, so the last few times, we got a cheap place for the Love Nest. He tells them it's till he gets back on his feet. He worried it might be too crummy and would turn them off, but . . . Do I have to say it? Nothing turns them off."

"Where is this Love Nest?" I asked.

"In Manhasset. It's not all *that* bad, except the toilet seat has a big chip on the side and it looks like—you know—caked-on poo."

"When does he use the Love Nest?"

"Not too often, but he has to show he has a place. And so I can call about repossessing his car." I waited. "See," she went on, "we have this thing. He goes to the bathroom at exactly nine twenty-five. That's when I call and leave a message on his answering machine, except the volume is way up: 'Mr. Whatever-name, this is Ms. McDonald, calling on behalf of Pinnacle Collections Agency.'" Mary's voice took on a clipped edge that was annoyed, almost angry. "'Listen, unless you can come up with the money for your car, it is going to be forfeited as per your former wife's judgment against you. We've been more than patient, Mr. Whatever-name.'"

Usually I'm pretty good at figuring out scams, but this one took me a minute, and I needed help. "The mark hears the message and . . ."

"Norman acts all embarrassed. But then he pretends to open up to her. He shows her a picture of his car. A Jaguar XJS convertible. Sometimes a Mercedes E320. We go out for test drives, and I take a picture of him with the top down."

Then I had it. "So the mark thinks he is in love with this car."

"Yes. Well, he does love cars. Really and truly. Anyway, he cries when he talks about his car. He tells them it symbolizes the whole divorce, everything he's lost."

"And so to make him happy, she knows she has to ante up thirty or forty thousand to get back his car for him?"

"Oh, they cost more than forty!" She smiled at my ignorance. "Buy them back or help him buy it back. But that doesn't happen that night or anything. I mean, he just keeps seeing them all the time. By the beginning of the third week, he says he wishes he was in a position to get serious with her. By the end of that week, she's ready to go to the bank. But he holds off. He says: 'I absolutely will not allow any such thing.'"

"So how long does it take before he lets himself be convinced?"

"Another two weeks." I must have shown surprise that it took that long, because she explained. "That way, they fall so hopelessly in love that when he gets the money and goes to get the car, they don't—you know—get it. He calls to say he's tied up with the paperwork and then—bingo! We're out of there. Meanwhile . . ." I think she understood that good taste would preclude a delighted grin, but it kept trying to break through. Her eyes sparkled. "They wait for *days* before they figure it out and call the cops."

I said: "I guess you know that with a marriage con, a lot

of marks never call the cops at all. They're too humiliated."

"Too in love!" she said brightly. "They can't believe that he'd run off because he's such a great actor. I mean, I tell him I think he half falls for each one of those turkeys, 'cause otherwise he couldn't convince them that it was so real." Her voice softened and grew silky. "I've never met a woman who didn't love him. I mean, even if they meet him for just a second. The lady in the Chinese laundry. The ticket lady at the movies." She eyed me as if she expected me to wave my hand in the air and shout: Me too! When I didn't oblige, she added: "It's like he has a magic wand. I remember something I read, like from a fairy tale. Or maybe from a paperback: 'She was powerless to resist him.' I mean, there's no women alive who can resist Norman. There are some men like that. With me, I fell in two seconds. He could have just tossed me aside after that night."

"But he didn't."

"He said he never knew what love meant till he met me." The gleam in her eyes turned to moisture. A single tear was detained by a mascara roadblock. Maybe this particular tear wasn't out of adoration, though, but out of fear. Mary's features froze as if she'd been on film and the final credits were meant to roll over that expression. Maybe she realized how brutal the con was, how it showed the depths of Norman's hatred of women. Did she honestly believe her beauty exempted her? Or did she sense that she, too, was Norman's victim? Had she been secretly afraid he would use her and then sneak out on her one night?

"Where were you going to get married?"

"The next city. He said Boston. He hadn't worked Boston for over ten years. I said: '*Boston?* Like maybe Miami Beach for a honeymoon?' He said all those rich old widows down there were too smart about cons. They almost expect it. But he said we'd just get away from Long Island after Bobette was done and figure it out."

"What did he do with Bobette's money?" I asked.

"He never got it! He was still working on her." But I knew that Bobette had taken out forty-eight thousand dollars the afternoon of the day she was murdered. Mary went on:

"Norman said Bobette was one tough nut, but once he got through her shell . . ."

"What?"

"He could tell. She was going to be real juicy!"

Six

Catholics say that a child of seven has attained the age of reason. Not being Catholic, there was no reason for Sylvia White to know of this milestone. Still, she was vaguely aware that a seventh birthday had significance. So she redecorated Lee's bedroom.

Down came the wallpaper with the pastel lambs, off came the yellow-and-white gingham bedspread. A shaggy persimmon carpet was laid. A couch covered in a heavy baby-pink cotton with a design of interlocking triangles of raspberry and burnt orange was brought in to serve as a bed.

For the prepubescent daughters of the aggressively upwardly mobile, a pink-and-orange palette was not unheard-of in the annals of 1950s interior decoration, but on the North Shore of Long Island, Lee's room was the first of its coloration. It earned Sylvia kudos from the group of fashionable suburban women who were her friends: "I'm speechless. Gorgeous!" "I couldn't believe . . . pink and orange! And it works. That Sylvia . . . gifted." "Beyond gifted: an artist!"

Aesthetics is rarely an issue with a second grader, but it had to be for Lee. She missed her pastel lambs. However, since she had, indeed, reached the age of reason, she understood what really mattered to her parents: clothes first, furniture second. She was a quick study. A stylistic faux pas would invariably provoke a fierce reaction—what she thought of as Mommy's Mad Breathing, a snort of annoyance amplified by smoker's phlegm. It didn't take her long to figure out how to avoid it. When her mother would thrust, say, a swatch of tangerine polished cotton under her nose and demand: "What do you think?," she learned first to check which expression Sylvia was wearing—the "Ick" or the "I love it"—and then to respond accordingly.

Not that Lee was a submissive child. Far from it. But having figured out that her mother cared primarily about appearances, all Lee needed to do to be deemed a dutiful daughter was to use her nailbrush, say "Thank you" frequently, smile a lot, and cede to Sylvia all decisions about clothes and interior design. Silence on the subject of the day's barrettes seemed not too great a price to pay for freedom. Then she was on her own. No clandestine nocturnal cookie retrievals for this kid. No oxygen deprivation under the covers to hide book and flash-light. Lee could gorge on Mallomars. No one would stop her from reading and rereading *The Bobbsey Twins' Merry Days Indoors and Out* till the wee hours in the bright circle of light from a one-hundred-watt bulb beneath a pumpkin-color glass shade shaped like a coolie hat that hung over her bed.

By age seven, Lee realized (as she sat on Sylvia's pièce de résistance, a lounge chair shaped like an amoeba, covered with an apricot-and-shocking-pink awning-stripe fabric) that deference to her mother's fashion whims was the best way, actually the only way, to have fun with her mother. A trip to the city to buy a new spring coat and Mary Janes could be a laugh-filled lark: a "just us girls" lunch in a restaurant with aqua tablecloths and hot popovers; making fun of Ick dresses, like the one with cherries pinned on the bosom at Best & Company; dropping in on Daddy's fur store, where Mommy tried on all the new styles and Dolly gave her a piece of chinchilla to stroke. She understood that saying "Gosh!" when her mother modeled a three-quarter-length silver fox was politically wise. It showed that Lee knew what was important in life—fur and style—and it made her whiny, I-want-to-go-home little sister look even worse.

At age four, Robin Renée White had traded in the infantile digestive irritability that had kept her awake and screaming twenty hours a day for a permanent colic of the personality. Nothing made her truly happy. She never giggled. The company of other children made her edgy. Playground noise gave her headaches. She could become agitated by a game of Candyland. Of course, there were times—listening to "Bibbidi-Bobbidi-Boo" on her *Cinderella* record, cutting out dresses for paper dolls—that Robin's lovely heart-shaped face took on a touchingly soft expression. Sylvia and Leonard would glance at each other and exhale a sigh of relief: Maybe the worst is over. Maybe now we can have the photographer come back and she'll smile and not wail in terror— "Oooo! Wooo!"—when the flashbulb goes off. (In fairness to Robin, it should be noted that on these rare occasions when her taut nerves relaxed and she began to smile, Lee was not beyond sneaking up from behind the moment Sylvia and Leonard's backs were turned and poking Robin hard and fast in the ribs, causing the little girl to lose the little equanimity she possessed and break into demented screams.)

Still, Robin was competition. No doubt about it. She was far prettier than Lee, if one's definition of pretty is huge eyes in a waiflike face, and a rosebud of a mouth. Her daintiness was memorable. Lee was the sturdy sort: Her body was saved from the inevitable consequences of Mallomars only because she had picked up a stray gene for athleticism. (That particular gene had last turned up in the girls' great-great-grandfather on their father's side, who was the fastest runner in exurban Pinsk—a not unwelcome talent, considering the proclivities of the neighboring peasants.) Otherwise, Lee was generic Girl. Her brown braided hair was neither straight enough to gleam in the sunlight nor curly enough to render her adorable. Her features were certainly pleasant but not singular enough to be remarked upon.

Robin was also smarter than Lee, if intelligence can be measured by standardized intelligence tests, age of onset of reading readiness, and ability to view long division as an intriguing process rather than an affliction. But that would come later. At four, smart little Robin had a tendency to make derisive tsk-tsk noises whenever her seven-year-old sister expressed an opinion— a frequent occurrence. That Lee merely ignored this scorn and kept on talking was an early, conspicuous, and of course unheeded sign that she was cut out to be a litigator.

From her lounge chair by the window, Lee could see the downward swoop of the lawn, the kidney-shaped swimming pool in its summer turquoise splendor. (The Whites' house itself, a not ungraceful assemblage of wood, fieldstone, and glass rectangles, designed by an architect who had studied under an architect who had worked for Frank Lloyd Wright in 1937, sat on two acres of velvet green lawn.) Lee could see, beyond the cabana—an overpriced shed with two changing rooms and a wet bar—that her mother was creating art. Or trying to.

Sylvia White was living disproof of the myth of Jewish intellectual superiority. She had scant imagination, hardly any curiosity, and only basic intuitive sense. What she had was style. She looked smart. She was always a pleasure to behold—even in rolled-up, paint-stained cut off khakis and the old white oxford shirt of Leonard's she used for painting. Her honey-colored hair was tied back in a blue bandanna, so if a stiff breeze came along, it would not blow her hair onto the wet canvas that stood on the easel before her.

The painting! From where Lee was sitting, it looked as if Sylvia was stabbing her picture. But Lee understood that her mother was making leaves on the sycamore she'd been attempting to capture for the last three months, stippling green on naked gray-brown branches with the flat of her brush. Pow, pow, pow, went the brush. Lee was too far away to make out the details of the canvas, although she had already seen enough of her mother's work to know the truth: lousy. Even a seven-year-old child with almost no artistic ability could tell that Sylvia's trees were flat, lifeless things. Ditto with Sylvia's still lifes—orange sections and a hammer, a vase of flowers beside a hatbox . . . to say nothing of her portrait of Duchess, the collie. Sylvia had hung that one over the fireplace in the living room. Lee watched her father sneaking fast, abashed glances at it. A couple of months later, it was taken down and replaced with a picture of black squiggles that she heard her father say, not without pride, cost enough to float a battleship.

Thus, at the age of reason, Lee had already grasped her mother's mediocrity and deduced that she cared deeply only about superficialities. Well, with one exception. Lee recognized that there was a single genuine passion in her mother's life: her father.

As Leonard's coolness toward Sylvia changed to complete detachment (on the way to coldness), as he turned his attention to Le Fourreur and his model/bookkeeper/lover, Dolly Young, his wife's ardor for him grew. It was a perfect inverse proportion. Lee observed her mother's eyes devouring her father as he brushed barbecue sauce on spare ribs—so many brush strokes that it was clear to Lee that his mind was on something other than pork. She observed her mother's coquettishness—her kiss on the back of his neck while he was watching his first *Meet the Press* on the new TV in the den, her curling up on the lounge chair beside him when he was reading the Sunday paper by the pool. All Sylvia's come-ons seemed to arouse was irritation. Still, the woman clearly could not help herself. Watching her mother get ready for her father's return from work, reworking her hairdo, putting on another dot of liquid rouge and spreading it over her cheek, like a caress, fiddling with the neckline of a peasant blouse—taking it off her shoulders, back up, letting it slip off one shoulder, tugging on it to bare a bit of bosom, Lee knew without a doubt that Sylvia was capable of feeling.

So how come she could not spare a little extra? Not that Lee consciously asked that question: Why is a privileged American woman incapable of the same devotion to her young as the average hyena? It was a good question. But at seven (and fourteen and probably even at twenty-one), even the most analytical child cannot answer it satisfactorily. It boils down to this: Her mother does not love her because she is, indeed, unlovable.

But at least there was some tenderness, a little physical affection in Lee's life. She received it once a month, during visits from her father's parents, Nat the Commie and Big Bella.

To be hugged by three-hundred-pound Grandma Bella ("How are you, my beautiful, vonderful tootsie-pie?") was to risk suffocation between those two monstrous marshmallows that were her grandmother's breasts. To have your hair tousled in gratitude by Grandpa Nat because you snuck upstairs and emptied your piggy bank (so, he explained, you could give your seventeen dollars and forty-four cents to Deserving Negro Children Down South) was to risk baldness.

It was worth the risk. Humans are, after all, warmth-seeking creatures. However, once a month is not enough, and the Weissbergs' visits to the Whites were marred by terrible tension: Leonard's face turning ashen, then livid, almost blue, at the sound of his mother's voice ("You're such a big shot, sveetheart, you can't kiss your mudder anymore?"). Sylvia's appalled expression upon spotting her father-in-law's white, hairless, skinny bowed legs in red Bermuda shorts. Inevitably, being a quick-witted girl, Lee realized she was not getting her birthright—love—from her elegant, well-modulated parents. Why not? Weren't they supposed to offer love without qualification? And how come her grandparents, who *were* willing to give it, made her parents almost sick?

But if the classical psychologists are correct, it is the mother who is the key figure in a child's life. Lee, while no stranger to self-examination as an adult, never had a clue as to how many stratagems she employed throughout her childhood to try and woo this woman who stood, at that moment in 1957, five hundred feet away, before a dreadful painting of a very beautiful tree.

For the sake of fairness and in the interests of feminism, however, let us not make Sylvia Bernstein Weissberg-Weiss-White the villain. First, there are worse people in this story. A lot worse. And second, even if we accept as true the notion that the mother is the star in a child's firmament, Sylvia was one of two parents. If she was dysfunctional, how come the other parent could not step in and function a little? Did Leonard think four trips to the zoo, an occasional excursion to Carvel, and bedtime readings of *Madeline* when Lee had chicken pox made him a good father?

Did he honestly believe that all he had to do to be a good family man was pay for his daughters' ballet lessons and not divorce his wife and marry his mistress? Leonard knew better. He *felt* better, experiencing occasional surges of love for his children that came straight from his heart. But those times, when Lee's prowess at crab-apple tree climbing filled him with great fear and greater elation, or when Robin's exegesis of Jerry Lewis's role in *The Delicate Delinquent* made him proud, and he grabbed her, hugged her and covered her with kisses, he unfailingly sensed a change in Sylvia. He'd look up: No, nothing, just a wide Isn't-that-just-the-sweetest? smile. But (was it his imagination?) the smile seemed a touch too broad, so even her back teeth were on display. So he merely unwrapped the little girl's arms from around his neck, gave her a friendly wink and a pat on the backside, and sent her off for another year or two.

Beyond Sylvia's easel, where the well-fertilized lawn ended, was a hundred-foot-wide strip of trees that, in full leaf, gave the illusion that the Whites' property was baronial, backing up onto a great forest. But from her second-story window, Lee could see it wasn't so. The land rose about forty feet, then leveled off at the beginning of Hart's Hill. Yes, a house with a name. Not that Lee could see it from her window, but she knew it was there. An estate. The estate next door.

Hart's Hill got its name in the late eighteenth century from the deer that roamed the north shore of Long Island. These noble mammals (albeit hopelessly tick-ridden) seemed drawn to that particular promontory. They grazed that very spot where, in 1757, 1820, and 1898, the manor house would be built. (The first house was destroyed by a fire in the hearth that claimed one Mrs. Rebecca Taylor as well as the rum syllabub she was preparing. The second was razed by a Mr. Arthur Taylor and the third erected by same after he made his second million in attorney's fees advising Edward Harriman during Harriman's acquisition of the Union Pacific Railroad.)

But before all this construction and upward mobility put an end to the noble hart, a real deer could wander right to that place. Its coat glowing red in the sunlight, a stag might gaze northward across the stern gray waters of Long Island Sound to look upon the dark-green forests of mainland America.

The Taylors of Hart's Hill themselves weren't much given to gazing, at least by the time their neighbor, young Lee White, became aware of them. They were too busy. Foster Taylor had left the Manhattan law firm of Willoughby, Crane and Buffet to serve on the United States Olympic Committee; he was also a trustee of the Boy Scouts of America, the American Bobsledding Association, the Iron Lung Alliance, and A Mighty Fortress, a traveling Episcopal goodwill choir. Georgina, his wife, was known as Ginger. It was said that if she hadn't gotten married in her sophomore year at Hollins and then gotten pregnant (the events actually occurred in reverse order), she could have been a professional tennis player. In addition to her daily workouts on the grass court at Hart's Hill, Ginger raised and showed basenjis, dogs that are inherently neighbor-pleasing since they do not bark. However, they do defecate, and entire broods of basenji puppies would often scamper down the hill and leave odoriferous brown lumps among the phlox in Sylvia's all-white garden.

Foster and Ginger were tall and lissome. Each carried two rare recessive genes that suppressed fat on thighs and upper arms, which they passed down to all their four children, so the younger

73

Taylors, too, grew up tall and lean-limbed. And handsome, with their mother's finely wrought features and their father's high color. Since Fos and Ginger were an effervescent couple, finding hilarity in everything from bobbing for apples to knock-knock jokes, they had a real belly laugh when they realized their initial initials were right next to each other in the alphabet. F for Foster! Ha-ha-ha! G for Georgina. Ho-ho-ho! So they named their children Hope, Irene, Jasper, and Kent. (They might have gone on to Lawrence, Melanie, and even Nathaniel, but Kent was born retarded, and Foster thought that sort of killed the fun, Kent's not getting the joke.)

Unlike the basenjis, the Taylors did not scamper down the hill. In fact, while they were vaguely aware that someone had built a modern house on the property beneath them, they remained happily unconscious of the Whites' existence.

The same cannot be said for the Whites. There was not one single day that Leonard did not think of the Taylors. As with a man haunted by a lost love, the most oblique reference could evoke their presence. Words: *athlete, hill, tennis, old money, lawyer, rich,* and *Olympic* made him dizzy with a mixture of desire and fury. Sights: a sailboat in the background of a Philip Morris ad; a church steeple; a dog (in fact, even Duchess, instead of barking and scaring away the little fuckers, seemed to view the basenjis' excretory activities with an admiration approaching awe). Fos Taylor, himself standing on the platform of the Shorehaven station, holding his *Herald Tribune* at arms' length to compensate for his farsightedness, or giving his train pals (whom Leonard thought of as the Taylor Boys) his idiosyncratic greeting, a stiff military salute, but using only his index finger. One time, he'd given that salute to Leonard—or so Leonard had thought. An explosion of joy went off inside Leonard, so powerful that it knocked him senseless. Somehow he managed a crisp salute in return. He thought: I've been tapped. (Tapped! what a wonderful word!) I'm one of the Boys. A second later, he saw Fos's eyes blink-blink-blink at the wrongness of his, Leonard's, behavior and he knew . . . Turning around, he spotted one of the Taylor Boys right behind him, the fat one, who looked like an overblown Audie Murphy balloon. "Sorry," Leonard began gamely, "I thought you were saying hello to . . ." Yes, he knew all about how crazy they were for acting as if nothing was bothering you even if you were in the middle of an A-bomb detonation, but by that time, Fos and Fat Boy had somehow managed to move off sideways. Not only that: They were saluting Paper Boy, the one who got on the train every day with the *Times*, the *Trib*, the *Journal-American*, and the *Wall Street Journal*. They were grinning too, as if they couldn't wait to tell him something hysterical.

Smells: The odor of dog shit enraged him. Once, he had to restrain himself from grabbing the leash of a toy poodle from a woman on Lexington Avenue, just down from Le Fourreur, and strangling her with it. In his mind, he could picture the skin of her neck reddening, puckering under the leather leash, and it gave him pleasure, as did imagining the squoosh sound as he pushed her dying body into the tiny brown pile her shitty little dog had made.

Sounds: The *thwomp!* of tennis balls from the Taylors' court moved him to melancholy to wrath and back again. The Taylors were a large family, and each member seemed to have a hundred friends who played, so *thwomp!* went on from seven on Saturday mornings to dusk on Sundays. Once, when Sylvia's parents were over for Mother's Day, the Judge had whispered: "Your neighbors play a lot of tennis, don't they?" Leonard became disconsolate. All he could do was nod. Then he excused himself and went into his bedroom, locked the door, and called Dolly, breaking his own No Contact on Weekends rule. They talked dirty for two and a half hours, until Sylvia banged on the door. "Leonard? What are you doing in there? Is anything wrong?" He didn't bother covering the mouthpiece. He never did. He had no secrets from Dolly. "It's Jack Feldman, Syl. You know, from Siberian Sable. They had a warehouse fire. Please, I can't get off the phone now." Sylvia apologized and went back to put on the charcoal herself.

Actually, Leonard did have one secret from Dolly. He knew she was game for anything, but although he was dying to play Mr. and Mrs. Taylor, he didn't have the courage to suggest it. How he wanted to put on that accent from Princeton or wherever and be Fos ("Ginger, dahling, I am not like all those other chaps on crew, am I?"). Dolly would be Ginger, which was not such a stretch, since she was actually slender as a reed. But as powerful as Leonard's desire was, so was his fear that, knowing this about

75

him, Dolly, if she turned against him, could blackmail him for everything he had. And he would give it to her, that's how horrible it would be if anyone found out his secret.

Of course, if he left Sylvia and married Dolly, they could play Fos and Ginger all the time. So how come he didn't? Ah! That was one more secret Leonard kept from Dolly: that he would never marry her. Even if he could get free without Sylvia killing herself, which he doubted, and even though he loved Dolly with all his heart, he knew she wasn't good enough for him. She was trying to be, taking French lessons at Hunter at night and going to matinees on Saturday; she had seen almost every play on Broadway and could discuss them very intelligently. She was taking riding lessons in Central Park. But if something terrible happened and Sylvia died and he was free, he wouldn't marry Dolly. He would want the real thing.

Seven-year-old Lee, of course, knew nothing about her father's affair, although in the intuitive way of smart children, she knew there was something fishy going on with Dolly. Why was Dolly so inexhaustibly wonderful to her? Dolly would practically gasp with delight on those rare occasions when Leonard brought Lee to work with him. "Lee! What a surprise!" she would gush, and then look toward Leonard: "Please, Mr. White, would it be okay if I took Lee out for an ice cream sundae?" And her father would consent. When they'd get to Schrafft's, Dolly would ask Lee what seemed like hundreds of questions about second grade and about Robin and her mother. And no matter what she said, Dolly was thrilled. Even if she said something stupid, like: "Uh, gee, I dunno what my favorite color is." Dolly was very sweet, and always looked beautiful and smelled like flowers, but the child wished she'd just shut up so Lee could concentrate on her sundae. Peach ice cream with hot fudge, whipped cream, and a cherry, although they were a little cheap with the fudge this time. Lee hoped Dolly would notice and ask her if she wanted more, and she'd say: Maybe just a teeny bit. But then the man behind the counter would think she looked like a real nice girl and felt awful she'd gotten so little hot fudge, so he'd give her two—no, three—of those big spoons full. But instead Dolly was waiting for her to say something. Oh. Favorite color. "Uh, yellow. No, red." Dolly would gasp: "Red! I can't believe it! I love red too!"

Actually, even though Lee knew Dolly's delight in her was, well, phony, she liked Dolly. It was wonderful to sit there with someone who felt you were important enough to fake pleasure in your presence. With her mother . . .

It had never been good. True, Lee was clever enough to know that when her mother brought home a box that said Tailored Woman and took out a suit or a dress, she had to say: "Mommy! That's beautiful!" Not only that: Having gone through all that trouble, Sylvia wasn't really satisfied unless her daughter added something original—and cute. But what qualified as cute? One time, as her mother took a yellow chiffon dress from its tissue-paper bed and held it up against her to model it, Lee asked: "Mommy, can I have that dress when you die?" Her parents thought that was very cute, or, her father's new word for cute, "droll." So the next time her mother got something—a Balenciaga coat—she asked if she could have the coat when her mother died. This time, though, her mother snapped: "Stop it!" So she had to think up something else cute. It was very tiring, or, as her father said, "wearing," to be droll all the time, because her mother bought something new nearly every day.

And if she wasn't cute, her mother wasn't happy with her. Not angry, to be fair. Not mean. Just . . . bored. Her mother found her boring because the things Lee found interesting—the collie, her new bike with training wheels, her *Madeline* book, and thinking about what she was going to get for lunch—her mother had no interest in.

But Lee was determined to win over her mother. Just then, gazing down from her window, she noticed her mother setting down the paintbrush. Why was she doing that? Oh, there: It was Ethel, the latest live-in maid, walking across the lawn, bringing out Robin after her nap. Through the open window, Lee could hear a faint "Mimmy," as Robin cried out for Sylvia. (Lee knew this was a bad sign for Ethel, because by forcing Robin onto Sylvia, Ethel was Not Taking Responsibility, which meant Sylvia would talk to Leonard and Leonard would fire Ethel first thing Saturday morning. Firing maids made him very crabby, so it would be a bad weekend.)

"Mimmy!" Robin's voice wasn't so high that it made you cover your ears, but its pitch worked its way through your semicircular canals and into your head and grated your nerves; a few more "Mimmy"'s, and Sylvia's and Ethel's teeth would start grinding. Nonetheless, Lee had to admit Robin's curls were golden. Even more ominous, Lee realized, Robin was showing dangerous signs of Fashion Smartness. Just the other day, sitting on the kitchen floor, she'd pulled on the ribbon of Sylvia's espadrilles and said: "Pretty!" Sylvia's color had gone all rosy, and she'd laughed and said: "Yes. Pretty and *very* expensive." Lee jumped out of the apricot-and-pink lounge chair and raced downstairs.

By the time she got across the backyard, Robin was sitting on the grass and whimpering. "What's wrong?" Sylvia was demanding, her hands on her hips, her brush dripping dark-green paint onto the grass. At the sound of her mother's displeasure, Robin's whimpering changed to whining. While this did not displease Lee, she did understand that the short, sharp spikes of grass on which Ethel had plopped her sister were prickling the little girl's legs. So Lee hauled Robin up, drew her over to the swing set, and sat her on the glider. "Thanks, sweetie," her mother called out, and went back to her painting.

It was a lazy August afternoon. Now and then a bird tweeted or a bee buzzed on its way to Sylvia's rose arbor. Lee sat across from her sister and glided, slowly, so as not to scare Robin. Day camp was over, third grade was two weeks away, her best friend, Dorie, was visiting her grandmother in New Jersey, and she'd torn up her paper dolls and flushed them away because her mother had said: No more toys. You have the nice paper dolls. Lee had come to her and said: I can't find the paper dolls. Unfortunately, her mother had found a paper leg (wearing paper Capri pants) floating in the toilet bowl and Lee was being punished with no Ed Sullivan on Sunday.

"Want to go inside and play with my dollhouse?" Lee asked Robin.

"No."

"Want to put on our bathing suits?" Lee tried to make it sound like the opportunity of a lifetime. "Turn on the sprinkler?" Her voice reached heights of delight. "Run in and—"

"No!"

"Want to color?"

"No."

"In my Peter Pan coloring book, Robin. You can use my crayons."

Robin started to climb off the glider. Quickly, Lee brought it to the fastest, smoothest halt she could. Still, Robin fell onto the ground and went screeching back to Sylvia. "Mimmy!" Sylvia slammed her brush into a can, threw Lee a dirty look, and, grabbing Robin by the wrist, half led, half dragged her to the patio.

The chairs, made of white wire mesh and resembling a cupped hand, were parts of an ensemble of metal outdoor furniture Leonard had ordered from France. They left funny marks on the backs of your legs if you were wearing shorts, Lee knew, but they were comfortable. Her mother lit up a cigarette, closed her eyes, and smoked. When she exhaled, she pursed her lips into a little bird mouth. Robin, seeing her mother's eyes safely shut, brought her foot up to her mouth and started biting her toenails. "Stop it!" Lee mouthed, but Robin ignored her. Lee closed her eyes, leaned back in the wire chair, and smoked an imaginary Pall Mall, breathing out a perfect thin column of smoke.

So neither Lee nor Sylvia noticed when Robin slipped out of her chair and headed toward the swimming pool. The gardener had finally oiled the gate of the white iron fence surrounding the pool (after receiving a nasty note from Leonard on the subject, enclosed with the monthly check), so neither Lee nor Sylvia heard a thing when Robin reached up and, with remarkable dexterity, flipped up the childproof latch. And of course, when Robin walked down the four steps into the pool, there was not a sound, because by the time her feet reached the bottom of the pool, the water was over her head.

Peril ought to be accompanied by the roar of a tidal wave or the screech of metal crushing metal in a car crash. Not by silence. Sylvia smoked on. But Lee opened her eyes. Something was not right. What? Oh, the absence of Robin crying, sniveling, or even shuffling. Lee swiveled her head, checking out the fieldstone wall of the house, the swings, the perennial garden, the woods that rose up the hill . . . But she couldn't spot the buttercup color of her sister's playsuit. Lee climbed out of the wire chair. "Mommy."

"Shhh."

"Mommy, where's Robin?" Sylvia, sluggish from the heat, listless with boredom occasioned by her own art, shrugged and inhaled deeply. It must be said that she did not comprehend the import of Lee's question. Without malice, it can be said Sylvia was in another world: picturing how to achieve the most drama in an arrangement of pineapples, grapes, and melons for a fruit platter she was planning for a Labor Day pool party. A flash of yellow caught Lee's eye.

In an instant, she flew across the crew-cut lawn to the pool. Before her mother had a clue that anything had gone wrong, Lee White opened the pool gate and took a step into the pool. Robin was in the shallow end, but too far to reach from the steps. Another step down. The water was overheated. It lapped around her calves and felt awful, almost hot. The stench of chlorine was so strong, as if it were masking some other, terrible smell. She should get out, call her mother. "You're not the boss of Robin," her mother was always telling her. "*I* am. Leave her alone." One more step, up to her waist. She could dog-paddle, but then what could she do about Robin? She couldn't grab her and swim with just one hand, could she? Robin was right at the spot where the shallow part got deep, over both their heads, so she'd be stuck out there too.

"Mommy!" Lee called, but Sylvia didn't hear her.

Robin was just floating there. No, not quite floating, because she was a little bit under the water. Not moving, her arms held out, limp, as if she were pretending to be a dead bird. Was this what drowning was? In the cartoons, you always hear "Heeeelp! Save me!" But not a sound, except the *glub-glub* of bubbles from the pool filter. Drowning? Yes!

And what could a seven-year-old child do? Run get her mother? Dial O and say, the way they taught you in school: "This is an emergency. My stupid sister is drowning"? There was nothing to do. Which was when the nascent trial lawyer took over and, nevertheless, *did*. Lee plunged forward into the water, swimming over to her sister. Dog-paddle, dog-paddle, she thought. Uh-oh, I'm in over my head. I could drown. I'm not allowed out this far. Keep going. Dog-paddle.

Like Lassie. So Lee thrust her head forward and, with her teeth, grabbed the yellow playsuit—and, in doing so, dragged her little sister out of the jaws of death.

Sylvia, roused by the splash of the paddling, was there when

Lee brought Robin up the stairs. "Oh God!" Sylvia screamed over and over. "My baby! Oh, God." Shut up, Lee thought, as her mother, shrieking, grabbed Robin away from Lee, as if Lee had done something wrong. "Oh, God in heaven!" Sobbing, Sylvia held the limp child so tight that, through sheer luck, she squeezed some of the water out of Robin's esophagus. The child regurgitated up the rest all over her mother, to Lee's satisfaction. "What happened?" Sylvia cried, a question directed toward God more than Lee, planting anguished kisses over the little girl's head and face.

"She went into the pool," Lee explained.

"Why didn't you stop her?"

"I didn't see her."

Now that Robin was coughing and gagging and clearly alive, Sylvia laid her gently on the flagstone pool deck and, weeping, almost silently, crouched over and dipped her forearms into the pool to wash off the vomitus. She rubbed and rubbed, then sniffed her skin and pulled her head back in disgust.

"Mim—" Robin gasped.

"Baby," Sylvia said, taking the child back into her arms, although admittedly averting her nose from the stench.

"Mimmy."

"Baby."

Lee turned and walked back into the house. Neither her mother nor her sister noted her departure or her absence. And that would have been that, except for Ethel, the eighth maid to whom Sylvia had said, upon hiring her: I hope you'll soon be a member of the family. On being fired by Leonard that Saturday, Ethel, twenty-three years old and up from Macon, Georgia, knowing there was more to the world than picking peaches, and not willing to take any guff from a white man who had just told her she was Not Willing to Do Her Fair Share, told him he was a mean ole dog with a ninny for a wife—

"I've heard enough!" Leonard shouted at her.

—and he should tell his girlfriend not to wear so much makeup because it came off on his shirts, even if the ninny didn't see it, and did he know Lee saved her little sister's life when the ninny fell asleep and the baby almost drowneded in the swimming pool. Huh? Did he know that?

"What happened?" Leonard was shouting at Sylvia.

She closed their bedroom door so he wouldn't wake the girls. "Nothing."

"She wasn't drowning?"

"No!"

"Goddamn it to hell, Sylvia. I'm sick and tired of having to deal with these maids, and if you can't make do with the next one, then you're stuck. *Stuck*. Either you train them properly or you make the beds yourself. Do you understand me?" His voice rose even louder, filling every inch of the room. There was no corner safe from his anger. "I will not fire another goddamn one of these stupid girls and have them open up a fat mouth to me and—" The knocking on the bedroom door must have been going on for some time, but Leonard and Sylvia didn't hear it until he paused for breath so he might continue his tirade. Instead he opened the door.

"Mommy? Daddy?" Lee wore a pale pink nightgown with tucking all over the chest. She would have preferred Little Lulu pajamas, but her mother had said no, this is much finer-looking, and besides, the pink is perfect in your room. She squinted to keep out the bright lights of her parents' room. "I heard yelling and I got scared."

"Lee," her father began.

"Stop it, Leonard," said Sylvia, trying to cut him off.

"Lee, did anything happen in the pool with Robin?" Lee was no dope. She knew her mother wanted her to keep quiet. But she had been like Lassie. Brave and keen. And no one had said: "You are a noble-hearted creature, Lily Rose," or even: "Thank you."

"Robin was drowning," she said, cocking her head to the side in order to look pert and putting on (it has to be conceded) an obnoxiously smug smile. "I saved her. Like Lassie."

"Where was Mommy?"

"Mommy was . . ." Too late, Lee realized this was a subject better left alone. She shrugged as if to say: Gee, I forgot what I was gonna say.

"Where was Mommy?" Her father's voice was so loud it shook the mirror over her mother's dresser. "Where?" She could feel the voice in her stomach. "*Where?*"

"On the patio," Lee whispered.

"What was she doing?" Lee looked to her mother. Her mother

82

looked away, as if there was something behind the bathroom door that was demanding her attention. *"WHAT WAS SHE DOING?"*

"Smoking." Lee mouthed the word rather than enunciated it. "Her eyes were closed for a second. That's why she didn't see. Just for a second."

Her father sent her away then, without asking to hear the details. That's what she had wanted to tell him about. The details. They were so wonderful: the too hot water, the dog-paddling, the chlorine taste when she grabbed Robin's soaking playsuit between her teeth, the water down her throat and up her nose, what a load Robin was, so don't think she's so skinny compared to me. And to hear her father say: Lee, you were brave and keen.

What she got instead was Greta Wolff, a thoroughly decent, indefatigable, ever vigilant, utterly humorless martinet from Frankfurt am Main, who served as a perpetual reminder to the entire White family that Sylvia was ineffectual and a liar, that Robin needed constant coddling, that Leonard was master of the house — and a merciless one.

And that Lee was a born troublemaker.

Seven

Believe me, I'm not in favor of coddling criminals. I don't want my purse snatched or my head bashed in any more than the next dame. But there's something more than justice we Americans dish out to people who violate our criminal laws. Take Norman Torkelson (or any one of my clients I can't spring on bail). Once they're locked up, we don't just take away their freedom. Nope. We humiliate them.

You want an example? Take the food. To call it unspeakable is to be kind. Three times a day, the inmates receive mounds and patties and globs of stuff the flat, gray-brown color of those splotches of year-old gum that adhere to city sidewalks.

A prison food digression: Years ago, when I was still prosecuting, I spent a day interviewing an inmate, a guy named Alfred Dunder, six feet two, three hundred pounds, with front teeth so buck they protruded almost perpendicular to his gums. Facing life without parole, Alfred had decided to cooperate in our investigation of a homicide—i.e., rat on his fellow murderers. Naturally, I wanted him to live long enough to testify, so our meeting had to be secret. He, Sam Franklin, and I sat in a room near the medical unit that was not much bigger than a stall shower. Around one o'clock, Sam's stomach grumbled, joining mine for a duet. Just then, one of the laughing boys from the sheriff's office brought in Alfred's lunch. He slammed down a tray on which was a plate with three different varieties of stuff Nassau County was calling food. Not only did it look revolting; I had to breathe through my mouth so as not to smell it. Alfred,

84

despite his eighty-five IQ, his brain damage from twelve years on smack and PCP and his total lack of empathy for his fellow human beings, picked up my disgust in two seconds flat. "Hey, Missus D.A., wanna—" he sneered at me, "—eat my lunch?"

But the food is not the most degrading aspect of prison life. If you really want to test-drive your gag reflex, give a look at the toilets in the adolescent men's cell blocks. Or if you find fear more compelling than nausea, take a peek at the inmates themselves. Well, not at them, since many of them are not at all unattractive; they work out and are well-muscled; some of them have lovely smiles and, despite an occasional missing tooth, appear no more malign than the average gas station attendant. No, the peek should be at their rap sheets. Or at their victims' statements—often made from hospital beds, sometimes from deathbeds. I'm not objecting that we put malefactors away. Why shouldn't we? Don't they deserve incarceration in order to garner the traditional benefits of a prison sentence: rehabilitation and deterrence? (That neither occurs very often is a point that should surprise no one in America.)

But if nobody is rehabilitated or deterred, something does happen in our jails. Just about everyone who stays in longer than a month comes out a career criminal. Less than four weeks, a first-timer may still be so staggered by what he experiences, and as yet unable to adjust to the brutishness, that he vows: Never again.

A hard-assed cop like Sam Franklin would say these bad guys are already past redemption when they go in. I don't buy that. I've seen enough eighteen-year-olds go to jail merely stupid or angry or cocky. Two years later, they emerge irreversibly vicious.

Maybe the food and the toilets and the stink and the total depravity of prison are society's way of getting even, as in: This is all you deserve, you thieving/murdering/check-kitting/dope-dealing bastard. Or the ugliness could be the prison authorities' expression of their own rage, as in: This is payback for me having to spend my life working in a jungle, keeping you animals under control. Of course, what makes a person want to be a prison guard is another story: One guy, with a round, cheery, freckled face, the kind of guy who leads everybody in another chorus of "Toorra-Loorra-Looral" on St. Patrick's Day, told me he used to be a Long Island Rail Road conductor, but being a guard paid two thousand bucks a year more. Two thousand extra bucks per annum to spend forty hours a week in hell? I can't believe it's the money that drives a man or woman to put on that uniform any more than the need for sex drives a rapist.

In any case, what we, as a society, do with our rotten eggs is a topic the man in my life (did I mention he's a lawyer too?) and I kick around every so often—like whenever there's a prison riot, or after some guard's finally prosecuted after sodomizing a hundred or so inmates.

I say our prisons have become our mad scientists' labs, in which we create our own monsters. My guy says that my sensibilities are too exquisite for me to be any judge of how the criminal class reacts to revolting accommodations and bad company, since I'd rather die of a ruptured bladder than go to the ladies' room at Shea Stadium. I say: "See? You said it yourself! Criminal *class*." And he says: "There's always been a criminal class, Lee. It's a criminology cliché—pickpockets working the crowd at public hangings of other pickpockets." And I say: "Name one thing we're doing in America to stop the growth of the violent criminal class we're perpetually hysterical about. We're breeding sociopaths as if we had a Department of Agriculture subsidy." And he pours himself another glass of red and says . . .

Forget what he says, because it only goes to show how perverse we must be: two litigators, people who earn their living by arguing, choosing each other.

But he's right about me and the ladies' room at Shea. That's just the point. If I were thrown into the slammer, I might recoil at the food, retch and heave mightily at the sight of the toilet, but sooner or later, I'd eat. I'd go to the bathroom. And after a time, ingesting and eliminating would simply become another part of my day and I'd have no reaction at all. How come? Well, my guy would say you can get used to anything. Inmates don't notice it, if they ever did. And I'd say back to him: They don't notice because their humanity is being ground down. Their senses get duller. Whatever standards of cleanliness and gentility they once possessed get worn away. Ergo, they lose that individual "you": As you are diminished, you become an undifferentiated member of the herd. You mean less. Human life means less.

Which brings us back, once more, to Norman Torkelson, who walked into the visitors' room looking less of a person than he had the day before. Part of it was the uniform, of course: those angry orange pants and the matching shirt that hung loose, like a maternity blouse. They drained his color and degraded his maleness. As he moved to sit in the molded plastic chair across the barrier from me, he braced his hands on the edges of the seat and, as if infirm or arthritic, slowly lowered himself.

"How are you holding up?" I asked.

"Not bad." His voice came out soft, a little weak, as if he hadn't had the strength to expand his lungs fully. "You saw Mary," he said.

"Yes." Then, seeing that he was waiting for more, I added: "She was very nice." That wasn't quite enough. "And so beautiful!"

Norman's face took on a bit of color. His spine straightened, till his posture was erect but nonchalant, displaying a pride of ownership similar to that of the possessor of a new BMW. "She's as beautiful inside as she is outside," he assured me.

"Then you're a very lucky man."

"She talked to you, didn't she?"

"About what?" I asked, looking him right in the eye.

"About my business." He sighed. "She tried to keep it a secret that she told you everything. That lasted about five seconds."

"Mary wants to help you, or help me help you. The last time you and I talked you told me she had nothing to do with your work. I guess it slipped your mind that what she was doing is something lawyers call aiding and abetting."

Norman offered me a boyish grin, one side of his mouth

breaking into a real smile, the other blasé, only mildly amused. I caught myself smiling back as if he'd just said something absolutely delicious.

"You'd be surprised. Mary's a good little actress," he remarked, as I worked on returning my face to its Lee White, Attorney-at-Law, unenchanted expression. "She can put on a whole bunch of different voices. You should hear her. Sweet as sugar in real life, but when she's calling about repossessing my car—it's like an icicle in the heart." He stopped short, made a fist, and started to gnaw on his knuckles. Something was eating at him. "Listen, she doesn't have any exposure on this, does she?"

I gave the knuckle on my index finger a quick, companionable chew. "Well, in your, um, what Mary called the Love Nest . . . Isn't that where she left a message about repossessing the car that Bobette was supposed to overhear?" Norman nodded. "If the cops somehow find out about the Love Nest and get a search warrant, they'll seize the tape from the answering machine. That would implicate her."

"Shit! Listen, do me a favor. They have one lousy pay phone for the whole cell block here. Make a call for me. Just tell Mary to go over—make sure she's not being followed—and get the tape and deep-six it."

I shook my head. "I can't tell anyone to destroy evidence."

I knew he'd be on the phone with her the second he could, saying: Rip it up, stomp on it, burn it. I couldn't stop him, but there's never a percentage in violating the canon of ethics for a criminal client. First of all, the law is a noble institution, if you'll pardon my mush, and lawyers should respect it. I'd much rather think of myself as a cog in the wheel of justice than as a scum bucket for hire. Besides, even if a client were to pay you a fortune to play a little dirty or simply to look the other way, you can't trust him not to turn around and rat on you—big time—the minute it's to his advantage.

"Norman, I understand that part of your business is protecting yourself and the people you work with. But I'm your lawyer. To the extent you keep me in the dark—like not telling me about Mary—you're making yourself vulnerable to attacks by the prosecution. If you're open with me, then

I can anticipate their attacks and be prepared to fight back."

"What do you want me to do? Confess to a murder I didn't commit?"

"Of course not. But if you're going to tell me something, don't con me. If you'd rather not talk about it, just say so and I'll move on." I realized that my chances of getting Norman Torkelson to be candid were as great as my ever getting my upper arms firm enough that I'd be able to wear a strapless gown. But a girl's got to try.

"What do you want to know?" he asked.

"Bobette. You said there was no sex the evening of the murder."

"That's the God's honest truth."

"Mary seems to believe you never had sex with your marks." I looked straight at him.

Norman leaned back in his chair, crossed his arms over his chest, and laughed. "What else am I supposed to tell her? Why hurt her? It's not fun; it's work: I have to make bells ring for ladies who may never have known that bells exist. Believe me, I don't push it, but I can't do business without it."

"How long were you having sex with Bobette?"

"For nine days. It's nine days with everybody. That's the ideal time: when they're starting to feel sure of you and before any doubts arise. I tried to make it shorter—"

"The time between beginning to have sex and the actual sting?"

"Precisely. Nine is the magic number."

"Do you have any set time you wait before initiating sex?"

"Oh, no," said Norman, a little surprised that I wasn't appreciating the subtleties of his operation. "That depends on the lady. I will say, even if it looks as though she doesn't have that much in the asset department, if I'm going to bother to take what she has, I wait at least two weeks before sex. You know, so she feels secure that she has a *relationship*."

"Women like that," I observed. "Relationships, I mean."

"Absolutely," said Norman. "They want to be cared about as a human being. That's what I give them. That, and then the sex. But what I said to Mary is a hundred percent true: It doesn't mean anything." He brought his chair back down on all four legs, and by the time he did, he wasn't laughing anymore. "She's had such a rough life."

"Mary?"

"Yeah. I met her, she was nineteen years old. She'd been out of the house from the time she was sixteen. Her parents beat her. Her old lady would bop her over the head with a broomstick until she was unconscious. The man she married—to get away from her family—he wasn't much better, so she ran out on him. Then she married an older man, but he died. His children screwed her out of everything. And she really loved him. When I met her, she was working as a chambermaid in a motel outside Phoenix. You wouldn't believe it! Her hands were bright red—almost purple—and all swollen from an allergy to the cleaning stuff. And in nineteen years, not one single person had ever behaved decently toward her." Norman looked down at the floor for a minute, then back at me, perplexed. "I don't get it," he said, so choked up his voice gurgled on the "get." "How could someone *not* want to do wonderful things for Mary?"

"Did you always have someone working with you?" I asked. "Making the call about the repossession, that sort of thing?"

"Not at the beginning," he murmured, clearly not liking the subject, wishing we could continue the Ode to Mary Dean. "I didn't want anyone getting messed up in this. I did okay working alone. You know, I had to relate the story of the car repossession myself, and that's not as credible"—he hesitated for an instant to check if I'd noted the "credible" and was appropriately impressed by his vocabulary—"as someone else calling up and putting the squeeze on me. But then I became involved with someone about ten years ago. She was the one who pushed me to be a part of it." Paled as he was by his uniform, pasty from prison food, fluorescent light, and recycled air, he didn't look as if he could attract anyone to a life of crime, much less get women to open their hearts and their savings accounts to him. At our first meeting, the dark hair on his forearms had been appealing. No, more

90

than that: erotic. Now he looked like a dying animal, its sickly skin shining through its thinning pelt.

"What happened with her?" I asked.

He shrugged, not wanting to answer. I waited. "Nothing. It didn't work out," he said finally.

"Any others?"

"Any others . . . what?"

"Did you work with any other woman besides this one and Mary?" He shifted in his seat but didn't answer. "Norman, I'm not your mother trying to pry out information about your girlfriends. I have to worry that on the off chance a story about this case goes out on the wire services or on some cable news program, someone will recognize your name or M.O. and be willing to give information. It wouldn't be a plus if the government put a witness on the stand who could recite the details of your business practices."

"I used different names with them."

" 'Them' meaning your lady friends, your accomplices—not just your marks."

"Right."

"So they don't know Norman Torkelson or Denton Wylie or . . . What name did you use for renting your apartment?"

"Robert McNulty. No, I never use the same name twice." Of course, once caught he was officially stuck with Norman Torkelson, since he had a record with fingerprints attached. Whether Norman was his true name or not I didn't know, but it was the one he was using when he was first booked in 1978 for possession of a forged instrument, having tried to cash a check from a checkbook he'd filched after a night of love with one Lorraine Krumholz, age forty-two, in West Quoddy Head, Maine. He was then eighteen.

"You must have a good memory, with all those names," I said.

"You know the old saying"—he smiled—"that a liar has to have a good memory. I have a *great* memory."

"Then do you remember receiving the forty-eight thousand that Bobette withdrew from her bank?" He didn't answer. "I don't have to tell you about the attorney-client privilege, do I? Whatever you tell me stays with me." I knew this was not exactly a major news item to him, and sure enough, he nodded. "And I'm not trying to find out how much cash you have so I can squeeze more money out of you. Remember, we both signed the retainer agreement."

"Bobette gave me the money."

"And then what?"

"I thanked her for her faith in me. Then I left."

"You never saw her again." Wearily, as if I was becoming stupefyingly boring, Norman shook his head: That's right—I never saw her again. "You know why I ask you that, Norman?"

"No," he muttered.

"Because if for any reason you came back to the apartment and, say, found her dead or dying, there might be some physical evidence of your presence *postmortem* that could link you to the crime. I hate to keep harping on it, but this is a murder charge, and the D.A. doesn't seem inclined to let me bargain this down to, say, manslaughter."

"I didn't kill her!"

"Then all the more reason that we may go to trial, and if we do, I don't want their serologist finding—um—let's say some of your skin cells under her fingernails, on the chance she tried to grab onto you for emotional support as she lay dying . . . if you happened to come upon her after she'd been attacked."

"There's none of my skin under her nails," he said sullenly.

"Good. I need that kind of information. The worst damage you can do to your case is to let me be surprised. I hate surprises. All criminal lawyers do." I tried to look him straight in the eye—in his lovely, limpid blue eyes, to be accurate—but he was staring over at the platform where the guards in charge of the closed-circuit TV monitors are stationed. "Do you have anything more to say on the subject, or should we move on?"

"After she gave me the money," Norman said quietly, "I went out to buy champagne. I always do. See, deep down, the marks are afraid I'll do exactly what I *do*: grab the money and never look back. Subconsciously, they know that my wanting them . . . it's too good to be true." He grinned.

"Well, it is. So if I just pick up and leave, some of them might start getting nervous after an hour or two. I can't afford second thoughts. I don't want them calling their bank or a relative or the police. So I go out, buy a bottle of champagne, and bring it back—surprise!—to celebrate. I offer a toast, something like: 'I love you for you. If it was possible to love you more—which I don't believe I can—I'd love you for your faith in me.'" Norman's big head turned up, heavenward, and as he delivered his lines, there was not a single trace of discernible slickness. For that moment, it really did look as if the light of God were shining through Norman Torkelson as well as upon him. "'I was so down-and-out,'" he continued his spiel. "'I thought: All right, I'll just have to live like this forever. Half a life. I can do it. I've got to do it, for my boys' sake. But then'"—together, Norman and I gulped with emotion—"'you gave me back my passion.'"

God's light flicked off. Norman cleaned under the nail of his index finger with the pinkie nail of his other hand. "When I got back with the champagne, she was dead."

"Did you touch her?"

"No," he said, glancing up from his nail grooming. "I could see she'd been murdered. Strangled. Her neck . . ." He leaned forward and, with great feeling, added: "Her face wore the mask of death!" Too loud. One row away, another lawyer—a blight on the profession whom I'd known for years—and his drug-dealer-to-junior-high-school-students client turned to check out Norman's violation of the unwritten etiquette of the lawyers' visiting hour: that all business shall be conducted in a mumble. And it wasn't only that Norman was too loud. His performance was way over the top. His already long face was stretched out by his high seriousness, as if he was playing up the Lincoln resemblance, trying to capture the Gettysburg moment—just after "shall not perish from the earth" and before the applause.

"You're positive you didn't touch her mask of death?" I probed. I might have phrased my question less sarcastically, but I'd been up late over at my guy's house (he had a lousy chest cold) and I was tired—both from lack of sleep and from Norman's relentless lying. I had to know. I did not relish the prospect of suddenly hearing Holly Nuñez introduce an addendum to the medical examiner's report that stated (to give you a for instance) that a half pint of Norman's saliva had collected in Bobette's cleavage as he drooled with delight while strangling her. "You didn't touch *any* part of her after you found her dead?"

Ethically, I felt I was walking a pretty slack tightrope here; it was hard to balance. I needed to gather all the information I could for Norman's defense, yet some of my questions would inevitably suggest to any person with an IQ higher than that of a Chicken McNugget that just in case he left some trace of himself on the body, he'd better say: Oh, yeah! I did touch her *postmortem*.

"Oh, yeah, I did touch her," Norman said. "I know I shouldn't have, but I was really shaken up. I mean, to walk in with a bottle of champagne and see *that*. I wanted to be absolutely sure she was dead. She *looked* dead, but what if she wasn't? I might have been able to do something."

"Do you remember what part of her you touched?"

"God, I'm not sure. I guess . . . her hand or her wrist, maybe, feeling for a pulse. And I guess her face too. You know . . ." He closed his eyes, I assumed to imagine the scene. "I put my face up close to hers, to see if I could hear her breathing."

"Do you think you might have touched her neck?" I asked.

"You mean, where she was . . ." Norman seemed to find swallowing difficult and, with his thumb and index finger, massaged the sides of his Adam's apple. ". . . choked?"

Clearly, this thought was distressing to him. As often happens, the girl in me began to fight the lawyer in me. The girl wanted to tell Norman: Never mind. Don't even think about those big ugly finger marks on Bobette's throat. So upsetting. However, he wasn't paying me two hundred fifty bucks an hour for being a girl. "Yes," I said, "where she was choked." Then I added: "You can see the marks left by the killer's fingers in the autopsy photos."

"Why would I touch her there?" Norman demanded, his

voice rising, as if I'd asked the stupidest, most impertinent question he'd ever heard.

"I have no idea. But in stressful situations, even the most rational, stiff-upper-lip people can react in strange ways."

"I don't know." Norman exhaled. "I may have reached out and just ... I think for a second, I may have put my finger on her throat. Kind of out of pity."

"Okay," I said coolly, as if my large intestine wasn't going to contract into a knot that would take three days to untie. "I'm glad you told me."

Right. Ladies and gentlemen of the jury. Those very large thumbprints you saw in the autopsy photos, the ones that make it seem as if some fiend had applied horrific force to the area over the larynx ... Those prints were left by the defendant after he found Ms. Frisch dead. They were a gesture of pity and—yes, ladies and gentlemen—love. (Why, you may ask, do I do this sort of work when I could be the Queen of Matrimonial Law and get home at five-thirty, in time to finish the ball fringe on an afghan I've been working on for the past eight months, poach a nice sea bass and reread *Great Expectations?* I really don't know.)

"I felt sincerely terrible," Norman was saying. "A terrible, brutal thing to happen to anyone. And I *liked* Bobette."

"What kind of a person was she?"

"Smart. Native smarts. She wasn't educated or anything. But she had a steel-trap mind when it came to money. Knew the rent for every apartment in the buildings she owned, who owed what, and how many more months they had to go on their lease. Never had to write a thing down."

"Would you say that she was a nice person?"

A small smile of embarrassment passed over Norman's lips at having to speak ill of the dead, but as I'd already graded him B-minus as a con man, it didn't surprise me that he was faking it—and poorly. "She wasn't very nice. In fact ... she wasn't like your typical lady, wanting to be liked. Wanting to be loved, actually. No, she was pretty unusual: going about her business, and if you didn't like her, it was fine with her."

95

"She sounds tough. How come you were able to touch her?" I inquired.

Naturally, Norman didn't buff his nails against his chest or make any other gesture of smugness, but the fluorescents in the visitors' room were too strong not to reveal the flush of pride that colored his forehead. "She was lonely."

"She was fifty-six years old. Presumably, she'd been lonely for years."

"But see"—Norman leaned forward, so his chin looked as if it were glued to the white Formica barrier between us— "the ladies I deal with preselect themselves! The fact that they answer my ad in the personals means they're lonely. Maybe even desperate, because they're not meeting other men."

"So this tough cookie was looking for love?"

"Hey, that's the headline in my ad that she answered! 'Looking for Love.' In her letter she said she just wanted companionship, but then she fell for me."

"Why? I mean, you're a nice-looking man and all that—"

"That's okay," Norman said generously. "Please don't apologize. You see, I play to their desires and their weaknesses. Bobette wanted love: that was her desire. And she was embarrassed about not having a good education: her weakness. So I quoted poetry to her—'Love is not love / Which alters when it alteration finds.' That's Shakespeare. And from Elizabeth Barrett Browning, a sonnet: 'How do I—'"

"I know it," I told him.

"I showed her a different world. A better, finer world. I took her on nature walks. You know, we'd go to a wooded area and I'd point out plants and stuff and give her the Latin names—"

"You know the scientific names of plants?"

"Are you kidding? I just use a few names I've made up: 'It *is* pretty, but it's a common gorse weed, Bobette, a *Rowinda numonica*.' That's where we were that last day, when that tenant of hers called the cops about my car. On a nature walk."

"Tell me about the tenant."

96

"I don't know his name," Norman said.

"Did you ever see him?"

"Yeah. He was foreign. Sort of dark. Not like Indian or anything. Probably from one of those countries that was behind the Iron Curtain. The way he said her name: 'Miss Frisch.' As if he had a big gob in his throat. But that's the way they pronounce things. Guttural."

"I know."

"Sorry," he muttered, trying to look boyish and abashed, not totally succeeding. However, I did feel my heart rise a few millimeters and wished I could find something to say to cheer him. That's what con men do, even the lousy ones. They bring out the best in you—your sweetness, your concern, your love, your passion—and then, when you're wafting about on your cloud of goodness, above mere mortal meanness . . . Whammo! They kick you off so you plummet to earth, headfirst.

"Did you ever have any encounters with this tenant before?"

"A couple of times. I pulled my car behind his crappy Hyundai and he had a fit."

"What kind of a fit? Yelling? Carrying on?" I was thinking: Ladies and gentlemen of the jury, you've seen Mr. Whosis on the witness stand. You've seen his hair-trigger temper. You've seen his clear bias against my client. No, strike that. His *hatred* of Norman Torkelson. His is the *only* testimony linking my client to that house on the day of the murder. But as His Honor will charge you, a witness's demeanor must be taken into account . . .

"No carrying on. Just had on a pissed-off expression. He kept saying: 'Damn it!' over and over. 'Dommit!'" Norman mimicked. "'Dommit! Dommit! Dommit!'"

Later, back in my office, I repeated "'Dommit! Dommit! Dommit!'" when I called my guy and told him about the morning's events and checked up on how he was feeling. "Any relief yet?"

"Well," he said, "my fever's gone down, but I'm still feeling pretty crummy. But you know us guys. Lousy patients."

"Want me to come over for lunch? Bring you something?"

"No. I'll be okay. So what do you think?"

"About what?"

"About your client, Norman."

"What do *you* think?" I asked, having revered his gut reactions in criminal cases for . . . God, nearly twenty years. "Is he guilty?"

"Lee, what do *you* think?" I got that low feeling, when first your stomach drops, then everything else seems to give in to the pull of gravity and falls as low as it can go.

"You tell me. What do *you* think?"

And my main man said: "Guilty as hell."

Eight

Greta Wolff, the housekeeper, clanged pots together and hummed a little ditty from *Der fliegende Holländer*. Not a hummer by nature, and far too deliberate to be a pot clanger, she was trying to drown out the sounds of Leonard and Sylvia's warfare upstairs so that Robin would eat her dinner. Ten-year-old Lee sat at the kitchen table also, but Greta did not concern herself about her. Lee would abandon a meal only if the house blew up and the ceiling collapsed onto her plate.

"I ask you just one thing, goddamn it to hell!" Leonard was raging. Some combination of materials in the house—stone and wood and the wool of their bedroom rug—had synergized and created a trumpet effect, so despite Leonard's deep-voiced fury, his tone descended to the kitchen as a nasal *whaa-whaa*. Greta stirred something vigorously. Lee suspected it was water. But the metal spoon clanging against the stockpot was merely an annoyance, not a distraction. "Be a mother to those kids. Is that too much to demand?"

"I was under so much pressure. I had too much to do—"

But he wouldn't let her finish. "I get a call from the school—"

"Sweetheart, Leonard, please, *please* keep it down," Sylvia shrieked.

Without realizing it, Lee brought her finger to her lips. "Shhh," she hushed.

"The goddamn door is closed," Leonard was hollering. "Now listen: I get a call from the school—"

"I know! I admit it. I made a mistake."

"Shut up and listen when I talk to you! 'Mr. White, we hate to bother you at your place of business, but Mrs. White was supposed

99

to pick up Robin. Her temperature's over one hundred.' *Over one hundred!* 'And she's complaining of a sore throat and earache.' "

"Don't be mad," Sylvia pleaded. She's going to cry, Lee thought.

She glanced over to her sister. Robin, now seven, was repeatedly plunging the tines of her fork into the liver and onions Greta had made for dinner. Apparently Robin hoped that by making enough holes, she would render the meat so porous it would lose its materiality and become invisible.

But on second glance, Lee observed Robin's head pulled, turtlelike, between her knobby shoulders, as if the confrontation upstairs was an attack on her, each word a bashing. The girl's white skin had turned ashen, her breathing rapid and shallow. Sensitive: That was the word for Robin, with family friends and Leonard's employees courteously omitting the "hyper-." If Lee's little sister had been a fictional character, she would have been the pretty princess who detected the pea while lying atop fifty mattresses—notwithstanding that before any consciousness of the legume, she probably would have been weeping and wheezing from an acrophobic attack.

"I apologize. What more can I say?" Sylvia asked. But of course she thought of more. "*Lists.* You say I have nothing to do, but—"

"You don't cook!" It galled him. Last Memorial Day, they'd gone to the annual Shorehaven Estates Beach Blast and he'd overheard Ginger Taylor telling two women that after she and Fos saw that foreign film at the Manhasset Cinema, *La Dolce Vita*, she had bought an Italian cookbook. Ginger had them doubled over with laughter: You can't believe the things I can do to spaghetti! The three of them were like Blonde, Blonder, and Blondest. All of them with beautiful, throaty laughs. And so perfectly got up for the Beach Blast. Dungarees cut off like Bermuda shorts, and sleeveless blouses. Sylvia had on a green linen trouser suit and an enormous straw hat and was pathetically overdressed. And all their neighbors had known exactly what they weren't, probably because of the way Sylvia looked. Shoes with a grosgrain bow and little heels, for Christ sake, for a party where you *know* you're going to stand in the sand! Makeup! None of them wore makeup—except red lipstick. Oh, God, the red lipstick with the streaky blonde hair! True, most of the neighbors had nodded or waved or even said

Hi, but the Whites wound up at a big round table for ten—except the only people sitting with them were a couple in their sixties named Turtletaub, and Frank and Louise Petullo from Harbor Road, the same Petullo the *New York Times* had informed him was Frankie "Salami" Petullo, the reputed brains behind the underworld's takeover of the sand and cement industry. Leonard had wanted to run, flee the horror, but he had to sit there making conversation with Beaky Turtletaub, who kept pushing for an offer of a silver fox wholesale.

"Tell me what you do!" Leonard yelled at the top of his lungs. "You don't clean! You don't—"

"How can I? You're always giving me lists. Get new garbage cans. Get a pegboard for the garage for your tools. *Why*? You never use tools. You bought that power drill set for fifty-four dollars and never once—"

"Shut the hell up!"

"Did someone tell you Foster Taylor has a pegboard and a power drill in *his* garage—"

"I'm warning you." Anger grabbed Leonard by the throat, squeezing his voice higher and higher until it was such a terrible, shrill cry that Robin had to cover her ears. "No more, Sylvia!"

"Leonard, just listen—"

"Shut up, or I'm leaving and not coming back!"

Lee's gut went into a sudden, agonizing spasm. She would always endure this pain in times of severe stress. However, unlike her more high-strung sister (hands over ears, chin aquiver, eyes swimming in unshed tears), Lee could take it on the chin—or in the gut—without falling apart. It was not that her suffering was any less intense than Robin's. The awful contraction just above and to the right of her navel hurt so that she could not catch her breath. However—except for once in her life—Lee had the strength to endure pain. While this may not have been the style of heroines in books—victimized beauties, or stouthearts who are allowed only moral courage, not physical valor or derring-do—this was Lee White. A hearty girl. A stand-up dame.

"They'll get over it, Robin," she said. Robin's hands, clapped over her ears, shook so badly her head bobbed up and down. Lee then tried a diversion. "Hey, Rob, you know next-door's new puppies?" Lee was referring, of course, to Ginger Taylor's latest brood of basenjis, but everyone in the house, even Woofer, the new weimaraner they had gotten after Duchess died, seemed to pick up on the waspishness that the name Taylor roused in Leonard, so they avoided mentioning it.

"So listen," Lee went on "Guess who got one of the puppies?"

"Who?" Robin hiccuped.

"Cathy Foti, in sixth grade. Her parents bought one from Mrs. Whatsis!" Robin blinked, and tears began to spill. Lee tried harder. "Those puppies! *So* adorable—okay, not when they're pooping. They got into Mommy's herb garden yesterday. Mommy had to pull out all her parsley. Anyway, Cathy's mother picked her up at school, and the puppy was in the car. You should have seen it!" Lee massaged Woofer's belly with the toe of her saddle shoe to soften the pain of her betrayal. "Teeny-weeny wrinkles in its little doggy forehead. Oh, and the itty-bitty curly tail."

The experts, having embraced the concept of sibling rivalry, are too quick to dismiss the force of sibling love. Lee, nuzzler of puppies, cuddler of kittens, could not fail to be moved by the fragility of seven-year-old Robin's frame, by the almost cartoonishly-big gray-green eyes that dominated the younger girl's dainty face, by the angelic softness of her pale hair. When not exasperated by Robin's excessive response to people and noises and smells, Lee wanted to protect her from reality.

"You made me take back Grape-Nuts Flakes," Sylvia was squawking.

"Don't make it sound like I held a gun to your head. I asked for Grape-*Nuts* and you bought *Flakes*. You know I hate them. Jesus H. Christ, is it such a big deal to return something to the A & P? What the hell else do you have to do all day?"

"*What else*? Pick up the black wing tips that were getting new heels. Take your gray tweed sports jacket to the cleaners for one-day service." She was probably enumerating, Lee thought, holding down each graceful, tapering finger, its nail perfectly polished—Cherries Jubilee this week—with the index finger of the other hand. "Pick up a baby gift for your accountant's sister—"

"How could you neglect your own child?" Leonard boomed. "How could you leave her in the nurse's office, in pain?"

Lee thought that if she were her mother, she would demand: How come *you* left her in the nurse's office in pain? You didn't exactly run to grab the next train back to Shorehaven. Her mother, Lee noted—with a clarity of thought that coexisted with the ripping pain in her gut—was a lousy arguer, never coming up with a good enough answer. And after these fights, her mother, shaken, ashamed, would take to bed for days, shutting the louvers of the blinds, refusing to come down for meals, not combing her hair or brushing her teeth. Her father, on the other hand, having blown off steam, invariably seemed lighter-hearted than usual, although that may have been because Sylvia was so despondent as to be mute and, thus, incapable of making any emotional demands of him.

But for the moment, Sylvia had not yet given up trying to win over the unwinnable. "Leonard, hon, Robin wasn't dying, for God's sake. It was just a sore throat. She gets sore throats all the time." She added vaguely: "I really should talk to Dr. Gould about her tonsils."

At last, Robin's tears fell. Lee was full of the envy and admiration she always felt. What dazzling crying! First, Robin's huge eyes would glisten. Then perfect, fat teardrops would meander down each cheek. No sobbing, though, although her reed of a body would jerk as if someone were screaming "Boo!" at her again and again. Miraculously, Robin's silent suffering brought her double—no, triple—the attention the average caterwauling child could get.

It wasn't only their parents' fighting that brought tears to Robin's eyes, however. Lee watched the little girl blanch as she took another peek at the liver. Any external event could cause an inner storm. Right that second, it had switched from her parents' fight to dinner. Robin was probably thinking: Doomed. There they were, sitting in the breakfast nook, with Greta just yards away alternately clanging pots and picking over the apples she was going to turn into applesauce. No way could Robin escape the dread liver. True, Greta's powerful back was turned toward them, but that meant nothing. A scrape of the chair leg at a decibel level so low that not even Woofer could hear it would make Greta spin around and blare: Ha! In any other house in Shorehaven Estates, children could flip food to the family dog, but Woofer was as awed by Greta's authority as Leonard and Sylvia were, so even though he lay right there under the table, he could not be relied upon to be the consummate disposal unit dogs by nature are.

Another thing about Robin's genius for crying, Lee mused. You'd think a kid who was such a bundle of nerves would always be grabbing wads of tissues, or wiping off her cheeks with her fingers, or blotting her nose with the back of her hand. But no, Robin never wiped away her tears; they accumulated around her nose or left shining trails until they dripped off her chin. They were mesmerizing, beautiful.

Robin's crying made Lee want to weep with jealousy. At the same time, it also forced Lee to come to her sister's aid—instantly. "Give me your plate," Lee commanded, but softly.

"What?"

"Pick it up quietly and hand it to me. Don't slide it. She'll hear. You take my plate. Don't be *too* quiet or she'll turn around."

"Why should I give you my plate?" asked Robin.

"You're too upset to eat your dinner. I'll eat it for you."

"You're kidding!" Robin's face reflected incredulity, then wonder.

"I'm serious."

"Oh, Lee-lee," Robin cried in her tiny high voice. Although not too loud. (Even as an adult, she would tend to sound like Tweety Bird.) "Thank you!"

"Welcome." Lee, naturally, played the liver for all it was worth, cringing at the taste, shuddering with revulsion at the texture. However, the truth was, she was crazy about liver and onions. In fact, after years of Sylvia's medium-rare meatballs and Chinese Jell-O—an ill-starred combination of lemon-flavored gelatin and julienned water chestnuts with a dash of soy sauce—there was nothing Greta cooked that Lee did not love. Although in later years Lee would refine her palate, her lifetime food preferences remained those of a Hessian day laborer.

"I'm done, Greta," Robin sang out.

At the exact same moment Leonard roared: "You went to Garden City, to a shoe sale at Saks, when your child was sick as a dog in the nurse's office!"

"I said I was sorry." Sylvia was screaming now. "What more do you want me to say?"

"I want you to say: 'I have no other responsibilities except to be a mother to my goddamn kids!'"

Greta set aside her apples and wheeled around for inspection of Robin's plate. "See?" Robin said. Her eyes were still wet. "All finished!" Her heart of a face was suffused with the light of grace under pressure: I have done my best under terribly trying circumstances.

Shrewd Greta turned her pale eyes to Lee's slick lips and shiny chin. "You think I was born yesterday, Miss Lee White? You think I don't know?"

Even way back then, in 1960, Lee would never cop a plea. "Know what?" she inquired, projecting genuine curiosity, even though she was beginning to feel a little nauseous from eating nearly a pound of liver—although not so distressed as to make her willing to forgo dessert.

"Know that you ate your sister's supper. Shame on you!"

"I didn't do anything!"

"No dessert tonight."

"Come on, Greta!" Lee protested. "That's not fair!"

"*I* decide what is fair!" Greta banged her fist down on the dish drainer; a colander rattled, and Robin shook.

Don't be too harsh on Greta here. True, she was a dreadful stiff, but her steel-rod spine grounded the White family. Because of her, floors were washed, dinner was served, Woofer got his rabies shot and the girls their polio boosters—all of which left Sylvia free to pursue her God-given talents: eyebrow-plucking, smoking, and creating bad art. And Greta never once complained, although working in other people's houses was a sad and wearying job.

(Greta had come to the United States in 1937 with her husband, who had determined that being a half-Jewish labor union organizer was perhaps not the ticket to a happy life in Nazi Germany. Although it was still the Depression, he managed to find a job operating a machine that sliced pumpernickel at a wholesale bakery in the Yorkville section of Manhattan. While he did not thrive, he did well, except for his high blood pressure, which he didn't know about. In any case, he dropped dead of a stroke a few days short of his first anniversary in America. Greta took the bit of money they had managed to save and enrolled in a secretarial course. But during the late thirties and early forties, her heavy German accent was an insurmountable obstacle to office employment. However, the same business big shots who would not let her take their dictation did not mind her scouring their bathtubs. In fact, the upper-middle-class families who employed her in the years before the Whites, as well as Sylvia and Leonard themselves, viewed her Teutonic style with approbation. They saw in her inflexible bearing and clipped consonants a benign personification of the efficient German war machine. Therefore, although she was a thoroughly decent person, her employers treated Greta as if she were more apparatus than human—that is, with all the warmth that would be accorded a well-oiled panzer.)

"The little one is all skin and bones!" Greta chided Lee. "How could you take the food from her mouth? *No fresh answers, Miss Lee White!*"

Just as a big grin began to spread across Lee's face, her mother screamed at her father: "Drop dead!"

"Ladies first!"

Lee's grin disappeared, but Robin, no fool, knowing she was off the hook in the dinner department, offered Greta her captivating waif smile. Then she climbed down from her chair and, purposefully, headed to her room. Lee realized: She's going to do it: Until Greta makes her go to bed, Robin will draw, color, and cut out yet another new wardrobe of paper doll furs, mink coats, Persian lamb ski jackets, and sable boas. And the second Mommy and Daddy's fight is over, Robin will be squeaking: "Ooh, Daddy, look!" And Leonard would cry "Fabulous, Robbie-my-baby!" Even Sylvia, in bed, would find enough energy to kiss the top of Robin's head and sigh: "Lovely, sweetheart."

It was going to be a lousy, lonesome night. For less than a second, Lee weighed the advantages of joining Robin and her paper fashions. But to watch Robin sharpen a crayon so the fur hairs wouldn't look too thick, then painstakingly cut out those stupid tiny paper coats in teeny-weeny nips with her mother's old manicure scissors, was too enraging to be borne. Robin's patience for detail was . . . shitty. And her love of style . . . Daddy, I like the way the sleeves go tight on the coat in your window. Is that sheared mink or mouton, Daddy? He lapped it up like a cat with a bowl of milk. He couldn't get enough. And, Mommy, doesn't it look prettier if I button the top button? Mommy would be in heaven, and they would talk about the vital importance of top-

106

button shittiness for a half hour! Shitty! Lee loved that word: *Shitty*!

She had learned it two years earlier at the school bus stop and had yet to say it out loud, but in her head she'd said it a thousand times. Shitty, Lee brooded. Lately, all Robin did was go to her mother's magazines and copy pictures of furs or clothes, and her parents kept having heart attacks of joy. "You have so much flair!" her father would cry. "If it was real sable, I could sell it to Mrs. Continental Can. Split the profits with you, Robbie-baby." Sylvia would sound reverent: "It almost looks like a Norell! I'm absolutely serious!" Lee thought: She's going to spend three damn hours drawing shitty little fur hairs one at a time, and if one doesn't look right she'll erase it! Shitty little brown-nose.

If Lee had been asked about it, she'd have sworn that word would never ever pass her lips. But the very next day, she actually shouted the word—and in defense of Robin. "Get your shitty lacrosse stick away from my sister's lunch box or I'll punch your fat nose in."

"Yeah?" snickered Jasper Taylor, the boy from the house next door. The really tall boy. Jasper, at age ten, the third of Fos and Ginger Taylor's four children, was already well over five feet tall and growing fast. Although slender, he had the powerful legs of a natural athlete and the presence of an all-star. Lee's mass was nowhere near as imposing as his, but at age ten, she had an inch on him. "You and who else?" Jasper demanded.

"I don't need anyone else," Lee growled, making a tight fist and holding it up in front of Jasper's face. "I can punch in your nose all by myself."

To which Jasper gave a raucous, derisive laugh. It made Robin wail with terror, a squeal so maddening that it mobilized both the armies that camped on opposite sides of the corner of North Road and Taylor Farm Lane. As Lee glared into Jasper's eyes— an uninteresting hazel, but quite thickly lashed—fist aloft, and Jasper glared back, two fellow fifth graders from the Shorehaven elementary school grabbed Lee and yanked her away. At the same time, three strapping boys, the entire midfield of the Wheatley Country Day lacrosse team, hauled Jasper back to their bus stop across the street—not without much ostentatious grunting as he fought being brought under control.

Normally, there were no hostilities. The two armies, the private

107

day school students and the public school kids, pretty much ignored each other. Oh, except for periodic spit fights. The origin of this particular form of belligerence is lost in time, but each new generation of schoolchildren on that particular street corner in America came to that place with seemingly innate knowledge of the rules of engagement of class warfare: The spitter has to cross the street and run the gauntlet among the spittee's schoolmates, who are free to try to trip or shove the spitter out of the way, although they may not grab onto the spitter's limbs or clothing and attempt to drag the spitter away. However, once the aggressor gets to his or her quarry, he or she is free to deliver the best shot as soon as the spittee's face is no more than a foot away.

Not that Jasper Taylor had targeted little Robin White for a gob of saliva. Far from it. His intended prey was Todd Lomax, a Shorehaven fourth grader, who had the gaunt, haunted look of a future poet. (In truth, Todd was coarse to the core and looked wretched simply because he had discovered the properties of airplane glue years before his contemporaries.) However, in Jasper's rush to expectorate, he forgot to lay down his lacrosse stick before charging; it accidentally banged Robin's lunch-box—*clunk*!—putting a slight dent in the picture of the Fairy God-mother, beaming as Cinderella stares down at herself amazed to see the ball gown just transmogrified from her rags by a touch of a wand. That was when Lee jumped forward in defense.

"Up your nose with a rubber hose," Lee yelled to him.

"Shut the fuck up," Jasper called back. He sounded bored.

Lee didn't follow him with her eyes. She didn't feel her heart beating faster. In fact, Jasper was out of her thoughts moments after he was back across the street. Unlike her father, she had almost no interest in the Taylors. True, she admired their puppies immensely, but Fos and Ginger's children left her cold. Any curiosity she had was aroused solely by her father's inexplicable response to anything Taylor.

Like last summer. When the sounds of "Sail Along, Silv'ry Moon" poured across the patio at Hart's Hill and down over the Whites' lawn, indicating that the Taylors were throwing still another party, Leonard did not react visibly. He did not stiffen in anger in his lounge chair or cover his face with his hands and weep in grief at once again going unnoticed and uninvited. No,

108

he lay motionless so as not to display to his wife his most sensitive area. Still, Sylvia had picked something up.

"Leonard? Want some lemonade, Leonard?"

"No."

"It's not too sweet."

"No."

"Greta made it."

"No."

"Anything wrong, Leonard?"

"*No.*"

Lee had sensed her father's turmoil as well. How? A slight movement, perhaps, a hollowing of his chest as if he had just received a knife in his heart as the music wafted over him. Or a change in his aura—if successful furriers reading the business section of the Sunday *Times* do indeed have auras—from a self-satisfied peachy beige to a thunderous gray. That the Taylors had the power, simply by playing a Billy Vaughn record, to drive her father to near insanity, even for an instant, made them an object of concern for his eldest child. But not dread. She had seen the Taylors: They were simply not scary.

Lee had seen Mr. Taylor only a couple of times. A creep, in her estimation. His chin was attached to his neck by a large, flappy patch of flesh, like a pelican's. His eyes were bulgy. He looked like a slow reader. Mrs. Taylor was blonde and pretty, except if you saw her walking down Main Street and she passed you up real close: You could see wrinkles crisscrossing every part of her face, hundreds of tiny tick-tack-toe patterns. And the kids: The two big girls now were away at boarding school. They were okay, except the one whose freckles were so close together it looked as though she had a brown butterfly tattooed on her face. She was always giggling. The other girl never smiled. Jasper, admittedly, may have been a jerk, but no worse than any of the Wheatley jerks in their stupid ties and jackets, like they were on their way to an office instead of fifth grade. There was a little Taylor brother, too young to go to school, who always waved at whoever he saw, flapping his hand back and forth in a floppy-wristed frenzy. "Hiya! Hiya! Hiya!" he'd call.

"How's your father, the goy?" her grandmother Bella inquired. The question could have been asked the following weekend, since it was one Bella invariably posed, but it was now two years later.

Lee was not perched on the brink of adolescence, as are many twelve-year-olds; she had gone over the edge. Her breasts were now larger than her biceps, and she had forsaken her tree climbing, her racing, and her roughhousing with the neighborhood boys for the lesser pleasures of the junior high school girls' tennis team. Coming of age as she had in 1962, at the height of the Jacqueline Kennedy mystique, and being Sylvia's daughter, Lee bore herself rather elegantly. She sat with her legs crossed only at the ankle, no matter how her body yearned to slump and tie itself into its comfy prepubescent knot. Lee's figure was fine, even noble, with the lovely shoulders and strong thighs of Winged Victory— although in a family of the small-boned and wasp-waisted, she felt too large, which she interpreted as being fat. She was beginning a lifetime crusade against an ever evolving list of wicked carbohydrates and satanic fats. Her face had lost its round girlish good looks and had yet to come into its bright-eyed, clear-skinned adult prettiness; every day at least one pimple popped up on one feature; her nose had bloomed faster than her cheekbones, forehead, or chin and would have totally dominated her face if not for the competition from her stick-out ears. Her hair had become her crowning glory, turning from plain brown into a thick chestnut mix—the warm gold of the nut mingled with the intense red-brown of the shell.

"Daddy? He's fine, Grandma," Lee replied absently, all her energies focused on a single loop of pink wool.

"Who's he fooling—*White*—with a schnozz like a knockwurst?"

Lee was tempted to ask what "schnozz" meant but, fearing it was yet another Yiddish word for "penis," kept silent. She was spending the weekend at her grandparents' apartment in Brooklyn and, as she always did, had taken over Bella's crocheting. This current project was an afghan comprising squares with a tricky rose design in the middle that required all her concentration.

"They fight?" Bella inquired, with a casualness that immediately caught Lee's attention. Bella always described herself as having retired from acting, but truth is, even in the Yiddish theater, where extravagant gestures were anticipated and overacting was applauded, Bella had been deemed lacking in subtlety. The truth was she had not jumped off the stage; she had been pushed. But as Bella did not find the truth appealing, she ignored it and created her own Biography of a Star (she had been too great to be a mere ingenue) who had left audiences weeping and critics gnashing their teeth in despair at her departure. And she did it all for the love of—as Bella always told it when relating the details—"a regular Joe named Nat."

"Fight? Who? My parents?"

"No, not your parents. Debbie and Eddie." Bella patted her hair, pleased with her show business allusion. She had a new hairdo, Lee noted, a bun of dyed red hair, a swollen thing, that looked like a bite from a huge and vicious insect, but her grandmother seemed quite pleased with her appearance. Then again, Bella believed herself to be a ringer for Rita Hayworth, demonstrating an exuberant ego not often found in three-hundred-pound, fifty-six-year-old working-class women in the outer boroughs of New York City. Satisfied with her hair, Bella let her left hand drift over to the coffee table, where it discovered a bowl of M&M's, and scooped up just three fewer than the critical mass of sugar-coated chocolate that would induce diabetic shock. "Of course I mean your parents. Hey, you're stretching the wool too tight, Miss Lily Weissberg."

"That's not my name."

"It's what your name oughta be. Now it's too slack; tighten up the littlest bit. Good. And you know it and I know it and your father, Mr. White, knows it. White! Like he's from Ohio, with a cow. 'Howdy, Farmer White. How's your alfalfa this year?' 'Not bad, if I say so myself.'"

Lee smiled and, abandoning what her mother called "proper carriage," wriggled deep into a corner of the couch: Ah, a perfect meeting of buttocks and cushion. The furniture in her grandparents' living room had been sold to them at a going-out-of-business sale by a salesman who swore the entire suite—couch, two club chairs, a side table, and a coffee table—would last forever, little knowing that for once he was telling the truth. Besides being rugged it was comfortable. And unusually hideous, a Brooklyn restatement of French Provincial style that might have been better left unsaid: painted white wood with flecks of gold, skinny legs, upholstered in royal blue. An odd choice, perhaps,

111

for a card-carrying Communist and his apolitical (but nominally fellow-traveling) wife, but the Weissbergs were blind to its pretensions and saw only its brightness. "Livens up the whole apartment!" Bella had decreed. Lee, whose aesthetic judgment had been honed by Sylvia, grasped that the suite was in the worst possible taste. Nevertheless, side by side with her certitude of its hideousness lay the contrary belief that her grandparents' furniture was the most regal anywhere. Besides, with its fat pillows filled with cheap, chopped-up foam-rubber, it was vastly more comfortable than the icy spareness of the Whites' Bauhaus furnishings.

"So?" Bella demanded.

"What?"

"Do they fight?"

"Once in a while."

"What about?"

"I don't know. They go upstairs and shut the door. I just . . . Their voices get louder, but I can't hear what they're saying."

"You think I was born yesterday?" Bella demanded. Her voice, easily capable of projecting from the Flatbush section of Brooklyn to an audience on the Lower East Side of Manhattan, resounded in Lee's ears. A second later, she softened her statement, smiling in kindly fashion, her mouth a tiny upturned crescent in her round moon of a face. "You don't gotta tell me nothing if you don't want to, toots."

"There's nothing much to tell, Grandma."

"Fine by me."

Two silent stitches, then: "There's nothing Mommy does that makes him happy. Even when she tries."

"So give me a for instance," Bella said, sitting back, crossing her arms and resting them on her shelf of a bosom.

"Like dinner parties. You know? Like they had twelve people over, and I helped her set the table. It looked beautiful, with the Georg Jensen silver—"

"Who?"

"Their good flatware."

"Flatware," Bella breathed. "God in heaven."

"Anyway, she made a centerpiece with a bunch of twigs and dead leaves and white roses." Catching her grandmother's about-to-curl lip, Lee added: "I know it sounds icky, but it was really

112

beautiful. Very ... What Mommy and Daddy call 'stark.' That means plain but in a very good way." Lee took a deep breath, hesitating to give her grandmother ammunition in her campaign against her son's life. "He came in, around six-thirty on Saturday. He'd been at the store all day. Mommy took him into the dining room, you know, to kind of show it off. And he said: 'Oh.' Just 'Oh.' And right away Mommy started acting too happy, the way she always gets when she's . . ."

"When she's what?"

"Afraid of him. No. I don't know. When she's . . . She wants him to love what she does, but the second he saw the centerpiece, he just stared at it. And she started acting even happier—laughing too much—ha-ha-ha!—telling about how she'd walked in the woods in back of the house to find the twigs and stuff and how she copied the idea from the dinner dance at the Museum of Modern Art . . . just blabbing away a mile a minute."

"And what did he say?"

"Nothing. No, wait. He said, 'They did those arrangements *two years ago*.' Then he said he had to go up and shower and change, but she kept hanging on to his arm and asking over and over 'Is anything wrong, Leonard?' So finally, he said: 'No. Everything's fine and dandy.' And then he just yanked his arm away and went up. Mommy sat down on one of the chairs and started crying, the way she always does."

"What way?"

"Putting her head all the way back. So her mascara on her bottom eyelashes doesn't run."

Bella took the crocheting out of Lee's hands and put her arm around the girl, pulling Lee into the shelter of her warm, fat body. "Is he like this with you, tootsie?"

"No."

"Is he okay with you kids?"

"I always kid around with him. He says I've got a big mouth, but he doesn't mean it in a bad way. He likes when I'm . . . what's the word? Spunky. And he likes that I'm good at tennis and get mostly A's at school. Robin gets A-pluses. She's a big cry-baby and can't do any sports. Daddy says learning sportsmanship is a key."

"Key for what?"

113

"For life. But he doesn't play any sports."

"So how does it come to be a key?"

"I don't know. So I tell him about all our games and what Coach says about my backhand—a killer backhand—and it makes him happy." Lee put the wool rose on her lap. "Happy in a kind of phony, excited way. He says: 'Super-duper!' I think he's happier when Robin draws designs for him." Lee's normally golden skin took on a yellowish hue, as if all the bitterness deep within had risen to the surface. "He's using one of her designs at his store. He's actually having it made up. A raccoon coat with a hood that zips on and off." Lee's mouth tightened until her lips disappeared. "I can't draw."

"Big damn deal. You got a killer backside, right?"

"Backhand."

"Whatever. And you know I love your sister, but if a tennis ball came flying at her, she'd piss in her pants."

"More than piss."

"Right. So you're very, very unique. Never forget that. You can play tennis and get A's and crochet like you was born with a hook in your hand. And you're a good girl too, nice through and through. *And* you're nobody's fool. Smart as a whip. Smart enough to know that nothing is ever going to make your father happy."

"Why not?" Lee asked.

"Because what he wants is to be whatever he's not. Mr. Joe College."

"How come he couldn't get a scholarship? He was smart, wasn't he?"

"It wasn't smartness. It was"—Bella touched an area around her solar plexus—"heart. I kept telling him: 'Lenny, you can be anything you want, Lenny. You're a brilliant kid, and you got a chance at the brass ring good as anybody's.' But he never believed that. He saw the deck stacked against him, with the plutocrats— you know, the haves—raking it in and the working-class getting *dreck*. That's always true, and don't you forget it. But now and then a person can make himself an exception. Something inside Lenny went bad, though. Like a disease that ate out the meat from his heart. Still and all, he did make a good business. Right? But he never got his true dreams. To be a big-shot lawyer in a three-piece suit. To be a sport. To be a goy. He got trapped in his own skin."

"And he didn't have the heart to fight his way out?" Lee asked softly.

"You got it in a nutshell."

"So why is he mad at my mother?"

"Because . . . Maybe you're too young for me to be talking to you like this, but you know what I always say? 'What the hell!' So here's what I think and I told your grandfather and he for once in his life didn't say, 'Bella, you're nuts.' Lenny is mad at Sylvia because the girl of his dreams don't want a furrier."

"But she keeps trying so hard to make him happy. It'll never work, will it?"

"I don't think so, toots."

"So I have one question."

"Shoot."

"If he doesn't like himself, and he doesn't like her, and they'll never be—you know—a fun couple . . . There's a fun couple next door, in that big house, up on the hill. But not my mother and father. They'll always be a pair of losers my father can't stand."

"Go on."

"Don't losers have loser kids?"

"No! Not on your life, toots."

"It's not what I think, Grandma. It's what Daddy thinks. He's got me and Robin. But if he had a son like . . ." The name Jasper Taylor choked her. She couldn't say it. She had watched her father standing transfixed, adoring, gawking up at Jasper racing along the perimeter of Hart's Hill's grounds with a huge kite shaped like a sailboat streaming behind him. Leonard had been so taken up with Jasper that he was oblivious that he had turned the pool backwash lever and that water was gushing out over his kidskin loafers.

And so Lee changed the subject and asked for a vanilla Coke. Thus, she never got to say Jasper's name to her beloved Grandma Bella, who died of a hot fudge sundae three months later.

Jasper disappeared from Lee's life the following September, when he went away to prep school, the same school Foster had attended, a prestigious, pedagogically third-rate institution named

115

for an Anglican saint so obscure the Archbishop of Canterbury would not have recognized his name. The next time she saw him was three years later, the summer of 1965, when they were both fifteen. She did not recognize him.

"Jazz!" one of his friends called from the counter of Dante's Pizza, and Jasper-now-Jazz slid out of his booth and ambled over, barefoot, to help his buddy carry the sodas.

It was his feet that drew Lee's attention away from the half-plain, half-sausage-mushroom-meatball pie that lay between her and Robin. Naked feet. "Ick!" Lee said. Going sockless was one thing: In Sylvia's book even that was tolerable only if accompanied by white duck yachting trousers, a striped boat-neck sweater, and a net income of over one hundred thousand dollars per annum. But a kid who went barefoot, even in his own house, was inviting society's condemnation and opportunistic infectious disease.

"Ooky-pukey," Robin agreed. Despite this comment, she was a much-improved child. The onset of menarche, which signals a period of tribulation for so many young women and their families, had actually calmed her. Some biochemical magic soothed her overstimulated dendrites, and while she was certainly still high-strung, she was no longer an identifiable basket case. "*Bare*foot!"

Jazz's feet were big, Lee noticed as he passed her table, with some light brown hair on the tops and the toes and black filth on the soles. His calves were hairy, although he was tan and the brown hair had turned gold. Muscular calves. She looked up. Blue-and-green madras Bermuda shorts and a blue golf shirt with an alligator on the breast. An alligator! *Mon dieu*, Lee actually said to herself. (She was at that time traveling with the Shorehaven High School intellectual set, and she let out a fast exhalation, a cross between a snort and a sneer.) His biceps looked predictably strong, but what aroused her interest, to say nothing of her libido, were his forearms. Clear muscular definition. Powerfully developed brachioradialis bulging under the tanned skin. And those curly golden hairs; she sensed she could lift one with the very tips of her fingers and it would spring back. Lee glanced up, but he was standing at the counter, beside his friend, a tall drink of water, kibitzing with Dante, Junior.

"I'm full," Robin announced.

"No shit, Ajax," Lee mumbled, her eyes on the forearms.

116

"I'm going to tell Mommy you said 'shit,'" Robin said, with less malice than a realization that her sister's attention was elsewhere and she wanted it back. Greta had taken one of her rare days off, and her parents had gone to a charity party in a tent somewhere far out on Long Island, at the "cottage" of one of Leonard's customers—which Lee knew was rich-talk for an estate on the ocean (unless the rich person happened to be referring to the hovel in the woods where his groundskeeper lived in degradation and squalor). Bred as Lee was by Sylvia and Leonard and molded by Galsworthy's novels (*The Silver Spoon* had fallen off the shelf at the library and hit Lee on the shoulder as she was browsing—at a time when she should have been studying for her plane geometry regents), her knowledge of upper-middle-class white Anglo-Saxon Protestant mores was near-encyclopedic, albeit wildly outdated and next to useless, unless an awareness of the proper livery for footmen is considered a good thing to know.

"I don't care what you tell Mommy," Lee told Robin. "Tell her I say 'shit.' Tell her I say 'fuck.'"

At this second, Jazz, passing her on his way back to the table with four paper cups filled with ice and a large bottle of Nedick's, startled. Then he looked at her and smiled. A lovely smile (although his teeth were slightly crooked from overcrowded conditions and a belief by Ginger that nice families do not send their children to orthodontists). He had a pleasing face too. Its contours had sharpened in a fine, masculine fashion, changing from rounded to rectangular. His strong jaw now joined his face at right angles.

Lee looked up at him. His smile, she could see, was neither a snotty smile nor a lascivious one, the kind a boy gives to the sort of girl who would say "fuck" in Dante's. It was . . .

"He heard you say it!" Robin whispered, aghast. "The F curse!"

Lee didn't deny it, but then, her attention was now focused on his receding back: more specifically, at the angle made by the bulges of muscle that were his buttocks as they tapered into the columnar solidity of his thighs. When he sat in the booth, he chose the seat that faced her. Thank you, she said to the God in Whom she already did not believe. But the boy wasn't smiling at her anymore, not even looking at her. That was good, though, because it gave her a chance to study him. His friends were rich dipshits, probably private school kids, as was he. But he was different. They made loud, stupid sports talk about someone being traded to Detroit and pulled long strings of mozzarella cheese from the pizza up into their mouths and made gross sucking noises. He just sat blowing on the slice he'd taken and looking pensive. No, serene. No, sensitive. That was it! He was so far above the morons he was with it wasn't funny.

"Lee!" Robin whined, demanding her attention. Lee hated this: being stuck with her sister on a weekend. "Lee!" It was an error, staring at the boy, because Robin turned and followed her gaze. "Why are you staring at him?"

And a bigger error to deny it so vehemently. "I am *not* staring at anyone, you infantile ass."

"You are too!"

"Shut up!" Lee snarled.

Robin fell into shocked silence, not comprehending the intensity of her sister's response. A second later, she did. "You have a crush on him," Robin taunted. "I can tell!"

"I do not!" Lee insisted, feeling her face, her neck, turning red, then purple, with mortification. Lee's throat felt constricted. Her chest tightened. She could barely get out the words because of the terrible feeling she was choking. "If you don't shut up, I'll kill you!"

"Ooh, I'm so scared!"

Lee flared her nostrils, which usually caused Robin to at least squirm in her seat, but this time it was a futile gesture. So she narrowed her eyes and glowered at Robin. "I'll tell Mommy where her three bars of Je Reviens soap went."

"Yeah?" Robin challenged her, although Lee picked up a quaver behind the resolution. "Where?"

"Over to Erica Johanson's for a slumber party, that's where. And if Mommy finds out . . ."

"You tell her that and I'll tell her you're madly in love with Jasper Taylor!"

"What?" Lee demanded, confused.

"With Jasper Taylor."

"Next-door's kid? Are you kidding? That's who he is?"

"That's him. Pizza boy."

Lee stared at the boy two booths down. "That's . . . ?" Even before Robin nodded triumphantly, she knew it was true. Well, he had been away at school someplace. She hadn't seen him since . . . God, it must have been elementary school. He'd changed so much.

His long leg was stretched out from the booth. His bare, dirty foot—did rich kids get some guarantee public school kids didn't, that germs wouldn't crawl into minuscule cuts and turn gangrenous, leaving them four-toed, unable to wear thongs for the rest of their lives?—extended into the aisle that led to the counter. This boy was Jasper Taylor? He wasn't that conceited idiot . . . although his eyes and the shiny brown hair . . . Yes! Someone had called him Jazz!

"You love Jasper Taylor!" Robin jeered. Too loud. He didn't hear her words, not consciously anyhow, but his name registered subliminally, and Lee saw his toes stop wiggling for one harrowing second. "You love—"

Lee grabbed her sister's bony wrist. "Shut up," she ordered. "Shut up or—" She was so agitated that for once she was at a loss for words. She couldn't think of any threat dreadful enough to stop Robin.

But Robin stopped herself. The look on her older sister's face: teeth clenched, mouth twisted downward into an anguished grimace, her brows coming together into a terrified V . . . "Okay," Robin soothed Lee. "I won't say it." Lee nodded, unable to speak—and also, Robin noticed, unable to withdraw her eyes from the Taylor boy's face. Lee's shoulders relaxed slightly, but she was still in the grip of some passion that would not release her, to return to being Lee, regular Lee, the big sister with the easy smile and the wise mouth. "Lee?"

"What?" Lee's eyes were on the boy as he licked a drop of tomato-tinged olive oil from his chin.

"Is he *that* good?"

"Yes," Lee told Robin, when she finally found her voice. "He's that good."

119

Nine

My private investigator, Terry Salazar, had a sweet, raspy tenor, the sort of voice heroin-addicted male blues singers with cult followings have: every word slow, provocative. His is the sound that makes every woman—semi-literate teen punks, Indiana Republicans—fantasize about writhing on rumpled sheets.

"Hello," I said into the speakerphone.

"Hey, Lee!" I didn't have to ask: Who is it? "You are fucked," he gloated.

"Badly?"

"No. Bad." Terry was a real American man. He guarded against any behavior that might remotely be considered feminine, like saying "please" or using the proper adverbial form. "You're fucked up the ass bad." I pushed the button to mute the speaker, lifted the receiver, and listened. "They got Bobette's tenant, his name is . . ." Terry paused, and I heard him riffling the pages of the small spiral notebook he kept on each of his cases. ". . . Eugene Pohl. Eugene got treated to a lineup yesterday afternoon. All five guys were six-three and over—just so you can't bitch about how long, tall Normie stood out."

"Was Pohl able to ID Norman?" I asked.

"It wasn't easy. It took him—Jesus—at least a tenth of a second."

Attorneys like me hire ex-Nassau County cops like Terry to do background on a case because of who they know—law enforcement types who never talk to a defense lawyer. But it's more than contacts: Smart cops know how to conduct an inquiry into a murder case. Terry had been a detective sergeant in Homicide and was a first-class investigator. He did more than just ask questions. Radiating rough charm when he felt it was necessary, he could get an enormous amount of information out of all but the most reticent of witnesses. Women would open up to Terry because they couldn't bear for him to leave. It wasn't that he was objectively handsome, but he was unequivocally masculine: A woman can sense when she is in the presence of erectile tissue. Men reacted to his gruff warmth. Although he didn't brag, they sensed his mastery of traditional male talents: hot-wiring a car, shooting a gun, deceiving his wife. They wanted Terry to approve of them, so they, too, kept talking.

Eugene Pohl, apparently, was one of the few exceptions. "He wouldn't say a word," Terry informed me. "What a pussy! You know, the kind who tucks his napkin in his collar so he won't get soup on his tie."

"Is he prissy, or is he what people imagine when they hear 'computer nerd'?"

"Computer nerd."

"Truly bizarre or just a little nerdy?"

"A big nerdy. Puny, and he's got a shiny bald dick-head. But, Lee, don't get your hopes up. He's definitely not someone you could make the jury believe is more of a killer than your pal Norman Torkelson."

"You have no idea what I can get a jury to believe," I snapped back.

I was angry at Terry for having doubts, for expressing them, but most of all, angry at myself for going along with his questioning my abilities. Even if only for a second, I'd let myself think: This case is too big for me. In all the years I'd known him, Terry had never given me a boost: Hey, you're going to *destroy* this guy on the stand! No, he was always negative. And my gut reaction always was: You must be right.

"Terry."

"What?"

"You really are a mean-spirited jerk. I'd call you misogynistic too, except you're too ignorant to know what that means."

"Lee, trust me on this. At most, he'll sweat a little. But you think he's going to start twitching on the stand and act real deranged in front of the jury once Holly Nuñez gets done preparing him? What the hell gives with her, anyway? Always so happy. 'Hi! You must be Terry! Grrreat to meet you, Terry!' "

"She's a little on the perky side."

"Doing her must be like fucking a white bread."

Which meant Terry was powerfully attracted to Holly and would make her his pet project over the next six months. I sighed, regretting the wisdom that comes with age, and switched the phone to the other ear. "Find out what you can about Eugene Pohl," I said, weary. "At Snapple—and ask around the neighborhood. Maybe someone knows something. Maybe he was trying to make time with Bobette himself, move up from the basement and become master of the house."

While I doubted this would be my defense strategy, I did not need to hear Terry's rollicking laugh. "Yeah, right, Lee. They'll come back with a 'not guilty' before the bailiff has time to take the lunch order. What are you going to say? Eugene Pohl was jealous of Norman's success with Bobette, so he set it up to make it look like Norman—"

As this was an accurate assessment of a strategy that had been flitting around the back of my mind, I slammed down the phone. I was regretting my childishness, when Terry called back to inform me Holly had told him that the discovery material on Torkelson was ready anytime I wanted it. Then he hooted: "Eugene Pohl and Bobette Frisch!" So I banged down the phone again.

The rest of that morning and afternoon, I got bogged down with a couple of other cases, including an unlawful use of scientific material and transportation of stolen property in interstate commerce, a crime I'd never tried before. My client, a secretary, had been fired from a small company in Lynbrook that did pharmaceutical testing. She admitted to me that she had stayed late one night, copied all their results on a new drug for treating hepatitis A, and mailed the secret data to the CEO of Upjohn—just so the Lynbrook people would "realize their systems weren't secure." The CEO, no lunkhead, called the FBI. My client was, frankly, nuts, so I spent half the day trying to arrange an appointment for me and her therapist (who concurred with my diagnosis) to try and talk the chief of the Criminal Division of the US Attorney's Office in the Eastern District out of prosecuting.

By the time I came up for air it was after five, so I left a message on Holly's voice mail that I was walking over. It was gorgeous out! I couldn't believe I'd missed it, holed up in an office building, the tenderest of spring days, with air that smelled so sweet you regretted the time it took to exhale. The grass around the courthouse was so new, so velvety, you wished you could forget you were an adult and simply roll around for a while on its softness, then lie on your back and let the late-afternoon sun warm your face.

"It's beautiful out there," I told Holly. "Makes me want to gambol in the grass."

In response, she handed me a file that had an ominous heft to it. Without being invited, I sat and started going through the material. At first glance, there was nothing to send me back outside with a song in my heart.

"Uh, Lee," Holly said, with regret so phony they'd be able to smell it twenty-four miles west, at the Fulton Fish Market, "I hate to bounce you, but I have *tons* of stuff I've got to do. Could you read it tonight or tomorrow? Then I'll clear the boards for you whenever you want to talk about it."

"In a second," I muttered, looking for something to get outraged about so I could accuse her of bad faith, put her on the defensive, and, with any luck, give her a bad night. Then, I actually found something! Another set of finger-prints—an unknown person's—all around the first floor of Bobette's house, including on the coffee table in the living room, right where her body had been found. "These prints!" I gasped. Really gasped. Luckily, the walk over to Holly's office with balmy May breezes wafting about had triggered my allergies, so my words came out in a giant wheeze, as though the finding had knocked the breath out of me. "There's somebody else's prints *inches* from where the body was found and *without any further investigation* you still arrest Norman and throw him right in the slammer."

"You know he would have run if we didn't," she said. But I could see the notion of the other prints were causing her a mite of concern, although, God knows, no discernible anguish.

"Why would he run? He didn't kill her."

"Oh, Lee!" she said, giving me one of those peppy-people smiles that display thirty-two teeth. "Give me a break."

"Why should I give you a break? Are you giving my client a break and trying to track down those prints?"

"He killed her. He doesn't deserve a break."

"How hard did you try?" I demanded, knowing the limited resources of the D.A.'s office. "You're holding what looks to me a lot like exculpatory evidence, and you let it lie here in the file?" Before she could arrange her face into still another sprightly expression, I said: "I want a copy of those prints."

"They could be anyone's," Holly objected.

"Like whose?"

"I don't know. The maid's."

"Holly, do you know for a fact that she had a maid?" Holly tried to look thoughtfully at her new acrylic nails, but I knew the answer was no. "Maybe they're the butler's prints," I suggested. She started buffing the shell-pink nail of her ring finger with her right thumb. "Did you check Eugene Pohl's prints, by any chance?"

"They're not his."

"I need those prints, Holly."

"I'll get them for you."

"I need them now."

"Lee, it's . . ." She made a big deal of looking at her watch and letting her mouth drop open. "I can't believe it! I really have to—"

"I'll wait," I told her.

Right before lunch the next day, I met Terry at the Love Nest and handed him a copy of the prints. He had pals

124

everywhere, and I was hoping the one he had in the state police could run a thorough computer check.

We stood on the sidewalk. Terry gazed at the exceedingly unlovely Love Nest, Norman's place of business, with amazement and respect. "He rented this place to take rich women to fuck?" To be a successful seducer in a depressing place like this was no small triumph.

"He must have done his romancing in their places first. After that, who knows? I guess love is blind."

" 'Love?' " he demanded, full of pity at my stupidity. "The guy must have had a schlong that went from here to Cleveland."

Though Norman's practice was to tell his marks the place was only temporary, till he could get back on his feet, I was still astounded any woman in her right mind would be willing to go inside. The apartment building, a cube of sand-colored brick, wasn't so bad in itself. Neither was the neighborhood, which appeared largely black and working class. But the site of the building: a mini-slum. Instead of a lawn, there was a packed-down dirt patch that sustained only a few pale-green sickly weeds. The dirt and the front walk were littered with cigarette wrappers that seemed to have blown in from all of Long Island. But that was just small-time litter. There was also a bicycle wheel from which the tire had been removed, a bouquet of pitted aluminum tubes from what once had been a folding chair, old beer cans crushed in the middle.

"Anything else besides the prints?" Terry inquired as he crouched to get a look at the make of the front-door lock. I reached past his shoulder and opened the door. Terry gave me a sour look, but the next second we were in a small hallway, an apartment on either side. On the door to the right, a business card was taped directly under the buzzer: Denton Wylie—the alias Norman had used with Bobette. Centered right beneath the name was printed: *INVEST-MENT*, and under that: "The Newsletter for the Venture Capitalist." In the lower-right-hand corner was an understated, lowercase "publisher and editor in chief." Terry eyed the lock on the apartment door. I motioned for him to go ahead; his key ring was so full it would put me on tilt, and sure enough, he got us inside in less than a minute.

The apartment was not as hideous as I'd expected, but that isn't saying a lot. Terry got busy in the kitchenette peering inside cabinets, looking for whatever it is private investigators hope to find: additional corpses or, more likely, unopened bags of Doritos.

I found a tissue in the pocket of my attaché case and used it to lift the lid of the answering machine that stood on a counter that separated the living room from the kitchenette. As I'd suspected, Norman had ordered Mary to get rid of the incoming message tape, which had her Repo Lady impersonation; it was gone. Terry followed me into the bedroom. "Wow!" I said. We stood silently and gazed at the bed: round and so huge that in order to get to what I assumed was the bathroom, you had to inch sideways, your back pressed against the wall. The bed was covered in a too shiny polyester throw that looked more like a tablecloth than a spread. Not that you'd want to eat off it; from its almost imperceptible odor, you knew it had not been laundered, or even vacuumed, for years. Plus it had a couple of pudendum-shaped stains near the circumference. Still, I understood why Norman had rented the apartment. The bed was as effective as a flashing neon sign advertising: HOT SEX! HOT SEX! THE SEX YOU DREAM ABOUT! HOT SEX!

Terry sidled along between bed and wall to go and check the bathroom. When he came back, unedified, he plopped down and patted the mattress beside him. "Have a seat."

"And get gonorrhea from that bedspread?" I leaned against the wall, slightly off to the side so that our knees wouldn't touch in the confined space. "Let me brief you on the discovery material." Terry reached into his inside jacket pocket and pulled out his notebook and a pen. I continued: "Their witness list has the usual cops, scientific experts. No DNA guy. That sounds as though they didn't find any of his skin cells under her nails or anything during the autopsy."

"Let me see the autopsy report," Terry said. Sandi, my secretary, had made copies of almost the entire discovery material for him. I took a fat manila folder from my attaché case and handed it to him. He'd been in Homicide for nine years and knew what to look for better than I did. "It says he didn't fuck her," he said after a few minutes' reading. "Poor bitch's last day on earth, and she didn't get laid."

"She ate a chocolate bar. She still had chocolate all over her mouth."

"I know you think that's as good as getting laid, but it's not."

He went back to the report. I watched him read. Terry looked like a cop, with a too flat hairstyle, slightly too tight blue suit—half an inch too much sock showing—and the kind of mustache that went out of fashion in 1973. He had quit the force three years earlier when he turned forty-one, the day his pension vested, and gone to work as head of security at a fairly upscale shopping center in Greenvale. But despite the big paycheck, the thrill of dealing with stolen Volvos and teenagers walking out of the Gap wearing three pairs of jeans palled after a few weeks. He stuck it out for a year, then opened his own agency, with himself as sole employee. My partner, Chuckie, and I threw what business we could his way, and within six months, Terry was thriving. He hired two other ex-cops to work for him. They were pretty good. Terry was terrific.

"Amazing," he said. "She gives him forty-eight thousand bucks. He gives her no sex."

"Nice work if you can get it."

"Listen, you got a block of cement like Bobette around, who can blame the guy? So listen, Lee, I don't see anything in the discovery material that'll hurt your little Normie any more than he's already hurt, except for the strangling itself: the size of the hands and the strength of the perpetrator." Terry was right. I couldn't stop the medical examiner from saying "very big hands" and "powerful," and the jury would look over at six-foot-five-inch, two-hundred-pound Norman Torkelson sitting at the defense table, his hands folded in his lap, and think: That's our boy. "Anything else in here I should worry about?" Terry asked. "Any nasty surprises?"

"Bobette's wallet appears to be missing."

127

"Maybe she left it in one of her bars or someplace," Terry said, for once not insisting on the worst-case scenario. But then I glanced over at him and saw he was not really paying attention. He was stroking the bedspread with his thumb, clearly thinking of all that was possible on a round bed. When you looked at his face in repose—past his bad tie, his mustache, and especially past his misogyny—you could understand how appealing he could be. Part Portuguese, part Irish, and part Italian, he had the long, lean, rugged face of an Iberian peasant farmer, soft blue Irish eyes, and a helmet of dark gladiator curls that he blew-dry into submission every day. However, although he was, on these rare occasions, a treat to look at, I wasn't paying him seventy-five dollars an hour and thirty-five cents a mile to contemplate the possibilities of a round bed and look dreamy.

"Terry, write this down." He peered up, slightly dazed at being summoned back to reality. "Check with your pals at MasterCard, Visa, and Amex. See if there were any Bobette Frisch charges starting with the Friday of the murder. Can you do that today?" He nodded and then, seeing that I was waiting for something, jotted a word or two in his notebook. "With any luck," I said, "somebody in San Antonio charged a thousand dollars' worth of chewing tobacco the day after Norman was arrested."

"And the Department will send a couple of detectives to Texas and they'll track the guy down and arrest him for Bobette's murder. Right?" He had a wolfish smile with very large white teeth. "You're dreaming."

The Love Nest offered up nothing more, so we headed down to Bobette's house to meet Sam Franklin. Holly had said he'd show us whatever we wanted to see, but I knew Sam would make it a miserable and difficult procedure. I followed Terry to Merrick in my own car. He would be destroyed psychologically if he had to ride as a passenger with a woman driving; and I would not drive with him: He fit the stereotype for cop slobs, and the car was a four-wheel garbage dump of unfolded, coffee-stained maps, oily Roy Rogers napkins, discarded straws and paper-wrapped, petrified gum globs. A vomitous air freshener in the shape of a banana hanging from his rearview mirror only made matters worse.

Sam Franklin's contempt for me was small potatoes compared to his loathing of Terry Salazar, an ex-cop who now worked for criminals. But Terry and Sam had never liked each other, even in the years when they had shared a desk in Homicide. They were different in every way: Gaunt / husky; introspective / superficial; puritan / libertine; devout evangelical Protestant / aggressively lapsed Catholic.

"Hey, Sammy, how're they hanging?" Terry inquired. He automatically gave all other men a diminutive ending just to show precisely who was the alpha dog in the pack.

"I have to be out of here in ten minutes," Sam responded. "You'd better get a move on."

Sam stood back and let us walk inside. His eyes didn't leave us for a minute. He was on the verge of protesting as I walked down the two steps from the front hall to the sunken living room over to check out the area between the couch and the coffee table, where Bobette's body had been found. However, Sam knew that I knew he had no grounds to stop me, so he clamped his jaw shut and refrained from grinding his teeth, aware that the sight of him all riled up not merely would delight Terry but could form the basis for a wicked imitation at old-boy cop gatherings: Sam Franklin Thrown into a Tizzy by Female Lawyer.

The crime scene photos, with their cruel light illuminating Bobette's body, had given her couch and coffee table the impersonality of furniture in a chain of economy hotels, so I'd expected a house that was as businesslike as Bobette. But it was so sweet that if the two men hadn't been there, I might have gotten all teary over the girl-at-heart who'd had the life choked out of her right where I was standing. Instead I swallowed the lump in my throat and perched on the arm of the couch, letting my leg swing back and forth to show them I was just as casual about this house of death as they were.

The couch wasn't beige, as it had appeared in the photos, but butter yellow, with a profusion of needlepoint pillows, the faultlessly stitched, innocuous ones offered in upscale catalogs: butterflies on a magnolia branch, a white Persian cat, a nosegay of violets, and the fourth, blue letters on a lemon background, which read: "Living well is the best revenge."

The room was so extravagantly girlish that it could have been conceived by a gay set designer as an *hommage* to old-fashioned femininity. A peach carpet, with a garland of blue and yellow flowers as a border. Yellow-and-pink-checked fabric on two armchairs, ruffled on the edges, so it looked as if Bobette had dressed them in pinafores. A collection of glass and ceramic cats on a side table, none taller than three inches.

"Did she have any cats?" I asked Sam.

"What?" I repeated the question, resisting the temptation to say it slowly, as if he were slow-witted. "We didn't find any."

"Are you sure? No litter box? No cat food dish?"

"No."

"A cat?" Terry asked. "Why would she have a cat?"

I turned back to him. "Why *wouldn't* she have a cat or two?"

"Because they're animals. They eat and they shit," he answered.

"So do you."

Unfazed, he took out a tape measure to determine the distance between the coffee table and a large picture book lying on the floor: *Fluff Balls: The Wonderful World of Angora Cats*. I wondered if Bobette's dream of romance had been so intensely cerebral that anything that would demand care—or even minimal attention—would have been a distraction. Just then an antimacassar in the shape of a valentine on a yellow wing chair caught my eye. Norman must have known, the second he stepped through the front door and saw that lacy heart, that her bank account was his for the asking.

We did a walk-through, Sam leading. Whenever we stopped, Sam stood legs apart, hands open and resting lightly on hips, as if any second he'd have to reach for his service revolver to prevent us from committing some felonious act. His eyes flitted from me to Terry and back to me, vigilant, as we looked around. What was there to see? Pot holders in the kitchen: one covered with daisies; another, a mitt, in the shape of a tabby cat. In the downstairs bathroom, a matching turquoise rug and toilet seat cover, each with an embroidered fleur-de-lis in the center; and a satin wrapper for an extra roll of toilet paper, in the shape of a Victorian bonnet.

Oh, and her bedroom! Entirely lavender: carpet, walls, bed linens. The floor-length curtains were tied back with a braided tassel of pale lavender and deep purple. On the wall were lavender-matted botanical prints of purple flowers: lilacs, irises, and lavender. The room was romantic—and erotic. Many women would shy away from such a baring of their soul's desire. Not Bobette, although maybe that was because she lived such a solitary life that she felt certain no one could ever discern, by a mere glance around her room, her sexual nature. At last, when Norman came along, she was thrilled to show him, because he was precisely what she'd been praying for all her life.

Sam, Terry, and I stood by the bed, a four-poster with a lace canopy, perfectly made. No sign of lovemaking. Terry checked the drawers of the nightstands. "Zilch," he reported.

"Did you take anything from the drawers?" I asked Sam.

"It should all be in your discovery material," he spat out, as if the question were so outrageous, so disgusting, that it nauseated him to answer.

"There is nothing in the material that refers to items taken from her nightstands," I said. "Therefore, I am assuming your answer is no, you did not take anything you did not record in the report. Naturally, I will ask Holly Nuñez to check up on this, since I cannot get an answer from you." Sam contemplated actually giving me a response—"no"— for a second, but decided against such humiliation. He crossed his arms and beat out a slow, jazzy rhythm on his elbows, as if he were all alone, listening to Coltrane. "You got a positive ID from the tenant, Eugene Pohl?" There was no sign Sam was hearing anything other than "Trane's

131

Blues." "Answer me, Sam, or I'm going after your ass!"

"Yes." The word was almost a hiss.

"And from the guy at the bank?"

"Which guy at the bank?" Sam asked innocently.

I thought fast. A teller doesn't simply hand over forty-eight thousand dollars. "The bank officer Bobette dealt with. And the guard near the door. They didn't see my client with her, did they?"

"No," he exhaled, telling me more about the status of Holly's case than I thought I would ever get.

"Your case is a fairy tale," I told him. "Right from the beginning, it was easier to sit back in your chair and tell yourself stories than it was to get out and investigate." I banged my fist against one of the bed's posts for emphasis, as if there were an invisible jury just off to my left. "No one else claims to have seen Norman Torkelson with Bobette except the tenant, and you know and I know—and the jury sure as hell is going to know—that Eugene Pohl is one very strange bird."

Then, before Terry could mouth off and thus once again antagonize Sam and thus dissipate the tiny cloud of uncertainty I'd managed to float, I grabbed him by the sleeve and yanked him out of Bobette Frisch's girlish dream of love.

Later that day, while Terry was around and about, checking the set of mystery prints that had appeared all over Bobette's house and trying to discover if anyone had charged anything to Bobette's missing credit cards, I went to court for the arraignment of a new client, a guy accused of selling counterfeit Donna Karan everything—shoes, suits, belts, sweaters, nightgowns. I was hoping he'd have an overpowering obsession, so I could at least play around with pleading insanity, but he was annoyingly sane and wanted to barter down part of his legal fee by trading my time for a new wardrobe: "I swear to Christ, Mrs. White. Would I stick you of all people with the fake Donnas? These are *real*, the ones I knocked off from. I'm talking six-ply cashmere." After the arraignment, I dropped in to watch a few minutes of Chuckie's arson trial, then, overcome by an irresistible impulse, spent my lunch hour in Bloomingdale's and wound up with a white cashmere shawl.

And a pair of sling-backs. Also, I bought a lip gloss and with it, for an extra $16.95, got one of those giant, useless makeup kits with circlets of cosmetics in colors designed for cheap hookers—not cheap hookers' legal counsel: hues like Papaya Sunset and Teal Twilight. So by the time I was in the elevator going back to my office, I was, naturally, giving myself a hard time, thinking that if I'd been a man I would have spent the hour and a half at the Bar Association library, looking up arcane case law. Or I would have invited some big-firm lawyer out to lunch so the next time one of his firm's hotshot corporate clients got picked up for statutory rape or vehicular homicide, "Lee White!" would leap to mind. Of course, being a lawyer, I sprang to my own defense, and as I was opening my office door, I was already arguing: So if I were a male lawyer, instead of Bloomingdale's I'd wind up at the Wiz, looking for a longer telephone cord, but instead I'd walk out with a Pentium computer with speakers the size of Mount McKinley and a quad-speed CD-ROM player, and therefore, wasn't my foray into cashmere relatively innocuous? Of course, a still, small voice began a siren song of a new computer, but I didn't hear it because as I walked inside, there in the reception area was Mary Dean.

"Hi!" she said brightly. She wore a red dress with polka dots the size of silver dollars. Its material was of some cheap synthetic so stiff it made crinkly noises when she moved. Her country-music hair was piled on top of her head and held by a big red plastic barrette in the shape of a bow. She was no less beautiful than she had been on her last visit. "Hope you don't mind that I dropped in."

"I'd prefer it if you'd call first," I said, demonstrating that the assertiveness-awareness seminar at the Women's Bar Association had not been a complete waste of time. Then I cast what I hoped was a withering glance at the receptionist who had allowed Mary to stay. She was the granddaughter of a guy in one of my partner Chuckie's poker games, a young woman with the spiritless serenity of a cloistered nun in a washed-up order.

"The reason I came back," Mary explained, after I closed my office door and we were both seated, "is that I remember something else."

"I see."

"You said it's *all* important, to help Norman."

"Anything you remember," I said. "You never know what will be helpful."

"I want to help!" She made a terrible gurgling noise. For a second, I thought she was choking, then I realized it was a sob. I felt for the box of tissues, pulled out a couple, and held them out to her across the desk. But her hands were covering her face so I put them back until she could see them. "I miss him so much," she wept, although it was difficult to hear through the tears and her hands. "It's like . . . without him . . . Oh, please! Get him out of that place!"

"I'm trying. And anything you can tell me . . . Sometimes the smallest detail can mean a lot."

She composed herself, wiping away her tears with her knuckles. She noticed the streaks of mascara on them, and I handed her the tissues. She wiped her fingers, then blotted the black smudges under her eyes, making tiny, dainty dabs, so as not to pull at the delicate skin. "You know how I told you I called up when Norman had a mark at the Love Nest, saying I was from the Pinnacle Collections Agency? You know, about repossessing his car."

"Right," I said briskly. Mary's voice was shaky, and I didn't want her to start bawling again. To be perfectly truthful, it was less out of compassion than from a desire to get rid of her; I sensed that she was about to tell me everything she knew about Norman, an encyclopedia's worth, and that would put a healthy bite into what was the not overly large retainer I'd charged him. "What else do you have to tell me?"

"I do other things too."

"What do you mean?"

"Like, if he thinks the mark isn't feeling sorry enough for

him, I call up and"—she smiled at some memory—"pretend I'm the ex-wife."

"Do you put that message on his answering machine as well?"

"No. Norman says more than one message on the machine would be, like, too obvious. No, I call up and scream my bloody head off: 'Norman, you fucking bastard!'" Mary squawked, clearly taking pleasure in her own performance. This voice, unlike the low-pitched, tough Repo Lady voice, was high, but not an ineffectual squeak. It was rough, mean, like an emery board abrading skin. "'I'm gonna make sure you're ruined. I'm gonna make sure you're so goddamn, pathetic broke you'll *never* get back on your feet again.'" Her pale skin took on an exhilarated flush from the tantrum. "Anyhow, I just keep screaming like the worst bitch in the world!"

"And you're so loud he holds the phone away from his ear, and the mark hears it."

"Yes! You know, you make me think, like, there's hope," Mary said. "You're so smart. As smart as Norman! I feel like, gee, you can handle this."

"Do you play any other roles?"

She laughed. "Doesn't roles always make you think of *rolls*? Like hamburger rolls—or those little curvy ones? They're in the dairy case, and they're triangles, and you roll them up and—"

"Right. But let's talk about acting roles."

"Well, I play his divorce lawyer's secretary. Like, 'Mr. Powers's office calling for Mr. Whatever-name-Norman's-using.' We arrange a time, and when the phone rings, he's busy someplace and asks the mark to get it and take a message."

"Did you play the ex-wife or the secretary with Bobette Frisch?" I asked.

"No," Mary said. A little tight-lipped, I thought.

"How come?"

"She was so crazy about him, I didn't have to."

I tried to sound casual. "Too crazy about him?"

"A clingy vine," Mary said, pushing out her overglossed lips into a pout. Not a cutesy pout: the real thing.

"In what way did she cling?"

"Like always begging him: 'Stay over. Don't go home, Norman. I can't stand it when you're not with me, Norman.'"

"Just the way you feel," I observed. Okay, not tactful, but it had been a long day.

"I have a right to him!" She was still wearing that pistachio-green eye shadow, and, with the red dress and lipstick, looked unseasonably Yulish.

"Of course you do."

"Who the hell does she think she is? I mean, I know it's Norman's job to make them feel he loves them, but she was acting like . . ." Mary shook her head; it was almost a shudder. "Like she really thought *he* couldn't stand being away from her. Like she was doing him a favor, letting him stay overnight in that stupid house."

"Did he spend the night there often?"

"Once or twice," she said, resuming her pout.

"Once or twice?"

"I don't know," she said, her volume control going out of whack, until she was almost shouting again. "Maybe three or four times. Okay? Like he would really get into that stupid purple bed of hers and do it to her. Fucking cow!"

"How did he avoid doing it?" I asked.

"Told her he wanted to wait till they were married. I mean, she was so old! Did she really think he could make himself do it without, like, puking?"

"Where did he stay when he spent the night there?" I asked.

"There's another bedroom right next to it. It's more an office, but it has a Hide-A-Bed." Mary was cooling down enough to give me a small smile. "At least it wasn't purple. I couldn't believe it!"

"I went there today. Even the botanical prints on the wall were all purple flowers."

"And did you see her dresser? That whole collection of purple perfume bottles?"

"Right," I said. We sat in silence for a few seconds. I buzzed Sandi and asked her for two glasses of water, hold the ice. "You seem really upset about Bobette."

"Why shouldn't I be?" Mary stopped, a theatrical pause, as if she were on a talk show, waiting for audience approval: Yeah! and Right! "Norman's in jail and——"

"I didn't mean about her murder. I meant about her relationship with Norman."

"No. I mean, I hated it when he slept over, but like he said: 'Unless you put in the man-hours, you don't get the profits.' He says a lot of business things like that. He has a great head for business." She got busy tugging at the hem of her polka-dot dress in order to get rid of the wrinkles around her lap, putting her weight first on one hip, then on the other. The dress was too short and much too tight, at least in terms of wrinkle-prevention. But with her long legs, it did look spectacular, and the dozen or so wrinkles didn't detract from it in the least. However, I felt she was avoiding my question and using the only means of obfuscation she had at her disposal: her sexuality.

"Mary," I said, "I don't buy it."

"Don't buy what?"

"Don't buy your act that you weren't upset about Bobette and Norman."

"What do you mean? Do you think, like, he fell in love with her or something?"

"No. But you tell me. Woman to woman. Something was bothering you."

Mary clasped her hands in her wrinkled lap. Finally, she said: "Swear to God you won't tell him?"

I nodded. That wasn't enough. I put up my right hand and said: "I swear."

"To God."

"I swear to God," I exhaled, thinking that I should double my hourly rates for dealings with my clients' sweet patooties.

"It's like, I've been so worried about him," Mary said. "He's tired. I mean, you have no idea how much his job takes out of him. The last few cities, when we have mail call—that's what we call it—it used to be so much fun getting all the answers to his ad in the personals. We'd drink our martinis and read them out loud to each other and laugh and laugh." She must have read something on my face,

137

because she quickly added, "Of course, we didn't laugh *all* the time. Some of them were kind of pitiful. But now, when he brings in the mail, it's like it weighs a ton."

"It's weighing him down," I suggested.

"Yes! He says he doesn't have the energy anymore to do the dance. Not a real dance. He means the con. He says it's draining him."

Sandi came in carrying a small tray with two glasses of water Mary declined hers. "It's bottled water," I reassured her.

"I'm not thirsty."

I waited for Sandi to go out and close the door. Then I prompted Mary: "You were saying how tired Norman is."

"He says: 'I'm bone-weary.' You know how tired *that* is. He says he wishes we had enough money to retire. Buy a condo in Florida or the Virgin Islands or someplace and just, like, spend the rest of our lives together."

Suddenly I asked: "You like being on the water?"

"I love looking at it. Being on the beach. Except it's not as much fun since sunblock." I walked over to the wall facing my desk and took one of the framed photographs off the wall, a shot of a house and dock that the man in my life had taken from a small boat in a canal: his house in Oceanside. I handed it to Mary. "Ooh! Isn't it adorable!" she exclaimed. "A little dream house."

"My boyfriend took the picture," I said, hanging it back in its place on the wall among his other work. He was a terrific photographer. "You know, you've spoken about all the pressures of Norman's job and how wiped out he was, but you still haven't made me understand why you felt Bobette was such a threat."

Mary's eyes were still on the picture. "I was afraid he would leave me for her," she said quietly.

"*What?*"

She seemed gratified by my incredulity. "Not 'cause he doesn't love me. But he's so exhausted. When you're tired of the con, what else is there? Like, on *Montel* or *Leeza*, there was this show: Men Who Get Depressed so They Run

138

Off with Older Women Because It's Like Their Mothers, or something. I remember thinking: Oh my God! Norman!"

"Did he ever indicate that he was thinking of leaving you and going with Bobette?"

"Of course not! But I could see sometimes how much it took out of him just to get up and go *meet* one of these old maids. I think there may have been a teeny-weeny part of him that was saying: 'Finally, here's one who's got more than money in the bank. Here's one that's got an *income*, who could support me.'"

I met up with Terry Salazar again a little before Happy Hour at Plumpie's, a bar that catered to the fringes of the criminal justice system: ex-cops, court reporters, bail bondsmen, an occasional disbarred lawyer. Its jolly name was misleading: Plumpie's was one of those dank, dark-wooded places in which you're grateful for the dismal lighting, because if they put in 150-watt bulbs, you'd see thirty years of unspeakable crud and a cross section of insect life that would haunt your dreams. Terry was drinking straight gin, which never did much for his disposition but mellowed his irresistible voice so it was even more compelling.

"Are you still coherent?" I asked.

Aggrieved, he answered: "It's my second."

I ordered one of the more esoteric light beers, one that Herman Oberndorfer, a.k.a. Plumpie, would not have on tap, so I wouldn't have to drink from one of his never-washed-properly steins. I lifted the bottle and took a swig. "Anything on Bobette's credit cards?" I asked.

"You're going to love this. Over six thousand dollars worth of stuff charged on the date of the murder."

"Maybe Bobette went on a shopping spree early in the day." I tried to sound confident, but I would have to work on it.

"I'm having my pal call a couple of the stores. They're all in that Americana Shopping Center. Like Louis Vuitton." He pronounced it perfectly, which led me to think that his wife had probably given up meditation once again and was shopping (once again) and I'd better make sure Terry wasn't padding his disbursements (once again). "Barney's," he went on. "Someone ran up three thousand bucks there."

"Probably bought two pairs of pantyhose. All right, try to get the information as soon as you can. Not just to time of day. Find out what they bought. My guess is, most of the men's stuff in an upscale place like that wouldn't fit Norman; he's way too tall."

"Maybe he bought something for someone."

"Right," I said, thinking of Mary. "Anything on the prints yet?"

"I had to pass my pal a hundred."

"Put it on your bill," I said, sure that what he passed was probably a couple of twenties. "Were they able to get a make on them?"

"No. Not yet. He can check with the Feebies, but that'll cost you more."

"Do you have a copy of the card I gave you, the one with those prints?"

"I gave it to my pal. I just have a Xerox."

"With you?" He patted all his pockets until he found it. "Do you still keep a fingerprint kit in your car?" I asked.

"Sure."

"Let's go."

Irked at having to pass up the thimbleful of gin still remaining in his glass, Terry followed me out to the street and got his print kit from a tackle box he kept in his trunk. We walked a half block more to my car. I handed him the framed photograph of my man's house that I'd taken down from the wall in my office. "Try for thumb prints on the two vertical sides of the glass," I told him.

Ten minutes later, he told me. "The thumb prints are from the same person who left the latents all over Bobette's place. How the hell did those prints get onto your picture? Who the hell is this guy?"

"Mary Dean."

Ten

The summer before her senior year of high school, Lee White contracted a vicious case of poison ivy when she ran up the hill behind her house to spy on Jazz Taylor playing tennis with his mother.

It wasn't as if she had planned such a mad act. No, she had just been lying on a chaise near the pool trying to catch her breath after swimming laps for forty-five minutes. Her eyes were closed. The sounds of the long, dull summer bubbled through the water in her ears: her own labored inhalation; the outrage of blue jays; the aggressive drone of the central air-conditioning unit; the interminable, cheery tinkle of her mother's Hawaiian wind chimes; the far-off *thunk! thunk!* of balls smacking against rackets on the Taylors' tennis court. Suddenly, out of this chorus of boring sounds, one youthful baritone descended from Hart's Hill: "Lucky shot, Mom!"

Lee was seized by a lunatic passion. Throwing off her towel, leaping from her chaise, clad only in a bathing suit, she charged up the steep rise that separated the Whites' from the Taylors'. Clearing a path, she pushed aside branches and tore away clinging vines with the fierce strength of a battle-crazed warrior. She had known for years that the entire incline was choked with nettles and poison ivy, but in that insane instant, she flung that knowledge out of her mind. Two whole years had passed since she had seen Jazz at Dante's Pizza. Not a single day had gone by that she hadn't thought about him.

When Lee reached the summit, she crouched low, darting in the serpentine fashion Charles Bronson had employed in *The Dirty Dozen* to dodge Nazi fire. She hunkered down behind one of the

141

junipers that screened the Taylors' tennis court. It was only then that she came to her senses. Well, somewhat. To be perfectly frank, Lee looked slightly moronic, glancing behind her as if to ask: What means of transportation got me here? But then the game took over.

Ginger was by far the better player. As much as Lee wished Jazz Taylor would be a god of tennis, wielding a Tad Davis Deluxe Imperial instead of a lightning bolt to strike his mother dead, she was too savvy about the game not to recognize which of the two was just a social player—and which might have once aspired to greatness. To Jazz, it really was a game; he relaxed between points, changing his grip on the racket, wiping his palm on his shorts, shaking out a crick in his leg, combing back his hair with his fingers, squinting into the sun, smiling across the net. But his mother played with an intensity that was almost scary. Ginger's tan, muscular arms and legs were bright with sweat. She was primed for every ball. Without taking her eyes off Jazz, she moved into position so she could cover the court no matter where her son hit the ball. For God's sake, Lee thought, he's not Billie Jean King! This is your son. Still, she was wowed by Ginger, and a little frightened. She had never seen a woman so intent on winning.

It was a half hour later, as the two Taylors were strolling off the court, when it suddenly occurred to Lee they might catch sight of her behind the juniper. Still, even then, when Jazz actually turned and looked back in her direction, as though homing in on the rays of desire beaming out from her, she stayed calm; her heart didn't pound, her mouth didn't go dry. No, all that was in her head was how extravagantly defined his thigh muscles were, like in those Da Vinci drawings in one of her mother's art books on the coffee table. Such thighs! Then a stray thought popped into her mind and grew and grew: If she were across the net from Jazz and slammed one with her backhand, he would say, "Holy . . . !" And Ginger, from the sidelines, would call out to her: "Nice shot!"

That was when it hit her, how alien these Taylors were from her own family. Not just that they had more money, what her father called old money, and were a different religion and sent their kids to private schools. No, they were alive. They had pep.

142

A nauseating word, Lee conceded, but that was what they had. Plain and simple vigor. Well, Ginger had pep squared. Okay, she was a killer who had no qualms about cutting out her own son's heart. But God, they were both so strong!

Whereas her family: Leonard, who hardly knew a tennis ball from a silver fox pom-pom, was a knob-kneed embarrassment in shorts. Winded by a stroll to the end of the driveway to pick up the Sunday papers, he could only gaze up the hill with his heart corroding with envy, pierced by desire. If her mother were here beside her, behind the spreading juniper, she would eye Ginger's grass-stained shorts and baggy, sweaty Lacoste shirt, sigh, then summon up barely enough energy to pat a stray platinum-on-gold-frosted hair into place, and decree: "Ick!" And Robin: At the first overhead smash, she would drop her racquet and shield her head. But from behind her bush, Lee now knew: *She could play their game.*

That night, Lee's shapely legs swelled until they looked like bowling pins. The tiny red dots that covered them, signaling her immune system's outrage, were so numerous that from the soles of her feet all the way up to her thighs she was a solid blaze of crimson. Her legs were so sensitive that it was agony when she covered them, even with a sheet. Greta had gone off to Frankfurt for a rare week's vacation, her mother was in one of her moods where she never got out of her bathrobe, so there was no one to look in on Lee. For forty-eight hours she lay shivering in the arctic air-conditioning, too sapped from antihistamines to get up and open a window.

But her espionage had been worth it. What memories! What treasures! Jazz's powerful forearms. His brawny wrists. And his shorts! He must have outgrown them, because when he lunged for a net ball she could see his hamstrings as they thickened into the pale crescents of his buttocks. Oh, and she didn't want to forget the bandanna he'd tied around his head as a sweatband. And more! When he and his mother changed over, and he was facing Lee; he looked so ... Okay, not handsome. But he had such a genuinely *nice* face, and when his mother aced a serve so hard he didn't even see the ball, he hadn't gotten defensive or temperamental. On the contrary! His wonderful face, his absolutely, totally good-natured face lit up with an appreciative grin.

143

It had been worth it! Jazz, she said to herself. Jasper. Jazz. If she ever met him, what would she call him? Of course, he might say: "Hi, I'm Jazz Taylor." Or: "How do you do? My name is Jasper Taylor. I believe we are neighbors," hopefully oblivious that in fifth grade she'd almost punched him in the suck.

Does all this sound like an obsession on Lee's part? It was. Not a dangerous fixation, the sort you hear of nowadays, where monomaniacs stalk their prey without rest or mercy. Actually, until her sortie up the hill, the extent of Lee's preoccupation with Jazz consisted of calling his prep school (from a pay phone so the call would not show up on her parents' bill) to ascertain when his spring break would be. She then spent an inordinate amount of time walking Woofer back and forth past the Taylors' driveway, hoping (in vain, it turned out) to get a glimpse of Jazz.

She kept hoping throughout her senior year of high school. Aware that they were both in the same grade, she fantasized every night about running into him at college interviews. ("Jasper, isn't that the girl who lives in that modern thing down the hill?" "I think it may be, Dad." Then, Jazz would turn to her: "Excuse me, are you from Shorehaven?") When Jazz didn't show up for the guided tours at Cornell or Brown, she felt cheated, as though she'd just missed him by seconds. She had even gone so far as to arrange interviews at Smith and Mount Holyoke, for the sole reason that, having studied an atlas, she'd calculated that the two colleges were a mere sixty miles from his prep school. In her mind's eye, she could see him waiting at a bus stop just outside snow-covered, Christmas-card Amherst on a frosty New England afternoon, anxious about getting back to be on time for afternoon tea or chapel or whatever. She'd spot him and turn to her mother: "Stop the car!" Then she'd lower the window and say: "Aren't you from Shorehaven?" They'd give him a lift back to school. With the cooperative illogic of fantasy, she was magically transported to the back seat beside him, while Sylvia chauffeured up front; by the time they got to his school, Jazz was slipping his class ring onto her finger. Of course it was much too big, but she knew exactly how to tape it so it would fit.

But the question remains: Was this obsession anything more than the standard teenage crush? Yes, it was.

Lee White clung to the image of Jazz Taylor's sliver of ass, to the remembrance of his vigorous baritone, far longer than might be considered healthy because she was a lonely girl. True, she had a lot going for her. She was a gifted (if not brilliant) student, a key member of the girls' tennis team, and managing editor of the Shorehaven High School *Beacon*, where she was a pillar of strength and fount of common sense for the temperamental reporters and the wild, impetuous photographers. She had a smart and lively best friend, Dorie Adler, three devoted pals, and at least ten acquaintances who thought of her in the warmest possible terms. But she had never had a boyfriend.

Of course, a seventeen-year-old girl who has never had a beau is not exactly a rarity. Still, almost every girl, even the most obnoxious adolescent, stands on the brink of womanhood with the reassuring knowledge that her family's love has always been (and will ever be) there for her. So it is no great loss if she does not yet have a pair of manly eighteen-year-old arms around her, because she knows—from her mother, father, sisters and brothers—that she is intrinsically lovable. In time, Mr. or Dr. Right will embrace her and whisper in her ear precisely what her family has been telling her all along: You are *wonderful*. I love you.

But Lee never got that from her parents. Not just those three little words: the feeling behind them. By the time she was finishing high school, Leonard was hardly home except on weekends. In 1967, there was no business like fur business. Well-off women wanted more than just their full-length minks. They wanted "fun furs"—ski jackets of dyed rabbit, trench coats lined in sheared beaver—plus serious furs to show that they were worthy of more than mere mink; they seized fox coats, sable cloaks, shearling tunics, off the racks at Le Fourreur as if they had been sentenced to decades of hard labor in Siberia. Leonard was becoming rich beyond even his wildest dreams.

So it was no problem for him to pay the rent on a one-bedroom apartment on East Seventy-eighth Street so he could have a place to stay weeknights. Obviously, Sylvia could not be there with him. The girls needed her. But he urged her: "Use it whenever you come in during the day. It's a great place to put your feet up for an hour or two before dinner if you've been shopping." (What Sylvia did not know, naturally, is that when she called the East Seventy-eighth Street apartment, the phone also rang in Dolly

Young's somewhat larger, more lavishly furnished co-op apartment on Central Park South which Leonard had also paid for and where he actually spent most Monday through Thursday nights.)

So Lee saw relatively little of her father. On school holidays, like Columbus Day or Veterans Day, he would often take her out to lunch, but their conversations were limited to safe subjects: school, polite inquiries about her friends and—the only area of her life that aroused his interest—the triumphs and travails of the Shorehaven tennis team.

"What's your won-loss record?" he inquired one day during Easter vacation of her senior year.

"You had to ask?" Lee laughed as she reached across the table at Miss Pansy's, a tearoom around the corner from her father's store. "We're one-five."

"Even with your backhand?"

"If it weren't for my backhand, we'd probably be five-one." Father and daughter exchanged smiles, each comfortable that this was not the case. Lee picked up a crustless triangle of her sandwich. "What's this gook inside?"

"Pecan cream cheese," Leonard answered, a little nervously. He never knew what Lee would say next. "A specialty of the house."

"Is it a big *goyishe* thing or something?"

"Shhh!"

"They're all *goyim* here. They don't know what I'm saying." Leonard glanced around nervously. "Dad, relax. We're in New York City. It's not against the law to say *goyim*."

"Where did you hear that word?"

"It's not *f-u-c-k* or anything," she said, smiling at his attempt to remain unperturbed. "Grandma used to say *goyishe* all the time." Leonard tried to appear as if this was a surprise to him; Lee made no effort to hide her amusement at his behavior. "And I heard it at Dorie Adler's."

"Oh." Leonard pretended to be absorbed in removing the gluey cream cheese coating from his teeth, following the dictates of good breeding—an impossible task.

"'Oh,'" Lee mimicked. "Okay, I'll put a help-wanted ad in the paper: Friend Wanted: Only Protestants need apply."

"I didn't mean—"

"Sure you did!" Lee retorted, but she smiled when she said it, and she had such a generous smile that it softened the censure.

"You know what's great about you?" her father demanded.

"No. What's great about me?"

"Your spunk. Men like that."

Lee put down her sandwich. "I don't think so."

"Sure they do," he insisted. "You don't think there are a lot of boys up at Cornell who want a girl with brains and . . ." He searched for a word. Lee waited for him to say "beauty" or at least "good looks." Finally he said: ". . . gumption. Listen, Lee, the most fashionable, beautiful—and wealthy—women in New York come into the salon. And you know what?"

"They don't have gumption."

"Right!"

"But I bet they had dates for their senior proms."

"Maybe. But they can't keep a man's interest. Their husbands— uh—stray, if you understand me. Because when a man comes home from a day's work, he doesn't want a bubblehead. He wants someone he can talk to." Loud silence: Leonard suddenly slammed on the conversational brakes, realizing that his uncommon honesty had almost brought them careening into the very walls of their home. Before it could last too long, he added: "You've got the brains to be someone special. You want to be a doctor? I'll pay for medical school." Considering that the worldview espoused in *The Feminine Mystique* had not yet made an impact on the psyches of male furriers, this was a remarkably decent offer. "A lawyer? A college professor? I'll be behind you a hundred percent." Then he patted her hand, and it was not a mere offhand caress; it was a pat replete with heartfelt warmth, the closest gesture to a genuine declaration of love she would receive from him in her life. "Lee, sweetheart, come on. You'll get your MRS degree too. Iron those wrinkles out of your forehead. Stop worrying. I guarantee it: You'll hook some guy."

Then Leonard waved to Olive, their waitress, a sourpuss he'd been trying to charm for a decade, and told her to bring his almost straight-A daughter who would be going to Cornell—that's one of the Ivy League colleges, Olive—next September a slice of Miss Pansy's famous Nesselrode pie.

* * *

147

The only guy Lee got that year was her prom date, Nestor "Baby" Langley, who weighed two hundred ninety-seven pounds. If his ironic moniker makes it sound as if Baby was a future tackle for the San Francisco 49ers, then it is doubly misleading. Baby got his nickname simply because he called everyone "Baby," believing it made him appear cosmopolitan. An amiable boy whose reputation for wit was based on his total recall of the epigrams of Oscar Wilde, he was as soft as the Ring Dings he was unable to resist. Baby, the editor in chief and movie critic of the *Beacon,* was the only boy in Lee's crowd who still could not find a prom date the week after Memorial Day—not even among the pathetically eager ninth graders in the fast crowd at Shorehaven Junior High. At the urging of a half score of their journalistic colleagues ("How can you *not* go to your senior prom? Even if it's with a friend. It's *better* with a friend, because you *know* how superficial high school relationships are and friendships last forever"), and after Dorie Adler drove over to Baby's house and stood beside him, holding his perspiring hand, as he phoned Lee and formally invited her, Lee and Baby became, ad hoc, an item.

Sylvia was elated. Not about Baby, of course (although Leonard was not displeased, somehow aware that Baby's father, Thaddeus Langley, was a member of Rolling Hills, the golf club to which Foster Taylor belonged). Sylvia was enraptured at the thought of shopping for a gown. "You need something very unique," Sylvia declared as she sat on the edge of Lee's bed.

"Not 'very unique.' 'Unique' means one of a kind." But Sylvia had become distracted. She scanned the room—now white and yellow, with a daisy-chain stencil painted high on the walls and around the edges of the oak floor. Hmm, she seemed to be saying to herself. Apparently, she had forgotten that she'd redecorated it a year earlier. Placing a Bougainvillea Pink enameled index fingertip on her one-shade-darker Appassionata Pink lower lip, Sylvia appeared lost in thought—although not so lost that Lee could not see where she was headed.

"Mom."

"What?"

"We're not doing my room now. We're doing me."

Sylvia offered an apologetic smile and even touched her daughter's cheek for an instant. "I made a list of places to look for prom dresses."

"Mom, I just want a plain, peasant-style—"

"Why? Are you a peasant?"

"We're not exactly descended from the Hapsburgs."

"Who are they?"

"They live on Driftwood Drive. He's an accountant."

"I don't think we know any Hapsburgs."

"I was just kidding. They were an aristocratic family."

"Well, your father is an aristocrat in the fur industry." Lee knew what was coming next. "How many furriers got mentioned in last August's *Vogue* and *Bazaar*?" Sylvia demanded. "We all have to keep up a fashion image . . . me, Daddy, Robin and *you*."

"The editors of *Vogue* aren't covering the Shorehaven High School prom. It's safe for me to wear a peasant dress."

"Do you want to wear work boots and carry a sack of potatoes out onto the dance floor?" Sylvia, no fool, quickly saw that the notion of work boots was not without its appeal, so she talked fast. "We won't look on the Island, because then you'll see yourself coming and going. But you want something classic. You're not Henri Bendel. I crossed that off my list. Too severe for you. You're Bonwit's. Saks. Bergdorf's too, but their stuff is so matronly this year you could throw up. Don't get me wrong: I'm not talking about anything sweetie-pie pastelly for you. You've got high coloring."

"I'm sallow." Lee didn't close her eyes, because she knew what she'd see in her mind's eye: Jazz Taylor at his prom, twirling a wisp of a girl, an ethereal violet-eyed gamin who had waist-length blonde hair, a letter of acceptance to Radcliffe, and a complexion somewhere between peaches-and-cream and porcelain.

"You are not sallow. You've got what they call a slight Oriental undertone to your skin—and you're the one who won't wear foundation, or even a little dab of rouge, so what do you expect?" It was not lack of rouge that made Lee a plain Jane, although this was one of the rare occasions when her mother was right: a little strategically-placed color would not have hurt. It was Lee's lack of sexual confidence that made her appear drab. Put her in front of an eligible boy, and the spark that fired her during a tennis game or in Honors English class flickered and died. She became mousy. But to defend herself against her mother's onslaughts, she had espoused a staunch No Makeup position. In her mind, the equation read: makeup=my mother=falseness. Too bad, because she had one of those fine, strong faces that cause readers of women's magazines to gush "*Un*believable!" when they compare a ravishing "after" photo to the ungainly, large-featured "before." It was not until two days before law school, when getting her hair cut at Bloomingdale's, she allowed the hairdresser—whose uncle was a judge in Minnesota and who claimed to have memorized every episode of *Perry Mason*—to talk her into an eyebrow tweezing, a facial, and a consultation with Miss Judi, who specialized in the Natural Look, that Lee began to allow herself to see that she was a damned good-looking dame.

"We have our work cut out for us," Sylvia said. "Can I safely assume Baby is going to wear black tie?"

"What else would he wear?"

"I don't know. Something beatnik."

"He's not a beatnik. No one's a beatnik anymore."

"What do you call your friend Dorie, with those black tights?"

"I call her my best friend. And Baby is wearing black tie." Lee leaned back. Her white wicker headboard whined in protest. The truth was Baby could not find a tuxedo to fit him anywhere on Long Island. He and Dorie finally made a desperate, secret trip to a king-size store in southwest Brooklyn, but all that the salesman at Big Barry's Formal Wear + Apparel could offer was an oxford-gray morning suit or a baby-blue tux that he swore had once been rented by Neil Sedaka's piano player.

Lee and Sylvia's shopping forays, while more upscale than Big Barry's, were certainly a lot less fun. Although mother and daughter, they were so different that to differentiate between them was not like comparing apples and oranges; it was comparing apples and catchers' mitts. In a dressing room in Bergdorf's (Bonwit's and Saks having failed them), Lee looked in the mirror and watched her mother watching her model in a navy-blue strapless silk sheath that brought the saleslady and Sylvia to the brink of ecstasy.

"Is it fabulous or fabulous?" the saleslady called from outside the cubicle. Sylvia withheld comment. She was staring at Lee's midsection. By any objective standard, it was not a ballooning midsection. Lee was in prime shape, it being tennis season, and her all-over muscle tone was quite fine. Still, there was a slight natural convexity to her tummy. "Mrs. White?" the saleslady called out again; her voice was tense, as if Sylvia's answer could hurt her. Lee fought down rage as her mother, ignoring the saleslady (and Lee as well), rested her tight, recently-operated-upon chin on the back of her hand so she could concentrate on studying Lee's flawed middle.

Stop it! Lee wanted to shriek. *Stop it*! Such noise as she would make had never been heard in Bergdorf Goodman since they drilled into solid bedrock to lay the foundation! Leave me the hell alone, you scrawny bitch! I hate this fucking dress!

But Lee also knew she was a disappointment to her mother. What more did the woman want, after all, than to have a pleasant mother-daughter day and buy her a gown that cost five times as much as anything her friends would be wearing?

So why can't she buy me . . . Okay, nothing peasant. Then a nice gown with a tulle skirt? Or something in chiffon, like that one in Bonwit's that was such a pale blue it was almost white? But Sylvia had grilled her: "You *like* that? You don't think it says 'Pittsburgh'? You like the way your bust looks with all that"—her voice curdled with contempt—tucking?"

It was late afternoon. Lee was worn down. She sucked in her mid-section. "Nice," Sylvia called out to the saleslady. Then she glanced up at Lee. "Do you love it?"

"It's fine."

"Because if you don't love it, we can come in again next Thursday and look in some nice little places on the Upper East Side."

"No. I love it," Lee said. She turned from the mirror and looked at her mother's flawlessly made-up face. It was still tense, unsatisfied. "Thanks for coming with me, Mom."

"You don't have to thank me!"

"I know," she said, "but you're an absolute saint for putting up with me. So patient."

Her mother's expression softened until it was almost benevolent. "Lee," Sylvia said, "don't forget. We have a lot of work ahead of us. Do I have to say the word? 'Accessorize.'"

Three months later, Lee arrived at Cornell University with a glorious wardrobe of pleated tartan skirts, coordinating knee socks, cashmere cardigans, Shetland crewnecks, flannel slacks, a camel-hair Chesterfield, a dark-green loden coat, and not one, not two, but three perfect-for-fraternity-parties little black dresses that of course looked marvelous with the gold Omega watch and double strand of seven-millimeter pearls that were part of her high school graduation gift.

By mid-October of her freshman year, when the leaves were turning such vivid reds and yellows that they looked like a kindergartner's painting of autumn, Lee had barely unpacked. In fact, during her four years of college, the stunningly expensive wardrobe remained just as Sylvia had left it, in its cocoon of flowered tissue paper in a trunk scented with lavender sachets. With the two hundred dollars she had realized from the sale of her eight-hundred-dollar watch, she bought a pair of jeans, a tie-dyed T-shirt, a denim shirt of the sort worn by share-croppers, and a pair of ankle-high shoes that might be issued to a marine on his first day on Parris Island. Of course, these purchases did not consume Lee's entire two-hundred-dollar profit; she donated ten bucks to Students for a Democratic Society and purchased six joints of excellent marijuana, which she shared with her boyfriend, Philip Mullen, or Flip, as he was called. Flip was a junior who had come all the way to Cornell from Denver, Colorado, to study physics, although in four years of college he probably learned less about quantum theory than Schrödinger's cat.

Flip learned a lot about women, though. He was a true believer in the antiwar slogan: "Make love, not war." And making love was easy, what with the sexual revolution of the late sixties dispelling both the Eisenhower era's peppy prudery and the Kennedy generation's insistence on a certain grace. A young man didn't even need clean fingernails, much less looks or personality or intelligence, to get laid. All he had to say was: "Wanna?"

Of course, Flip was pretty bright. And almost handsome. He looked like a sane Rasputin. His shoulder-length hair was the color of top-grade mahogany, and he had an impressive beard, smoldering black eyes, and a large and lively penis. Flip was a late sixties version of the Big Man on Campus. If he was not the leader of Cornell's anti-war movement (that role being taken by a senior far more organized and much less sexually animated than Flip), he was at least its preeminent follower. The first time Lee saw him, her second day of classes, he was cutting Elementary Real Analysis and working for peace, handing out signs that pledged: "No more men! No more money! No more killing!"

It had been a long day for Lee. Overwhelmed by the vast greenness of the campus, by the disdain of her roommate—a girl who had gone to boarding school in Switzerland and had actually laughed in Lee's face when Lee said: "*Ça me rend heureuse de vous voir*"—and by the difficulty of her chemistry class, Lee only noticed the first exclamation on the sign. "No more men"? She thought: What did that mean? She felt that light-headedness that precedes nausea. *No more men.* Her worst fear: During the darkest part of the night, she terrified herself by thinking about how the world was not precisely half male, half female, but rather, forty-nine percent male to fifty-one percent female. What if she was in that two percent damned to eternal spinsterhood, to birthdays celebrated in her parents' kitchen with Greta's carrot cake and its inch-thick cream cheese frosting? Sylvia and Leonard would be there, dressed for the evening, on their way to the city for dinner, Sylvia in Guy Laroche, perfuming the whole first floor with Mitsouko, Leonard in a navy-blue suit made (he'd inform her for the fourteenth time, while ostensibly picking a thread off the lapel— but in fact mesmerized by the near-invisible hand stitching) by the bespoke tailor who made suits for *the president of the Bank of New York and John Hay Whitney*. Robin would be sneaking looks at the clock, letting Lee know how she was dying to get out and meet her boyfriend, not wanting to ask him to the birthday celebration because that would be cruel, his presence emphasizing Lee's unremitting manlessness. Then one day Greta would die, and the cakes would come from Loaves and Kisses, three blocks from her father's store, because Long Island bakeries made sickeningly sweet ick-looking cakes, so now the cakes would be in chic Manhattan flavors, like pistachio-cognac. And then Robin wouldn't be able to come, because she and her husband and their three stunning children would be vacationing on the French Riviera. And then her parents would die and she'd be all alone, because the teachers in Shorehaven Junior High—that's where she'd wind up, teaching social studies and coaching girls' softball because someone else was already coaching tennis—wouldn't want to call attention to the fact that Lee was forty-three or fifty-seven and living alone, her only companions a declawed, neutered cat and the seven fur coats that hadn't been sold after Leonard's lawyers arranged for a going-out-of-business-due-to-death sale. "No more men!" the sign said. She did not even notice Flip. Of course, her apparent indifference fascinated him.

"Hi," Flip said meaningfully.

"Hi," Lee said apathetically, wanting to get away from this bearded person whom she thought must be either a hermit or a Hasid.

"Are you a freshman?"

"Yes," she said, realizing by his persistence and his clear, western accent that he was probably neither of the above. However, her mother's influence still exerted its pull from the north shore of Long Island all the way up to Ithaca; thus an involuntary "Yuck, beard" response kicked in. "Excuse me," she said, trying to get around him and his signs. "I have to get to the library."

"Isn't there something that's more important than the library?" he asked, trying to burn her with his hot eyes.

The right answer, naturally, was: The war in Vietnam is more important than the library. For Lee, who was smart as a whip but (to be totally truthful) no great shakes as an intellectual, the issue of "Are We Fighting in a Really Stupid War?" genuinely was more interesting than "What Were the Philosophical Underpinnings of the Council of Trent?" To her pragmatic mind, the Domino Theory as a justification for intervention in Vietnam made no sense. "Domino" was not the operative word: "Theory" was. In Lee's short life, she had never found a theory that could explain or serve as a guide to all human behavior. And if Marx and Freud couldn't satisfy her, a couple of guys in wire-rimmed glasses in the Pentagon certainly were not likely to either. Besides, propping up a corrupt government headed by a debauched playboy did not appear to Lee to be an effective way to halt the spread of totalitarianism.

However, there was an alternate answer to Flip's question, "Isn't there something that's more important than the library?"—for which equal credit would be given. That answer was: Yes. You and your incredible broad shoulders under that tight, faded T-shirt are more important than the library. Thus, aflame from moral outrage and from Flip Mullen's smoldering-ember eyes, she reached for a sign and began her real college education. Good for her.

And too bad. While Lee and thousands like her changed the course of American history, she missed out on the historic joys of undergraduate life. No shy glances as she and Flip stood on line in the cafeteria. No stolen kisses in the stacks at Uris: On the second night of their acquaintance, they were engaged in exuberant sexual intercourse on a stained mattress beneath a poster of Che Guevera. She missed out, too, on the intimacy of campus life, heady discussions with professors, close friendships with other girls, thrilling late night disputes as to whether essence precedes existence or vice versa. Within a week, Lee moved into Flip's off-campus apartment, a down-at-the-heels place he had transformed into a slum. Not merely her lover, he became her professor, her friend, her political mentor, her atheist priest.

So she got a lousy education. Although Flip was not stupid, he lacked the two qualities that most appealed to Lee: curiosity and humor. While he knew the degree of ineffectiveness of Operation Phoenix in neutralizing the Vietcong infrastructure better than the assistant secretary of state for Southeast Asian Affairs, he never took her to a concert. They never discussed a book. Lee spent the first two years of college doing pretty much what she had done in second grade: drawing jumbo letters with Magic Markers— STOP THE WAR! BOMB SAIGON! The rest of the time, she cooked vats of spaghetti so she could feed Flip and his friends when they sat around the kitchen table planning protests. (While the feminist movement was surging, it had not yet raised many consciousnesses among the antiwar set at Cornell University.) On occasion she read one of the books required for her courses; now and then she handed in a research paper. But since exams were periodically canceled in the face of student strikes and many beleaguered professors were willing to negotiate final grades, Lee achieved a stellar grade point average for only a C-minus effort. By the end of her sophomore year, she knew a great deal about making marinara sauce and a bit about the subjects on which she had written papers: "The Roots of Anarchist Thought in Eighteenth Century England," "Mao Tse-tung and the Peasant Movement in Hunan Province," and "Weather Imagery in *Bleak House*." She read a lot of Shakespeare and all of Austen. She read the assigned books of the Old Testament for a Bible as Literature course, but all she came away with was that God was not very nice and that her Hebrew name, Leah, belonged to a zero, a born loser, a woman whose husband was disappointed in her from the moment he lifted her bridal veil and who only wanted her sister.

"I'm going," Flip murmured late one night in April 1970. Although May was just a week away, it was still damp and nasty cold in the apartment. A stiff wind rattled the windows and insinuated itself through the cracks in the splintered wood sash. "To Canada."

"Mmm," Lee said in response. It was not that she was uncaring, but Flip had wakened her. She was exhausted. The Cadre of Eight, the leaders of the various antiwar groups on campus, had been eating and drinking and debating whether to take over the student union building until two in the morning, and she had not gotten to bed until after three. She had been busy cleaning up after them, discarding cigarette butts and marijuana roaches, picking up the balled-up papers from the floor, washing dishes and, for half an hour, scouring a black crust of burned tomatoes off the bottom of her sauce pot after one of them, inexplicably, had turned up the burner as high as it would go. Also, Lee did not see Canada as an immediate threat. The night before, Flip had announced that he fully expected to go to jail rather than concede the legitimacy of the draft. Two nights prior to that, he had been musing about joining up with some old movement friends in Sweden.

"I'm leaving right after graduation." She pulled up the blanket—one of her Grandma Bella's afghans which she had brought up to college—so it covered her cold shoulder. He'd change his plans a thousand times more. She was rolling over onto her right side, her most comfortable position, when Flip added: "I got a job in Saskatoon."

Lee froze on her right side, her back toward him. This sounded serious: a real plan. "Doing what?" she asked, doing her best to sound interested but not anxious.

"Teaching math." She felt his heated breath on the back of her head.

She tried to swallow, but her mouth was too dry. "Saskatoon?" she managed to say. "Up in Canada somewhere?"

"Saskatchewan," he said.

"Where is that?" She was dying to turn around and see his expression, but she was positive she had morning breath.

"I don't know. Up there. Above North Dakota or something."

Knowing Flip, any question she asked would be interpreted as grilling, and she was fearful of offending him further when he was under so much pressure. "Is it definite?"

He exhaled a badgered breath at even this. "Is *what* definite?"

"The job."

"Yes."

"Do you want to tell me about it?"

"Not particularly. Do you think I'm happy about it? Did I go to Cornell so I could teach trigonometry to a bunch of idiot teenagers whose fathers work in a fucking meat-packing plant?" He lapsed into an angry silence. She heard the rapid, dry sound of his rubbing his beard between his fingers.

She knew a really devoted girlfriend would just join him in silence at this moment. But the words spilled out of her mouth. "How long have you been planning this?"

"Jesus!"

"Flip, why couldn't you just have—"

"Wonderful. Let's have a discussion about the relationship."

"No, please, I'm sorry. It's just that . . . I understand this must have been too painful to discuss with me." He didn't put his arm around her and pull her close, but at least he stopped playing with his beard. She slid down the mattress a couple of inches so that when she turned over, her breath would be on his breastbone, not in his nose. "Flip," she said softly when she was facing him.

"What?"

"I love you." He said nothing, but she could feel his exasperation. She had vowed only three days earlier not to bring that subject up again, and here she was, once again, breaking her promise. "I know I'm not supposed to say it."

"Then why do you?" He turned on his back and reached for his Marlboros.

"I don't know. I swear, I don't mean to put pressure on you. I just . . ." She took the matches from him and lit his cigarette. He smoked and stared at the dark ceiling. (Three years later, Lee would announce in her consciousness-raising group that this had been a masochistic relationship and that she cringed every time she thought of how she had walked down College Avenue carrying a Santa-sized sack of Flip's dirty clothes to the laundromat, where she waited so when they came out of the dryer she could fold them before they got wrinkled. But at that moment, all she felt was ennobled by her love of this martyr for peace.) "I love you so much. You have no idea. You're my life. I'd do anything for you."

"Then leave me alone!"

Lee tried to console herself with the thought that at least there was no anger in his words, only weariness. But the words themselves hurt, and she began to cry. Flip crushed out his cigarette in the saucer he'd taken from the cafeteria to use as an ashtray, but it smoldered and filled the room with a bitter stench. "Please, Flip."

"Please *what*?"

"Let me come with you."

"I knew you'd say something like that."

"Please."

"No."

"Why not?"

"You know why not."

"I don't."

"There's nothing for you up there."

"*You're* there. That's all—"

"You know what you're doing, Lee, don't you?"

"What?" she asked in a small voice, wanting more than anything not to hear his answer.

"Trying to get me to marry you."

"I swear . . ."

He grabbed the Malboros and, snatching the matches out of her hand, lit another. "You are bourgeois to your core. There isn't an inch of you that isn't your mother's daughter. I'll go to Canada and rot and you'll finish school and get a mink coat for graduation and you'll marry some guy with golf clubs. And you'll live happily ever after."

"No I won't!"

"You will," Flip said, with the blasé certainty of an omniscient god. He blew an imperfect smoke ring.

Lee rested her head on his shoulder, relishing the warmth of his body on her cheek. "Never," she insisted. "I'll love you for the rest of my life."

Not quite. By the time he got around to calling her from his rooming house three and a half weeks later to ask her to join him in Saskatoon, she had moved in with a ¡Puerto Rico Ahora! insurgent named Jorge.

Eleven

Pinstripes rubbed up against pinstripes in the Nassau County Correctional Center. If you took a deep breath (never really advisable in the visitors' room), you got blasted by the expensive musk of lawyers' aftershave fusing with the raw stink of locked-up men. There were too damn many suits that day. It felt as if every attorney ever admitted to the bar in New York State was conferring with a client under the brutal fluorescence.

Down the row from Norman, a kid with the oily ears of someone who hadn't seen the inside of a shower for too long was asking counsel about the significance of his third conviction for first-degree robbery. In the row ahead of ours, a blond-haired, blue-eyed Christmas-tree angel of a teenager turned out to be awaiting trial for shooting a nun point-blank in the head. The crimes perpetrated by these young felons were always a double whammy, not only devastating their victims' lives but diminishing their own souls. Even if they managed not to get in the way of a bullet, even if they avoided heroin and crack and eluded AIDS, even if they lived another fifty or sixty years, most of them were, already, dead men.

There were a few older, white-collar white men in the slammer that day too. Since they could buy justice that the poor couldn't afford, these guys were stuck in the clink for a reason: Their deeds were so appalling—first-degree assaults with nauseating consequences, like bitten-off ear lobes, or aggravated sexual abuse on a minor—that no magistrate could let them loose on bail. Or they had grown so rich on economic crimes that they were adjudged likely, when their trial date came up, to be sailing off the coast of a tropical paradise that did not enjoy the benefits of an extradition treaty with the U.S. Since the correctional center was, as I have mentioned, the stuff from which nightmares are made, these upper-middle-class malefactors were desperate to buy protection from the horror—or at least distraction from it. Guys like these were always requesting conferences with counsel, and they usually found the sound of "my attorneys" far more bracing than "my attorney."

One of them, directly to my left, had actually been my client. "Call Me King of the Sea!" was the owner of a small chain of unhygienic seafood restaurants. He deserved the death penalty solely on the basis of his cable TV commercials, on which he wore a crown, carried a scepter in one of the lobster-claw gloves he wore, and screeched: "Eat me for just $12.95!" But it wasn't his unmitigated coarseness that got him into trouble; it was his viciousness. I had talked the D.A.'s office into dropping the assault charges against King of the Sea on two occasions but had passed on representing him the third time around. Now, for what must have been the tenth time, he was accused of battering one of his employees, this time a woman who now had a flattened disk of cartilage where her nose had been. Unlike most of the other times, he could not buy his victim's silence. The beating had been near-fatal—with the dishwasher as an eyewitness—and *Newsday* was on his case. So despite King of the Sea's largesse to the Republican party, not even Woodleigh Huber, our county's utterly conscienceless district attorney, could let him pass the time before trial playing billiards in his estate in Upper Brookville.

The room was so congested with legal talent that Terry had to yank two chairs out from under a team of Manhattan lawyers. They grumbled a lot—impressive, four-hundred-dollar-an-hour grumbles—but they didn't try to stop him. They all had magnificent haircuts, and they all wore worried Park Avenue forehead wrinkles as they huddled across from an abortion-mill owner accused of massive Medicaid fraud.

Having won two seats, we were finally able to inquire of

Norman how come his girlfriend Mary's fingerprints happened to turn up all over Bobette Frisch's house when he had stated unequivocally that Mary had never been at Bobette's. "Mary's never been arrested," Norman assured me.

"What does that have to do with the price of tomatoes?" I asked.

Norman looked as if he were trying to gauge the depth of my stupidity. "I'm sure she's never been arrested," he explained patiently. "The cops couldn't have her fingerprints on file. Whosever fingerprints they are, they aren't hers. It must be a mistake."

"It's no mistake," Terry chimed in, ominously drawing out each word. Having intimidated the Manhattan lawyers, he was on a roll.

"As of now, the police don't realize those fingerprints are Mary's," I explained. "They don't know whose they are, and so far they don't care."

Norman swallowed hard. "But it's only a matter of time?"

"It may be."

He blanched. Each time I visited, he looked less imposing. Not in size of course. In luminosity. He had lost his glow; his magic was dying. A thick blue vein pulsed nervously on his left temple. Just below it, a rash shaped like Florida dotted his cheek, its redness clashing with his orange prison uniform. In addition, Terry, glowering beside me, was spooking Norman more than I would have believed possible; that diminished him even more. Of course, when I thought about it, I realized why someone as blatantly, crudely masculine as Terry was so disturbing. Norman's entire world revolved around women: He charmed them, he conquered them, he destroyed them. He was not used to dealing with men. Or maybe he was afraid of them and had carefully crafted a universe in which he was the only male.

"Listen," I said. "If the police decide to investigate Bobette's murder any further, it *will* be only a matter of time before they ask Mary if she'd mind coming with them to headquarters for a little chat. But the way things stand now, there's not going to be any chat. As far as they're concerned, you're it. The D.A. is completely satisfied that Holly Nuñez has a strong circumstantial case against you and can get a guilty verdict."

Norman rested his head against his open palm. Not weary, I thought. The man had made a meticulous study of how he appeared to others. He knew how that pulsing vein on the side of his head could give him away: Over and over again, it throbbed a message: Nervous! Nervous! "Do *you* think they've got a strong case?" he asked.

"I think I've indicated before that it may not be strong, but it is ... I'd call it solid. If I were the prosecutor, I wouldn't hesitate to go to trial."

"Oh," was all Norman could say.

"I've been straight with you right from the beginning. The way things stand, I can't get you a very good deal. The assistant D.A. says she won't plea-bargain now—although she probably will eventually. But the deal she'll offer will be so lousy that I don't see any choice but to go to trial. Either way, you're looking at a minimum of twenty years."

"I see," Norman replied. I don't know if he actually said it; the visitors' room had become very loud. No shouts, but a deep, angry hum, the most ominous male sound, the noise that might rise from a band of wild creatures just before a rampage.

"Do you see that from our point of view," I said, louder, "finding someone else's fingerprints at the crime scene is the first break we've had in the case?"

"But you say they're *Mary's* prints," Norman said. "She's not the murderer. There's got to be an innocent explanation. She couldn't hurt a fly."

"Are you sure she couldn't have hurt Bobette?"

"Positive! The whole idea is ridiculous!" He shook his head sadly. The fleeting half smile of someone faced with monumental idiocy curled his lips. "More than ridiculous. It's insane. *Mary?*"

Yes, I knew Norman was a con man, but I could also see he could not believe that Mary could have had anything to do with homicide. Of course, it was easy for him to have that sort of confidence if he knew himself to be the killer. "Well," I said patiently, "an eyewitness puts you there that day, right around the time of Bobette's murder. You say you did not kill her. Okay. So how did she die? She didn't put her own hands around her neck and strangle herself. Someone else was there. And now Mary's fingerprints put her in that house."

"Listen . . . ," Norman began. But he didn't know what to say.

"Are you a hundred percent sure you didn't know she'd been at Bobette's?" Terry demanded, his slow, husky voice so controlled he was starting to sound maniacal. I gave his shoe a tap with mine, signaling him to ease off a little. He was going over the top with the intimidation business and, instead of being scary, was beginning to sound like Boris Karloff. Norman would laugh in his face.

But Norman answered fast, as if desperate to mollify Terry. "No, I swear I didn't know. Mary never told me she was there. But there *had* to have been a reason."

"Come on," Terry demanded. "Like what?"

"I don't know," Norman said, directing his answer to me, as if I'd posed the question. "Like maybe Mary got insecure about me. I mean, it's crazy, but . . . I stayed over at Bobette's a couple of times. Bobette really wanted it, *expected* it, wouldn't take no for an answer, and I didn't want to queer the deal. It was too close to the big finish. Maybe Mary thought . . ." His voice trailed off.

"What did she think?" I asked. Norman shrugged, so I repeated the question.

"Maybe she thought I might actually go through with it this time. You know."

"Know what?"

"That I would marry Bobette."

"Did you give Mary any indication you were going to?" I asked.

He laughed. "Are you kidding? Of course not!"

"Because you weren't going to marry Bobette? Or because you didn't want Mary to know what you were thinking?" Norman looked down at his big hands, noticing them as if for the first time. His nails had grown long. Their unkempt length was highlighted by arcs of greenish dirt beneath them.

He folded his fingers to hide the nails but continued to stare down at them in something approaching horror, as if the first two joints had suddenly been lopped off. "Norman, try and answer my question."

He crossed his arms over his chest, hiding his fingers under his armpits. Looking above the crowd, he stared up into the glassy eye of the guards' closed-circuit camera. He didn't speak for almost a minute. Finally, he said: "Look, you know what I do, what I am. So my word probably doesn't mean anything to you. But I swear to God, I would never have left Mary for anyone." He took a deep, agonized breath. "I admit"—another breath—"I thought of it. Bobette had around fifty thou stashed in the bank. Over two hundred in a brokerage account. And she netted around a hundred twenty-five a year from the bars and a couple of buildings she owned. I could have managed her holdings for her. She was dying to give up all that responsibility and just stay home, be taken care of. But I only considered it for . . . seconds, just seconds. You know why?"

"Why?" I asked.

"I didn't *like* her." His eyes drifted toward Terry, but he pulled them back to me. "I know that may sound funny to you, but I honestly like some of my marks. Some of them are really sweet. But Bobette was a pain in the butt most of the time. And when she wasn't"—a shiver of disgust went through him—"she would act cute. 'Am I your bunny, Denton?'" he mimicked. "Marry that loser? Not for all the money in the world! Not when I have someone like Mary!"

"So what was Mary doing at Bobette's?" Terry asked.

"Have you met her?" Norman inquired, his chest puffing with anticipatory pride.

"Mary? Not yet." Terry bunched his features together, angry with Norman's attempt at male camaraderie. Not truly angry: Whenever Terry wanted to move things along, he'd frightened someone. On a busy day, he could put on his scary face ten or twenty times. He leaned forward as if ready to spring. On the other side of the barrier, Norman pressed his spine as hard as he could against the back of his chair. "You didn't answer my question," Terry persisted. "I want an answer now. *Why are Mary Dean's fingerprints all over that house?*"

"Maybe she was looking for . . ." But Norman Torkelson couldn't think of a thing.

A half hour later, Mary stood in her living room, held up her left hand, and swore: "Honest to God, I wasn't in her house!" I watched as Terry Salazar's hard features softened into that squishy, low-IQ expression of the sexually besotted male.

"If you weren't there," I snapped, "then someone borrowed your fingers and put your prints all over Bobette Frisch's house."

The furnished apartment Mary shared with Norman wasn't as bad as the Love Nest, although all the furniture was grim, covered in variations of institutional-strength nubby beige and brown. In her kelly green silk bathrobe, Mary was far too dazzling for such a dreary place. "Well . . . ," she said, trying to buy time.

But I wasn't selling it. "When were you at Bobette's?"

She glanced over at Terry, hoping to be rescued, but he was still wearing that moronic smile and was useless. So she turned back to me: "*Please.* Don't tell Norman."

"When were you at Bobette's?"

"Oh, God," she squeaked. I waited. "It was . . . It turns out . . ." Mary flashed an apologetic smile to Terry. I was hoping he had come to his senses enough to flash back his hard-boiled private-eye piercing stare, but not only did he beam back at her, but the beam—goofy-grinned, glazed-eyed—was proof that the sight of her had transformed his brain to butterscotch custard. Mary went on: "The day I was there . . . It turned out to be the day she got killed."

"It turned out?" I asked.

"Yes."

"What a coincidence."

"I know."

"What time were you there?"

"Not *when* she got killed."

"What time, Mary?"

"Like, um, most of the afternoon."

"You were in her house?"

"No! Outside."

"What were you doing outside?"

"Watching." She pretended to adjust the cuff of her robe. "I was, like, jealous. Okay? I watched the house. They were inside the whole day."

"Where were you when you were doing your watching?"

"Just hanging out. Walking around the block. I couldn't just stand out in front and look. And I don't drive, so I couldn't rent a car or anything and sit and wait there. But around three o'clock, my feet hurt. I was scared if they came out, you know, that Norman would spot me and have, like, a total shit fit. So I went and I sat . . ." She hung her head and mumbled the rest: "I sat on her back stoop."

"Did you look inside?"

"Every once in a while."

"From the rear of the house?"

"Yes. And from the sides too. But I was scared her neighbor would see me. Her neighbor on one side. On the other side there's big bushes. Then, when I stopped looking, I went back to the back stoop." She sighed. "I shouldn't have worn heels."

I told Terry to find out if the cops had checked for footprints and if there was any indication of high-heel marks. Then I turned back to Mary: "Weren't you afraid Bobette would come out and spot you?"

"No. It was super-cloudy. Very chilly too. She wouldn't want to sit out in back."

"What if she'd left something outside? What if she wanted to empty her garbage?" Mary clearly had not thought of that. "What if her tenant saw you?"

"I didn't remember about him. He came out, though, and I heard him on the other side of the house, giving Norman a lot of grief. You know, about his car blocking the driveway."

"What time was this?"

"Late. I was starved. I kept thinking about fajitas. It was after they got back from their nature walk. Must have been after six. Then the tenant drove away and Norman and Bobette went back in. Chicken fajitas. The beef ones are too greasy."

"So how did you get inside?" I asked her.

"I heard the front door open and someone come out. So I kind of snuck around and peeked. It was Norman. Then he drove off, and then I heard the shower. So with him being gone, I went around to the front. He always presses that teeny little button on the lock of the door of our apartment because he always forgets his key. Sure enough, the door was open! He must have done it. Or maybe Fatso unlocked it for him to get back in. Or maybe she forgot about it. Anyway, I walked right in."

"What did you plan to do?"

"I don't know. I didn't have any plan."

"Come on, Mary," I said, my patience running out. Also, I was experiencing a near-irresistible urge for chicken fajitas. "You must have had something on your mind, going into Bobette's."

"Well, you can imagine what I was thinking."

Out of the corner of my eye, I noticed Terry nodding like a lunatic. "I'm sorry," I replied, not at all snidely. "I can't imagine what you were thinking."

"I wanted to see . . . Like maybe Bobette bought plane tickets 'cause they were going to go away for a honeymoon. Or something. I just wanted to *know*." She hugged her green robe tighter against her. "I can't help it. I get jealous."

"Did you search the house?"

"I went upstairs first, to her bedroom. I figured it would be safe with her in the shower." I waited. "I went through her drawers. Nothing. Just her stupid, ugly fat-bras. Then the shower went off. I almost had a heart attack, I was so scared." She put her hand over her left breast and gave it a series of rapid pats. I deliberately avoided looking at Terry looking at Mary. "I didn't have time for her closet. I ran back down."

"And?"

"Oh, God, my heart was pounding! Boom! Boom! I could

hear her footsteps upstairs! Clomp! Clomp! Clomp! And then I got even scareder, because I thought: Oh God, what if Norman comes back and finds me?"

"So what did you do next?"

"I just ran out."

"You didn't look around anymore?"

"Maybe for, like, a second, before I got totally petrified. But I didn't find anything."

"Did you take anything?"

"No!"

"You didn't, for example, take Bobette's wallet?" Mary's tongue darted back and forth over her lower lip. "You didn't then take a local cab or a bus and go up to the Americana Shopping Center? Maybe buy a bag at Louis Vuitton?"

Mary's eyes filled up. "How did you find out?" she managed to ask. Then she started to weep.

"You want to help Norman, don't you?"

Mary was sobbing too hard to answer. Terry eyed me as if I'd committed a major human rights violation. Finally, I heard a hiccupy "Of *course* I want to help him. I love him."

"Do you want him to go to prison for a crime he didn't commit?" She shook her head. "So, Mary, we have to get at the truth."

She lifted her tear-drenched face. Terry looked as if his heart would explode. "I bought a shoulder bag," Mary admitted, wiping away a mascara-blackened tear. "The big one. And a cocktail dress at another store." Suddenly she tore away from us. She seemed to be rushing headlong toward the bedroom. I realized that if she could climb out the window, she'd disappear along with Norman's small shot at freedom. I followed her. Terry started to follow me, probably to protect her, but suddenly Mary was hurrying back to us—carrying a shirred white cocktail dress with spaghetti straps, a minuscule thing about the size of a hand towel. "Isn't it, like, *the* best dress ever?" she demanded. "Feel it. It's the silkiest silk." I kept my hands at my sides. But I watched her hands as her fingers caressed the fabric.

"Mary . . ."

"I know I shouldn't have. But it was sooo silky. I mean,

169

how should I know she'd go and get murdered? I thought: Well, Norman's going to score, and why shouldn't I get something nice for myself from her? Not what Norman would give me: something straight from her. I mean, look what she has! Her own house. She can buy all kinds of clothes, that fatso pig, and she has *two* VCRs. So big deal: Why can't I have a little shopping spree before we leave town?"

"But I thought you were afraid that he might stay and actually marry Bobette."

"Not deep, deep down."

"Deep down enough to sneak into her house when she was there and risk getting caught."

"I was just . . . you know. Wanting to reassure myself. And the wallet just happened to be there. You know, that old blobbo had an American Express *and* a Visa *and* a MasterCard! I've been dying for one of those Vuitton bags for, you know, about a hundred years. And when I saw that dress, it had, like, my name on it! It said: Mary, this is yours. Your dream dress for when you go to some really, really expensive club to celebrate after you and Norman get married."

Little Chuckie Phalen was attached to a big tan machine by a clear plastic hose. The machine extracted oxygen from the air and pumped it straight up his nose. He kept the thing right beside his desk; that way, he could, with a quick flip of his scuffed cordovan shoe, turn off the flow of oxygen so he could light up a Camel.

My partner, Chuckie, had always been an affable man. Despite his diminutive size, he was the rare sort who could break off a bar fight with a few good-humored words. He was a great storyteller, too, and was always being asked to emcee some judge's retirement party, or to say a few words on behalf of So-and-so, who was being honored by the Nassau County Guild for Something Legal and/or Catholic. Being so outgoing, Chuckie had naturally chosen the most sociable means of suicide, and I had no doubt there were bets among the boys at TJ's Tap-room as to what would get him first: his smoked-out lungs or his Scotch-saturated liver.

He used oxygen only in the office, convinced that whatever compassion points he could score with a jury by being hooked up to a portable tank would be offset by their annoyance at having to feel sympathy for a sick man. "It's not a good handicap, like being blind. Or having a leg off and being able to roll right up to them in a wheelchair," he'd informed me. We tried to meet at the end of every day for a drink, a Sam Adams for me, a J&B for him, and to shoot the breeze about our cases and office matters before I went home to meet the man in my life and he to the boys at TJ's.

"My heart is in smithereens," Chuckie commented, after I'd told him about my day on the Torkelson case. "You don't think it *really* could have been the beauti-full girl who killed the old maid, do you? I hate the thought of beauty behind bars."

"What if she were ugly?"

"Throw 'er in the clink!"

"Her killing Bobette does sound pretty improbable," I mused, "at least when you first think about it. But Mary has very big hands. Like the hands that left those marks on Bobette's throat. And she certainly has the size and strength to strangle someone."

"She's a *big*, beauti-full girl?" The glimmer in his eye suggested he was recalling something specific: In Chuckie's case, it was probably a porn film he'd seen in 1947.

"She's tall, not big. But she looks pretty strong to me."

"Happen to notice any marks on her forearms? I mean, if she strangled the old maid—"

"Bobette."

"Right. Bobette. If she strangled her, and if the old maid was no weakling—"

"The autopsy report puts her at five-four, a hundred and sixty-one pounds. She was what you could call solid."

"—then Beauti-full would likely have had scratches or bruises on her hands or arms, where the old maid would've tried to pull her off."

"Possibly. But then again, Norman didn't, either, right after he was arrested."

"So what are you saying: Someone else did it?"

I sipped my Sam Adams from a blue plastic beer stein, a grotesque thing with football helmets embossed on it. Sandi, my secretary, had bought it for me at a flea market. For all its hideousness, it was a great find, with a freezy liquid trapped in its innards that kept the beer at ice-cold perfection. "No, it would really be pushing it to say someone else did it. I mean, there's a tenant, but from what Terry could find out, he's just a creep, not a psycho. But what about Mary Dean? She had motive—in her mind, anyway. She was terrified Norman would stay with Bobette, marry her. Maybe she felt she *had* to get rid of her. And she knew the layout of Bobette's house amazingly well. My guess is Mary had been stalking them for some time, not just the day of the murder. And I bet you anything it wasn't the first time she'd broken into Bobette's house. She wanted the threat of marriage to Bobette eliminated. *There's* your motive. Now think about this: Norman had no motive."

"Lee, you're talking to me, Charles Michael Phalen, your partner," Chuckie wheezed. "Or do you think I've lost all sense?"

"Listen, what could have motivated Norman to commit murder? He has an absolutely predictable M.O. He gets their money, goes out to buy champagne, brings it back, and toasts the mark—so the mark feels confident he's not running off with her life savings. At which point he runs off with her life savings. He doesn't have a violent nature."

"Then why were you so sure up to now that he did it?" Chuckie asked.

I was dying for another beer, but I allow myself only one, and a glass of wine at dinner. For that pleasure, I have to run three miles a day, forgo dessert eternally, and eat more fish than is necessary for human happiness. If I had even a single extra sip, I would gain so much weight so fast that I would make Bobette look like Audrey Hepburn. "This is what I thought happened," I said slowly, "when I still was convinced Norman did it: He was at Bobette's. She'd taken

172

the money out of the bank, but maybe she wouldn't let him have it. She wasn't a born patsy. She was a shrewd businesswoman; she might have had second thoughts. Or maybe . . . I don't know why I think this, but maybe she expected fireworks along with the champagne and Norman wasn't able to perform. He was really turned off by her. I know he found her very demanding, insisting he sleep over."

"But why would he kill her?"

"I just had a gut feeling she may have taunted or condescended to him and she did it at the wrong moment. He's a worn-out man. Tired of the game. Wants desperately to be a big shot to this beautiful young woman he's in love with and senses she suspects he's getting weary. So he has this— what do you call it?—performance anxiety. And so if Bobette ridiculed him, he might have snapped."

"Are you defending him? It sounds like you're prosecuting him."

"I'm ruminating, Chuckie."

"Ruminate away, dearie."

"My guess is, Norman was afraid that if he showed Mary how exhausted he really was, she'd run. He was also afraid that Bobette would figure out he was just going through the motions."

"Why? Wasn't he good at the con?"

"Sure, but no one's at his best when he's tired, and Norman was so exhausted he might not have had the energy to be a great lover. I'm not just talking about the sex part; I'm talking about the stamina it takes to be charming to someone you're either indifferent to or you can't stand. But the irony of it is, that's all he's equipped to do. He couldn't hold down a real job. And he sure as hell can't live off his investments. He's in his mid-thirties. He's been doing the con since he was a teenager. Want to bet that he's never saved any money?"

"Those guys never do. They piss it away. That way, they have a perfect excuse to pull the con again."

"Exactly. So all Norman wanted was to make a quick score and move on. But he's not the man he was."

"Maybe it's because he's actually in love with Beauti-full. I mean, real love."

"I think he is. On the other hand, he does admit he considered actually marrying Bobette. The guy is desperate to stop."

"So, Lee," Chuckie said, swirling the scotch around his glass, "you're not prosecuting him now? You're back to defending him?"

"Right."

"So it was Beauti-full who done it, because she was afraid Norman would marry the old maid."

"Right."

"But are you *sure* Norman didn't do it? The old maid may have laughed at him and he snapped. Remember? Or she figured out it was a con and he snapped. Or she held the money back in some way and he snapped."

"Maybe Bobette wasn't onto him. Maybe she was just kidding around. Like, 'I'm not going to give you the money until you kiss my . . . whatever.'"

Chuckie shuddered. "Dreadful notion."

"It's not a dreadful notion, Chuckie. You're antediluvian."

"I'm not antediluvian. I'm Irish, and it's dreadful. Anyone can see that's why the poor fella snapped." I shook my head, but I started picturing Norman's powerful hands around Bobette's throat. Then the next second, in my mind's eye those hands tapered and grew soft and it was Mary who was strangling Bobette. "I can see that the sixty-four-dollar question remains unanswered in your mind," Chuckie said.

"Who done it?"

"Pre-cisely!" Chuckie slammed his glass down on the desk for emphasis. A few drops of liquid sprinkled his hand. "Who done it?" He brought his hand to his mouth and licked off the drops.

I replied: "I still don't know."

As I rose to go back to my office, pack up my attaché case, and go home, Chuckie huffed: "One more sixty-four-dollar question, partner."

"What's that?"

"If she did do it—which strains what little is left of an old man's credulity—is it conceivable that a fella with Norman's character would actually take the rap for her?"

*　　*　　*

174

The next morning, I was the first lawyer at the correctional center. But not the first caller. I was chatting up one of the guards outside the visitors' room, asking about her son, a kid I'd once represented for carrying a concealed weapon; I'd gotten him off and he was now studying to be an X-ray technician. Suddenly I smelled a familiar gardenia fragrance. At that same instant, a flash of canary yellow registered at the edge of my peripheral vision. I looked in the direction of the odor and color. Sure enough, it was Mary Dean, in a minidress that looked as if someone had taken a bolt of yellow polyester, wrapped it tight around her body, and then, on a whim, added sleeves the size of volley balls. The odd thing was, no one looking at her too-made-up face and trashy dress would say: Boy, does she look cheap. No, there as something about Mary that engendered goodwill. People would think: Aw, isn't it sad that glorious-looking woman can't afford expensive clothes?

"Hi!" she said, too cheerfully.

"How are you, Mary?"

She teetered on her high heels, not because she couldn't balance in them, but because her weight was on the balls of her feet; she looked ready to run—and I got the feeling it was from me. "Me?" she said. "I'm fine!"

"Good."

She teetered some more. "I hate to, like, insult you or anything, but I've got an appointment and I'm already late."

"What kind of appointment?" I asked.

Naturally, she didn't have an answer and it took so long for her to come up with one that even she knew she shouldn't have bothered. "A-uh-a, you know. Doctor."

"Did you just see Norman?"

"Yes," she said, unconsciously slipping her hand under her hair and tossing it lightly. Norman must have just complimented her on it.

"How does he seem to you?"

"Um . . . Listen, I really have to get going. Give him a kiss for me." I must have looked unnerved, because as she hurried off to retrieve her handbag from the lockers and get

175

away from me, she called out: "I mean, tell him Mary sent him a big, juicy kiss."

Norman was not in the mood to receive a kiss. The second the guard who brought him over to me left, Norman snapped: "Leave Mary the hell alone!"

"Norman, I know you're very protective of her. I admire that. But she was in Bobette's house the day of the murder. She stole Bobette's wallet."

"No she didn't!" His brows drew so close together they became one.

"She admitted it to me," I said.

"She lied."

"No, she didn't lie," I replied calmly. "She stole it."

"Listen," Norman hissed, "she did not take the goddamn wallet. She wasn't even in the house the day of the murder. It was another day that she was there. She's confused. Maybe she's covering up for me."

"I'm sorry, but I don't buy that. I think she—"

"*I* stole the wallet. I gave it to her. I said: 'Go ahead. Buy out a store or two.'"

"When did you have time to give her the wallet? She made those purchases late afternoon or early evening the day of the murder, when you say you were still with Bobette, or going out to buy the champagne."

"There was time. And she did not kill Bobette! Okay? Get off that!"

"Then who did? You?" Norman didn't answer. He scowled, and although it looked like an adolescent's sullen expression at first, it was clear his compressed lips were a grown man's attempt to keep from screaming words of rage. "I know this is a terrible situation for you," I went on. "You want to take care of Mary. The last thing you want is to implicate her in a murder. I admire that. But her presence at Bobette's is your only hope."

"Let me tell you something," Norman said. He spoke so softly that I had to move close to the barrier between us. His face was just inches away from mine. I could see bunches of red capillaries in the inside corners of his eyes. "You leave her out of this. She is a sweet, innocent girl."

"Then you're saying she had nothing to do with the murder of Bobette Frisch?"

"I'm saying if you don't leave her alone, you're fucking fired."

Twelve

Graduation day did not start out all *that* badly. A single powder puff of a cloud was all that marred the sky's blue perfection. True, Robin had promised—sworn, in fact—that she would meet the family at nine-thirty on the dot in front of Barton Hall, where Cornell's commencement exercises would take place. By ten o'clock, she still had not shown. Also true, Sylvia's first act upon seeing her elder daughter in cap and gown was to lift a handful of Lee's long, lank hair in her open palm, examine it, and inquire, after a tsk loud enough to be heard at UCLA: "I *know* it's the style, but couldn't you have pulled it back into a ponytail, so it's off your face?"

Lee, who had spent three-quarters of an hour ironing her hair so it would meet her mother's rigid Hair Sleekness Criterion yet still conform to proper student radical standards, snapped: "No. I could not have pulled it back in a ponytail."

"Fine." Wearily, Sylvia upended her palm; Lee's hair dropped from her hand. "You're the one who's going to have to look at your graduation pictures ten years from now."

Lee had taken Psych 1. While not introspective, she was hardly a bubblehead. She had to have known there was nothing she could do, short of marrying Yves Saint Laurent, that would make her mother happy with her. In fact, in her heart of hearts, Lee probably knew that even Yves would not please Sylvia, for when it came to Lee, her mother was unpleasable. Yet for all her pot-smoking, revolution-fomenting rebellion, Lee could not stop trying. Intent on giving peace a chance this day, she even smiled at her mother. But Sylvia, concentrating on the untweezed inch between Lee's brows, did not notice.

178

"Girls." Leonard cut into the silence. "Let's make it a happy day."

He was not taking his own advice. To begin with, he was stewing over Robin's failure to appear, although this should not have surprised him. Failure had become Robin's vocation. She had dropped out of the University of Pennsylvania, having failed every course she took her first semester. She then failed to complete applications to any of the other, more tolerant institutions of higher learning that a pricey college adviser had suggested. Following that, Robin failed to show up for work at the Revillon showroom at Saks Fifth Avenue, where Leonard, after much obsequious pleading and pledging of future favors, had succeeded in landing her a trainee's job. The man was at his wits' end. During spring break, he had even confided to Lee that Sylvia suspected Robin might be smoking pot. Lee, subduing an urge to whoop with mean-spirited laughter, merely mumbled: "She never talked to me about pot." Technically, that was no lie. As far as Lee could see, Robin was not much interested in such a namby-pamby hallucinogen as marijuana, preferring lysergic acid diethylamide.

A happy day? Not for Leonard. It wasn't only Robin. In fact, for him, Robin was mere irritation. No, his misery was on a grander scale. He knew now: He was doomed to be forever locked out of the world he yearned to enter. His elder daughter could feel at home in the Ivy League. He could only pay the bills. For some reason, it had taken him forty-seven years to finally comprehend this simple fact of American life: He would never be one of them! Now, as he trudged up the seemingly endless hill that was the Cornell campus, his legs ached. His knees felt as if someone had bisected them with a hatchet. The hammering in his chest made him feel that his heart was trying to crash through his rib cage and roll on the grass in shame. Also, he could not get his wind and had to clamp his mouth shut and concentrate on breathing through his nose in order that all the Old Boys and Old Girls so at home at this place wouldn't think the Ivy League was too much for him.

Now he pulled out his handkerchief and dabbed his forehead: gentlemanly dabs. "I'm a bit overheated," he remarked.

Lee observed her father. He wasn't a bit overheated at all. He was sweating like a pig. Perspiration streamed from Leonard's

179

clipped sideburns down his shaven-to-raw cheeks. It splashed off his jaw onto his starched shirt collar. It dribbled from his chin onto the camera.

"Stand closer together!" he commanded his wife and daughter, trying to pretend he was a man in charge, the family photographer, and that his face was dry and his shirt wasn't soaked. But his order came out harsh and loud. "Closer, goddamn it!"

Suddenly, Leonard saw a passerby, a snooty-looking horse-face in a slub-linen suit, turn and give him a slit-eyed glance. He felt she had peered into his soul—and learned it had been born in Brooklyn. Actually, the woman, an assistant manager of a Big Boy hamburger drive-in in Cincinnati, had noticed neither him nor his disagreeableness, as all her attention was focused in her myopic search for her soon-to-be-graduating grandson. But her glance made Leonard change his tone. His words became cultured pearls: "Let me see some smiles! Syl, dear." Sylvia, however, didn't realize the voice she was hearing was her husband's. "Syl, over here, sweetheart! Give me a smile."

Clearly, money had been no object when it came to presenting himself and his wife to the Eastern Establishment. And—looking through the hideously expensive Hasselblad camera he had bought for the occasion—he couldn't believe he could have been so blind: He had been so positive that he knew exactly how that presentation should go. For one thing, he had ruled out Sylvia's customary darkly chic French or Italian ensembles. Instead she was decked out the way he'd told her he wanted her decked out: "A tweed suit. English. Don't worry if it itches. It's supposed to itch. That means it's good quality. And stout walking shoes. Remember, tell them 'stout.'" Her fashionable frosted hair, customarily an amalgam of bronzes, coppers, and platinums, had overnight, at his directive, lightened into ash blond. She had drawn it back, the way he urged, post-post-debutante fashion, and tied it with a folded Hermès scarf. (Had Sylvia been the devoted Taylor-watcher her husband was, she would have known instantly that her hair was now the exact hue and style of Ginger Taylor's.)

This is what Leonard saw; irony of ironies, that while Sylvia could pass, he could not. He looked so *wrong*. Inadvertently, his hand smoothed his lapels, stroked his tie. *Wrong*. Oh, God, he had tried. His navy blazer was exquisitely tailored. Gray flannel slacks. Egyptian-cotton button-down-collar shirt. Silk rep tie. Loafers burnished until they gleamed the consummate loafer tone between mahogany and umber. *He* gleamed. In full East Coast Establishment regalia, he could almost have passed for an alum—"Hello, there, '47." Almost. Unlike Leonard, none of the genuine alumni gleamed. Their blazers and slacks and loafers looked as if they had been making the rounds of garden weddings and restricted clubs since the end of the first half of the century. Leonard's own flagrant newness made him a marked man. He bowed his head in shame. In grief. He tried to fake total immersion in focusing the camera, but his face was too wet. And some of the wet stuff was tears at his own gauche sheen.

Lee glanced around, longing for a friend, or even an acquaintance, to dilute her parents' presence. But the few graduating seniors still lingering outside Barton Hall were engaged in agonizing psychodramas with their own families and were thus too exhausted to come to her aid.

Lee looked back at her parents. Oh, God—her father! His hands holding the camera were trembling. And her mother: "Do you think Robin might be waiting someplace else?" Sylvia's voice barely rose above a whisper, but the "else" careened out of control, rising to a high note of incipient hysteria.

"How the hell should I know," Leonard muttered, trying to appear nonchalant, a difficult look to achieve when one is purple-faced and sweating bullets.

So Lee was graduated from Cornell University with absolutely no one paying attention to her. Her father, in his eight-hundred-dollar lightweight wool blazer, was beside himself. Actually, it was Sylvia who was beside him, but she was beside herself too, swiveling her head, trying to cover all the entrances to the cavernous building so she could wave Robin over the instant Robin came through the door. But Robin never appeared in Barton Hall.

However, there she was, waiting outside, when they emerged. Robin's fair, heart-shaped face was clear as fine bone china, her features were small and delicate, her slender body was forever poised between youthful androgyny and womanhood. She squinted into the sunlight and offered her family a feeble wave, more a flick of the wrist than a real salute. An outsider, noticing her pale frailness, might have thought her ill. Her mouth, however, tight with the rage endemic to adolescent offspring of the haute bourgeoisie in the early years of the 1970s, gave her away.

"Hi," Robin said to Lee, her tone sarcastic, as if Lee had done something that merited bitter derision.

"Hi," Lee replied. She did not expect her sister to offer an apology for being late, which was wise, since she did not get one.

"Is it over?" Robin inquired.

"You missed it." Lee had known Robin would pull something on graduation day. Without consciously rehearsing, she had prepared herself to react with aggressive neutrality. Still, she knew that Robin knew she was seething inside. Well, why shouldn't she fucking seethe? Here she was, finally getting her goddamn degree. Headed for law school, for God's sake! She had taken her law boards only as a lark, but they had been so stellar that she felt compelled to apply. True, her average was barely over a B+. She had no extracurricular activities, excluding indiscriminate sex and helping set fires in three ROTC file cabinets. Yet with those spectacular LSATs, she had been offered admission to every school to which she had applied: NYU, the University of Virginia, Georgetown, the University of Michigan.

But this day was not turning out to be a celebration of Lee's achievement. Like every other occasion when the Whites got together, it had become Robin's Day, a time for forced smiles and spastic colons.

"Where *were* you, for God's sake?" Sylvia's voice, usually barely audible, was much too loud. Leonard made a hysterical "Shhh!" sound that lasted until he ran out of breath. But Sylvia wouldn't shush. "You *swore* you'd be here!" she yelled at Robin.

"So? I'm here," Robin replied, and waved to someone in the throng.

Sylvia stared at her then. They all did. But only Sylvia cracked. Why? It wasn't so much that Robin had not washed her face, or that she was wearing tattered—in actual shreds!—polyester bell bottoms in a hideous rust-colored floral print, and a short top that exposed half her stomach and midriff, and a cheap, fake-pewter peace symbol on a leather thong, that made Sylvia start to sob. It wasn't her dilated pupils that caused Leonard to gnash his teeth in rage and humiliation. No, it was that Robin had summoned over a man. Not a boy: He was in his early thirties. At least. Now she clung to his arm.

The man had a matted black beard; what looked like a strand of albumen from a soft-boiled egg bisected its width. His dark eyes were hooded. His nose was hooked. His blemished skin managed to be swarthy and pasty at the same time. If he had been wearing a long black coat instead of a torn T-shirt and what appeared to be bathing trunks, he would have looked like an anti-Semitic caricature.

"Aren't you going to say something?" Sylvia shrieked at Robin.

"Shhhhh!" Leonard hissed.

"What do you want me to say?" Robin sounded like the soundtrack of a movie being played in slow motion.

"Like 'congratulations' to your sister!" Sylvia's voice seemed to echo through the hills and across Lake Cayuga and come back, louder and brassier, for everyone to hear.

"Shhhhhhh!" Leonard was nearly crazed with embarrassment.

"Don't bother," Lee said to Robin.

Robin gave a coy smile. "How about 'congratulations' to me?"

The Whites stood together in the comfort of not-knowing for a moment. Then Leonard, the head of the family, was forced to speak. "Congratulations"—his deep breath was almost a gasp—"for what?"

Robin rubbed up against the dirty elbow of the man by her side. "Congratulations on my *marriage*," she said, her voice sluggish and coquettish at the same time. "Mom, Daddy . . . oh, and Lee. This is my *husband*." She lifted the man's arm and put it around her shoulder. Then, leaning forward, she grabbed his other hand in hers. The man slid it out of her grip and placed his hand—his hirsute yet disturbingly delicate hand—in proprietary fashion on Robin's naked stomach. Sylvia clapped her own hand over her mouth to stifle a scream. But the scream did not come because she started to faint. Leonard might have keeled over, too, but he leaned against his wife to keep her from flopping sideways onto the grass, which would, of course, have underscored their utter humiliation in front of hundreds of Protestants. The Whites, tilting against each other like two tent poles, were unable to move without humiliating themselves.

Maybe it was the glaring midday sun, but Lee's eyes were drawn to the man's arm that was wrapped around her sister. In the crook, on the pallid, vulnerable skin, she could see a scattering of dark dots. Birthmarks? she wondered. No. Blackheads. Blackheads on the inner arm? she had to ask herself. With this slobbo, why not? Still, she knew, even as she tried other, hopefully better explanations—spattered paint, bites from a small but spiteful insect—that the dots were the tiny scabs of intravenous injections.

Robin laughed an insolent barbiturate laugh. "Isn't he cute?" Her parents remained tipped and dumbstruck. Lee felt the man's eyes upon her. She gazed back into his face; it had absolutely no expression. Her fury at Robin was momentarily replaced by a shiver of dread. Despite his counterculture getup, this man was no aging hippie. He was . . . Lee's heart began to flutter erratically under her gown. He was bad. She knew if she averted her glance he would discern her fear, so she kept staring into his empty eyes. "We're Mr. and Mrs. Ira Kleinberg. Ira, say something." Ira said nothing but at last turned his gaze from Lee to Sylvia. Robin laughed again. Then, with a seductive roll of her hips, she sauntered over to her father. "Daddy," she said. Leonard did not move or speak. "*Daddy.*"

Leonard's mouth formed "What?"

Robin whispered loud enough for all of them to hear: "We need money for a honeymoon."

In later years, Lee would laughingly refer to it as the Summer from Hell. Too bad: She had been counting on that summer between college and law school. First of all, she was going to defeat Richard Nixon. Then, in her spare time, she would read *The Magic Mountain*, listen to Corelli's concerti grossi, visit every museum in Manhattan, and, in short, get the liberal education she would have gotten at Cornell had she not been protesting the war, challenging racism, and cooking pasta for radicals. Admittedly, in the back of her mind, she also knew that she would drive by Jazz Taylor's house a few times a day. Not that she was obsessed anymore, but the memory of him—his well-muscled thighs, the sunlight on his hair, his niceness—remained, her valentine, her most romantic memory.

But by the time Lee said goodbye to her friends after graduation, loaded her clothes and books and stereo in her car, and drove back to Long Island, she discovered that Robin and Ira were already there, having moved into Robin's room. Not that they had asked if Sylvia and Leonard minded. They had simply bumped upstairs the two plastic garbage bags that contained Ira's worldly possessions, pushed together the twin beds with their wicker headboards, and locked the door.

Then the summer began.

"Ask Robin what the hell happened to the thousand dollars I gave them for their honeymoon," Leonard ordered Lee.

"Go tell Robin they have to get out of the room so Greta can change the linens," Sylvia instructed her.

"Please inform your sister that I am doing a white wash today," Greta commanded, "and that if she wants clean underwear, to leave a pile outside her door."

No one mentioned Ira, but they all knew he was there. They all seemed to fear him. Leonard and Sylvia would rush past Robin's room on tiptoes, as if trying not to disturb the fiend within, who, if angered, would come crashing through the door and rip their limbs from their bodies. Even Greta's equanimity deserted her. She began making three or four desserts at night, offerings to placate the demon Ira, who appeared to feed only between the hours of midnight and dawn, leaving crumbs and crusts on the floor and dirty dishes on the kitchen table.

"Lee, ask Robin if she needs to renew the prescription for her asthma inhaler."

"Find out if it's okay if Jerry from Gold Coast Carpets comes in to clean her rug."

"Would you *please* remind Robin that we have a septic tank system here and she *cannot* run the shower for a half hour."

"I want you to tell her that playing that music at three in the morning is unacceptable! Do you hear me? *Un-ac-ceptable*!"

The Summer from Hell. Sylvia could no longer be relied upon to take to her bed for weeks on end and stay out of the way. Her usual melancholia gave way to agitation. She sat all day and into the night at the kitchen table, sucking on Parliaments, drinking endless cups of black coffee and hyperventilating, her exhalations coming out as mewling sounds.

Leonard was drawn back to his house with the reluctant fascination of a driver passing a bloody crash on the highway. Some workweeks, he came home every single night. None of Dolly Young's considerable tricks could keep him in the city. "Anything happen today?" he would demand of Sylvia, his voice croaking, choking with emotion. Sylvia would shake her head back and forth very fast and fill her lungs with more smoke. "Nothing," she would rasp, clutching her bathrobe tighter against her chest. Her hand was a claw, her neck bones made a pitiful V. She was getting thinner and thinner but could only bring herself to eat a bite of the carrot muffins Greta baked fresh every morning to tempt her. "They didn't come down at all."

"They never come down until we're asleep."

"What are they *doing* up there?"

Lee would get home from her summer job, working on the petitions drive at McGovern headquarters in Manhattan, and find her parents standing by the door, awaiting her, as she came into the kitchen from the garage.

"Is Robin taking drugs? What do you think?"

"Go upstairs, knock on her door, and see if she wants to talk to somebody. You know, a doctor."

"Speak to your sister!" they ordered Lee. Tell her: The third overdue notice for *Steppenwolf;* a funny smell, like bad cheese, coming through the door of her bedroom; that girl who's in that *Last Tango* movie with Marlon Brando is on *Johnny Carson* tonight and she might want to see her; Grandma Eva is in the hospital; Grandma Eva is in a coma; does she know where my bone Ferragamo flats are; Grandma Eva died and the funeral is tomorrow at eleven o'clock at Schwartz Brothers.

During June, Lee, dutifully, would knock on Robin's door. Her sister would open it a crack. The room was always dark and stank of pot and body odor; Ira was never in sight. "Yeah?" Robin would demand. Lee would deliver the message. Robin would invariably respond with "Fuck you, fuck them," and shut the door.

Then, for the first two weeks of July, Lee simply jotted down her parents' entreaties and slipped pieces of paper under Robin's door.

After that she began a lackadaisical affair with one of McGovern's advisers on fiscal reform, a forty-eight-year-old corporate lawyer from the second-biggest Wall Street law firm, who had a wife and four children in New Canaan, Connecticut, and a pied-à-terre facing Gramercy Park.

Lee did not return home for the rest of the summer.

You would think, since at least a quarter of the fibers of Lee's being were dedicated solely to Jazz Taylor, that she might have found something familiar about the finely built young man with the square jaw and cascading brown hair—gorgeous, sun-kissed hair—who sat, in New York University Law School's alphabetic tradition, five seats before her. At least, his smile—broad, his high cheeks pushing up his eyes into twin crescents—might have reminded her of someone she had spied upon while hiding behind a spreading juniper. Barring that, you would think, surely, that in the second week of classes, when that mad genius of torts, Professor Myron Blumenthal, actually bellowed "Jasper Taylor!" she would gasp in recognition, or that her heart would leap or her head would spin. But no: nothing, zero, no reaction at all.

Lee was too frightened to notice. The summer had drained her: not being able to go home for fear of either being grabbed by her frenzied parents or, if she could steal upstairs unhassled, having to listen to the bumping of a headboard against the wall as Robin and Ira engaged in one seemingly endless honeymoon hump; the doomed McGovern campaign; the dreary love affair of convenience, made even more burdensome when the corporate lawyer proposed to leave his wife and children and begin life anew with Lee in what he referred to as "a Village pad."

And law school! Could there have been some terrible mistake when they mailed out the scores of the LSATs? Could she have been given some legal genius's number, while some other White—the legal genius—got hers and gave up hopes of a seat on the Supreme Court and was now a junior buyer in the notions and trimmings department at Ohrbach's? The more Lee studied, the more she did not know. She was awed by the penetrating intelligence of her teachers, frightened by the aggressive cleverness of her classmates. No matter how much work she did that first terrible week, she could not make sense of anything that had to do with the law. She searched the faces of the students in her section, hoping to discover fear in their eyes, but more disquieting still, she saw none.

She noticed the young man only because of the manner in which he failed to answer Professor Blumenthal's question: "Can the same act be both a tort and a crime?"

"I really don't know," the young man said. What made her look down the row at him was his air of casual regret. It said: Gee, that's an awfully good question. I wish I knew the answer. He was sitting back comfortably in his seat, looking Blumenthal straight in the eye. He displayed neither the white-lipped, dry-mouthed fear nor the bogus sangfroid that never hid a student's mortification at being caught not knowing.

"You don't know?" Blumenthal boomed. He was a massive man, with a bald head so huge he looked like a monstrous, hydrocephalic baby. "*You do not know?*"

The young man shook his head, and his shoulder-length hair moved with soft grace. "No, I don't." Now everyone was looking at the young man. They were riveted. Lee could see why: He was simply not terrified. What was wrong with him? Did he lack a nervous system?

"May I ask why you do not know?"

"I guess I didn't comprehend the reading."

"You did read it?" Blumenthal snorted a cruel laugh that implied doubt and derision.

"Yes, I did." Not even a hint of panic. Mild regret, and perhaps the onset of the most trifling irritation that Blumenthal was carrying on so.

Blumenthal, poised at the bottom of the amphitheater of a lecture hall, began to vibrate like a tuning fork, unable to decide whether to attack or merely to dismiss the young man disdainfully. To do the latter might be construed as retreat, even cowardice. Blumenthal filled his large chest with air. Lee felt sick for the young man. But then Blumenthal did not strike. Instead he was lowering his enormous head. He was scrutinizing his seating chart. Now he was looking up, ready to attack anew. His voice rang out: "Mr. White!" She looked around, hoping. No Mr. White. "Lee White!" Her guts liquefied.

"What?" was all she could say, because she could not for the life of her remember the question.

"Answer, please, *Miss* White."

She stared at Blumenthal, but there was not a hint on his mask of a face. Torts, she told herself. This is my Torts class, so the question has to be . . . "The same act can be both a tort and a crime," she heard herself saying.

The professor began to shake his head, as if in utter weariness with the human condition. But her answer was right! She remembered reading . . . Oh, right. He wanted the details. "Take the case of an assault," she went on. "It's a tort because it is an offense against an individual." She swallowed. Her throat hurt so much she didn't know if she could go on. And she felt feverish. And her stomach! Any second, she could get diarrhea standing there, and no matter what she did with the rest of her life, anyone at NYU Law School would remember her as the Girl Who Had Diarrhea in Blumenthal's Section. "But it's a crime too, because it's an offense against society."

Blumenthal nodded, but his expression was bitter, as if what she'd said was not merely inadequate but vile. "Can a tort arise out of contractual relations?" he asked, as if not expecting an answer.

"Yes."

"Yes?"

"Like if a person is induced by fraudulent representations to purchase stuff."

"*Stuff?*"

"Merchandise," Lee clarified. Then she saw Blumenthal had begun to breathe another weary sigh. Her words shot out like bullets. "An act can actually be three things: a breach of contract, a tort, and a crime. For instance, the misappropriation of funds by a trustee is a breach of the contract of trust, the tort of conversion, and the crime of embezzlement."

Blumenthal looked away from her, back at the man with the glorious brown hair. "Did you hear that, Mr. . . . ." He consulted his seating chart. "Taylor?"

"Yes," the young man said. He leaned forward and looked down the row at Lee. "Thanks," he said, and gave her a grin that was not merely genuine, not merely good-natured, but heartfelt. It filled her with warmth. She smiled back, more girlishly than in all the years since she had become a student revolutionary and stopped shaving under her arms. And in that second, when at last she was able to avert her eyes from his, his name rang out in her head: Taylor. Taylor? Trembling inside, wishing she were numb, she turned back. Taylor! He was still smiling at her.

"Jazz Taylor," he said, after class.

"Lee White." Shit! she chided herself. She should have said "Jazz?" Why hadn't she sounded at least mildly curious about such a singular name? "Jazz? Are you a musician?" she could have asked. No, too contrived. How about: "Is Jazz short for something?" Now, of course, he'd figure out that somehow she knew him. Not just knew him: He'd put two and two together and realize that she was the girl in the Dodge Dart who kept obsessively driving by Hart's Hill throughout his senior year and even during college vacations. Very likely he knew exactly who she was! She was probably the laughingstock of his whole family. Jazz's girlfriend in that dreadful Dart, ho-ho-ho.

"God, you were cool in there," he said. Up close, his skin was fair but weathered, with the sandy texture and rich red undertone of a born outdoorsman.

"Cool?" she asked. She heard her own voice coming out cold, snotty: like her mother talking to a salesgirl who was wearing cheap shoes. But the words kept coming, and she was powerless to stop them. "Cool like 'Hey, that's cool'? Or cool as in unruffled?"

And now what was she doing? Flirting with him! Shit-ass-rat-fuck! If she were a bystander, watching herself, she would puke. Looking up at him with a starlet's you-great-big-hunk-of-man gaze. Surely in half a second he'd check out his watch and make some pathetic excuse and rush off. Or maybe he was too polite to cut and run, but he definitely had to want to scream with laughter at the sight of her combing back her hair slowly, erotically, with her fingers. Quickly, she stuffed her hand deep into the pocket of her bell-bottom jeans.

"Cool as in unruffled," he replied. "I was so damned ruffled I couldn't remember whether I read that part and forgot it—or just didn't read it."

"You had to have read it," Lee said. "It was assigned—" She stopped because now he was laughing—at her earnestness. Maybe he was one of those Learned Hand-type prodigies who merely had to sit in a classroom in which a few legal notions were bandied about and—Bingo!—all matters juristical became clearer than crystal. She was annoyed at not being able to repress the fast, follow-up realization that if Torts had been clearer than crystal, then Jazz Taylor would not have been caught short by Myron Blumenthal. "Doesn't it scare you *not* to read it?" she asked him. "I mean, every night when I start getting tired, I think: What if Blumenthal calls on me?"

"And so you keep studying?"

"Till I drop," Lee said, now laughing with him. She realized they had walked through the halls of the law school and out the front door only when a gust of hot-dog-scented wind from Washington Square Park hit her in the face. "There's so much intellectual rigor here," she told him. "I'm not just afraid of not doing well. I'm afraid of not . . ." She paused. He was waiting, and doing what no one else in law school had the time to do: listen.

"Afraid of not what?" he urged.

"I'm afraid of not *getting* it. I mean, even if I could memorize each individual case, I may not comprehend what the cases mean in relation to each other, in relation to the law."

"In relation to God too?" He was smiling, but not in fun. In compassion. "For someone in her first month of law school, you're aiming kind of high. Do you really think you have to comprehend the entire history and meaning of jurisprudence? Couldn't you settle for a B in Torts?"

"But it could be an F!" she exclaimed.

"Come on," Jazz said, shaking his head. "You're incapable of getting an F in anything."

She was about to demand: How do you know? But as she strolled alongside him across the park on this bracing gray day—somehow he had led her across the street without her even knowing it—he seemed so certain. For the first time since she began law school, her jaw unclenched. She would pass Torts. In fact, as she stood beside Jazz Taylor on line at the hot dog cart, she suddenly knew she would get at least a B from the bully Blumenthal.

"Mustard?" the man at the cart was asking. Higher than a B if she kept working the way she had been.

"Lee?" Jazz asked.

"Umm . . ." Jazz was going to think she was an idiot. A person either likes mustard or doesn't. She doesn't stand there with a stupid, apologetic grin on her face, assessing the pros and cons of mustardhood.

But the September air felt cool on her face. The people in the park—undergraduates, mothers and toddlers, junkies—all looked radiant. The first fallen leaves, the litter, even the dog shit, appeared to be the perfect examples of their kind. Isn't this the most gorgeous day ever? she wanted to ask him. Red stems brought out the vivid beauty of yellow leaves on the pavement; a Yoo-Hoo bottle resting against the crumpled sports page of the *Daily News* might have been arranged by Renoir; a Newfoundland puppy left a proud, steaming heap of feces. Lee felt something rising inside her. Exhilaration. She was not going to fail. She was going to be a lawyer! Jazz Taylor had made her see that.

"Lee?" And he was saying her name! This wasn't any exceptionally cute-looking guy, slender (but with powerful arms bulging out of his army-green T-shirt). This was literally the man of her dreams, saying her name! "Lee." Jazz Taylor!

"Mustard," she told the hot dog man. "And tons of sauerkraut."

Life is rarely as thrilling as fantasy, or as well scripted, so it was a double pleasure that two days after Halloween, after they had already sipped seven cups of coffee together and enjoyed two dinners in each other's company, Jazz finally got around to asking: "Where are you from?"

"Long Island," Lee responded casually.

"No! You're kidding! Me too. What part?"

The revelation was precisely as she had imagined it. Well, not precisely. They were friends, not lovers. And the sad fact about the pressures of law school was that Jazz was still the only close friend she had made. She didn't yet know any woman in her class with whom she could share the do-you-think-it's-that-he's-secretly-shy-or-that-he's-only-interested-in-me-as-a-friend? conversation and get reassured that he was indeed secretly shy. So unlike in her dreams, Jazz wasn't kissing her fingertips at the very moment he found out where she lived. He was sitting across from her, sipping his usual half-coffee, half-cream concoction—cream

192

of coffee soup, he called it. She said, offhandedly, as if he probably never heard of the place: "Shorehaven."

"No kidding! Me too!" His enthusiasm, as always, was boundless. It seemed that no matter what the circumstance, Jazz was filled with a happy energy. Streaks of exhilaration shot out of him and zapped whoever was in his presence. Lee had watched him outside of class, in the hall in the dorm; anyplace Jazz was became a party. What was remarkable, she decided, was that unlike many individuals with gregarious natures, he was not Class Clown. In fact, he was more Most Popular Boy, which in the fall of 1972 meant that he managed to maintain an air of Jack Nicholson—like perpetual irony. His conviviality was always in perfect balance with his cool.

"Right," Lee said, with the tolerant look of amusement she had practiced so often in fantasy. "You live in Shorehaven too."

"I do! I swear I do!"

She shook her head. "I went to elementary school, junior high, high school and I never saw—"

Jazz put down his mug and leaned toward her. "I went to private school! *That's* why you never saw me. Now tell me where you live."

"No. You'll tell me you live right next door."

"Okay," Jazz said, clearly delighted that he was about to convince her of the validity of his Shorehaven credentials. "I live on Taylor Farm Lane." Lee had practiced so often she knew not to gape; a mouth wide open into an O! would have been too theatrical. But she let her eyes open wide. She puckered her brow, as if she were trying to resolve a most perplexing dilemma. "Do you know where that is?" he asked, although he could tell she did.

"There's only one house on Taylor Farm Lane," she said slowly.

"Right! Mine."

"You're . . ."

"Come on, Lee. What's so funny?"

"Your house . . . what do they call it?"

"Hart's Hill."

"Down the street from there, right near North Road, there's a modern house. Fieldstone front." He nodded. He knew the place. Lee was relieved he had not pretended to retch in revulsion. "That's *my* house."

"No."

"Yes."

"No."

"I swear."

"You're making it up."

"Jazz, how would I make up something that specific? I mean, I know the street name, what the house looks like."

"If you're kidding me . . ."

"Why would I kid about being your neighbor, neighbor?"

And just like in her fantasy, Jazz Taylor finally comprehended that he was the boy next door, and he beamed with unadulterated delight.

Lee and Jazz became the best of friends, a delightful relationship but one Lee hoped was remediable. It was also a friendship with certain limits. They had not yet met each other's families.

In Jazz's case, this was because the Taylors, after the requisite exhausting one-day celebrations of Christmas and Easter, would board the basenjis and fly away to their vacation house just south of St. Petersburg, a stucco-and-Spanish-tile affair they called (with the lack of originality that often goes hand in hand with inherited wealth) Casa Mildew.

For Lee's part, she told Jazz quite openly that she did not want him at her house. Her sister and brother-in-law had remained ensconced in Robin's bedroom in a hostile fog of sex and drugs, thus causing Sylvia to have a nervous breakdown—the ambulatory variety, where she could still, on a good day, go for her manicure. The situation was so excruciating that the stalwart Greta began to suffer what she designated tummyaches but which were, in fact, the pains of peptic ulcers.

Furthermore, Lee could not tell Jazz that she couldn't bring herself to invite him home, because she feared her father would suffer a major coronary, or at least a paralyzing stroke, from the sheer excitement of having a Taylor in the house. Or, worse, that Leonard might make an ass of himself, saying "cahn't" for "can't." "Cahn't" first emerged the summer between her junior and senior years at Cornell: Upon any annoyance, her father would say, "I cahn't abide it," as if he were a character in a bedroom farce. A shiver of dread went through her at each "cahn't."

194

However, by the end of her first year of law school, as she was packing to go to Washington for the summer, her father came into her room and, in his alluding to what he now called the "Situation"—the seizure and occupation of the house by Robin and Ira—Lee noticed another change in his diction. "I can't take it anymore," he was saying. Lee noticed not just the loss of "cahn't" but the acquisition of a new, cosmopolitan manner of speech: still a little world-weary, yet, despite the solemn words, not upper class. Snappy. He sounded like any successful Manhattan man: a tabloid reporter, a urologist, a (and this surprised her) prosperous furrier.

"So tell them to get out," Lee replied, a little absentmindedly, since she was engaged in a furious internal debate as to whether she should bring a pair of heels to Washington. She was now, after all, an editor of the *Law Review*. And she was going to be an intern at the Kroll Institute for Justice, a prestigious left-wing think tank where great ideas were mulled over by people in denim and where no one wasted a neuron of brainpower on a subject as frivolous as patent-leather heels.

"It's easy for you to say, 'Tell them to get out,'" Leonard said, in his snappy new manner. "I happen to be her father. I'm the one who would have to deal with the consequences."

"What consequences?" Lee asked. If she took the heels, she'd have to buy panty hose. She sighed, went to her closet, and brought a pair of never-worn heels over to her suitcase. But even if there was a place she could go to where heels were required, would she *want* to be in such a place?

"Consequences like . . . Who knows what can happen to Robin with that putz?" Lee, who had never before heard a word of Yiddish coming from her father's lips, turned to scrutinize him. Despite his anguish over the Situation, he looked good. Well, except for the trendy wide tie with an Op Art black bull's-eye on a white background and his new long, fluffy sideburns. "We've got to get *him* out."

"How are you going to do that? He'd be crazy to get out. Free meals. Clean laundry—not that it matters to him. All the money he can steal. All the silver he can pawn."

"We don't know for sure . . . ," her father began, but then gave up, knowing that the Frank Lloyd Wright silver tea service had been taken not by a burglar with splendid taste, but by their very own in-house junkie. "Listen, I have a plan to get rid of him."

Lee, who was about to take her heels back to her closet, stopped in her tracks. Her father's dark eyes were sparkling, moist with almost lunatic anticipation. Her first thought was: Oh, God, he's hired a hit man to rub out Ira. "How are you going to do that?" she asked, keeping her voice steady so as not to agitate him.

"Move."

"Move?"

"Sell the house," he explained. "Look, I've had it with commuting. All these years." He did not mention that he'd also had it with staying with Dolly four nights a week. What had begun as wild sexual revelry on an antique iron bed they had bought together had ended up as three obligatory screws a week, and he looked forward to the one night with her—usually Wednesdays—when he could just sit in front of the TV with his Chinese food takeout dinner on a tray and watch Mery Griffin. If he had Sylvia in the city, he'd be able to cut Dolly down to one or two nights a week, plus have the perfect excuse not to sleep over at all. "It'll do your mother a world of good, being in the city." Seeing Lee's dubious expression, he added: "You have no idea how many things would open up to us if we were there. Socialwise, living on Long Island is the KOD."

"What's KOD?"

"Kiss of death," he replied, in the casual manner of the true insider. "We can't throw a dinner party out here, because no one would come. No one who matters. No one from Manhattan. We could buy a co-op on Park or Fifth with a big entrance gallery and a formal dining room and have people over and get invited"—his eyes grew even more luminous; his chest puffed up—"everywhere!" Leonard, catching his daughter's wary expression, took pains to dampen his fervor. "Look, I'm not talking about being social butterflies. You know I wouldn't go for that shallow kind of life. But why shouldn't I have some fun? I've made a modest success." He paused until Lee smiled at his understatement. "And your mother was born with a great sense of style. She'd be fine, once she got a little self-confidence." He tried an insouciant wink, but all that happened was that his cheek twitched and his upper lip curled, exposing his newly capped canine tooth. "Can you imagine what your mother could do for the gross national product, shopping for a really full social life?"

"Dad," Lee said, "I don't know if she's in any shape for a really full anything."

"That's because she's stuck here, with *them*, with this . . . this unbearable Situation. If we lived in the city, had dinner parties to go to, believe me, she'd be high as a kite."

"She'd be high as a kite if someone told Robin and her husband to get out."

"Where would they go? What would they live on?"

"Whatever they could earn."

He shook his head hard, angry to be yanked away from the dinner party in his head. "You're being simple." Simplistic, Lee wanted to correct him. "You're the one who's going to be the lawyer," he went on. "She'd go out and sell drugs. Do you know how long she could wind up in jail for?"

"That's how she's keeping you under her thumb! Keeping you in fear of all the terrible things that can happen unless she gets her way. Do you honestly think that you can get rid of the problem by selling the house out from under her?"

"That's not the only reason I'm selling it."

"Don't you think she'd move into the apartment?"

"We wouldn't have a room for her!" Leonard said triumphantly. He walked to the window and pulled aside the curtain. In the twilight, all he could see was the backyard and the land rising up toward Hart's Hill. "I've had it with the suburbs, with boring *goyim*. This isn't for me. I spend my business life dealing with the most successful people in the city. They *like* me. And I'm not just talking about the fur business, or even fashion. I could be going to parties with the most fascinating people! Journalists. With movers and shakers in big business. Wall Street. With people in show business, for crissakes. Did you know that your mother and I could have been at a dinner party last Thursday with the producer of *Pippin*?"

Without thinking, Lee shoved the high heels into her suitcase. The next morning, she left for the nation's capital.

She did not wear the shoes all summer. As her Constitutional Law professor had promised, the Kroll Institute was a place for pro-

197

found thought, so Lee spent June, July, and August in a pair of handmade sandals she had bought at a crafts fair in Ithaca in 1969, and not a single Kroll fellow even glanced at her feet. They were interested—to the degree that they were interested in any of the legal interns—only in her mind. So for fourteen hours a day, six days a week, she researched defective grand jury proceedings in Jackson County, Missouri, for one of the resident thinkers, a man who could not remember her name but instead called her Rita. She countered with "Lee," eleven or twelve times, then gave up for a day or two. But working in the belligerent stillness of the institute and living with a roommate who worked for the Federal Mediation and Conciliation Service, an agency that apparently required a vow of silence, she had a great deal of time to think.

So she thought: If I give up and let him call me Rita, all that will happen is that I'll show myself that I back down easily. Not from direct confrontation. I'm okay at that. But I have a tendency to get wounded by oblique hits: a raised eyebrow by an intern from Harvard at the way I footnote; an invitation to have lunch in the park that I almost said yes to until I realized it was meant for the guy across from me at my table in the law library; not making enough of an impact to have my name remembered. So if I'm going to be a lawyer, I've got to watch out for the indirect thrusts. That's where I'm vulnerable. If I let myself go to pieces when someone mocks my case citations or doesn't ask me to join him for a reading of the Magna Carta at George Washington University, I can't fall apart. Well, I can't let them see me fall apart.

So every time the great thinker called her "Rita," she responded with "My name is Lee White." That made her feel better. But not much.

She missed Jazz so much that thinking of him brought her to the verge of tears. Since she thought about him almost constantly—defective grand jury proceedings in Jackson County not being as fascinating to her as perhaps they should have been—she spent a great deal of time swallowing the lump in her throat and opening her eyes wide, so that even if she blinked she would not cry.

He missed her, Jazz told her when they spoke, usually once or twice a week. Of course, he said it in a friendly way, as in: I miss my great pal. Clearly, Jazz was having a wonderful summer. Through his uncle, the senior corporate partner, he had gotten a summer job at Matthison, Appleby on Wall Street, a plum usually reserved for second-year students with averages a point higher than his. The work, he informed her, was the dullest in the world, and the partner for whom he was working was a drag, a man whose sole passion in life was his role as peacekeeper in the unending internecine war at International-Hudson Machine Tools. But he was sharing an apartment on the Upper East Side with three of his college fraternity brothers, and they were having a blast. "And don't think I'm not getting culture," he told her. "I saw *Two Gentlemen of Verona* and a play about an English soccer team where the guys come onstage naked. What a pathetic collection of peckers! And I went to a couple of rock concerts in the East Village. So what have you been doing?"

"This week?" Making sure not to crinkle the pages, she leafed through the *Washington Post* until she came upon the calendar of events and reported having seen *Six Characters in Search of an Author* and gone on a picnic.

"Sounds great!" Jazz said.

"Well . . ."

"It isn't?" His voice was so filled with solicitude that he seemed to Lee not only to understand her loneliness but even to know the details of it: the bologna-lettuce-and-tomato sandwiches on the park bench at lunch, the solitary nights trying to read *Dubliners* so she wouldn't be too limited as a human being but instead falling asleep.

"No. The work . . . I'm okay at it. Not good, though. And I have a sneaking suspicion that I'm not an intellectual." She laughed, trying to sound lighthearted.

But there was no echoing laughter. Jazz could tell how miserable she was. "You don't like the work you're doing?"

"No."

"Why not?"

"I keep telling myself every case I'm reading is a human life, but it doesn't feel that way. It just feels . . . like words. And the words are ideas; and ideas *qua* ideas . . . to tell you the truth, I don't give a flying fuck about ideas. I never did. Even in college, all my antiwar stuff stemmed from seeing pictures of people burned by napalm, not from any serious intellectual objection to warfare."

"Okay, so what *do* you give a flying fuck about?" Jazz asked.

A small smile played across Lee's lips: Could I tell you a thing or two about flying fucks! she thought. "People. I care about people."

"See? You've learned something this summer."

"Right. I should have been a social worker."

"No. You learned you're not an academic type. You don't belong in a think tank. And you probably shouldn't think about a big law firm, because let me tell you, all you do for the first twenty years is research one tiny aspect of one big and boring case."

"So? Where does that leave me?"

"It leaves you as a practicing lawyer who represents *people*."

"Ah," said Lee. "I'm going to law school to be a lawyer." She felt as if Jazz had removed a great weight. Her shoulders relaxed. She rotated her head from side to side and had to marvel at the sudden easing of the muscles in her neck. But with that burden gone, she was able to feel something else: desolation. Alone not only in Washington but in life.

She had no man, and—just as bad, she thought, or maybe worse—no purpose. Sure, she would graduate law school in the top ten percent of her class, but then what? Join a law firm and get the job women lawyers always got: trusts and estates, or matrimonial work? Do something meaningful for society, like researching amicus curiae briefs for redwoods? She could, but those prospects shriveled her soul. With nothing she cared to do, she would probably wind up on the legal staff of some dreadful person who called himself the Ralph Nader of Brooklyn and who picked at his ingrown beard hairs. And she would read in the *Cornell Magazine* about all her friends' wonderful lives: "Philip 'Flip' Mullen and his wife, Astor 'Pooky' Gibson, '71, are thrilled that their twins, Albert and Max, will be freshmen at Cornell next September. Flip, who admits to being a former 'peacenik,' is a fellow in physics at the Institute for Advanced Science in Princeton and is renowned for his work in fluid dynamics. Besides being a judge on the United States Court of Appeals for the Third Circuit, Pooky assists emerging nations in drafting their constitutions."

"Jazz," Lee said.

"Hey, you sound gruesome. I thought I cheered you up."

"I miss . . ." She imagined him slung over a chair in his apartment, his jacket off, his tie loosened, sipping some Wall Street law firm beverage: a martini, a Dewar's straight up. Then she changed him into a pair of shorts and a T-shirt and stuck a joint between his thumb and index finger.

"What do you miss?" Jazz asked.

"I miss"—Lee's voice broke—"New York."

By the end of the third month of the second year of law school, Lee decided she was not cut out to be a victim of love. She longed to be like the other women in her class, waking up to thoughts of Property, jogging around the park while musing about the impact of the Warren Court on criminal procedure, sleeping with dreams of Clifford Trusts swirling about her head. Jazz Taylor was a perpetual presence and a constant intrusion and she resolved, sitting in Tax, to get him out of her life, or at least out of her heart. If a thought of him entered her mind, she was going to heed the advice she had read in *Glamour* or *Mademoiselle* years earlier. Tell yourself "Stop it!" and *immediately* think of something else. Just as the article had suggested, she lined up her replacement topics: school, of course; getting a wok and a cookbook and learning to cook Chinese food on the illegal hot plate she had in her dorm room; recollecting her grandmother Bella; calling Dorie Adler and asking her high school friend to arrange a blind date with one of her brother's friends at Columbia Medical School.

So the Wednesday before Thanksgiving, Lee sat on the Long Island Rail Road with something approaching relief. Not that she was anticipating any pleasure in the holiday. Greta would make her traditional twenty-pound turkey, but this year, Leonard had told Sylvia not to pad the guest list. Forget your cousins from Rockland County, he told her. And no lonely new neighbors. Just us. And Sylvia agreed. God only knew in what state Robin and Ira would come to the table, and now they had their friends Bonnie and Nikki with them, sharing the bedroom, eating the Whites out of house and home, and showing no signs of leaving. Company might ask: What are those girls with dirty hair doing there? Who are they?

But Lee felt good, because she had not thought about Jazz in three or four days . . . Stop it! Lee made herself think about a guy in Tax class, Rob Reynolds. Short, which was okay. But awfully small-boned. A mini-man. Would she look like a balloon in the Macy's parade beside him? Was he interested in her? Well, he kept finding a reason to come up after class and—

At which point, Jazz Taylor took the seat beside hers, squeezed her nose, and made a loud honking sound. "Hi."

"Hi," Lee said, not quite knowing how to behave. Part of her resolve to evict Jazz from her consciousness was to let the friendship cool. Having breakfast, lunch, and dinner with him, even in the company of their growing circle of friends, was not the way to get rid of him. Sitting carrel-to-carrel in the library was not a help either, nor was sharing a Coke and a popcorn every Sunday night at the Waverly.

"Where have you been?" Jazz inquired.

Lee pulled out her exclusionary, elitist card. "Hanging out at the *Law Review* office," she said, heaving her book bag onto her lap and rummaging through it, as if driven to find a particular book crucial to her legal education. Her hands raced through notebooks and casebooks, pushed aside a small bottle of aspirin, a plastic case for tampons, a Chap Stick, a disintegrating recipe for Mongolian lamb she'd torn out from a magazine in the dentist's office months before.

"What's wrong with you?" Jazz asked.

"Nothing."

"Bullshit." She shook her head, denying anything was amiss, and pulled out a monograph on Crummey Trusts that her Tax professor had suggested she would find scintillating. "Did I do something?" he persisted.

"Of course not."

"Then . . . ?"

"Then nothing," Lee said, realizing that instead of the proper playful inflection she wanted, her intonation was funereal. She had to sound cheerier. Jazz's greatest gift was his understanding. Already he knew she was avoiding company—specifically, his. If she did not start sounding blithe right away, he would figure out exactly what was bothering her; he was that empathetic. "Listen," she said, her voice almost manic with ersatz merriment.

"I'm being driven mad by *Law Review*. I mean, I'm barely managing all my course work and then this article on executive clemency in capital cases. It's so . . . vast! And then on top of that, having to go home and face what passes in our house for family life . . ."

Lee stopped only because he put his hand on hers as if to say: Cut it out. That's not the cause of your ignoring me. She tried to go on but could not think of a thing to say. She wasn't used to Jazz's touch. Sure, he would routinely give her a preadolescent greeting: honking her nose, poking her arm. Once, when they were standing on line for *Soylent Green* and it had been bitter cold, he had hugged her, but it was a jock's bear hug, insulated by the six layers of wool between them. Now, though, it was skin to skin, and the rough warmth of his palm heated the back of her hand. Oh, God, she had to come up with something to say, fast, and she couldn't. A lawyer is supposed to be able to think on her feet, but all she could think of was how hot his hand was. Should she pull her hand away? Give him a fast, chummy poke with her elbow? And what was wrong with him, anyway? Why didn't he take his goddamn hand away?

In truth, Jazz was considering doing precisely that, but at that very instant, the train's electrical system went through a routine malfunction just as the train was accelerating into the tunnel under the East River, and their car was plunged into blackness. Before either of them had another thought, his hand began to caress hers and somehow, despite the absolute lack of light, their lips managed to find each other and Jazz said: "I love you, Lee."

And the lights blazed back on as Lee was saying: "I love you too."

Thirteen

"I'm letting Norman Torkelson stew in his own juices," I announced to the man in my life.

"Not a bad idea."

Since he was the best litigator on Long Island, and probably in the world, I was more than pleased with his concurrence. "Thanks," I replied, debating whether to simply pat myself on the back or open a bottle from the case of Dom Perignon I'd received as a bonus after getting a mob guy off on a charge of criminal possession of a machine gun with intent to use same unlawfully against the person of another. "In fact, thanks a lot."

"Except you seem to have jumped into the same pot."

"What pot?"

"The one Norman's in. You're really stewing." As usual, he was right.

As a criminal defense lawyer, life was simple: Most of my clients were guilty. Especially, and obviously, Norman Torkelson. But suddenly I was not only having doubts but experiencing every clichéd symptom of twentieth-century *angst*—clenched teeth, roiling stomach, lower back pain (with sciatica, naturally), and aching head. Those symptoms then set off my first hot flash. So I figured if I was miserable, why should Norman get a free ride? Since he had threatened to fire me for doing my job—trying to find a way to beat the murder rap that was facing him—I decided to let him stew in stir for three days.

However, considering my aptitude for anxiety, this current distress could not be called one of my major stews. During those three days I managed to work on my transportation-of-stolen-property-in-interstate-commerce case. I also pushed around some papers for a sentencing memo, interviewed witnesses for a vehicular homicide trial I had coming up, edited a court of appeals brief Chuckie had written, met with a new client—a college kid who had knocked down a security guard and torn out of Tower Records with twenty-two CDs shoved under her denim skirt—and bought a seven-hundred-pound cast-iron birdbath at an antique store's going-out-of-garden-ornaments-and-into-art-moderne-furniture sale.

If you're going to defend people on criminal charges, you're going to stew. Period. You make your living dealing with people who commit dreadful crimes, or at least wreak havoc for very cheap thrills. As their lawyer, you learn to put your own morality in a bag and stick it on a high shelf. Yes, the suffering that the person you represent causes to their victims, their own families, and themselves ought to break your heart. But after the first twenty or thirty sleepless nights, you begin to realize how little you can do. You comprehend that many of your clients *need* their problems. They live mainly to bring chaos out of order. And you, their lawyer, cannot change their lives. Also, you can't repair the damage they do and you cannot obtain Justice, at least not the highfalutin kind with a capital J. All you can do is work your ass off to see that they get the best deal the system will allow.

So I kept myself busy, which was easy. Since Chuckie was a god-awful writer, I got so involved with editing his brief that I decided to give Norman still another day to stew. But then Norman called the office, pleading with Sandi to have me come to see him. He told her he was "conscious stricken" and "full of remorse" over his "shoddy behavior." So I left Chuckie's "Defendant-Appellant seeks this Court's review of his unconscionable conviction for illegal and unlawful possession (with intent to sell) of a certain quantity of a controlled substance" and drove over to the Nassau County Correctional Center.

"How can I tell you how sorry I am?" Norman said from his side of the partition.

"Forget it. This place is a hellhole. It gets to people."

"That it does. Let me explain about Mary. Please. You may view her as a tough little cookie"—I started to make a pro forma objection but Norman cut me off—"but get past her facade. She's terribly fragile."

"I understand."

"I know by your standards I'm no bargain," Norman went on, "but it so happens I'm the best thing that ever happened to Mary." With its calculated lack of expression, a poker face would have given me away even more than the guffaw I felt coming on. So I just nodded stiffly and concentrated on studying the crumbs on the side of his mouth. There were also a few trapped in the chest hair that peeked out of the V of his prison uniform. Yellow-brown crumbs, which meant the correctional center had served its culinary masterpiece for dessert: chocolate-chip cookies—without the chips, as mandated by the latest round of Republican budget cuts. "She's a magnificent creature," he went on. "I know: You might be thinking that thousands of men would want her. And you'd be right. But they would want her merely as an ornament."

Now that he'd gone and apologized, I couldn't be rude and cut him off. But it was like sitting in a lecture hall for some awful required course: Mary Dean 201: The Postpubescent Years. As he kept on, I felt I was coming close to telling him to stuff it.

"In practical terms, Mary cannot sustain a relationship with any of these men. You may ask why. It is because they need her only in a libidinous way. They do not *need* her, so to speak, as a human being or as a conventional wife. Mary has little utilitarian value."

"What does that mean?" I asked before I could stop myself, thereby dooming myself to another hit of Norman's verbiage.

"It means she cannot cook. She is too flighty to be able to care for children. She cannot be trusted to take a simple phone message. She cannot do anything, really. *Except* be a good person."

"A good person," I echoed, thinking about the almost

sexual pleasure she'd taken in aiding and abetting Norman in the con, playing the Repo Lady, his matrimonial lawyer, and his ex-wife and thus helping destroy the lives of all the women he preyed on.

"I know I'm *not* good," Norman conceded. "I know that I've lured Mary—very skillfully, I might add—into being complicitous in my work . . . in my crimes. But at least I care about her goodness, which other men don't. And I sincerely want to make her happy—if only for the egocentric reason that she makes me happy. I mean, I don't need someone to cook me dinner. Any one of the marks would have been delighted to be, as it were, my willing slave, but Mary—"

If I waited for him to finish talking about her, Norman and I would be celebrating my Diamond Jubilee together in the visitors' room. So I asked: "How come you got so upset when I suggested Mary might have had something to do with Bobette's death?"

"Because she didn't do it!" Norman spit out. He was losing it again, leaning toward me, his eyes bulging with rage.

I looked straight at him till he abandoned his hostile posture and, after another few seconds, averted his eyes. Then I let him have a minute to get back to himself. Meanwhile, I checked out the visitors room. A colleague, Louie Pacheco, a guy I'd been in the D.A.'s Office with, was strolling my way in the row ahead, getting ready to meet with a client. I noticed Louie was sporting a fancy new suit, with gargantuan shoulder pads tailored to fool the eye into thinking his middle-age pear shape was a young, athletic inverted triangle. Louie, normally the color of boiled chicken, now had a tan one shade darker than a Brown & Serve sausage. A new hairstyle too: a ponytail. Clearly, he had a new, young girl-friend. From the look of him, she had taken charge. From the completeness of his transformation, it looked as if she would be his second wife—although from the fact of his wedding band I concluded that Louie hadn't informed his first about his change of plans. And he probably hadn't mentioned it to any of his four children—none of whom could be over twelve years old.

"Take it easy," I said, turning back to Norman. "I understand you love Mary. I understand your wanting to protect her. But you seem to be overprotective, and that leads me to believe you're fearful for her. As your lawyer, it would help me to know why." He clasped his hands together and rested his chin on the tops of his knuckles. His eyes closed. I understood this was a Meditative Moment, so I looked back at Louie and regarded his ponytail. Gray, limp, it hung dejectedly down the broad back of his dark-blue suit. I offered what might have been—had I been the praying type—a little prayer that the second wife would give him a major myocardial infarction on their honeymoon. "Norman, when I told you about the fingerprints at the crime scene being Mary's: That seemed to scare you."

"I suppose," he said, addressing the ceiling.

"Let's forget for a minute what she did or did not do at Bobette Frisch's house. Does Mary have a record? Is that why you were afraid?" He seemed to be taking a count of the acoustical tile overhead. "The truth would be of interest, Norman."

Norman looked back at me. "A couple of arrests for shoplifting. One conviction. Suspended sentence. No big deal. She likes pretty things and sometimes . . . You know, when someone like Mary is raised in an environment devoid of nurturance, she needs . . . objects. Talismans, if you will, to ward off privation. But if the police were to find out, they'd be all over her in a minute. They'd trump up some charge and arrest her. And let me tell you, one night in a place like this . . . It would destroy her. I can't let that happen! I love her. But even more, I'm . . ." He swallowed hard. Just when I was thinking he was a lousy actor, his eyes squeezed shut. Tears began to leak out of the corners. "I'm a flawed human being," he managed to whisper. I waited the moment it took him to begin speaking again. "I need Mary to make me whole, or as close to whole as someone like me can get. Dear God, I'm so terrified of life without her. *That's* why I have to protect her. No matter what the cost."

* * *

In the movies, private detectives always have offices with linoleum floors (on which click the spike heels of sexy clients), milky glass partitions, and overflowing ashtrays. Terry Salazar's had ivory wall-to-wall carpeting, an ivory sectional sofa, and two ivory pull-up chairs beside an ivory Art Deco-style desk. He had taken over the lease of a skin-care products company that had sunk all its assets into a slickly expensive infomercial featuring a porcelain-skinned soap-opera star who was supposed to appear genteel; instead she came across as so snooty that almost all the calls to the 800 number were not orders but denunciations of the bitch. For an additional five thousand bucks, Terry had purchased the furniture, a Packard Bell computer and, it turned out, a closetful of Satin-Skin Exfoliating Granules.

In Terry's mind, he was simply buying a white office. It was not until one of his cop buddies started ribbing him about how he must know an interior decorator that he realized his office was—what a nightmare!—*feminine*. For a time, he tried to nullify the place's atmosphere by rolling up his sleeves to display his arm hair and puffing offensive cigars, but in the end he did most of his business in Plumpie's or another extravagantly dirty bar, Big Nick's, and kept clients away from his office.

But he made an exception for me, largely because I'd once sworn never to make a snide remark about his ladylike furnishings or let on to anyone else in the entire criminal justice system about them. I kept my word. Other than the stink of cigars, living and dead, and the dark ink smears from fingerprint kits, it was an appealing place, and I often dropped by. As comfortable as my own office was, I hated being stuck in one place. If a day went by without a court appearance, I'd find an excuse to go to Terry's or the library at the Bar Association or even drop by police headquarters on ostensible business and shoot the breeze for a half hour.

At Terry's, I always took the same spot on the sectional, kicking off my shoes and putting my feet up on the white marble coffee table, a practice he encouraged because it was so distinctly uncouth. "If Mary has a record," I asked, "how come the cops didn't ID her when they checked those prints in Bobette's living room?"

Terry, leaning back in his ivory leather chair, *his* feet up on his desk, puffed his cigar and said: "Two possibilities." He took his cigar out of his mouth and examined its length, not without satisfaction.

"I'm paying you seventy-five bucks an hour to be a detective, not to look at your surrogate penis in thoughtful silence."

"What the fuck are you talking about, Lee?"

"Two possibilities," I snapped. "What are they? Come on. I don't have all day."

He shook his head sadly at my lack of civility. "One: If Mary had just one arrest, something could have happened with the paperwork and the prints never made it to the computer."

"Does that happen often?"

"More than anyone wants to admit."

"Or . . . ?" I encouraged him.

"'Or' what?"

"You said two possibilities."

"Cute little Holly forgot to run the prints."

I sat up and put my feet on the floor. "*Forgot?*"

"Why should she?" Terry asked, still sitting back comfortably, licking the tip of his cigar in the usual way guys lick cigars—i.e., the way a dog licks its genitals. He did not seem in the least perturbed about Holly's laxity. "If she checks the prints, then she has to go out and find whoever they belong to, haul him in for questioning. It would only cloud up her case."

"It's her professional responsibility . . ." I began. But instead of offering a speech on ethics, I told him to call his friend and see if the FBI check had come up with anything.

"I can't hurry him," Terry protested.

"Yes you can. I'm paying you and you're paying him and I want an answer."

"You know, when you talk like that, you're so fucking masculine. It's a real turnoff, Lee."

"Good," I said, and sat back while he made the phone

call. Naturally, he gave away nothing as he was talking. A few manly chuckles, inquiries about each other's wives, and then a lot of uh-huhs and hmms. He reached over, picked up a pad and pen, and made a few notes.

"So?" I said, the second he hung up. "Come on. You're suppressing a self-satisfied grin. You're thrilled with yourself."

"I'm always thrilled with myself."

"Come on, Terry!"

"Mary Dean has a record."

"For what?"

"Not shoplifting."

"So?"

"A long—and I mean *long*—record for prostitution."

The record didn't surprise me. The "long" did.

"How long?"

"Twenty-seven arrests."

"Gee," I said. "She's a real pro."

"I bet she is." Terry wore his reflexive lascivious leer, but it was clear he was disappointed in Mary. Hurt, even.

"Do you think Norman knows?" I asked him.

"How could he not?" He furrowed his brow, the way bad actors do on movies of the week, when they want to show they are cogitating. In Terry's case, however, his brain actually was working. "I bet Norman goes out of his way *not* to remind her that she was a hooker. You know, treats her like a princess. I guarantee you, that would make her a hundred times more loyal. I mean, I'll bet he's set it up so she sees only two choices. Being worshiped and taken care of—or getting twenty bucks a blow job for a bunch of guys in the back of a Dodge Ram." Every time I start getting completely disgusted with Terry, he comes up with insights like that.

"Where were the arrests?" I asked.

He peered at his notes. "California, Nevada, Arizona, New Mexico."

"Did she serve any time?" I asked.

Terry smiled. "Five suspended sentences. She sure in hell never got a woman judge. What guy would have the heart to put her in jail?" Just as I was starting to step back into my shoes, Terry announced: "One more arrest."

"What for?"

"Assault."

"Assault?" My foot remained poised over my shoe. "What? Tell me about it."

"Eight months ago. In Annapolis, Maryland. Her alias was Marissa Shaw. She beat the hell out of a sixty-year-old woman. A widow. Facial contusions, concussion, two cracked ribs."

"You're kidding!"

"Mary claimed the woman attacked her. The judge allowed bail, and guess what?"

"Mary ran."

"Of course." Terry leaned back his head and blew a smug stream of smoke toward his ivory ceiling. "She ran."

It took only a few minutes more to find out the sixty-year-old woman's name: Carolyn Knowles. I didn't need a detective to find her; a quick call to 410 Information got me her number. As soon as I heard the click of connection, I signaled Terry to pick up his extension and take notes. She answered my call on the second ring, as if she'd been circling the phone, waiting for someone to call. I explained I had heard about her case from Maryland authorities.

"Are you a policewoman?" she asked. Her voice was overly cultured, her "Are" coming out as "Ah," and every syllable carefully enunciated. Just for the diction alone, I could see why someone would want to give her a contusion or two.

"No, but I've been hired to investigate . . . Well, to tell you the truth, Ms. Knowles, the woman who assaulted you, the woman who was using the alias . . . ." I paused, hoping she'd think I was looking at my notes and oblige by giving me the name.

And she did. "Marissa Shaw," she said, her pearly tones making it sound as if Marissa Shaw were someone who'd stopped by for a water-cress sandwich and a cup of Darjeeling instead of someone who beat the shit out of her.

"Marissa Shaw is only a collateral part of my investi-

212

gation. The person I'm really trying to get information on is"—I heard her quick intake of breath—"is known to change his name frequently. However, I can describe him to you. He is six feet, five inches tall—"

"Have you found him?" she gasped.

"I have a pretty good idea of where he is, Ms. Knowles, although right now I'm not at liberty to discuss the matter. Now, as far as you know, was there any connection between . . . Under what name did you know him?"

"Arthur Berringer," she said, tenderly, slowly, as if the name still held magic.

"And did he ever give you any indication that he knew this Marissa Shaw?"

"No." A definite no. "In fact . . ." She hesitated.

"Anything you can tell me would be deeply appreciated, Ms. Knowles," I said, as Terry mimicked the male autoerotic gesture that signaled a major jerk-off was in progress.

"He definitely did *not* know her," Carolyn Knowles replied. "When it happened, he tried to pull her off and kept saying: 'Who are you? Stop!'" Her voice rose. "'Stop!'"

"Where did the attack occur?" I asked.

"In my car. We drove up to my house in my car. I have a LeBaron convertible and the top was down. We just sat there for a moment. Arthur—my fiancé—took my hand." Then, almost shyly, she added: "We had just come from getting our marriage license." As she paused to compose her thoughts, and probably to keep from crying, I paused too: to reflect that Carolyn Knowles was born to be a mark. Here she was, giving me her entire story—without ever having asked my name. "All of a sudden, from out of nowhere, this woman came and pulled open the door."

"Driver's or passenger's?"

"Passenger. Arthur was driving."

"And then what happened?" I asked, as delicately as I could.

"She must have unlatched my seat belt. Before I knew what was happening, she pulled me out of the car. I literally was dragged onto the sidewalk."

It sounded like a series of sniffles, but I knew she was crying silently. "What a horrible thing," I said.

"Horrible, horrible."

"But Arthur tried to stop her?"

"Yes, but she was amazingly strong. He came around and tried to hold back her arms or pull her off. He was yelling 'Stop it!' and she kept yelling 'Stop it!' back to him—that he should stop trying to stop her."

"Did she give you any indication what the attack was about?"

A huge sob came across the phone. A moment later, she said "No. She didn't say a word. Just kept punching me. With her fists, like a man. Then she took my head and"— the cultured voice broke, only to be replaced by a high, confused inflection that sounded like an injured child's— "banged it against the pavement."

"Do you remember anything else, Ms. Knowles?"

"No, I passed out. Not for too long, I think, but when I came to, the girl was gone. Arthur was holding me in his arms. When he saw I was . . . well, not all right, but at least conscious, he said: 'I'll run in and call the police and an ambulance.'"

"And did he?"

"Yes."

I knew the answer to my question, but I had to ask it anyway: "Was he there when the police arrived?" I asked.

"No."

"Did you ever see him again?"

"No."

"But you saw her?"

"In a lineup. The police found her an hour later near a shopping center about three miles from my house. A fluke, really. They broadcast the description I'd given—the hair, the heavy, heavy makeup, the cheap sundress, turquoise— and a passing patrol car spotted her. The next day, they brought me from the hospital to the building where the jail is, and I identified her. They thanked me and said the state attorney's office would contact me before the trial. And then, two days later, a judge let her go on bail!"

"And she took off?" I asked.

"She did indeed."

"And you never heard from Arthur again?"

"No. I filed a missing persons report. But in my heart of hearts I knew . . . Arthur must have had some trouble earlier in his life. Things hadn't gone well. His marriage had failed, his wife was a monster, tormenting him. But there must have been trouble with the police as well, because he could not face them. His last words, just before he went into my house to call them, were: 'Carolyn. I love you with all my heart. Never doubt that.'"

"And you didn't?"

"I did not!"

"One final question, Ms. Knowles."

"What's your name?" she demanded.

"Lily," I said quickly. "Did you find anything missing?"

"Missing?"

"Yes."

"Some jewelry."

"Such as?"

"Everything I had."

"And you reported it to the police?"

"Of course. And to the insurance company as well."

"And did they investigate?"

"What was there to investigate?" she asked. "Marissa Shaw—what do they call that—oh, jumped bail. Even if they find her, do you think she will still have the pearl choker and the diamond-and-ruby brooch and the diamond ring and the platinum-and-diamond watch and the—"

"The jewelry wasn't on Marissa Shaw when the police picked her up?"

"No."

"Did the police think that Arthur Berringer may have had something to do with the disappearance of the jewelry?"

"No!" she boomed. "It was perfectly clear that Marissa Shaw had been in my house. They found her fingerprints in there." I glanced over at Terry: So Bobette was not the first mark Mary had spied on. "And I *knew* Arthur as I knew myself. Know, as I know myself. And he would never take what is not his."

"And so you never mentioned him to the police?"

Just as Terry was shaking his head, as in "You've gone too far," Carolyn Knowles slammed down the phone.

"Lee," Terry said, taking his feet off his desk, "if you were a guy I'd call you a schmuck. How could you ask her that?"

"I'll tell you how, schmuck. I wanted to find out for sure if Holly had the cops check out the mystery prints—Mary's prints—near the body. Clearly, they didn't, or they would have found out the prints were associated with a middle-aged woman who had been viciously assaulted. And I'll bet in that file down in Annapolis are all the other latents they found when they dusted Carolyn Knowles's house—the plumber's, the pizza delivery boy's, and Norman Torkelson's. Ergo, schmuck, if I can convince Norman to cooperate, we have priors on Mary Dean that ought to be very convincing to the D.A. And if not to the D.A., then the jury."

"You don't have a chance in hell of getting Norman to cooperate," Terry said. "He's going to protect that girl."

"But she's a known batterer! And it's the same pattern! She thinks he's getting too close to marrying one of his marks, and whomp! She attacks. And not girl stuff—hair pulling and a smack or two. She goes out of control."

"There are no other marks on Bobette except the ones around her neck."

"What other marks were necessary? The ones around the neck did the trick. This time, Mary cut out the preliminaries."

"You just can't stand to lose, Lee."

"Not this one. Because Norman Torkelson did not commit this murder."

Terry Salazar shook his head sadly and, not without warmth, said: "Schmuck."

Fourteen

It was certainly not that browbeater Professor Blumenthal and his torts that finally captured Lee's imagination. Nor was it the charismatic Nestor P. Von Hassel, who unraveled the tangles of corporate law not only for the secretary of commerce but for the hosts of the *Today* show and, thus, for all America. It was not even Kevin McTeague, the Errol Flynn of evidence, with his flowing ebony hair and his swashbuckling presentation of the Excited Utterance exception to the Hearsay Rule. No, in the first semester of her second year at NYU Law School, the one who really made Lee a lawyer was Professor Lucille Poole.

She was a sallow-skinned woman with hair dyed shoe-polish black. Her nose was so long and pointy that, had it been orange, people would have thought she'd snatched it off a snowman. If Sylvia had ever seen the professor, she would have been too sickened to mock her; Professor Poole's wardrobe consisted solely of cheap, shapeless black dresses, as if her clothes were hand-me-downs from working-class Italian widows.

Upon seeing her, people thought: Ah, with those looks, she must be a charmer. Hardly. Each semester, Professor Poole brought nearly every student in her Criminal Law classes to the brink of nervous collapse by lecturing in a double-time monotone. In fact, there was nothing she did not say too flat and too fast: "Swiss on my burger, please," in the cafeteria came out like Swzzbr, plis. Her introductory "Since my time is limited, I assume Your Honors are familiar with the facts and the prior proceedings in this case," to the entire bench of the Supreme Court of the United States of America, became a mere whir of sound. And if you said hello to her in the corridors of the law school, you were never certain if the reply you heard was her reciprocal greeting or simply a rush of air passing over a crack in the wall.

However, despite Professor Poole's next-to-unintelligible speech and her lack of anything that might be construed as a personality, she routinely won the appeals she argued on the issue of police coercion of prisoners. Some of her colleagues muttered that her success was due to her briefs; her writing was so simple a third grader could understand it. Others claimed she won so often because she was a woman in a man's field, or because she was so ugly the appellate judges pitied her. A few asserted it was because she was a manipulator, forcing judges to strain to understand her jabber, thereby capturing their complete attention. What these carpers seemed unable to acknowledge was that while all the above was true, Lucille Poole, that black crow, stood before the bench with the fire of legal brilliance burning within her.

"MsWhi," Professor Poole called out as she entered the suite, the words hurtling past lips that were puckered like a long-forgotten prune. "Good point you made about the statute of limitations in noncapital offenses."

Lee, working at a table in the Regina and Stanley Farbman International Center for Criminal Justice—a two-room suite in a fleabag hotel on West Twenty-second Street—did not hear the entire sentence. What came through was "G' point" and "statute of." So, with a reasonable degree of confidence, Lee replied: "Thank you," and suppressed the shiver of pleasure that passed through her. This was the work Lee loved best, so much better than the dry, dead stuff at law school. Here she was, exposing the system's stupidity, duplicity, and cruelty where it really counted: in matters of crime and punishment. The real thing, where a person's life or liberty was at stake. To hell with trusts and estates. Screw copyrights. Fuck corporations. *This* is what was important. And how she loved it! "Thank you very much."

"Welc."

The suite resembled Professor Poole: unattractive and cheerless. What had been a living room was now crammed with four collapsible bridge tables, bowing under the weight of books and papers, and dark-brown filing cabinets that resembled upright coffins. In the adjoining room, a plywood bed board resting upon the mattress of a double bed formed the giant desk where the professor,

218

hunched over, did her writing and ate what she ate every single lunch and dinner (and, for all anyone knew, breakfast as well)—ground beef. The rich, fatty scent of hamburger or meat loaf sandwich or meatball hero was always in the air at the Regina and Stanley Farbman International Center for Criminal Justice.

To Lee's surprise, Lucille Poole took a folding chair from another bridge table and sat beside her. "Wha' doing?" she inquired. Lee lifted the yellow legal pad she had been scribbling on, but before she could launch on a spiel about the exercise of reasonable prosecutorial diligence in *New York v. Wu*, the professor added: "Not Wu. Summer."

Lee's heart fluttered, then throbbed. A summer job offer? The chance to be Lucille Poole's research assistant! To help draft the reply brief for the Quinones case, which would be argued—Lee swallowed hard—before the Supreme Court of the United States of America in the fall. For just an instant, she could hear Chief Justice Burger saying "Interesting point," and Professor Poole, for once, speaking slowly enough for all to hear: "Credit where credit is due. My student assistant, Lee White, came up with that." Her name in the Court record *before she was even out of law school*. And Jazz would probably do something wonderful, like putting that page of the transcript in a silver frame as her Christmas gift. Although, in truth, she'd rather have an engagement ring, but that appeared too much to hope for. He loved her. He had told her that. But he had said not one single word about the future beyond suggesting they get tickets to *The Ritz* for sometime in the spring. Could it be possible that he would just love her forever without ever asking her to marry him? She could be seventy-two, still without a ring on her ropy-veined left hand. No, worse: On her thirtieth or fortieth birthday—whenever she'd finally get up the courage—she would confront Jazz and ask him if he was ever going to marry her. Looking surprised and, worse, pained, he would explain that while he really and truly loved her, and the last thing in the world he wanted to do was hurt her, she—how could he put it without seeming like a total bastard?—she wasn't what he imagined when he thought of a wife. He would probably do better with . . . not a lawyer. You know, someone less challenging. More traditional. More—don't take this the wrong way—feminine. A teacher or something.

"I don't have any summer plans," Lee told Professor Poole. "I want to stay in New York." She was going to add something about wanting to be with her boyfriend but decided that might make Professor Poole think her frivolous, not the solemn sort who would work eighteen hours a day in mortal combat with Injustice.

"I cannot use you as a research assistant," Professor Poole announced. The awful thing was, every word was clear. Lee hugged the legal pad against her chest, close, like a teddy bear. What was she seeing in her mentor's eyes? Pity? "Not an academic, y'know." Not sorrow. Disdain?

"Oh," was all Lee could think to say. Not the rapid-fire response one might expect from a prospective litigator, but an understandable one, as she was concentrating on holding back a cascade of tears.

"Not that you haven't w . . ."

"I beg your pardon?"

"It's not that you have not worked hard this entire semester," Professor Poole said, pronouncing each word as if it were a separate sentence.

"Uh-huh," Lee replied.

"You're dedicated . . . to put in the hours." So? "But your talent . . . not in scholarship." What are you talking about? I have an A-minus average! I made *Law Review*. Where the fuck else does my talent lie? "It lies in being fast on your feet," Professor Poole went on. That means I'm shallow. Unoriginal. Unimaginative. "You were born to be a criminal lawyer."

"But not to argue before the Supreme Court?"

"You might. Never know. Solid student. If a case should bring you before the Court . . . Few lawyers could deny themselves . . ." Lee waited. "But you aren't . . ." Professor Poole's voice evaporated.

"A legal scholar."

". . . good trial lawyer. Do you know how rare . . . ?"

"So this summer?" Lee was so ashamed. No, humiliated. No. She wanted to quit law school. She wished she could get married. "Do you have any suggestions, Professor Poole?" Lee inquired, her manner as casual as a customer asking a drugstore clerk for advice on choosing a lipstick. "I'd like something challenging." She wanted to add: you egomaniacal hag, letting me work nights,

220

weekends. Sending me down to pick up your fucking bacon-mushroom-Swiss burgers because you think the delivery guy takes too long and they get cold.

"Yes." Something Lee could not hear, and then: ". . . Manhattan District Attorney's office."

"*What?*"

Professor Poole rose. "A good lawyer . . . argue both sides. Manhattan D.A. . . . best place . . . I'll . . . phone call."

Since Lee could not come up with another response, she said: "Thank you."

"That is, if you want . . . If you have other . . ."

"Your calling would be great," Lee answered. "I appreciate it." Oh, God, she thought, what the hell am I doing?

". . . like it," Professor Poole said.

In fact, Lee loved it. By the end of her third week in the Rackets Bureau, she was working six days a week on the prosecution of one Howard "Howie the Hose" Fogelman for extortion: to wit, threatening seven kosher butchers on the Upper West Side of Manhattan with firebombing unless their stores carried the Gan Eden brand of knockwurst.

To Lee, the Manhattan D.A.'s Office resembled a late forties black-and-white crime buster—except it wasn't a movie. It was real and, miraculously, she was playing a supporting role. Forget being a star; she was thrilled to be welcomed, with an offhand "Hiya," as part of the cast. She belonged. No questions asked. Lee treasured every detail of the hard-boiled life: the endless cardboard cups of overperked coffee; the dented metal desks; the rough-talking cops from Hell's Kitchen and Harlem; the world-weary secretaries. She thrilled to the gruff, New York—accented banter of the assistant district attorneys out of St. John's and Brooklyn Law; the eager-beaver preppy enthusiasm of the A.D.A.'s out of Yale and Columbia as they mimicked the jargon and the hunchbacked slouch of the toughest of the cops. Most of all, she loved her colleagues' unspoken love for each other. She would gladly have worked seven days a week to see that Howie—whom, with the rest of the cops and A.D.A.'s, she referred to as "scum-bag" or "that piece of shit"—got what was coming to him, but she knew it would upset Jazz.

They were living together for the summer in a sublet on University Place, a studio with a rain forest of plants and a narrow Murphy bed on which, after making passionate, athletic, and benevolent love, they slept, arms and legs entwined. But it was not the sex Lee marveled at. It was Jazz's sweetness. "Hi," he would say all of a sudden, at a moment in the act when all that the other boys with whom she had slept could manage was, at best, a grunt of encouragement best translated as: Hump harder. But as Lee and Jazz lay together, sweaty bodies sliding against each other in humid currents exhaled by an air conditioner not equipped to handle heated sex, Jazz would somehow find the tenderness to say "I love you so much." And he would gaze into her eyes as if he could see something breathtaking right behind them.

Lee felt beautiful that entire summer, even in dark, lawyerly skirts and businesslike white shirts. Her skin glowed a rosy gold; her hair—pulled back into compliance by a tortoiseshell barrette, looked as if it wanted to break free and fall, thick and wanton, over her shoulders. "I love the way you look," Jazz would tell her. And it wasn't only in bed that he admired her. That was the nicest part: his tributes offered beside the Saran Wrap and aluminum foil in Marty's Superette, or in front of the Abyssinian kittens in the window of Village Pets.

Lee noticed, too, that for the first time, strange men were eyeing her with admiration. Not because she was exhausting herself being charming, clever, amusing, but simply because living with Jazz had transformed her into a love goddess. The guy in the subway token booth gave her the once-over, then the twice-over. The cop who stood by the elevator in the D.A.'s actually winked. Construction men on a scaffolding across Centre Street discovered new adjectives, and an elderly man in a seersucker suit walking his Doberman down Tenth Street doffed his panama hat.

So while many in the D.A.'s Office gave up their Sundays to go in to work simply because they could not bear to be away from the pursuit of justice or the company of their colleagues, Lee kept her day of rest because she wanted to be with Jazz.

He needed her company. His summer job was less enthralling than hers. Through his father's connections at the U.S. Olympic Committee, he was working in the office of the general counsel of the National Hockey League. Sports law, Foster decreed. It's getting bigger every day. Get yourself in on the ground floor, buddy-boy. You'll thank me. But by the end of the first week of July, Lee became aware that—as he was the previous summer, at the job his uncle had gotten for him at Matthison, Appleby—Jazz was bored. She could see it in his eyes, which lit up when she walked through the door each night. Thrilled by the very fact of her, true, but, even more, almost pathetically grateful for a friend to play with.

"All you keep saying is that it's boring. What specifically don't you like about it?" she asked him the first week in August. They stood on the platform at Penn Station. Only nine in the morning, but the heat rising from the tracks was already so wetly oppressive that the few Sunday travelers had the glistening red faces of foundry workers.

"I don't know. It's just boring."

"But you like hockey. I know a couple of people who can name all the presidents, but you're the only one I know who can name all the Stanley Cup winners since 1704 or whenever."

"Since 1927."

"The fact is, you *love* hockey. So how can your job be boring?"

He smiled, and for the hundredth or thousandth time, she marveled at his sunny temperament, which did not alter with adversity or foul weather or bad news. And Jazz's optimism was contagious. With him at her side, she could face the Black Plague or a nuclear firestorm, knowing they would emerge unscathed and smiling. "You're badgering the witness, Miss White," he joshed.

"I'm not badgering. This is what's called probing. And I'm probing because I care about you, you fool. I want to see you happy."

He crossed his arms tight over his chest, as he always did when he was reflective, a mannerism Lee found utterly charming. Despite the sapping heat, she moved closer to him and immediately felt better. "I guess it's boring because the job isn't about hockey," he explained. "It's about law."

"Is that it, Jazz?"

"Is what it?"

"Do you feel pressured? Because your father and all the Taylors back to Peking Man were lawyers: Does that mean you're doomed to be one? I mean, if you truly don't like it . . ."

"No. Law's okay. I mean, I don't wake up every morning all hot to discuss due process—"

"You're telling me!"

"—but I want to be a lawyer."

"Is it that you *want* to practice law or you can't think of anything else you'd rather do?"

"That's a big question for a Sunday morning."

"I know. You don't have to answer it if you don't want to."

She could tell Jazz did not want to give a glib response. He was considering her question, for both their benefits. "I honestly don't know the answer to that. I look at you, loving what you do at the D.A.'s. But if it weren't the D.A.'s, it would be the A.C.L.U. or the N.A.A.C.P. you'd be gung-ho about. You get wrapped up in stuff. I'm not like that. But maybe there's something out there for me. I think to myself: Maybe somewhere there's a job that'll make me jump out of bed every morning and say; 'Hey, I'm lucky! I get to go to work today!' Or lots of jobs. It's just that *this* job is boring."

Lee was very tired. In truth, standing on the platform waiting for the train to Shorehaven, having this meaningful discussion, she wanted nothing more than to lean against Jazz's strong shoulder and close her eyes, save her strength for going home to Long Island. To Jazz's home, actually.

For the first time, he had suggested that they spend the day with his family. A milestone. Their relationship seemed to exist solely in Manhattan, as if he had come from a place like Bombay, she from, say, Montevideo, and there they were, alone together in New York. True, they appraised and analyzed their families often (Lee having taken Introduction to Psychology at Cornell and Jazz Introduction to Sociology at Colgate). But they spoke of their parents and siblings as if they were dead or at least in a different hemisphere.

But the previous evening, Saturday night, Jazz confided that his old lady was bugging him: She never saw him anymore. Lee suggested he could visit his family alone, half hoping he would, but grateful when he demanded: Are you kidding? Miss my one day of the week with you? So she could not have said no, even if she had wanted to. And part of her wanted to, most desperately. Part of her dreaded that the Taylors would not approve. Within seconds after the introduction, with a mere frozen smile from Ginger or a too stiff handshake from Foster, her relationship with Jasper Taylor would come to an end. And that would be even before they learned she came from the family who lived in the modern house that lay beneath Hart's Hill. In Lee's secret heart, she regretted telling Jazz the truth about being White. True, he seemed to have found the Weissberg-Weiss connection both exotic and amusing. But what if it was secretly disturbing to him? What if, unable to admit to a touch of anti-Semitism in himself, he just happened to mention the fact of her Jewishness to his parents, knowing that they would do the job—getting rid of Lee—that he was not quite man enough to handle?

But around three that afternoon, as Lee was passing the kitchen on her way out to help Ginger feed the basenjis, she overheard Fos, back from his golf game, telling Jazz: "Nice girl you've got there, pal." And since Jazz said "Thanks" and not "She's one of the Jews from next-door," Lee felt somewhat reassured.

The Taylors's life, however, was less reassuring. Take Hart's Hill. It was, to be sure, a great house, perhaps even a mansion. Its ceilings were impossibly high, its rooms noble in dimension. Arthur Taylor, who had built it in 1898, had given his architect an open purse and his full confidence: Lay on the moldings, my dear fellow! Panel those walls with the finest hardwoods! Don't stint on the leaded glass, old chap! But Hart's Hill looked as if it had fallen on hard times half a century ago.

Lee glanced around the grounds as she hurried to the doghouse. She staggered slightly under the new twenty-five-pound bag of Blue Ribbon Champion Chow. Ginger had forgotten to bring it from the garage. The grass tennis court was in beautiful shape, Lee noted, rolled every day. But the back lawn looked as if it had not been mown all summer. It wasn't even a lawn anymore. Weeds and stiff yellow reeds had grown so high that the legs of the ornate wrought-iron garden furniture were completely hidden; a bench and four chairs appeared to be floating on amber waves of grain.

The doghouse was not what Lee had imagined—a mini-Tudor manor house designed by the original architect of Hart's Hill. Instead it was scraps of nailed-together lumber, a doggy-size Tobacco Road hovel. "Over here!" Ginger called out to her.

Ginger was hunched over the mother dog, searching its coat for something Lee knew she would not want to see. "They eat and poop out here," she explained. "Otherwise, they're with us all the time." Turning to the puppies, Ginger spoke in the squeaky baby voice the childless employ with small children. "You're really little piggies, aren't you? Making big, doody piles in the house!"

Kent, Jazz's younger brother, looked up from the dam's coat and smiled at Lee, a radiant smile. Had it been an illustration in an old-fashioned children's book, it would have been labeled: A Delightful Surprise. He had fine, tawny skin and golden-brown hair, along with the flattened features and epicanthic eye fold of Down's syndrome. "Hi," he said, "What's your name?"

"Lee."

"I'm Kent." He smiled, pleased that their interchange had gone so well. While Jazz, with his long, angular, well-chiseled features, was clearly his mother's son, Kent bore more of a resemblance to the middle-aged man Foster Taylor had become. However, Kent's rounded face, with its baggy double chin, was redeemed by blue eyes so bright they could indeed be called sparkling.

But his clothes! Okay, Lee told herself, even Sylvia White wouldn't expect a retarded fifteen-year-old to be a fashion plate, but it was not simply that Kent's red-and-blue-striped pullover did not match his brown plaid shorts. They were far too tight, the shirt's stripes making waves over his thick chest; they were clothes for a large boy rather than a good-size young man. The hem on one leg of the shorts had unraveled, and threads dangled down behind his knee. Kent kept slapping them away, but of course they continued to annoy him with their tickling.

Ginger seemed oblivious to her son's discomfort. And she appeared to be unaware of the ripped shoulder seam of his pullover, so the short sleeve hung down over his biceps like a striped armband. Yet she did not seem to be a cruel or an uncaring parent. She and Kent played what was evidently a familiar game: He picked up the pieces of kibble that had not made it into the dogs' bowls, as she counted. "Thirty-seven," Ginger pronounced, exhaling with only slightly weary finality. Kent appeared gratified by the total, although whether it was a high or a low number for them, or if he would be thrilled no matter what the tally, Lee could not determine.

Still, despite the counting game, Lee couldn't stop herself from scrutinizing mother and son as they headed back to the house: Ginger's tennis clothes could have been called grays rather than whites; the seat of Kent's shorts was black with what detergent commercials refer to, ominously, as ground-in dirt. Not just today's dirt, Lee perceived. She wished she could keep from knowing. She longed to think well of the Taylors. After all, she had expected them to be perfect. Okay, perhaps a little too casual about money, about each other, but essentially the best family in America. Yet here she was, dragging her feet through the high, scratchy weeds that were the back lawn, forestalling the disillusionment that she knew was inevitable once she got into the house again and—this time—allowed herself to really see.

It wasn't just the run-down condition of the house. Lee, who had been raised by Leonard to revere—if not worship—the upper-class god of genteel shabbiness, could not stop herself from noting that there was a profound difference between a threadbare Chippendale settee and a toilet dripping brown water onto a rust stain that had eaten through the tile floor. That single two-by-two-inch tile told Lee the story: The Taylors were either cheap or poor—poor meaning not rich enough to maintain an estate as grand as Hart's Hill. Her heart was heavy. She had wanted them to be inexhaustibly wealthy, to say nothing of benevolent and eccentric and effervescent—like characters in a thirties screwball comedy. However, what disturbed Lee most was not the lack of money.

It was the lack of care: breakfast dishes with bits of bacon stuck in gluey maple syrup never cleared from the table in the kitchen; moisture-beaded highball glasses exuding a stale liquor smell in the living room; the *Times* from the previous Sunday still spread out on the unvacuumed rug in the library. It was more than just mess, however. Taylor did not care about Taylor.

After saying "Nice girl you've got there, pal" Fos clomped up the grand staircase in his golf shoes. By the time Lee returned from the doghouse and passed the library, Fos was seated, barefoot, on a leather sofa. His toes, splayed out on the rug, were fat, shaped like a collection of tablespoons. He was scraping the cleats of his shoes with an ivory-handled letter opener. Scrape, scrape, and bits of grass and tiny clumps of dirt fell onto the rug. Later, when Jazz brought her into the library to show her his grandfather's maps of Shorehaven, Fos, hunched over the newspaper reading sports statistics, a smoldering cigarette held between his thumb and index finger, cupped in his hand, did not even look up.

"Looking for Granddad Toby's maps," Jazz muttered, and his father muttered back something like "Nnn" or "Mmm." Lee couldn't be certain because his head was twisted at an odd angle as he scrutinized a list of American League pitchers' earned-run averages.

Fos's conversation at dinner (pizza Jazz had volunteered to pick up, an offer for which Lee was pathetically grateful, sensing the alternative might be tuna-basenji-hair casserole) was not much more stimulating. The kitchen table around which they sat was an oblong of cherry wood more imposing than most people's dining room tables. Ginger, from the foot of the table, called out to her husband at the head: "Fos, Lee's working for the D.A. in Manhattan this summer."

Fos stopped flattening the fluting on the edges of his paper plate and squinted in Lee's direction. "Manhattan D.A.'s?" he said.

"Yes," Lee responded.

She must have looked pathetically eager for a response, because he sighed and came up with one further observation. "The senior litigating partner at my old law firm was there. Years ago. Cap Malcolm."

"Chester Malcolm," Ginger elaborated, sliding the pizza box across the wood to Jazz.

"Oh," replied Lee, a little too brightly, she realized. She wished she had heard something wonderful about good ole Cap Malcolm so she could have something to say to the Taylors. They seemed to have no need to say anything to one another, and hardly any to say anything to her. She wished Jazz's sisters were there. Maybe they would talk. But Hope, the eldest, was married to a golf pro and living in Palm Springs and Irene, a year older than Jazz, was on a commune in Oregon.

The Taylors ate slice after slice of the two large pizzas Jazz had brought home. Each chewed with intense concentration, as if he or she were dining alone in a tiny Neapolitan café and trying this dish for the first time. Jazz, usually full of bright observations or intelligent questions, fell into a silence she wished was not so comfortable. In fact, engrossed as he was with the elasticity of his mozzarella cheese, he seemed to have forgotten she was his guest/girlfriend and that he was in love with her. And they all ignored Kent, despite the fact that the boy was having problems separating his slice of pizza from the pie and, then, from the box.

Lee held back from helping, thinking that it was some family decision, or possibly a principle of Down's syndrome child psychology: Let the child fend for himself. But as Fos was reaching for his third slice, Lee could no longer bear the desperate, hungry look on Kent's face. She disengaged a slice from the box and handed it to the boy. Glancing around, fearful of a rebuke, or at least a scathing look, she saw Jazz was studying a cross-section of pepperoni and Ginger wiping off the olive oil that had dribbled down her arm. Fos, head thrown back, chins quivering, drank from his can of Coke with soft glugging sounds.

"Thank you!" Kent said to Lee, his gloriously blue eyes shining brighter than ever. With a shudder of anticipated pleasure, he stuffed the triangular tip of the pizza in his mouth.

"You're welcome." Realizing that might be the end of the dinner conversation, she asked him: "Do you like pizza?"

"Yes," Kent replied, charmed by her question. "I like pizza."

"I like pizza too."

"I like pizza," Kent said, his words filtered through a jumble of crust and tomato sauce. "I *like* pizza." For a frightened instant, she was afraid he would repeat the sentence over and over, and Jazz—to say nothing of his parents—would be irate with her for having set Kent off: Doesn't the girl have the brains to know how to behave with someone like that? But Jazz was now engrossed in the take-out menu taped to the cover of the pizza box, Ginger was breaking her crusts into tiny pieces and Fos was once again defluting his paper plate. "I like pizza." Suddenly Lee realized that Kent was making conversation, being hospitable, trying to put her at ease.

"I like pizza," she confided. "And Coke."

"I like Coke," Kent responded, amazed and gladdened by the coincidence. "I like . . ." He paused. No one noticed the hesitation; certainly no one jumped in to help him. "I like . . ." Abruptly he slapped his hand down on the table: I've got it! "I like chocolate milk!"

"Me too!" Lee answered. "And ice cream."

"Cake!"

"Hamburgers."

"Hot dogs!"

They might have gone from macaroni and cheese through Cocoa Puffs to Twinkies except Fos left the table. Then Ginger called in the basenjis and began flinging the bits of crust into their midst. Then Jazz told Lee it was getting late. They had work the next day. They really ought to get back to the city.

On the ride back, Lee read *Gideon's Trumpet*, while Jazz read a golf magazine he had fished out of his father's attaché case. As the train crept through Queens, he looked up and said: "What can I tell you? My old man isn't a laugh a minute." She felt she waited a second too long before responding: "Wait till you meet mine." The hesitation came because she had fully expected Jazz to add: "And my mother's not going to win the *Better Homes & Gardens* gracious hostess award either," as well as to offer an apology for the terrible condition of the house—or at least for the neglect of his kid brother. Kent had looked so bereft at her leaving that she'd wanted to grab him up in her arms, bring him back to their studio apartment. She would buy him new shorts and a T-shirt and a big box of Froot Loops, give him a bath and scrub his neck. Or if Jazz could not offer an apology, she mused, what about an explanation for his parents' behavior? But Jazz did not notice her concern, because he went back to reading an editorial about driving ranges in Maui.

Well, Lee had to concede, if he had been a visitor at her house, would she have spent the next thirty-six hours apologizing for her family's defects? True, her father had stopped trying to pass for what he thought the Taylors were. But now he had taken to acting as if he were Noël Coward's houseguest—kiss-kiss, dahling, a Beautiful People peck on each cheek. Would he kiss-kiss Jazz? Or would he shift back into High Wasp mode for the occasion and, in a voice pitched mortifyingly low, boom out: Glad to meet-cha! What could she possibly say? Uh, my dad's a little affected. And gee, sorry that my mother just sat there picking on the nubs of her Chanel suit and not talking. And oh, yeah—my sister has a serious drug problem—and she's married to a junkie and a thief.

So they went back to their sublet apartment and, exhausted, went to sleep without making love. The next morning, they returned to work. Then, before they knew it, they were caught up in their third and final year of law school. So Jazz Taylor never got to meet Lee's family until . . . well, in fact, until the day after he married her.

Now, that might make it sound as though a long time passed, but it happened quite soon, sooner than either of them expected it would. And it was all because of Christmas.

A week before, Ginger called Jazz in his dorm room. As she had not phoned him since the beginning of law school, he thought (as he later explained to Lee) that something terrible had happened: The canine equivalent of Dutch elm disease wiping out all the basenjis. Or his sister Irene getting fatally mangled in some malevolent piece of farm machinery on her commune. What's wrong? Jazz had asked, and his mother responded: Your father had to fly down to St. Petersburg to play golf with Mr. Whosis from the Atlantic Citrus Council who is having a conniption about something your father forgot to do so please get yourself home in time to buy the tree and set it up—damn, I forgot to buy the ham—because I'm in charge of the entire dessert table at the Kennel Club's Yappy Yule party and Kent ate something funny and has the trotsies and I *cannot* get out of the house.

The next caller was Leonard White, who telephoned a mere hour and a half later. Jazz was still in Lee's room, expounding to her how profound his dread of Christmas was. Chaos. His father was always someplace else and always arrived late. His mother was perpetually overwhelmed. Two years earlier, she had given him a roll of gift paper and three stick-on bows along with the presents she had not had time to wrap.

Leonard sounded far less frazzled than had Ginger. In fact, Leonard sounded like a million bucks (which at that moment happened to be one-quarter of his net worth, part of the reason for his ebullience). But for the young couple, his call was even greater cause for apprehension than Ginger's had been.

"I've rented a house in St. Bart's for the holidays!" Leonard

exulted. Lee got so irritated at his pronunciation, "holly-days"—
an attempt to sound educated-at-Oxford? a non-sectarian Christmas euphemism among pro-Semitic jet-setters? a playful reference
to the evergreen?—she did not at first understand what he was
saying. "When are your finals over?" Leonard inquired.

"My last one's the twentieth."

"Then you'll have to meet us there."

"Where?"

"St. Bart's."

"*Where?*"

"St. Bart's. An island in the Caribbean. Everyone says it's very
in. But not overrun, if you know what I mean."

Lee covered the mouthpiece of the phone and whispered: "St.
Bart's?"

"A nickname for the church?" Jazz murmured back, knowing
all about Leonard's Episcopaliphilia.

"An island," Lee whispered.

"Never heard of it."

"Lee?" her father demanded.

She turned away from Jazz so she could focus on her argument.
"Why can't we stay home?"

"Because we have a magnificent villa right on the ocean, with
a butler, a cook, and two housemaids, and I'd rather spend the
holidays there with fun people than on Long Island with no one
and Greta's greasy goose."

"But I made plans with my boyfriend—"

"Unmake them."

"Dad, I can't." Her parents knew there was someone in her
life. However, preoccupied as they were with their troubles, the
continuing occupation of their house by Robin and Ira, Lee had
never found the right moment for telling them just who the fellow
was, much less bringing him home to introduce them. Sometimes
she was afraid that her father, having forsworn his Taylor fixation,
would treat Jazz badly just to prove how little Protestants meant
to him. At other times, she feared Leonard hadn't gotten over the
Taylors at all, that he would grovel before Jazz in such a sickening,
relentless manner—Can I get you a glass of Veuve Clicquot? A
snifter of Rémy XO? A sable coat for your mother?—that even
good-natured Jazz would recoil.

"Look, Lee," her father said, "I know people your age don't want to hang around with a bunch of old farts like us. But I've invited some terrific people. Bright. Movers and shakers. People who if you're going to be a lawyer you should meet."

"Dad—"

"Bob and Bobbie Prager. He's going to be Lindsay's next consumer affairs commissioner. *Very* well respected. And Bobbie's mother was part of the Frick family. From the museum. She's been a customer for years. And Polly and Lloyd Gilliam. The journalists. She's a contributing editor for *Vogue* and he—"

"Dad, please. I've been working like a madwoman—"

"And I haven't?"

"Dad, I know how hard you work, but I need time—"

"This is what St. Bart's is all about!" Leonard roared. "Relaxing!"

"Not for me!"

"Well, how about doing something for the family for a change? Or is it all right by you just to have me pay for your tuition, your room and board, your clothes, your whatever? You know damn well your mother is a little shaky."

"So why are you taking her down to the Caribbean and loading her up with houseguests?"

"Because the house comes with plenty of help. I'm entitled to a little fun! Have you ever heard me say that before? No. You haven't. But *I am entitled.* I work like a dog, and I'm entitled to a little life in my life. I wanted to move to the city. No. Your mother's not up to it. Okay, fine. I want to go on a buying trip to Copenhagen, stop over in London, see some theater, and Greta— the maid!—comes crying to me that she's afraid to stay in the house alone with Ira. Don't worry, Greta. I won't go. But don't I *ever* get a turn?"

"Are Robin and Ira coming to St. Bart's?" Lee asked, imagining Ira's silhouette blackening the sun as the Fun Couples lunched on the terrace; Ira passing them on his way to sneak into their rooms and rip off their suitcases.

"I offered to send them to California, so they can visit with their friends. I really think . . . it looks like . . . I'm hoping they'll take me up on it."

"I can stay home with Greta."

"You can come with us. That's where you belong on the holidays. With your family."

Lee did not slam down the phone. She hung it up and turned to Jazz. "He wants me to be with them for Christmas. Translated, that means if he can't terrorize my mother into getting out of bed once they get down there, he'll do the old 'Sylvia has the flu' routine. She's pretty good at it. Once she coughs on cue, she's off the hook. Then he'll put his arm around me and say, 'Lee will fill in, won't you, dahling. Lee, have the girl bring the coffee out to the terrazzo.'" Jazz put an arm around Lee, she put an arm around him, and they stood beside her desk, rocking side to side, comforting each other.

A few days later, with final examinations behind her, Lee was back in her dorm room, getting ready for St. Bart's. More precisely, she was folding and refolding a blue cotton T-shirt as if expecting a grade in packing skills to be computed into her cumulative average. For the fourth time, she aligned the shoulder seams only to have a gigantic wrinkle pop up front and center. No matter what clothes she packed, she knew, her mother would be prepared with a fashion antidote. Lee would get to St. Bart's and there would be, God help her, a closet full of cruise wear in her room. Shocking-pink two-piece bathing suits with matching jackets or, worse, sarongs. Sun-yellow jumpsuits with palazzo pants legs. Lime-green shorts and halter tops, the sort of thing Robin could wear and look like an elf-queen, but that would make Lee look like a troll. Lee felt a lump midthroat. It's only for ten days, she soothed herself. At worst, I'll get a tan, and at best . . . Who knows? Maybe the fun people really will be fun.

She knew she was getting overemotional. It was not as if Jazz would meet some limpid-eyed beauty at the country club's New Year's Eve dance and immediately realize the error of his ways. Actually, Lee conceded, that *was* it. The lump in her throat grew so large it forced tears out of her eyes. A drop slipped from her cheek onto the T-shirt and made a sad little mark. All fumpfed up, that's what she was. Fumpfed—or something like it—was a Greta word. It seemed to mean something like filled with grief. It was a word she and Robin could never pronounce. But when one of them got upset, the other used to say, in a cruelly comic German accent: You are all fumpfed up.

234

Lee was so fumpfed up she did not notice that Jazz had come in. When he sat beside her on the bed—on top of her T-shirt, actually—she gave a too loud hoot of surprise.

"Sorry," he said. "I thought you heard me come in."

"No. I was so spaced out . . ." Her voice was excessively husky, she noticed, a combination of a constricted throat and a need to fight fire with fire and best the blonde hussy from Rolling Hills Country Club.

But such tactics were not necessary. When Jazz saw her tears, his eyes filled as well. They sat beside each other on the single, lumpy dormitory bed. Then they wept. "It's only for ten days," Lee managed to say. Not two seconds later, Jazz said the same thing back to her. "Why are we carrying on like this?" she demanded.

"Beats the hell out of me," he said, checking out the ceiling in the embarrassed way men do when they discover themselves crying. After a second, he added: "Maybe . . ."

"Maybe what?"

"Maybe we're all upset because our being apart is a crime against nature." Lee started to laugh, but her nose began dripping so fiercely she settled for a fast guffaw. "I'm serious," Jazz continued. "We were meant to be with each other. You and I . . . we're a given in natural law."

"Lee and Jazz. Axiomatic."

"Exactly," he agreed, without her irony. "And to be apart on Christmas is the worst. You know why?"

"Why?"

"Because the two of us, we're more family to each other than our own families are."

From there, it seemed only logical that the following afternoon, as soon as Jazz finished his Antitrust final, they visited Dr. Donald Humm, an internist known to the students around NYU for his fondness for writing prescriptions. He did the blood test. And a mere three telephone calls later, Judge Susan Margules Steinhardt, the august, cerebral New York State Supreme Court justice presiding in the Howie the Hose extortion proceedings, said that indeed she did remember Lee as the student intern from the previous summer—first-rate demeanor, so rare these days—and yes, she would be delighted to marry the couple Monday at noon in chambers and wasn't it, um, adventurous that the two of them were eloping and—no problem at all—she'd be pleased to read Shakespeare's one hundred sixteenth sonnet (her husband had in fact recited it to her while they were courting) and wasn't it romantic that they were going to spend their honeymoon in St. Bart's. Romantic and lovely. Just lovely.

It looked lovely: tropical twilight of Christmas Eve, coconut palms arching protectively over the pink villa with a red tile roof. An instant later, there was Sylvia meeting them at the front door, looking crisper than crisp in a white trouser suit with gold braiding—an officer in the world's most *au courant* navy. Her sleek champagne hair, now cut Cleopatra style, gleamed in the light of a chandelier consisting of six frosted-glass pineapples. Her flawlessly mascaraed lashes fluttered instinctively at the sight of Jazz, square-jawed and breathtakingly broad-shouldered in a well-worn blue blazer. Sylvia's lips, a juicy mango, pursed to kiss Lee, although she did not apply them to her daughter's cheek; instead she touched the side of her face lightly against Lee's and tweeted in the direction of the back of the house. Then, as if responding to some sharp command, she stepped back precisely eighteen inches: the perfect distance so her outfit could be observed in full, yet not a detail missed. Only then did she extend her hand to Jazz. "Jasper," she whispered tenderly.

"I hope you don't mind my horning in on your Christmas, Mrs. White." Lee looked up at him, at the sharp angles of his jaw, at his clear eyes and slightly-smaller-than-average nose, and knew, instantly, that had he had a Ph.D. in psychology and written his dissertation on the convolutions of the psyche of Sylvia Bernstein White, he could not have articulated a better sentence than the one he had just spoken. "Horning in" was something you could really get away with only after your tenth generation in America. "Christmas" of course was a word only his kind could pronounce perfectly, with that loving familiarity: their word. And the "Mrs. White" was masterful icing on the wedding cake: incredibly courteous, inviting immediate correction.

"Please! Call me Mom." Suddenly the woman Lee had known all her life disappeared. Snooty flared nostrils and puckered lips were replaced by soft diffidence. "Unless you'd rather call me Sylvia."

"I'd love to call you Mom," Jazz replied. Simultaneously, they moved in to kiss each other, then took a perfectly choreographed step back and smiled. In that same instant, Sylvia took her daughter's hand and stroked it. What amazed Lee was her mother's velvety warmth. She had expected a body temperature that was degrees cooler than normal human flesh.

Sylvia gave her daughter a benevolent smile and Lee found herself beaming back so broadly that for all she knew, her uvula was exposed. She could not help the peace that touched every part of her. Such utter peace that it made the transcendental meditative state she had managed to achieve twice in her junior year seem like a Led Zeppelin concert. Her every nerve felt soothed, her every muscle slack. For that moment, Lee no longer had to stand watch. She was protected.

Then, as the hand drew away, serenity vanished abruptly. Looking at her mother, Lee marveled that the bliss of seconds before could have come from that hand, that woman. There was her familiar mother, cheeks sucked in, stomach concave. "How was your flight, lovie?" Sylvia asked.

Lee realized that with Jazz by her side, she was now lovie, so she answered: "Not bad. But the little plane we had to change to . . ." She saw she had lost her mother's interest and rubbed her middle and little fingers against the solidity of her brand-new wedding band. Golden magic: She could face anything. But what was there to face? Sylvia was thrilled with her new son-in-law: For the Jew who prays for a Christmas gift, could there be any present better?

But, Lee conceded, her mother did not look well. True, Sylvia appeared normal standing in the foyer, regarding Jazz's scuffed loafers and, not unpredictably, gratified by them. Freshly polished shoes would have shown weakness, a pathetic need to please. Lee studied her mother as she stood, lightly brushing the outside corners of her mouth with the tips of her pinkies as if smoothing out some minuscule flaw in her lip liner. But her left eye had a staccato tic. Blink, blink, blink. It couldn't stay open. And she was swaying slightly, first left, then right, then back again. Was she dizzy from medication? Reeling from shock: How could you betray me like this? Elope! Deprive me of consultations with the caterer at the St. Regis and Jackie Onassis's calligrapher!

Blink, blink, blink. Left, right, left. But then the next sway to the right was greater than the one before. Sylvia would have crashed against the doorpost and cracked her head if Jazz had not been quick. In a single balletic motion, he was by her side, grabbing her elbow, rotating her one hundred eighty degrees, escorting her into the living room. "A piano" he was saying, while he lowered her into a bamboo chair with giant pink hibiscuses printed on the white cushions. "If you want to get rid of your houseguests, I can play my famous Christmas carol medley. They'll swim home."

"Oh, God!" Sylvia suddenly cried, as if he had made whatever pain she was in ten times worse. Behind her, by the picture window facing an inner courtyard, a Christmas tree, brilliant with thousands of tiny lights, was hung with hibiscus and frangipani blossoms. Real flowers. They were dying, their petals drooping and brown-edged.

Jazz, stunned by the drama of her outburst, tried to make a joke of it. "All right, I swear. No Christmas carols."

"You have no idea," Sylvia said, staring up into his eyes. "This is a disaster."

Understandably, Lee thought she had retracted her initial welcome and was now referring to the marriage. Pressure built up on the sides of her head until it felt her skull was about to explode. So she could not make a quick comeback, or any comeback at all. It was Jazz who asked: "What's a disaster?" clearly secure that whatever the nature of the catastrophe, it had nothing to do with him.

In fact, it did not. "Bob and Bobbie Prager canceled at the last minute," Sylvia said. "They didn't even call. They just didn't show up at the airport. And the Gilliams were there with us, waiting at the gate. We were the only people who hadn't boarded. Leonard was trying not to show that he wasn't . . ." Sylvia lifted her hands. They were trembling. She could not find words to describe the depth of her husband's horror. "He called their apartment and the man—houseman, butler—said they were in Sun Valley. Skiing. And he had to come back and put on a good face to the Gilliams. 'Bob and Bobbie can't make it. Some last minute hitch.'

I thought he was going to have a stroke. Two first-class tickets wasted."

"Daddy paid for their tickets?" Lee asked.

"That's how it's done," Sylvia explained, unwilling to meet Lee's eyes. "For a minute," she told the giant ceiling fan, "I swear to God, I thought the Gilliams were going to cancel."

"But they're here," Jazz said soothingly.

Sylvia kept her head tilted back. "In the dining room. With Daddy—and Ira. Ira! We tried to get them to go to California, but they wouldn't. And Ira is here. Oh God in heaven, Polly Gilliam writes about outerwear for *Vogue* and he has a goatee and is very important."

"Where's Robin?"

"Not feeling well."

Sylvia's face, made poreless and flawless by exorbitantly-priced foundation extracted from the placentas of white lambs, remained trained on the laconic revolving blades of the fan, although several times she did manage to turn her eyes back to Jazz. The point of her tongue slid out to moisten her lips, but it too was dry.

"Sylvia!" Leonard's voice called out. Even a stranger could hear the desperation behind the near-hysterical bonhomie. "Is that Lee-lee and Jasper?"

Sylvia nodded slowly and carefully, as though her head weighed several hundred pounds. Lee, who had not called herself Lee-lee since before her third birthday and who could recall no previous instance of either parent using that name, was so agitated she could not respond. How could she get herself and Jazz out of this nightmare? More to the point, the incipient prosecutor within her demanded, how could she have been so demented as to think Christmas week in St. Bart's with her family should be the place to begin a marriage?

"Lee-lee?"

Jazz answered for her. "We're here!" he called brightly.

And Leonard, as if blasted from a rocket launcher, shot into the living room. "Lee!" he called, flinging out his arms in a come-my-children flourish. "Jasper!" Jazz, watching what Lee did, the way a person faced with eating snails for the first time observes a tablemate, leaned in toward Leonard and allowed himself to be gathered into a desperate embrace. "Wonderful!"

"Hi," Jazz said. Because Jazz was significantly taller, his father-in-law was still saying "Wonderful!" into his neck. "I don't know exactly what to say," Jazz went on. "I mean, dropping in on you. It's not just like for a drink. It's like: Oh, hello and Merry Christmas and so nice of you to let us have our honeymoon here."

"Wonderful!" Leonard was still saying as Lee and Jazz managed to pull themselves out of his hug. "Couldn't be happier. So glad you came." With Jazz now a couple of feet away, Leonard was able to look up at him. Soak him in. His face began to flush with pleasure. And then he spotted his wife. His color ebbed. "Sylvia!"

"What?"

"They're waiting."

"I know." But her eyes darted left and right, searching for what they were waiting for.

"Well . . . ?"

"Um," she responded.

"Sylvia!"

"*What?*" she begged him, clearly at a loss.

"'*What?*'" Leonard repeated. "Oh, God, don't tell me. Oh, God!" His hands clutched at his fashionable thick sideburns. He might have actually pulled them out had he not caught sight of Jazz. "I'm so sorry you have to be here at a time—"

"It's okay," Jazz smiled. Could nothing affect his easygoing nature? Why wasn't he saying to himself: How the hell can I extricate myself from this lunatic family—Lee included? Can I get a fucking annulment in time to get home to Christmas dinner with people who have as their birthright the competence to decorate a tree properly? Je-sus! Dead flowers! Lee watched in wonder as Jazz rested his hand on her father's shoulder, the reassuring masculine touch a catcher would offer a rattled pitcher. Leonard stopped yanking on his hair and dropped his hands to his sides. Still, he remained agitated and looked from Jazz to Sylvia, his expression changing from longing to loathing.

"Dad?" Leonard glanced in Lee's direction, surprised, as if he had forgotten she had come to St. Bart's with Jazz.

"You have no idea," was all he could say.

"Robin?" Lee asked.

"The tip of the iceberg." Leonard rammed his hands deep into the pockets of his white linen trousers.

"Those people who didn't show up?"

Leonard's dark eyes narrowed into menacing slits at this reminder. "They're nothing," he said, trying to sound dismissive and, of course, not succeeding. His eyes narrowed even more, so that all light in them was cut off; he was furious at Lee for such a bitter reminder. "Social climbers," he mumbled to Jazz. "You know?"

Jazz nodded in weary commiseration, as if this were something he and his father-in-law were doomed to suffer every day. "What's going on?" he inquired. *Don't!*, Lee wanted to shout. Don't set him off! "Something wrong down here?"

But Leonard looked grateful for the query, as if he'd been waiting days for someone to ask it. "No servants," he managed to say. For an instant, he seemed so frail, so old, even, that Lee was afraid he would collapse into Jazz's arms. But then Leonard glimpsed Sylvia in the bamboo chair, wringing her exquisitely manicured hands. Immediately, he was filled with savage energy.

"Four goddamn help were supposed to be here," he growled. "One—the driver, fellow who shops for groceries—was supposed to pick us up at the airport." He clenched his teeth so tight it seemed the enamel of the uppers and lowers had fused. Finally, he was able to pry them apart. "He never showed. Okay, I'm cool, calm, collected. I call the house. *No one is there!* Okay, I tell myself. It's the goddamn Caribbean. The phones aren't working. I get three cabs. No one speaks English for crissake." Suddenly, realizing "crissake," like Christmas, had Christ in it, he stopped his diatribe. "Sorry," he apologized to Jazz. "Anyway, finally I got Robin to look alive and tell the cabdrivers where to go in French, so we got here. And what happens? It's empty! An empty house! An empty refrigerator! I manage to grab one of the cabs before he takes off. I go to the local gendarmes. They call the guy who's the butler. He says he's off for Christmas! What? I say. What? I have a house full of people. Sorry, he says. Monsieur de Valois—that's the French bastard who owns this place—said they could have the week off. *Paid* them. Two weeks vacation pay."

"Did you—"Lee began.

"Please!" her father said, angrily, contemptuously. "I offered him twice that. Three times that. I told him: Name your price. He says: Sorry, we wish to be with our families for the holidays. So I called de Valois."

"And?" Lee asked.

"And he's off hunting something. Bear. Boar. I couldn't get what his wife was saying, with her stupid Frog accent and Robin was sleeping and I couldn't get her up to come to the phone. Won't be back till 'le tent of January,' she says. Sorry, a little misunderstanding. January tenth! When we'll be back in New York for four goddamn days!"

"I'll call her tomorrow," Lee said, waiting for her father to be grateful.

But he was glaring at her mother with an animus beyond hate. "I'm sorry," Sylvia cried, covering her face with her hands. "I just forgot!"

"Forgot what?" Lee asked.

"Dinner," Sylvia whispered.

The Whites' houseguests, Polly and Lloyd Gilliam, sat under a huge canvas umbrella, breathing in the sweet, soft Caribbean air, waves lapping near their feet. They sipped iced tea and looked put out. Actually, that is an understatement, for as Lee was slogging through the sand, bringing out a plate of cookies—which her father and the Gilliams insisted on calling biscuits—she overheard Polly grousing to her husband: "I am so supremely pissed I can't even discuss it." From the waist up, Polly was built the way she wanted to be, thin and breastless like Twiggy. From the waist down, however, she was heavy, bell-bottomed, like an accessory made for a boat, weighted not to tip over in rough weather. Thus shaped, she had wrapped a giant chiffon scarf around the waist of her bathing suit, but a random breeze had uncovered a hefty hip and a huge, dimpled thigh.

"Pissed?" Lloyd said. "Pissed? My dear, I am beyond pissed. I am in utter *extremis*. You, on the other hand, have no right to be pissed since it was *you*, love, who said, and I quote: 'No, not Mustique. We've been invited by Mr. Fur himself'—Mr. Fuh, as he would pronounce it—'who's having all *sorts* of marvelous people to St. Bart's—'"

The Whites, Lee thought, did not think in terms of family honor. Still, at this moment, she wished they did, so she could avenge it. Punch that snotty prick in the snoot he tanned at other people's second houses. Jerk his well-stroked goatee. Pretentious asshole. At dinner the night before, he pontificated on Whither Henry Kissinger? as if he were James Reston. But it hadn't taken much cross-examination to reveal that the articles he wrote were celebrity profiles for magazines like *New York* and *Esquire*—"Maria Schneider's Two-Step: What the *Tango* Star Won't Say." Lloyd stopped talking as Lee's shadow fell over them.

"Ah," Lloyd said, because he could not remember her name, "the Bringer of Biscuits." He scrutinized the proffered plate, then shook his head. Not good enough, was the unsaid message. Polly, unable to accept a cookie judged inferior by a cultural arbiter of her husband's stature, would have had to refuse as well. But before Lee could offer them, a hideous scream—a woman's shriek merging with a man's howl—burst forth from the pink villa, shattering a perfect Christmas peace.

"Stop it!" Lee shouted at her parents. "Be quiet, for God's sake!" It was not that she wanted decorum. It was that someone needed to think, and since her parents were standing in Robin and Ira's room, watching their younger daughter convulsing on the bed— naked, sweating, pale legs jerking, mouth foaming, eyes rolling back—and wailing at the horror of such a sight, Lee was going to be the one who had to think. Oh God, why hadn't she taken the MCATs instead of the LSATs? She could have gone to medical school; she'd know what to do now. When the shit really hit the fan, who the hell needed a lawyer?

Convulsion: Fever? She put her hands on Robin's forehead and neck. Drenched, but cool to the touch. "What is it?" Leonard cried out. Sylvia made terrible squeaking sounds, as if she were pretending to be a mouse: "Eeee. Eeee," over and over again. Could Robin be having some sort of allergic reaction? Lee turned to Ira. He was standing in a corner between the bed and the window, trying to fit his back into the right angle where the walls met. In black briefs: the bad boy, head hung. His arms and legs were as scrawny as a child's. Only the few hairs growing around his small, pale nipples showed he had passed puberty. "What did she have to eat today?" Lee snapped at him. "Ira!"

It took him what seemed forever to lift his head and say: "I

243

don't know." But then Lee understood. Her sister was now on heroin. Too much? Too little? Oh, God, where was Jazz? Driving all over the damn island, looking for tonic for Polly's vodka. What? Polly had whined. No Schweppes? Don't they have Schweppes on St. Bart's? Isn't this civilization? I'll go on a search and destroy mission for tonic, Jazz told Polly, charming her. She'd actually smiled, and Leonard had been so grateful he'd walked Jazz to the rented jeep, saying, Thank you, thank you, thank you, practically sobbing with relief and gratitude. But now Jazz had been gone for over an hour. All right: Think. Okay, Robin was having either d.t.'s or convulsions, and that would suggest withdrawal. Didn't it? Jesus, what the hell did Lee know about heroin? She—all her friends—had ingested a pharmacopoeia of drugs, but not heroin. Who the hell would be so stupid as to take heroin? Robin.

"Out!" she barked at her parents. Paralyzed, they stood by the bed, her mother still making mouse sounds, but softer now. "Get out!" she said even louder, and to her amazement, they about-faced and double-timed out. A little too eagerly. Lee realized that now, if anything happened—if Robin died—she would be blamed. It was too silent. Then she heard the rumble of the jeep and then Jazz's voice: "Hey, I found this little store with gallons of tonic!"

"In here!" she called. "In Robin's room."

Ira shuffled his feet, probably meaning to move out as well, but he was too stoned to actually ambulate. "What the hell is going on with her?" Lee yelled at him. In slow motion, Ira raised his narrow shoulders into a shrug. She raced around the bed and stood right before him. He smelled musty, like a dank basement. "I know it's heroin. Is it an overdose or is it withdrawal?" Ira managed to hoist his head so he could look directly at Lee, but all he did was look; he had nothing to say. "Overdose or with-drawal?" she bellowed. Still nothing. She grabbed his throat in her hand and squeezed. His Adam's apple bobbed about in terror. He clutched her wrist and tried to pull it away, but he lacked the strength or the coordination. "Tell me, you son-of-a-bitch, or I'll squeeze tighter. I'll choke you to death and bury you in the sand, and no one except the fucking crabs will know about it. Overdose or withdrawal?"

Ira managed to get out a tiny sound: "Withdrawal."

"Why? Did she want to stop?" When he didn't respond, Lee slammed him against the wall. "Did she want to stop or did you just take too much?"

"Me," he said.

"How do the two of you take it? Intravenously?"

"Yeah." It was less a word than an exhalation.

"Do you have any more? Answer me."

"Not much."

Jazz came into the room, bouncing in his sneakers. Then he saw Robin and froze. "What . . . ?"

"Heroin," Lee said. She waited, expecting Jazz to do something, but he just stood there, hands at his sides, staring at Robin's naked, sweat-drenched body. Lee separated the sheet from the blanket that lay twisted on the floor and covered her sister.

"Listen to me," Lee said to Ira. "You're going to get the heroin right now and show me everything: the stuff itself, the needles, all the shit you use. So I'll know exactly what you have. Then you're going to put the smallest possible amount in the needle and give it to her so she comes out of this convulsion."

"Okay."

She looked over to Jazz, but he was looking down at the floor. "You're going to give it all to me," she told Ira. "I'll be first-vice-president in charge of heroin. If we can avoid going to a hospital here I'd like to, because I don't know if they're any good with drug problems. And I don't know anything about the island's drug laws. I don't want my sister winding up with a life sentence on St. Bart's. So if you can get her stabilized, we're going to hire a plane and get her to a hospital back in the States and get her detoxified properly." She took a deep breath. "If she needs another shot, you'll give it to her. How often does she"—Lee squeezed Ira's throat until his tongue bulged out—"shoot up?"

"Four, five times."

"A day?" He nodded. "Right before we land, we'll have to get rid of the drugs. We can't risk bringing them in. You're going to stay with us until she gets wheeled into the emergency room. Then you get a hundred bucks. You get your clothes. You get out of her life permanently. If you don't, I will personally take a knife and slit your throat. Do you understand me, Ira?"

"Yes."

"Do you think I mean what I say?"

Ira hesitated, but at last, wiping his nose on the back of his hand, he said: "Yeah."

"Then let's move it." She moved in front of Jazz, staying with Ira as he knelt down and pulled a leather shaving kit from under the bed. She watched as he prepared the drug and filled a syringe. His fingers seemed flaccid, and she winced as he fumbled with the drug paraphernalia. "Ira, if you give her too much, you're dead too. You understand that, don't you?"

"Yeah."

He took a length of rubber tubing, the sort that would be used in a hospital, and made a tourniquet around Robin's thin arm. Then, with a casualness more appropriate to handing someone a cup of coffee, he ran his finger over her skin until he found an accessible vein and injected her. Within seconds, the convulsion stopped. Robin's lashes fluttered as if she were a belle flirting with a new beau. She began to smile at Ira, but then she spotted her sister. "Hey," Robin said, the smile vanishing. She dabbed away at the dried white foam on her chin. "You don't belong in here. Out. I mean it, Lee. Haul ass!" Then she closed her eyes again.

It was only after Lee sent Jazz out to have her father hire a plane—now!—to fly to Miami that she came up on the side of the bed and smacked her sister across the face.

Fifteen

My secretary, Sandi Zimmerman, was born with a happy face. Add to her button nose, round brown eyes, and congenitally upturned mouth a ponytail that curled up at the end into a cheery little smile-shape, and you had a person strangers wanted to meet.

People who knew her, however, avoided her whenever they could. It wasn't that Sandi was obnoxious or even mean; it was that beyond her two good qualities, honesty and diligence, she had no redeeming social value. Give her a friendly "Hi" and she'd act perplexed. "*Hi?*" she seemed to be wondering; how peculiar; how alienating. Finally, after a too long pause, Sandi would respond with an edgy "Oh. Uh . . . hi." Invite her to join you for a cup of coffee, inquire if she'd watched the Oscars the night before, ask her what her vacation plans were—in short, treat her as you would any casual acquaintance—and Sandi would stiffen, jerking back her head as if you had suggested she join you and a quadruped in a bizarre sexual practice.

Then there was her nerves. From font changes on the office's word-processing program to the introduction of the four-digit suffix for zip codes—everything rattled her: There was nothing about which Sandi was not anxious. Every client walking into the office was a maniac about to pull out a machete and cut us down—or, if not slaughter us, at least set us up by means of a subtle and nefarious ruse so we'd be easy pickings for a malpractice suit. Although she had been working for me for fifteen years, I had no idea how she'd come to be so strange since questions about her family or her childhood made her even more apprehensive. All I really knew about Sandi was that she was my age, lived with a divorced sister and a bachelor brother in Huntington, was a terrific stenographer and typist, and had a fondness bordering on fixation for Celestial Seasonings Lemon Zinger tea.

Naturally, in the back of my mind, I sensed that a decade or two on the couch probably wouldn't hurt her. But in an office relationship, it's easier to assume the weird person you are dealing with is eccentric rather than a fellow human being in terrible pain. But Sandi kept getting stranger and stranger.

Being a forty-five myself, and a feminist, I was reluctant to blame her increasing oddness on menopause. But I overcame my reluctance. About three months before Norman became a client, she had started going nuts about dirty telephones: The only phone in the office she would use was the one at her desk; arriving in the morning or coming back from the ladies' room or lunch, she would spray the entire receiver—mouthpiece, handpiece, earpiece—with Lysol. A couple of weeks after that, she began to spend her lunch hour in the conference room, where, after glugging down one can of vanilla Ensure and one can of Diet Slice, she cut out elaborate doilies from old copies of the *Law Journal*. I was tempted to ask her what the doilies were for, but I was afraid my question might set her off on a psychotic voyage from which she'd never return and I would then become one of those lawyers who get ten years taken off their life by having to deal with temp agencies.

Still, it did come as a surprise to discover (as I was dictating a memo to files *in re* Torkelson) that Sandi had fallen madly in love with Mary Dean. "It is worth noting," I was saying, "that in a conversation with me on May ninth of this year— several days before Mary Dean admitted to having been in Bobette Frisch's house—Ms. Dean showed a familiarity with the layout and furnishings of the premises that indicated she had spent a considerable amount of time there." I swiveled around in my chair a few times as I constructed the next sentence and noted that the patent leather on my pumps was looking dull. Then I noted that Sandi was writing with her right hand—her usual practice, but toying with her bangs with her left. God knows why, but she must have curled her bangs; the rest of her hair was straight. It looked as if she had glued a piece of poodle to the top of her forehead. Nervously, over and over, she kept sticking her finger into the center of each curl. "The observations Mary Dean made—about a collection of purple perfume bottles on Ms. Frisch's dresser, the furnishings of a second bedroom next to Ms. Frisch's—suggest that far more than the hurried glimpse she has admitted to, she has a detailed knowledge of the house—"

"Because Norman *described* it to her!" Sandi broke in.

In all the years she had worked for me, she had never commented on anything I dictated. In fact, although her transcriptions were astoundingly accurate, I had always felt that while she got the words, she didn't hear the music. So I was stunned. My mouth may have dropped open in quintessential stupnagel fashion. Not that my reaction mattered to Sandi. Her face was flushed dark red. I could sense her outrage, although with her strange, upturned smiley mouth and round cheeks, she just looked happy.

"No, it was not something she heard," I responded slowly. "Mary said something like 'I couldn't believe my eyes.' She *saw* the place. She was in there."

"He's a con man!" Sandi insisted, a hysterical screech creeping into her voice. "He made it seem so real it became real to her."

"Boy, I'm glad you're not on my jury," I said. "Anyway, since when have you become a Mary Dean fan?"

Sandi set down her pen and steno pad. "My heart goes out to her. She's so good. You can see it!" Her lips parted. Her eyes shone. I sensed I was watching something that ought to have been private. "Oh, I know with those kind of clothes you think she's tawdry. Not a good person. *I* was put off by it at the beginning. But under all the makeup, she's so innocent." Sandi placed her palms together as if she were about to pray. "A saint, that's what she is! You can see it in her eyes." What I was seeing in Sandi's eyes was a moist, mad glow. "And she's been dragged down by that man, dragged into the gutter—"

"Before Mary Dean met that man she had twenty-seven arrests for prostitution, which might lead one to believe the gutter was not exactly terra incognita," I commented.

I was shaken by Sandi's outburst. Sure, there'd been plenty of emotion in the office, but it had come from my clients or their wives and girlfriends. Weeping, wailing, fainting, pounding on the desk—or on the client's head. Once, I billed the Perich brothers, two contractors I was representing for tax fraud, an extra two hundred bucks for a carpet cleaning to remove bloodstains after Frankie hit Billy in the gut and Billy socked Frankie in the face and Frankie had a nosebleed all over my rug. But it was easy to keep a distance from my clients' craziness. They were *supposed* to go off the wall.

Well, that makes it sound so easy: dealing with people who didn't feel obliged to keep a stiff upper lip. It wasn't. Even viewed from the objective distance I had trained myself to maintain, it often exhausted me. So what I needed to protect me from those client storms was tranquillity, peace in the workplace. That's why I found Sandi's explosion terribly jarring. Just as I depended on our receptionist to be obtuse, on our associate to try to act cool while walking up the courthouse steps, on Chuckie to be droll, I relied on Sandi to be reassuringly, perpetually dull.

"I'll tell you what," I announced. "Take a break. Then you can finish up the paperwork on that Eastern District case, that transportation of stolen property." I got up. "See you later." And I bolted.

For about half a minute I considered putting on the sneakers I keep in the trunk of my car and going for a five-mile walk to clear my head. But in the next half minute, I got into the car and headed toward Mary Dean's. Was she, as Sandi was maintaining, an innocent? Or was she guilty of murder and, perhaps, a con of her own?

"I don't want to talk to you," Mary announced. She stood in the doorway, blocking entrance to the apartment. Not inviting, but not belligerent either. She was wearing matching shorts and crop top in a peach so vivid it was almost a new color. Her hair, tossed on top of her head, was held in place with a banana clip. As I'd suspected, her complexion without makeup was without blemish. Her skin's only flaw was a patch of blue, a dried-up piece of facial mask, that was stuck between ear and jaw.

"I wish you would talk to me," I said. "I'd really like to see things from your point of view."

"Sorry." Inside the apartment, a TV was on, a talk show. One guest was shrieking at another, who kept hooting back: "I'm laughing in your face."

"I bought us cappuccino," I said, holding up the white paper bag. "One with cinnamon, one without. Which do you want?"

"Uh," she said.

"Either one's fine with me."

"Cinnamon," she said, standing back so I could walk into the house. "But I don't have any cookies or anything."

"I have a couple of biscotti. Those hard cookies."

"I was always scared I was going to break a tooth on one of those," Mary said, turning off the TV, clearing off a small round table on the far side of the living room. She had been clipping supermarket coupons. "Then I learned to dunk"—a coupon for Dove soap fell to the floor—"so it's better, except when you dunk for, like, one second too long. Then it gets all gooky and falls into the coffee."

We sat across from each other. The atmosphere was companionable, two hausfraus having a kaffeeklatsch. Mary, who was able to sit in shorts and a crop top without even a millimeter of flab showing anywhere, said she wished she and Norman could settle down in one place; there was a coupon-clippers newsletter she was dying to subscribe to, but since they were never in any town longer than three months, it didn't pay. Since we were getting on so well— she showed me the box in which she kept her coupons filed, a green metal thing decorated with rolling pins and egg beaters—I did not mention I was more than half hoping that her only long-term address would be in care of an upstate maximum-security facility.

"You know who I spoke to?" I asked, taking what I hoped

was a casual sip of cappuccino. "Carolyn Knowles. The woman you had that altercation with in Annapolis."

"Oh," Mary said, a wispy sound. "Gee."

"She said you smashed her head against the sidewalk." Mary stretched out her hands in a gesture that said: I can't remember *what* happened. "Want to tell me about it?" I asked.

"How did you find out?"

"It wasn't hard."

"Do the police know?"

"I don't think so. If they knew the fingerprints at Bobette's were the same as those made in another instance of an attack on an older woman, they might have a few questions for you."

Mary toyed with a drip of coffee meandering its way down the Styrofoam cup. "Like what?"

"Like what happened? What set you off down there in Annapolis?"

"She said, 'Get out of here, you whore.' She didn't even know who I was! She kept looking at my dress like it was cheap. It wasn't!"

I tried to look shocked and distressed. "Tell me about it."

"I was just hanging around—"

"Her house?"

"Yes. I mean, just checking it out. Norman said it was gorgeous. You should see it, he said. It's called a landmark! She couldn't paint it a different color without permission because it was history."

"Were she and Norman there at the time?"

"No."

"Where were they?"

"They went for a drive. She had a convertible." She shook her head. "Why is it that when you *should* have a convertible you can't afford it, and every time you see a really great car, some old poop-head is driving it?" As I had just recently been wavering between a financially secure old age and buying a BMW 325i ragtop, I merely shrugged. "So I walked around her house. She had gardens. That's what you call it when rich people have, like, a place for roses and another place for vegetables and another place for tulips or whatever. Not a garden. Gardens, even if it's all in the same backyard."

"So you looked at her gardens."

"Yuck. Lots of little, low things. If you wanted to smell the flowers, you'd have to crawl around on your hands and knees."

"Did you go inside, Mary?"

She sat up straight, alert. "No."

"No? You didn't even try to get in?" She shook her head vehemently. "Mary," I said, giving her what I hoped looked like an indulgent look. "Come on."

She came back with a sheepish smile. "It was locked."

"Did you try the windows?" She chewed the inside of her cheek for a while. "Mary, I'm Norman's lawyer. You can tell me."

"I tried."

"Did you get in?" She nodded, not without a gleam of triumph in her eye. "And found some jewelry?"

"Yes. *So* great."

"What made you take the jewelry? Weren't you afraid you'd ruin Norman's chances of a score with her?"

"How would she know a robber had anything to do with Norman?"

"That's true," I conceded.

"She didn't even have, like, a safe or anything. It was in a jewelry box in her closet. A walk-in closet. With built-in shelves for everything. Baskets to pull out for sweaters, and a thing you hung scarves on."

"Where's the jewelry now?"

"I gave it to Norm. He said it was too hot to sell. He put it in a safety deposit box he has."

"Where is that?"

"In Atlanta."

"Why in Atlanta?"

"Beats me," Mary said.

"Didn't you keep any of it to wear?"

She screwed up her mouth and shook her head. "He wouldn't let me. I tried to hide the ruby pin. So gorgeous, I couldn't believe it. Like a firework: fat in the middle, with

253

all those spray lines going out. I stuck it in the bottom of my Tampax box, but he found it. He said it was too . . . some word that means it would, you know, point the finger at me."

"Is that usual for you, Mary? Breaking in and taking jewelry. Something tells me . . . It doesn't sound like you."

She rested her chin in her hands. The blue dab of facial mask fell off. "It isn't like me," she said gratefully.

"So what made you do it?" I played a hunch. "Did something set you off to want to hurt her in some way?" She took our cups and napkins and stuffed them into the paper bag. "What was it?"

"Tickets."

I remembered her saying that she had gone into Bobette's house looking for airplane tickets for a honeymoon. It had been such a strong and specific image that it was jarring to me at the time. "You found plane tickets?" I asked.

"Yes."

"For Carolyn Knowles and . . . What name was Norman using then?"

"Arthur."

"Right. Arthur Berringer. Where were the tickets for?"

"Paris." She closed her eyes and took a deep breath. "I knew he could go with her. See, he had an Arthur passport. Usually he just has a driver's license and some credit cards, but for Arthur . . . for some reason, he got the works."

"And you thought he was going to marry her."

"He had a weak moment."

"Right. So you saved him, in a way. I mean, by beating her up, with him as a witness, he would have to make the choice right there: her or you. And he wouldn't choose her." Mary nodded, an agreement and a thank-you. But what I had meant was that Norman would not dare risk dealing with the police, even as a mere witness to a crime. He had too long a record; he would have known that a first-rate cop—like Terry Salazar had been—in two seconds flat could make him as a guy who had done time. "So you ran?"

"Yes. He was holding her and saying, 'Carolyn! Darling!'

But he whispered to me, 'Get out. I'll meet you back at the apartment.' Except I was all, like, shook up. I went to the apartment, but it was such an awful place, in someone's basement, with no rug or anything. So I thought: Well, he'll be a couple of hours. So I left the jewelry there and went to a shopping center, just to pass the time."

"You had Carolyn Knowles's credit cards?" I asked casually.

"Yes. I only bought a camisole. Oh, and then I was walking over to a place where they had leather coats—just to look—and that's where the cops picked me up."

"You must have been scared."

"Was I ever! I thought: Oh, shit. I'll be thirty before I get out of jail, what with bopping her and taking her jewelry. I mean, thank goodness I had left all the stuff back at the apartment, but they'd know it was me."

"Did they charge you with robbery as well as assault?"

"Yes. Uh-oh, I thought. That's what my lawyer thought too. But the judge was such a sweetie. He said: 'I want your word that if I grant bail, you'll be back.' So I said: 'Oh, Your Honor, I swear I won't let you down.'"

"And then you were out of there."

Mary winked. "Straight to Baltimore. No bathroom stops, no frozen yogurt stops. Then the first plane out to anywhere. We wound up in Pittsburgh. Not bad."

"I've never been there."

"No, I mean, Norm made a forty-two-thousand score in less than three weeks. He said she was so easy, he hated to take the money."

"And all was well between the two of you?"

"Fine!" But she looked away, shamed by a memory, and tried to hide her chagrin by staring at a coupon for Joy.

"What was the problem?"

"He was so hurt that I hadn't trusted him."

When we first started seeing so much of each other, the man in my life and I recognized that such an alliance of two trial lawyers could be problematical. Unless we invited a judge along to hand down rulings on the almost daily basis we saw each other, our friendship could become one endless litigation, the first thing in the day one of us would say to the other being: Now, about the issue you raised on January fifteenth last. Let me enumerate the reasons why you were so pathetically misguided, to say nothing of lamentably wrong.

So we made a pact to listen to each other: really sit and hear, without structuring a response. We'd each get five minutes or whatever to state our case and after we'd both spoken, we'd work together to find a solution. This worked pretty well, except for occasional moments. Like when he threw a fit because I'd planned a vacation without consulting him. Without inviting him, to be perfectly honest, but it truly had not occurred to me that he would want to go to Disneyland. Or when I took one of the many, many jars of his mother's heinous corn relish that, like his mother, seemed threatening to take over my pantry, my dinner table, and my life, and threw it—at him.

Our other resolution was not to talk too much law, on the theory that, inevitably, my neighbors would report a strange smell and the medical examiner would rule that our deaths were simultaneous, due to acute boredom. So while we kept each other up to speed on our more interesting or troublesome cases, we usually spent our evenings doing normal-people things: watching TV, listening to music, reading, talking about life outside the law.

But that night, I was so upset about the Torkelson case I couldn't have talked about it even if I had wanted to. I made a lovely salmon tandoori style and basmati rice and couldn't eat a thing. Believe me, I had never been one to lose my appetite when under stress. With me, one small worry equals one thousand calories. And I was worried, big time. I couldn't distract myself. I picked up the novel I was reading and kept reading the same paragraph over and over; I tried crocheting but kept dropping stitches. I felt as if I had a tuning fork inside me, and its barely discernible, relentless hum was agitating every cell in my body.

"Lee? Where did you hide those oat bran pretzels?" my guy called out. He had just come in from the garage, where he was sanding an antique music stand he'd bought at a yard sale. Then I entered the kitchen. "What's wrong?"

"Nothing," I told him. I opened the pantry door and handed him the pretzels, which, naturally, were right in the front, at eye level.

"Torkelson case?"

"Yes, but I'm so . . . I don't know. I can't talk about it." If he had tried to pull it out of me, I might have spilled everything, but he said he understood, and was off like a shot, back to his sandpaper. So I spent the evening leafing through old copies of *Gourmet* magazine from 1987, when I had a subscription, looking at recipes I would never try. Then he left to go back to his house, and I spent the night in bed, staring out into the dark.

Could Mary Dean have killed Bobette? She had a pattern of moving against women she perceived as rivals for Norman. There were strong parallels between her behavior at Carolyn Knowles's and Bobette Frisch's houses: breaking in, stealing. Were there others in this category? Or were these two so well-heeled and Norman so weary of the con that they presented a special danger that his other marks hadn't? If Terry's analysis was right, Norman, in Mary's eyes, was not merely the love of her life. He had taken her, a whore, and bestowed upon her coupon-clipping respectability. More, he gave her a home. He became her family. Wouldn't she do anything to preserve what she had with him?

The problem was, all the evidence—from fingerprints at the crime scene to marks on Bobette's neck to the probable time frame of the murder—pointed to Norman as much as it did to Mary. So which one of them had killed her? Was he covering up for her? Was her insistence on his innocence a cover-up for her knowledge of his guilt?

The next morning, first thing, I was knocking on Mary's door, sure I would have to pound away for a half hour before she would wake up and hear me. But she opened it on the third knock. "Hi," she said, and a moment later, reluctantly, she invited me in. Seeing that the goodwill I had established the day before had dissipated, I regretted not bringing more cappuccino.

257

The ironing board was set up in the middle of the living room and she was working on a pile of laundry: sheets and pillowcases, Norman's shirts, her clothes. She saw me staring at a pair of his undershorts that was on the board. For an instant, her manner eased, her mouth moved toward a smile as she picked up the iron. "He says not to bother, but ironing makes things so much softer. Doesn't it?" I nodded enthusiastic agreement. She ran the iron over the hems of the legs of the shorts, shooting small bursts of steam. It was an elaborate appliance, loaded with gauges and dials. Before her lips could part into a genuine smile, she remembered something. "How come you were asking me all those questions about Carolyn in Annapolis?"

Since I hadn't slept more than an hour, I couldn't come up with a decent answer. However, a lawyer has to appear— if not actually be—unbowed and uncowed at all times. I had learned to throw questions back on the questioner. "Why do *you* think I was asking them?"

"You think, like, because I beat up Carolyn maybe I"— she set down the iron but continued holding the hem of the shorts flat—"did, you know, the same thing to fatso Bobette."

"The thought crossed my mind."

"Except the report, the autopsy report . . . Didn't it say she wasn't beat up?"

"That's right."

"So I didn't! The report proves it."

"You didn't beat her up. I believe you." Mary, apparently feeling vindicated, took up her iron again. "Did you kill her?" I asked.

"*What?*" She stood there motionless, then slowly raised the iron off Norman's shorts and stared, stupidly, at its flat, shiny surface.

"Did you kill Bobette?" Drawn into the mirrored depths of the iron, she did not seem to have heard me. So I repeated the question once more, slower and louder.

"No! Of course not. Are you totally nuts?"

"Okay, I just wanted to know." Mary was either incensed or frightened. Whatever it was, she was so overcome by emotion that she could not do what she clearly wanted to do: throw the iron at me. "The reason I asked is that you seem so positive Norman didn't kill Bobette."

"I am positive!" Mary set down the iron and made a quick cross over her left breast. "I swear to God, my mother's life to die! Norman couldn't hurt anyone."

"Well, there are only two sets of fingerprints there, yours and his. And the marks on her throat . . . they were made by someone with big hands."

We both looked at the large, long-fingered hand holding down the hem of the shorts. "But I didn't touch her," Mary said. "I was never in the same room with her, ever. Do you think I could strangle somebody?"

"It's not what I think that matters. It's what the authorities think, and they think Norman strangled her. But you say Norman couldn't do it. I wish I could convince Holly Nuñez of that. She knows he has no history of violence, but she still won't believe me."

"It was someone else!" I made a motion halfway between a nod and a shrug and got up to go. "I didn't do it. Norman didn't do it."

"Even if that's true, it looks as if he's going to go to jail for the crime."

"For how long?"

"If we're lucky? Twenty years."

She braced both hands on the ironing board. "No," she whispered. "I hear people get out . . . much sooner than that."

"Not these days. Especially not with his record." Her white face went from porcelain to sickly pale. "He didn't tell you how long?" She managed to shake her head once: No. "I'm sorry, Mary," I told her.

And I was.

Chuckie was the social butterfly of our firm, sitting on the secretaries' desks and passing the time of day, taking out our associate and paralegal for a Welcome to Phalen & White drink at TJ's, dropping into my office to talk about a case or simply to shoot the breeze if he got bored. So he knew something was up when I walked into his office and closed the door behind me. "What's the matter?"

"I just thought I'd say hi."

"Good!" he said. "Take a load off your feet."

"You're trying to sound hearty and it's not working."

"Well, missy, you're trying to sound jaunty but you're not Irish and you never will be and it's not working. What's up?"

"It's Torkelson. Torkelson's girlfriend, actually. Mary, the one I told you about."

He turned off his oxygen machine. "Hate that damn hum it makes. Can't hear myself think with it on. Talk to me. I'm your partner."

"I'm losing sleep. My stomach . . . Don't ask."

"You keep having doubts that Norman actually did it?" I think Chuckie may have been surprised that I was still in such a twit over Norman's possible innocence, but he's got the gift smart trial lawyers have. The unreadable face. Not quite a poker face. It's an expression somewhere between mild amusement and serenity—easy, pleasant, giving away nothing.

"I can't be at peace with myself if I have to go to trial on this one."

"Look, over the years you've tried—what?—two or three cases where you were convinced one of your clients was innocent. I agree it's a big burden, but it's nothing you haven't been able to handle in the past."

"But this is different. What if Norman didn't do it but he *wants* to go to jail for it, to protect Mary? Sure, he'll go to trial, because what does he have to lose? I could conceivably get him off. But the more I look at the case against her, the more persuasive it is."

"Lay it out for me."

"Do you have time?"

"Lee, cut the gracious lady act. Give me your case against Mary."

So I went over all the Carolyn Knowles business, how Mary had robbed her, beat her up. "The details in Bobette's case appear to be the same. A robbery and attack on an older

260

woman who was a real threat, someone she was convinced Norman was going to marry."

"Was he?"

"I'm not sure. On one hand, I'm convinced he is genuinely, madly in love with Mary. On the other hand, he wants out of what he's doing—the con. But it's not as if he could get some other job to support them. A confidence man doesn't suddenly become a shoe salesman, does he? He doesn't say: Gee, I think I'll go get a master's in social work and begin a whole new career. And my guess is, Mary is too scattered or dumb or something to hold a regular job. The only way she could support Norman would be if she started turning tricks again. But that's why she loves him and is so full of gratitude: He gave her Tupperware."

"Any physical evidence that she was inside the house— beyond her own admission to you?"

"Fingerprints. That's how we found out about her record." Chuckie's mouth turned down; his expression turned sour. He didn't like the "we." Like me, he used Terry Salazar because he was a first-rate investigator, but he didn't approve of Terry's ways. "Fingerprints all over the house, including the site of the murder. And there's the stuff she bought with Bobette's credit cards. She showed us an expensive dress. She hadn't worn it yet; it may have still had the tag."

"Hmm," he said, and uncrossed his arms. "You're not there yet."

"Listen. In all his years of criminal activity, there was never one single instance of Norman Torkelson committing any act of violence. On the contrary: In all the witness reports I've read, the marks talk about what a gentleman he was, how sensitive. Now, Mary, on the other hand . . ."

"So she knocked somebody's head against the sidewalk a couple of times. That's not a pattern of violence. It's a single incident. Come on, Lee. You know the assistant in the case . . ."

"Holly Nuñez."

"Holly Nuñez isn't going to drop charges against Norman and haul this sweet, beautiful creature before the grand

261

jury and say: 'She once hit a rich old lady. You can hand up the indictment, ladies and gentlemen.' Forget it, Lee."

"I can't. I keep thinking of him spending the rest of his life in jail—"

"For a crime he may have committed."

"But what if he didn't?"

"Then at least he'll spend the rest of his life feeling that he performed a single act that was fine and brave."

"But is that justice?" I demanded. "Is it?"

"You're in the justice business now?"

"I'm a lawyer!"

And for the first time in all the years I'd known him, my partner laughed at me. Not with me. At me.

Sixteen

Students rarely live in luxury. Still, for a girl from a rich family, Lee had spent a considerable part of her adult life in wretched circumstances, beginning with the student-radical dump she shared with Flip Mullen. Her next year at Cornell, it was an apartment designated as off-campus housing but that, objectively, was a tenement so mouse-infested that when she and her roommates stopped talking or turned off their tape deck, they could hear a glee club of squeaks. She laughed about it, but in her heart the squalor frightened her and she wished someone would come and take care of her. No one did.

In her first year at law school, her dormitory room was clean enough; it even had a window overlooking Washington Square Park. But the woman next door had an illegal hot plate, and when she was not reading cases, she experimented with the cuisines of obscure ethnic groups, all of which had garlic as their principal ingredient. Complaining to the woman directly resulted in a raised middle finger and a fortnight of curried fish. The dean of student life promised a remedy but in the end did nothing, perhaps fearing that all the ethnic groups represented on the hot plate would take offense and, armed to the teeth, hold a sit-in on law school property.

So Lee pleaded with Leonard to let her get an apartment. Nothing fancy: There were walk-ups in the East Village that were really cheap. However, at that particular time he was feeling put upon by women. Sylvia had just redecorated the house; Robin was shoplifting and on four different occasions he had had to buy the silence of merchants; Greta was threatening to retire unless he converted to gas and bought her a stove with a salamander; and

Dolly Young, having hinted broadly, had been given a top-of-the-line Jaguar. So Leonard drew the line. Don't be ridiculous, he told Lee. The smell couldn't be *that* bad. Dad, you want to wish you didn't have a nose? she challenged him. Come on up, any hour, day or night. Leonard did not take her up on the invitation; instead he suggested that she learn to breathe through her mouth.

Ah, but she breathed easier as Mrs. Jasper Taylor. Upon their marriage, Leonard told them: Stay in the married students' dorm? How can I let my kids live in a dorm? On lower Fifth Avenue, he bought them a co-op in an upscale building, where the doormen called Lee "Madam." Although modest in size, the place had all the requisite luxuries New Yorkers ooh and ah over: parquet floors, twelve-foot ceilings, crown moldings. When Leonard and the real estate broker showed them inside for the first time and all but said "Voilà!" Lee waited for Jazz to protest: Sorry, very generous of you, but we can't accept this. What he said was: Hey, this is terrific! Thanks!

More than the fact of Hart's Hill, more than the way he pronounced "tomato," this was the moment she became cognizant of the class difference between herself and her husband. She was the daughter of nouveau riche parents who, now that she had married so well, were impatient to indulge her. But where she came from, the passing down of privilege was an option, not a governing principle.

In Jazz's world, it was the natural order of things. True, the Taylors were upset that they had eloped, upset that their son had married a girl whose forebears did not play golf, but not so upset that Ginger did not unload a mammoth chest of Victorian flatware monogrammed with a *T*, an embarrassment of old linens, and two Hepplewhite chairs. They themselves might have set up the young couple in an apartment, but they were, as Jazz revealed—with not a trace of shame or bitterness—dead broke. Fos's work for the U.S. Olympic Committee, although prestigious, paid just slightly more than nothing, and the cost of maintaining Hart's Hill, his accountant kept informing him, was eating away the capital he had inherited.

Still, as the firstborn son, Jazz was the beneficiary of his parents' connections. He had been admitted to prep school on the basis of a telephone call. When he decided that Colgate was the college for him, his father said a few words to one of his then law partners. The partner had a chat with President Barnett; the following week, the word came down that Jasper Taylor would be a member of Colgate's class of '71. Every summer job Jazz ever held was the result of someone lifting a phone on his behalf. So while the apartment Leonard bought was beyond the young man's expectations, the fact that his father-in-law was supporting him came as absolutely no surprise. It was the way things were supposed to be. That's what parents were for.

Accordingly, while Jazz was busy studying for the bar examination, Foster Taylor made a couple of phone calls; the men whom he called did likewise. Not long after, Jasper Taylor, Attorney-at-Law, was obliged to get what he and Lee called his Establishment Pig haircut; he had his long, glossy hair clipped to a reactionary three-quarters of an inch. Then he donned a pin-striped suit and dark red tie and began working down on Wall Street at the eminent law firm of Johnson, Bonadies and Eagle.

When Leonard heard how Foster had gotten Jazz a job, he was galvanized and told Lee he was going to call his own lawyer, Seymour Breitbart, of Breitbart, Wasserman, Mishkin, Schwartz and Oshinsky, to see if there was a spot for her. They represent half of Seventh Avenue, Leonard ballyhooed. Two-thirds. The best designers. If you worked there, you could walk right into any of the showrooms—even the French places: Lapidus, Patou—and tell them, "I'm a lawyer at Breitbart, Wasserman," and get to-the-trade prices.

But she told him not to bother. She knew that she did not require a phone call. While not at the top of her law school class, Lee was close enough. True, in 1974, old-line law firms still subjected women to a remarkable array of insults and inequities. And the fact was, they rarely broke out the champagne upon the hiring of a Jew. Even so, she still could have gotten a job at Johnson, Bonadies and Eagle, or at Matthison, Appleby, or, for that matter, at the National Hockey League. Strictly on the merits. But Lee's first job as a lawyer was at the place where she had been happier than ever before in her life: the Manhattan District Attorney's Office.

*   *   *

Her first case as an assistant was a third-degree sexual abuse. She prepared for it as if she were lead prosecutor in the Rape of the Sabines trial.

"Look," Jazz said, during her second week of preparation. "There's such a thing as working too hard. I know you want to run with this thing, but it's not the crime of the century."

Lee laughed. "It's not?" Frankly, she did not feel like laughing about her trial, although objectively she realized that the case of *People* v. *Robert Steven McCarthy* was not a blot on the landscape of American civilization. It was merely a misdemeanor, to wit, the feeling up of one Joyce-Ann Goldenson on a northbound number 6 subway shortly after it pulled out of the Fifty-ninth Street station, a charge Robert Steven McCarthy vigorously denied. Not the crime of the century, but her crime. Nevertheless, Lee laughed along with Jazz, because here it was, one of the rare Saturday nights she didn't have to be a complaint assistant and spend from eight o'clock to midnight in court. But she was still working. She should have been playing—with her husband. A good-looking husband, lean, well-muscled, lying right there beside her on the bed, naked.

"Why don't you just let the poor sucker go?" Jazz asked with a grin. For at least the millionth time, Lee marveled at his natural happiness. He instinctively looked at the bright side. That, combined with his fine looks and inborn kindness, guaranteed that he would always be Most Popular Boy. "Seriously. Why not?"

"You're kidding."

"No. Come on, babe, be serious. It was a feel, not a homicide."

"If you give me 'She should have been grateful' . . ."

"No! You know I'm not some stupid Neanderthal."

"You're a smart Neanderthal."

"Right! Do you know what she should have done? Hauled off and smacked him. What was so terrible that she had to pull the emergency cord and call the cops?"

"Because he pressed up against her side and started humping her. And then he pretended to get jostled and—what do you know!—his hand happened to get pushed up onto her left breast."

"That's a crime?" Jazz asked, reaching up and letting his hand drift over both Lee's breasts.

She tried to relax, get back into the mood. She should be the one to initiate the next round of lovemaking. Hadn't the last one, an hour before, been truly fine? So why didn't she want more? But instead of tossing aside her yellow legal pad and stretching out along Jazz's length, Lee found herself quoting the law: "'A person is guilty of sexual abuse in the third degree when he subjects another person to sexual contact without the latter's consent.'" Even as she said it, she could hear how prissy she sounded.

"I know, I know," Jazz said, getting into an even more comfortable position on the linen sheets his mother had given them. The sheets were monogrammed *KVT*. Another Taylor bride, although when Lee had asked Fos and Ginger who she was, neither had a clue.

"I feel bad, being preoccupied like this," Lee said, trying to sound tender. To feel tender. But she couldn't. Jazz knew perfectly well she had to work late. Yet nearly every night for the past two weeks he had thrown some temptation her way: a movie, a Sly and the Family Stone concert, dim sum in Chinatown, a Rangers game. And each time she said no, sorry, the length of her apology grew. Jazz seemed surprised. He would say, in his usual sunny manner: Just thought I'd ask.

But what was he doing, asking? Where did he get so much free time? That was what Lee wanted to ask him. More than half their classmates from NYU were doing what Jazz was: working as first-year associates at big law firms. None of them were going to Rangers games. Not a single one had time to see a movie during the week—not when they were working until nine or nine-thirty every night, then dragging themselves home, praying they had clean underwear for the next day, and flopping, exhausted, into bed. How come only Jazz had time to play? Was there some secret footnote to the law firm work ethic that exempted prep school boys from the institutional nine-to-nine grind?

"Don't feel bad," Jazz said good-naturedly. "It's just that you never let up. Your father called the other day, worried. No, more concerned. Said you had circles under your eyes the last two times he saw you."

"I don't have circles!"

"That's what I told him. It's just that he doesn't get it."

"Get what?"

"Your . . . you know. Your ambition. In his world, a woman

267

marries a professional and she quits her job—gladly—and devotes the rest of her life to picking out wallpaper."

"It's not that I'm ambitious. It's just that I love what I do."

"I know. Listen, stop apologizing. You're a perfect wife and a great fuck and I love you and you can go back to your work with a clear conscience. You knocked me out. I'd probably need a crane to get it up. This way, it's all your fault"—he grinned—"and I get to do exactly what I was dying to do, which is go to sleep." He blew her a kiss, slid under the covers, and turned over.

But what was he so tired from? Soon after the bar exam, when they both started working, she would call him at Johnson, Bonadies and Eagle in the early evening. Except he wasn't there. Uh, one of the other associates would say, I, uh, think he left already. Or (another might add, more charitably) maybe he's in the twenty-eighth-floor library. Not there at seven-thirty? She—making a third of what he was at her government job—was sitting in front of a mile-high pile of paper at her mud-green desk at seven-thirty, in the cubicle she shared with two other assistant D.A.'s, both of whom were also hard at work. Hesitantly those first few weeks, not wanting to embarrass him, she would call the apartment, and Jazz would answer: Hi! He was always in a bright mood, ready to chat. How's crime paying? he would ask.

Lee was so afraid for him. How could he just pick up and leave his office? Wasn't he terrified of being fired? But he didn't sound terrified: How did it go in court today, babe? Nice and easy. She'd chitchat for a minute or two, not wanting to seem as if she had something better to do than talk to her husband of eleven months. But the fact was, she had. Work. Or if work wasn't better than Jazz—and it wasn't, she assured herself—it was at least necessary. The first few years of being a lawyer were all about paying your dues.

Well, her first payment was *People v. Robert Steven McCarthy* and she was going to get the little son-of-a-bitch for groping Joyce-Ann on the IRT.

It wasn't going to be easy. Robert gave a great impression; he had the bantamweight charm of a Mickey Rooney combined with an endearing deep, dumb voice—a little like Smokey the Bear's. Joyce-Ann, on the other hand, came across like one of Freud's case studies in hysteria. She was so tense she did not speak so much as yelp, so tense that when being questioned about her allegations, she crossed her arms over her chest and rocked her breasts as if they were foundlings. I think she's going to make a lousy impression, Lee told the assistant supposedly supervising her trial, a man who had been a lawyer a year longer than she had. Do your best, he told her, not looking up from the lab analysis he was reading. Lee had a feeling that if he did look up, he would have no idea who she was.

But he did soon enough. Lee won *People v. Robert Steven McCarthy*, the case everyone who thought about it—and there were not many—thought was a real loser. She did so the way all good trial lawyers do, with thorough preparation and natural talent. Lee's gift was not for podium-pounding harangues or withering cross-examination, but for credibility. The very directness that had so often alienated her family worked in the courtroom. She did her best with what she had: intelligence, intuition, and common sense. If Joyce-Ann was tense, make her feel comfortable—or at least as close to comfortable as a Manhattan hysteric can feel. Lee spoke to her in a gentle voice and spent patient hours going over her testimony, until Joyce-Ann did not cringe at the word "erection." True, she did flinch a bit, but Lee decided rightly that the jury would find this understandable, even laudatory.

And if Robert sounded dopey like Smokey, it was just common sense to try and trip him up on some complicated question. So Lee probed: "You say you did not rub yourself against Ms. Goldenson that day. If you touched her at all, it was simply because you were jostled and fell against her. So then how can you explain your hand reaching around and squeezing her left breast?" I *didn't* squeeze it, he insisted, as Lee knew he would. "Well," she went on, "all right. You just touched it then." Right, the defendant agreed, and he agreed to her next question as well, that yes, he did in fact remember touching her left breast, but it was an accident, definitely not a squeeze. And then Lee (having rehearsed the scenario at least ten times with a crouching Jazz playing the much shorter Robert) asked him to come off the stand and demonstrate how it happened. Pretend I'm Joyce-Ann Goldenson, Lee suggested. Robert's lawyer objected. The judge overruled. Lee said: Okay, you grabbed for the subway pole in your right hand. That's right, make believe you're holding the pole. Now, if you were facing the direction both you and the complainant agreed you were facing . . . She positioned herself in front of him. Were you like this? she asked. Yes, he conceded. Then without actually touching me, show me how when you were jostled you came to rub up against Ms. Goldenson's side. And while you're at it, how your hand and Ms. Goldenson's breast came into contact.

The jury was out for just thirty-five minutes. When they returned with a guilty verdict, the first thing Lee did was race back to her desk and call Jazz. Fantastic! he'd exclaimed, and she could tell by his voice that he was truly thrilled for her. Brilliant! I mean it, Lee. All the courtroom stories are about great defense lawyers. Ever think of that? They're going to have to start a whole new category for you: Genius D.A.'s.

The truth was that Lee was good, quite good. But not a genius. There were two real geniuses in the District Attorney's Office. One was a bland-looking man five years older than she, who tried homicide cases. He was half-Polish, half-German, born in a cold-water flat on East Eighty-seventh Street, out of Brooklyn Law School. His heart was so malleable it could assume the shape of any or all the jurors' hearts. He barely needed an opening statement: That great heart of his told them all they had to know. Whenever she had time, Lee sat in on his trials. At the beginning she had hoped to learn something: the way he related to the jury or handled cross or how he spoke to the judge. All she learned was that whatever it was he had, she did not.

But the following year, the other office genius, Melanie Tucker, the deputy chief of the Supreme Court bureau, had a great deal to teach her. "You ought to use your femininity more."

"*What?*" Lee asked, convinced she had not heard right. True, Melanie herself often seemed as if she had been sucked up by a cyclone from the tea party she had been hostessing and plunked down in the D.A.'s Office. A dainty perfumed handkerchief always peeked out of one of her modest long sleeves. Melanie was known as a genius strategist, the greatest teacher of advocacy ever. Lee, however, was appalled. This was 1975! The very idea of using

270

feminine wiles to achieve a goal was disgraceful. "Use my *what?*"

"Your femininity," Melanie replied. She sounded so genteel that she should have been sitting before a silver tea service, offering clotted cream and marmalade, not at a desk with a stack of crime scene photos of a victim shot in the nose at close range. Her desk was a great and clumsy gray metal affair, but the photos were arrayed in a delicate fan shape, and all her papers were in folders on either side of a cream-colored blotter set in a tan leather holder. "The problem with women trial lawyers is this: They try to be men." She gestured to Lee to be seated, a gracious roll of the wrist.

"I'm not trying to be a man," Lee said, thinking back to the day before, her second trial in the Supreme Court unit. Simple. A one-witness robbery. Where could she have acted mannishly? A bodega owner in East Harlem claimed the defendant held a gun on him and then ran out with the three hundred dollars from the cash register and a carton of Camels. "Are you talking about the Suarez case?" she asked.

"I am." Melanie picked up a petal that had fallen from the single white rose she always kept in a bud vase on her desk and, with delicacy, sniffed it. She had gone to Radcliffe.

"But I won!" Lee exclaimed. "The jury came back about four-thirty."

"I know."

"So where was I mannish?"

Lee really didn't want to hear Melanie's answer. She dreaded it. It would be something humiliating—like telling her she should use lip wax because juror number eight seemed to be staring at the area directly under her nose. And indeed, he had, all during her summation. Or the answer could be something more profound—like she was acting so masculine that people would think her wedding ring was a phony.

Sometimes she actually felt like the man of the house, coming home late, neck stiff, muscles sore, bones aching, only to find that Jazz had prepared a big dinner. Why? They could have gotten a sandwich from the deli. He could have been working as late as she was. He should have been. Jazz said everything was fine. What was she worried about? And in truth, he had not been fired.

But she had seen with her own eyes, at his law firm's outing the previous June, how the partners did not take him seriously. Hello! they would call to him, a little too heartily, without stopping to make conversation. Jazz didn't seem to care, though, or even notice. Boring, was all he could say about the partners. Workaholics, he remarked of his fellow associates. Not me. So he left the office while others still had three or four hours more work, while Lee herself still had three or four hours. He came back to the apartment, watched the news, listened to the radio, cleaned, did the laundry. And cooked. Then he showered to be fresh when she came home. Well, this was the wave of the future; that's what all the articles on the New Feminism told her. Forget sex roles. Be what you want to be. And if you have a husband willing to take on household responsibilities, then be grateful and give him a great big kiss as he hands you your pipe and slippers.

"I didn't say you were *mannish*," Melanie explained. "I said you are using tactics that are associated with men. Yelling, for instance."

"When was I yelling?"

"During most of your summation." She rubbed the rose petal between her thumb and forefinger.

"I wasn't yelling," Lee retorted. "I was trying to sound strong."

"But your talent is for being direct, down-to-earth. You're likable. I admit I was in and out of the courtroom, but I must have seen about an hour of the trial. You were very easy to take. You asked a question—a well-thought-out question—and you knew just what to do with the answer. You were polite to witnesses, to the judge, to Suarez's idiot lawyer. When you made an objection, your voice was firm but under control. Excellent."

"Thank you."

"But you almost blew it during summation."

"I wanted to be forceful."

"Be forceful for Lee White, then. You were forceful for some hairy-chested Italian guy out of St. John's. Sweeping gestures. Big voice. They could have heard you in Bronx Supreme. And that banging on the podium!" Melanie let the petal drift from her fingers. Then she crashed her fist on her desk. "Does that seem natural?"

272

"No, but I'm not like you," Lee explained, trying not to stare at the lace hem of Melanie's handkerchief.

"Granted. But you are not a stevedore either. You seem to be a bright, energetic young woman from . . . Where?"

"Long Island."

"Do they bang podia on Long Island?"

"It's not a local custom," Lee admitted

"And the women there: Do they speak forcefully and directly? Or do they shout?"

"They don't shout," Lee admitted.

"If you came from a long line of female shouters, it might be another story. I assume you do not?"

"I had one grandmother who was in the Yiddish theater. She had a healthy set of lungs, but no, I don't think she shouted."

"Nor do you."

"Right."

"You see, juries know that about you," Melanie said, looking at her short but perfectly buffed nails. "They watch you. During your opening. Walking up to the sidebar for conferences. Taking out a Life Saver during his lawyer's cross of the transit cop. You, the judge, the defense lawyers . . . All of you represent the law to them. Justice. For many of them, this trial will be one of the most memorable events of their lives. So they are riveted on you and everything you do."

"Sorry about the Life Saver."

"Perfectly all right. The jury understands reaching into a pocket or handbag surreptitiously and popping a Life Saver into a dry mouth. It also reinforces what they already know about you: a nice, normal person. A young woman from Long Island who was probably brought up *not* to shout."

"But this is a *trial*. I'm a prosecutor!"

"This is a trial, and more than anything, they have to believe you. During your summation, several jurors were sitting back and going: Huh? What's going on here? What's she yelling about? This isn't the assistant D.A. we've come to know and like. This is someone emoting. Being false. Can we trust her? Were we wrong about her being so nice?"

"But I won," Lee argued.

"Yes, but look what you had going for you. The bodega owner was a great witness. And the defendant looked like the punk he is; he didn't dare testify. The jury was out almost a full day. They shouldn't have taken longer than a couple of hours. That means you almost lost them."

"I didn't realize . . . I thought because they were out so long, I had done a great job."

"A good job. The summation . . . well, you made them doubt *you* and therefore they doubted your case. But as you say, Lee, you did win it. Congratulations."

The Whites and the Taylors got along amazingly well. That was because all four of them—Leonard, Sylvia, Foster, and Ginger—had good manners. If they hadn't, Lee and Jazz's third anniversary celebration at the Whites' might have ended with words, or even a "Well, I *never!*" followed by a slammed door. Each set of parents despised the other individually and collectively.

Sylvia stood by the Frank Lloyd Wright-style chrome and glass bar where Leonard was pouring drinks and whispered in a not very *sotto voce* about Ginger's outfit: "It's a slap in the face! Baggy cotton pants and an old sweater, like she was going out to mow her lawn . . . which would be nice for a change."

"She probably thought it was casual," Leonard replied. "Sunday afternoon, just to celebrate the kids' anniversary."

But Sylvia wasn't having any: "It's either a deliberate smack in the face or she's the dumbest of the dumb goys, which—believe you me—is pretty dumb."

At that same instant, Ginger was staring at the food on the dining room table—a turkey that looked as if it had been designed by Ralph Lauren, a glistening glazed ham, a jewel of a cranberry mold, a cornucopia of baby vegetables, a cheese platter that would cause the American Dairy Association to shout Hallelujah—and Sylvia's triumph, which she had ordered two months earlier: gingerbread models of the Whites' house and Hart's Hill. Ginger murmured to her husband in a voice accustomed to summoning dogs from several acres away: "Who does she think is coming for dinner? The whole Israeli army?"

"Not with that ham," Fos countered. "Anyway, it's just us."

"I hate to say it, but it's true what they say about them: They know the price of everything and the value of nothing. They *wanted* us to figure how much it cost. Have you ever *seen* such a display?"

Since both mothers were talking at the same moment, they did not hear each other. The fathers kept their feelings to themselves, although Leonard, once enamored of Foster Taylor, then respectful, had been shaken to his core when Fos asked him for rye and ginger ale. Rye and ginger ale! A 1940s low-class woman's drink. Or was Fos kidding? Was it some Rolling Hills Country Club in-joke, where you ask for rye and ginger ale and everybody hoots with laughter and the bartender hands you an Absolut on the rocks with a wedge of lime. Leonard had tried an experimental chuckle when Fos asked for the drink, but there had been no corresponding laugh back.

Foster, in worn corduroys and a cotton turtleneck—which covered about a third of his sagging pelican chin—couldn't think of a thing to say to his in-law, this slim, platinum-at-the-temples man mixing drinks and wearing a double-breasted nipped-waist suit and one of those dime-thin gold watches . . . on a Sunday! Who the hell gets dressed up like that in his own house? Can you talk about the Giants with a guy like that? Politics? There was no doubt in Foster's mind that Leonard was a knee-jerk Democrat, and he'd wind up puking if he had to listen to him go on about liberal crap, like how Gerald Ford deserved to lose and how that liver-lipped cracker Carter was so great.

The elder Taylors were perched on the edge of one of Sylvia's decorating epiphanies, a leather and chrome daybed that sat, plunk, right in the middle of the Whites' living room. They were sipping their drinks, tiny bird sips, as if waiting for a moment when the Whites would turn away and they could bolt.

The Whites, standing by the bar, appeared almost paralyzed, their lips barely able to move. Lee assumed her mother was saying: Let's serve dinner now, and her father was replying angrily: It's only three o'clock. We can't serve until four-thirty—at the earliest. How the hell could you ask them to come at two for a four-thirty supper?

"I don't know," Jazz said to Lee, with that irreverent, irresistible, and decidedly sexual half smile she loved. "Doesn't look promising, does it?"

"God knows why. Two Fun Couples like them, they should be whooping it up."

"What's so amusing, you two?" Ginger called out so cheerfully it was clear she was desperate.

"What's so amusing?" Kent echoed, sounding a sour note. His parents had stuck him with Lee's sister, who was trying too hard to find something interesting for him to do. He was tired of drawing pictures of his family for her and making Play-Doh out of flour and water and salt. It *wasn't* Play-Doh, and he'd told her he was too old for Play-Doh, and she hadn't listened to him. He wanted to be with Lee and Jazz. He wanted to eat. There it was, all set out on the table and they wouldn't let him even go near it.

"You two look happy!" said Robin, using her ebullient voice. After six months in rehabilitation, she had returned to Shorehaven for four-times-a-week therapy and a volunteer job at a day care center. She was trying very hard to show the Taylors a good time and, while she was at it, to show she was not a thieving junkie. She was aware that was her reputation around town, a reputation—she had learned to own up to in group—she had earned. But it was exhausting having to act so animated and to keep Kent amused.

Jazz and Lee waved her over. As Lee knew he would, Kent leaped up and came along. "Hi!" he said. He put his arm around her, laid his head on her shoulder, and heaved a satisfied sigh.

"Hi!" Lee smoothed his hair back from his forehead. Too shaggy again. Deciding not to ask herself why her mother-in-law could spend hours every day grooming her dogs but couldn't take the only child she had left at home for a haircut once every six months, Lee made a mental note to take him to the barber the following weekend.

"Hi!" Kent said again.

"Hi!" She turned to Robin. "I know this isn't exactly scintillating for you. You're being wonderful."

"Stop it! Wonderful is having you guys here in the house. I mean, Mom and Dad have been great—especially considering how I made their lives a living hell. But they're so nervous with me. If I'm not constantly smiling, they're nervous wrecks."

Lee reached out and put her other arm around her sister. Physically, Robin appeared more fragile than ever. Her dark-blonde hair was swept straight back from her forehead and temples,

276

accentuating the heart shape of her face with its pointed chin. She would have been beautiful or close to it—thin as a whisper, with whiter-than-white skin and eyes the color of an overcast sky—but the drugs she had taken for so many years had taken their toll. She had dreadful dental problems. To hide her unattractive teeth and bad gums, she puffed out her lips. While this made her mouth pretty and pouty in repose, when she spoke it looked as if she were imitating a fish.

Jazz stared at the sisters and, as people invariably did, marveled at their differences. Forget that they seemed to have come from separate families: They might have belonged to separate races. Although the same height, Lee was sturdy, with strong shoulders and hips verging on generosity. Her hair was thick and chestnut brown, her skin golden. In her walks through Greenwich Village, tourists would stop her and ask directions in French, Spanish, Italian, or Greek, believing she was one of their own. "The two of you . . ." he said, shaking his head in amazement.

"Night and day," Robin said.

"Rich and poor," Lee added.

"Black and white," Robin continued.

"Christian and Jew," Jazz chimed in. As if on cue, the sisters looked from Fos and Ginger to Leonard and Sylvia—and began to laugh. It was only then that Jazz could see the resemblance: heads leaning to the right at the precise same angle, cheeks red and shiny. They wiped tears of laughter from their eyes at the same instant with the exact same motion, an outward flick with their middle fingers.

"What's so funny?" Ginger asked too eagerly. She sounded beyond desperate now, so with Robin and Kent in tow, Lee hurried over to her in-laws to try and make them think they were having fun. This was no simple job. She became a jurisprudential Scheherazade, regaling them with one whimsical courtroom tale after another. Finally, after three-quarters of an hour, she succeeded. Sylvia had joined them in good-natured chuckling, and then Fos took the floor, telling horror stories of pushy parents of would-be Olympic competitors. It was only then that Lee looked around for Jazz and found him gone.

"In the den with Daddy," Robin informed her. Lee pictured Jazz and her father watching football, her father mimicking Jazz's

"Yeah!" and "Asshole!" after various plays. Her father admired men who admired sports, and though he himself knew little and cared nothing about athletics, she was aware he was shamed by this defect in himself. Still, after another hour, Lee was astounded at her father's tenacity. True, she realized Leonard idolized everything about Jazz, from his Platonic ideal of a nose to the way he said thank you to busboys in restaurants when they refilled his water glass. Nevertheless, she wondered how Leonard could last through so much football. Of course, she admitted to herself, she could be wrong; there might be a documentary on Channel 13 on the history of the mink stole.

The two men came out moments later in high spirits, Leonard calling to Sylvia that he was starved and Jazz putting up his fists for a round of mock boxing with Kent. Sylvia whipped yards of Saran off the spread on the table. Leonard uncorked two bottles of wine Lee sensed were embarrassingly expensive, and the Whites and the Taylors dug into the buffet as if they had spent years in caloric deprivation.

"Mmm! Great turkey," Ginger said.

"Good vino, Len," Fos remarked.

Everyone, even Robin, had at least two portions of everything and at the end, they all applauded as Sylvia cut the gingerbread White house into slices.

"Yum!" said Fos.

"I can't believe something that looks so good can taste so delish!" Ginger remarked.

Sylvia insisted the Taylors take home the model of Hart's Hill. They made a brief, bogus protest, grabbed the cake, and, with an overenthusiastic chorus of "Thank you!" and ecumenical "Happy holidays!" they rushed out the door, forgetting Kent.

"Don't worry," Jazz assured Lee as she made for the door to call after them. "They know he's in good hands. I'll drop him off later. Sit down." He glanced over at Leonard who, as if by design, was sitting back expansively on one of Sylvia's newly acquired Corbusier love-seats, his arm resting on the back, legs crossed in leisurely *Gentleman's Quarterly* style. Jazz led Lee to the matching love seat, across from his father-in-law's. Leonard, meantime, patted the spot beside his own, inviting Sylvia to sit. When she took no notice, preoccupied as she was with watching Greta clear the table, he called out: "Sylvia! Over here. Sit down. We have something to tell you."

Lee interpreted the "you" as meaning her mother, so she snuggled against Jazz, her cheek enjoying the incredible softness of the vicuña sweater Sylvia and Leonard had given him the previous Christmas. She half closed her eyes, the better to luxuriate in the blended scents of Woolite and Jazz's own virile odor. But then she opened them. He was not circling his arm around her in their customary marital embrace. No, he looked casual, legs stretched out before him, crossed at the ankles, but his torso remained erect, and the arm that always crooked so comfortably around her stayed on the back of the love seat. She sat straight up.

Her father cleared his throat, then Jazz his, even louder. Deep, manly sounds. But then Leonard met Jazz's eye, and the next sounds out of them were boyish chuckles. Lee couldn't be sure. Were they We've Got a Secret chuckles or Bad Boy sniggers? Had they planned something? A surprise New Year's Eve black-tie dinner at some four-star restaurant? God forbid, she thought, having to ring in the bicentennial year with her parents and Robin over mountains of shaved truffles and oversolicitous waiters instead of over a six-foot hero and Chianti with their friends. Or worse, had her father gotten Jazz involved in planning a lavish vacation the five of them could share in some exorbitant tropical paradise? She wished she could be certain that Jazz's increasing closeness with her father—the twice-weekly lunches, the frequent exchange of jokey notes accompanied with *Wall Street Journal* or *Forbes* clippings—arose out of Jazz's inability to hurt anyone's feelings and not from any commonality of interests.

"Lee," Jazz began. But then he stopped and looked to Leonard. "Honey," her father said. Out of the corner of her eye, Lee saw Robin sitting Indian-style on the daybed with Kent, folding the *Times* into hat shapes, straining to hear what was being said. "Jazz and I have been talking," Leonard said. Jazz nodded, as if to quell any doubts that this was the truth. "We've come to a decision." For some reason, Lee suddenly remembered what Melanie Tucker had been saying when they had a drink a few weeks earlier, about never giving the other side any help in putting a knife in your back: I've seen too many women lawyers smiling supportively or murmuring comforting, maternal uh-huhs. Don't get caught in that trap. Just sit there with a neutral expression and let them get out the bad news as best they can. Sometimes they'll trip themselves up. "It affects all of us," her father was saying. This is crazy, Lee thought, my thinking like this. I'm not in court. I'm with my family. But her face could not move itself out of its frozen neutrality.

"What?" Sylvia demanded. "*What* is going on?" Her cajoling was so girlish it demanded a ruffled petticoat and a hair bow, not the sleek black velvet condom of an at-home dress she was wearing. "Come on. *Please*. I can't stand secrets."

Both men ignored her. Their eyes were on Lee. "Babe," Jazz said, "don't react. Just listen." An entirely unnecessary statement, since Lee was sitting as unyielding as a petrified tree. "This is going to be great for all of us."

"I can't take the tension!" Sylvia protested. "Pretty please!"

"This is the story, honey," Leonard said to Lee, ignoring his wife. "You know what's been happening with Le Fourreur. Can I say it? Can I brag? An unqualified success. A success beyond my wildest dreams." When his satisfied smile did not elicit the same from Lee, he looked across the huge block of pink-veined marble that was the coffee table and winked at Jazz, bolstering and boyish. Lee did not have to look to know her husband was winking back.

"You men!" Sylvia declared. "Tell us!"

"Success brings rewards, enormous rewards, but it brings problems too. Dealing with top-of-the-line designers who have armies—I'm serious—of advisers. Dealing with suppliers, with foreign governments, for God's sake. Do I have to tell you who the number one importer of Russian golden sable into this country is? I mean, I should have my own embassy in Moscow."

Jazz let out a deep breath, reluctant to join the conversation, but he realized Leonard had stopped and was waiting for him. "You know how I've been trying to help," he told Lee. "Serving as a sounding board, really, so your dad can check out what his lawyers have been telling him. And in general, trying to be there for him." Lee was close enough to smell sweat-drenched vicuña. "But this is the thing: We talked. We went out to lunch. You know. Got to know each other."

"More than father-in-law and son-in-law," Leonard interjected. "More like peers."

"Peers," Leonard echoed. "And friends, I hope."

"Friends," Jazz said, as if it could not be otherwise. "And besides that, I realized one thing. No. Two things. One, I was able to help your father."

"It was incredible!" Leonard said. "I had a whole law firm working for me. You wouldn't believe the fees they were charging. And what was I getting? A lot of 'On one hand, but on the other hand.' No one could make a decision. Until Jazz. He'd say: 'This is what I think you ought to do. Here are the pluses. And so you can reach a balanced decision, here are the minuses as well.'"

At that moment, Lee regretted being a lawyer, because she understood what was going on: What Jazz was telling her father was no different from what Breitbart, Wasserman, Mishkin, Schwartz and Oshinsky was telling him. But she kept stone-faced and stony silent. Because she thought she knew what was coming next—and she was right.

"It wasn't just that I liked helping your father," Jazz continued. "You know, being useful to him. I found out that all the times I was working with him, I was having fun. I mean, sometimes we'd have lunch uptown and then I'd go back to the salon with him and look at whatever needed looking at, and it was *fun*. Challenging. Interesting." (Naturally, Jazz did not mention, then or ever, that it had taken him about twenty minutes in Leonard's mahogany-paneled office to realize that his father-in-law and Dolly Young were longtime paramours, a state of affairs Leonard confessed to him anyway, at their next lunch.) "But then I found out something else. That when I was finished and had to go back to the office, I was . . . well, I felt really, really low."

"I sensed it," Leonard went on. Listening, Lee was somehow reminded of the oft-repeated stories married couples tell of how they met and fell in love. "And I thought about it. I mean, heavy thinking. I knew how much Jazz liked working with me, and it goes without saying that I was getting more and more . . . well, dependent is not too strong a word. Dependent on him. His advice was always great. And whoever I introduced him to at the place: my insurance man, the employees, the customers—my God, the customers!—they were crazy about him. So . . ."

281

"So . . . your father made me an offer, Lee."

They waited for her to ask what it was. When she didn't, Leonard finally said: "I offered him the presidency of Le Fourreur."

Sylvia clapped her hands together with joy, but she bit her lip. "What about you?" she asked her husband.

"I'll be chairman of the board," he said proudly. "And founder. I'll do the buying of skins. I'll deal with the designers. Sell to customers who need special handling. Work on bringing in bigger names. But Jazz is going to take over running the show."

Lee sensed she should be angry, but she felt nothing. Nothing. No matter that the term "absolute zero" had a scientific meaning; that is what she felt. "You're going to leave Johnson, Bonadies?" she asked.

"Yes. Of course." Then Jazz added: "I already told them."

"You already told them?"

"You *know* I wasn't happy there."

"I asked you over and over again whether you were happy there, whether you would be better off someplace else, and you said—" She cut herself off because she realized there was no point in going on. Jazz was leaving the law. Unlike the five previous generations of Taylor men, he did not have the stuff. And there was another reason for her not going on. As any smart corporate wife knows, it is counterproductive to belittle one's husband in front of his boss.

The following year, the two hundredth anniversary of the birth of the nation, Lee successfully prosecuted an organized-crime figure on kidnapping and assault charges, shut down a major heroin wholesaler by going after him—nine times in four months—for building code violations, and convinced a notoriously lenient judge to sentence a pimp to the maximum seven years for the vehicular assault of a fifteen-year-old prostitute. As a reward for her achievements, she became part of the District Attorney's elite group, the lawyers who got to try homicide cases. The D.A. himself told her she not only was a natural in court; she had great judgment out of court.

True. Perhaps it had to do with growing up within Leonard and Sylvia's house. Whatever, Lee White had developed what the streetwise refer to as a built-in bullshit detector. Thus she was able to take the measure of her colleagues, judges, police, and others in the criminal justice system with a fair degree of accuracy. Her passionate soul—the part of her that could be captured at Dante's Pizza by Jasper Taylor, or that thrilled with anticipation and pride each morning as she walked through the hideously ugly D.A.'s Office at 100 Centre Street—did not get in her way at all. Rather, it helped. It kept her from becoming cynical; it kept her believing her efforts were, truly, on behalf of the People.

Her work was painful at times, all the more so because Jazz's was now so . . . well, the only word that came to her mind was "frivolous." Here was someone with the best education money could buy, and he was now spending his days taking department store executives out to long, extravagant lunches, cajoling them to carry Le Fourreur's exclusive sheared beaver ski jackets. Or poring over contracts with chinchilla ranchers. But she had to admit, he was happier than ever. His normal good cheer had given way to exuberance, now that he was liberated from what he thought was his life sentence at Johnson, Bonadies and Eagle. He loved his new job, loved his huge salary, loved being loved— adored, actually—by everyone from his father-in-law to the wealthy customers to the young man who swept fur scraps in the back room. He loved the leisure he now had. He took a wine appreciation course. He bought two seats at center court for Knicks games and a box for the Rangers. He arranged for their vacations, bought their theater and concert tickets, and began to keep up with art gallery openings. And he seemed to love Lee all the more for being the means by which he had secured everything he had ever dreamed of.

So with what little energy she had to spare, she took pains to hide her disapproval of his life. In fairness, if she did not love Jazz's choice, she still loved Jazz. It wasn't hard: In his custom-made suits, his gleaming brown hair growing fashionably long once more, he had gone from being good-looking to being devil-ishly handsome. Coming home from the D.A.'s, she was some-times startled to discover the beauty of the man waiting for her. He remained an ardent and attentive lover. If he was not particularly inventive, at least he now had the time to read, and he bought books and videotapes and studied the arts and sciences of Eros so he might knock Lee's socks off. And when she was not in the mood—as she usually was not during the height of a homicide trial—he was the warmest and tenderest friend.

But her work was such a contrast to his. Unlike some of her male colleagues, Lee did not want a bubbly spouse to jolly her out of the black moods brought on by the horrors of the crimes she prosecuted. Rather than talk things out, and thus relive what she wanted to forget, she preferred to suffer in silence. There were nights, however, when she tiptoed out of bed, went into the bathroom, closed the door, and sobbed at the viciousness of what she had seen: tortured corpses, some of them women her age; photographs of children brutalized by the very people who were supposed to love them. Sometimes, though, she forced herself to remember. She would take a crime scene photo home with her to look at it last thing every night and first thing every morning while she was on trial—to remind her what she was fighting for. This isn't necessary, Jazz told her. It is, she said sadly. It is.

For the first half of 1976, his first six months with Le Fourreur, Jazz seemed content to live as they always had, albeit with better seats at sporting events. But by June, it was clear to Lee he wanted some changes made. Already drifting away from their classmates, he laid down the law on the matter of the Fourth of July: He absolutely did not want to go to a big, noisy keg party in someone's tiny apartment overlooking the Hudson River and watch fireworks. And he definitely did not want to trek to a mildewy house out in the Hamptons someone was renting for the month, to sleep in sleeping bags and get bagged on crappy Chablis. Okay, he was just twenty-six and maybe he was sounding like an old geezer but he was the president of a multimillion-dollar company. Not his, and—he was the first to admit it—he could never have done it on his own, and he didn't deserve it, but there it was. The fact: He was different from their old friends at law school and really didn't have that much in common with them anymore. At least, not enough to spend the Fourth of July of a lifetime with, the celebration he and Lee and the rest of America would always remember. Unless she really and truly *wanted* to go, and then of course he would, for her.

Lee did truly want to be with her law school pals, or with a group of assistant D.A.'s and cops who were planning a bash on Liberty Island, in the shadow of the Statue. But she knew Jazz now felt uncomfortable among lawyers. He saw himself through their eyes as a loser, a guy who couldn't cut it. Conspicuous by his comparative wealth. Made a target of gossip among their old classmates by his move out of the world of men and into the world of women—a move made more humiliating by his wife's success among the toughest of the tough guys.

They spent the Fourth with Leonard, Sylvia, Robin, the fur buyer from Lord & Taylor and a fashion writer from the *New York Times* and her whining husband and two sniveling children. Leonard hired a forty-foot sailboat and crew for the day at a stunning price, and they cruised along, watching the flotilla of tall ships and getting drunk on fresh salt air. That night, Greta made an all-American barbecue based on Sylvia's instructions for red and white food served on blue dishes. Lee did not have one moment of fun.

The following morning, Jazz drove her to the station for her train back into the city. She had a trial coming up, witnesses to prepare. Over and over she apologized for having to leave him, after she'd promised to take a few days off, stay out in Shorehaven, and play tennis at his folks' house.

"Don't apologize," Jazz told her as he pulled Leonard's Mercedes convertible into the parking lot. Even Lee thought he was being too tolerant. She had been the one who had made the big speech about having some balance in life, vowing she would take more time off. No more working on weekends, she had pledged. And if I don't get it done by eight or eight-thirty at night, it's not worth doing. Here she was, however, the only lawyer in America not on vacation, going back to Manhattan to interview a pickpocket, a chicken-hearted, mean-spirited liar who was her one eyewitness in what was going to be a miserable case to try.

"I can't *not* apologize," she said. "I feel terrible. But if I can't get this guy to tell a straight story, then there's no point bringing this to trial. So I'm sorry. And you're being absolutely wonderful about it."

"Thanks," Jazz said, a little absently.

"What's the matter?"

He glanced at his watch. "Your train is in two minutes. Better get going."

"Jazz . . ."

"We'll talk tonight. I'll come back in around seven or eight. Maybe you can break away, and we can go out for dinner."

"Fine," Lee said. The door handle was in her grasp, but she let it go. "What's up?"

"Your train—"

"Forget it. I'll get the next one." Naturally, her stomach responded to her easygoing offer by immediately going into a spasm. The cop, the witness, everybody waiting for her, looking at their watches. "What's bothering you, Jazz?"

"I love it out here."

"I know." She smiled, indulgently. "Especially in the summer. But you love the city, too. Eight million stories, eight million movies, the theater, the Knicks—"

"Please, Lee." He took her hand between his and held it tight. "I want to *live* here."

"What?"

"I've made the best of the city, but I'm not a city guy."

"But, Jazz, I can't. Not now. I can't live here and be an A.D.A. in Manhattan. I have to reside in the jurisdiction. You know—"

But he wasn't listening. Or perhaps he knew so well what her objections would be that he didn't have to hear them. "I'm so miserable in New York. I want to be able to come home at night and breathe air that doesn't stink and see trees that aren't stunted. I need a break from the workaday grind. I know you think I've got it easy compared to you—"

"No, not at all."

"—but believe me, I feel I have to prove my worth every single day. And I'm good, really good. But it takes a toll. Why can't we come out here—"

"Don't you think commuting would take a toll?"

"Millions of people do it every day. You get to read the paper, do some work; it goes by like that." He snapped his fingers. It made a loud sound and she sat up straighter. "Your dad and I even talked a little about getting a driver, take the pressure off. So we wouldn't have to cope with sitting behind the wheel in traffic, and wouldn't have to be dependent on the Long Island Rail Road's whims. It would be the best thing in the world for me. And also, it would mean we could be near our families. I know, I know how much of your folks you can tolerate. The same with me and mine. But at least you'd be near Robin, now that she's a human being. And Kent. I know you worry about him a lot, and it kills me too, the way my parents ignore him. We could be there for him." He lifted her hand to his lips and kissed it. "I know it would mean a sacrifice to you. Your job. But you know you can't do the work you're doing and have a family. Isn't that something you want?"

"But we're only twenty-six!"

"So?"

"Do we have to do this now?"

"When, then?" He let go of her hand. His voice took on a harsh, aggrieved edge she had never heard before. "Next year? Next decade? When will you have time for me?" She touched him on the shoulder, but he jerked away. "I've tried to support you in every way I can. But I need to know there's some mutuality at work, that I'm not the only one who gives and gives and gives."

"You think I'm crazy," Lee said to Melanie Tucker.

"Not at all," Melanie replied, rearranging her handkerchief in her cuff. "I think you're a fool."

"Oh," was all Lee could think to say.

They had deliberately chosen a deserted spot for dinner, a trendy place in TriBeCa where the chairs were made of rubber tubing. It was too expensive for cops and prosecutors. And at seven in the evening, it was far too early for the chic set who came for twenty-dollar variations on the sun-dried tomato.

"I don't see you rising to your own defense," Melanie observed.

"I'm too used to being the prosecutor. I'm cross-examining myself: How could you leave the best job in the world to be a furrier's wife on Long Island?"

"And your answer?"

"I have none." Lee moved an oily vegetable—on the menu it was called Sliced Sauteed Summer Squash in the Umbrian Manner—around her plate with a fork that resembled a hoe. "Well, maybe I'll find something in one of the law firms out there."

"That might be challenging," Melanie said in the upbeat manner of women who were girls in the fifties—with a rising lilt in a dead voice. A second later, she recovered; all she had learned since 1959 prevailed. "Personally, I don't think defending companies who corporately defecate in Long Island Sound will challenge you. But that isn't why I called you a fool."

Lee's fork pierced the squash. "All right? Why?"

"Because you are giving up everything you fought for and care about for a man."

"For a *marriage*."

"For a man who is eaten up by jealousy and for a marriage that—I'll understand if you never talk to me again—a marriage that will come to no good. Why move? You'll only want to come back. But then it will be too late."

Seventeen

I had watched Norman Torkelson go from being the Cary Grant of the Nassau County Correctional Center to being just another dirty-nailed, unshaven con. Now he was at the third step: exactly where anyone in his right mind would be in similar circumstances: depressed. Not suburban depressed, with the standard loss of appetite or sleep troubles, the sort of malaise a little Prozac, a little therapy, or a new girlfriend can cure. No, this was the big-time despondency of a guy who was going to spend the next couple of decades in hell and emerge, somewhere around age fifty-five, an old man.

"Norman," I said, "we've got a trial date set."

"Okay." Just a wisp of the word came out; the rest lay heavy inside him. Sitting across the Formica barrier from me, slumped, round-shouldered, his head hanging down, you couldn't tell what a big man he was. Norman was fading, as prisoners do, out of the land of the living. No matter how long I practiced, I couldn't get used to seeing this kind of suffering. I guess it was the absolute loneliness of it that got to me. Sure, I knew many of my clients had inflicted much worse pain than this on their victims. Norman himself, even if he hadn't killed Bobette, had destroyed enough women's lives to deserve eternity in the worst jail there was. Nevertheless, part of me wished I could reach through the opening in the barrier and pat his cheek—just to let him feel human warmth.

But what I said was: "I think we should talk about whether or not you're going to take the stand." I waited for him to nod or give some indication he was hearing me. He just sat there, sagging, lifeless, as if he were the homicide victim. So I went on. "The reasons for you not to testify are obvious. You have a long record. And the sort of crimes you've been accused and convicted of aren't particularly sympathetic." That was putting it mildly. The twelve jurors would probably be shouting "Whoopee!" and giving each other high fives two minutes into deliberation—after their unanimous guilty vote. "Other than Mary—who I don't think would do well under cross-examination—is there anyone who could serve as a character witness for you?"

"No," he breathed. I waited for him to add something about moving too often to form close relationships, but he didn't seem to care anymore. He was beyond making excuses.

"I've been debating with myself whether we should risk trying to use your record to our advantage. I'd put you on the stand, have you admit to everything, tell them everything bad you've ever done. All to make one point: You never laid a hand on anybody. Of course," I added, thinking out loud, "what Holly Nuñez is going to say is that there's a first time for everything, that something went wrong with Bobette—"

"I didn't kill her," Norman said softly. Then he lifted his head and said it again. Tears were flooding down his face.

"I understand," I said, wishing he would wipe them away, or at least sniffle. "You've maintained your innocence all along. But if you didn't kill her, who did? Every time I bring up Mary's name you get furious. So I've stopped bringing it up. I'll do my best for you, but I can't hold out too much hope. I'm sorry."

"I know you're doing all that can be done, given these circumstances." He lifted a shoulder and used it to dry one of his cheeks, then did the same with the other side.

"I appreciate your confidence."

"I want to tell you what really happened."

I realized Norman was prepared to tell me something big, something new. I got that strange, anticipatory feeling I experience at moments of great drama. My senses grew sharper: I could eavesdrop on every lawyer-client conversation, all the guards' gossip, in the visitors' room and not miss a word; read the entire "Visitors May Not Touch Inmates" sign, even the fine print; I could smell the menthol cough drop the lawyer three seats down was sucking. "I'm listening," I said.

"I know who killed Bobette," he said. I waited. I couldn't breathe. Then he whispered, "Mary," and began to cry again.

"Were you there when it happened?" I finally said. He shook his head slowly. Come on! I wanted to yell at him. Get a grip! *Talk* for God's sake! "No rush, Norman. Whenever you're ready."

"It was like I told you," he said at last. "I went out to buy the champagne. I told you that, didn't I? Like I always do. I leave and then come back. That calms their worst fear, that I am who I really am, that I'll take their money and leave town. So I went out, bought the champagne—"

"Do you remember where you bought it?"

"What? No, not the name of the store. But it was in a little shopping center about a mile away."

"You could tell me how to get there?" He nodded. "Do you think anyone there might remember you?"

"Maybe. Because of my height. And when I bought the champagne, it was expensive and the guy said something like 'This must be an important celebration.'" Norman started to cry again. No sobs this time, just a quiet dribble of tears. "I'm just telling you this because I . . . Who the hell knows? I can't stand having it inside me. But understand: you can't do anything about this. Even if you wanted to, what could be done? Even if I wanted to betray Mary—and I'm telling you, I don't—no one would believe me. Sure, her prints are there, but so are mine. And the marks on her neck. Even if I swore 'She did it,' they'd think I was full of it because of what I am." He swallowed. "I'm a con man. A professional liar. So what I'm saying is just for you."

"Go on," I said, trying to recall if the autopsy report mentioned anything about skin cells under Bobette's nails or any possible DNA evidence that would corroborate Norman's statement.

"Just for you," he repeated. "You're my lawyer. Anything

291

I say to you is confidential." He wiped the tears away, this time with his hands. "Anyhow, I got back and went into the house."

"You had a key?"

"No. I'd pushed the little gizmo on the side of the door so it wouldn't lock. The door was open. I went in. I remember, I was calling out, 'Bunny'—that was my nickname for her. 'Bunny, if you have two glasses, I have a bottle of champagne.' Except I never finished the sentence." He rubbed his chin. I could hear the rough scratch of his beard.

"She was dead?"

"Yes. I knew right away."

"And Mary?"

"Standing there. Hysterical. Trying to talk."

"What was she trying to say?"

"I'm sorry! I'm sorry!"

"To Bobette?"

"No, to me. I started saying, 'Why? Why?' But then I realized I had to get her out of there. I didn't know if she'd fought with Bobette and if there had been a ruckus someone could have heard. Even just her hysterics. She was getting louder and louder: If someone was passing by the house, or if for some reason the tenant came home . . . I *had* to move, so I grabbed her and pulled her out of the house."

"You didn't touch anything?"

He closed his eyes as if viewing the scene. "I bent over to see if there was a chance Bobette was still alive. Objectively, I knew she was dead. But I thought, well, maybe if the breathing was suppressed or something, I could call 911 and get out of there before they came. I may . . . I think I may have held her face in my hands." He shuddered. "Already, it was colder than a face should be. You know?"

"You didn't touch her neck?"

"I don't think so."

"Then what?"

"I took Mary by the arm and I pulled her toward the door."

"The front door?"

"Initially. But then—I couldn't believe this. She sticks her

292

hand in her pocketbook, one of those shoulder bags, and takes out a tissue and starts wiping the doorknob and the thing where you turn on the lights."

"The switch plate?"

"Right. I knew the more we did, the longer we stayed there, the more chance there'd be for leaving some trace. So I grabbed the tissue. I was going to use it to open the door, but then I realized it would be stupid for us to be seen walking out the front together. Mary's—you know—noticeable. I was already thinking I didn't want anyone to think in terms of the, uh, crime committed by a man with a woman. I wanted Mary completely out of the picture. So I led her out the back door. I used the tissue to open and close it."

"Then what?"

"Then I went toward the front. I took a quick look around. No one was there. So I got her into my car and we drove home."

I waited. What was I expecting to hear? We lived happily ever after? Norman did look better for having opened up, that much I noticed. The crying had stopped, and some color had returned to his face. Still, he seemed feeble, as if trying to get back his strength after a terrible illness.

"When did you talk to Mary?"

"When we got home. She was too hysterical in the car."

"What did she say?"

"That Bobette had come down and surprised her. Started shouting at her: 'Get out!' That's the one thing that sets Mary off. Shouting."

"It makes her violent?"

"No. Not with me, anyway. We've had a couple of fights, and I've raised my voice, and all that happens is she"—he swallowed hard at some sad memory—"falls apart. But I think if someone else is yelling . . . I mean, that incident in Maryland."

"That incident where she beat up Carolyn Knowles," I elaborated. "Brain concussion, a couple of cracked ribs, facial contusions."

"Yes."

"Did Mary and Bobette argue? Did Bobette know her connection with you?"

"I don't know. I don't think so. All Mary told me was about the yelling, that all of a sudden she was on a different planet or something. She didn't know what she was doing until . . ." His hand drifted up and softly touched his Adam's apple. "Until she looked down and saw the thing she was holding between her hands and shaking was Bobette's neck. I probably walked in a few minutes later."

"How long were you away when you went to get the champagne?" I asked.

"Fifteen, twenty minutes."

"You drove away. Mary probably went in right after you left. She surprised Bobette. Right? Strangled her. Bobette's strong, but so is Mary—taller, in much better shape. Did she have any bruises, by the way?"

"Bobette? I didn't notice any."

"No, Mary. Any signs of a struggle, of Bobette fighting back? Black-and-blue marks—"

"On her wrists," Norman admitted sorrowfully.

"So what happened next? You're back home. Is Mary still hysterical?"

"Close. I calmed her down a little. I kept saying: 'I know it's not your fault.'" I thought—as I often do when listening to accounts of my clients' lives—how pleasant it must be to receive such easy absolution. "Finally, she stopped crying," Norman continued. "I put her to bed, tried to give her a sleeping pill—"

"You have trouble sleeping? Or does she?"

Norman shook his head. "Neither of us. It's just some-times . . . Sometimes I slip a pill—a capsule I open up—into whatever the lady I'm working on is drinking. I mean, if she's staying up late and being boring and I want to get home. I always carry a couple in my wallet. Anyway, Mary is very antidrug and said no. So I sat with her until she dozed off."

"Then what?"

"Then . . . nothing."

"You stayed home? Watched TV?"

"No. I went out and drove around. Tried to think."

"How long were you gone?"

"I don't know. Hours. It was pretty early—around six-thirty, seven, at night—when I found Mary at Bobette's. But by the time I got back home it was already getting light."

"Where did you drive?"

"I don't remember. I know I wound up on the New York Thruway. Finally, I got so exhausted, I pulled off into one of those service areas, where the Dunkin' Donuts and Burger Kings are all in one building, and had some coffee. Then I turned around and came home."

"And then?"

"Nothing. I told her we had to get out of town. Not that they could trace me, but why hang around Long Island longer than necessary. I wanted to leave then, but Mary was so shaken—she kept falling apart, crying hysterically. Then she got a bad period. So I made the mistake of letting her rest. We were going to leave first thing Tuesday morning, like at five-thirty, and go somewhere warm. San Diego, I was thinking. Once we got out of New York, we'd ditch the car I was driving and buy a new one."

"You had the cash Bobette drew out of the bank?"

"Yes."

"You opened the envelopes the cash was in?" He nodded. I was relieved to see he wasn't lying; his fingerprints had been on the tape that had sealed the bank envelopes. "Where did you open them?"

"At Bobette's."

"How come?"

"Just to make sure she gave me what she said she would. I always do that. Hold up the envelope and make some little joke about can't wait to see the money that's going to change my life. Ninety-nine times out of a hundred, the lady will say: 'Open it.' Sometimes they're nervous about me. They go to the bank but only take out part of what they promised. But I always check. If I catch them, believe me, they're always ready to run back and get the rest."

I was feeling uneasy. Tales of masochistic women always make me uneasy, and unease makes me think of food. I had a little bag with a yogurt and a plastic spoon in my attaché case. Vanilla. I kept wishing I could open it up and gobble it down. "So, Norman," I said, trying very hard to forget the yogurt, "unless I can get you an acquittal or keep hanging juries until Holly Nuñez gets worn out, you're going to go to jail for a crime you didn't commit."

"Yes." His spine seemed to crumple, but he did not cry again.

I sat quietly for a minute and looked down at my hands, trying to assimilate everything Norman had told me and trying to forget I wanted to eat. My latest diet book said hunger pangs last only ten to twelve minutes. Think of something else: I noticed that I had chipped the nail on my right index finger, that I had what appeared to be a smudge of breakfast cottage cheese on my watchband, and that even under the harsh prison lights, I still did not have any brown age spots. By the time I looked back at him, I knew: "You're not telling me the whole story, Norman."

He didn't pretend to be stunned, and he didn't act as though I'd hurt him to the quick. "What do you think I didn't tell you?"

"Look, you and I seem to be playing poker now. So I'm not going to show you my hand. You tell me what you left out." It would be nice to say I knew precisely what he was holding back, but I didn't. I just had a strong sense that Bobette didn't simply surprise Mary, yell at her to get out, and then get strangled. It was too pointless. Yes, I know homicide often is pointless, to say nothing of stupid, but this story didn't quite add up to the usual senselessness.

"I think they must have had words."

"About what? You?" Norman nodded yes. "Somehow, Bobette found out that this intruder was connected to you?" When he didn't respond, I asked: "What were the words they had about?"

"Getting married," he muttered.

And then I was sure I knew. "You *were* going to marry Bobette, weren't you?"

"Yes," he said softly. "We got the license that day, before we went to the bank."

"If you were marrying her, why did you want the cash?"

"I just wanted it, free and clear. For all I knew, she could turn out to be a cheapskate. I mean, she kept saying she wanted me to take over everything for her so she could be— you know—a housewife. I'd oversee the bars, collect the rents and manage the properties. But I couldn't be sure. I figured if it turned out she wouldn't let me take over, I'd know in a couple of weeks. That way, I wouldn't have to hang around waiting for crumbs. I could leave and still have close to fifty thou."

"What were you planning on doing with Mary?"

"Nothing. I mean, we'd keep on like always. I'd be out all day, tell Bobette I was seeing to business. But I'd spend the whole day with Mary—and whatever nights I could. It wouldn't be ideal but . . ." He wrapped his arms around himself. "I needed to rest for a year or two. To put my life on hold. I love Mary with all my heart, but I couldn't keep running around the country doing what I was doing, like I was still a kid. Being World's Greatest Lover to a bunch of ladies who . . . forgive me, but who I didn't give a shit about. Setting up the Love Nest over and over in every damn new town. Wading through the responses to my personals ads. I had been doing it so long. There was no fun left. Maybe because I really was in love. That's the kicker, isn't it? I'm in love with Mary, in love for the first time in my life. So what do I do? Get ready to marry someone else."

"Did Mary know?"

"I told her the night before." He looked away and mumbled to the floor: "I guess that was a mistake."

"I guess so."

"But listen, I swore to her nothing would change. All it would mean was that for a while she'd have to spend the nights without me. But in terms of real time, I'd be with her *more* than ever before. And then, in a year or two, I'd start making it so tough on Bobette that she'd pay me big bucks just to get out. Then Mary and I could go someplace, and I'd never have to work the ladies again." His eyes grew filmy. "We could have had a beautiful life."

"Except Mary didn't see it that way."

"No. She didn't believe me when I told her I would always be true to her." Norman looked me right in the eye. "But I will be."

"You could've knocked me over with a feather!" Terry Salazar said the next morning. Terry's life is a series of brief but passionate romances with clichés; he meets a new one, hangs around awhile, then moves on to the next. He'd been getting knocked over by feathers for the past couple of months, and it was starting to irritate me. "There I was, in the county clerk's office, looking at this piece of paper that actually says that Bobette Frisch and Denton Wylie are okay to get married in New York State, and I'm thinking: Holy shit! Haul out the smelling salts! The guy told the truth for once in his life."

"All right," I said, swiveling back and forth in my desk chair. It's the sort of motion you see in the movies, big tycoons twirling from side to side, a phone in one hand, a cigar in the other. But it soothes me and helps me think when I'm feeling pressured. "This makes me so nervous. I hate it when I think a client is innocent. I mean, not guilty is different; that I can deal with. I *like* knowing someone has a real defense for the crime he's accused of, that I don't have to get overly creative. But actually innocent?" I shuddered. It was only part pretense.

"You think he's conning you, Lee?"

"How would I know? That's the whole point, isn't it?"

"Take me with you to see him. I'll let you know." Terry noticed I was looking on my desk for something to throw at him. "I'm not saying you're not smart. You are."

"Especially compared to present company."

Terry seemed to think I was engaging in banter, not truth telling, so he gave me his wink-grin combo. "But you're a *woman*," he insisted. "That's his specialty. Conning women."

"Stop it. I'm a criminal defense lawyer. I can't get through a day without someone trying to con me. Let's just dope this out." Terry looked agreeable. He loved long, meandering discussions—and why shouldn't he have, at his hourly rate? "Norman Torkelson used the name Denton Wylie with Bobette."

"Right," he said.

"Is there any possibility at all that there was a real Denton, that Norman is or was pulling some sort of scam involving a real person—or a dead person—that's beyond my ability to comprehend?"

"I can't see how. This Denton who applied for the marriage license gave his age as thirty-five, which is what Norman says he is. Now, objectively, Norman looks about thirty-five, doesn't he?"

"Somewhere around there," I agreed.

"And the lovely Bobette gave her real age: fifty-four. That is not your usual age difference: a dried-up old prune with a guy nineteen years younger, so already it sounds for real." Since by his standards I would be a dried-prune in nine years, I gave him a dirty look, which of course delighted him. "Also, there's the whole section of the marriage license application form that has to be filled in on former spouses. Bobette's is blank. Our pal Denton has one former." Terry consulted his little spiral notepad. "Lorinda Maddox Wylie in Westchester. Salem. It matches perfectly with his story about having a rich-bitch ex up in Westchester, except I checked. Lorinda—Maddox or Wylie or both—doesn't exist. The address he gave, White Horse Farm on Winding Way, doesn't exist. Winding Way doesn't even exist." Most investigators could have come up with this information, but it would take them two weeks. Terry had gotten it in a couple of hours, which was one of the reasons I put up with him. "You want me to bottom-line it, Lee?"

"Go ahead."

"Norman made Lorinda up. He made Denton Wylie up. So Denton Wylie does equal Norman Torkelson."

"Would you put money on that?" I asked him. "*Your* money?"

"Yeah." Terry took out his wallet. Instead of the five-dollar bill I expected, he counted out five twenties and slapped them on my desk. Then I was sure Norman Torkelson and Denton Wylie were one and the same.

* * *

I worked on some other cases the rest of the morning. Instead of going over to the Bar Association for lunch, I ordered in and went into Chuckie's office and watched my cooking shows on his TV. There was a French guy I was in love with—he got very passionate about using veal bones in chicken stock—but I had also taken a shine to an extroverted Chinese guy who was really cute with his cleaver. I was mulling over dinner, what to stew in a clay pot, when I realized I had one big fat ethical problem: What do you do if you believe a client is innocent but he is insisting on taking the rap for the guilty party and ordering you, his attorney, to keep quiet? Abide by lawyer-client confidentiality? Or figure that a larger principle is at stake—Justice—and that your first duty as an officer of the court is not to let an innocent man pay for a crime he didn't commit. Or try something sneaky. I called Holly Nuñez.

"Lee! Hi!" Now that a trial day was set and she was convinced she was going to nail Norman but good, her bubbliness knew no limits. "How *are* you? God, won't it be great to go out and have a drink together when all this is over?"

I admit I did stick my index finger into my mouth and made a gagging gesture, but I said: "I look forward to it. Speaking of the Torkelson case, I was wondering if you ever ran that other set of prints."

"We did!"

"Good!" I enthused back, thinking that if I actually did go to trial, I'd have to start hormone replacement therapy immediately. "What did you find?"

"They belong to a woman named"—I waited while she made noises with paper, pretending to look—"Marissa Shaw."

"The thing is, Holly, you're supposed to tell me about this."

"You beat me to the punch! I was going to call you this afternoon!" She read me all the stuff I already knew from Terry's investigation about the altercation in Maryland, with Mary as Marissa beating up Carolyn Knowles.

"Do you know who Marissa Shaw is?" I inquired.

300

"Do you have something to tell me?" Holly countered, with perky anticipation, as if I were about to impart some marvelous cheerleading secret.

So I told her that Mary/Marissa was a single dame. And what do you know, the man who bolted, the man whom Carolyn Knowles was set to marry, known as Arthur Berringer, was none other than six-foot-five Norman Torkelson. "Do you see a parallel, Holly?"

"Between what and what?" she asked.

I finished explaining twenty minutes later, and as I'd feared, it got me absolutely nowhere. She remained convinced Norman killed Bobette. The fact that he had a girlfriend who had once, as Holly put it, "blown her top" was of no interest to her. I urged her, then begged her, to at least interview Mary, but all she said was that she was "crazed, absolutely crazed" with work and couldn't find the time.

I put in a call to the chair of the Bar Association's Ethics Committee to sound him out about being able to tell Holly that Norman had admitted to me that Mary killed Bobette, but I had little hope on that score. He'd probably tell me to withdraw from the case and hint to Norman not to confide in his next lawyer. Even if he said to go ahead, you can talk, the chance that Holly would buy Norman's Mary-did-it confession was nil. And I knew the chance of my going over her head to the D.A., Woodleigh Huber, who not only was stupid, ambitious, and venal but couldn't stand me, was nil squared.

I left the office and picked up a cold bottle of Chardonnay and a corkscrew, then two cappuccinos. I figured one or the other would get me into Mary's apartment. Sure enough, the wine worked. "We don't have wineglasses. Just champagne glasses." She took out a couple of the old-style ones, the kind that are shaped like birdbaths. "I told Norman, we can't keep doing this forever, you know." She had just given herself a pedicure. The smell of polish permeated the room. A rolled-up sheet of paper towel, wound between her toes, was keeping them apart and the raspberry polish from smudging. "I want my own things. I want my own dishes. I want to pick out the pattern."

"It's nice to be settled in one place, with things you like, people you love."

"Silverware. And wineglasses, all the different kinds. You ever see when they show fancy tables in magazines? They have three or four different glasses. And a water goblet too." She was wearing a denim minidress with a lot of industrial zippers in what seemed to me to be useless places. Her hair was held back with a matching denim headband. "Do you want some honey-roasted peanuts?" I shook my head. "Pringles?"

"No thanks. How are you doing, Mary?"

"Fine," she said, but she was edgy. She couldn't seem to concentrate on anything, or to sit still. She showed me a project she was working on, a fabric-covered shoebox she was decorating with miniature fake seashells and a glue gun. She lost interest in it quickly and moved over to a laundry basket and began folding washcloths and towels, but that didn't last long. Then she searched the living room and the little galley kitchen for a bag of cheddar popcorn she was positive she'd bought. "I *know* I bought it," she told me. "It's a black, shiny bag. I didn't eat it, and I bought it after Norman . . ." All of a sudden, like a balloon losing air, she rushed around the room until finally, spent, she collapsed in an armchair.

"It's such a strain, isn't it, Mary . . ."

"Yes," she said, in a peculiar, high-pitched tone, as if she had something more to add to the sentence.

Then I realized it was because she didn't want to hear what I was going to say next: ". . . knowing Norman is going to be in prison for such a long, long time."

"Don't you think you can get him off?"

"It's possible. Not at all likely."

"I love him," she explained, as if letting me in on this for the first time.

"I know you do. I know it's breaking your heart to see him cooped up in that jail for a crime he may not have committed."

"He didn't!"

"I can't get anyone to believe that, Mary. I wish I could.

302

But his record is working against him. And worse, all the facts are against him."

"What facts?" she demanded angrily. "There aren't any *facts*."

"There's an eyewitness who puts him at the scene very near the time of the murder. Now, I know you were there, too, but no one knows about it. And for all I know, there may have been other people there, but no one knows about them either. Only about Norman. And then there are his fingerprints."

"But mine are there too!"

"But no one thinks you did it, Mary. They all think Norman did it."

"But he'll get on the stand and swear—"

"He has a long record for fraud. As a con man. Even if I let him take the stand, there's very little hope anyone would believe him." I took a deep breath. "Of course, he has no history of ever hurting anyone."

"He wouldn't touch a fly!"

"But you . . . you have a history." For a moment, I thought she was going to spring out of her chair and go for me. Her eyes flashed: How dare you! I regretted all the adult-ed self-defense courses I never took. But the fire left her eyes, and she simply sat back in the big chair looking weary, somewhere between a tired child and an exhausted hooker. "You lost it with Carolyn Knowles." She bowed her head slightly: Yes. "And you lost it with Bobette." Her head came up. Her eyes widened. "Didn't you, Mary? Didn't you panic because you knew Norman was actually going to marry her? You waited till he left, and when you went in you lost it. You must have been overwhelmed with feeling, and you just fell apart."

"No!"

"I think it's 'yes.'" She turned her head away from me fast, and looked out past her shoulder. But she was staring at a blank wall. "It must have been an awful feeling."

Just when I thought I would be talking till I was blue in the face, she whispered, "Yes."

I forced myself not to move, not even to breathe. I kept

my voice as soft as I could. "And it must be hell, every day. Thinking that Norman is getting blamed for something you did. Thinking how deeply he loves you, and how much he must be suffering for that love."

"Oh, Jesus God!" she cried out, and covered her face.

"I know you want to help him."

"I do!" she said, her voice muffled by her big hands.

I walked over and sat beside her on the arm of her chair. I wanted to pat her on the head, but I was afraid that she'd get upset if I messed up her hairdo. So rather awkwardly, I patted her shoulder. "There's only one way you can help the man who loves you so much."

It took her a moment, but she finally said: "By telling the truth."

"That's right. By telling the truth. That you killed Bobette Frisch." She nodded. Yes. I did. But I had to hear it. No, I had to make her say it. If I couldn't convince her to get it out at that moment, she would never do it in front of Holly. "It must be so awful for you, to have this burden. You're such a wonderful, sweet young woman."

"Thank you," she said in a little voice.

"Tell me what happened that evening."

"Like I told you. I was there that afternoon, watching them through a window. Not that I really saw anything much. Norman just opened up the envelopes from the bank. Those brown envelopes they give you." I waited. "He took out the money. It made a big wad. Then he kissed her." She shivered, as if recalling something hideous, unnatural.

"Was it more of a kiss than you expected?" I asked, keeping my tone as soothing as I could.

"Yes. And . . . I mean, it was like he was *enjoying* it. I know he's a good actor with them. He has to be. He told me: 'Sometimes they make me want to vomit, but they think I'm wild for them.' But I *know* him."

"And this time he didn't want to vomit?"

"No! He kept kissing her, and kissing her and finally *she* pushed him away. But he kept going after her. And then . . ." She couldn't speak.

"Did they have sex?" I recalled there was no evidence of intercourse on the autopsy report.

"No. She sat back on the couch, that cow, and *let* him kiss her for a while. Like she was doing him a favor. Then she pushed him off again and got up. He got up and followed her into the kitchen. Like he couldn't stand to let her out of his sight. I couldn't see them in the kitchen, because there's a big window there and they would have seen me out there. Anyway, the next thing I know, I heard him go out."

"That's when he went to get the champagne?"

"Yes."

"Did you go right in?"

"After his car left, I counted to two minutes. One-chimpanzee, two-chimpanzee . . . Then I went in."

"Which door?"

"The front. I told you, he doodled the button."

"I remember. Where was she?"

"I heard her clomping up the stairs to take a shower. So then, you know, I went through her things."

"Took her credit cards."

"Her whole wallet. She had over seven hundred dollars in cash, besides the cards! And then I heard her, so I ran downstairs."

"And she came down?"

"A little later. Wearing this ugly negligee. I mean, can you picture a cow in a lavender negligee? I mean, it got me so mad! How could he marry her? She's old enough to be his mother. How could he want to . . . I saw the way he kissed her. It was like it didn't bother him. Like he . . . liked it! Like he wanted more. And then I was standing in this little, like, vestibule, right by the front door, kind of peeking out but hiding and she's in the living room, and all of a sudden she says: 'Who's there?' In this big, scary voice. You wouldn't believe how scared I was! And then she comes running over and sees me and grabs me by the arm. She hurt me! She was screaming: 'Who the hell are you? What do you want in my house?' "

Mary started to shake violently, almost as though she was going through it all over again. "Take it easy," I soothed. "You're doing fine. What happened next?"

305

"I pushed her away, and she went, you know, like back-wards into the living room. I felt better, because I'd been so scared she was going to beat me up. Or kill me."

I assumed this was Mary's way of testing to see if a self-defense theory would fly. I just said: "It must have been terrible. What happened? Did you follow her into the living room?"

"I guess I must have. I mean, all of a sudden there I was, standing right in front of her. By the couch. She was scream-ing that she didn't have the money anymore, that someone had taken it. I guess she thought that's why I was there. That some way I found out that she took all the money out of the bank. Then she started screaming at me again to get out. And louder, because I was right next to her. And she had this pukey bad breath, and I was thinking: How could he kiss her? And then all of a sudden she stopped screaming and moved back. She was trying to run away. But I grabbed her." So much for a self-defense theory, I thought. "And she got all panicked. I mean, you could see it in her eyes. Like I was going to hurt her. And she started begging me: "Please, please, I'll give you anything you want. I can get money—'"

Mary started to shake again, and this time she gulped huge, terrified mouthfuls of air.

I knew I had to get her through, to the end. "She offered you money," I said, as though this was a terrible affront.

"I said, 'I don't want your fucky money, you fat old bitch." Then she started acting real scared. And like, instead of that awful, scary voice, she sounded so pathetic. 'Please don't hurt me! Please!' I swear, I wasn't going to hurt her. But she kept begging me and begging me and finally I just wanted to shut her up. So I grabbed her.'

'Her neck?'

'And the next thing I knew, her tongue was out, and then I put her down on the floor 'cause she was so heavy and she was . . .''

"Say it, Mary."

"Dead."

Eighteen

"How *nice*," said the real estate agent as he drove Lee and Jazz around the Estates section of Shorehaven. "That is what I call a *love* story." Mr. Chadman, for that was his name, then sang a few bars of "The Boy Next Door." He liked to think of himself as a late-twentieth-century incarnation of a Victorian eccentric, whimsical yet lovable.

When they passed the modern stone and glass house that Sylvia, Leonard and Robin White lived in, he nodded in its direction and decreed: "An important house." Its importance had to do not with the family that lived inside or the house's architectural distinction but with the fact that in that year, 1976, it would have brought at least half a million dollars had it been put up for sale.

"Important," of course, was too small a word for Hart's Hill. Mr. Chadman stopped his car in front of the driveway, gazed greedily through the trees that obscured the house, and remarked: "What *can* one say?" He twisted around to pay homage to Jazz, who was sitting in the back seat.

"One can say we're looking in the wrong neighborhood," Lee remarked. All right: Her temper was a little short. But there she was, stuck in the passenger seat beside the agent—a place she did not want to be. To be honest, Shorehaven was a place she did not want to be. But Jazz, of all people, had pronounced Connecticut too Wasp and Westchester too pretend-Wasp. New Jersey, he declared, was overrun with unassimilated members of obscure ethnic groups—none of whom could be trusted behind the wheel of a car. As for Long Island, all the towns other than Shorehaven were either glitzy or overly quaint or rundown. In the end, Lee had let him have his way. She knew she had lost the Battle of Manhattan and, as prisoner of war, her fate was in the hands of her captor. Nevertheless, she realized he was a captor who was generous in victory. Whatever you want, he kept telling her. Colonial. Tudor. Ranch. What she didn't want was a house within shouting distance of his and her parents—not that she could picture any of them shouting. "We really can't afford—" she tried to explain to Mr. Chadman, trying for honeyed tones to soothe whatever raw spot her last outburst had left.

"Trust me, my dear, if I may say 'my dear' without sounding like one of those male chauvinist pigs. 'Afford' is not the issue here." Lee and Jazz each suppressed a smile and took comfort in knowing that the other was doing likewise. "I have your dream house. Just on the market. Part of the old Howell estate. Finally subdivided now that old Mr. Howell passed on, may his soul find eternal rest. It was his estate manager's cottage." He made a quick right after Hart's Hill, then another, and bounced up a badly rutted road. "On the high end of your budget, maybe a tad over. But one must pay for charm."

"I don't think—" Jazz began as they drove under a canopy of elms.

"We don't want to live quite so close to where we grew up," Lee explained diplomatically as they passed a flame euonymus, so brilliant that its redness made her turn away. "We were thinking that some other area of Shorehaven—"

But they fell into silence as the car pulled up before their dream house. "Hey," Jazz said softly. "I never knew this existed."

"This place, it's . . ." Lee was going to say "perfect," but Mr. Chadman sat beside her, his chin raised in smug triumph, and she could not bear to give him the satisfaction. She turned back to the house. Not very big, built entirely of large, irregularly shaped stones held in place by gold-colored mortar. Nestled in a grassy glen, circled by ancient oaks and sycamores, it looked like an illustration for a fairy tale—a cheery, revisionist, non-Grimm tale, to be sure—with its quirky tilted chimney, windows like shining eyes, and a wide, welcoming red wood door. Rambling ruby roses climbed up the right side of the house. Nice, she decided to say to Mr. Chadman. No: Charming. Or maybe give the pompous ass Sweet. But before she could stop it, "Beautiful!"

fell out of her mouth. Three months later, after the painters and floor sanders left and the carpenter screwed the final knob onto the last kitchen cabinet, they moved into the most wonderful house in the world.

Right before they moved, Lee made it clear to Jazz that she would not give up the law. Furthermore, she was not interested in some tame suburban lady-lawyer position—assisting a matrimonial specialist or pushing papers across a table at real-estate closings. No, she wanted to be in court. As a prosecutor. However, the district attorney of Nassau County was a Republican. So without even consulting Jazz, Lee went directly to her father-in-law and asked him to use his influence in securing her an appointment as token Democrat.

Fos told Ginger he was at least grateful someone connected with the Taylors was an attorney. What Jazz had done rankled him. He had not expected much from his daughters, and he had not gotten it: One did little but play tennis and golf and, at thirty-two, had skin like that on her brown alligator pumps. The other was becoming a hunchback, picking cucumbers on a commune. Kent was useless. But his Jasper! Fos was not merely anguished but infuriated by his son's new life: Leaving Wall Street! To take up with garment center types. He could not for the life of him understand it.

While ten generations of Long Island inbreeding may have diminished the once soaring Taylor IQ, Fos was no dummy. He was smart enough to realize that his favor-seeking daughter-in-law was not a party to Jazz's idiot decision. Further, Fos sensed that Lee might be an ally. Woo Jazz back to where he belonged. It would be such a relief, when the fellows on the Committee or at Rolling Hills inquired, How's that fine son of yours coming along?, not to have to go mumble mumble . . . fur coats . . . mumble, feeling he would die of humiliation. Accordingly, he was not only vaguely fond of Lee but also not unwilling to help her. In addition, while not a bighearted man, Fos was worldly enough to know that there are certain requests that cannot be denied. Since he could not dream of telling the future mother of his grandchildren to go stuff it, he picked up the phone and spent half a morning being jovial to a few of his fellow Republicans who, only recently,

309

had been badgering him for myriad courtesies at the games in Montreal—and who owed him. He hated to waste his IOUs on a cause not his own, but that could not be helped. And so, two days later, Lee was face-to-face with the district attorney of Nassau County, Woodleigh Huber, in his office.

And what an office! Oak-paneled, with a desk so monumental it seemed that nothing less than a manned rocket to Mars or the D-day invasion should be launched from it. Behind it, three eight-foot flags, representing the county, the State of New York, and the United States of America, stood proudly against a blue-draped wall.

"Homicide?" Huber inquired.

"Homicide," Lee affirmed. That was what she wanted. And she had done her homework: The Nassau District Attorney's Office was considered middling to good—except for its Homicide unit. That was reported to be first-rate.

"Homicide," Huber sighed. If he was not incredulous, he was at least dismayed. "It isn't that I don't think you're up to it. I hear nothing but good things about you: smart, straightforward, no fancy footwork, but delivers the goods. What you've got to understand, though, is that this is not New York City." He nodded his agreement with himself, and his shock of white hair flapped in approval. Huber was a handsome fellow, high-colored and square-jawed. He looked like an actor hired to play the President of the United States for a television movie of the week. Seated as he was between his grand old flags and his important desk, his every action seemed calculated for a photo op. But if his moves appeared false and contrived that was not the entire Woodleigh Huber story. He did care that the District Attorney's Office was perceived as a fine one and, in fact, worked hard, if not entirely successfully, to achieve that goal. "Our jurors aren't so—shall we say—sophisticated as the ones you're used to."

Lee smiled. "I guess you haven't seen a Manhattan petit jury recently."

"I think what the Boss is getting at," Jerry McCloskey interpreted, "is that it might be too *upsetting* to a suburban-type jury to have a woman representing the People in a homicide trial." He was a squat pale mushroom of a man, who appeared to be the quintessential political gofer, existing solely to say or do anything his patron found unpleasant. "I don't have to tell you homicides can get pretty gory."

"So can rape. I hear you have a woman in your Sex Crimes unit."

"We do indeed!" Woodleigh Huber said, in the powerful voice he dreamed would be heard on a segment of *60 Minutes*. "Portrait of a Crime Fighter" he imagined it would be called. "Bonnie Brinkerhoff. Soft as a marshmallow outside but when she walks into that courtroom ... hard as nails. A hell of a lawyer. I mean that." Lee nodded. She had heard Brinkerhoff was, on her occasional good days, mediocre and had inherited the job when the man who had previously held it was run over by his lawn mower. "Believe me, we welcome you women. We think you're a tremendous addition to the team. Tremendous."

"Except this is the thing," McCloskey explained. He smelled a little stale, as if he or his suit was overdue for a cleaning. "We're full up in our Homicide unit right now." Like Lee, McCloskey sat in a straight-backed chair before Huber's desk. Unlike Lee, McCloskey was perched on the edge of the hard seat, as if not high enough in rank to have the right to rest his entire backside. "Full up to the gills." Huber nodded.

Lee thought fast. If they were full up in Homicide, that meant they were going to put her someplace else, some less plummy unit. But she was in, it seemed. Hired! A prosecutor again! Foster Taylor had come through for her! He'd had the clout. And if he had the clout to get her—a Democrat, a woman—the job, he must have been owed some big favors. So big, she suddenly realized, that the job had probably been hers before she set foot in the office. Before she could get cold feet, Lee turned from McCloskey to his master and blurted: "Give me a month's trial in Homicide."

"As Jerry mentioned—"

She cut him off. "I know how competitive it is, getting a spot in the unit." Huber's mouth compressed in annoyance until his near-lipless mouth was merely the width of a paper cut. "And because Homicide is so good, so public, that's all the more reason to give me a shot. If I can't cut it, I'll be glad to try cases elsewhere. But if I'm as capable as your background check suggests I am, then I can make the unit's statistics look even better."

311

"Well . . ." Huber mused.

Out of the corner of her eye, Lee saw McCloskey inch even closer to the edge of the seat. Had she gone too far? Had he gotten some signal and was he getting ready to show her the door? McCloskey didn't like her, she could tell. Why should he? She did not belong in his scheme of things, in which deserving people got what they deserved—and Woodleigh Huber received chits from them for future favors. True, Huber must have owed Foster Taylor or a Foster Taylor friend something major and had to pay up. But Lee understood that a two-bit pol like McCloskey would know in his bones that no further benefit would accrue from putting her in Homicide: Lee White would feel she owed the District Attorney her best efforts, nothing more. *Ipso facto*, a stinko deal. "Listen, Boss," McCloskey began.

But the Boss had already filled his lungs to declaim, and McCloskey lost his chance. "You've got one month, Lee," Huber said resonantly, imagining introducing her to Ed Bradley or Mike Wallace. A younger member of our Homicide unit. Nonpartisan. As you can see for yourself, it doesn't matter here if you're male or female, black or white or green. What matters is what you *do*. And this girl's won major cases. Toughies. He could hear Lee saying, I may be a Democrat, Ed, but this man is beyond politics. "Jer," Huber commanded, "bring her downstairs."

"Downstairs, Boss?" McCloskey asked, but without much hope.

"To Homicide. To Will Stewart."

William Hibbets Stewart was definitely not handsome, even though everyone would give you an argument that he was. He had a round face that lacked even a single arresting angle; small, undistinguished eyes; and a too awesome nose, big and down curving, a signal that one of his African ancestors had gotten quite friendly with an individual of Arab descent. But as she stood where she and McCloskey had run into him, right outside his office, Lee judged he was well over six feet tall. Imposingly built too, with shoulders so broad they were parallel to the floor. His skin was richly dark, somewhere between ebony and mahogany. His body, the ideal male V, was slim and muscular, and his carriage was so regal that even one of his most culturally illiterate colleagues had been heard to say: Will's like one of those, uh, African statues or somethin'.

What made Will Stewart a standout, however, was his elegance. It was the real thing. He was beautifully dressed, in a gray suit, white shirt, and burgundy tie, all so simple and yet somehow she knew: the best there was. Yet his bearing had nothing to do with money. Leonard's Savile Row suits and hand-stitched shoes made her father look like nothing more than a rich businessman. Even Jazz's new wardrobe showed him to be a good-looking guy with nice taste and a Hong Kong tailor. Will's elegance came from within.

"Hi," he said. "Good to meet you." He had a thrilling basso that could have been singing "Il lacerato spirito" at the Met, or moving huge congregations to leap into the aisles and shout "Praise the Lord!" To Lee, it was a huge, nineteenth-century orator's voice—a courtroom voice. "Good to meet you."

"Good to meet you."

"Will," McCloskey said. "Could I have a quick word with you, Will?"

With a sinking heart, Lee watched Will enter his office. McCloskey, clearly nervous, followed and closed the door. No one had prepared Will Stewart for her. He would be furious. Like hell I will! he would boom. McCloskey, terrified, would race back up to Huber, who would be forced to change his mind. Lee saw herself taking "Basic Puff Pastry" in the Shorehaven School District's adult ed program several decades sooner than she'd expected. No, it could even be worse. Will would view her as a party hack and treat her with contempt. It would take her years to gain his respect. If she ever could: Eager to prove herself, she'd screw up case after case so badly that not only would she get tossed out of Homicide; they wouldn't even let her try misdemeanor cases.

It was taking too long. She strained to hear shouts, but all was silent behind Will's door. Attorneys passed and glanced at her curiously. She should not have worn a beige suit. It was too late into the fall. She felt so wrong and wished that someone had mentioned the fact that Will Stewart was black and infinitely suave. The door opened. Will stuck his head out. "Who can I call about you?" he asked pleasantly, even warmly, as if he was

313

so pleased with her that he couldn't wait to hear more good things. She realized that he was a smarter politician than Huber and McCloskey put together.

"You mean from the Manhattan D.A.'s?" she asked. What a moron she sounded like! What did she think he wanted? References from the eight million guys at Cornell she'd fucked?

"Right," he said.

"Well, the D.A. himself. Or the head of the Supreme Court bureau—"

"Melanie Tucker?" he asked congenially. At least, he seemed congenial. For all she knew, he loathed Melanie and any recommendation from her would mean automatic rejection. Yes, she nodded, her head bobbing like a fool's, Melanie Tucker. "Sorry to keep you waiting like this," he said.

"That's all right," Lee replied, but he had already closed the door. All right, she thought, as long as her tortured gut did not cause her to writhe and double up, groaning in agony. She held her handbag in front of her and pressed her forearms against her raging stomach. How much longer? She couldn't stand it. Maybe he would hate her because her last name was White. She could knock, say Excuse me, it's really Weissberg. Except maybe, despite all those rabbis on the March on Selma, he was an anti-Semite.

The door jerked open, and Jerry McCloskey flew out. "See ya," he muttered, and tore down the hall.

"Come in," Will called.

Although his name was on the door, Will Stewart's office had nothing to do with him. It was standard government issue, newer than its Manhattan equivalent and just as lifeless. But he had done nothing to make it his: no pictures, no mementos, no bound appellate briefs, no knickknacks. His pen was a twenty-nine-cent Bic. "Come *in*," he repeated. Lee took a deep breath and then, propelled by the exhalation, went into his office. He was standing behind his desk, but instead of the expected forefinger pointed toward the door, he was extending his hand. "Welcome," he said. She felt a little dizzy but noticed he had sat back down and seemed to be suggesting that she do the same. "Sorry to put you through all that."

"No problem," she said cheerfully.

"Lee," he said. With his voice, it sounded like a summons from

314

God. He sat back comfortably in his chair, his hands clasped behind his head.

"What?"

"I'm your boss. Don't bullshit me: 'No problem.' "

"Okay. I had terrible stomach cramps, and I was afraid I'd embarrass myself in some particularly disgusting way. Or else I'd go into shock and convulse, and my head would bang rhythmically against your door and you'd think I was interrupting your discussion with Jerry McCloskey."

"I wasn't discussing with him. I was torturing him by not accepting you as a fait accompli. I sat here for a couple of minutes looking dubious. Then I called Melanie. She thinks the world of you, by the way."

"That's what I think of her."

"So do I. We testified together before a House committee." He did not smile, but his face softened. "She'd be my mother's dream girl, with those hankies up her sleeve. And pearls. The only way she could be more perfect would be if she were black." He continued to look faintly amused—either at his mother or at some recollection of Melanie, but he did not smile. Then he leaned forward. "The stomach business. Do you get nervous in court?"

No, she was going to say, but heard herself saying: "Most of the time. Right before I open and when I sum up. But once I start talking, it disappears."

"Too bad they can't bottle that," he said.

"Do you ever get that way?" she asked. A second later, she shrank back, nearly crazed by her audacity.

"I used to. Not my stomach. I used to sweat, which is worse, I think, because everyone can see it. But it hasn't happened in years. I guess I've been doing it too long. You get numb to it, and that's not good. You lose your competitive edge." She nodded, suddenly exhilarated, realizing they were having a conversation. "I don't know, though. Maybe being numb is better than being scared shitless. Now, let's see: I've got to get someone to find you a desk. You want a chair too?"

"While they're at it." She smiled at him. Her infectious smile, Jazz called it. Or contagious. Whatever. You smile at someone and they light up, Lee. I'm telling you, it's true.

Will did not smile back. In fact, he looked away and opened

315

a folder on his desk, passing a quick glance over the papers inside. "Okay, you get settled. Then you'll have to fill out all the forms. We Republicans say we don't want big government, but don't believe us. It will take you hours. Come back around . . . whenever. Five, six." He picked up what looked like a Justice Department newsletter and immediately became engrossed.

"Thanks!" Lee said. She waited a fraction of a second too long, hoping he would glance up and smile. Not a big smile, just something quick, spontaneous. Or at least say, You're welcome.

But she got nothing more from Will Stewart until seven-fifteen that night, when he handed her five eight-by-ten photographs of Nicky "The Rooster" Gaudioso in the trunk of his Lincoln Continental—which had been found in the woods in Eisenhower Park. He was at least two weeks dead, his throat slit, his testicles stuffed into his mouth. "I think you'll have fun with this," Will said. Her parents, her sister, Jazz—any civilian—would have recoiled. But Lee nodded. She knew exactly what Will meant, and she knew he was right.

She took the photos home, and after dinner, while Jazz watched the Yankees getting creamed by Cincinnati in the Series, she spread them out on the kitchen table. With a flashlight in one hand and a magnifying glass in the other, she bent over them, studying Nicky and the trunk that had been his grave. Not much, she thought, although it might make a good ad for the Continental: Check out our roomy trunk! A few minutes later, she noticed: There was something pale and squiggly in the right-hand corner. What was it? More important, was it what she thought it was? She called the detective sergeant on the case, a guy named Brody. Yeah, he said, it's rubber gloves. You know it's after ten o'clock? Lee ignored his question and asked if he'd brought in the gloves to the lab to check for prints. Prints? Brody asked, as if it were a strange new concept. The perpetrator might have used the gloves to put Nicky in the car and simply forgotten them, Lee explained. Gotcha, Brody said wearily. I'm sure the gloves went in. It's automatic. Good, Lee said. Then let's not give the killer time to remember he forgot his gloves and skip town—unless you think it was Nicky who kept them there in case he had to perform emergency microsurgery. I'd like the answer by noon tomorrow.

316

When Eddie Marcantonio, whose fingerprints were found inside and outside the gloves, was arrested for the murder of Nicky Gaudioso, he claimed that he was a salesman for Sunshine Garden Supplies. While he did collect a check from Sunshine, however, he would not have known a pile of manure from a hot rock. As Detective Sergeant Brody told Lee, his real profession was hit man for the Gambino family. His job required patience and not imagination or intelligence, so Eddie did quite well. He was not the sort who minded spending his working life sitting in a car, waiting hours for one of his subjects to emerge from a dinner of *cervelli fritti* at Vincente's restaurant or from a visit to his girl-friend's. He was patient, looking straight ahead, not listening to the radio, not reading a newspaper, with only his knife or his gun for company. Then he would do what he'd been sent to do: commit murder. Eddie knew, naturally, to try and avoid crowds, but if his business was ever observed, he did not worry. Should the terror of the moment not frighten an eyewitness, the notion of the cruel death that would follow a court appearance to identify Eddie as the killer worked wonders.

"Eddie didn't do it!" his lawyer, Chuckie Phalen, announced to Lee. "He uses rubber gloves all the time. In the garden supply business. Doesn't like dirt getting under his fingernails." Chuckie wheezed as he spoke. His pallor was almost as bad as Nicky Gaudioso's.

"This is your defense?" Lee asked. She neither liked nor disliked Phalen. He was one of the Old Boys, criminal lawyers who con-sidered themselves archliberals in those rare instances when they managed to refrain from calling a female attorney "honey."

"Just because he has an Italian last name doesn't make him Mafia." Despite his breathing problems, Chuckie spoke with an energy that was rare for an Old Boy on a routine murder case.

"No," Lee agreed, already hearing his summation in her mind. She hated to admit it, she had told Jazz the night before, but it wasn't so terrible working out here—and don't say I told you so. He'd been thrilled, and his hug had been full of joy. Well, it wasn't *that* terrible. Lawyers waited until she finished her sentence before beginning theirs. The cops didn't pal around with the assis-tant D.A.'s the way they did in New York, but they were cordial enough. Brody had even shaken her hand when the fingerprints on the gloves proved to be Eddie Marcantonio's and then, for good measure, patted her on the back and announced: You're hot shit. "There happen to be three drops of Nicky's blood on Eddie's rubber glove," Lee informed Chuckie Phalen. "That doesn't exactly paint a picture of Mr. Sunshine Garden Supplies planting petunias, does it?"

"I like your stuff," Chuckie said. It was, on the surface, a predictable compliment, the old pro patting the rookie on the back, hoping the rookie would feel enough of a personal tie to give his client a break. But Lee sensed it was sincere, and she wanted to smile and give him a warm thank-you, maybe even—after the trial—say something about her liking his stuff. But she could be wrong, he could be setting her up, so she just offered him a slight incline of the head that said: I heard you. "Aah, you think I'm buttering you up. I can tell. That's okay, I understand. Now listen, sis—"

"Lee."

"Lee, what I have here is a family man. Wife, two kids. A dog, even. So maybe we can talk."

"They don't allow dogs in Attica. The wife and kids can visit."

"You're a real softie."

"I keep trying."

"You want to check with Will on this?"

"No."

"Will is tough but fair."

"Good. That's how I want to be."

"So how's about five to seven?" Chuckie asked, the air creating a whistling sound every time he inhaled.

"That's what I'm hoping he'll get for illegally parking the Continental on county property." For the first week, she kept saying "city," and she was only now getting accustomed to glimpses of green outside and being greeted with actual hellos instead of grunts by the unit's secretaries. "The murder charge is extra. I can offer you something less if he's willing to discuss who asked him to kill Nicky and send a message."

"What message?"

"The message that this is what happens to guys who talk."

"You mean, the you-know-whats in Nicky's mouth?" Chuckie

asked, with such false innocence that Lee couldn't help it. She threw back her head and laughed.

But she stopped laughing six months later, in court.

Chuckie was good, very good. The way he cut into the credibility of her expert witnesses: not with eye-rolling, give-me-a-break mockery or go-for-the-throat attack, but by respectful solicitation of their views seeking ever more amplification until the experts were drowning in rolling seas of their own jargon. In addition, Chuckie had the New York-Irish equivalent of courtly Southern charm, calling prospective jurors "Ma'am" and "Sir" during voir dire, wheezing to the judge phrases like: "I respectfully submit to Your Honor" and "I would beg the Court's indulgence." There was not a hint of blarney. A gentleman, the jury was obviously thinking, and Chuckie's dignity subsumed the man beside him at the defense table, Eddie Marcantonio—who, after a Chuckie wardrobe consultation—was looking like a deacon of an extremely sincere church.

But Chuckie's being good was only half the problem. It was that Lee was not. She could tell it by the way the judge listened to her motions; no matter how reasonable her arguments were, he reacted as if she were being not merely frivolous but sneaky. And the jury. For them, Chuckie was a good show and she was the commercials. They kept tuning out.

"What's happening?" Lee demanded of Will. She threw up her hands. Several shreds of coleslaw flew off her plastic fork and landed on his office rug. She reached over and picked them up. "You sat in yesterday. You saw. They're not with me, and don't tell me they are."

He put down the huge, drippy corned beef and pastrami combo she had been coveting. "I won't tell you they are, because they're not."

"You could at least be a little less eager to give me the bad news."

"No. I'm giving it to you where it has to go: right between the eyes. You're screwing up." But he said it with affection.

In her half year in the D.A.'s Office, she had gone from awe of Will Stewart to having a slight crush on him, then a large crush, then to a realization that what he was, above all else, was a great

319

friend—although in truth the crush never disappeared. Will had grown up less than ten miles from her, in Glen Cove. His parents had worked on one of the great Gold Coast estates, his father as head groom in the stables, his mother as a laundress. The owner of the estate had taken a shine to him and paid for his education at Columbia. Will had gone on to Columbia Law School on scholarship. She found him a fascinating mix, a kid from a blue-collar family who had grown up to be a down-to-earth working stiff—civil service division. Yet hand in hand with his lack of airs and his nose-to-the-grindstone work ethic, he comported himself with the polish of someone born to great wealth. It went far beyond his impeccable clothes and physical grace.

Time and again, Lee got annoyed with herself for comparing Jazz and Will, but she could not stop. She was dazzled at the differences between two men whose lives had been molded by old money. Jazz, at twenty-seven, was still the bright-eyed, high-spirited preppy who viewed the world as a fun place and Long Island as his own special playground. Will, at thirty-seven, was not the least bit bright-eyed. Lee could not imagine him that way, even as a child. He behaved as if he had seen it all and was faintly amused by it. But only faintly. He had a nice mouth, but it never smiled. She sensed there was sadness behind his elegant and wry facade, but since he played his personal cards so close to his exquisitely-fitting vest, she had no idea what the sadness was—or whether it was simply a romantic notion she had.

What she couldn't get over is that he seemed made for her. Not the way Jazz was. Taylor made, she called Jazz, the way he cheered her by his very nature, the way his own self-assurance gave her a confidence in herself she had never before had—because why would such a man pick her unless she was, in fact, as wonderful as he kept telling her she was? And of course, the way he made love: Taylor made. Still, once they finished the business of marriage, the routine recounting of their day, the gossip about their extended families, they had very little to talk about.

But based on their common interests, she and Will Stewart could have sprung from the same egg. They discovered they listened to the same radio shows driving to and from the office. They were passionate about music. Lee gave Will a tape of Fats Waller playing stride piano, which he loved, and he introduced her to one of his favorites, the late-Renaissance composer Fresco-baldi, and after she heard it, she told him: I owe you for this. They both cooked and gardened; they enjoyed obscure off-off Broadway plays; they were intensely political, and while she was a Democrat and he a Republican, they were moderates, so their arguments over lunch were more about style than ideology. One weekend, shortly after she had once again taken up the crocheting she had learned from her Grandma Bella, she realized that making afghans was the sole interest she had that Will Stewart did not share, and that his abiding love of the New York Mets—he was at that moment at a game—was not going to be hers, ever.

Still, however close, theirs was an office friendship, and Will was her boss. Lee set down the plastic platter of tuna salad. "*How* am I screwing up?" she asked. Her answer was his glance, right at her stomach. She was barely six months pregnant but looked as though she was about to give birth to twin sumo wrestlers. "Being pregnant?"

"You don't want to hear it."

"Yes I do."

"You're not dealing with Manhattan juries anymore. Out here, they don't like to see women in court trying murder cases. Okay, Huber told you that, you didn't like it, and you fought him on it. Good. I'm glad you did. But they really don't want to see pregnant women in court trying a case where she has to talk about a guy's balls getting whacked off and shoved between his teeth."

"But I'm being feminine!" Lee made a sweeping gesture with her hand, indicating her soft silk blouse and small, antique locket. "I don't fucking shout!"

"You just did."

"I mean in court. I'm polite, nice. You saw how feminine I was yesterday, didn't you? What the hell else do they want from me?"

"They want you out of the courtroom and home taking care of your baby."

"I don't have a baby yet!" She rested her hand protectively on her mound of a stomach and felt a friendly kick of acknowledg-ment. "Look, Will, give it to me straight. Are you telling me I should stay out of court?"

"No."

"Good, because if you did, I'd fight you on it."

"I'm telling you that you have to adapt better. You're not just another lawyer. You're a pregnant woman in a traditional, middle-American community, and if you want them to approve of you, you need more than a little heart on a gold chain."

"What do I need? A gingham pinafore?" She felt weary. Pregnancy exhaustion, trial fatigue, as well as the cosmic weariness that comes with the fear that you have made the wrong choice in life. Maybe she was not good enough for the job, and the whole time in Manhattan she had been flying with Melanie Tucker's wings.

"You need to show the jury you're one of them. The judge too."

"I *am* one of them. There are seven women on the jury, and six of them have kids."

"And not one of them spends her days going after a ball-chopping mob guy. So you've got to show them what you have in common with them. Not your locket. Your values. You and I both know we have to be strong to stomach what we see in this job, and we help ourselves by keeping an emotional distance by being cynical. Nothing surprises us, nothing gets to us. But there's a difference between being strong and being tough. You're not tough. Deep down, you're shocked by what Eddie Marcantonio did to Nicky. Aren't you?"

She did not want to give him the easy answer he was looking for. But when she thought about it, letting him finish his sandwich in silence, she had to answer: "Yes. It's horrible."

"Then let the judge and jury see that. You don't have to go into a phony feminine swoon. Let them see the person who grew up around here and is appalled to find Mafiosi butchering each other and then—just as bad—*driving on the grass* in Eisenhower Park to leave the body. Your shock is real, and you've got to use everything you have. Use your shock. Use your normal, human response: Yuck! And I'd like to hear one reference during the trial to the fact that you were born and grew up here on the Island, and one more during your summation. More than that would be overkill. Trust me, Lee, I do it all the time. It calms their prejudices: Oh, local kid made good. Not some slick piece of work from the city. One of us. Makes them feel safe."

"Thank you," she said.

322

"Don't thank me. I'm here for more than lunch."

"You know," Lee said to her witness that afternoon in court, Detective-Sergeant Brody, "when I was growing up here"—she would have sworn the twelve jurors and two alternates sat up straighter—"we used to go to Eisenhower Park and run in the wooded area all the time. Wasn't it a terrible risk that some child would find Nicky Gaudioso's Lincoln Continental?" She wrapped her arms protectively on her pregnant belly. "And if they opened the trunk . . ." She closed her eyes, and thought of one particular close-up of Nicky's face, and a genuine shudder passed through her.

Use everything you have, Will Stewart had said. Chuckie Phalen lost *People v. Marcantonio.*

Lee was due to give birth on June 21, 1977, and since by the weekend following the trial she needed either Jazz or a derrick to pull her out of a chair, she began her maternity leave. In truth, her only regret in leaving the office was not being able to see Will every day. While she liked some of her colleagues and the cops she dealt with, the camaraderie she had felt in Manhattan, that elation that filled her at ten-thirty at night when some Homicide detective came in carrying a couple of sixpacks and everyone gathered around to shoot the shit, did not come to pass in the Nassau County D.A.'s. No, this was the suburbs. Lawyers worked hard and went home to their wives to discuss whether to invest in an underground sprinkler system, while they waited for the charcoal to heat up so they could grill their marinated chicken thighs and vegetable kebabs.

Jazz called her almost hourly. Anything yet? Nothing, just Braxton Hicks contractions, she reported. They had been to natural childbirth classes and took comfort that by breathing properly and knowing what would happen, they would be in control. She did not feel in control. There was so much pressure on her bladder that if she sneezed or laughed she wet her pants. Not that she was laughing much. The start of the tenth month of pregnancy is not a good time to begin asking oneself: Have I made a mistake?

She never felt that way at night, when Jazz came flying through the door, all smiles and kisses, telling her to stop it, she did *not* look like a manatee; she was still a fantastic piece of ass. As they watched TV together, he would massage her feet and ankles on their brand-new cushy couch, and she would think: This is what love is.

But days were different. She had too much time to think. It bothered her a little that she, an ex-radical, had gotten co-opted into the system without even a peep from her conscience. Living in a rose-covered cottage and leafing through books of afghan patterns. Working for the government. If her conscience was not sticking it to her, then shouldn't her pride be giving her the business? Had her beliefs in her college years been that shallow? Or was she being too hard on herself? Was the lawyer who stood up and said "Lee White for the People, Your Honor" indeed the woman the Cornell revolutionary once dreamed of becoming?

What bothered her even more during those endless daylight hours was Jazz. When he was not with her, she wondered: Who is he? She had fallen in love first with a barefoot boy in a pizza parlor and, second, with a man utterly at ease with himself. How she had marveled at his simple acceptance of the fact that the world was his oyster and, then, at his invitation to come join him on the half-shell and spend her life with him. Come on, the invitation read. You don't have to prove yourself all the time. You don't have to push. You're with me. We're in like Flynn. More in, because Flynn is an arriviste and you and I, babe, belong.

"Don't you think," Lee asked Robin, "that Mom and Dad won?"

"Won what?"

"Won the war with us. We've become everything they wanted us to be."

Robin bit her rose petal of a lower lip. Her work at the day care center was voluntary, and she had stopped going in afternoons in order to be with Lee. When Robin announced her decision, Lee had been first appalled, then fearful of wounding her sister by explaining her need for privacy. After that she became angry, because she always had to tread softly where Robin was concerned; any serious obstacle to what sensitive Robin wanted might catapult her back into the darkness of drugs. But in the end, Lee found herself grateful for her sister's company. She was lonely, and frightened about going into labor alone. She had a recurring daydream of experiencing a fierce contraction and running for the phone to call Jazz and the obstetrician but stumbling, crashing to the floor, striking her head or breaking both legs, and lying, helpless, screaming out in pain for hours—and having the baby come out stillborn. So she felt safe with her sister in the house. Also, she found it fun to have a friend to talk to, especially a nonlawyer who was smart but who didn't always have a smart rejoinder.

"They didn't win with me," Robin said. "I'm not what they want me to be."

"Sure you are," Lee said.

"No. Only to the extent that I'm not a junkie now. I didn't finish college. I have a menial job—"

"It's a good job. You love being with kids."

"Not to wipe fifteen asses three times a day. That sounds terrible. I *do* like the job, and I know that if I went back to school, I'd major in education. But right now . . . I guess I'm doing the best I can."

"You're doing wonderfully."

Robin retied the ribbons of her cork-platform espadrilles. She had become her mother's shopping companion. Lee had observed to Jazz that her sister was the best-dressed day care worker in America.

Certainly the best-looking, Lee ruminated. Now that Robin was off drugs and had had her teeth capped, her fragile prettiness had bloomed into beauty. She had her mother's willowy figure and fair coloring, but with finer, sweeter features, as if a Pre-Raphaelite painter had given Sylvia a makeover. "I'm doing all right," Robin said. "*You're* doing wonderfully. You have it all."

"All by Mom and Dad's standards. A husband, a house in the suburbs. I mean, what was the point of all my rebellion? I married the man of their dreams, and I'm about to give them a grandchild who they're praying won't have a nose like Grandpa Nat, and I'm living in a rosecovered cottage two and a half minutes from their house. If they had given me a blueprint, I couldn't have met their specifications any better."

"You became a lawyer."

"I had to do *something* after college. No one was pounding on my door, shouting marriage proposals."

"Give me a break!" Robin said. "You could have gotten some

normal kind of job." Having arranged the bows on her espadrilles to droop with the proper degree of casualness, Robin was now running her fingers up her shin, over and over, searching for a near-invisible blonde hair her razor might have missed. Lee could not get over how someone as intelligent as her sister could be so utterly serious about fluff. "Anyway, you're the one who chose this life, with Jazz, living here. You're just pissed off that it's what Mom and Daddy wanted for you. But you shouldn't be."

"Why not?"

"Because it's what everyone in the world wants. Love, marriage, a beautiful house. Ask yourself this: What would I rather have than love, marriage, and a beautiful house?"

"Nothing," Lee admitted. She glanced around the living room, with its comfortable overstuffed chairs and warm wood tables. The afternoon sun streamed through windows framed by ruby roses. "I can't believe we lucked into this place, can you?" Robin smiled, a fuller smile than in the past. Besides her teeth being fixed, she was also happier. "What's so amusing?"

"You're so sophisticated," Robin said.

"Sophisticated? Every time Mom looks at me, it's like she can't decide who to call first: a wardrobe consultant or a plastic surgeon. I mean, I'm one notch above dowdy."

"I mean intellectually sophisticated. You question everything. And whenever you talk about your job, you always wind up talking about how you didn't trust what some cop swore up and down to, or you didn't trust some lawyer, or even—before you started doing only murder cases—that you didn't believe what the victim of a crime was saying."

"So?"

"So you're funny." Robin lowered her head and chuckled. Then she looked back up at Lee. "Listen. This is just between us, okay? But do you think a gem like this house just *happens* to become available the day you decide Okay, fine, I'll move to the suburbs?"

Lee felt neither a shiver of foreboding nor an all-senses alert. All she experienced was the slightest shift in sensation, so that instead of feeling normal she felt nothing. "It was prearranged?" she asked offhandedly, as though she had suspected sly doings all along.

"I'm sorry. I probably shouldn't have said anything."

"It's okay. Tell me."

"Mom and Daddy went looking every weekend in the spring. Not this spring. Last. I don't know if it was even for you that much; it just gave them something to do. Anyway, the Howell estate had been up for sale forever, but no one was buying it, so it was being broken up."

Lee tried to fill in the blanks. "They negotiated for this house?" Robin nodded. "Without us ever seeing it?"

"Of course not! Daddy took Jazz over. He fell in love with it too. It *is* irresistible. But he knew you didn't want to move, so he said he'd have to convince you first, because otherwise showing you the house would be meaningless. But while all that was happening, Daddy was afraid it would get away. He wanted to make sure no one else got it. So he and Jazz did something financial, with money from the business—and they bought it."

Lee felt her belly growing rigid with a contraction. At first, it seemed like the ones she had been experiencing for weeks: awesome when you felt the strength of the muscle getting itself into shape, but certainly not painful or even uncomfortable. But this one! "My God!" She gasped at its violence. "I'm not sure if I can take this."

Valerie Belinda Taylor was named for two great-grandmothers, Valentine MacDougal and Bella Weissberg. Born on the fifth of July, she would tell her friends when she grew older: Even then I was slightly perverse. By the time she uttered that statement she was studying acting at Juilliard, and thus, hyperbole was not a stranger to her tongue. But the truth was, from day one, despite a tendency to make even the opening of a bag of potato chips an occasion of theater, Val was a good-natured, reasonable child.

A good thing too, because for the first few months of her life, her parents were feeling anything but good-natured. "How could you?" Lee demanded from her bed in the maternity wing at North Shore Hospital. She kept her voice down, because just beyond the drawn curtain, the woman in the next bed was having trouble nursing and a gynecologist and two nurses were standing around the bed, discussing nipples. "It's such a betrayal."

"What the hell are you talking about?" Jazz asked. Since the floor was made of hard tiles, and he could not dig his heels in and thus demonstrate his determination to fight this one to the finish, he simply crossed his arms tight across his chest. "You are blowing this way out of proportion. It was a business deal, for God's sake."

"You bought the house before I even agreed to leave the city!"

"Your father and I bought it because it happened to be an excellent investment opportunity."

"You're full of shit!" she said, obviously too loud, since the nipple committee beyond the curtain fell into quivering silence.

"Keep your voice down."

"How can I?" she demanded, although in a whisper. "You lied to me!"

"I did not! I went into a deal with your father, who happens to be my business partner. Okay, I admit this was—is—a great house for a young couple. A little gem."

"You know who you sound like? That oozing-charm jerk of a real estate agent. 'Little gem!' And don't tell me you didn't lie. We went to his office and you shook his hand as if it was the first time you'd ever met him. Then we drove to the house, and you looked around like Wow, gee, what a place, and you said you never even knew it existed." Lee could tell from the slump of Jazz's shoulders that she had scored. "If that's not a lie, what is it?"

"I did it for you."

"You did it for yourself. If you were doing something for me, you would have let me stay in the job I loved." He stood and walked to the foot of the bed, putting distance between them. "In the city I loved. What do you want? To grow up and become our parents?"

"We're not our parents," Jazz said, leaning toward her over the foot of the bed. Lee could hear him trying to remain calm, trying to get the anger out of his voice by substituting the tone of benign understanding that he knew from natural childbirth class one ought to use when dealing with a woman who is four hours postpartum. "And Valerie isn't going to grow up to be us."

Lee was about to demand: But what about your lying to me? It was too big a matter to let drop. But just then a nurse came in holding Val, and the tug at her heartstrings as well as the tug of the stitches in her episiotomy incision made her feel particularly vulnerable. So she reached up for her baby and put her to her breast and a moment later she was nursing for the first time and Jazz was back beside her on the bed, running his finger over his daughter's perfect pink cheek and smiling beatifically. They looked for all the world like a picture of paradise, so when Jazz whispered, "I'm sorry," Lee nodded and decided to let it be for the time being.

The time being moved very slowly when Lee came home from the hospital. Having spent all her adult life being overstimulated, she found that the peacefulness of maternity made her edgy. She held Val a great deal, unable to get over the wonder of all the tiny parts parents traditionally wonder at. She luxuriated in the serene lassitude breast-feeding induced and understood why cows were so content. She started to reread *Jane Eyre* but found it too rousing, so she put it down and picked up *Emma*. She wrote thank-you notes for all the little pink gifts friends of their parents had sent and for gender-neutral yellow and green gifts from their own friends.

Kent came over to check out his new niece and was so pleased by all the activity—the baby's diaper being changed, the interviews with prospective nannies, opening gifts, helping Lee make dinner and set the table, the new large-screen TV and videocassette player in their den—that he stayed. In her fourth week home, Lee sat across from Kent playing checkers—a game he did not quite comprehend but which he nevertheless enjoyed, trusting Lee to help him move his pieces and tell him who won. She realized he was now part of their household. What do you think? she asked Jazz, who replied, I don't know. What do *you* think? She thought it wasn't so bad having Kent around. He was really doing well. Not that she necessarily wanted the responsibility, but the thought of sending him home to her in-laws', where he would be, if not ill-housed, then surely ill-clothed, ill-fed, and ignored, disturbed her. So she said: Let him stay—if it's okay with your parents. They laughed, Jazz did a fine imitation of his parents celebrating, and they turned out the light; and since it was too soon after birth to have intercourse and since it didn't really pay to start fooling around on a Sunday night if nothing was going to happen, they went to sleep.

*   *   *

In Lee's fifth week home, Will Stewart came for lunch, bringing with him a silver cup with Val's initials and an autopsy report and crime scene photos of a double homicide in Hewlett Harbor—a banker and his girlfriend shot dead in the banker's sauna. "Beautiful," Lee said, holding up the cup to the sunlight.

"To go with the silver spoon she was born with," Will explained. "It's not quite an antique. It's from the 1880s or '90s. The dealer had a fit when I asked him to monogram it, but I told him this is for a very special young woman." He bent over Val's carriage and touched her nose and ran his finger lightly over her downy scalp, but he declined Lee's offer to pick her up. "Not for single guys," he said, sounding slightly nervous, as if by holding her he would then be held liable for anything that went wrong for the rest of her life.

They sat under an old linden in the backyard. Lee had spent the morning on a salmon mousse and was still edgy over the suspense of unmolding it. It looked beautiful, she had to admit, surrounded by translucent slices of cucumber and toothpick-thin curlicues of carrots scattered capriciously about. She had set the redwood picnic table with some of her Taylor linens, and although it was almost like falling on the point of a sword, she asked to borrow some of her mother's English china. Too showy, she had fretted, moments before Will arrived, rearranging an allegedly casual centerpiece. But there was something about him that made the gracious gesture seem all right—not ostentatious but a grand idea—and now she was glad she had fussed.

"This could have been your case," Will remarked, buttering his roll, watching Lee read through the medical examiner's notes. "Not that you have time to watch TV or read a paper, but it's all over the news."

"What should I have done? Stuck my uterus in a shopping bag and come to work right from the hospital?"

"If you were really dedicated."

"How's the office?" she inquired. For a quarter hour, they discussed the case he had brought to show her. Then he regaled her with amusing war stories of other cases Homicide was working on and added a few horror stories about Jerry McCloskey's increasing attempts to interfere with his running of the unit—and Woodleigh Huber's reluctance to put an end to McCloskey's political maneuvering. "Why are they doing this to you?" Lee asked.

"Because I fired one of their boys and refused to hire another."

"But you hired me. I was a political contract."

"You were different. You were good. The guys they sent me were consummate party hacks. Huber genuinely wants me to run the best Homicide unit in the state, but he also wants me to staff it with his imbeciles, so he sends McCloskey down to try and get me to comply."

Will looked wonderful, Lee thought. He sat relaxed in a lawn chair, the plate and napkin resting casually on his lap, his dark skin shining in the glimmers of sunlight that shot through the thick leaves of the linden. The only man on whom a seersucker suit was not baggy. Of course, Will Stewart could wear the salmon mousse on his head and look elegant.

"When are you coming back, Lee?"

"Soon."

"Define soon."

"Another six to eight weeks." They both turned to Val. She was fast asleep, but her tiny mouth was busy making nursing movements.

"She's a beaut," he observed. "Hard to leave." He set his plate and napkin on the table. "Are you thinking of not coming back?" Lee froze, thinking perhaps something had gone wrong and Will did not want her back. Or if not Will, maybe Woodleigh Huber had determined that her father-in-law did not deserve such a big plum as her job. "Now stop it," Will admonished. "I see you going off the deep end, and there's no reason for it. I want you back. So does everyone. Okay? But every time I call you about one of your cases and ask, Hey, when do you see yourself getting back here? you start obfuscating: I'm not sure. I have to speak to the doctor. I have to check a nanny's references. Can I call you back, I'm rolling out a pie crust."

"Well, I just told you," she said, wishing she had not made peach pie for dessert. "Six to eight weeks."

Will studied her. "Forget I'm your boss and you live and die by my whim," he said. "Talk to me. Is something wrong? I sense . . . I don't know. I sense something."

"I feel a certain pressure to stay home."

"From your husband?"

"From my whole family. I'm out of sync with them. Definitely with my mother and sister. My mother tries on shoes for a living, and my sister works as a volunteer in a day care center. You couldn't find two more traditional women's roles if you looked for them."

"Okay, so you feel pressure to be a housewife?"

"Yes. But there's a lot about being a housewife that I like. There's a part of me that would love to win a Pillsbury Bake-Off or learn to cut a dress pattern. But I want to be a lawyer too, more than I want immortality for my blueberry-ricotta cheese tartlets. Much more. Actually, the pressure isn't just from my mother and sister. It's more from the men. Here they are, Jazz and my father, going off to work. And what do they do there? Talk about sleeve lengths. Have coffee with rich ladies and butter them up—'Indulge me. Try on the lynx. I have a feeling it's right on the money with your coloring.' And what do I do? Hang out with a bunch of hairy-chested cops and criminal lawyers. Strategize how to demolish a witness on cross."

"So they're doing traditional women's work too?"

"Yes, in a sense, even though it's business. I think *they* see what they do as not quite manly enough. Girl stuff. And I'm sure as hell doing the boy stuff."

"So you feel you don't fit in anymore?"

Lee nodded. Even though Val had not made a peep, she picked her up from the carriage and held the baby close against her. "It's not what I *do* at home that I don't like—the cooking, the crocheting, and all that. It's how I *am* that bothers me. I hear myself sometimes, and I'm talking half an octave higher than I do at the office. So girlish, so sweet, so unball-busting. I never talk about work anymore. Just 'Whew, had a hard day,' or something like that. Nothing of substance. Because nobody wants to hear it."

"Are you sure it's not just you feeling guilty about how much you love being a lawyer because your husband . . . couldn't cut it?"

"No, I don't think so. Does how much I love it show?"

"Sure, blatantly and flagrantly. For all your blueberry things, there's a part of you that loves a fight, *has* to contend. And isn't what we do a much more civilized way to deal with aggression than the way our defendants get rid of their hostilities? So if you're thinking of quitting . . ." Will reached out for Val. Lee draped a cloth diaper over his seersucker shoulder and handed him the baby. Although he did not smile, he looked extremely content with what he was doing. "Don't quit. You need a safe arena to fight in."

"I'm begging you," Jazz said, following Lee into the bathroom. "Please, just put it on hold for a year or two."

"We agreed—"

"Don't you want to spend time with Val?"

"Don't you? What kind of question is that?"

"You're the mother." She squeezed the toothpaste too hard, and a strand of aqua paste squiggled onto her hand. "I know it's not fair, but for thousands of years, mothers are the ones who stay home. I'm not saying give it up. I'm saying put it—"

"—on hold. Well, the answer is no. N-o. I know my being away all day is not a perfect solution, but I can't help it. I hired a great nanny. *You* said she was great." What Jazz actually had said was that the nanny, a woman from Iowa named Cherry Berke-meyer, was "a dream," and he had sounded so much like Leonard at his trendy worst that Lee had felt something fairly close to nausea.

"It's not just Val. We have responsibility for Kent now. You're the one who wanted to take him on."

"*We* were the ones who agreed to take him on, and if you'd like, I can quote back that conversation verbatim." She brushed her teeth with such force that her gums began to bleed. She wished she could put her hand right in the middle of his chest and shove Jazz out of the bathroom. Instead she rinsed her mouth as discreetly as she could. "And when I hired Cherry, it was with the clear understanding that Kent is part of the package, even though he's away all day. When he comes home, he's hers as much as Val is."

"What if Cherry leaves?"

"She was at her last job for seven years. We're paying her the national debt. Where is she going?" Jazz shrugged and turned to leave the bathroom. He was wearing pajamas that had his initials on the breast pocket. "Jazz," Lee said.

"What?" he said, exhaling slowly to show his patience.

"You're not the man I married." Before he could say that she was not the woman either, she continued. "You've become a middle-aged Jewish furrier. What the hell has happened to you? Wanting me to stay home . . . where I belong! Where is the man I went to law school with, the man who was so proud of me—of what I did?"

"I was proud of you then. I admired your drive, your guts. But I think it would take a hundred times more courage to quit and not do the knee-jerk feminist thing and abandon your kids to someone else to raise."

She flung her toothbrush onto the counter. "Then let me make a suggestion. If you don't want your child abandoned to a perfectly competent and very nice woman, then you stay home. Quit the fur biz. I'll stay with the D.A.'s another year, then I'll go into private practice. Who knows, maybe we can even afford to keep the house. In any case, I'll make something we can live on, if not here, then someplace else that isn't a hellhole. Okay?"

"No," Jazz said very quietly. "It's not okay. But I see I have no say in the matter, do I?"

"In terms of my work, no. In terms of your own, yes."

"Then I'm sorry if I upset you." He turned and walked back into the bedroom.

"I'm sorry if I upset you," Lee replied to his retreating back.

"I guess we'll have to agree to disagree," Jazz called out as he kicked off his slippers and lifted the blanket.

"I guess so." Lee looked into the vanity mirror, feeling there was something more she had to do in the bathroom. But she could not think what.

The next day she returned to work.

Nineteen

Before Norman Torkelson and Mary Dean came into my life, I had tried fifty or sixty murder cases. So did I know what went on in killers' heads in the days and weeks following a murder? Not a clue. Elation? Maybe. Anguish? Could be. Or did they simply revert to regular life, thinking: Hmm, I've got to buy more oatmeal, or: Gosh, I'd better get to the bathroom, because *Seinfeld* will be on in two minutes? After more than twenty years as a prosecutor and a defender, all I knew was that killers keep their crimes to themselves. Except for the random teenage sociopath who brags to his friends, hardly anyone admits to murder.

An example: Take those times when the circumstantial evidence is overwhelming that X shot Y right between the eyes. Overwhelming means nothing: X will deny it. *What*? Me kill Y? Outrageous! If there are actual eyewitnesses—an entire order of nuns willing to testify that, yes, they saw X come over and whack out Y (who at the moment of his death was on his knees, saying his rosary)—then X will have to admit, Okay, I did it. But he will swear on a stack of Bibles that it was in self-defense.

So now that Mary Dean had actually offered me that uncommon gift, a confession—*I killed Bobette Frisch*—I wasn't about to throw it away. Forget about telling Norman. He would only fire me. And if he had half the brains I credited him with, he'd have his new lawyer start proceedings to keep me from talking about the case—if not to shut me up permanently, then at least to hassle me until Norman could get Mary out of harm's way. Or Norman would simply shove aside everyone in line at the jail pay phone, call Holly Nuñez, and claim that Mary was confessing to save him. Don't believe a word she says! I did it. And Holly would respond: Not to worry, Norman. I believe you.

So sitting there with Mary in the furnished apartment she and Norman had shared, I knew my only course of action was to keep her from talking to him. I sensed that with this case, considering all the webs a con artist could spin, any fancy footwork on my part would be counter-productive. Simple, direct action was best. So I invited Mary to come with me to talk to the assistant district attorney in charge of the case.

"You mean now?" Mary inquired, bending over to unplug a vacuum, one of those low, expensive chrome models fitted with tools for cleaning venetian blinds and upholstery. Too sleek to have come with the apartment. I wondered if she and Norman schlepped it from city to city on their travels or if they sprang for a new one in each place they stopped for a scam. "You really think I should?"

"You're the one who has to make that decision," I said, sounding like any proper, mealy-mouthed lawyer. Come *on*, I was thinking. Let's get this thing rolling! But my words came out as soft and sugary as cotton candy. "If what you tell me is true, Mary, that you want to help Norman, then . . ."

"I'll go," she said quietly.

"I'm glad," I told her. Mary wheeled the vacuum into a utility closet crammed with an awesome array of mops, brooms, brushes, spray cans, bottles of scary-colored cleaning liquids and two pairs of rubber gloves. "Just get on a pair of shoes. I'll call a colleague of mine. A lawyer. I can't represent you, because I'm Norman's lawyer, but I'll stick by you and this woman will see you through it. We'll stop by her office, then go on to the D.A.'s. I'll drive you down there." I did not tell her to bring her toothbrush while she was at it; there was no point in putting her good intentions to the test.

Mary peered down at her denim minidress. "Is this okay to wear to the D.A.'s?" It was a mistake for me even to think about it, because in that microsecond, she was off to her bedroom closet, going through the rack, no easy task, since the clothes were packed in so tight, hangers were just an impediment. She eased out a black dress, only to reject it as "too evening-y, don't you think?" Then came three green dresses: olive, emerald, and bottle green. After a conversation longer than the ones I usually have to explain every single nuance of the plea bargaining process, we agreed the olive was best for such a serious occasion.

I was half expecting her to consult with me on her choice of shoes and bag. When she didn't and, instead, hopped into a pair of gold sandals, I found myself let down. Why? I suppose because I didn't want to face having to see Mary face the music. Yet that was precisely what I'd been working toward: fairness, justice, whatever you want to call it. The killer should be the one punished for the crime of murder. No matter what kind of louse Norman was, it was wrong for him to pay for what Mary had done. Walking over to the telephone, though, I felt low, that logy premenstrual feeling. Just moving the three feet was almost beyond my capacity; I was slogging through a substance thicker than mere air.

While Mary put on makeup, I called Holly and announced I was bringing someone in to see her on urgent business. Before she could tell me she didn't have time for me, I hung up. I watched Mary at the bathroom sink, a magnifying mirror in one hand and a mascara wand in the other. Time trudged forward. It was taking so long, as if she were coating one lash at a time and letting it dry before starting the next. For all I knew, she was. When at last she picked up a blush brush I said: "It's better if you look a little pale, Mary."

I had met Barbara Duberstein in the Mommy Room—these days apparently called the Mommy-Daddy Room—on the first day of our children's nursery school. A five-foot-tall powerhouse—her husband called her The Little Engine That Could—she had just started at Hofstra Law School. We hit it off, getting into a fairly emotional discussion about the Eleventh Amendment and the limits on the jurisdiction of the Federal judiciary, while her son and my daughter watched

337

the class guinea pig move its bowels—an apparently enthralling experience. She was now a single practitioner in Mineola with a solid general practice, doing everything from wills to matrimonials to an occasional criminal case. She was smart and savvy, one of the rising stars of the County's G.O.P., and I wanted her for Mary because I knew she had clout, in case clout would be called for.

But I knew, and so did Barbara, that clout couldn't do much for a client who wanted only one thing: to confess to murder. She tried getting Holly to agree to use immunity, in which we could go in for a single interview and nothing Mary would say could be used against her. But as we figured, Holly wasn't giving out anything, not to someone who is determined to confess to a homicide the D.A. already thinks has been solved. Are you *sure* this is what you want to do? Barbara asked Mary. Once we get there, you won't be able to take it back. And Mary replied: Let's get it over with.

Mary was staring at Holly's perfect oval pale-pink acrylic nails. Understandable. Nail-staring was definitely less distressing than looking into the lens of the video camera looking down at her, taping her confession. Earlier, she had tried to alleviate the awfulness of this brown, plasticwood room by making goo-goo eyes at Sam Franklin, who was sitting on Holly's side of the table in the D.A.'s small conference room. But he had regarded Mary with such indifference that, wounded, she had turned away. It was strange sitting in that windowless, airless room: three women lawyers with shoulder pads, an about-to-confess killer in a halter-top dress, and a cop who kept looking from one of us to another, as if fearful of contracting estrogen poisoning.

Holly, unlike Mary, was not checking out nails. No, it only looked that way. For the last hour, she had been studying Mary's powerful-looking hands and long, strong fingers. "What happened when you choked her?" Holly was asking. "Did she die right away?"

"No," she said. "Not right away." At first, I had been furious with Mary. What a birdbrain, that she would be more interested in an assistant district attorney's manicure than in the fact the A.D.A. was going to send her for many years to a place where lack of emery boards would be the least of her problems. But then I saw how Mary was sitting: bolt upright, her hands clutching the brown metal arms of her chair, fingers curved rigidly, like claws, toes curled tight in the open sandals. All I could think of was that her posture was that of a condemned woman strapped into the electric chair, waiting for the juice.

"Tell me about it," Holly prompted. "The choking." Her usual cheerleader's perkiness was absent, but she couldn't fight her nature. Congenitally buoyant she was: chin up, shoulders back. Her hands, fingers loosely laced, rested on the edge of the table, but every once in a while they would flutter, as if seeking the crepe-paper pom-poms they were born to wave. From a professional point of view, I had to admit, she was handling the interview with the right balance of skepticism and encouragement. For Mary's sake, I was relieved Holly was prosecuting, and not one of Woodleigh Huber's other new assistants in the Homicide unit, two guys my partner, Chuckie, and I referred to as Venom and Spite. Holly, for once not looking as if she had something better to do, was making Mary go over her account again and again, each time seeking more detail. She got everything out of Mary that I had, and more: like the fact that Mary had been stalking Bobette and Norman for three days prior to the murder, peering into the windows of Bobette's house. Once, the day before, she had watched them as they made love on the couch in the living room.

"I'm waiting," Holly said. "I need you to tell me about it."

"You mean the neck thing?" Mary asked.

"You bet. The strangulation," Holly responded, a little too brightly for my taste.

"I don't know. I was, like, in this daze. But she kept trying to pull my hands off of her. Grabbing me here . . ." She lifted her right hand and brought it over, gingerly massaging her left wrist.

"She was grabbing you around your wrists," Holly said for the record. "Is that right?"

339

"Yes, she was trying to pull my hands away. She kept doing it, but I was stronger and she kept getting . . . you know." Mary looked away from Holly's nails, embarrassed.

"No, I don't know. Please tell me."

"She was getting weaker. So then she started making these noises." Mary croaked four times, brief, staccato froggy sounds. "I mean, it was awful, but not *really* like choking. More like she was trying to tell me something but couldn't."

"Were you saying anything to her?" Sam asked.

Mary turned to me and Barbara. We signaled it was all right to answer his question, so she turned back to him. Her expression eased: a man. The enemy, hostile, but still a man. "No," Mary told him, "I didn't say a thing." He and Holly sensed what I sensed, that this was a lie. He waited, fiddling with the clip of his photo ID on his breast pocket. "I *may* have said something about her getting out of Norman's life," Mary finally conceded.

"Be more specific," Holly ordered.

"That, like, Norman was in love with me and was going to marry me and the only reason he said he would marry her was for her money because she was . . ." She lowered her head and mumbled something.

"Talk a little louder," Barbara prompted her.

"She was a fat pig," Mary said defiantly, staring right into the glass eye of the video cam.

"Did she die right then?" Holly asked. Naturally, she knew from reading the autopsy report pretty much how death had occurred. She was trying to make sure that Mary's account concurred with the objective findings.

"Not that second. But the"—Mary made the choking sound again, but softer this time—"finally stopped. And her eyeballs got yucky. Then she shut her eyes and I let her down." She turned to Sam. "She was very heavy. I couldn't hold her."

Before he could make a nasty comment and rattle her, Barbara Duberstein asked: "Mary, remember when we started, how Ms. Nuñez asked you if you were making this statement of your own free will? You said yes, you were." Mary said yes, quietly and, for her, quite seriously, as if for once she truly comprehended the import of what she was saying. "Did anyone put undue pressure on you to make this statement?"

"No."

"Did you discuss making this statement with Norman Torkelson?" I asked.

Mary gave a loud, fast laugh. "Are you kidding?"

"Is that a no?"

"Of course it's a no. He'd kill me if he knew I was doing this!" She happened to glance at Sam as she said this, and shrank back. "I don't mean, like, really kill," she explained to him. Almost as if it were beyond Sam's control, his eyes changed from cold dead cop eyes to sympathetic eyes, and almost instantly, into the misty eyes of soap opera close-ups. Holly glanced at me as Sam's face began an unfamiliar journey into softness. I shrugged, as in: What did you expect? Holly shrugged back, as in: Another one bites the dust. Barbara merely looked heavenward and exhaled. "But see," Mary continued, addressing only Sam Franklin now, "Norman said he should be the one to go to jail. Because he started the whole business and dragged me into it—which isn't true. I love him. It was my idea we should work together, not his. But he said it would be easier if he went, because he's been away before." Still looking at Sam, she explained: "To jail. Away to jail." He nodded his gratitude for her elucidation—passionate, all-out nodding that might never have stopped if Mary hadn't started talking again. "See, Norman knew the ropes about jails. But he said, like, it wouldn't be that long, with time off for good behavior. He told me: Just sit tight. But I can't! Not now. I didn't know they"—she turned from Sam to look at Holly—"were going to throw the book at him." Her beautiful green eyes filled with tears then, and in total disregard of her mascara, Mary began to weep.

"Well," Holly began when we were back in her office. She had called in a policewoman to baby-sit for Mary while she, Sam, Barbara, and I talked. But Sam had made some excuse about pressing business at a crime scene in Plainview. The last we saw of him, however, he was no closer to Plainview than Mary's chair. "I have to admit: You told me so, Lee."

"So now what?" I asked, crossing my legs, thinking about the inevitable call I would make to my guy to tell him I had no idea how late I'd be and would he be so good as to start thinking creatively about the defrosted chicken breasts in my refrigerator. This was going to be one long day.

"There's just one little problem," Holly said.

"What's that?" I asked.

"I don't believe her." Her voice was effervescent, like one of those bubblehead quiz show dames who think their co-host might be putting over a fast one on them.

"What are you talking about, Holly?"

"It doesn't play for me."

I hate hip new uses for old verbs. "It doesn't matter if it plays for you. It's not a record, it's not a movie; it's a confession in a homicide case."

"It's something they cooked up, some scam."

"Holly, they haven't connected on this. Norman doesn't know she's opened up to me. He sure in hell doesn't know she's here."

"I'll have to ask Jerry."

Terrific. Jerry McCloskey, the head of the Homicide Bureau, was so ineffectual that he'd probably want to commission a poll before deciding. "Go ahead," I told her. "There's really nothing much to discuss. You have a confession. You have physical evidence to corroborate the confession. Whether it plays to you or not is not a matter of law."

"I'll get back to you."

"No," I said. "I'm not leaving until you make a decision." So she went to speak to Jerry McCloskey.

While she was gone, Barbara and I discussed how it never fails to amaze us that even the most assertive people will knuckle under to outrageous behavior. How come it did not occur to Holly to say: "What do you mean you're not leaving? Get out of my office. I'll call you when I'm good and ready." Throughout my legal career, all I had to do was cross my arms and dig in my metaphoric heels. Okay, now

342

and then a lawyer would tell me to take a hike, but if I'd sit there, unmoving, and maybe glance at my watch to let them know how much I resented their obstinence, they'd get up from their desk or pick up the phone and do whatever it was I wanted them to do.

The question neither Barbara nor I addressed was that if we were both such hotshot tough lawyers, how come we so often turned into wimpettes in our personal lives?

Holly returned in about fifteen minutes. "Jerry says okay."

"Good," I said, curbing a desire to leap up and shout with joy and do a jig.

"I want it clear that we're not disposed toward anything approaching leniency," Holly said to Barbara.

"Pray you get a female judge," Barbara replied. "Otherwise, you're going to get leniency up the wazoo."

"You're dead if it's a man, Holly," I concurred. "Did you check out Sam Franklin?"

"I know! Did you ever see such total mush?"

"Terry Salazar," I told her. "My investigator. Mr. Hard-Ass."

"He's kind of cute," Holly said.

"If you got to know him, you'd realize he's the most uncute man in America. Except when he met Mary: She turned him into marshmallow fluff. And the last judge she appeared before, the one in Maryland who granted bail after Mary smiled . . ."

"A man," Holly guessed. "Well, wouldn't you know it!" She laughed brightly. Too brightly.

For God's sake, I thought. It's one thing to be relieved that a matter is resolved. But she's just lost the chance at a big, fat, juicy trial that she was going to win. If this had been my case as an A.D.A., I'd be pretty depressed about that. Okay, she was doing what I wanted her to do, being decent, fair-minded, but Holly had gone for the easy out so damned fast. Barbara didn't seem troubled by Holly's cheery mood, but she really wasn't involved in the case. I had expected at least four or five hours of brawling, though, with Holly pounding her desk a couple of times, telling me that Norman wasn't off the hook yet, that he might have been an accomplice, or at least an accessory. Holly should have put up a fight, if only to save face, because her judgment had been wrong when I'd tried to get her to listen to my theory that Norman might have been innocent of Bobette's murder. But here she was, sitting back, yukking it up, having a high old time. Wasn't she in the least surprised at Mary's confession? Or at least thoughtful about the case: After all, she had almost sent the wrong person away for life.

She told Barbara she would do serious thinking about a sentence recommendation, which I doubted. Then Barbara left, to allow me to talk about my own client. "When can you spring Norman?" I inquired.

"I don't know that he can get sprung. We may be holding him as an accessory."

"Holly, give me a damn break! There is nothing in Mary's confession that puts him there at the time of the murder, nothing that connects him in any way to the homicide. You know there isn't a judge around who's going to keep him in, so why do we have to go through all this?"

"I'll see," she said, making a little note to herself. She used a pen with aqua ink. "I would have to have his release approved upstairs."

"Huber will be thrilled."

"He'll be okay." Holly was chirping again. "Jerry's been putting tons o' pressure on us to push those cases through, so they're going to be *real* glad we can close the books on this one."

"It's not fair to Norman to have to stay on ice while you're waiting for your paperwork to go through. That could take weeks."

"It won't take weeks, Lee," Holly said, laughingly. I all but expected her to add: You old silly. "Days at most. I'll do my best to see to it that it gets moved through channels as fast as humanly possible." This last offer did not spring from Holly's usual chipperness. Having been caught prosecuting the wrong person for murder, she wanted to keep the case as quiet as possible. If she locked Norman in the cooler for too long, she knew perfectly well I would have to start making a loud and public fuss. "Okay?"

"Okay," I said. But I was reluctant to leave. I told myself that if Holly wasn't down about not going to trial, I was. Sure, I'd known *People* vs. *Torkelson* would be almost impossible to win. That didn't matter. I needed to try; I needed the fight.

"I can't believe I won't have to stay late tonight," she enthused. "I'm going to call up my boyfriend and say, 'Hey, let's have dinner.' I hope he doesn't die of shock that I'm actually free."

But this was a big deal, damn it! Didn't Holly have any emotion about it? Or was she some new breed of woman, so smart about the ways of the world that nothing got to her? Had she experienced everything—or seen so much on television—that she had no innocence left? No euphoria? No despair? Something important had just happened. Or was "important" just a word in her vocabulary, a tool in prioritizing? For Holly, life seemed to hold no surprises.

"Speak to you tomorrow!" she promised, trying to pry me out of my chair. Then she began leafing through her papers, searching for her next case.

Sam was the one watching over Mary. The policewoman, a cinder block in a blue uniform, was leaning against the wall opposite them, checking out the scaly skin on her elbows, now that it was Department-decreed short-sleeve season. Sam, leaning toward Mary, was saying God knows what into her ear. He was trying to soothe her. But all Mary seemed to hear was some tragic song in her own head. She did not even look Sam's way. She stared straight ahead, her eyes swollen, ringed black with dissolved eye makeup. But she was no longer crying.

"Mary," I said softly. I gave Sam a Get-away-I'm-a-lawyer look, but he wouldn't budge from her side. In fact, I was not her lawyer. And I was not on her side. I was the reason she was about to be fingerprinted, photographed from the front and in profile, and given the baggy blue female inmate's uniform. "Do you want me to get Barbara back here for you? Or do you want to discuss things with Norman?"

Suddenly Mary came back to life. She seemed to expand

in her chair, a parched plant getting water. "I can see him?" she asked.

"I don't think so. But maybe I can talk them into finding a room for you up here, so you can have a private phone conversation." She slumped back down. "Barbara is quite good." I found myself wanting desperately to cheer her up. I gave her an encouraging smile that all but said: Help is right around the corner. Except it wasn't. What was wrong with me? I had done more than my duty. I had done the right thing. Except I felt like hell. God, how I hate ambivalence—and there's so damn much of it.

Mary looked down at her gold sandals, which would, in a matter of an hour or so, be replaced by a pair of often-worn, smelly, ill-fitting prison shoes. My heart went out to her. Not because she was a gorgeous-looking girl going into an ugly place. In the whole scheme of things, I told myself, why shouldn't she be going? She didn't deserve my pity. She had committed the ultimate crime. Taking away her gold sandals, her eyeliner, and her freedom would still not make up for the cut-off life of Bobette Frisch.

But what in God's name had brought Mary Dean to this place? What kind of home had she come from? What sort of family life turns a girl into a hooker at age sixteen? She was so beautiful. She had such a capacity for love. And, okay, she was dumb and coarse and selfish, but as even Sam Franklin had discovered, she was so sweet.

And any chance she might have had for a life was now lost forever.

Twenty

Naturally, Lee had heard stories around the office about Will Stewart's lady friend, Maria. So upper class that she was called Ma-rye-a, not Ma-ree-a. Maria Parkhurst. Half black, half white. Her father was either a rich Socialist or a surgeon, and her mother a dancer for someone—one person mentioned Martha Graham, another said no, Agnes de Mille, and a third was positive she had been the only black Ziegfeld Girl. Whoever her parents had been, Maria Parkhurst had inherited good looks. "Stunning" seemed to be the adjective favored by the lawyers, while one of the homicide detectives who had been invited to the previous year's Nassau County District Attorney's Office picnic preferred "like nothing I've ever seen before."

"You've never met her?" Jazz asked, surprised.

"No." Lee craned her head, looking over her colleagues spread out on blankets on the sand at a private club in Atlantic Beach, a low-key, relatively proletarian club the office had taken over for the day. She spotted someone tall and brown in a lime-green playsuit at the volley-ball net, but when the woman turned around, Lee realized it was Wanda, the law librarian, who looked like Louis Armstrong with a wig. "Maria lives in the city, so she's not about to drop into the office. And Will is so close-mouthed about his life he'll only tell you something if you ask. Right around Easter, when he went to Greece, I asked him if he was going alone. He looked at me like I was asking him to see his privates, but he finally said no, he was going with Maria. 'My friend Maria.' Ha! Like they were going to take separate rooms."

"What does she do?"

"She's the assistant headmistress at a girls' school in the city.

The Barton School. She teaches history there. It's supposed to be very exclusive, very—"

"It is," Jazz informed her as he returned Woodleigh Huber's wave and exhaled a small but patient sigh as Huber, his white hair rigid in its pompadour despite a brisk ocean breeze, jogged through the sand to greet him. "I guess my old man's party credentials are still okay."

Lee smiled at him. Why not? After the three months of discord following Valerie's birth, Jazz had gone out of his way to be a good and generous husband. Generous in gifts: a ruby ring for Christmas, a big Ford station wagon for her birthday. Part of her was mortified, feeling they were presents for a completely different kind of woman, someone decorative, useless. Certainly they were not presents people still in their twenties should be giving each other. Yet another part could not take her eyes off the sizzling red sparkle on her finger—and cried "Hot damn!" at the classic wood side panels of the wagon, grabbed the key, and went for a ride.

But forget largesse: Jazz had grown generous in understanding. He told Lee he was trying not to view each night she worked late as a personal affront. And as for having asked her to quit work, well, he'd done a lot of thinking about how his mother had stayed at home—and how thoroughly she'd neglected all four of her children. He had been wrong about pressuring her not to go back to the D.A.'s, and he was really snowed by the way she was handling it all. He hoped she would accept his apology.

Added to Jazz's reawakened good nature was the fact that he was now more attractive than ever. The sleek, self-satisfied sheen of young wealth that Lee found profoundly unappealing was being tempered by the loss of his boyish softness, the emergence of sharper, more manly features. To her and, evidently, to the female lawyers and the secretaries on the beach who trekked across the sand in Woodleigh Huber's wake in order to be introduced.

Of course, a woman's having a winner for a husband does not mean her heart freezes in the presence of other men. When Lee finally spotted Will and Maria on the wood steps that led to the beach, she was chagrined at the insistent *thump-thump-thump* in her chest. *Thump!* Will's here! In white shorts, no less—wow, does he have great legs!—and a yellow shirt, with a blue sweater

348

tied with casual perfection around his broad shoulders. He looked as if he had stepped out of the pages of one of the debonair men's magazines Jazz read but had neither the guts nor the panache to emulate. *Thump,* too, because of the woman beside him.

An exasperated *thump,* because Maria really was as advertised. A knockout. No, more. She looked like someone wonderful to know. White pedal pushers, simple white shirt, a plain straw hat, holding Will's arm with practiced intimacy. A warm smile. Will waved. Lee waved back.

"That's got to be him," Jazz said.

"Who else?" she replied, smiling.

"And *her,*" he added. "Holy shit!"

Lee behaved as if she were amused by her husband's reaction to Maria Parkhurst. But it is hard to be truly amused at the sight of one's husband googly-eyed over a six-foot-tall, amber-colored, hollow-cheeked beauty, especially when that beauty is on the arm of your great pal, your boss, the second man you think of as, somehow, yours.

Up close, however, Maria was not beautiful, merely fabulous, with almond-shaped hazel eyes and full lips that thrust forward slightly, as if in a kiss. Lee was nervous that Jazz, smitten by Maria, might act foolish, but his manner was perfect and his patter above reproach. She should have known better than to doubt Jazz's social skills, she later reprimanded herself. She did note, however, that he was aiming an inordinate number of four- and five-syllable words at the headmistress when shorter ones would have done fine. Their discussion was fairly straightforward and—so as not to affront Will's Republican sensibilities—innocuous about what the G.O.P. campaign strategy might be against Jimmy Carter. Such purposely inoffensive conversation did not require "eventuate" and "dissimilitude" on Jazz's part.

Fortunately, he calmed down later, reverting to short, friendly words, as the four of them made their way to tables set up on an awninged patio where an early dinner was being served. "How long have you two known each other?" he asked Will and Maria. Lee wanted to pat him on the back: Good work! Will, not surprisingly, remained mum.

Maria answered: "It seems forever, doesn't it?" Will managed to incline his head: Yes, it does. "Let me think. Twelve years, I believe." Her elocution was so perfect it made everyone else sound as if they were talking through huge globs of mashed potatoes. Upper class, but brisk, not with elongated, isn't-life-too-too-tedious vowels. Every word she uttered sounded perfect. And to make it worse, Lee thought—as she stood beside Maria, feeling excessively squat—the woman was nice. Maria disengaged her arm from Will's, turned away from the men, and focused on Lee. "I'm so glad to have the chance to meet you. Will is enormously fond of you."

Lee was about to say, The feeling is mutual, but felt that would be too corny, so she settled for: "Thank you," even though she knew she should have come up with a more graceful response, considering the company she was in.

Maria, meanwhile, was peering along the length of the buffet table. Lee assumed she would turn up her nose at the plebeian food—hot dogs, burgers and a vat of chili—but Maria grabbed a plate. "He used to feel terribly isolated." She plopped two hot dogs onto buns, added sauerkraut and mustard, then helped herself to a hamburger. Why did Will feel isolated? That's what Lee was dying to ask. Because beneath his savoir faire he was shy? "How do you think chili will look on my shirt?" Maria asked. "Oh, what the hell: I'll chance it." Isolated because he was a black working in a largely white world? "Could you pass me a spoonful of those chopped onions, please? Thanks. Oh, look! German potato salad! You know, you're his first friend in that office. I'm not talking about the usual collegial relationships. You're a real friend."

Lee was so thrilled to hear that her feelings about Will were returned and so grateful that the formidable Maria had chosen to be cordial that it was only near midnight, leaving Val's room after watching her sleep for about fifteen minutes, then searching for an antacid to combat the effects of the chili, that she realized Maria and Will were perfectly matched. Together they dazzled. Together they were interesting, substantive, articulate. Both were decent and courteous well past the point of genuine kindness. And neither gave the slightest hint of what he or she was really feeling.

"Wait," Lee said as she climbed into bed. "Don't go to sleep yet. Tell me what you think about Will Stewart and Maria."

"I think she should buy a sable coat. She'd look magnificent."

"She looks magnificent without it." Lee did not even wait for the loyal, husbandly You look magnificent too. "Do you think they're in love?"

Jazz kept his teeth together, but she could tell by his flaring nostrils that he was stifling a yawn. "I can't tell."

"What do you *think*?" she insisted.

"I think she's awesome."

"But does he?"

Jazz turned over onto his side to face her, acknowledging that sleep was not to be his until the conversation was finished. "I can't tell. For two people who aren't all that demonstrative, they're very affectionate with each other. Holding hands, giving each other private looks when they think no one is watching. I guess they're in love."

"So why don't they get married?"

"I don't know. He works out here and she works in the city."

"Come on! That's twenty-five, thirty miles. And they spend a lot of time together. Weekends. She has a house somewhere up in Connecticut, and he's always going there. And vacations too." Then she added, in a voice she could hear was too emotional, "They're going on a photographic safari in Kenya in September!"

Jazz could not suppress his next yawn. "Can we talk about this tomorrow?"

Two days later, Lee took her five o'clock cup of yogurt into Will's office. He responded by getting a cup of coffee. "How's the *Yancy* appeal coming?" he asked.

"Fine." She stirred up the fruit on the bottom a little too vehemently. "I liked Maria."

"Good," Will said. Knowing something more of an intimate nature was required, he added: "She liked you and Jazz." He waited a fraction of a second and gave her: "I liked Jazz too."

The following week, they went out to a Chinese restaurant, ostensibly to discuss whether she had any thoughts on training the new assistant D.A.s. But she and Will had been finding some excuse each Wednesday or Thursday for months. Just dinner: Lee could not acknowledge to herself that these evenings were the high points of her week. Their discussions covered a lot of ground:

351

They bickered about politics and delved into legal issues. They discussed everything from how to marinate salmon to their personal lives, although "personal" was a relative term.

Will spoke with respect and affection and some degree of annoyance of his parents, of their ambition for him, and how he felt that no matter how much he accomplished, they were never quite satisfied. He went into some detail about the pain of growing up smart and black but isolated from any black community, a child of servants on the Giddings estate; and of being pressured by his parents to take whatever guff Mr. Giddings' twin sons, boys his age, dished out. To Lee, the twins sounded like everything Will was not: white, stupid, and incredibly mean-spirited. That was as revealing as he got. When he talked about Maria, it was more travelogue than disclosure: We went here; We ate in this restaurant; We heard this orchestra.

Lee, on the other hand, held nothing back, in part because for the first time, she had a friend who truly wanted to listen and had the time to do so and whom she trusted. She told Will about her early life, not just the outline of it but the texture, about her parents and sister and how she had always felt both her I.Q. and her weight were twenty points too high to allow her to be loved by her family. She confided in him all about her early obsession with Jazz, and they talked about what it meant in the marriage. Will was not just a polite listener; he was a rapt audience. He even relished all Lee's updates on Valerie: standing up by herself, sitting beside Lee and pretending to read The New Yorker aloud—in her baby gibberish—and the gleeful, devilish look in Val's eyes when she first tasted chocolate.

"Will," she said, so quietly he looked up from his hot and sour soup. "What about you and Maria?" The couple at the next table turned to stare, but whether it was because Lee and Will were white woman with black man or because they sensed an important turn in the conversation, Lee could not tell.

"What's there to talk about?" he asked.

"You know, we're friends. I don't hold back. Now maybe the average mature woman or the average shrewd lawyer wouldn't be so open. But I have absolute confidence in your friendship."

"Good," he said, and crumbled the crispy, greasy noodles he usually disdained into his soup.

"I wish you had the same confidence in mine."

"Lee, you're making a big deal over nothing. What you see is what you get with me. I don't have any secrets. There's no mystery."

"What about you and Maria?"

He took a slow sip of soup. "I love her."

"Does she love you?"

He thought about it for a moment. "Yes. But I don't think we've ever gotten to the point where we're *in* love with each other, at least not at the same time. That's why we never married. I guess deep down, we're a couple of romantic saps. We want it all. That's that."

"That's not that. That can't be."

"It is."

"I want to know how you *feel?*"

"About what?"

"I don't know. About anything. About not being married. About not having children. About being a Republican, for God's sake. How could you have retained your sanity during all those years of Silent Majority crap?"

"It's not that I don't think about things," he said cautiously.

"Are you the only person in the world who doesn't have an inner life?"

"What are you talking about?"

"I want to *know* you. Tell me something I don't know about you."

Will put down his soup spoon. "My biggest regret is that I've never had children. My secret ambition is to write a book about a case the NAACP brought in '38, where the Supreme Court ordered the admission of a black into the University of Missouri Law School because the state hadn't provided a law school for blacks. You want something else? I think tarragon is an overrated herb."

"You know all that isn't what I'm talking about."

"I had a brother who died when he was nine. I was six. Leukemia."

"I'm so sorry. Was it painful for you?"

"What kind of question is that? Of course it was. His name was Timothy. Timmy." He looked away.

So they talked about other things throughout the meal, especially about cooking, as they often did, and Will told her how much he liked shopping for food in Chinatown. After they paid the check, he mentioned that he was very serious about going to China for a couple of months to study cooking. Lee was amused. "When are you going to be free for a couple of months?"

"Soon."

"What do you mean? I can't believe you're actually going to take the time—"

"I'm leaving the office, Lee."

"What?" She didn't get it. "Leaving the D.A.'s?"

"Yes."

"*Why?*" He did not answer right away. Lee hugged herself as if she were cold, but it was summer. She felt frightened. I don't want to be left alone. Don't go! Ridiculous! Would any male lawyer feel like this? *Don't leave me! Don't leave me!* she wanted to plead. What's going to happen to the two of us? How could Will want to go someplace she wasn't?

Crazy, her reaction. She knew that. But she could not imagine a morning without Will opening the door of his office at nine-thirty on the dot and her strolling in with a bag with two cups of coffee and the one buttered sesame bagel they shared. Why, after spending his entire legal career at the D.A.'s, would he choose to quit? Especially now that she was there? "What made you decide to leave?" she managed to ask.

"There's a new chief of Homicide."

"What? Who?"

"Jerry McCloskey."

"I don't believe it!"

"I suggest you do believe it. Huber wants to run for governor in '82. I'm the one person getting in the way of his patronage plans. With Jerry in there—"

"The man's a nincompoop, for God's sake!"

"Well, Lee," Will said, and he reached out and took her hand, something he had never done before, "he's going to be your nincompoop."

The first six months after Will left the office were utter misery, and the next six months were so bad that Lee considered quitting the law altogether. However, she did not want to give Woodleigh Huber the pleasure of replacing her with one of his dum-dum cronies. Also, she sensed neither she nor Val would thrive if she became a full-time homemaker. Oh, it was tempting, but in her heart she knew she would come to loathe fresh-baked bread. She would never finish the complete works of Dickens. And a girl can crochet just so many afghans.

So she stuck to it, trying to compensate for her loss of spirit by throwing herself into her cases with increased vigor. Which is how she and Chuckie Phalen wound up screaming at each other. He was defending the owner of a cesspool service company, one Jimmy Durk, whom the grand jury had indicted for beating to death Marlon "Buck" Toomey, a service station owner who had refused to do any more work on Durk's truck until an outstanding bill had been paid. The beating had been witnessed by Durk's assistant, an eighteen-year-old with a history of drug use.

The fight had begun with Chuckie's outrage that Lee was charging his client with murder, not manslaughter. "There was no intent to cause death!" he shouted. It was not too loud a shout because his lungs were constricted with emphysema. It was, however, angry and antagonistic to the extreme.

"Of course there was. The kid saw Durk banging Buck's head against the car lift over and over and shouting at the top of his lungs—"

"'I'm gonna kill you' is just an expression, and you know it!"

"Murder in the second degree, Chuckie."

The fight had gotten worse when Chuckie discovered that Lee had taken the eighteen-year-old witness under her wing, getting him enrolled in a drug rehabilitation program, arranging with the minister of his mother's church to pay for tutoring so the young man could earn his high school equivalency diploma, getting him a part-time job as a janitor with a furrier in Cedarhurst, a man Jazz and her father knew from the Furriers Industry Council.

Chuckie stormed over to Lee's desk two days later. "You baked the kid cookies!"

"Brownies. So what?"

"'So what?' she says! 'So what?' You're buying his testimony against my client. So what about that, Mzzzz. White?"

"I'll make you a batch when the case is over, Chuckie," she

replied, not even bothering to look up. "Now stop it. You're not going to change my mind." If she had looked up, she would have seen that her opponent had gone from purple-faced to white with rage, and that his jaw was set in stone.

So it did not occur to her an hour later, when Woodleigh Huber's secretary called and said the Boss wanted to see her, that it had anything to do with Chuckie Phalen and *People v. Durk*. She only knew that she hated every sprayed-in-place white hair on Huber's head, hated his pale blue telegenic shirts, hated him for putting an incompetent, time-wasting, jurisprudential know-nothing bootlicker like Jerry McCloskey behind Will's desk.

"Come in!" Huber called out in his big, *60 Minutes* voice.

Lee opened the door and saw Huber positioned before his flags and, standing across the desk from him, Chuckie Phalen. She gave Chuckie the beginnings of a you've-got-to-be-kidding smile before turning her attention toward the man all the assistant D.A.s except her called Boss. "You wanted to see me, Mr. Huber?"

"*Are you out of your mind?*" Huber roared. Shaken by his vehemence, Lee took a step backward. "Making all sorts of calls on a cooperating witness's behalf? Getting him a *job?*"

"What's wrong with getting him a job?" she inquired.

"What's *wrong?*" Huber cried out.

"It's like giving him money," Chuckie prompted.

"Shut up, Chuckie," Lee said. She was no longer mildly amused by his running to tattle. She was angry, so angry that for once her stomach did not hurt. She turned back to Huber. "What I did was entirely proper."

"Then you're even worse off than I imagined, if you don't get what was wrong! What you did was *outrageous*! You stepped over the bounds of proper prosecutorial conduct." He was booming, as if speaking to a great gathering without a microphone. Lee understood, then, that it was a performance. In part for Chuckie. More, to show her he had no loyalty to her. She was not part of the team. He could not fire her for cause, but he could make her want to quit. "What you did is a discredit to law enforcement!"

She started to say: I'm sorry, but I don't see it that way, but all she got out was "I'm sorry—"

"Being sorry is not enough!" Huber must have moved, because

the flag of the State of New York fluttered. "You're off this case!"

"Mr. Huber, this is—"

"One more word out of you . . ." He let the threat hover in the air, then turned to Chuckie. For Huber, Lee was no longer in the room. "Chuckie, Jerry will call you the minute he's reassigned the case. You have my profound apologies—"

Lee slammed out of his office.

The following day, Jerry McCloskey told her she was no longer in Homicide. If she wanted to, she could remain in the office, but because she had shown such a lack of plain old common sense, they did not think she should be trying murder cases. Or even felony cases. The following day, she was assigned an unlawful-dealing-in-fireworks trial.

A week later, she walked out of the District Attorney's Office.

Chuckie Phalen must have heard Lee was packing up because he was waiting on the courthouse steps, breathing hard. "I'm sorry this happened."

She knew the Old Boys liked lady lawyers to be ladies, so she said: "Fuck you. Fuck the horse you rode in on." Then she added "Ass-kissing snitch," and kept walking.

"What you posit is not without merit," Chuckie conceded. She turned. He fluttered a not-very-white handkerchief. "See? Now listen to me, Lee—and notice I didn't call you 'Sis.' I know you don't like that. I blew my cork and went up to Huber's to blow off a little more steam. I had no idea he'd lace into you like that, especially in front of me, that self-serving windbag. You know what that was all about last week, don't you?"

"Yes, I do," Lee replied coldly. "And he got what he wanted, didn't he? I quit. Maybe he's not such a moron after all." She walked away from Chuckie, but when she saw he was trying to catch up with her and the effort was too much for him, she slowed her pace.

"Buy you lunch?" he inquired, nodding in the direction of the silvery lunch truck parked around the corner.

"No, thank you."

Chuckie was gazing down at the framed photos poking out of her overstuffed tote bag. One that she herself had taken, Jazz and Kent at a Knicks game. Another of her and Jazz with the five pups of Ginger's latest litter. And a picture of Val, queen of the jungle, amid her stuffed animals. "Beautiful. How old is she?"

"Almost two." She could see him working very hard to hide his discomfort: a mother leaving a child that age to go to work.

"Wonderful age. Lovely child. Don't suppose you want to go over to TJ's, have a snort with me?" Lee knew the Old Boys meant by that a jigger of Scotch; cocaine was merely something their clients trafficked in.

"No, thanks. Too early for a snort. And even if it weren't, Chuckie, I don't want to drink with you right now."

"I understand," he said, and let her walk away. But he was waiting as she turned back to see if he was all right. "Lee!" he called out in his reedy voice. "Stick around. We'll open a bottle of glue." Weighed down by her attaché case, her tote bag, her shoulder bag, and a Saks Fifth Avenue shopping bag filled with copies of her appellate briefs and extra pairs of panty hose, she found herself returning to him. "Come in with me." At first, she thought he was suggesting TJ's Taproom again. "Come work for me, Lee. It'll be fun."

"I don't want to work for you, Chuckie. I don't want to work for anybody."

"Come on, Sis, wake up and smell the coffee. You know how many firms will hire a female to do trial work? You should jump up and down and clap your hands and say 'Goody-goody' that I'm making you an offer."

"I'll find something. Or I'll go out on my own." Her possessions felt very heavy, and she had to prevent herself from looking over at the courthouse, in the direction of the District Attorney's Office, wondering if there was a way she could talk her way back in, knowing there was not.

"And who's going to refer cases to you?"

"I hope you will, Chuckie. And I have a few pals." Lee knew Chuckie was aware that she was considered Will Stewart's protégée, and she had no doubt there were rumors of another sort of relationship between them as well. After a six-week trip to China, Will had returned to become a name partner at one of the biggest firms—and certainly the best—on Long Island.

"Will Stewart's doing civil stuff. Is that what you want to do? Rake in the money doing corporate litigation? Is that the kind of law you want to practice, each side trying to suffocate the other under reams of paper? Working ten years on a case, never getting into court? I don't see how your pal stands it. With me, you won't get rich, but you'll get the real McCoy."

"I can get the real McCoy without you."

"Bushwa!"

She knew she would never go to Will with her hat in her hands. She wanted him as a friend, not a patron. And Chuckie was right. How many lawyers would refer criminal cases to her? Corporate? The thought of doing corporate litigation made her want to take a nap. "Thanks, Chuckie. I appreciate your—"

"Aw, don't give me that hooey. Put down your things, would you, so's we can talk properly." She set down her shopping bag, tote bag and attaché case. This was nuts, she thought. Out of a job for five minutes and dickering over a new one on the courthouse steps. Take time to smell the roses. Get a subscription to *Foreign Affairs.* Go to the Frick and look at Dutch masters. "What do you want?" he inquired.

"A partnership."

"A partnership? You're talking through your hat! You're still a kid. You just got your walking papers from the D.A. You're not being realistic. Here I was thinking: This girl's got a head on her shoulders. I guess I was wrong. You're living in a dream world."

"We try it out for a year. You pay me fifty thousand dollars."

"*What?* That's crazy."

"That's a bargain. You've got a huge practice, Chuckie." She did not mention that he was ill and it was common knowledge that he desperately needed help with his caseload. She did not have to. "After a year, we're partners."

"What'll you be asking? Ninety percent of the take?"

"What do you think is fair?"

"Twenty," he muttered. "I'm the founder. I built it up."

She really was embarrassed about haggling with him. After all, she didn't need the money. Everyone knew she had a successful husband. Allow an Old Boy like Chuckie his male pride.

Not if she was going to be his partner. "Thirty percent, and fifty percent of any work I bring in."

"You've been smoking that funny stuff, Sis."

"Call me 'Sis' one more time and it's off."

"Lee," he sighed, and put out his hand.

She shook it and said "Chuckie."

While Will celebrated her decision to join Chuckie Phalen as if she had just been appointed attorney general, sending not merely a case of champagne to Lee's new office but a six-foot-tall flowering hibiscus tree, Jazz reacted as if she'd told him she had bought new towels for the guest bathroom. "Great," he said, bisecting his baked potato and hiding it under a dollop of sour cream only a person with a vigorous metabolism could consider. "I look forward to meeting him." Lee ground some pepper on her half potato and waited for questions about their deal. Jazz wasn't just her husband; he was a smart businessman as well as a lawyer. But he had no questions.

Lee was furious at his reaction: I have to listen to a two-hour diatribe about what the fur buyer at Bonwit Teller said about the button-holes on raccoon jackets and then prove I'm listening by asking questions for another hour, and he can't even ask: Hey, where's your new office? But as she was doing with increasing frequency, she quickly transformed her anger to hurt, and then almost immediately transmuted her wounded feelings into sympathy. I understand Jazz is having trouble dealing with my career because he was brought up in such a hidebound, male-dominated world and because the whole subject of lawyering is painful to him. He's trying so hard to be supportive, and he's really thoughtful about everything else.

This was true. When she was on trial, he took over completely, coming home early from work, often giving their nanny a night off to be with her boyfriend, making dinner for two—him and Val. While Lee still fulfilled many of the usual female functions—buying birthday and Christmas gifts, keeping the social calendar and the family checkbook, gardening—Jazz took over the grocery shopping and stacked and emptied the dishwasher.

And he did it with such good nature. Lee could never get over his best quality, his innate cheer, and realized that it would have been wasted in the solemn halls of Johnson, Bonadies and Eagle. But in the retail business, his buoyancy, blue-blood manners, and brilliant smile brought him nothing but success. Where Leonard was insecure, Jazz was confident. The younger man was the one who decided to approach chichi department stores around the country and soon had them carrying Le Fourreur's line of fun furs—jackets and coats designed for everyday wear. Emboldened by his success in the upscale market, Jazz, subtly and diplomatically, convinced his father-in-law to overcome his snobbery and go out for the low-priced trade as well; there were now three Furhavens in New York and New Jersey, with a fourth and fifth on the drawing boards.

So before their thirtieth birthdays, Mr. and Mrs. Jasper Taylor—as the place cards at the Fashion Congress's annual Luxe Awards dinner had them—were already a well-to-do young couple.

"Turn around," Sylvia said to Lee, eyes narrowing as she assessed her daughter's outfit, a classic ivory strapless ball gown that gleamed, like the pearl choker she was wearing, against Lee's golden skin. "Nice. Whose is it?"

"Valentino."

"Impeccable. When did you get it?"

"Last month sometime." Then she added, because she knew it would annoy her mother. "I went one day during my lunch hour."

Sylvia sighed and shook her head at Robin, but fairly good naturedly. Now that her younger daughter was drug-free and dressed in a four-thousand-dollar blue-and-green Saint Laurent peasant gown, she was easier about granting her elder daughter the right to be eccentric. "And I'll bet you bought this because it didn't need any alterations," Sylvia said indulgently.

"Absolutely. My fashion philosophy is: If it zips up, I buy it."

"I knew it!" Sylvia crowed. "See? I know you, Lee!"

The Penthouse at the St. Regis was filled with men in their black and white tuxedos and with their women, gorgeous peacocks strutting their colors in silks and jewels. Even in the soft dimness meant to approximate candlelight, Lee was nearly overcome by the beauty of so much smooth, bare skin against lustrous fabric, by the sweet and spicy scents of extravagant perfumes, by these people's casual acceptance of their own incredible wealth. So different from her working world, from the savagery and sewer stench of the holding pens in criminal court to the wood-paneled, leather-chaired austerity of fine old law firms like Will's.

"Are you okay, Lee?" Robin asked.

"Fine," she said, as she watched Jazz dazzle a department store dowager agleam in emeralds and diamonds, the diamonds far whiter than the smile the woman was flashing back at Jazz. "I love to watch him work the room."

"He's not bad," Robin said, then flung back her head and burst out laughing at her own understatement. Her long blonde hair, held only by a velvet ribbon, shone in the pale light. Jazz glanced in their direction and waved at them. "He's a social genius is what he is. Can you imagine anyone feeling that at ease with themselves?"

Lee shook her head. She was glad Robin was there, because she certainly did not feel at ease. The cocktail hour was already stretched to nearly two, and no one except her seemed wiped out by the continuing parade of magnificence and the paucity of hors d'oeuvres. She needed her sister. Yet she wished Robin were elsewhere. It disturbed her that her sister's life had not changed. Twenty-seven years old and still a volunteer at a day care center, still a college dropout, still living at home and vacationing with her parents. But Robin herself had changed, Lee knew, from her old self-absorption to being the most loving and reliable sister, an adoring aunt, a fond sister-in-law. Lee and Jazz often included her in their plans not out of familial obligation but because Robin was good company.

Jazz came over and put an arm around each of them. "Bearing up?" he asked, just as the lights flickered, signaling dinner.

"We're fine!" Robin said happily.

"Fine," Lee assured him. He shepherded them into the perfectly proportioned ballroom to their table, keeping perfect pace with the rest of the graceful crowd. Not an elbow was jostled, not a hem stepped on. He held out a chair for each of them and Lee watched as Leonard mimicked his courtesy and did the same for Sylvia. Several men at other tables followed suit, until a contagion of chair-pulling overcame the ballroom. "See what you started?" she asked Jazz, delighted. She took his hand until the banquet was served, a menu chosen less for taste than for its lack of drippiness.

She ate and watched her husband pick at his food, too busy being the Golden Boy to eat. He waved, he stood to chat with table-hoppers. He shook hands, kissed cheeks, accepted compliments with sweet modesty, and laughed. It was only when Jazz sat back down that she caught a glimpse of him pressing his tired back against the rear of his chair, closing his eyes for an instant. When he opened them, there was not a sign of laughter. His eyes seemed as old as those of the ninety-year-old shoe mogul in a wheelchair at the next table. Older, because the shoe mogul was swiveling his head, taking everything in, tearing off bits of his roll and stuffing them into his mouth, greedy for now and for banquets to come. It was only then that she understood that Jazz was just as miserable in this splendiferous company as she was.

She kept busy with the cases Chuckie handed over to her: a criminal possession of stolen property here, a grand larceny there. But although Lee received a few referrals from the attorneys she had come up against as a prosecutor, they were relatively minor matters. She knew she had to prove herself as a defense lawyer. It was easy for the Old Boys, and the younger ones as well, to brush her off with the explanation that anyone can win when representing the People; the facts are on the People's side.

How do I get a big case? she asked Will during one of their daily phone calls. I want a showcase case, where they can see what I can do. Will said simply: Ask for it. What do you mean, *ask for it?* Start taking lawyers to lunch, he advised her. Tell them you're looking to build up your own practice, that you don't feel it's right to rely solely on Chuckie. Talk shop with them. Let them see you as a colleague, not as a girl lawyer. If someone has a big-mother case, ask if you can be second seat. *Ask?* she practically gasped. This is your professional livelihood—okay, Lee? It's not like asking a boy out on a date. It's permissible. It's also permissible, if you hear of a big, fat, juicy crime, to try to get there before anyone else does.

The eleven o'clock Sunday-night news is really a no-news broadcast. Politicians announce nothing new on Sundays. Not a single press release is issued, and no one marches to protest anything. So on that night, television journalists elaborate on sports and weather and offer horrific reports of fires, rapes, and murders. On a cold and sleety Sunday night in February, she heard that Eddie Urquhart of Locust Valley had been savagely beaten that morning as he slept late. He was in a coma, and although a spokesman would not comment, a source at Glen Cove Hospital said he was not expected to recover. Lee, who had spent the day making Valentine decorations with Val and Kent, organizing her scarves and sweaters by color, making love with Jazz during Val's nap, and going out to a new and mediocre Northern Italian restaurant with her parents and Robin, sat up in her bed. "Did you hear that?" she asked Jazz. "Beaten to death in his bed this morning. A million bucks it wasn't a burglar. What burglar sneaks into a house on a Sunday morning?"

He glanced over the top of the business section of the *New York Times.* "What?"

"Shhh," she said, as the barely postpubescent reporter, his face shiny with sleet, stood before a grand colonial house with white pillars and told her that Urquhart was the owner of Spectacle, a chain of eye-glass and contact lens stores located—"On Long Island!" Lee crowed. Nassau County police were said to be questioning Mrs. Urquhart for a description of the intruder. "She did it!" Lee announced.

"Who?"

"The wife." Her pulse was racing.

"How do you know?" Jazz asked. Not waiting for an answer, he went back to an article on regional customs unions.

"I feel it," she said, putting both hands over her heart.

At seven the following morning, she called and woke Chuckie, to find out who represented Spectacle. He didn't know. At eight, she called Will at home, who said it wasn't De Ruyter, Lefkowitz and Stewart, but he'd check when he got to the office, first thing, to see if anyone knew. At nine-twenty, she found out it was Keelan and Stern, Woodleigh Huber's former law firm. Damn! she said. Will said, You're going to worry if he bad-mouths you? His former partners probably don't trust his opinion any more than we do. Okay, Lee said. Let me give it a shot. Will wished her bon voyage and extracted a promise that she would call immediately if anything happened.

At ten-thirty, she was sitting in the office of one of Keelan and Stern's senior partners, Peter Pappas, a contemporary of Huber's, a man given to high Victorian-style collars that hid his entire neck. Thus his large, bald head was a giant bubble emerging from his shirt.

"You don't have to give me your curriculum vitae," he told Lee. "I've heard of you."

"From Woodleigh Huber?" she asked, prepared to defend herself.

"Nah!" he snapped, rather viciously, she thought. "Around. Grapevine."

"Good," she said. "I appreciate your seeing me on such short notice. I don't want to waste your time." Pappas nodded: good idea. "I understand you represent Eddie Urquhart. I'm sorry to hear about his troubles. But it's his wife I'm interested in."

"Why?"

"It sounds as if she might need a criminal lawyer. I'd like an introduction. For a woman of her background, I think I'd be the ideal choice."

"You do?"

"Let me tell you why."

At noon, Lee was in Locust Valley talking with Paula Urquhart, gathering information, finding out precisely how much the woman had already told the police. Two hours later, Paula Urquhart took Lee into the library, a low-ceilinged room filled with leather-bound unread books. It smelled like a crypt. Paula drew the dusty damask curtains and showed Lee the myriad lumps, concavities, and scars all over her body that were the result of the beatings Eddie inflicted during twenty-two years of married life. At a quarter to three, Paula signed a check for Lee's ten-thousand-dollar retainer. Then she made a pot of coffee, and they sat around until the police came to arrest Paula for assault with intent to kill.

"You're not giving me a hell of a lot to work with," Terry Salazar told Lee. He had just opened his own investigative agency. In a blue suit just slightly too bright to be called navy and crepe-soled brown suede shoes, he still looked more like a cop than a capitalist.

"I don't have a hell of a lot," Lee responded. "Paula told the precinct cops that she'd been downstairs, reading the paper. When she came back upstairs around eleven, to shower, the window was open and Eddie had his head bashed in. She thought he was dead."

"Except he wasn't."

"Right. Just comatose. The first cop on the scene noticed that the window was only open about nine inches. It would have to have been a pretty skinny burglar."

"Who, by the by," Chuckie added from the couch in Lee's office, "was so busy bashing Eddie's head in that he forgot to burgle anything."

"This Paula babe doesn't sound like a criminal genius," Terry observed.

"I think Eddie bopped her on the head one too many times," Lee said.

"Insanity defense?" Chuckie inquired politely.

"I'm not sure yet, but I don't think so. She doesn't seem at all nuts. Nice as nice can be. She put up a pot of coffee and defrosted a Mrs. Smith apple pie for the crime scene crew. Anyway, insanity is a real desperation defense. It hardly ever works."

"Almost never," Chuckie concurred.

Lee rubbed her face, trying to erase the fatigue. Now that she had the Urquhart case, she had no idea what she was going to do with it. Still, she finally had her own client, and a client who could afford to hire Terry. And Chuckie Phalen was sitting in her office, not she in his. It was all—she smiled to herself—exhilarating.

"What was the weapon?" Terry asked.

"One of her kids' old ice skates. The blade." Both men barely suppressed a shudder. "She says she was up in the attic going through the old sporting goods stuff, looking for a baseball bat, but then the bulb started to flicker, and she got scared so she grabbed the first thing she could. She knew it wasn't as good as a baseball bat, so she made sure that her first hit was a hard one, and right between the eyes."

"He's a vegetable?"

"Now and forever." She closed her eyes for an instant, trying to imagine Paula Urquhart as she made her first hit with the blade of the ice skate. Then she pictured the scarred, misshapen mess that was her client's body. "She was deathly afraid," Lee explained when she opened her eyes. "That's why she tried to kill him."

"Self-defense?" Terry asked with a chuckle.

"I hear it's worked in a couple of states," Chuckie said, squelching Terry's chuckle. Then he turned to Lee. "Wasn't Eddie sleeping at the time?"

"It's still self-defense," Lee told him. "He beat her, he terrorized her for years. She lived in that big house on the sound. Alone. No house-keeper, no nothing. After the second kid went off to college, he took away her car. He said it was because she'd dented the fender twice and couldn't be trusted. He would not let her out of that damned house! The only time she left in the last year was for her two trips to the emergency room. He was holding her prisoner. She knew it was only a matter of time until he killed her. And she had to save her own life."

So this is the problem, Terry reported to Lee. I checked out all the hospitals she's been to over the years, all the doctors. And she never once said, Hey, my husband is beating the shit out of me, punching me in the stomach till I'm puking up blood. Paula tells them she was in a car accident, or she had her steam iron fall on her—she used that one a lot—or she was in the garden and got hit by a rake, or she was cleaning out a closet and all the stuff fell onto her. There's no record of her ever accusing Eddie of laying a hand on her. One doctor said he asked her: Is your old man beating you up? And you know what she said?: How dare you!

Go back, Lee told him. Find out if the doctors felt the injuries were more consistent with a beating than with an accident. And don't let your hospital contacts read her medical records to you. I want you to look at them yourself. Somewhere, someone must have made a little note about isn't it odd how her left wrist keeps breaking. Three times, as if someone twisted it and twisted it till it snapped. Ask if they're willing to testify. If they're not, tell them we'll subpoena them. Speak to all his employees at the Spectacle stores: Has he ever flown off the handle at work? Gotten into any fights?

She spoke with social workers, psychologists, psychiatrists and academic experts in the still burgeoning field of domestic violence and hired expert witnesses. She employed a photographer who specialized in medical malpractice cases to photograph Paula Urquhart's disfigured body. And she met daily with her client.

Paula Urquhart, unfortunately, looked perfectly capable of fending off whatever blows came her way. At forty-three, she was of slightly above average height and appeared solid, as if she was even larger but had been compacted. Her hair was light enough that the gray was not at first noticeable. She wore it off her face and seemed shaken when they took away her plastic tortoiseshell headband in the Nassau County Correctional Center. She was neither pretty nor homely, but totally forgettable. It was only when you stared at her, searching her bland face for the wielder of the ice skate, that you noticed one cheek was higher than the other, which had been flattened by repeated blows to the face.

"Paula, was there a telephone in the house?" Lee asked. They spoke in a small room in the women's section of the jail, an area referred to as the Waldorf, where inmates charged with highly publicized cases were held. The Waldorf had a common room for meals and TV, a few cells, and a small, square interrogation room, which was used for lawyers' conferences. It was furnished rather luxuriously for the center, with two chairs that were not nailed down and a couch covered in artificial blue leather. In her blue uniform, Paula seemed part of the furniture.

"A telephone?" Paula repeated, not seeing the point of the question. "Of course we had a telephone." She counted on her fingers. "Six extensions. No, wait, seven. There's one in the basement."

"And Eddie went to work . . . how often?"

"Six days a week." Her voice was strong yet sweet, like that of a teacher of early primary grades.

"If I put you on the stand, the prosecutor is going to ask why—in all those years—you didn't call for help."

"He said he'd kill me if I talked about our private matters. That's what he called it all the time: 'a private matter.' He'd come home and if he was feeling mean . . . it was hard to tell from looking at him, because he's got such a nice face. Friendly. With freckles. People always think freckles are friendly."

"'A private matter'?"

"Yes. He'd come in and put down his briefcase and hand me his coat and I'd hang it up. When I came back, if he'd say: 'Paula, I have a private matter to discuss with you,' then I knew I was in trouble."

"And then? He'd start hitting you?"

"No. He'd talk to me, tell me what I did wrong. Like he felt

368

sorry for me and wanted to help me see where I was making a mistake. Then he'd get angry and say I wasn't paying attention or something. And then he'd yell, and pretty soon he'd start hitting."

"Did he hit you with his hands?" Lee observed Paula closely, looking for emotion, but could find none; she spoke as if what she was describing had happened to a woman she had never met. Lee knew her expert witnesses could explain this seemingly dispassionate account, this distancing of herself from the horror she had experienced, in order to survive. But come on, Lee thought. Cry a little, for God's sake. Help me out. Give me some tears for the jury.

"Usually he punched me, but if something was around, he'd use that."

"Like what?"

"Like anything. A wooden hanger. A pot. A Dustbuster."

"You have two children, twenty-one and nineteen. Right?" Paula nodded. Lee did not see the instinctive smile most mothers display when their children are mentioned. "Are you on good terms with them?"

"Oh yes. Very good."

"Did they ever see Eddie beat you?"

Paula's forehead creased. She touched her ring finger, probably to twirl her wedding ring around, but it was in an envelope in a safe in the correctional center's basement. "Not really."

"What do you mean?"

"They saw him get angry and shove me. Maybe smack me once or twice. But he was good about keeping his temper around them. He'd wait till after dinner and till I cleaned up. Then he'd say: 'Excuse me, kids. Mom and I have a private matter to discuss.'"

"But he beat you severely. Don't you think they heard anything?"

"I hope not. I tried very hard to keep quiet. I didn't want to frighten them."

"Ladies and gentlemen of the jury, good morning. My name is Lee White, and I am the lawyer for Paula Urquhart. Mrs. Urquhart is accused of a vicious crime: assault with intent to kill. As the prosecutor has told you, on Sunday morning, February tenth, someone entered the bedroom in the Urquharts' mansion in

369

Locust Valley and beat Eddie Urquhart so badly that he is now in a coma and not expected to recover. That someone was not a homicidal maniac, not a burglar whom Eddie surprised, but his wife, Paula, whom you see there at the defense table in the pink shirtwaist. You may be asking yourselves: How come, if we admit to this crime, we're here pleading not guilty?"

The courtroom was packed. Chuckie, Will and a couple of his partners, Barbara Duberstein and a score of past and present assistant district attorneys sat comfortably, their arms draped on the backs of the wooden benches to display their proprietorship of the halls of justice. They were not there only to root for Lee or the prosecutor, however; this was one of the first invocations of the battered wife defense in the county, and they wanted to see it. Terry Salazar was right behind the defense table, wearing a new suit. He had been foul-mouthed and obnoxious but brilliant. Lee was amazed when he discovered how many people were aware of what Eddie was doing to Paula, and even more amazed at how many Terry had been able to convince to testify.

The press was there too, as were everybody's relatives, from the judge's incredibly fecund extended Italian family, which took up three rows, to Eddie and Paula Urquhart's—sitting on separate sides of the courtroom—to Lee's. Ginger and Fos fit right in, but Sylvia, Leonard, Robin, and Jazz were so glaringly attractive, so fashionably turned out, that they might have been VIP's in the first row for Thierry Mugler's latest collection. Lee made sure not to glance in their direction so as not to align herself with the overprivileged and, by doing so, alienate the jury. However, even without looking, she could feel, hanging heavily in the air, her mother's disapproval of her gray dress with white collar and cuffs. The few remaining seats were taken by courtroom buffs, including a retired mailman who watched all Lee's trials. When he took his seat, the mailman had pointed to his lapel: a white carnation. "White," he had called out, and winked.

"We're here because for twenty years of their twenty-two-year marriage, Eddie Urquhart beat this woman, sometimes once a week. Not shoved, not smacked, not even hit. Beat her with his fists, with broomsticks, with a lamp. The first time that he broke her nose and cheekbone, he did it by hitting her full force in the face with a telephone. Not just once, but over and over again."

Lee stopped and took a deep breath. Oxygen, fuel so she could be propelled onward to talk about something so revolting she could hardly bear it. She, not Paula, would be the one to show the judge and jury the terrible toll of Eddie Urquhart's violence, since nothing—not even Lee's not very veiled suggestion that it was all right to show some emotion—could wipe the pleasant expression from Paula's face. She prayed that by the end of the trial, the jury would understand that this was one of the cruelest scars of all.

"The first question that came to my mind when I heard about this case was this: How come she didn't call the police if it was so bad? Eddie was a successful businessman, and he worked every day but Sunday. Paula had a phone. For a while, before he took it away, she even had a car. If she was too proud or too fearful to call the police, she could have taken her children, escaped. She could have told one of the emergency room doctors bandaging her fractured ribs: My husband did this to me. She could have called her brother or her sister and cried: Help me! Hide me! And if she was totally desperate, she could have armed herself, and the next time Eddie brutalized her, she could have shot him in self-defense. If she had done that, she would not be in this courtroom today. Well, in order to find her not guilty, you'll have to understand in your hearts just why Paula could not cry out for help, why she had to wait and strike at her husband the only time when he was not her personal terrorist, her very own torturer: when he was asleep."

Lee outlined for the jury the witnesses who would testify to Eddie's brutality: the frighteningly polite Urquhart children and an oil-burner serviceman. Paula was the perfect housewife, with a list of repairmen and a file of their bills. Every one of those people had been contacted by Terry. Only one had observed friendly-faced, freckled Eddie out of control, but the man could tell how Eddie had banged Paula's head against a wall near the thermostat six times. Then, moving the length of the jury box, Lee summarized the testimony her expert witnesses would give. "You will hear, ladies and gentlemen, that Paula was a prisoner of terror. The one reality in her life was that this all-powerful man would hurt her if he was displeased. It was not a fear: It was fact. He inflicted terrible pain on this woman two and three and four times a month. And he was displeased so easily. If a shirt button was loose, she got punched in the mouth so hard she lost three teeth. When she dared to serve him a steak that he said was overcooked, he broke a bottle of wine over her head. It took two hours in the emergency room for them to get all the pieces of glass out of her scalp. She told the doctor she and Eddie had been having a drink in a bar and somehow she got hit when two men began to fight. If those were the punishments for the crimes of a loose shirt button and a well-done steak, can you imagine how she feared the punishment for telling the truth? The lawyer for the District Attorney's Office is going to try and make it sound easy. 'Dial 911. What was the big deal?' By the end of this trial, you will understand with terrible clarity what the big deal was."

After her opening, Jazz kissed her and said: "There are no words." Then he found one: "Amazing." Robin echoed "Amazing," and Sylvia and Leonard held back for a moment before embracing her, as if waiting for permission. They were not just proud, she sensed, but a little frightened of her.

"Good opening," Chuckie said, and pinched her cheek.

"A-plus, Whitey!" the mailman called out.

"I can't believe it," Barbara Duberstein said. "Me, buying this defense. But you got me."

Will waited for her by the water fountain. He seemed both amused and pleased by the fuss over her. She left the others and approached him. He had such grace, such stature, that he made everyone else in the hall outside the courtroom appear dim. "Well?"

"A great opening. Really. You're on your way."

"But not there yet. Did you see juror—"

"Number four?" Will asked. "With his mouth all screwed up, like he's saying 'Give me a break. Had to save her own life by cracking his head open with an ice skate while the poor guy was asleep. Ha!' Number four's a rough one, Lee. You're going to have to fight for his soul." But he said it with spirit, indicating it would be a good fight, one that would be worth something whether she won or lost.

"Any advice?" she asked.

He thought for a moment. "It's just a case. You've tried hundreds. Don't blow this up too much. Don't think this is going to make or break your career. If you lose, people will know you did a fine job, and you'll get some referrals. If you win, you'll get a lot of nice phone calls and a few more referrals but you won't make the cover of *Time*." She nodded, knowing objectively that he was right although not quite believing it. Then she began to go over the pros and cons of a particular line of questioning she was thinking of using with the government's expert on domestic violence—all the while wishing that instead of telling her it had been a great opening, Will had hugged her.

Nothing could have prepared her. She was so exhausted after the first week of trial that she wished she could have hired someone to brush her teeth for her. On Sunday morning, she sat at the kitchen table beside Kent, showing him how to hull strawberries. His hands and arms were covered with red juice. Val, in her high chair, was throwing slices of apple about in a spiteful manner, as if she had saved her entire quota of Terrible Twos egregious behavior for this hour.

Jazz had come in minutes before and was unpacking groceries, humming a sappy old song. He seemed so happy that she did not feel too guilty that she was not paying attention to him. She turned from Val—clutching the last apple slice in her hand, debating whether to fling it or eat it—to Kent. Now he had crushed strawberries in his hair. "How about a shower, kiddo?" she asked him.

"No."

"And a shampoo."

"No."

"New soap, new shampoo."

Kent considered her offer and decided to yield to temptation. Whenever they went on vacation, Lee saved the complimentary toileteries the hotels gave out, knowing that nothing made Kent happier than his own new cake of soap. She decided to go along with him to make sure he did not transfer strawberries to the wallpaper as he climbed the stairs. "You'll watch Val, Jazz?"

"Sure," he said. Lee glanced up at the clock. Nearly eleven. She was trying not to think about the trial. But it was at nearly that very hour, on another Sunday, that Paula Urquhart told herself that if she did not act soon, Eddie would be waking up.

Lee found a cake of soap—The Breakers, Palm Beach—where

they had spent a week the previous winter watching rain on the ocean. But although there were four bottles of hair conditioner left in the box she kept in the linen closet, there was no shampoo. "Here," she said to Kent. "You start your shower and I'll go find shampoo."

"I'll wait," he said, clearly thinking she was trying to pull a fast one. She laughed at his suspicious expression and walked into the bedroom, to Jazz's closet. Stretching to reach the top shelf, she got down his travel kit. Beside the mini-can of Gillette Foamy and the smallest bottle of Tylenol was a miniature bottle of shampoo from a hotel. She sighed, relieved. Confrontation averted. She zipped up his case and returned it to the shelf. "See?" she said to Kent. "Would I kid you about new shampoo?" She glanced at the bottle. Hotel Carlyle. New York. New York? Why would Jazz have shampoo from a New York hotel?

"Give me it!" Kent was irate at her holding back. Lee checked it again, thinking she had misread it. Hotel Carlyle. New York. Kent grabbed it from her hand and went to shower.

All right, maybe the Carlyle was part of some chain and Jazz had really gotten the shampoo in Toronto, where he had gone for some big fur fashion show. Or it could have been from when they'd traveled out West and stayed in Portland for a long weekend to spend time with his sister Irene.

But in her heart she knew how the shampoo had got from the Hotel Carlyle into her husband's overnight kit.

The prosecutor waited until Jazz had been asleep for nearly an hour. Around midnight, she got out of bed. He did not stir. Methodically, she went through his closet. In a pocket in his camera bag, she found one of the miniature books sold at the counters of bookstores: Elizabeth Barrett Browning's *Sonnets from the Portuguese*. The tiny red ribbon bookmark was placed on what Lee knew to be the most overquoted poem in the English language: "How do I love thee? Let me count the ways." She searched, heart pounding, but found no inscription, no "To JT with love from Whomever." Careful. They were being careful. She realized the sappy song he had been humming that morning was "Secret Love."

You've gone off the deep end, the defense lawyer in her declared. He bought the book in a sentimental moment on some business trip and forgot it in his camera bag. And the shampoo? An out-of-town department store buyer visiting New York could have given it to him. Do you honestly believe that? the prosecutor demanded. No, she did not.

She tiptoed downstairs. She knew Jazz would not be so stupid as to charge an extramarital affair on their joint American Express card, but she went through the receipts for the past twelve months: no evidence. At twelve-twenty, she woke Terry Salazar and told him she had a confidential matter she wanted handled. He understood that when she said "handled," she did not mean handled the following morning. When she called him back at one-thirty, he told her that a J. Taylor from a company called Le Fourreur had stayed at the Carlyle twenty-two times in the past year. She wrote down the dates. Thank you, she said to Terry. Please hand-deliver your bill. Don't send it to the firm. There's no bill, he said. And listen, Lee, I've already forgotten what I just found out. She thanked him and he told her he was sorry for her troubles and it sucked the big one, didn't it, learning shit like this when she was on trial.

She had forgotten she was in the middle of the Urquhart case. Absolutely forgotten. Twenty-two times. So he was seeing her twice a month. Was she from out of town? From New York and married? He traveled only about two or three nights a month. Except on buying trips to Scandinavia and the U.S.S.R. And for industry conferences. Or if a store executive needed special handling. Actually, he was away more than she had realized.

She took the list of dates she had written down and the little book of sonnets, and retrieved the bottle of shampoo from the floor of Kent's shower. She hid the evidence in the toe of her L. L. Bean Maine hunting shoe. Then she went back to bed, where the man who had betrayed her slept in perfect peace.

"Not now," Will told her.

"I have to," Lee insisted.

"Of course you have to. But you're on trial for two or three more weeks." At eight-fifteen the next morning, they were sitting in the empty courtroom. Lee realized that Will had simply assumed she wanted company, or was getting cold feet and needed bucking up; he arrived with a heartening greeting and a bag with two coffees and a sesame bagel. Still, when she told him of her discovery, he did not flinch or appear in any way surprised. She did not want to ask if there had been something about Jazz she had not seen, if Will had felt all along that he was a heel. For the time being, she took comfort in telling herself that Will was the worldliest man she knew and, therefore, nothing surprised him. "If you deal with your marriage now," he told her, "you won't have the energy to deal with Paula Urquhart."

"How can I not think about it?" she asked, staring into the tan depths of her coffee.

"I'm not saying not to think. I'm saying not to act—unless you feel there is some need for immediate action."

"Who could it be?" she asked. "*Why*? What did I do—"

"I'll take the day off right after your jury comes in. We'll sit down and talk about everything for the entire day. I'll even throw in lunch. Okay? Right now, tell me: What's your biggest problem in the case?"

"You're trying to get my mind off Jazz."

"Yes."

Lee was not sure if she had managed a smile or if her face had merely twisted. "My biggest problem?"

"That's right."

"It's that I am totally convinced of my self-defense theory when I'm in court. This woman was so terrified that she felt her husband was in sole control of her fate. She wasn't able to call for help because somehow Eddie would find out. He was her whole universe. He was God, and he was omnipotent."

"Why is that a problem?" Will asked.

"Because when I'm not in court, when I'm driving home or shaving my legs I start to think: This woman is full of shit."

"You do?"

"My own experts testify under oath that she could not have picked up the phone and called the cops or a priest or someone for help. They swear there was no way she could have told the truth about what hit her all those times she went to the doctors and the hospital. They say, sure, the kids heard what was going on, and yes, they're quite damaged, but she did the best she could, protecting them from seeing the worst of it by going upstairs. And

376

you know what? I can't buy it. There's a voice inside me saying: No matter what, you have to take responsibility for yourself. It may take everything you've got, it may kill you, but ordinary people act with amazing courage every day. And even if she couldn't stop the abuse for herself, how could she not protect her children from living in that hell?"

"You don't think the killing was self-defense?"

"I think she did have to get rid of him. I think she could have done it two ways: with a call to a local cab company, saying come and get me—or with an ice skate. I think she hated him. With good reason. He did terrible things to her. He took away joy and he took away hope. She hated what she had become. I have no doubt that she was a victim of a terrible, continuing crime. And if I were on my jury, I'd tell myself: Self-defense? Bullshit! She murdered him in cold blood."

"How does the jury find the defendant Paula Urquhart on the count of assault in the first degree with intent to kill?"

"The jury finds the defendant not guilty, Your Honor."

The night after the jury came in, Lee slept for thirteen hours. The second night, she told the nanny to go out, visit her boyfriend, enjoy herself. She sent Kent for a visit with his parents. She sent Val to her parents' house with five stuffed animals. She knew Robin could be trusted to keep Val happy.

Jazz flew into the house at seven o'clock, a huge bouquet of white roses mixed with white lilies and a bottle of fine red wine to celebrate her victory. When he heard Kent and Val were spending the night away from home, he could not hang up his trench coat fast enough. He raced back into the kitchen, but Lee was not there. When he rushed into the living room and found her sitting at the end of the couch, feet primly on the floor, he said: "Hey, the flowers are still in the kitchen. You forgot to put them in water."

"I don't care about the flowers."

"What's wrong, honey?" He sat beside her, his brow creased with concern. She knew he was waiting to hear how exhausted she was, or that after all the adrenaline of the trial, she was let down. Lee could feel the warmth of his arm through the sleeve of his suit, so she got up and sat in a chair catercornered to his. "Something's the matter?" he asked.

"You are having an affair." He got out the "Wh—" of "What are you talking about" but she cut him off. "On nights that you were supposedly out of town on business, you stayed at the Carlyle. Thirty-five East Seventy-sixth, corner Madison." It is said that when people are shocked, they look as if they have been hit in the stomach. To Lee, Jazz looked as if he'd been hit in the face. His features went slack and so soft that the bones underneath could have been shattered into smithereens. "But then, I don't have to give you the address, do I? You found it twenty-two times." She watched as he tried to come back with something, but he could not find anything to say. He put his head in his hands. His wedding band looked dull in the lamplight, as if it had a film of soap scum over it.

Finally, he spoke through his fingers. "When did you find out?"

She wanted to tell him what a horrible blow it had been, seeing that little shampoo bottle. Twelve days I held it in! You know how they say in stories: She thought her heart would break? Well, my chest hurt on the left side for almost two weeks. A terrible, piercing pain sometimes. It would spread out and it would zing me, in the middle of the day as I was rising to object, in the middle of the night. But I'm too much the trial lawyer to give away my case, she told herself. And with that, she gave away her case. "Who is she?" she cried out, unable to stop herself from showing how little she really knew. He sat there, his head still in his hands, saying nothing. "Damn it, I have a right to know who she is!"

"No, you don't." He stood and walked across the room and poured himself a tumbler of vodka. He did not ask if she wanted anything.

"Do you love her?" she demanded of his back.

In his own good time he turned around. "I don't know," he said quietly. Then he added: "Yes."

It was worse than she had thought. In all her imaginings, he always started crying and begged for another chance, that the woman was nothing, stupid, not worth throwing away a beautiful marriage for. Please, Lee, forgive me. "What do you want to do?" she asked.

378

"I don't know."

"Do you want to end the marriage? Or do you want to give her up?"

"I wish I knew what I wanted. I wish I knew what would be the right thing."

"How could you sleep with me when you're sleeping with someone else?"

"Don't."

"Don't *what*?" she shouted. "Don't imagine you fucking your brains out at the Carlyle and stealing teeny bottles of shampoo, you cheap bastard!"

"Oh," he said. "Is that how you found out?"

She was not going to let him think he had been caught on that one false move. "One of many clues. You didn't cover your trail very well." She waited for him to hang his head, or put down his drink and run to her, kneel before her and cry how hurting her seared his soul. But he just sipped his vodka slowly and methodically, as if he were at a boring fraternity party at Colgate, trying to get drunk without getting sick. "I'll give you till tomorrow morning to make up your mind," she told him.

He whirled around the liquid in his glass. "I need more time than that, Lee."

"You don't have it. I've had all the pain I can tolerate. If you don't choose me by tomorrow, you've chosen her."

At seven-thirty the following morning, Jazz told Lee he wanted to stay with her.

Late that afternoon, when he had gone to pick up Val and Kent, it occurred to Lee that she had never even asked herself whether she wanted to stay with him.

Twenty-one

There were gaps in my education. Take Spanish. For example, I can to this day have a conversation in Spanish, as long as no complex ideas intrude and it stays in the present tense. I can even quote several key lines of dialogue from *La casa de Bernarda Alba*. However, it took five years of visiting the Nassau County Correctional Center before I realized that a sign I'd thought was a rather menacing warning aimed discriminately at Latino inmates, EL VATO, was the result of someone's pinching the E and the R from the elevator sign in Building C.

Another gap? I had taken Psych 1, to say nothing of Criminal Law, but I hadn't the foggiest notion of how to deal with a client who refuses to get out of jail. So I just said: "Norman, you can't stay here anymore."

"Go to hell," he growled at me. He couldn't say much more because he was busy scuffling with two correction officers, who were trying to turn him over to me for the short walk through the door and out to the parking lot and freedom. Being six foot five, Norman was much taller than either of them, but as they were built along the lines of *corrida* bulls, his progress from the Return Uniforms Here window to the exit door, where I was waiting, was fairly swift. "You're making a terrible mistake!" he cried to his escorts, trying to pull his arms out of their powerful grips.

"Get your ass outta here," the beefier one of them grunted, displaying not the slightest intellectual curiosity about why an inmate would be so intent on remaining on the premises.

"Listen," Norman gasped at them, breathless from his

380

struggle. He was not more than five feet from where I was standing, and getting closer, "I killed Bobette Frisch! Don't let me out." The smaller of the officers—but a guy who could lead the running of the bulls in Pamplona—seemed to hesitate.

"Check the paperwork," I advised the cop. "They want him out of here. Someone else confessed. They arrested her. He's trying to protect her."

"I choked Bobette to death!" Norman stretched out his fingers to demonstrate strangulation, but as his arms were so tightly held so far apart, he could not get his point across. "It was *me*. I did it."

"The one they arrested is his girlfriend," I explained. Unimpressed by Norman's gallantry, the guards heaved him in my direction.

The fluorescent lights in the jail are pretty strong, so I'm not sure that there is a physiological reason why every person who is released squeezes shut his eyes momentarily, as if to keep them from getting scorched by the sun's fierceness. Norman stood outside the closed door of the Center, using his hand as a visor. His red and white checked shirt and gray slacks—the clothes he'd been wearing at the time of his arrest—were now too big for him. Seamed with stiff creases from being folded into a plastic bag, the shirt and slacks looked shabby as well, as if they had contracted some nasty fabric infection that was out of control in the Clothing Storage Room.

I don't know what I expected for getting Norman out of jail and the murder charges against him dropped. Certainly not a thank you, as what I had done was explicitly against his wishes. Not a physical attack either, because the one thing I felt confident about was that Norman did not express his anger in a violent way. I figured I'd hear a big-time chewing out, really nasty, with bellowing and maybe some fist-banging on the trunk of someone's car, a diatribe that would end with one of the guards in the parking lot strolling over and threatening to arrest him for first-degree harassment.

What I did not expect was to be ignored. Once Norman

got used to the sunlight, he stuck his hands in his pockets and walked away. "Norman." I tried to catch up with him, but with his long legs, he was taking two steps for my one. So it was not until he stopped, apparently confounded by the number and ugliness of the jail's pale, bloodless brick buildings, that I was able to apologize. "I'm sorry," I said. "This was not what you wanted—"

"Quite the opposite." Because he was so tall, it was easy for him to pretend I wasn't there. He kept his head high and moved it back and forth, trying to home in on some elusive target.

"Where do you want to go?" I asked.

He shot me a what-kind-of-stupid-question-is-that look. "To see Mary."

I realized he'd been in the Visitors' Center as an insider, not an outsider, and hadn't a clue to where it was. "I'll take you over." When I had left my house, it had been a sweet suburban spring Friday, but the vast concrete parking lot in East Meadow seemed to draw down all the sun's heat. We made our way toward the entrance of the Visitors' Center slowly, trudging like hikers lost in a malevolent desert. "Do you have any identification on you?" I asked.

"Leave me alone."

"Norman, they won't let you see her without your showing a driver's license or a birth certificate." He stopped beside an old car, dark green, filthy. In its grime, someone had drawn the opposite of a smiley face: a circle with two dots for eyes and an upside-down U for a mouth. "They're pretty strict about regulations here," I explained. "But then, you know that." He nodded, barely, a single shake of his head. "I'll be glad to drive you back to your place, although to be perfectly honest, I think the cops were probably over there with a search warrant after they arrested Mary, and if you had a pile of phony ID's, I can't guarantee they weren't seized."

He considered his options, pressing the top of his beaky little nose, right between his eyes, with his thumb and forefinger. "You can take me there. I'll change, then I can go get a birth certificate."

"If you have your choice of a name," I advised him, having seen in my years in criminal law a pretty fair selection of counterfeit documents from dealers in the area, "get something with Norman Torkelson on it. The guards at the Visitors' Center know you by that name. It takes them about a week to forget an inmate your size, so you don't want to show up being Irving Schwartz—at least not today."

By the time I dropped him off, he was speaking to me, although not happily. I understand, he told me. You were faced with an ethical issue and you resolved it as best you could. However, he added, I must say that ethics or morality in the larger sense was *not* served by what you did.

On one hand, I thought he was beyond annoying. A con man spouting off on morality? On the other hand, I felt so sad for him. What a loss! Mary had allowed him to do something he had never been able to do before: love a woman. Everything about her had been perfect for him: her beauty, her sweet dopiness, her larcenous heart. Even her crime had worked for Norman, because it had enabled him to be noble, to offer himself up to save her. What a shock to his system those foreign two emotions—love and self-sacrifice—must have been to a rat like him. But after a while, I thought, he'd gotten used to feeling virtuous. It suited him. I considered it remarkable that this professional slimeball had not once tried to weasel out of taking the punishment that should have been hers.

Now, though, all his goodness had been for nothing. Sure, he was free. And justice had triumphed. But what did he care about justice? The one and only person who had given his life meaning—Mary Dean—was locked up in Building D, waiting to be processed so she could make the trip to Bedford Hills, where she'd stay for the next fifteen to twenty years.

I was not about to be an accessory to a felony and drive him to a date with criminal possession of a forged instrument, so I dropped him in front of the apartment he and Mary had been so happy in. On the spur of the moment, I told him I'd buy him dinner so if he had any questions about Mary's case I could answer them. He did not seem surprised—or seem anything else, to tell the truth. He was operating on automatic pilot, so in a monotone he said all right and asked what time he should be at my office. I was tempted to blare a trumpet and announce: Hey, I've never invited any client out to dinner, ever! But I just said seven-thirty—and make it casual.

Norman showed up in a tie and pin-striped suit, a little more Al Capone than Wall Street. But he seemed to feel Establishment, if not downright lawyerly, in it. With him so dolled up, I scratched plans for the glorified hamburger joint-salad bar I'd planned on and took him to a restaurant in the Garden City Hotel, a place with a great deal of soft light, pink marble, and waiters so terribly worried about your welfare that you fear for their blood pressure.

"I want the best lawyer for Mary," he told me.

"The one she has is fine."

"I'm talking about someone with a national reputation." I noticed that for a guy who would have to fill in a blank after "Occupation" with "Criminal," Norman had un-usually genteel table manners. He had ordered snails and was managing the pincer with masterful dexterity. I won-dered if he honestly liked snails or if ordering them was part of his routine, to display to his marks how culti-vated he was. "I have the money," he said. "I can pay for it."

"Look," I told him, setting down my salad fork. "You can get anyone you want. And I'm sure with all the time Mary is facing, it's tempting to imagine a prince on a white steed coming in and, abracadabra, making everything all right. The problem is this: She won't be having a trial, so you don't need someone who has the reputation of mesmerizing juries. And there are no complicated issues, so you don't need a brilliant legal mind."

"But if someone can convince a judge—"

"Do you know someone who can do it better than Barbara Duberstein, the lawyer she has now? I don't. She's been practicing here for ten years. She's good and the judges like her, and even more, they trust her. You want my opinion?

You're much better off with good local counsel than with some city slicker the sentencing judge knows has been brought in just to bamboozle him."

"How much will this cost?" Norman asked. Two middle-aged women at another table—considerably more middle-aged than I—were watching him. I thought I saw longing in their eyes. "Not that cost matters."

"I'm not sure. You can can check with Ms. Duberstein."

"A rough estimate."

"A couple of thousand."

He seemed surprised. "That's like nothing." He looked around, and he caught the gaze of the two women on him. He seemed more saddened than pleased: He didn't want the game anymore. He only wanted Mary. "Isn't there some way, with, say, a six-figure number, that we can find a judge—"

"No."

"I know that's what you're supposed to tell me—"

"I have no doubt that you know all the fine points of what I'm supposed to tell you. So I'll save my breath. But it might be useful for you to know that from my experience practicing here—as a prosecutor and a defense lawyer—that your six-figure bribe will buy you a ticket back into the slammer. Now, I may be wrong. There may be a State Supreme Court justice sitting in Nassau County who can be or has been bought. I honestly don't know of any. And I don't know any lawyer here who would be willing to try and negotiate that kind of a purchase." While this was not strict truth—I had my suspicions about one or two of my fellow members of the bar—it was true enough to tell some-one like Norman.

We were well into our entrée—prime rib for him, monkfish for me—when I started wondering why he had been asking how much Mary's lawyer would charge. "What happened to the forty-eight thousand you got from Bobette?" I asked, knowing that these days, the more intrusive a question, the more people seem willing to answer it.

"I sent most of it down to the place where I keep my money. That's why I needed to know what sort of expenses

I'll be incurring with Mary's defense . . . or representation, to be more accurate."

"Atlanta?" I inquired, vaguely remembering something Mary had said. Norman laughed too heartily. Then he seemed embarrassed. I couldn't tell if it was because I'd caught him in a phony laugh or if some memory was making him uncomfortable. "Do people in your business now have Atlanta accounts the way they used to have numbered Swiss accounts?"

"Atlanta is just something I made up for Mary," he admitted. "I have to go to Grand Cayman Island." The Caymans were in the Caribbean, not far from Jamaica, and had become a center for international funny money. I was surprised, because most con men I knew were spenders, not savers. Their lives were a never-ending cycle of scam and squander and scam again.

"Are you going to spend any time down there?" I asked. Not that I was curious, but even if we passed on dessert, we still had to finish our petits pois with mint and get the check. I was afraid of running out of conversation. "Don't you want to relax, get a little sun?"

"I can't afford that luxury. I want to see Mary again tomorrow. I'll see if I can get a flight out on Sunday and do business first thing Monday and get back here by midday to visit." He sighed and got lost in playing hockey with his fork and a pea. His goal seemed to be a curlicue of carrot, but before he got there he looked up. "Is there any chance of bail?"

"No, Norman. Try to understand: she isn't awaiting trial. She's confessed to a murder, and she'll be sentenced by the end of next week. Early the following week, she'll be off to Bedford Hills."

"I'm taking out a fair amount of money," he told me. "I'm buying a house."

"A house?"

"Yes. Up there, not far from the prison. I've already talked to a real estate broker in Katonah. She says she has a lot in my price range. A modest little house. That's all I need, because it will just be I. I'm viewing it as an investment.

When Mary gets out, we can sell it and go to someplace warm."

"What are you going to do in Katonah?" I asked.

"Visit Mary in Bedford Hills every day I can." He patted his mouth with his napkin, a little too daintily for my taste. "I won't try to con you. At this stage of my life, what do you think I'm going to do? Get a nine-to-five job? Do you think I'm like all of you"—he swooped his hand around, indicating everyone else in the restaurant—"needing someplace to go to, something to do every single day? I've always enjoyed my leisure. Reading the financial pages, watching a little TV, working out. I like to read. I read an enormous amount of books. If I told anyone I talked to for more than five minutes that I didn't go to college, they wouldn't believe me." He was waiting for me to confirm this was true, so I nodded. "In any case, I have the wherewithal. I can live pretty nicely on what I've got socked away."

"You're a rarity," I told him.

He knew what I meant. "You mean most men working the con—I hope you'll pardon my language—piss it away."

"That's right."

"Not me. I have plenty for now, and I'll have a nice chunk left for Florida or wherever we wind up."

I signaled to the waiter for the check. "What about the con?" I asked.

"What about it?"

"You sound like you're thinking of retiring."

"Let me tell you something," Norman said, leaning forward, looking me straight in the eye. "I didn't do it just for money. You must know that. I used to love it. The travel, the setup, playing out the game. And the ladies: All you legal types and all the shrinks think it's just because I want to fuck them or, more to the point, fuck them over, if you'll excuse the vernacular. You're right in that the money is incidental, although I made a pretty penny. What you don't get is that every single time, it was a thrill. A *thrill*. I got to fall in love over and over again. You have no idea. What a rush!" He sat back. "But then I met Mary. And sure, we moved around, I did the con. She even assisted me. But from

387

the second I saw her, I knew the game was over for me. I could never fall in love again with one of my marks. Because this time I was truly and forever in love." He folded his napkin and put it beside his plate. "I lost my gift. I was hardly able to go through the motions. I can't believe how I pulled it off with the last few ladies. Especially with a smart cookie like Bobette. She must have been so desperate." He shook his head. "Poor, pathetic thing."

Having gotten Norman off, I didn't shout "Whee!" and run around, giddy and gay. But I did feel relieved. Except just when I thought I was finished with the Torkelson case, I started getting calls from Mary Dean. I refused to accept them, telling Sandi, my secretary, to refer them to Barbara Duberstein. That should have been that, but Sandi was still unhinged on the subject. She would not let go of the idea that Mary was an innocent. Please, she begged me, *please* speak to her. I told her Mary might indeed be innocent of a great many things, but the crime of murder was not one of them. Mary called twice Wednesday morning and once Wednesday afternoon.

Tuesday and Wednesday, Norman called too. Mary was in a bad way, he reported. Very upset. Not depressed. Angry. She was being irrational, screaming. They had to haul her out of the visitors' room and put her in Administrative Lock-in. She kept begging Norman to get her out. He knew he couldn't do that, he said to me, but was there anything— anything at all—he could do? Could he get her into some mental hospital? A private one would be fine. He had the money. I told him that Mary had already said she would plead guilty to murder. If she wanted to change her mind and plead not guilty by reason of mental disease or defect, he'd have to get in touch with Barbara. But I suggested that given Mary's videotaped confession, I didn't think it likely that kind of defense would succeed. It sounded, though, as if Norman was so deeply disturbed by Mary's behavior that he'd half conned himself into believing she might still wind up in a sanitarium with a rose garden.

By Mary's third phone call that afternoon, my secretary

was in such a froth of distress over Mary and fury at me that I suggested she go home. She told me she didn't want to. I told her I wanted her to—and not to come back the following day if the pressures of the job were getting to her. Vacation time was due her, and what a beautiful time of year to get away.

Naturally, she was in the office before I was Thursday morning. But she left of her own accord before lunch. She had tears in her eyes: I can't take it, she said. If you could only hear that girl's voice. She's so sweet, so truly innocent, so . . .

The thought of getting away was beginning to appeal to me. My guy, the lawyer, was about to sum up in a trial in federal court, and was therefore unavailable, to say nothing of useless in terms of human companionship. I called my daughter, who is studying acting (and slinging hash in a restaurant in Tribeca) and asked if she was interested in a long, luxurious, and free weekend at a spa in the Berkshires. Usually she jumped at anything preceded by the word "free." But she actually had an acting job starting the following Monday, two scenes in a cable TV movie being shot on Staten Island, and she had to prepare. So I decided to settle for an evening in the city and called an old friend of mine at the Manhattan D.A.'s. We agreed on a restaurant in Little Italy.

As I was about to leave, around six, the phone rang. I picked it up, an act that I invariably discover is folly. "Lee?" It was Barbara Duberstein, and she sounded wiped out. Of course, I thought: It's the end of the workday, and she still has two adolescent children at home.

"How's it going?" I asked.

"Did you hear about it?"

"About what?"

"Mary."

In a theatrical gesture my daughter would have abhorred, I slapped my forehead. But I sensed this was drama. Maybe tragedy. "What happened?"

"She tried to hang herself." I couldn't find a thing to say. "They found her just in time."

"Did she say why she did it?"

"No." I could hear Barbara take a deep breath. "All she said is that she wanted you."

Twenty-two

Take any group of associates—girlfriends, the National Conference of Catholic Bishops, professional bowlers—and set them to talking about treachery. A single truth emerges: Once someone betrays you, you can never trust him again. You can try to understand the reasons behind the double dealing, of course. Forgive it, even. (You really don't have much choice if you're a bishop.) But you can never forget, not entirely.

Hogwash. Maybe in those troubled, dark-souled nations where widows wear black the rest of their lives, they tend perfidy like a living flame. But Americans, those optimists who clothe themselves in bright team colors, are always ready for a do-over. Certainly, in the days and weeks following the discovery of defalcation or adultery, the torment seems unbearable; there is no hurt like being stabbed in the back by someone you trust. But then it is allowed to subside, so superficial relations can resume. In the months to follow, the absence of acute pain feels so good that you begin, now and then, like any good American, to let a smile be your umbrella. And your compatriots, seeing you happy, relieved that you are no longer a loser, pat you on the back and take you out to lunch, and pretty soon—providing the lying, cheating, unprincipled bastard doesn't act up—you are your old self again.

This is not to say that Lily Rose White would not have been wounded if someone had given her *The Collected Works of Elizabeth Barrett Browning* for her birthday. And Jazz had enough sense, when they spent the evening in Manhattan, not to drive up Madison Avenue; that would have brought them right past the Hotel Carlyle. However, by October of 1980, six months after her terrible discovery, Lee was a happy wife again. Sex, if not as frequent, was again becoming lively and satisfying. Jazz was, she had to admit, a devoted father, coming home early to take pictures of three-year-old Val dressed up for Halloween, in a garish pink costume Lee had tried to talk her out of. But Val had insisted on being Strawberry Shortcake, and so she was. Jazz joined Lee in taking the little girl around the neighborhood trick-or-treating. As they stayed back to allow Val to stand on tiptoes and try to ring each doorbell by herself, their shoulders touched and their hands sought each other out. After the neighbors stopped oohing and aahing over Strawberry, they beamed at her young and, obviously, very much in love parents.

By the beginning of November, Lee was thinking it was time to have another child. She even mentioned something to Chuckie Phalen: You know, at some point I'll probably have another kid. Chuckie said: I thought as much. A little concerned, Lee could tell, and when she told him she planned on taking no more than a three-month maternity leave, he seemed more comforted by the reassurance that everything would be hunky-dory with Phalen & White than dismayed that she was capable of leaving not just one but two little tykes.

A week later, on a Sunday night, sitting on their living room floor before a roaring fire, the first of the season, Lee kissed Jazz and whispered: Do you think it's time we had a burn-the-diaphragm party? He took her in his arms and said: "Wonderful!" Just like that. No hesitation, no catch in his voice to suggest reluctance. She heard what she wanted to hear, total agreement. "Wonderful!" offered with Jazz's typical exclamation point. Lee did not allow herself to think: Gee, he's being pretty casual about such a big decision. Or that "Wonderful!" was the same lyric, the same tune he used with department store buyers from Milwaukee when they upped their order (Wonderful! You'll see how they'll fly off the floor!) and with old customers who allowed him to charm them into fun fox for those occasions when their new mink was too serious (Wonderful! Call me in February and tell me how much you're enjoying it!).

Wonderful? So? She was right between periods. Ripe and ready. But the next night, Monday, was football, played on the West Coast. She understood that. Tuesday and Wednesday, Jazz had to go to Minneapolis and Detroit. They were big accounts, he told her proudly. Now they're bigger. And Thursday, Friday, Saturday, and now, Sunday, he was exhausted, enervated, fluish, finally just plain out of sorts. Not himself.

So by the time she got a good look at him the following Thursday across her parents' Thanksgiving table, handsome, broad-shouldered in a cashmered interpretation of a Harris Tweed sports jacket, beaming up at Greta as she served her pineapple-sweet potato casserole, Lee could see: Definitely not himself. "Wonderful!" he enthused to Greta. Yes, Jazz was being the movie star, putting on the shine for the plainest girl in his fan club, but as Greta moved on, Jazz's light went out. He was not a good enough actor to sustain his role.

Not himself? Then who was he?

Weary. Irritable, losing patience with Kent, insisting on getting rid of him for the holiday. His own brother, who made his home with them: Get rid of him for a few days, he commanded Lee. She had complied, but she felt sick at having double-crossed Kent, sticking him with his parents who did not want him.

Lee watched Jazz staring at his plate. Why wasn't he able to look into the eyes of her family? Leonard, stroking the sleeve of his double-breasted blazer, a new design by the latest *enfant terrible* of European menswear. Sylvia, holding her knife and fork daintily between the pads of her fingertips so as not to chip her nail polish: Pure Pomegranate, the latest tropical shade, so she could leave for Palm Beach the next morning and not be seen with northern nails. And Robin, pale and absolutely lovely in layer upon layer of intricate Italian knits, her exquisite little purple and blue and green vest alone costing more than the average day care aide's monthly salary, waving at Val across the table.

Jazz could not keep his eyes off the food mounded on his plate. He seemed defeated by a glob of cranberry-raspberry relish the size of a human heart. Not himself. This feast was a torment for him. It was only then that Lee permitted herself to understand: Jazz was indeed himself. And that self was a cheat and a liar. But a passionate one. The cause of his terrible pain was deep, deep emotion. Not an emotion like guilt over mere fornication: No, the biggest of all emotions. Her husband was in love. Not with her.

*   *   *

393

"You're sure?" Will Stewart inquired. He added more brandy to her snifter so discreetly that she did not notice until she took the next sip.

"Yes." She set down the brandy.

"Don't worry. I'll drive you home. I'll figure out how to get your car back tomorrow." She had left Jazz in front of the television, a dead man watching the Giants. When she told him she was running over to the office for an hour or two, his "Fine" was replete with relief.

"He wants out," Lee said. "That's what all his pain is about."

"Pain about getting divorced?"

She heard herself laugh—Ha!—the harsh, snorting noise lonely women make. "Are you kidding? No, he's in the fashion business. He's nothing if not *au courant*. Being divorced once or twice shows you're not a home-loving, uncool schmuck." She would have to watch herself. She was sounding so bitter. On the other side of his small living room, Will was observing her with concern. "Jazz has got a bigger problem," she went on. "Even if he'd made a fabulous impression at his old law firm—which he didn't—he hasn't practiced in almost five years. For a good reason; he hates the law. It would be very hard for him to get back to being a lawyer, even with his father's help."

"But he's doing so well in the fur business—" Will stopped and corrected himself. "Your father's fur business."

"It's not that he couldn't get another job. They're so thrilled to have someone like him in the industry, they all but raise the Episcopal flag every time he walks into a room."

Will got up from his chair and threw a couple more logs into his wood-burning stove and poked them in place. Not a plain black iron stove, of course, but a tall ceramic one, yellow and white, an antique he had bought in Sweden. His whole house, on an inlet of Middle Bay on the south shore of Long Island, was like that: modest, manly but simply beautiful, a home for one—but one with very good taste. She had been there only once before, for a Chinese banquet Will cooked for his old crew from the Homicide unit, but she had fallen in love with the place. "So Jazz can leave your father's company, but wherever else he goes, he's not going to be the son-in-law."

"I don't think it's only the money that made him hold back so long—although he is getting about three times what he could make elsewhere. It's the perks. The best restaurants, the best seats in town to whatever he wants to see, the car and driver: He goes in every day with my father, and before they get picked up, the driver buys two *New York Timeses*, two *Wall Street Journals* and two *Women's Wear Dailys*—so they don't have to lower themselves to read already fingered newsprint. It's a whole way of life he has to give up. He can charge anything he wants to the business . . ." She stopped and closed her eyes, listening to the never ceasing rush of water outside Will's back door.

"You mean his charging his entire affair?"

"Yes," she whispered, not trusting her voice. Lee was less afraid of crying than of making some hideous gargling sound that would repulse yet another man. Not that Will ever seemed unrepulsed. He was her friend. Her best friend. Not a day went by now that they did not speak at least twice. But not a glimmer, not the faintest undercurrent, at least not on Will's part. Maybe, Lee thought, sitting up straighter, trying to swirl her brandy in a sophisticated gesture, hoping it did not slop over the rim of the snifter, if I looked more like Maria—a bust of Nefertiti, not an Easter Island statue—he'd want to poke something white beside the damn stove.

She must be drunk, she realized. She did not feel drunk, yet she sensed that under normal circumstances, she would not be so aware that she had nostrils. Jazz loved someone else. She had loved him from the time she was fifteen years old and miraculously, he had married her. He loved someone else. Another woman would be getting dressed and she'd feel Jazz pressing against her back. She'd drop her panties and turn around and kiss him and then lower herself, her tongue trailing down his neck, his chest, his belly.

She might be drunk. She was sensing ears on the sides of her head. Lee fingered her earlobe. Soft, as soft as Valerie's sweet skin. Soft as a rose petal. Her middle name: Rose.

"Will?"

"What?"

"Do you know what my real name is, the one I was born with?"

He shrugged. She had to admit he was not exhibiting a pressing need to know. Fuck it, she'd tell him anyway. "Lily."

"Oh," he said politely. But then he must have said her name to himself: Lily White. He threw back his head, and for the first time since she'd known him, he laughed out loud. "Lily White." A deep and wonderful roar. "No shit!"

And she threw back her head to join him, but it didn't work, because she had already begun to weep.

Lee was not thinking clearly, but Will was. He drove her almost home but let her off a little more than halfway up the rutted hill to her house. Your car died, he coached her. Since you knew Jazz was watching the game, you called a cab. It's better if he doesn't see you get out of my car. When you open discussions about the possibility of splitting up, you don't want him to think: Hmm, she said she was going to her office Sunday. How come her close male friend drove her home? Don't give him an excuse to feel less guilty.

Okay, Lee said.

Obviously, Will went on, you only have to offer the whole broken-down-car-cab story if he notices you didn't get home under your own steam.

Obviously, she said. It wasn't obvious to her at all. She was relieved that Will was advising her. She wanted to be told exactly what to do and what to say, because otherwise she would be too afraid to go home.

You can handle this, Will assured her.

I know. She did not know.

Will made her promise—swear, insisting she actually raise her right hand—that she keep mum. You are Unfit to Think, he decreed. Wait till tomorrow. Then, when you're calmer—to say nothing of sober—you'll speak to my partner, Joe Clark. He handles our matrimonial work. Then Will waited while Lee trudged up to the house, his headlights illuminating her way, his Porsche purring like a protective mother cat.

Lee walked around the house so she could enter through the side entrance, as if coming from the garage. Evening was becoming night, and a cold wind was blowing in from the sound, but it was still crisp, perfect Thanksgiving weekend football weather. Twigs crackled under her feet. She inhaled the pungent rot of the leaves, smoke from the fire Jazz must have built. She hugged her blazer around her. Good smells. Before her mind could censor, her body reacted to the late-autumn air: Ah, how lovely. A night to cuddle up and keep warm. Then she shivered.

As she passed the den, she saw Jazz where she had left him, sitting on the couch staring at the television set. Concerned because Cherry, the nanny, had the day off, Lee was immediately relieved when she walked into the kitchen and found Robin sitting with Val, patiently watching the little girl interact with a bowl of the chicken noodle soup Lee had made that morning. A moment later, Val was in her arms. Lee went over to Robin and, as she usually did, touched her cheek to her sister's and chirped into the air, in their standard mockery of their mother's kisses.

"Jazz is in the den," Robin told her.

"Bad mood?" Lee asked, sidestepping so her sister would not sniff brandy breath.

Robin shrugged. "Not a good mood, I would have to say."

Too damn bad, Lee thought, setting Val back down so she could swish around the soup pot. She found a small piece of chicken and a carrot to cut up.

"No!" Val announced, shaking her head so ferociously at the carrot that her glossy pigtails whipped back and forth. In all honesty, Lee admitted to herself, repressing a smile, she loved that her nay-saying daughter was such an ornery pain in the ass. "Yucky peas!" To Val, every vegetable was a pea.

"Okay," Lee said, "I'll eat it," knowing her offer would immediately stimulate Val's appetite. She picked up a circle of carrot. Val immediately stuck out her hand. "What do you say?" Lee demanded, depositing it in the child's tiny palm.

"T'anks."

" 'T'anks,' " Lee repeated to Robin. "She sounds like Grandma Bella. Next thing you know, she'll say, 'You're velcome, dahlink.' "

"I really don't remember her too well." Robin had gone to the stove and was peering into the pot as if she had made the soup. "Listen, I'll keep an eye on Val. You ought to let Jazz know you're home. He keeps popping in, wanting to know if you're here yet."

Will was right, Lee mused as she walked toward the den. Unfit to think. She ought to be concentrating on keeping her face bland, unreadable, but her mind kept jumping: a cold-water washload with her burgundy sweater and black panty hose; that article on women playwrights she had torn out two Sundays ago, still on her night-stand; oh, and she had to add a protein conditioner to the drugstore list. The blue light of the television flickered inside the den. Lee stood beside the open door. She wished she had passed up Will's brandy because she really wanted a tranquilizer. No, general anesthesia: if only she could be put out until it was all over. She forced herself through the door.

"I'm home." Her weight rested on the balls of her feet. She was primed to pivot and get out.

"Come in," Jazz said, rising from the couch. He switched on a lamp and turned off the TV.

"I've got a ton of stuff to do."

"Please. I want to talk."

"Go ahead," Lee replied. Since she made no move to sit, Jazz remained standing. But he kept glancing back to the couch. Lee sensed he had rehearsed this scene in his mind, and this was not the way it had played. Her head hurt. Drunk. What was Will's theory about preventing hangovers? Water. Drink huge amounts of water. She wondered if it was too late.

"It's like this," Jazz began. Then he fell silent. She waited, but it seemed as if he was expecting her to speak. When she did not, he finally said: "I don't know how to say this."

"Say it," Lee snapped. She crossed her arms but felt awkward, unable to decide whether to rest them on top of her bust or beneath it. She glanced at Jazz to see if he had noticed her difficulty. No. He was looking past her. Lee turned. Robin was at the door, carrying Val as if she were an infant. "I'll be with you in a minute," Lee told her sister. But Robin merely stood there. Lee sighed. If she said: Excuse me, Robin, but Jazz and I need some privacy, Robin would say: Oh, sure, sorry. But for the next few days—just when Lee would need her sister most—Robin would sulk, answering all attempts to engage her in conversation with monosyllables.

"Come in," Jazz invited, making an arcing my-house-is-your-house gesture. Before Lee could think of a diplomatic way to bounce her, Robin, still holding Val, plopped into the biggest seat in the room, a high, fat-armed wing chair.

"When you found out," Jazz said to Lee, "I swore to you I would end it. And then I told you it was all over."

For a moment, Lee did not understand what he was talking about or, at least, could not believe he was speaking of it in front of her sister. And Val! She was too young to understand the words, but to have such a conversation in front of your own child? "Are you insane?" she hissed at him.

"It was *never* over."

"Would you be quiet, for God's sake." She could see Val struggling to climb off her aunt's lap and get closer to her parents.

"I'm in love," Jazz insisted. Lee shoved him away. The push said: Shut up! End this conversation now! Too hard a push. Jazz would have fallen backward if, in one swift movement, Robin had not set Val aside, vaulted from the big chair, and held him by his shoulders, steadying him. "I'm in love," he insisted.

"No," Robin corrected him. "*We're* in love."

Before Lee's mind could absorb the shock, her body did. It crumpled. Her legs turned from sturdy limbs into flesh without bones. She aimed herself toward the couch and, mercifully, fell into it.

"Mommy?"

"I'm okay. I just tripped."

A shudder passed through Lee's body, and immediately another. Oh my God, she thought, I'm having a convulsion. I've got to get Val out of here so she doesn't see me. She looked over at her child. Only three, but Val was no fool. Robin was attempting to distract her, offering the TV remote control, but Val knew there was a better show being broadcast. Emphatically, she shook her head: No.

In the ensuing silence, Jazz and Robin came together before Lee in such a fluid motion it might have been choreographed. Jazz and Robin, so close to each other that Lee's eyes were forced to see them as a couple. Beside him, Robin appeared so fine and fragile that she, not strapping, red-cheeked Valerie, might have been his little girl. Horrible: They looked so beautiful together. "We've been in love for a long time," Jazz began.

"Of course," Robin said, taking up the story, "we couldn't even admit it to ourselves for a while, much less each other." Lee was surprised to discover that she could stand. She went to Val and drew the child to her, putting her hands on the little girl's head, smoothing her silken hair. She mouthed: Stop! to her sister. "Lee," Robin sighed, exasperated, "a child that age does not have the language. She cannot comprehend. Okay?" Jazz flushed. A mustache of perspiration grew on his upper lip. Robin, though, was not in a sweat. She seemed to grow calmer. Lovelier, too, and stronger with each passing second, as though she were being transfused with magic nutrients. "You have to listen, Lee. Because if you walk out now, it will still be there when you get back. It is *not* going to go away."

Robin wore a white angora sweater and white wool slacks, and looked as though she had materialized from a cloud. Lee realized her sister had shopped for an outfit appropriate for the annunciation: I need something in an angelic fabric but that shows off my waist. Oh, and please, tight around the rear and the crotch. When did this begin? Lee cried, although not aloud. Still, her sister answered as if the question had been screamed out. "It happened the first time we saw each other." A quickly suppressed sound, something that might have been the start of a delicious giggle of reminiscence. "Well, not the first time, because I was at the worst of my drug problem, when I was in"—Robin took a big, brave breath and came out with it—"heroin withdrawal." That was in St. Bart's, Lee thought. What is she talking about? Why doesn't he interrupt her, correct her: No, no, St. Bart's was right after Lee and I got married. Except there was Jazz beside Robin, his head moving up and down: Yes, yes, that was the very moment I fell in love.

Lee was astounded at her own clarity, that a part of her—the lawyer, the wronged wife—was taking notes while the rest of her crumbled into pieces, like the dying leaves she had crushed just minutes earlier. She understood why Jazz had sent Kent back to the Taylors. This performance had been meticulously planned, and he and Robin wanted no unruly members in their audience. Robin, head high, hands on her hips, lips bright red against her white face, pressed on with rawmeat energy. "Jazz said that day he first saw me, he thought he was happy, that he knew where his life was going. Then there I was, on the bed. I'm sure I was

400

pale as a ghost"—Jazz nodded his confirmation—"and naked. And he said his heart stood still."

"Too bad for all of us it started again," Lee said softly.

"Robin," Jazz said hesitantly. He spoke the name with a tenderness, a passionate doting that Lee had never even dreamed was part of his repertoire. "This probably isn't the time."

"No . . . Jazz," Robin said, faltering right before his name, so it was clear she had been about to call him Darling, or Love. "It has to come out."

"You're right," he agreed.

What kind of a lawyer is he, Lee thought, that he doesn't shut her up, blabbing on and on about the chronology of their adultery? "It was when we landed in New York," Robin continued, "and Jazz was carrying me out of the plane so the ambulance drivers who came to meet us could get me. I looked up"—Robin swallowed hard at the memory—"and there was this beautiful man I had never seen before. And I knew I would love him for the rest of my life."

"But we never said anything to each other," Jazz interjected. "Not for the longest time. I swear. And we didn't do anything until . . ." He gazed down at Val, who had taken a seat on the rug. "Until after . . ."

Lee knelt and hugged her daughter.

"I told you she'd use the baby as a weapon," Robin said to Jazz.

"Val," Lee said to the little girl, "I know you want to stay here, but this is grown-up talk. So I'll make you a deal. If you can get into your pj's all by yourself, no bath tonight"—she could see her daughter growing intrigued—"I'll give you two scoops of vanilla fudge." With less reluctance than Lee had imagined, Val hurried from the room, but then, two scoops were a bribe beyond Val's greediest imaginings.

With Valerie gone, the room's atmosphere altered. More danger here. Ominous silence until the wind rattled a window. Lee sensed Robin waiting for Jazz to take over, but when, looking expectant, Robin turned his way, he hunkered down and began to align the Sunday papers that had been scattered on the floor around an ottoman. Lee knelt beside him. "You didn't have the guts to face me alone," she whispered.

"What?" Robin demanded. "This isn't fair." Jazz stood. "What did she say?"

"Nothing," he replied.

Lee tried, and failed, to rise in a single fluid motion.

"Come on, Jazz," Robin said, a note of exasperation mixing with the sexual teasing. "Tell me what she said."

"Shut up, Robin," Lee barked.

"Don't tell me to shut up!"

Lee turned to the man she could not believe was still her husband, so thoroughly did he seem to belong to and with her sister. She noticed that he, also, was wearing a white sweater. "What do you want to do, Jazz?"

"I think it's clear that we have to end the marriage."

"Perfectly clear." Perfectly clear? she asked herself. She sounded crisp, like a character talking to Sir Alec Guinness in a not very serious English movie. How could she not be howling in pain? "I assume you already have a lawyer?" Unlike Robin, who started nodding, Jazz had enough breeding to look ashamed. But not too ashamed. Abashed only at having sought legal counsel so quickly. Not about adultery, not about the terrible betrayal of her, of his daughter. "I'll need a day or so to find proper representation," Lee told him.

"Take all the time—"

"Don't give me your gracious prep school manners. You're a cheap piece of work." Lee glanced at her sister, half expecting the old Robin—washed out, exhausted by the tension. But Robin looked radiant, so Lee turned back to Jazz. "Both of you: nice hair, great clothes, but cheap to the core. You were made for each other." She turned to go. "Even if there is no God, you'll get what you deserve."

It would have been a fine exit line, but as Lee passed through the threshold of the room, Robin called out: "We want custody of Valerie."

Lee did not freeze for more than a second. Then she whirled around and grabbed her sister by the front of her sweater, shaking Robin until Jazz grabbed Lee around the neck with a wrestling hold and pulled her back. "No!" Lee shouted. "Never! Over my dead body you'll get custody."

"I'm just as good a parent as you are!" Jazz shouted. "Better."

"Much better," Robin corrected him. "Much." She looked at her sister. "You're never home."

"What are you talking about?" Lee cried, sick at heart, knowing she had worked late two nights that week. "I love that child. I'm a wonderful mother."

"You consort with criminals," Jazz shot back.

"You're quoting your idiot girlfriend now," Lee snapped at him. "I don't 'consort,' you dipshit. I represent. You used to be a lawyer. A lousy one, but at least you used to know the difference." Tiny tufts of the white angora from Robin's sweater clung to her fingers. She tried to pull them off, but they stuck.

"I told you she'd bring up that you're not practicing law anymore," Robin practically sang to Jazz.

"I have spoken with my attorney," Jazz said to Lee, taking Robin's hand. "If we have to litigate, we'll litigate. Believe me, he won't shrink from it. It's his life's blood. But think about it. We have no intention of driving you out of Val's life. She just would do better living with us. With me. We have time for her."

"Sure. Because neither of you has a grown-up job. You don't have to work. Daddy takes care of you."

"I hope you don't think just because you're the mother you'll automatically get custody. Things are not what they were."

Lee wanted to curl into a ball on the couch and cry. No, howl. She was so frightened, thinking of some of the idiot judges she knew on the Family Court bench. How easy for them to rule for a smiling, handsome, rich, come-home-early father from a centuries-old Long Island family and against someone just like her. "You don't have a leg to stand on, you turkey."

"He *does* have a leg to stand on," Robin said, making it clear that she was tired of being understanding. "He has a damn good chance—"

Lee left them. As she rushed away, toward Valerie's room, she heard Jazz reassuring Robin with what she knew were his attorney's words. "She's going to find that custody rulings have changed since she went to . . ."

Valerie was not in her room. Oh, dear God, Lee thought, they've arranged to have her . . . But she heard a high "Mommy?" and there was Val, in the kitchen, standing before the freezer. "Two scoops."

403

"Not here, Val," Lee said, and she grabbed her daughter and her handbag and was out so fast that Jazz still had not finished his discourse on matrimonial law when he and Robin heard his Mercedes pulling down the driveway and racing down the hill.

By the time Lee got to her parents' new house in Palm Beach late the following morning, she looked as bad as she felt. Her hair was unkempt in the manner peculiar to distraught people—sticking out in clumps from her head, each individual strand frizzled to a fare-thee-well. Her skin, if not blotchy, at least looked as if she were suffering from a vitamin deficiency and she was certain her eyes had grown smaller. Her clothes looked slept in.

They had been. She had been afraid Jazz would call the police and the cops would come pounding in the night at her office door. She dared not spend the night there. So she drove out of the county, into Queens, and checked into a motel near the airport, paying cash and giving her name as Lily Rose. The moment they entered the room, she gave Val the two pints of ice cream—chocolate and vanilla—she had bought at an all-night convenience store. She was so ashamed of herself, using food as a bribe. Nevertheless, to Val, the payoff wasn't good enough. Chocolate and vanilla did not equal her beloved vanilla fudge. The child began to wail. But she yawned mid-protest and two minutes later was sound asleep on the dubious sheets of the motel bed. Lee joined her, snuggling next to the warm little body, knowing that from now on, this was to be her only comfort. She knew, too, that she would not be able to sleep, yet she felt comforted by Val's nearness. Amazingly, her eyes next opened at precisely six-thirty the following morning, her usual wake-up time.

The trip to Florida was hellish, the entire plane jammed with people over sixty-five who did not try to hide their disapproval of a disheveled woman who would let her child out of the house in pajamas. As the plane emerged from the clouds, the first glimpse of palm trees buoyed her, until they reminded her of her honeymoon in St. Bart's. Why am I doing this, running home to Mommy and Daddy? To squeal on Robin? Mommy, guess what Robin did! To find solace? Maybe, but experience told Lee that Sylvia and Leonard were not likely to be listed in any Who's Who of great consolers.

The truth, she admitted to herself in the taxi, was that she needed someone to share more than her outrage. Will might have done that, but she had not been able to bring herself to call him. He could not share her shame.

"Little girl sick?" the taxi driver asked, looking at Val's pajamas in his rearview mirror.

"No. It's just more comfortable for traveling," Lee told him.

"Nice neighborhood you're going to. You live there?"

"No." He was waiting for something more. "My parents do."

Shame. They had indulged Robin for so long. All of them, Lee included. And instead of indulgence leading to mere sloth, it had bred viciousness. How could Robin have done this vile thing to the family, tearing herself off from them irreparably, taking her sister's husband and, not content with that theft alone, trying to grab her sister's child? Give me what Lee has. Give me! *Give me!*

But forget what Robin had done to Lee and Valerie: How could she have been so heartless about her parents, her father especially? Leonard had come to full life only in the sunshine spread by Jazz. Now that light would go out. And Kent. Robin wanted smart and pretty and bright-eyed Val, but Lee bet her sister and Jazz were planning to put a stamp on Kent's head and mail him back to his negligent parents.

"Once you get past the Palm Hacienda turnoff, do you know how to find the place?" the driver asked.

"Sorry, I don't remember." In truth, Lee had never been there. Her parents were only days in their new house. Old house. Not one of the major mansions, but still grand enough to have a name: La Luna. They had bought it from the social butterfly scion of a Pittsburgh corrugated box fortune, and while they laughingly said they had been merely looking for a nice place with a pool and a water view, it had been clear to Lee they were using the place to launch an incursion into Palm Beach society.

What would her father do now? More and more, he had been relying on Jazz. And Jazz had indeed proved himself reliable. At Thanksgiving dinner, Leonard had assuaged his guilt at leaving the salon for three months by chuckling: I'm just a phone call or a plane ride away. And, to give equal time, what would her mother do? Take to bed for months, as she had done so often in the pre-Jazz era? Would she sneak out for secret shopping trysts

405

with Robin? Or would there now be inexorable pressure on Lee to become someone whose name, measurements, and style preferences were known to the salespeople in every boutique from East Fifty-ninth to East Seventy-ninth Streets?

"*Very* nice, ma'am," the driver said as they pulled up in front of La Luna, and Lee felt obliged to overtip him. As he was thanking her and as Val, barely toilet trained, was yelling "Pee!" the huge front door with its crescent moon knocker jerked open. Lee had expected a white-coated, brown-skinned butler. Indeed, one was hovering in the background. But in the foreground were her parents, looking almost as agitated as Lee herself.

"You're here!" Sylvia was crying, although on close inspection, Lee could see no actual moisture around her mother's eyes.

"Thank God!" Leonard bent down and took Val into his arms. "We were frantic!"

"Panicked!"

"Terrified!"

"Pee!"

"Lee, how could you have just taken the baby—" her mother demanded.

"Stop it, Sylvia," Leonard directed.

"—in the middle of the night—"

Lee grabbed Val and, with the help of the man in the white jacket, found a bathroom just feet away. Black marble with black fixtures. It looks like a toilet in hell, Lee thought. She squatted before her daughter, holding her up for lack of a potty seat. She could not believe that Jazz had actually called her parents. Could he be so stupid as to believe she would hurt Val? "What a big girl you are!" she told her daughter, pulling off a length of toilet paper. "I am so proud of you!"

As Lee and Val emerged from the bathroom, the white-coated butler was gone. So was Sylvia. "Where's Mom?"

"Sending the housekeeper out to buy clothes for Valerie."

"Thank you," Lee said, and allowed her father to take her arm and gently lead her, as he would someone suffering a terrible illness, to the back of the house. A huge porch overlooked a pool and, beyond it, a body of water that was not the ocean. "Beautiful," she said.

"Shwim?" Val asked.

"Later," Lee promised.

Her mother came out with the butler, who was bearing a tray of sandwiches, a pitcher of iced tea, and a smaller pitcher of milk for Val. To Lee, it was such an act of kindness that she felt herself choking up. That is, until she caught her mother eyeing her slacks and blazer. All that could be wrong with them was: wrinkled, a mismatched plaid on the seam of the sleeve—a red plaid, no less. "Why don't I bring you upstairs so you can take a shower?" Sylvia said. "I can lend you an outfit. I know I have a Vivienne Westwood that has a little give to it."

"Later," Lee said. "Thanks." She cut Val's sandwich into the finger-length shapes the child preferred. "What did Jazz tell you?" she asked her parents.

"It wasn't Jazz," Sylvia began. She stopped as Leonard cleared his throat.

"Robin called you?" Lee asked.

"She said there had been some disagreement," Leonard explained. "That you were very upset and you grabbed the baby and ran out in the middle of the night—"

"It was a little before seven o'clock in the evening."

"Oh. Well, you know your sister," he said. "High drama and all that." He paused. "You should have called, Lee."

"What would you have done at that hour on a Sunday night?" From a Fun! Sun! Florida! shopping bag, Lee pulled out a Weebles toy fire truck filled with little round Weebles firemen. She had bought it at the Palm Beach airport. She placed it on the grass below them, out of hearing distance.

"Well?" she asked Val. "Come here. It's all yours."

"T'anks, Ma!" Beside the truck, Lee set down a coloring book and a large box of crayons, more colors than Val had ever had. "Wow!"

"I mean," Sylvia was saying, "you should have called just so they weren't so worried—"

"*They*?" Lee inquired. Too loud, she realized. Her parents did not yet know what she did. "I have something to tell you," she said. Something very painful." Leonard edged forward in his chair. Sylvia, though, just sat back and crossed her waxed legs. Her Pure Pomegranate toenails blended perfectly with her reddish-gold thongs. She did not look as though she wanted to hear anything painful. But whoever does want to, especially in a paradisiacal place like La Luna? And certainly not on this, Sylvia's second day as a probationary jet-setter. "Jazz and I are going to get a divorce," Lee said, trying to give them the good news first.

"Uh-huh," said her father.

"Oh," said her mother.

"He's been having an affair." To this they said nothing. "He wants to marry the woman." Her parents were more motionless than the palm trees in giant terra-cotta pots that ran the length of the great porch. Shock, Lee thought. What a blow. She looked to her father, knowing how Leonard adored Jazz. Driving to and from work with him every day. Popping in and out of each other's offices all the time. Chatting on the phone at night, on weekends. Shock. And he didn't even know about Robin yet. Just wait. The pain, the disgrace, the—

The butler appeared in the doorway. "Do you need anything more, Mrs. White?"

"No, thank you, Gibbons," Sylvia said sweetly.

Sweetly? Wait a second, Lee thought. It was one thing not to want to mess with a butler named Gibbons. Another for her mother to be able to keep up her gracious-lady act in the face of such awful news. Unless it was not news. "Dad?"

"Yes, sweetie?"

"Do me a favor and call my office, tell them I'm here. I don't want them to worry." She did not say that nothing short of reading in *Newsday* that the mutilated body of a thirty-year-old female had been found with a "Lee White, Attorney-at-Law," business card clamped between its teeth would cause anyone in her office to worry. Leonard, however, looked as if he was about to delegate such a potentially secretarial duty to Sylvia, so Lee added: "I'd like you to speak directly to Chuckie Phalen, Dad. He deals better with men. Don't give any details. Just that I had to come down on an important family matter."

"Sure, honey."

Leonard went off into the house. Lee waved at Val on the lawn, but the child was too busy with her fire truck to notice. Sylvia smiled at her daughter. "I know. One of those nonsexist toys. But why firemen? Ick. Oh, now's a good time. Want to try the Vivienne Westwood?"

"Sure!" Lee smiled back, then allowed her face to dissolve into sadness befitting the occasion. "In a minute. Mom, did Robin tell you the whole thing?" Sylvia's eyes darted around searching for Leonard, which answered Lee's question. "She told you about her and Jazz?"

"Yes. Lee, let's be honest: I know you feel it's the end of the world, but it isn't." Lee had been a criminal lawyer too long not to know the witness was not telling the complete truth. Check the demeanor. Brow drawn. Okay, was a drawn brow appropriate to the news that your younger daughter had been sleeping with your older daughter's husband? "You're still young, attractive—"

"I can't think about that now."

"I know. I can't tell you what this is doing to me."

A drawn brow. That was all. Was that a response to learning hours earlier from a phone call that your younger daughter was planning on marrying your older daughter's husband and had joined with him in demanding custody of your only grandchild? Lee did not want to know. And yet she did: That was precisely why she had sent her father to call Chuckie. "You've known about this for a while, Mom."

Since it came out as a statement and not a question, Sylvia was perplexed about how to respond. Lee looked at her mother: curious. So her mother said: "Not for *that* long."

"Dad kept it from you?"

"He didn't want me to get upset."

"I can understand that," Lee said. "It *is* upsetting."

"I know this must be such a shock for you, Lee. I'm so sorry."

"Thank you. It's been awful." Did she hear footsteps? "So Jazz will stay in the business?"

"Well, you know . . ."

"Dad's come to rely on him so much."

"Well, he has made a difference."

"And he'll still be married to a daughter, so it won't be that different than before." It was only then that Sylvia comprehended Lee had trapped her. And just as her mouth dropped open, her husband walked in, and her eyes filled with fear as well.

"What's wrong?" Leonard asked. "What is wrong?"

Before her mother could say anything, Lee said: "I'm here telling you my husband has left me, and you're asking what's wrong?"

"Sorry," Leonard breathed. "I spoke to Mr. Phalen. Some character! He says to tell you—"

"You knew goddamn well they were going to demand custody of Val, didn't you?" Lee snarled at him. Her father was literally taken aback. He retreated two steps toward the safety of the house. "Didn't you?" she demanded louder.

"Shhh!" Sylvia pleaded.

Lee ignored her mother and walked over to her father. "If you don't tell me what I want to know, I'm going to start screaming. Terrible things. The servants will hear." She paused. "The neighbors will hear. I will accuse you of the most vile crimes. I hear horror stories every damn day in my office, in the courts, and I'll accuse you of everything I've ever heard." She took her index finger and stabbed her father in the chest. "You knew they were going to demand custody?"

"Please, Lee, it's better for us all—"

At the top of her lungs, Lee boomed: "How would Gibbons like to know about the time you—"

"I knew," Leonard whispered. "I knew."

"How long?"

"That?" If there was a "that," Lee knew, there was also a "this." "A few weeks. Jazz told me after he spoke to a divorce lawyer."

She got to the "this" with another poke. "And how long have you known they've been lovers?"

"Just a few weeks more."

"You're lying!" Lee blared.

"Lee, *please*," her mother begged. "We love you. We're so sorry you have to go through all this terrible—"

Lee flipped her hand in her mother's direction: You're dismissed. "How long have you known about Robin and Jazz? Don't think you can lie to me. I ferret out the truth for a living. I'll get it from you no matter how long it takes and how loud I have to yell."

"Don't threaten me, Lee," Leonard said, setting his jaw firm.

"What do you want to be accused of first? Embezzlement? Insurance fraud? No, that's boring. Why don't we jump right into a really interesting sex offense?"

"Let's stop the theatrics. They won't get you anywhere." He

glanced toward the house and the unseen Gibbons. "I found out soon after it started."

"Which was . . ."

"When you were pregnant. The accountant was troubled by some charges Jazz had made to the business. So was I. I went and talked to him."

"And he said: 'It's okay, Dad. I was just fucking—'"

"Don't use that word!" Sylvia called out.

" 'I was just having illicit sexual congress with your younger daughter while your older one was pregnant with your grandchild. Don't worry about the charges. It's all in the family.'"

"Do you think I was happy about it?"

"What did you do about it?"

"What do you think? I spoke to him. I spoke to Robin, heart to heart. I told her: It isn't right."

"Did you at any point threaten to throw him out of the business if he couldn't keep his pecker in his pocket?"

"Lee!" Sylvia called, getting up from her chair.

"Do you honestly think my threatening him like that would have stopped it?" Leonard inquired.

"Yes. If you had threatened to fire him. Or to kick that slut out of the house so she would have to earn her own living. Yes, indeed. But you couldn't, could you?" Leonard looked past her, as if waiting for a ship to come in. "Because you're afraid of Robin. But that's not the prime reason. It's not fear. It's love. You love Jazz more than any of us, more than all of us put together. If you had a third daughter and Jazz wanted her, you would condone that too. You would choose him over her. Protect him over her."

"You have your crazy theory," Leonard said quietly. "Nothing I say can stop you."

"That's right. So give your boy a message. He's not getting custody." She turned to her mother. "Call me a cab."

Sylvia looked to Leonard. "Go ahead," he told her.

"I don't know who to call," she replied.

"Tell Gibbons," Leonard said harshly. "He'll do it." She hurried into the house.

"Tell Gibbons," Lee repeated, an unexpected smile forcing itself onto her face.

She hurried down to the lawn to pick up Val. "Shwim?" asked the little girl.

"Soon, Lee said, brushing off the grass from her pajamas.

"Shwim *please*?"

Lee looked down at Val, all thirty-seven inches of her poised to leap into her grandparents' pool and splash. Right on the spot, Lee determined she would not be on the next plane to New York. What was she rushing back to? All she had left was right there beside her. Chuckie could cover for her at the office. She could call the matrimonial lawyer at Will's firm and set him to work. And she could find a hotel with a pool—and allow herself and her daughter a day or two to shwim.

Joe Clark, Lee's divorce lawyer, was a tall, trim, broad-shouldered man in his forties, with a blond crewcut. He and Will, side by side in De Ruyter, Lefkowitz and Stewart's oak conference room, looked like photographic negatives of each other.

"Can he get custody?" Lee asked. Looking tanned and healthy, she felt embarrassed. She should be wan, frail, maybe trembling a little. That's how she felt. She had kept Val in Florida for a week, and every night after the child went to sleep in the middle of their king-size bed in the Miami Beach hotel room, Lee would stand over her and weep in silence, terrified that Jazz would win custody.

She finally forced herself back to New York, but there was no comfort there. Jazz's attorney was not what she had imagined— a sleek, shiny counselor to upper-class Manhattan husbands. No, much worse: Jazz had chosen Manny Plotkin, a short, bald, sputtering Long Island lawyer, a human torpedo who was fast making a reputation for himself demanding—and often winning—rights for men in child custody suits.

"Realistically?" Joe said. "It's the exception rather than the rule for fathers to get custody. Especially where the child is a little girl. It's just not done."

"They're going to say I'm an unfit mother."

"That's nuts!" Will said.

"You've got him on adultery charges," added Joe. "With your sister. Who's unfit?"

She could tell they were losing patience with her. "Look, I've

412

read some of the case law," she explained. "There's a trend. Mothers don't automatically get custody anymore. And it's not as if he's bringing in some New York slicko to represent him. Everyone says this Manny has won a lot of cases out here and . . ." Fear overcame her, and she could not speak. She pictured all the nights she had worked late, how often Jazz had given the nanny, Cherry, the night off. He had said: I don't mind being home. I love puttering around the house, making dinner. Robin had been there every one of those nights. She fit in so well, as if she was one of the family. Which she was, someone whose presence Val would never question. The judge would bring Val into chambers, and Jazz and Robin would be sitting there, and before the judge could ask the little girl how she felt, she'd be racing over to climb onto Robin's lap.

And what could she offer? Jazz had taken Cherry away. Hired her to work for him and Robin. At first, Lee, although furious, was amused at his chutzpah, but then she realized how confident he was that he would win. Did he know something about the judge that she and Joe Clark and Will did not? Jazz was pushing this case with demented energy. He wanted it over. He wanted to win. Every day brought a new shower of paper from Manny's office, details—dates, times—of nights worked, meals missed, dinners Lee had had with Will.

"Do you think he had a detective following me the times I met Will for dinner?" she asked Joe quietly. Her hands were like ice.

"Sounds like it." With his close-cropped hair, rasping voice, and jutting jaw, he appeared to be the ex-marine he actually was.

"But that works for our side," Will added. "Nothing happened. I've been involved with Maria for years. He knows you and I are just friends."

They both looked at Joe. "In that case, nothing to worry about," Joe told them. "What can any picture show? A man eating a bowl of spaghetti talking to a woman eating a meatball?"

"How about a black man and a white woman standing in front of the woman's car talking?" Lee answered.

"You *are* nuts," Joe told her, nodding apologetically to Will for having doubted him.

"Not totally nuts," Will responded after a moment. "What she's

413

getting at is that it depends on what the judge feels in his gut when he's faced with an interracial relationship. Legally it's meaningless. Practically, if his gut goes into a knot at the sight of a white woman with a black man, it won't help." He rested his elbows on the conference table and gazed across at Lee. "But I can't believe that's going to be a deciding factor in this case. Look, this has been a nightmare for you. The man you loved betrayed your trust. That's a terrible thing, but you know what? It happens. Somewhere in the back of your mind, Lee, you know that in marriages, it is sometimes possible for a man to be unfaithful to his wife. It is even possible that he might want to leave her for another woman. So while this is a bad blow, it's something that you can deal with."

"I'm so damn tired of being strong," Lee said.

"I know. What I'm telling you is that nobody's strong enough for what you have to handle now. It's one thing for you to acknowledge that, okay, the marital contract might be violated. But there are certain social contracts that are assumed to be honored by everyone. The family: parent and child; brothers and sisters. Your husband can screw you forty ways till Sunday, but don't worry—there's always your family. They'll be there for you. So what I'm saying is that you've had the rug pulled out from under you in new and unexpected ways. The fact you're sitting here, brave enough to be able to talk about what happened—"

"What the hell choice do I have?" Lee cried out. "Don't you think I'm up every night, sick with fear about Val and sick with thinking how I'd like to kill them? Some nights, I'm running over Robin with my car. Some nights, I'm taking one of those knives they use to cut fur and slashing my father's . . ."

"Understandable," Joe said with such placidity that she realized his practice was as permeated with threats of murder as hers was filled with the actual deeds.

"All that's keeping me sane is Valerie. And they want to take her away from me."

"We won't let them," Will said.

Lee pushed back her chair and stood. "Can you give me a guarantee?"

Will hesitated, then turned to his partner to speak. "No," Joe

Clark said. "Wish I could, but I never give guarantees. Sorry. Especially not with a lawyer like Manny Plotkin on the other side."

"You're fucking crazy, Lee," Terry Salazar told her.

"I could take her anyplace. Ohio . . . Iowa . . ."

"Yeah? And how would you earn a living?"

"I don't have to be a lawyer."

She could say to Terry what she could not say to Will. That with the trial date set in the custody suit, she was growing sicker and sicker with fear. Joe Clark's rational "Highly unlikely" and "Not to worry, I can be as tough as it takes" did not bring her ease. Nor did Will's continual reassurance and his attempts to help her understand why she was so terribly scared: Was she frightened by the fury blazing up in herself? Racked with guilt about being a working mother—not just a mother who had to work, but a mother who loved her work almost as much as she loved her daughter? Did she feel that somehow, Robin—pretty, clothes-buying, don't-want-to-work-for-money Robin—deserved Jazz more than she did because Robin was what a real woman should be and Lee was not? Or that she owed Robin something because she was a success and Robin a failure?

She was getting so tired of Will's constant company and loyalty and thoughtful analysis that she was actually relieved when he went off to be with Maria. Well, not so relieved. Lee told herself she did not expect him to end a years-long love affair now that she was free, that she was perfectly content with his deep and devoted friendship, with his incredible sweetness, now not only to Val, but to Kent also. But in her heart, that was precisely what she had hoped for: Will for herself.

"Listen, you want to be treated like an equal, but you're talking like a real dumb broad," Terry told her. "You got your head so high up your ass you can't see daylight. You run with the kid, he'll find you. The bastard's got nothing but resources to squander on guys like me, to say nothing of the cops and the Feebies who would be looking for you if you went on the lam. You know what this Jazz guy's worth?" He grabbed the papers on his desk, looking for the figures he had gotten, with a hundred-dollar bribe and a great deal of charm, from a secretary in Jazz's accountant's office.

415

"The mil he showed you and Uncle Sam and almost two mil more."

Lee sat on the white couch in Terry's all-white office, for once blending in. She was pale, almost colorless. When she looked at herself in the mirror that morning in the house she was renting, she felt sure she had faded, that she was already less. Jazz was winning. She might even die. She was so tired she could barely speak. "Then what should I do?"

"Do? You got a good lawyer. You got evidence up the ass. I got you that waiter who quit the Carlyle, who's willing to testify about him and her. What other detective could have come up with that, especially considering that I'm working for you on such a discount it's practically nothing? You've got his own admission, for Christ's sake. He's fucking living with your sister in your house. Jesus, you folded on that like a fucking wimp. All you had to say was 'Hey, get your cheating ass out of here and—'"

"It didn't matter. I couldn't stand the place anymore. He bought it under false pretenses, so right from the start . . ."

Lee stopped because Terry began playing an imaginary violin. She did not tell him to go to hell, because she knew he was expecting her to. "You know what gets me about you?" Terry demanded. "You're so tough. I'm not talking about butch. You're not. You're okay, if somebody likes ball-busting women. But look at you now: a fucking basket case. And over what? What are you scared of? A Wasp who was born to run the whole goddamn country and he winds up selling fur coats? What kind of a man do you think that is? For Christ's sake, Lee, you're a powerhouse. He's a pussy! What's with you?"

"What should I do?"

"'What should I do?'" he whimpered. His hands dangled from limp wrists. He pretended to cringe. "'Oh, what should I—'"

Rage propelled her across the office. It was only when Terry grabbed her arm and held it out to the side that she realized her fist was clenched tight and that she had been about to punch him. Not a stop-that-you-bully sock in the shoulder. A hard punch in the mouth. They stood there, facing each other, arms stretched out, perpendicular and stiff, as if in some travesty of a tango.

"Get rid of the fist and I'll let you go."

"Stop it, you jerk."

"I don't think so," Terry said. His voice was soft, velvet. Not the rest of him.

"Come on," she said lightly, as if this coming together were a mere annoyance, and that she could not feel his heat through his shirt.

He stretched out her arm even farther, bringer her closer to him. Her face pressed against his, damp with excitement at their dance. "Come on," he said, rocking his hips into hers. "Come on." He kissed her, not a gentle suitor's kiss. Inflamed, right away, with teeth and tongue working on her. She pulled her wrist out of his grip only to put her arms around him, to try to see if she could draw him in even closer.

Terry was good. Better than good. No finesse, no technique, no sweet words. Hot and hard and didn't stop: That was all she wanted.

That was all she got.

Jazz refused to meet without their lawyers present. Too emotional, for all of us. Sorry. That's what he said when she called to say she would like to come over, to speak to him and Robin. Too emotional? Terry laughed. That's not the reason. After another week on the case, tailing Jazz—just for practice, Terry told her— he had followed him and Robin to a doctor's office. A gynecologist. Oh, obstetricians too. A little charm, no bribe necessary this time for the cute little technician in the medical laboratory the doctor sent his work to. No, charm was all it took to discover that, indeed, an R. R. White, age twenty-eight, was pregnant. It's not "too emotional," Terry said. "The skinny bitch is probably showing."

Lee pushed her way past the two French-accented junior sales-men at Le Fourreur, past five astounded customers, past Dolly Young, past her father who pleaded, "I beg you, Lee, please don't—" into Jazz's office and slammed the door. "You've made my life a living hell!" she told him.

"Get out. This will count against you, you know, your not having the self-restraint—"

"I will make your life a living hell."

"You already did. For years. You can't anymore."

"Item one: My sister is pregnant. She can have an abortion—"

"Stop that!"

"—or she can be an unmarried mother, because I will drag on this litigation forever. Living hell. When I can no longer afford my own lawyer, I will appear *pro se,* and by that time I'll be such a genius at matrimonial law that I'll make mincemeat out of that shyster you've retained. It will drag on for *years.*"

"Stop it!"

"You'll be on your third illegitimate child by that time. And that's just the beginning. I'll bankrupt you. I'll kill you with paper. You won't have a dime left and Manny's wife will have five sable coats and you'll still owe him hundreds of thousands."

"Do you think you can scare me?" Jazz demanded.

"I hope so, because if you're not trembling in your Guccis now, you're a fool. I don't want alimony. This is what I want: I want you to speak to your parents. They don't want Kent. Do you?" Jazz said nothing. "Well, I do. I want them to agree to name me guardian. I want him to live with me. As far as Val goes, I want child support and a guarantee you'll split her educational costs with me fifty-fifty. I get custody." She paused. "I get what I want. Or you get a life that won't be worth living."

On the first day of 1981, Lee and Will went to the beach, a spot not too far from Will's house. The air was cold—freezing, in fact—but there was hardly any wind, so they hunkered down against the dunes, looked across the powder sand to the churning gray ocean, and ate their sausage and pepper sandwiches with their gloves on.

"Brisk," Will said. "Good for the head, good for the soul."

"Brisk? You call this brisk? I call this glacial." She picked up her coffee. "My face is too numb to tell if it's dribbling down my chin and giving me second-degree burns, so let me know." She took a sip.

"You're fine so far." He lifted his Styrofoam cup and touched it to hers. "Happy New Year, kid."

"Happy New Year," she said. "I'm not going to say anything self-pitying and small-minded about this year being better than last."

"I admire your restraint."

They set their cups in the sand and went back to their sandwiches, huge, drippy, comforting things. After a while, Lee felt warmer, heartier. She could be one of those Polar Bears, those mad, jolly people who dive into the Atlantic every winter at Coney Island, racing across the sand, rushing through the surf, and going under, only to emerge with a cheer and a huge grin. She turned to Will. "Did you have fun at the New Year's Eve party last night with Maria?"

He set down his sandwich. "I wasn't with Maria."

"You told me . . ." He had mentioned in early December that he and Maria went to the same party every year for New Year's Eve. Casual conversation, but meant, she knew, so she would not hold out false hopes.

"I know what I told you. It wasn't the truth."

"It wasn't the truth?" She knew it was an odd question for a criminal lawyer to ask. She was trained to doubt. Yet she had never doubted that every word Will uttered was the absolute truth. "Where were you?"

"That's a long story," he said quietly. "A long and difficult story."

Lee's heart began to beat faster. Perhaps Maria had only gone out of town or come down with the flu, but the "difficult story" was that they had finally decided to marry. Not now, she prayed. Please, plan a June wedding and tell me about it in May. "Are you going to tell me the story?" she asked him.

"Yes. That's why I thought we'd come here. No interruptions."

"Okay."

"You know how much you mean to me, Lee. Your friendship." Uhoh, she thought. It's coming. She nodded, trying to seem pleased that Will valued her enough to really hurt her. "For me anyway, it's a lifelong friendship."

"For me, too," she said.

"So let me tell you." She waited, but he did not say anything. Clearly, this was going to be painful for him. She could leave now, rush away, not have to listen, but he had driven his car to the beach, and he had the keys. And it was a stick shift. She wondered if it would be rude to take another bite of her sandwich. She laid her fingers on the warm, greasy, paper-wrapped mess and decided it would be. "I'm gay," Will said.

"Gay?"

"As in homosexual."

Gay, she thought. Oh. No wonder his sports clothes are always so perfect. Suits are one thing, but those slacks, those sweaters. Then a wave of grief crashed down upon her, the realization that she would never have what she now most wanted. What a man! She could love him. She already did.

Suddenly she became aware of what a horrible moment this must be for him, waiting to see how she would react. "I didn't know," she said brightly.

Too brightly. "Lee? Tell me what you're thinking."

"I'm very, very surprised."

"Surprised or shocked?"

"Shocked." Will looked out at the ocean. "Don't be sorry you told me. You're my friend and I love you. I understand how courageous it was for you to confide in me." She rubbed his sleeve with her glove: I'm with you, pal. She left a blotch that looked suspiciously like a mushed-up string of red pepper. "I assume this is absolutely confidential, that I'm not Step One in your plan to come out?"

"God, no!"

"Then I will keep it in absolute confidence for the rest of my life."

Again, Will's eyes searched the ocean. They looked watery to her, but it might have been the cold. "I started college in 1958. No one came out then, or at least, hardly anyone."

"Did you know you were gay then?"

"I knew I was gay by the time I was twelve. I didn't know what to call it. I didn't know it had a name, and to tell you the truth, I didn't know there was anybody else in the world who felt the way I did."

"It must have been a terrible burden."

"It was. But on the other hand, I was this bright, healthy kid. Not a great athlete, not what they expected from a black kid in Glen Cove in those days. But good enough not to feel I stood out. And I was smart. Very smart, very reflective. When you're a teenager, that's a blessing and a curse, but at least I was able to begin to understand what I was and realize I wasn't the first boy in the world who didn't care what the girls were wearing underneath their outfits."

"But you checked out the outfits."

"Yes, I did."

"When did you first have sex?"

"I was fifteen."

"And? Was it okay? Traumatic?"

"It was fine. Very romantic. A lot of candles and massage oil. It was an affair that continued for four years. That's why I went to Columbia. So I could stay in New York, be near him."

"Who was he?"

"My parents' employer." Will came close to smiling as Lee's mouth widened into a huge O. "Clement Giddings. Clem. It sounds like a banjo player, but he was the most urbane man I ever met."

"I don't buy it!" she said angrily. "He was using his power and position to get a boy—"

"Grow up, Lily. He didn't seduce me. I seduced him. Not that he wasn't open to seduction."

"You were still a kid."

"I was. And he was very good to me. Not a great lover, but you're not looking for finesse at fifteen. And a decent man. Not a warm man, not a friendly man, but decent. He paid for college, even after I told him I'd found someone else."

"Who was that?"

"No one. A lot of different guys. I didn't want to be stuck with a forty-eight-year-old man who had never worked for a living except to catalogue his wine collection and who had a wife and two really stinky, obnoxious kids. He offered to pay for graduate school, too, by the way."

"You must have been something."

"I was. His white dream come true."

"Your parents . . . ?"

"They didn't have a clue. They still don't."

"I didn't have a clue."

"I know. I'm good at what I do. I'm sorry I have to do it. But by the time it was no longer necessary—in terms of cultural acceptance of men living an openly gay lifestyle—I was stuck in a suburban subculture where if I came out . . ." He paused to collect his thoughts. "Not completely stuck. I could have left, gone to the city. It was my choice not to. I like it here."

"So do I."

"But there are drawbacks. You can understand, being a woman who works in what is largely a man's sphere: You have to be twice as good as any man to get anything close to equal credit."

"That is a drawback."

"As a black man, twice as good isn't enough. I have to be four times as good. I really believe that. I've *lived* that. And I knew that, practicing law on Long Island, being in the D.A.'s Office, dealing with the cops and all, if I came out, four times as good wouldn't be enough. I'd have to be eight times as good as any white lawyer. And you know what? I'm just not that good."

"Yes you are."

"Thank you. But not eight times. A flash of sheer brilliance once or twice a year, yes, but nothing I could sustain."

Lee glanced down at her sandwich. It was probably cold. She took a bite. Cold but good. "What about Maria?" she asked.

"She's a professional educator in a private girls' school. She's a lesbian. She lives with a woman. We met at a gay Valentine's Day party in the city one of my friends threw. She's wonderfully intelligent, cultured, attractive, and black. The minute we looked at each other, we knew."

"The perfect couple."

"The perfect black couple. 'Aren't they stunning together? Aren't they nice? And *so* well-spoken!'"

"So you don't really love her?"

"No, but I like her enormously. She's an amazing person."

"And last night?"

"What? Oh, New Year's Eve. I was home. Alone. I stuffed a Cornish hen and opened a split of champagne and had a party."

"You don't have anyone in particular?"

"I have someone in particular. Unfortunately, he has someone in particular, someone he's been living with for ten years, so I suppose that makes me his little bonbon on the side. I have a studio in the city. We see each other one or two nights a week. Usually one."

"What does he do?"

"He's an architect. Very arty. Long, flowing hair, quivering nostrils. I can laugh about him when I'm not with him."

"Thank you for telling me, Will." He nodded and got busy

putting their lunch in the plastic bag it had come in. She had not finished her sandwich but decided it would be churlish to stick her hand in the bag and grab it back. "I know you felt you had to say something because you sensed I had a crush on you and you didn't want it to ruin the friendship." He looked at her, almost boyishly embarrassed at being caught. "Well, I had—or have—a crush. I'll get over it. And thank you for valuing our friendship so much. I realize what a risk you took."

"Lee."

"What?"

"I know you. It was never a risk."

On February 29, 1981, the Honorable Anthony J. Paterno of Nassau County's Domestic Relations Court ruled, in the matter of *Taylor* v. *White*, that inasmuch as both parties agree that Ms. Lee White will be the custodial parent, all issues arising from the pending litigation are rendered moot and that custody of Valerie Belinda Taylor, an infant, will be with the child's mother. So Ordered. Submit Judgment.

Twenty-three

Prisons are harrowing places. At night, amid the snores and sleep screams of fellow inmates, I don't know anyone who's so strong that she wouldn't think, even for a moment: I would be better off dead. And the days aren't a hell of a lot better. With no sharp objects, no pills, no tall buildings from which to jump, no car exhaust to inhale, the inevitable jailhouse means to the end is hanging. So Mary Dean was not exceptional. Suicide attempts are so common in jails that most places have a supersharp blade called a 911 tool, which cuts through the bedsheets inmates use to hang themselves. The guards are so accustomed to these incidents they refer to them casually as "hang-ups." If there is no damage—I'm not talking emotional here, I'm talking if the inmate can breathe and walk—he or she is expected to be in line when the next meal rolls around.

There was no way I could be casual about it. That Thursday, right after Barbara Duberstein's call, I sat at my desk, shaking inside. What had gone wrong? Mary had not been pushed into confessing, had she? She had jumped. She had insisted, damn it! But had she insisted because I'd manipulated her into insisting? I tried to soothe myself by thinking she had to have known what she was getting into: Between the assault charge in Maryland and her various arrests for prostitution, she was no stranger to the inside of a cell. There were no surprises here for her. Were there? No, Norman had been innocent and she was guilty. Justice had been served. I had done what I had to do, period.

My serenity lasted about three seconds. Sooner or later, most criminal lawyers come across a client who tries to kill himself. And you have to be either stupid or a first-class putz if you don't ask yourself: Could I have done anything at all to stop it? Your heart is a stone if an incident like that doesn't summon up a time in your own life when you felt death might be preferable to the pain of living. But what made me tremble so was that of all the people who had sat in that armchair on the other side of my desk, Mary was the most likely to want to live. Sweet and stupid and blissfully amoral, delighted by her own beauty, by flamboyant dresses and ten-cents-off coupons for Niagara Spray Starch, madly in love with Norman, Mary was all loud colors and bright sunshine. Of course, I knew she wouldn't thrive in jail. No one would. But to try to hang herself?

My door opened. Chuckie Phalen, as he did every evening, stuck in his head to say goodbye before toddling off to TJ's Taproom. My face must have stopped him. He told me I looked like the wrath of God. When I didn't give him an argument, he knew something was wrong and came in. I told him what had happened. Both of us could hear the tremor in my voice. What are you going to do? he asked me. I'm meeting Barbara Duberstein. I'll play it by ear.

Mary looked as if her suicide attempt had been successful. Dead eyes, although still stunningly green and accentuated by thick black lashes. She did not walk toward us as much as allowed her body to be conveyed by a female corrections officer. The officer was either extraordinarily compassionate or in awe of Mary's beauty. She escorted her across the huge room not with the usual antagonistic impatience—Come on! Move it!—but with a degree of deference that might have been shown a queen on coronation day. Far from being pushed, Mary was being escorted by the officer: Turn here, good, that's right, and They're right over there. Mary was as unaware of the special treatment as she was of the officer herself, even when the woman supported her elbow and helped lower her into her chair.

"Mary," I said, "I had to ask Barbara to come along. I want to do everything I can for you, but because I was

425

representing Norman, there are some things that need doing that I can't do."

"How are you doing, Mary?" Barbara asked.

"I'm sorry," she whispered to me.

I wasn't sure if she was apologizing for trying to hang herself or for asking me to visit her. "Don't be sorry. You must have been in a bad way to try what you did."

She covered her face with her big hands because she started to cry. Still, I could hear: "Norman."

"What about Norman?" Barbara asked, taking out her fountain pen and a small leather book she always carried. In all the years I'd known her, she had never run out of space in the thing. "I'll just make a note or two."

"Tell us about Norman," I suggested after a minute of watching her cry. Shoulders heaving, she sobbed whole-heartedly, gulping huge, noisy mouthfuls of air.

"He's gone," Mary finally said "Gone." She was hoarse, as would anyone be whose larynx had been compressed by a noose.

"Gone?" I said, relieved. I could ease her anxiety. Norman had called my office Tuesday and Wednesday, alarmed about her, trying to see if there was a way to get her out of jail, into some fancy mental hospital. He'd sounded very much *not* gone, very much involved. "He didn't come to see you today?" I was already kicking myself for having been so responsive to her suicide attempt. What a sucker I was! "Is that what got you so upset, Norman's not showing up today?"

"He didn't come to see me"—the tears started to flow again—"since last Friday."

I was stopped cold. "Last Friday?" Either she was lying or confused. Very confused. Or when Norman had called me, yesterday and the day before that . . . "Are you sure, Mary? Today is Thursday, right?"

"Don't you think I know what day it is?" she asked, her voice rising, echoing off the walls of the cavernous space. "Don't you think I've been counting every day since he left?"

"All right, then," I said, trying to soothe her. "Help me

426

understand so I can try and help you. When did Norman leave?"

"Last Friday."

"And where did he go?" I asked, although I knew the answer.

"Atlanta, Georgia," Mary said. "He has his money there. He was going to go to where he hides the key to his safe-deposit box. Then, Monday, he'd go to the bank."

"Cayman Islands," I murmured to Barbara. "But the time-table's the same."

"What was the money for?" Barbara inquired. Mary did not answer right away. As far as I knew from Norman, he was going to get money for Barbara's retainer as well as for the house he was buying near the prison Mary was going to be transferred to. Nevertheless, Mary's silence spoke to me. It said that Norman had told her to keep quiet. She was torn between that obedience and five-foot-nothing Barbara Duberstein's natural authority. "Speak up. We have to know what the money was for."

"He said he needed it to pay a better lawyer."

"Better than me?" Barbara asked.

"Better than you and . . ."

"And what?" I prodded her. "Don't hold back, Mary. Do you mean a lawyer better than Barbara and better than I?"

"'Better than I,'" she repeated. "Norman would like that."

"Norman thought he would find a better lawyer? More aggressive? More *what?*"

"More . . . better. I'm sorry."

"It's okay."

"He said he already called some famous lawyer in Texas and the lawyer was probably going to take my case."

"Do you know this lawyer's name?" Barbara asked, putting her pen to the paper. Mary shook her head. "All right, so Norman got the money—"

"That's what he was going to do!" Mary cried. "I haven't heard anything from him, not since Friday! That's what I've been telling you."

"Wait a second," I said. "He called me. Yesterday, and

427

the day before. He said he'd been with you, that you were going through a bad time. He was looking for ways to help you."

"He wasn't with me," Mary said patiently, the teacher with a slow student.

"He wasn't here? With you?"

"No. Monday, I knew he'd be at the bank in Atlanta. Then Tuesday, I thought maybe there's some holiday down there on Monday, a Georgia thing or a South thing, so that's when he went to the bank. And then after visiting hours in the morning on Wednesday, I thought: Oh, sweet Jesus, maybe he's hurt. Or dead. Maybe a bank robber could've been there and shot him. That's when I called you the first time. I was, like, starting to get hysterical. But then, today, I knew."

"Knew what?" I asked. Mary covered her mouth with her fingertips. A speak-no-evil gesture, and also, I sensed, a signal that said how humiliated she was to have come before us with no lipstick. It did not take much to distract her, and right then it was Barbara's rose-colored mouth. Mary had begun longing for makeup, and I took that as a sign of hope, that even if she did not know it, she did want to live. "What did you know, Mary?" I repeated.

"I knew that Norman wasn't coming back. And that's why I tried to . . ." Her fingers slid down to her throat. Her neck was striped with a red burn mark where the twisted bedsheet had throttled her.

"But then why would Norman call me?" I demanded, turning to Barbara. "Why would he say he'd seen her when he hadn't?"

"Well . . ." Barbara hesitated, but it was clear she knew and was simply reluctant to have to tell me.

"Don't hold back," I told her.

"Because he was conning you."

"Conning *me*?"

"He got you to think he was here, doing the right thing by her, so you would feel easy about him. He was buying a little extra insurance. Didn't want you thinking he might be disappearing into the night."

"But why?" I persisted. "What's his motive?"

It was Mary, not Barbara, who answered, with a calm voice and dry eyes. "Because he didn't want anything to get in the way of my pleading guilty. I knew it today. I *knew* it."

"What did you know?" I demanded.

"Norman conned me too."

The visitors' room seemed so frightening, now that all the dangerous inmates were safely in their cells. Just their odors lingered to prove that they had been there—and would be back. Not the raw smell of gyms or men's locker rooms: a meaner stink. And it was dangerously quiet. No movement except one officer patrolling the floor, her shoes making no sound. Another, cleaning his nails with his front teeth, monitored the closed-circuit TV. A prison movie without a sound track.

"How did Norman con you?" I managed to ask.

"He told me . . ." Mary closed her eyes, unable to bear reality any longer.

"Please, Mary. Tell us." I was sick. I already knew.

"Norman said you thought I did it. That gave him an idea."

No. It was worse than that: I didn't just give Norman an idea. He manipulated me. He made me think that here was a man who had killed, who had led a life without worth, who richly deserved whatever punishment he would get. A defense lawyer's nightmare, but also a defense lawyer's dream. The unwinnable case: To be able to turn that around! He must have started planning the moment he was arrested for Bobette's death.

"Oh, my God," I said. Barbara reached over and squeezed my hand. It did not reassure me. "Tell me about his idea."

"That I should say I killed Bobette."

"Did you kill her?" Barbara asked.

Mary turned to her, insulted, incredulous. "No. Of course not."

"Who did, then?"

429

Mary's liquid emerald eyes took us both in, pitying us for our lack of insight. "Norman killed her."

"But then why were you willing to say you did it?" I demanded. "Didn't you know it was a murder charge?"

"Why? 'Cause I love him."

"He asked you to do this?"

"No! Of course not." Mary ran her fingers through her hair. It lay oily and lifeless on her shoulders. She lifted a tress and stared at it, not believing it could be hers. "He told me what he was facing. All those years. He said: 'You can't wait for me, Mary. It would be like . . .'" Embarrassed at revealing such intimacy, she fell into uneasy silence and began to chew the inside of her cheek.

"What did he say?" Barbara asked. "Please, don't be shy with us. We came here because we care about your welfare."

Mary allowed herself to be persuaded. "He said if I waited, it would be like leaving a beautiful flower in the desert to die. He wouldn't let me. He didn't even want me to visit him in jail. He said: 'Let's end it now, because otherwise it'll be agony.' But I couldn't. How could I leave the one man in the world God meant for me? That's when I started to think about what he was telling me, about how people with long records get life, and how he was so sorry he had a record 'cause people who really haven't done anything much get off easy. I thought: Hey, it wouldn't be that bad for me, not like it would for him. And I knew he would wait for me. So I told him."

"Told him what?" Barbara asked.

"Told him I'd take the fall. And he said: 'Not on your life!' But I begged him. I said, 'Please, let me do this for you, Norman. I mean, I don't really have a record. Not a bad one, anyway. Not like yours.' And finally he said let him think about it. He's a very deep thinker, so it took him a couple of days, but he figured it out. With all his money, he was going to get this very famous lawyer from Texas. He's never lost a case. He's always on TV, Norman says, on all the news shows. And even if he lost, you know, if the jury said I was guilty, if it's the first time you ever did anything, like a violent crime, you don't go to prison long. Like, your sentence can sound long, but you don't *stay* long."

"Did Norman tell you how much time you'd be away for?" I asked.

"He said the lawyer—the Texas lawyer—told him four years tops. But see, with this lawyer, even if he did lose, it wouldn't be more than two."

"Two years?" Barbara and I said together.

"And then, like, it might not even be *that* long, because the lawyer thought he could get me off on appeal." Mary made it sound so reasonable, so inevitable, that I could see she still had not stopped believing it entirely.

Barbara was staring at her. "And you believed him?"

"Norman loves me." She pressed against the barrier that separated us and asked me: "Didn't he? Tell her. Didn't he love me?" I was so sick at heart. Before I could think of something kind to say, Mary slumped backward. "So?" she asked us. "How many years is it going to be?"

"In this case?" Barbara said. "Actual time? I guess somewhere between eight and twenty years." She looked to me for confirmation.

"Mary," I said, "you can fight this. You can—"

She shook her head. "It doesn't matter," she said very calmly. "In jail, out of jail. He's gone. I'm going to die either way."

"No! Listen to me," I said, so harshly that she flinched and Barbara dropped her pen. "You want to die. You think you're going to die because there's no reason to live. When the only man you love suddenly whips around and sticks a knife into you—and then walks away because he's too sensitive to watch you bleed—you say: 'Okay. I'm giving up. Let me bleed to death, because I cannot stand the pain. And besides, it's what he wants. Maybe my dying will somehow make him love me again.' Screw that! I've been there. You *can* stand the pain. You and I are going to pull that goddamn knife out of your heart. Whatever happens—and I can't guarantee anything—you're going to live. You're going to have a big, ugly scar, but you're going to live."

Mary's eyes went from me to her lovely high-rise bosom.

431

"You're just kidding about the ugly scar, aren't you?" she whispered.

I didn't know if it was the worst night of my life, but it was definitely one of my top two. Conned by my own personal con man. I, the one person under no delusions about Norman Torkelson, had been totally bamboozled by him. How he had picked up on what I had wanted! Not love: He knew he couldn't work that scam with me. I was far too wary of him. And where he was, in jail, what good would my going nuts for him do? No, he wanted me sane. At peak efficiency. Norman knew precisely what I was and what I yearned for: I was an ordinary criminal defense lawyer who desired, from the top of her head to the soles of her not too high suburban heels, to be special. To stand beside Justice as her sister. To save an innocent man.

And so he had set me up to save him. He knew that Mary had been in Bobette's house, knew her fingerprints were everywhere. He was probably outraged at the shoddy police work. How dare they not even mention a second set of prints! How dare they arrest him without investigating further! (And oh, how he must have hated Mary, blamed her for his arrest because she had stupidly registered his car in the name that led the police straight to his door!) So he set to work, dropping his poison into my ear drop by drop. And when it began to work, when I started to suspect Mary might have been at Bobette's, he grew so defensive, so protective, that my suspicions had to grow: not only had Mary been there, but *she* was the killer. Not my client. Not my client, whom I was going to get off!

And when I built such a brilliant case against her, he could deny it no more. All right, yes, Mary did it. But you can't do a thing about it. I'm going to take the rap. I, the con artist, the criminal, the moral leper, deserve this one chance to be redeemed. Allow me my humanity.

How poetic! How noble! How I fell for it! How much like all those piteous marks of his I turned out to be. Norman conned me and sent me out to con Holly Nuñez, and I did not disappoint him. I was so ready to believe him.

I took him out to dinner, and he ordered prime ribs of beef!

Forty-five years old: There had been a lot of water under my bridge. I was one street-smart dame, wasn't I? Who would have believed someone like me could be conned? A con man. Who else?

Forget my ego: What would this do to my career? Would my partner ever trust my judgment again? For that matter, could I trust Chuckie not to yuck it up with the boys at TJ's over how I'd been conned? ("Would a fella ever fall for a hoax like that? I ask you?") And what about Holly and her bosses at the D.A.'s? There wasn't much love for me in that office, but at least there was universal acceptance that I was a straight arrow. My credibility was my stock in trade. Now that it was shot, what did I have? And when word went around the Bar Association? Who would ever refer another case to me?

And Barbara? She had not yet been paid. I asked her—almost begged her—to let me split my retainer from Norman with her. Don't be ridiculous, she chided me. A right and graceful response. But a case that had looked like a few hours of easy work, watching over some killer desperate to confess, had turned into a misery that was eating up time from the rest of her practice.

And the worst of my nightmare: My guy. Not just a fine lawyer. There was nothing he did that he did not do well. What would he make of such a screwup? I had no doubt he would show me incredible compassion. He would say: It's understandable. Don't give yourself such a hard time. You're human. It could have happened to me, Lee.

In my heart I did not believe it could have happened to him. It had happened to *me*. Now he would know that I was not as good as he'd always sworn to me I was. What we had would never be the same again.

I had made a pretty good speech to Mary about pulling out the knife. Well, I couldn't get the thought of that knife out of my head. And I thought about twisting a bedsheet into a rope.

It was not a good night.

*　　*　　*

Holly Nuñez's young forehead was wrinkled. She squinted as if she was dying to be in a dark room. Basically, she looked like a dame with one hell of a headache, and when she looked at me, she acted as if I was the one who had given it to her. Well, basically that was right. And Barbara's forehead wasn't exactly smooth. If she wasn't acting as if I'd given her a headache, she could not hide the fact that she was under heavy-duty stress. After all, she was the lawyer in a case she never had control of—and never would have.

"So you're saying that once Norman allowed himself to be convinced to let you take the rap, he coached you on what to say to Ms. White and me?" Holly was asking.

"Yes," Mary said.

"All right," Holly said. "Tell me what he told you."

"Well, see, he told me what happened. Like, he described it. He said if I could see it through his eyes, it would be like seeing it for myself."

"So you're telling me he described the murder of Bobette Frisch to you?"

"Yes," said Mary, a little impatiently. Clearly, she did not think much of Holly's powers of comprehension. But Holly was comprehending, and she knew she had a terrible problem on her hands. She had tried, without any success, to trip Mary up in the hopes that Mary's story itself was a con, part of a labyrinthine scheme concocted by Norman with the aim of forcing the district attorney to let them both go. But in the end, Holly, Barbara, and I all understood: It was Norman Torkelson alone who had killed Bobette.

Holly was wearing a pink suit that looked like a major Easter mistake. Or perhaps it looked so awful, so Pepto-Bismolish, because its wearer was not her usual pink-cheeked, pink-lipped perky self. As she interrogated Mary, I could see her trying to figure out how she could manipulate this whole situation so she would not look bad. She couldn't seem to find a way. To her credit, she hung in there. She was of a new generation of women, one that admitted no obstacles to its upward march. It was not a matter of age so much as temperament: Holly Nuñez wanted to go to the head of the American Dream line. Well, why shouldn't she, now that the Establishment Wasps had become marginal and the Jews were fast becoming the new Wasps? Except in all her dreams, this was the one career move she hadn't planned on: humiliation.

"Tell me how Norman Torkelson described the murder," Holly ordered Mary.

"Like he was really tired. And crabby. She had been all over him before they went to the bank. He couldn't say: 'Hey, get off of me, Fatso.' Could he?"

"Did they have sex?" Holly asked.

"No, and that was part of the problem. 'Cause he couldn't, you know, get it up for her."

"You told me in your taped confession that you saw them having sexual relations," Holly said.

"Not that day, the day she got killed. The day before. I think. So do you want to hear about how she got killed or not?"

Considering that Mary's entire life hung on the slender thread of Holly's cooperation, I thought she was being a little imprudent. I considered a wink or a hint, but knowing Mary, I said: "Don't get angry with Holly. She's the only one who can help you, and if she walks out of here, you're going to be spending a lot of years in Bedford Hills."

"Sorry," Mary said, her voice still a little hoarse from her suicide attempt. Still she did not begin her account.

"What's the matter, Mary?" Barbara asked.

"Will this get Norman in trouble?" She had stopped her edgy cheek-chewing and was now openly nervous, biting her lower lip.

We three lawyers glanced at each other. She was still protecting him. "Let's put it this way," I suggested. "What kind of trouble can you get him in? What do you think the odds are that Norman is hanging around here, waiting for the police to come?"

"He's out of here," Mary said quietly.

"And do you think he's going to take risks that could lead to an arrest, knowing that with you facing twenty years in jail, the only sane thing for you to do would be to tell the truth? Do you think he's going to allow himself to get caught once he becomes a murder suspect again? His fingerprints are in the computer. If he got picked up, he'd be back here in a day or two. He's going to lie low for a long time. So you tell me, do you think you can get Norman in trouble, even if you wanted to?"

"No."

"Then please tell Holly everything he told you," Barbara told her.

"Where was I?" Mary asked.

"His not getting it up," I reminded her.

"Oh, right. He couldn't get it up, and all the way to the bank she kept saying things like: 'Maybe I'm making a mistake. Maybe I'm buying a pig in a poke.' On account of his not being able to."

"Did he ever have that trouble before?" Holly asked, a question I sensed was posed not for prosecutorial reasons but because she was dying to know.

"Not with me!"

"With Bobette?"

"I don't know. See, he didn't know that I knew about him doing it with her. I don't think there was any problem, because if it happened before, she wouldn't have gone to the bank at all, would she? Anyways, she was making these crummy remarks. And then she took a real long time at the bank, and he could see through the window this guy in a suit was talking to her. Norman was, like, pissed. Because of the pig in a poke thing and because marks *never* talk to anyone in their banks or anything. I'll tell you why. Norman says they don't want to be stopped. Deep down, they know, but they really don't want to, if you get my drift."

"Did he know what the man in the bank was saying to Bobette?" Holly inquired. I had never gotten to the point of reading the bank officer's account in the discovery material, but I was sure she already knew the answer.

"Not then, 'cause Norman was outside. But later. They got home and Bobette wanted to try again. Norman made some excuse about being real tired and also so excited that she was giving him this opportunity to start his life all over again. That's when she says the guy in the bank told her: Hey, this is an awful lot of money, and she told him it was an investment and he made some remark about being careful. About how there are con men all over the place! So Norman starts to laugh it off, and she just walks away."

"And then what?" Holly asked.

"She came back. She was stuffing her yap with a Snickers and saying: 'Maybe you are a con man,' with Snicker goo all over her mouth, and her teeth were, like, brown. Like teasing him, but he knew it wasn't only teasing. So he said that's where he made his mistake."

"Killing her?"

"No. Taking the bank envelopes with the money. He said if he'd left them there and walked out, insulted that she was saying he was a con man, she would have come running after him. But he took them. And she tried to grab them back."

"And?" Barbara said.

"And so they sort of started fighting, and she was pretty strong so he stopped her."

"How?" I asked.

"By choking her." All three of us looked at Mary's hands at the same moment. Big, yes. But not as big as Norman's. With tapering, feminine fingers. Mary thought we were looking at her bitten nails and folded her arms so her hands were hidden.

"When you described the murder," Holly said, "you talked about Bobette's tongue sticking out, about how heavy she was. A lot of detail. It made it seem as though you'd gone through it."

"I did. Not in real life. But like when I played Norman's ex-wife, or Ms. McDonald from Pinnacle Collections. We rehearsed. A lot. Norman said I had to do it over and over until it didn't just sound good: It had to *feel* natural. And that's what we did with the Bobette business. Over and over. He gave me the story and he played Bobette. You know, like he pretended to be scared when he saw me, and he's so good, I really *believe* he's scared. And then we moved around our place like it was her place—going into her living room.

It was so real. Like when Norman was saying, 'Please, please, I'll give you anything you want. I can get money,' I was so mad at her. But it was him! Except it felt like it was her." A nervous spasm made her head quiver. "A couple of times, like the night I tried . . . you know, with the sheet. I got this real oogy feeling. Like I had done it. Except it was worse, because I *remembered* I did it. Except I really didn't. Norman did."

"Well," I said, "do you think Norman feels oogy about it?"

"Norman?" Mary said. She almost smiled. Then she shook her head: No.

Before Holly was willing to sign off on the case, she had the police lab make prints of Mary's hand. It took two days, but they finally determined the hands were too small and the fingers too thin to have strangled Bobette Frisch. By that time, I was a wreck, so exhausted from saying "I'm sorry," so ashamed of the whole Torkelson mess, that I was taking refuge in extralegal fantasies: Start a catering business featuring home-cooked meals harassed working women could pass off as their own: Gee, Mom, that was great meat loaf! Or open a little storefront wool-market-cum-crocheting school and blanket Long Island in afghans. I had fantasies of my daughter striking it so big in a television series that she'd say: You've worked long and hard enough, Ma. It's time for you to retire and enjoy life. But Barbara and I had a conference call with Holly, who finally conceded, albeit grudgingly, that we had a deal. Mary would go free. A warrant would be issued for Norman Torkelson, wanted for murder. And once again, for only the fiftieth time, I apologized.

Holly called me back an hour later. "I'm sorry, Lee," she began.

"What?"

"Woodleigh Huber won't let her go."

"*What?*"

"He says he doesn't believe her recantation. He thinks she's guilty."

"That's impossible. The hand prints! Did you—"

"He says it's a judgment call. He says the lab is wrong. It's his duty to stand firm."

I told her I would be down in her office in a few minutes. I hung up the phone, thinking: This case will never be over. And just moments before, I had been at the bank and withdrawn a thousand dollars to give to Mary so she could take some time and think about what to do with her life. I had a feeling that given the choice between hustling and dental hygienist school, she would go for hustling every time. Still, I had already called my across-the-street neighbor who owned a few franchise beauty parlors; he agreed that if she would go for her hairdresser's license, he'd hire her as a shampoo girl so she could have a foot in the door. In my mind, I was already assuring her that I'd pay for beauty school tuition.

"What the hell are you doing?" I asked Jerry McCloskey, who was head of the Homicide unit and Woodleigh Huber's chief toady. "We had a deal." I did not yell at him. He was wringing his hands, and I could see he was being pulled between Holly and Huber. What amazed me was that he was even considering Holly's position. And that Holly, legs crossed, arms crossed, and determined as hell, was still on my side. "We made a deal," I told Jerry.

"Calm down, Lee."

"You've known me for years, Jerry. This is calm for me. Now, off the record, what is this about?" McCloskey peered around his office as if he suspected I'd hidden a camera crew. "I said off the record."

"The Boss was fair with you, Lee. No partisan crap, no nothing. You got your guy off fair and square. But this time . . . No. She did it. And the Boss feels used. You have one success, and now—"

I cut him off. "Look, I apologized. I was conned. You were conned. But worst of all, Mary Dean was conned, and she's facing twenty years for murder. For the life of me, I don't understand why."

I thought this was between me and McCloskey, but Holly spoke up. "The 'why' is that Woodleigh Huber can't admit he was conned. He'd rather have her rot in jail than come out and say he made a mistake. There's an election coming up in less than a year."

"Holly!" McCloskey practically gasped.

"Oh, stop jerking us off, Jerry," she said. I truly did a double take. Her words, of course, were delivered with their usual happy gee-whizness, but she was standing tough—for me. "That woman was the victim of a clever and vicious criminal. You and the Boss should have some humanity, for heaven's sake!" She was making my argument, so I sat back and let her.

"This 'victim,'" he shot back, "besides being a hooker, has a record for assault."

"This victim has been used and abused by men for years," Holly retorted. I thought she might be stretching things a little. Maybe Mary was a victim, but she'd also been a pretty willing accomplice. Still, I was Mary Dean's advocate, not Woodleigh Huber's. Holly went on: "You and the Boss are sure flying the old male flag. "A hooker!" She's twenty-two years old! Are you going to sacrifice her to the Boss's political ambitions?" Holly uncrossed her legs and leaned forward. "Come on, Jerry. This doesn't have to happen."

"You're overruled!" McCloskey barked. Then he flapped his hand to us: Out!

"If I have to," Holly told him, "I'll go to the press."

"You go to the press, Ms. Nuñez, and you're out of this office. As it is, you're skating on thin ice. Very, very thin." He jerked his head in the direction of the door: Get out! I waited to hear Holly's response. I didn't. I saw it: She left.

"Reconsider, Jerry," I pleaded.

"There's nothing to reconsider."

"To do this to someone for politics? How can you? It's not even good politics."

"Nothing the Boss does is good politics to you, and believe you me, he's well aware of it."

"Jerry, don't take it out on Mary Dean. Take it out on me."

He rose from his desk, strode more manfully than he ever had in his life and yanked open the door. "We are," he said, smiling.

440

Twenty-four

They were only three: herself, Val, and Kent. Nevertheless, Lee bought a frame house in Port Washington so spacious that during the presidency of William Howard Taft, its first owners—a family by the name of Palmer—lived there with their five children; after a few years, they invited Mrs. Palmer's twin sister and her husband and their twin boys to move in, and then Mr. Palmer's bachelor twin as well. During the Depression, its second owner, Mrs. Schottland, a widow with three children, took in four boarders.

The first time Lee walked through the place with the real estate agent, she could almost hear the contemptuous questions people would ask: Lee, are you crazy? A white elephant like this? It's you and Kent and Valerie. However, she first saw the house on a late afternoon. Sun passed through a stained-glass window and broke into rich and melting colors on the wide-planked oak floor. She realized that although the objections were prudent, no one was making them. She was alone. And she wanted this house.

So she told the realtor the place was not for her. Sorry, I know I did say Victorian. But the size of this thing! Out of the question. It makes no sense for a divorcée. The following day, the sellers— Bill and Mopsy Tuccio, who were moving to Santa Fe in two weeks—came down another ten percent. The next day, they all shook hands and Lee bought their dining room table, which could seat twenty, and the five turn-of-the-century rocking chairs on the great wraparound porch. The Tuccios threw in their glider. We always sat in it after dinner in the summer, Bill told her. The whole family in that old thing. Back and forth, back and forth. Great being all together, the family. Mopsy gave him a subtle cut-it-out poke and Lee a too sunny smile. Family.

441

Americans are often uneasy about family. Occasionally unhinged. Give them a holiday gathering of their nearest and dearest, and a strong minority will renew their prescriptions for Xanax. Offer them more than a modicum of mother love, and thirty percent of them will move cross-country. Yet the moment Americans acquire their fifth freedom—from family—what do they do? Of course: seek out a family.

The aroma of turkey must be inhaled by a large group. A chorale of "Ooh"'s is a necessary accompaniment to fireworks. And there is little to equal the comfort of being shoulder to shoulder to shoulder to shoulder around a bowl of eggnog. Cro-Magnons did not huddle around fires merely to form an alliance against saber-toothed tigers. They needed to feel they were a clan. For Americans, reared on Hallmark commercials, preferring as they do sentimentality to sentiment, to be simply one or two or three is not only to lack the crucial support of community. No: Painful as isolation itself feels, it is nearly as disturbing to be perceived as being alone. The question must arise: What have you done to make yourself unpopular?

So for her own sake and sanity as well as Val's and Kent's, Lee bought a house that demanded to be filled. For their first Thanksgiving, she invited Will, Chuckie Phalen, two of Chuckie's bachelor pals from TJ's, Melanie Tucker from the Manhattan D.A.'s Office, as well as Lee's new next-door neighbors, the Rothenbergs, and Lulu Martin, an emergency room nurse she met and with whom she became friendly when Kent, trying to help the movers, dropped a carton of books and broke his foot.

Hearing Lee was searching for a full-time housekeeper, a colleague who also did pro bono work for the county's coalition against domestic abuse introduced her to Puella Thorne, a former battered housewife. Puella, in addition to pressing criminal charges, had sued her husband so effectively that he had skipped town—leaving her with a seven-month-old son and a twenty-thousand-dollar debt. She and her baby, Harley, joined Lee's family at the table for Christmas dinner

Lee might have been able to pull off a Chanukah party that year too, but she had by then pretty much forgotten that she had a religion. However, right after New Year's, she got to chatting with a couple ahead of her on line at the movie on Main Street.

They had a son Val's age and mentioned he was enrolled in Sunday school at the local synagogue and actually looked forward to going. The following morning, Lee walked into a Jewish house of worship for the first time in her life. After a surprisingly lively discussion with the rabbi on medieval codifications of rabbinic law, she enrolled Valerie Weissberg-Weiss-White Taylor.

The Sunday school pleased not only the daughter but the mother, not least because Lee knew that not only would Jazz have to pick up Val at a synagogue—dressed, at Purim, as Queen Esther—but that the child, theatrical to the core of her almost-five-year-old soul, would perform Hebrew ditties for Grandpa Leonard and Grandma Sylvia, singing not just well but loud. Over and over. That Passover, Lee attended her first Seder: her own. Twenty-six people squeezed around the table for twenty. Later, she confided to Will that as she lit the candles, she thought about her grandmother. There was a grin on Bella's face. Not from pious pleasure—she hadn't been so pious—but because through her granddaughter Ms. White she had finally outfoxed her husband, Nat the Commie, who had hated God and wouldn't allow Him in the house.

There were too few feasts, though, and too many endless days, spent rushing from court to office and home to dinner, then racing out to a Bar Association program, a PTA emergency session on drinking fountains, or a support group for families of Down's syndrome adults. In the years after Jazz left her for Robin, what Lee missed most was not the conversation, not the sex, definitely not the fur, but the very fact of marriage: a union of two adults. Another body at whom to direct a casual comment while watching the evening news. Someone willing to take responsibility for choosing a new car or a plumber. Someone to share the burdens. True, Puella could drive car pools, offer milk and cookies after school, even prepare dinner when Lee was on trial—a luxury Lee was well aware most single mothers could not afford. True, Will became Val's confidant about her dreams of acting. And he spent so much time with her family that Kent took to calling him "Daddy." Yet Lee knew she was solely in charge of Val and Kent. No days off: Except for alternate weekends and two weeks vacation, she had to put in the time.

There was no: Hey, how about taking Val to the park for an

443

hour so I can do the crossword puzzle? No: Why don't you take Kent with you when you're looking at snow-blowers so I can soak in the tub without someone banging at my door?

For an entire decade, Lee was always tired and usually exhausted. She took to wearing black panty hose because she often did not have the energy to shave her legs. She had time to read only half of the *Times*, so she relied on public radio to inform her about foreign affairs and Will Stewart to keep her informed of business and economic news, a proposition she knew was risky; even though he was a moderate, he was still a Republican. She lacked the concentration to read fiction. She went to museums only with Val and Kent, so she saw too many dinosaur bones, too much Matisse. She, the music lover, the Bach buff, the jazz aficionado, the rock and roller who could at one time quote every word of "Midnight Train to Georgia" and "Pride and Joy" and thum-thum the bass line to "Lucy in the Sky with Diamonds," did not even hear of Bob Marley's death until nine years after it had occurred.

Some nights, Lee was so weary she fell into bed without taking off her makeup or brushing her teeth or even getting into a nightgown. Yet once under the covers, she would turn from her left to her right, then back again, trying to recall which was her good side, unable to sleep for hours. She heard the wind, the scratching of a blue spruce against her window, the almost inaudible whir of her alarm clock, the snorts and deep sleep-breathing of her three dogs. Those nights, she thought of nothing, or everything. Her heart banged as if a momentous occasion were seconds away. Or if sleep was kind enough to take her before midnight, it never held her long. She would wake at four in the morning, her mind ragingly alert, racing from stir-frying parboiled carrots to the laws governing extradition from Canada to buying paper hats for Val's birthday party in school. Winter, summer, year after year, she played and replayed every scene in her marriage that featured a joint appearance by Robin and Jazz. Had those memories been a videotape, it would have disintegrated into shreds.

Every night, she thought about Will.

Now and then she thought about Terry Salazar. A little more than a year after their affair began, she read an article in a magazine in the dentist's office, yet another of those how-to-stop-humiliating-yourself-over-a-worthless-man advisories. Flushed with assertiveness, pumped with nitrous oxide and novocaine, Lee drove to Terry's office and gave him an ultimatum: No more sex on his white couch or white rug or white desk. If he wanted to see her, it would be at a nonsleazy motel. Naturally—being a feminist—she would pay half. Fine, Terry said, glancing at his watch. But shit, we only have an hour. Got a stakeout in Roslyn Harbor. Husband onto dyke wife and aerobics instructor. Hey, he added, inserting his hand between the buttons of her silk blouse, running his fingers along the edge of her bra, why don't we go to the Regal Motor Inn. About seven minutes from here. She realized from his very exactness what a patsy she had been, willing to abrade her knees, her ass, on his stiff, dry polyester rug. He had not dared been so cheap with his other women. He had probably used the Regal for so many other extramarital assignations they all but hung a plaque with his name on it over Room 204.

Terry was neither interesting nor nice. He was, however, a fine lover. Or—as Lee realized in the fourth year of their affair, not precisely a lover. A sex partner. He was always ready, usually raunchy, never not in the mood. And while not genuinely intelligent, Terry was shrewd enough to allow Lee to separate their work from their play. While he was working on one of her cases, he was all business. Or mostly business. He might stare at her thighs if her suit skirt was snug, or find an excuse to read a report over her shoulder, standing too close for propriety, but he never touched her unless she signaled that she was ready to begin. Nonetheless, after five years, he displayed a casualness with Lee, a comfortable slouch when sitting in her office, a lack of the hired hand's deference, that suggested a familiarity beyond the usual criminal lawyer-detective informality. Lee realized that Chuckie had guessed. So had Sandi. And although they said nothing, she knew that they did not approve.

In the sixth year of their affair, after three hours at the Regal that left them amazed at their prowess and barely able to stand, Terry finally offered to leave his wife. "Listen, the marriage stinks. It's stunk for years. We don't have to be doing it at a place like this. We could be together."

"You cheat on me now, when we're only having an affair."

"I do not!"

"You lie too. If you married me, you'd feel obligated to screw around twice as much. You'd be a lox. Totally useless. And I'd be stuck with your dirty laundry."

"This is what you'd be stuck with," he said, grabbing her hand, putting it on his penis, which once again, miraculously, was showing signs of life. "Think about it. We could have a lot of fun."

Driving home that evening, she was amused: Think about it. She could find only two pros about marriage to Terry: She could get regular sex and have an excuse to buy new pots. The cons? As if she would let him live under the same roof as Val and Kent. Puella would watch him swagger into the house and would quit five minutes later. The entire bar of the County of Nassau would laugh itself sick. Will . . . She couldn't even bring herself to contemplate Will's reaction. Think about it!

Indeed, she thought about it for more than a year. She had twice fallen asleep in Terry's arms, and he was surprisingly nice to wake up to. He kissed the top of her head and said "Hi!" as if he hadn't seen her in ages. She liked his easy, masculine competence: He could change a tire in three minutes, fix a sparking electrical outlet, pacify an armed opponent with easy words or a karate kick. It pleased her immensely that he was the sort of man who always carried a Swiss Army knife. But in the end it came down to this: She did not love him. She did not want him to sit at the head of her table, with all the people in the world she loved gathered round, and carve her Thanksgiving turkey. Telling Terry her decision was not a problem, because after that brief offer in the motel, he never again alluded to any marriage except his own dysfunctional one.

She tried to find a man. Really tried. She was certain that somewhere out there was someone just right for her. Well, in order to face grim-faced judges and glowering jurors, even the most cynical trial lawyer must, at heart, be an optimist. Lee was. She accepted every blind date arranged by friends, neighbors, and colleagues. You never know when it will happen, she told herself. She cut no corners on these occasions, always flossing first, always making up before a magnifying mirror in bright light, always opening the door with a welcoming smile. Thus she spent evenings with a drunken physicist, a cocaine-addicted journalist, an anti-Semitic swimming pool contractor, a forty-seven-year-old endodontist who referred to his mother as Mommy. She met men who became nasty when she refused to have sex with them after a three-hour acquaintance, men who told her she was too smart for her own good, men so busy fulminating over their former wives that they never asked her a single question about her life. True, she was introduced to a number of men who were decent and courteous, but few of them interested her. One of them, a veterinarian, admired her beagle and reminded her of John Lennon. But after three dates he stopped calling. When she screwed up the courage to phone him, he sheepishly explained he had, uh, um, gotten engaged. One of those love-at-first-sight things. His fiancée, Lee later found out, was twenty-six.

For a little more than a year, in the mid-eighties, Lee went out with Robert Mandelbaum, a pathologist from New Jersey whom she met when he was testifying for Chuckie as an expert witness in a murder case. For the first few months she was so grateful that, unlike many medical examiners, Robert did not expound on putrefying limbs over dinner that she was able to ignore the fact that she did not enjoy his company. He's perfect, she reported to Will. A widower, so there's no ex-wife he hates. I'm so tired of going out and hearing about some greedy, self-involved, manipulative, shitty mother-bitch-whore. Robert's a genuinely nice guy. We go hiking a lot. He's going to teach me and Val to cross-country ski. He loves music. He plays the cello in an amateur string quartet. He has a wonderful dog, a sweet, stupid Irish setter. A few weeks later, Will observed: You talk more about the dog than you do about the guy. Lee tried very hard to love Robert, or even to like him. She could not. During sex, she twice caught herself yawning and tried to hide it by rolling her head and moaning, pretending she was writhing in passion. She found herself faking ardor and could not believe that a doctor trained to notice the most minute evidence on the human body could not pick up that he left her cold. Will told her: All he probably notices is you're not dead, which ipso facto makes you hot stuff. After a year, she admitted to herself and then to Will that Robert's wife must have died of boredom.

I have to face facts, she told Will shortly after she stopped seeing Robert. I'm no bargain. She was grateful that Will immediately sprang to her defense, telling her how intelligent, pretty, good-natured, and fun—You're a good time, Lee!—she was. So she prosecuted. Just imagine you're a man telling a friend about me: She's a lawyer, so she can never let you have the best of an argument. A real ball-breaker. She makes a decent living, but that house! Crazy, huge old place that sucks money out of her checking account. And who lives there with her? Her kid. Pretty but, you know, wants to be an actress and has a scene every fifteen minutes. Then there's her ex-husband's something . . . brother I think. How she got stuck with him I don't know. A re-tard. Big guy, too, but he can't stay home alone. Needs a baby-sitter the times she goes out with the daughter. Then she's got this maid, this scrawny, white-trash woman who's always blasting Pentecostal preachers on the radio. The maid lives there full-time with her son, nine or ten years old, who's got Coke-bottle glasses and keeps bumping into walls because he's looking down at his accordion all the time. He's not bad, but who the hell wants to hear an accordion eighteen hours a day? Oh, and she's got three dogs: One of them has only three legs. A stray she found, hit by a car. Ugly! You should see the way it hops around: freaky, disgusting.

Will, Lee said, name me one man who would want to marry all that.

"All that" isn't who they'd be marrying. It's you. And you're going to find someone, he assured her. Don't worry.

Do you think I stacked the deck against myself? I mean, subconsciously created a situation that no man in his right mind could possibly want?

I think you've created something for yourself. Something you had to have: a family. Look, happily ever after doesn't happen all the time. So what are you supposed to do when it doesn't? Keep looking at your watch until you're eighty, saying: Gee, he should be coming any second—I'll be glad when he does, because then my life can have meaning? Or do you make a life that has meaning for you?

But what has meaning for me could be a turnoff to some guy.

That's right, Will agreed. It could be. So what are you going to do? Create a life for yourself that's so man-pleasing that any guy in the world would fit in? Keep an electric drill and a jigsaw in the garage and a tape of NFL highlights on top of the VCR?

448

Meanwhile, she kept seeing Terry Salazar: sometimes once a month, sometimes four or five times a week.

And she saw Will. For his social events, he occasionally still escorted Maria. Lee went to weddings, bar mitzvahs, christenings, and lawyers' dinner dances alone. But he began coming to her house for dinner once a week, then four or five nights. They tried cooking together, but they had too many fights, so he often chased her out of the kitchen and cooked himself. They saw almost every movie that came to town. They bought a Philharmonic subscription together. They played tennis twice a week. He was the one who persuaded her to take Val's acting abilities seriously and did the research on acting classes in the city, and dramatics camp for the summers. They took Val to the theater and Kent to the petting zoo he loved. They spoke on the phone first thing in the morning, from their offices, and last thing at night, after Will got back to his house.

After ten years of friendship, he finally introduced her to his parents. His father had worked with horses all his life, and with Will's financial help, he and his wife had retired to a condominium near Virginia horse country. They were an imposing couple, dark brown, broad-shouldered, and big-nosed like their son. Jack Stewart looked as if he could tame a stallion with a withering glance, and Marjory, in her own way, was equally impressive; her palms were stained purple from the fruits and berries she was perpetually putting up. Except for the four hours a night she slept, she was never without something to pickle or preserve.

The elder Stewarts wore only plaid. Or, as they corrected Lee, tartan. The colors of the clan Stewart. Dress Stewart. A slightly larger variation of the pattern: Muted Dress Stewart. Then there was Gray Stewart. Black Stewart—which Will never failed to comment upon. Oh, I see we're in Black Stewart today, he'd say to his father. How apt. Quiet, William! his mother would command, coming between the two men. Will told Lee it was not until high school that he realized how odd it was for people to wear plaid every day of their lives. Plaid shirts, plaid skirts, plaid jackets. Plaid bathrobes. Plaid slippers. Plaid ties to church. Plaid seats on their dinette chairs. Only the Stewart tartan, of course, which made each sighting of a Gray Stewart raincoat or Black Stewart bathing trunks all the sweeter. In his sophomore year at Columbia, it hit him that the closest his parents had ever come to Scotland was the eighteenth-century farmer who had owned and perhaps sired Jack's ancestor. Again and again, Will asked his parents why, or more to the point, how could they. What were they trying to be? Why don't you wear a dashiki if you want to show what you are? Or all those ropes of beads, the way they do in Kenya? They became furious at his brass: We're Stewarts!

"Hey, Dad," Will said. His parents were visiting him from Virginia, and he had invited Lee, Val, and Kent to go with them to a Mets game. He and his father were fervid fans, transferring their Brooklyn Dodgers-Jackie Robinson fanaticism to the newer National League New York team. "Gray Stewart today!"

"Shut your fresh mouth!" his father barked.

Kent smiled in commiseration with either Will or Jack Stewart. Lee could not be certain. Or he might be happy simply because he was sitting in a box seat close to first, right over the Mets dugout. It was a sunny day, and he was devouring the two hot dogs Will had bought him and being allowed to sip Lee's beer. Valerie, at fourteen, was not eating or sipping anything. On a diet, she had brought along a bag of raw vegetables and was resting her carrot entirely too suggestively on her lips while making eyes at the first baseman, a fellow who looked like a descendant of the Jukes and the Kallikaks. Between batters, he seemed to be ogling her back. Marjory Stewart eyed the plastic bag of vegetables hungrily, as if she wanted to snatch it from Val's unappreciative grip and make a fast chutney.

Lee smiled in Will's direction but knew he would not notice her. He and his father rarely took their eyes off the field, as if they, and not Mets management, were responsible for any success the team might enjoy. To look at them, plaid-jacketed father and blue-blazered son—with mother in a plaid shirtwaist beaming on—was to think: Ah, *there* is the great American family.

In fact, they took no joy in each other. The Stewart men merely shared a love of the national pastime. And while both parents might enjoy a fine afternoon in box seats provided by one of their son's corporate clients, they were not happy with their son. Nor was he with them.

In Jack and Marjory's view, Will had let them down. He had

not married and given them grandchildren. Bad enough, all those little plaid dresses and tiny plaid baseball caps going to waste. Worse, he was not the first black president of the United States. He had not even tried.

Will thought he had. He had bought them their condo and their Subaru station wagon, sent them on luxurious senior citizen bus tours all over the country, given them their dream, a first-class trip to the Kentucky Derby. He spoke to his father's cardiologist so often they were on a first-name basis. He donated such a hefty sum each year to their church that whenever Will visited Virginia, the minister came to the airport to greet him. He even tried to take his parents to Scotland: I'll *go* with you. But they declined, not approving of Europe. He told Lee that they might have accepted the trip if he could have flown them there on Air Force One. Back in 1980, his father had urged him to run, telling him it was a Republican year. Will, Jack counseled, the country is ready for a Negro president.

Nothing Will accomplished—*Law Review* at Columbia, getting into the D.A.'s Office, heading the Homicide unit, becoming a name partner in the most prestigious law firm on Long Island—was enough for his parents. We expect the best from you, they had warned him when he went off to Columbia. He thought he had given it.

It's not that they want the best from you, Lee told him. It's that they want everything.

They're always disappointed, he'd replied.

As long as you're not. Will had nodded, but it was one of the few times his face turned sour. His expression was crabbed, angry.

But looking at those plaid people, Lee thought: better to want everything for your child than to want nothing, the way my parents did.

Well, when she thought about it, her mother at least had wanted something from her: better taste. Or maybe a more bubbly child, one who was fun to buy shoes for, one who could jolly her out of a clinical depression. In the years since her divorce, Lee often ruminated on the myth of the ever-loving, overprotective Jewish matriarch. How come she hadn't had one? Where were all those self-sacrificing mamas hiding? Was the Jewish mother a myth perpetuated by male writers and filmmakers—they being the boys, the chosen children who actually got the love and protection? Or in becoming White, did Sylvia make some final break with her heritage, taking on Anglo-Saxon Protestant restraint without the concomitant sense of duty, strength of will, and grace under pressure?

Still, every time Lee considered her mother's failings, she could not help but wonder what it was that formed the woman. A lifeless, unloving household? Lee had only a vague memory of her grandparents Bernstein, two pallid whisperers who, in their last years, when she was a little girl, seemed to murmur only about the Judge's gas. Was her mother a casualty of these two people, dead decades before they died? Was there something incomplete inside Sylvia, a spark that ought to have caught fire but never did, so she never received sufficient heat to make her truly human?

Yet could Sylvia truly be pronounced dead? Wasn't she capable of passion? To be sure, it was passion for furniture, passion for clothes, passion for appearances, but still, she cared deeply about something. If mother love did not come naturally, could she have worked at caring deeply about her own child? And if she could not have cared, what had kept her from behaving with a little common decency all those years? Or like Paula Urquhart, could Sylvia White mount a defense by claiming to be a victim who could not help herself?

Maybe the jury had found her client not guilty, but Lee did not believe she was innocent. And she did not believe it of her mother either.

She could find no excuses for her father. He knew his wife was more than defective; she was hurting Lee by malign neglect. Why hadn't he fought for his daughter? What made him feel he had the right to now and then shake his head over his wife's indifference—Too bad—and then wrap himself up in his own furry world in Manhattan? Would he have stuck around a little more if it had been a son who was being damaged?

It was not as if Leonard was ignorant of what a father was supposed to do. He had had two lively parents. True, Nat the Commie had not been the most supportive father, but he was not an unfeeling louse. He had wanted the best for his son and pulled all the threadbare strings he could on Leonard's behalf. And Bella,

452

that loud, loving realist, would have done anything for him.

But as with so many children of immigrants, the world outside had meant more to Leonard than the world in his parents' one-bedroom railroad flat. To be part of that outside world, he needed to destroy everything of Bella and Nat that was inside him, for he lacked the imagination and the spirit to keep them with him as he refined himself. So Leonard grew whiter than white, so white he became invisible. But it was not only himself and his parents he obliterated. Lee came to believe that if you are willing to do away with your parents, you will then be willing to destroy anyone else in your family who gets in the way of how you want to be perceived.

So while Lee no longer saw her parents, she understood that for Valerie's sake and her own she could not kill them off. She had to let them live. She never spoke ill of them in front of the child. When Val came home from her weekends with Jazz and Robin and her two half-brothers/first cousins with reports on them and on her grandparents, Lee listened with interest and suppressed every hateful remark that came to mind. She never lied and told the child she loved Sylvia and Leonard, but she did tell her daughter: I know how much they love you. She did not add: Because you are Jasper Taylor's child.

She also searched her memory and found enough decent moments to use for show-and-tell with Val. Sylvia fussing over what Lee would wear to the prom. Leonard celebrating her acceptance to Cornell. Planting sunflowers. Going with Mom to buy new Mary Janes for the Young People's Concerts in the city. Going with Dad to buy our dog Woofer. Being allowed to buy all the paperbacks she could hold in her arms.

Lee looked at her companions basking in the gorgeous July sun in the box at Shea Stadium. The Stewarts, who were incapable of taking pride in their extraordinary son. Will, who could not give up trying to make them proud. Kent, whose parents had not inquired as to his welfare in seven years. Herself.

She turned to her daughter. "Hey, Val," Lee said softly.

"What?" The teenager's eyes remained on first base.

"I love you."

Val was wary. Fearful. But no, thank God, the first baseman had not heard her mother. Quickly, because she could not divert her attention for too long, she turned to Lee and removed the carrot from her lips. "I *know* you love me, Ma."

A half hour later, after the first baseman had struck out and the Mets shortstop slammed what looked like an in-the-park home run and the crowd stood up and roared, Val once again put down the carrot and murmured, just above the din: "Love you too, Ma."

Twenty-five

Despair. Remorse. Anguish. Misery. No one word in the language can express what I felt about Woodleigh Huber's decision to go ahead with the prosecution of Mary Dean. Sickened comes close, but that doesn't take into account the rage I felt at the injustice, or the shame I felt that I had allowed myself to be conned.

"The worst thing about it," I told Will Stewart as we sat rocking on my front porch, "is that I can't think of any way to put the scales of justice back into balance—short of running Huber over with my Jeep."

Will put his hand on my shoulder. "Stop trying to keep an ironic distance. You're a mess."

"Yes."

Will was a lawyer, and before Jerry McCloskey was sent in to degrade and dishonor the Homicide unit, Will had run it. Now he was a hotshot civil litigator, so his hand wasn't resting on my shoulder just because he was being Mr. Empathy. He knew precisely what I had done: come up with an alternate version of Bobette's murder that showed my client to be innocent. Okay, lawyers do that all the time. They tell a once-upon-a-time story that views the facts of the case in a soft pink light. If it's a really captivating fairy tale, some juries will buy it. Sometimes even the lawyer buys it.

But I just didn't think: Hmm, good argument. Better than what the government has. I bewitched myself—with Norman Torkelson's help. And then, because I believed in the story so completely—Love Triumphs over Wickedness! No-Good, Rotten Con Man Seeks Expiation Through Sacrifice!—my belief, my passion, gave me the power to enchant everyone else. Will Stewart knew: I hadn't been a lawyer; I'd tried to grab Justice's toga and wear it myself. Except it didn't fit. I was in large part responsible for a killer's taking a walk and an innocent person's paying for the crime. Earlier that day, a bus had rolled of out of the Nassau County Correctional Center taking Mary Dean and twelve other female prisoners up to Bedford Hills.

"Don't run Huber over," Will advised. "You'd be the prime suspect. The minute the lab ran tests comparing the tread marks on his face with your Jeep tires, you'd . . ." His voice trailed off.

"Go ahead. Say it: I'd be sharing a cell with Mary."

"No. I'm not going to remind you she's in jail and Norman is probably sitting back, sipping a margarita in some Sun Belt state. I came over to cheer you up."

"Consider another line of work."

"No. And I'm not leaving until you're okay."

"Then you're in for a life sentence." I tried to keep my voice light, so Will wouldn't know how appealing his never leaving sounded to me. We rocked back and forth for a while in familiar silence, two old fogies on the front porch watching the twilight. Stars were coming out, and a gibbous moon. I caught the season's first hint of honeysuckle. "Will?"

"What?"

"Are there any other cute moves I could make to force Huber to let Mary go? Anything I haven't thought of? Because there are no more tricks left in my bag—not even ineffective tricks I could use just to piss him off."

"Nothing beyond what you're doing now—spinning your wheels with the habeas corpus petition."

"But we both know that's not going to work."

"Correct." Will leaned his head against the spindles of the rocker and closed his eyes, pretending to take in the honeysuckle. Except I knew him too well to be suckered by a deep sniff. He was thinking, so for a few minutes I got hopeful. He was such a fine lawyer. A clever strategist. A smooth negotiator: The other side never got up from the table feeling screwed, even if they had been, royally. But more than that, Will was creative. When he couldn't win by logic or law, he often won through sheer surprise. "Lee."

I rocked forward and stayed that way, ready, I suppose, to jump up and act. "What?"

"Lean on me for this."

"You have an idea?"

"For springing Mary Dean? No. Nothing comes to mind." I let the chair rock back. "Not right off the bat, anyway. But you're going off the deep end and you don't want anyone to stop you. That's crazy. You're not responsible for her being in jail. At worst, you made a mistake. Lawyers make mistakes every day."

"Not like this."

"Yes. Like this and worse."

"Everyone knows I was conned. Everyone knows that poor girl is spending the better part of her life in prison because I thought I was being such a hero."

"Everyone knows you misjudged Norman Torkelson. So did Holly Nuñez. Is she sitting in a rocking chair right now having a psychotic episode?"

"No. She's trying to figure out a way to put a hundred miles between her and me. So is everyone else, except you."

"You're always telling me how smart I am."

I looked at him, so dark he was almost a shadow in the nightfall. "You are. The smartest."

"So if it's my assessment that you made a mistake but not a fatal one, why can't you accept it? Or do you think my intellect has limits, in that the only thing I can't evaluate is how badly you fucked up?"

"I don't know."

"Trust me, Lee. What do you think is going to happen? You're going to walk into the Bar Association and all conversation will stop? And then—like in one of those old westerns—someone will spit on the floor? I hate to tell you this, kid, but you're a one-week wonder and your week is up tomorrow."

"You're wrong, Will." I was in a bad way. Sure, I would slog on and finish out my life, maybe chalk up a couple of big wins, maybe have a grandchild or two, but I felt a deep dullness, a sense that I would never again know pleasure.

"I don't know if it's because you're a woman or what, but you feel you've got to have the biggest balls in town. Everyone else can screw up: not Lee White. Or maybe because you got conned by that schmuck husband—"

"Ex."

"—ex-husband, you can't accept that it could happen again."

I got off my rocker and leaned against a post, looking out at the street, away from Will. "Give me truth or pretense, and what do I wind up going for every time?"

"Truth," he said.

"Like hell I do."

"You're a woman of the world. Why does it come as a shock to you that some men get away with murder?"

I turned back to face Will. "I let it happen."

"Come off it, Lee! You didn't *let* it happen. It happened. You see injustice every day of the week in your work. You think you're immune? Who the hell inoculated you?"

"I couldn't see past the surface. I thought I could. I thought I *knew*. That's what gets me. I believed I was different, that I had depth. If I gave my heart to a person, or to a cause, it would be someone or something worth fighting for. And what happened? I was duped."

"Yes, you were."

"So?"

"So why don't you go off and shoot yourself because you believed what appeared to be the truth twice in your life? Come on, Lee. What have you ever done that you feel obligated to give yourself such a bad time? Not even Woodleigh Huber, that shitheel, would dare to do to you what you're doing to yourself."

"So I should just forget it?"

He got up from his rocker and stood right beside me. "No. Not quite yet."

My daughter, Valerie, was a marvel to look at: cascades of auburn hair, peachy skin, and huge, intelligent hazel eyes that dominated her face—and any room she happened to be in. At two in the afternoon that Sunday, she happened to be dominating the kitchen and laundry room. She had invited a fellow actor—a tall girl from Chicago, who was trying to look like a born tragedian—to spend the weekend. It appeared that they had taken in laundry from the entire cast and crew of the cable TV movie they had bit parts in. Between wash loads, they watched the entire filmography of Maggie Smith. Val had said: Want to be a patron of the arts? So I'd paid for the video rentals as well as their foray into Ben & Jerry's—this a half hour after I had watched Val tearing a head of lettuce into tiny pieces, dicing a zucchini and slicing mushrooms and meticulously measuring out a quarter teaspoon of Parmesan cheese, agonizing over its fat content.

"Where are you going, Ma?" she asked, her spoon poised to dive into the ice cream again.

"No place special," I said, hoping she'd say: Hey, you paid for this stuff. Why not join us? Come on, dig in.

Chicago was working on Chunky Monkey while maintaining a sour expression that should have curdled the cream. Maybe she was involved in her process, as my daughter would say. Probably daydreaming about being Medea killing her children. I liked most of my daughter's friends, but this dame was a heavy piece of furniture. I wasn't in the mood for moods.

Val, I could see, had gone for her usual, a pint of New York Super Fudge Chunk. "If you're going to be passing the video store, we forgot *The V.I.P.'s*."

"I'm not sure what I'm doing. I want to plant some nasturtiums, but if I do go out, I'll—"

Val smiled at me, a wide, incredibly friendly smile, so unexpected on a classic pretty face. Part of her charm, I thought for the millionth time. Surprise. That this lovely young woman was still entrancing with fudge chunk on her teeth and a chocolate ice cream coating on her chin—Suddenly I didn't fall into my usual isn't-she-a-marvel reverie. Something wasn't wonderful. Something was wrong. My maternal instincts are pretty good. "Ma, you're looking at me funny."

"No I'm not."

"Yes you are." But no, it wasn't Val.

It was the chocolate.

I was rushing around, looking for my car keys. "It was the chocolate," I said. "I've got to go."

"What?" She knew my leaving would mean she was going to have to fold her own laundry. She might be an actor, but she was not a lawyer's daughter for nothing. If she could not win one point, she'd try for another: "Do you want to take us out for sushi when you get back?"

"Very much. But now . . . Hate to rush out on you, but . . ." I was picturing Bobette's mouth and lips, thick with chocolate from the Snickers bar. "I've got to get to the women's prison in Bedford Hills before visiting hours are over."

On the drive up to Bedford Hills, I was thinking that I should have taken Chicago with me, to show her what a really tragic face looked like. Except even before Mary Dean spotted me and broke out into a big smile and a two-handed wave, she looked happy. All right, if not happy, then at least something between untroubled and carefree.

"Hi!" she enthused. "It was *so* sweet of you to come and see me. I was talking to one of the girls and saying, 'It's gonna be a bummer on visiting day 'cause I'm not from New York and I don't know anybody so how can anybody come and visit,' and the next thing, here you are!"

"You sound pretty cheerful," I said. "Considering the circumstances."

"Yeah, well, what can you do?" The blue uniforms of Nassau County were gone. New York State, for some reason, was pushing a deep green, a more flattering color for Mary because it matched the dark-green glints in her emerald eyes. "You know what? I'm going to finish high school. You can do that here. To tell you the truth, they kind of push you. I mean, you can't just go to work in the laundry or in the kitchen. No, before they even talk to you about a job, you gotta take all that English and history and—jeez, I hope not math. But that's New York for you. A very smart state."

I could see by the way Mary flashed little smiles at the other inmates, or made ooh-isn't-he-cute faces at their boyfriends or children, that she was knocking herself out being congenial. She was right to want to build up some credit. Beauty like hers was a liability in the slammer. If someone took a dislike to her and a fight broke out, they would go for her face. Bruise it the first time, disfigure it the second. In fact, her whole ebullient manner—upbeat smile, happy babbling—was a front. I was at least relieved to see the other inmates wave back with a reasonable degree of warmth, noting, I had no doubt, that Mary was obeying the unwritten law: scrupulously avoid eye contact with their men.

I handed her a bag of grapes I'd brought from home, red, purple, and green. "I wasn't sure what you needed."

"This is *so* nice," she said. "All they give you here is oranges. Sometimes bananas for breakfast, but they're . . ." She made a fairly hideous guttural sound in the back of her throat.

"Mushy brown spots?"

"Brown all over!" Her too cheery behavior was replaced by a sweeter, more genuine manner; she was getting into a real conversation. If I could stay on yucky bananas or a comparative analysis of eye makeup remover pads, we could have a fine visit. "I mean, if you really went like this"—she squinted—"you could find maybe one banana-color little teeny spot in all that brown ook."

"Mary." She saw something serious coming on, and her eyes darted left-right-left: Let me outta here. "I'm going to try and keep this conversation light, okay?" I assured her. "I know you're worried you'll start crying, and you probably don't want the other women to know how emotional it is for you right now." She nodded. "Okay," I said, offering her a big, phony grin. "If the discussion gets too rough on you, rub your nose. I'll go into a long song and dance about my boyfriend or something."

"Is he cute?"

"Who? Oh, my boyfriend?" She nodded. "Yes, pretty cute. And a really nice guy."

"Good, 'cause I was worried about you. I mean, your age, no wedding ring. I figured, Uh-oh, something must've happened. I remember I said to . . ." She looked toward the red Exit sign over the door.

"Now that you mention him, Mary: There were a couple of days between the time Bobette was killed and her body was discovered."

"Uh-huh."

"When the police came and arrested . . ."

"Go ahead. You can say his name. I don't care."

I smiled. "Thank you. When they arrested Norman, he wasn't wearing the same clothes as when he killed Bobette. Right?"

"Uh . . . No."

"It might be helpful if you could remember what he was wearing that Friday, the day he went to the bank, the day Bobette was killed." Mary screwed up her mouth and drew her lovely arched brows together in deep thought. Or maybe she was practicing looking cerebral for her high school equivalency diploma classes. But nothing was happening behind that beautiful forehead. I was such a New York knee-jerk liberal that I was always thinking: Hmm, this person must have had an emotionally deprived childhood to appear this dull-witted. Or, this person must have been dropped on her head. Maybe I was right. I certainly never thought: Holy shit, is she dumb! until that moment in Bedford Hills. "Did Norman say anything about ripping anything during the murder? Or about Bobette trying to fight him off, or just moving around and possibly getting something on his clothes?"

"Chocolate!"

"Chocolate," I repeated.

"On his sleeve. Like right on the top of the cuff. A teeny doodle of chocolate."

"From Bobette. From the Snickers bar she was eating."

"Right!"

"Did you notice the spot or did Norman?"

"Well, I *would* have, because I always check before I do a laundry or send stuff to the dry cleaner 'cause stains have to be specially treated. I have a Mary Ellen book, and it tells what to do for each one."

"But Norman saw it?"

"Did he ever! I mean, he came home and he was, like, crazy. It was right by the DW. The initials on his cuff. Denton Wylie. Well, I mean, I don't know whose initials they really were. Norman lifted this expensive suitcase in a little airport, Santa Barbara. He just picked it up and walked out with it. He said the guy was his size—and that didn't happen every day, a rich guy that tall, 'cause most rich guys are little teeny men with little teeny . . . Do I have to tell you? You're a lawyer. What happened was, the rich guy gave it to a skycap and the skycap put it down and when the skycap got busy doing something, Norman picked it up. And there were five shirts with initials and a whole bunch of ties in a leather case with a gold *DW*. A case just for ties! The shirts were silk, except they were so expensive they looked like cotton. Anyhow, that night, after Bobette. He tore off the shirt. I mean *tore*. A couple of buttons came off."

"And then?"

"And then? I forget. I guess he must have told me what happened. No, wait, he wanted a drink. Chivas over ice. You don't say 'on the rocks.' It's not classy. I made it for him, but he went right back to the bottle and poured, like, a cup more. Right up to the top of the glass."

"And the shirt?"

"Oh, he said: 'Get rid of it.' "

"Right then?"

She gave that a minute's thought. "Later. He drank so much so fast. I mean, both of us like to have a drink, but you know . . . Sip. He was the one who taught me about sipping, but he wasn't sipping. He was glugging it down and telling me what happened."

"And he told you to get rid of the shirt?"

"Yes. He was pretty drunk, but Norman wouldn't ever get that drunk that he couldn't think. He said: 'Get rid of it,' and then he went to sleep. And when he got up, he said: 'Did you get rid of it?' "

"Did you?" I asked.

"You're asking too? Jeez! No one gives me credit for anything. I told him: Norman, relax. I told him I walked about half a mile to a used car lot—he knew which one—but naturally it wasn't open. It was spooky at night, I told him. And I used up a whole book of matches, but I finally burned it and stomped the gray stuff, ashes, into the ground." I suppose I must have looked as if my life was over, because Mary bent forward to look at me with a mixture of pity and curiosity. "I shouldn't have burned the shirt?"

"It doesn't matter." The guards were moving around. Inmates were starting to say goodbye to their families. It was easy to tell which were the troublemakers. For them the guards enforced the no-touching rule, but they bent it for the others. Mothers kissed their children, touched the cheeks of their parents. Women patted their hair, or moistened their lips, so their men would have someone pretty to remember after that last look. I stood to go. "Please don't worry about the shirt," I told her. "It might have been helpful if it was still around, but probably not. Don't give it another thought."

"Okay," she said, only too pleased to comply. Then she added: "Because I didn't."

"Didn't what?"

"Didn't burn it." I sat back down. "It was *silk*. White silk. Norman loved those shirts. You give it to the dry cleaner, you know what you get? A spot. They get the chocolate out, but leave a little drippy-looking raindrop thing. And he did say: 'Don't even think of giving it to the cleaners. Get *rid* of it.' Except I figured, what the hay: With some silk—not all, but some—you wash them on the cold, gentle cycle and then you pull it out. Don't let it go through the spin, just pull it out wet—"

"Mary, did you wash it?"

"I'm trying to think. I remember thinking: If it comes out nice, he won't know it's the Bobette shirt because they're all the same. White silk. But they were so expensive and beautiful and all with *DW* initials. We could've kept using them. There are lots of D names. Dennis and Dwayne and Dick—"

"Picture what you did with the shirt, Mary. Tell me what you see."

She closed her eyes. "I put it in a net bag. Like what you put your panties in. And then . . ." I waited. "I zipped it. It's one of the ones with a zipper."

"And then?"

"I put it in the washing machine."

I took a deep breath. "Did you turn on the machine? Do you remember taking out the wet silk shirt, letting it drip dry?"

"No. Oh, I know why. 'Cause Norman was home that whole weekend. Really bad. Drinking. Didn't want to have any fun. Kept sleeping and drinking and sleeping. So I wasn't going to do a wash, not with him there. I had to wait." She sighed. "That's not good to do with a stain. And now I'm up here for twenty years."

"You didn't wash the shirt once Norman went to jail?"

"No. Isn't that weird? Oh, I know why. I did some washes, but I took it out of the machine because, like why not wait till I had a few more things for a cold water wash? I mean, if it was like her blood or something I would have done it separate. Or maybe I really would've burned it. But it was just Snickers."

"Where is the shirt?"

"In the net bag."

"And where is the net bag, Mary?"

"Let's see. I stuck in some panties and a teddy and . . . It should be right where I left it." She closed her eyes and lifted her left arm high, making a patting motion with her hand. "Right up there on that shelf, in the broom closet. Next to the Endust."

Next to the Endust! I tried to keep myself calm going home. I didn't go more than ten miles over the speed limit. Fifteen. When I got to the Throgs Neck Bridge, I called my investigator, Terry Salazar, and told him to meet me at Mary's apartment. It hadn't been a full week since she'd been arrested, and I prayed that even if Jerry McCloskey ordered a complete search of the premises, the cops would have overlooked a silk shirt stuffed under panties and a teddy on a shelf in a broom closet. Since Mary had confessed and pleaded guilty, they wouldn't have had to seize the contents of the apartment. Would they?

Except I didn't get a chance to find out, because when I pulled over to the curb, I saw Terry making a thumbs-down sign. "What's the matter?"

"Sealed," he said.

"Sealed?" I didn't want to believe him. I got out of the car and ran to the building. Sure enough, the cops had pasted their Sealed by the Order sign onto the door and jamb of the apartment.

"Want me to break in through one of the windows?" Terry asked.

"No!" I snapped.

"You on the rag?"

"What good will your breaking in do? I'd have gotten the shirt illegally. It's no use saying Mary authorized me to search the apartment now that it's sealed. Anyway, knowing Huber, he'd accuse me of faking evidence."

"If it has Bobette's saliva with her DNA—"

"What if it doesn't? What if it just has some Snickers juice and that's it? He'll say I got a silk shirt—"

"You're going off the wall, Lee. Calm down. I'm sure during the whole investigation with Norman they took samples from him. Didn't they?"

"Yes."

"So if we find some of his hairs with roots on the shirt, body hair, whatever, that shows it's Norman's. That you didn't plant it." I got back into my car and slammed the door. "Hey, now that you screwed up my Sunday, getting me over here," Terry said, "why don't we go for a drink or something?"

I turned the key in the ignition and left Terry behind. I went home to take Val and Chicago out for sushi. Home to figure out a way to get my hands on the shirt Norman was wearing when he choked Bobette Frisch to death.

I would have spent the whole night on the phone with Will, but at eleven-thirty, he said he wanted to get a good night's sleep. "You're going to ask me: 'How can you possibly sleep?' " he said. "So I'll tell you. I'm tired. But I can also tell you right now you're not going to change Huber's mind, because he's decided that letting Mary go would show that he was conned, ergo a dupe, ergo not fit to hold public office. I've crossed him off my to-do list. As far as any other avenues leading to the shirt, the only one I can think of is Holly Nuñez. She did back down at the end but she was on your side for a while. She went head to head with McCloskey."

"She lost."

"The point is, at least she had the guts to go stand up to that pathetic piece of white trash."

"Should I call her?"

"I think you should do nothing. Let me be your lawyer on this."

"You want a retainer?"

"No. I want a good night's sleep so my head can be clear. Is it a deal?"

"Deal," I acknowledged, and hung up the phone for the night.

De Ruyter, Lefkowitz and Stewart looked as if it had been designed by Thomas Jefferson on a bad day. It was a two-story red-brick building trimmed with white wood, with a Greek portico in front. It even had a Monticello-style Roman dome. But contrary to the usual Georgian symmetry, the building's right side had been overextended to accommodate the three senior partners' sudden, irresistible whim—after half the structure had been erected—to each have a private bathroom with a shower. The whim became a request, then a demand. The architect, a macho type with a chest-length beard and work boots, wept. The contractor all but swooned from joy at the cost overruns. What it came to was this: De Ruyter, Lefkowitz and Stewart, although not ugly, always looked unbalanced, as if it were about to slide down the hillock on which it stood.

I had been to the firm a few times for depositions or meetings, and once as Will's date, to an impromptu champagne celebration after he'd won a big case for a defense contractor, a guy who had faced thirty years in jail and ten million in fines for selling gyroscopes used in fighter planes to Iraq. "Oh," said the receptionist when she saw me, glancing at the brass carriage clock on her desk. It wasn't even ten in the morning. Her "Oh" came out as "Ew," because she barely separated her lips when she spoke, De Ruyter, Lefkowitz and Stewart was such a tony firm. "Ms. White. Do you have a meeting today, or are you . . . ?"

"I'm here to see Mr. Stewart."

"Ew." I'm sure she was dying to know why, because she hesitated, as if expecting me to confide something fascinating about my relationship with Will. When I didn't, she punched a few numbers and murmured my name to his secretary in a refined but disappointed tone.

Instead of the secretary, Will came striding out. "Hi," he said, and led me to his office.

"You don't seem surprised that I dropped in on you."

"What surprises me is that you were able to hold off until ten o'clock."

Instead of sitting behind his desk, he took a seat on his couch and patted the cushion next to his. It was a very plain couch. His whole office was plain. Beautiful, simple, and austere, the sort of working space God would have. Will had perfect taste.

"Do you have any thoughts?" I asked. "Or thought? For what I'm paying you, I can't ask for too much."

"I got off the phone with Holly Nuñez about fifteen minutes ago."

"You spoke to her? About the Torkelson case? Do you know her? Have you ever met her?"

"Yes, yes, no, no. But she knew who I was." There was no false modesty and no genuine modesty in Will's remark: a simple statement of fact. "We spoke for nearly an hour."

"And?"

"And we're meeting for lunch today. At a little place near my house, where we won't be seen."

"What is this? A new chapter in your life?"

"I'm giving Holly Nuñez the chance to be a champion of justice and a defender of democracy."

468

"Are you nuts? She has acrylic nails and she wimped out to Jerry McCloskey."

"Lee, what do you say to your clients when they start to second-guess you?"

"Something like 'You hired me because you trust my judgment and know that all my years of experience count for something. You have to be willing to let me be the lawyer.'"

"Okay. You hired me because you trust my judgment and know that all my years of experience count for something. You have to be willing to let me be the lawyer."

I said: "So what time will you be back from lunch?"

Will did not seem surprised to find me waiting in his reception area when he strolled into his office a little before three. "What did you have?" I demanded. "A five-course meal?" He ushered me into his office. The receptionist looked so crazed with curiosity I thought she was going to leap over her desk, grab us, beg us: What is going on here? Which is what I wanted to know. The second he closed his office door, I said: "Everything. The tone of your voice when you said hello. Was her handshake warm or not so warm? From the first minute she walked into—"

"As we speak, she is taking Sam Franklin over to Mary's apartment. They're going to break the seal, look for the shirt, and if they find it, bring it to the lab. They should have preliminary findings by Wednesday or Thursday."

I sat there flummoxed. For the life of me, I could not imagine how he had done it. "How did you convince her? What issue did you raise that would make her take such a huge risk? She's going to lose her job!"

Will said: "She won't be needing it. She's going to run for district attorney on the Democratic ticket."

I clapped my hands to my face. I must have looked like some Disney version of amazement. "*What?*"

"I pointed out that she knew what you had asked for was fair and just. Mary Dean did not kill Bobette Frisch. There is no reason for her to be paying for the crime. I also pointed out to Holly that all that was stopping her from following her instincts—her fine, commendable instincts—was Woodleigh Huber and his flunky, White Trash."

"And the only way to stop him is for Holly to run against him?" Will knocked me out; I couldn't believe the audacity of what he was doing.

"Right."

"But she's a Republican."

"That can easily be remedied. Huber runs every four years with no real challenge because everyone's convinced he's a shoo-in. Big voice, no controversy, all that white hair. Well, Holly wants to see to it that there is controversy. Mary Dean: She was the victim of one man, Norman. And now the victim of a second man."

"Huber?"

"Yes. He's pulling off Justice's blindfold and spitting in her eye."

"My God!" I said. "You gave Holly that line and she's going to use it."

"She probably will."

"I could use a hit of Chuckie's oxygen now. This whole thing . . . It leaves me breathless."

"It should leave Huber breathless. Holly wants to make the point that he's so stuck on image—on the old politics—that he can't admit he was conned. He's willing to let someone serve a fifteen-to-twenty-year sentence just to save his political ass. She knows he's going to fire her the minute he finds out that she authorized lifting the seal on the apartment. She *wants* to be fired."

"And the Democrats will want her?"

"Lee," Will said patiently.

"They'll be thrilled," I acknowledged.

"Exactly. And they'll be ecstatic when they find out I'm breaking with my party to fund-raise for her. I'm going to get her big bucks. She's going to give that slick piece of work a run for his money—and then some." He took my hand in his. "I'm doing this because I think Woodleigh Huber is profoundly fourth rate, and anyone below second rate is dangerous when he has prosecutorial powers. I'm doing it for Mary Dean, because I'm a sucker for the grand gesture.

To sacrifice yourself in the name of love! At the very least, she deserves to get her life back. I'm doing it for myself too, because I have achieved everything I ever dreamed of achieving—and to tell you the truth, it's a little boring. I need a cheap thrill. Well, this campaign won't come that cheap. That's okay. But mainly, Lee, you know why I'm doing this."

"For me."

"Yes. For you."

It took quite a big longer than Thursday, but the lab confirmed that the chocolate on Norman's cuff was like that of chocolate from a Snickers candy bar. Further, the saliva found on that same spot matched the DNA of Bobette Frances Frisch, deceased. Additionally, an almost microscopic smear of blood along the rim of the collar of the white silk shirt, consistent with a shaving nick beneath the jaw, matched the blood specimen taken from Inmate 1025567–95, Norman Torkelson.

I was planning on going to Holly Nuñez's press conference, but I had a sentencing. My client had been caught by the state police after his truck hydroplaned off the Long Island Expressway during a downpour and hit an embankment, causing many of the crates that contained the six-hundred-forty ducks he had stolen from a farm on the North Fork to break apart and set off a cataclysm of bloody feathers on the median, as well as drumsticks beating on the windshields of passing Range Rovers. It was his third duck-rustling offense. The assistant D.A., a new kid who had clearly read his animal rights literature, was annoyingly graphic on the subject of my client's genocidal proclivities when it came to poultry, and the judge refused to hear my argument for a suspended sentence with community service.

It wasn't until I got back and turned on the TV in Chuckie's office for the five o'clock news that I was able to see Holly announce her candidacy for district attorney of Nassau County. She had a new hairstyle, straight-cut with bangs, something between Cleopatra and Betty Boop—

though instead of vampish, it made her look pure, a Madonna in a Puerto Rican church. She was wearing a navy suit and a crisp white blouse, so she appeared sufficiently lawyerly for the job. Whether she'd been coached to be low key or it was a natural television genius, I don't know, but instead of perky—her prosecutorial correlative of an *Entertainment Tonight* cohost—she merely looked bright and energetic. I kept waiting for the cameras to turn to her supporters so I could get a glimpse of Will, but the cameras liked her too much.

Naturally, I didn't get to hear everything she said, just a sound bite or two on the various local newscasts. She spoke about the Bobette Frisch case and how Bobette was the victim of one man, Norman Torkelson, but how Mary Dean, the woman serving time for the murder, was the victim of two men: Norman—and Woodleigh Huber.

"It's easy to *look* tough," she told the cameras. Holly seemed so much the genuine article they all but nodded back. "We need someone who has the guts and the integrity to *be* tough, and that means standing up for justice no matter what the political cost." Her dark-brown eyes moved from lens to lens, giving each station its share. "It's *wrong* to run a D.A.'s Office by taking polls and holding press conferences and wearing hair spray. Nassau County deserves better than pretty-boy politics. That's why I'm running against Woodleigh Huber."

Will came for dinner and stayed for the ten o'clock news, and then the eleven. By that time, a couple of reporters had caught up with Woodleigh Huber as he was coming out of the Nassau County chapter of the B'nai B'rith Anti-Defamation League's annual black-tie fundraiser, where he had no doubt been giving his usual Jews Are Good speech. He was looking spiffy, a blue silk handkerchief in his tuxedo pocket, his hair looking as if Michelangelo had carved it out of Carrara marble. "I have no comment at this present time," he commented. "All I can say is that Holly Nuñez"—he paused for effect—"was fired from the District Attorney's Office for *cause*." Not a particularly effective statement, or a terrible one. Or at least not until the same idea popped into every late-night news producer's head: a close shot of Huber's face, his luxuriant white hair frozen in the brilliant TV lights, followed by a clip of Holly declaring: "It's wrong to run a D.A.'s office by taking polls and holding press conferences and wearing hair spray."

I looked over at Will, sitting in a Papa Bear chair, his feet up on an ottoman. He was actually smiling. "She's better than I thought she'd be."

"Does she have a chance?" I asked.

"In this county, against one of the most proven Republican votegetters? A guy with Conservative, Liberal, and Right-to-Life endorsements?" He thought for a moment. "When the press conference was over this afternoon, I told Holly how good she was. Know what she did? Took her hand and mussed up her hair a little. She said: 'No hair spray. In case any of the reporters asked.' Interesting: I was the one who suggested she run. But when I did, it didn't come as any surprise to her. None of that 'Who, me, run?' stuff. She said great, she'd use the Mary Dean business—woman-as-victim and all that—but she wanted to nail Huber on what she called the Politics of Fatigue: how he plays to the cameras but doesn't have the energy or the imagination to get to the root of crime."

"What does 'get to the root of crime' mean?" I asked.

"Damned if I know. She's big on the word 'proactive.' I told her to find a synonym. What was amazing is that she had the entire campaign against Huber already mapped out in her mind. True, she'd probably been thinking of a Republican primary challenge, not bolting and running as a Democrat. But I was just a catalyst, a guy who could raise money so she could do it four years earlier than she'd originally planned."

"If she wins, will she be any better than Huber?"

"Let's put it this way. She's smart. Smart enough. And she's a woman and a Hispanic, and she's enormously ambitious. Based on that alone, she's got to be at least two or three times as good as Huber."

"And now she's a Democrat, so she won't trample on people's Fifth and Sixth Amendment rights."

473

Will moved his feet from the ottoman to the floor. "Did anyone ever tell you that you're a political imbecile?" He stood and put on his jacket. "In my life, I've never heard such idiot stereotyping as comes out of your mouth every single election campaign."

"Fine," I said. "Be the Clarence Thomas of Long Island. That's your business. Just wait till your party pals learn you're supporting a Democrat."

"Please. They already know."

"So how many times this summer do you think you're going to be playing golf at their lily-white country clubs, big boy?"

"With any luck? Not a single goddamn one." He patted the top of my head. "Lily White," he said, and he went home.

Some men get away with murder. But some of their victims can come back to life. Not Bobette Frisch, of course. Mary Dean was a different story.

The day after Holly Nuñez's news conference, Woodleigh Huber held one of his own. He said he would not deign to address his opponent's hair spray remarks, except to say categorically that he did not use hair spray. That day he was telling the truth, but he made the mistake of speaking from the courthouse steps. Somber, pin-striped, every inch Mr. District Attorney. A breeze toyed with his hair, first lifting it up so it appeared electrified, then tossing it to the left, so it looked like the hair of a mad genius. Huber patted it back down once, then again. In the end, the only information most people watching him on television registered from his appearance was that the district attorney of the County of Nassau was horribly upset about his hair.

This is what he said that did not register. He welcomed the opportunity to debate the issues with Ms. Nuñez. He was proud of his record, darn proud, and was not afraid to run on it. And contrary to his opponent's blatantly false and spurious assertions, he was not keeping an innocent woman in prison because he was ashamed to admit he'd been conned. "The buck stops here," Huber announced. "I don't just take

474

credit for all the successes of this office. I am willing to take full responsibility for my misjudgments. Now, there haven't been many, but in this case, like every single lawyer and public official involved, I believed Mary Dean's confession. However, subsequent information proved to me that she had been used by Norman Torkelson, a notorious con artist. The moment I heard the truth, I knew she had to be released. However, unlike my opponent, I do not shoot from the hip. I do not speak rashly or act rashly. There is a procedure to follow in these cases, and I had to follow it. *I am sworn to uphold the law.* I have devoted my life to upholding the law. And now that the procedure has been followed"—he patted down his hair and broke out his *60 Minutes* voice—"I am ordering Mary Dean to be released forthwith!"

I picked Mary up at Bedford Hills the next morning and drove her back to her apartment on Long Island. "Jeez," she said, opening the car window and letting the wind stream into her face. "A couple of weeks cooped up, you forget air. It feels so good."

When we turned off the Sprain Brook Parkway to the Bronx River, I asked: "Do you have any plans?"

"Like, for lunch?"

"I really meant plans for your life." The subject seemed to be of no particular interest to her, so I added: "But I was hoping you'd let me buy you lunch."

"You mean, you would buy?"

"Yes."

"I should be taking you out for a champagne dinner, getting me out of there. I swear to God, I thought I'd be stuck there till I was, you know, forty or something." Her eyes closed, and she turned her face to catch the sun.

When we got back, she told me she couldn't go to a restaurant looking the way she did. With her skin clean of the mask of makeup she usually wore and her hair deflated, she looked far more beautiful than anyone else on Long Island. But I understood her need to re-create the Mary she wanted to be, so I agreed to give her an hour before picking her up.

"We'll just have fun," I promised her. "No serious discussions about your future. No pressure."

"If I don't feel like going for my high school diploma, I don't have to?"

"Of course not. I told you: We'll just be two ladies out for a nice lunch."

I didn't mention that I had a few plans in place for her if she was interested. Beauty school, waitressing. I couldn't help find her a job in a bar, because the state liquor authority would run her prints and find out about her record. As far as that went, I had already spoken to a lawyer I'd once dealt with in Baltimore who had recommended someone in Annapolis; he was going to look into getting the assault and fugitive charges against her reduced. I'd spoken to a pal in the probation department who knew a social worker in Queens who had a grant to work with prostitutes, offering them alternatives to the life; I'd set that in motion too.

I was interested in Mary's past and her future. Ladies who lunch open up to each other. What had her family been like? What had turned her into a hooker? And was there any way to change her path so she wouldn't about-face and go right back to it?

And all right, I was not without hope that somewhere in an hour and a half of her ditsy chatter I'd find a glimmer, a hint that she herself hadn't picked up on, of where Norman Torkelson might have gone.

"What should I wear?" she asked as I pulled up to the apartment building. She took in my gray linen suit, then looked into my eyes with something that might have been pity. "I don't have anything like that."

"Anything other than shorts or jeans," I told her. "It doesn't matter. You always look wonderful."

"Thanks," she said, pleased by the compliment but not thrilled: It had not come from a man. The second she climbed out of the car, she was rubbing a lock of hair between her fingers, checking what conditioning it would need. "Oh, and thanks a million for getting me out." She laughed. "I wish I could pay you a million."

"You wouldn't have to," I said. "I'd give you a discount."

Mary laughed. "A big fat one, I hope!"

"A big fat one."

I drove to my office to check my mail and returned to Mary's an hour later. She was gone. I never heard from her again.

When I think about the case and I'm in an upbeat mood, I imagine Mary on some Amtrak train out of New York, sitting next to a nice guy in a suit who knows she's not the kind of girl Mama wants him to bring home, but nonetheless, he's going to bring her home. I see her in a pretty house with a central vacuum system, pregnant, clipping coupons for Wisk and Just Right. When I'm feeling low, I see her punched in the face, kicked in the head by some drunken pig of a john who grabs back the fifty bucks he gave her.

And now and then, late at night, I think she knew all along where Norman was, and they are together again.

Twenty-six

Of course, the Torkelson case wasn't even the half of it. To finish Lily White's story, it is necessary to backtrack a few years, before Lee met Norman in the visitors' room at the Nassau County Correctional center, even before Mary Dean met Norman when she was working the bar at the Paloverde Cocktail Lounge in the Maricopa Motor Inn in Phoenix. We have to return to the early spring of 1991, shortly after Lee's forty-first birthday.

Sandi Zimmerman slid into Lee's office and closed the door. She kept her hands behind her on the knob and narrowed her eyes in the furtive manner of minor characters in Humphrey Bogart vehicles. "There's a man outside who says he's your father," she said. "His name is Leonard White." Blood rushed to Lee's head. She felt dizzy. She calmed herself: Great emotion—how could it not be? Or was this something beyond emotion? A stroke? "Is it?" she heard Sandi asking.

"Is it *what*?" Lee snapped. Her skull was expanding against her scalp, desperate to escape the pressure inside her head. By the time Sandi brought her father in, she'd be aphasic, trying to make the *D* sound—Dad—but she wouldn't be able to move her paralyzed tongue up behind her teeth, and the only sound that would emerge would be a feral growl.

"Is it really your father?"

"Sandi, you're standing in front of a closed door. I can't see him." Lee realized then that Sandi was probably frightened the man was not her father at all, but a dissatisfied ex-client packing a semiautomatic rifle under his raincoat. She was irritated that everyone else got carte blanche to be crazy and she had to be the sane one. Reluctantly, she put her massive cerebral hemorrhage on hold. "If he's a spiffy-looking man in his mid-sixties, he's probably my father."

The man who came through the door was indeed her father. He did not look spiffy, however. Leonard had gone from slim to thin, but his trousers had not. They were held up by a pair of expensive suspenders—pearl-gray, with a black design. Plumes? No, bushy-tailed foxes. The suspenders held up his trousers, but he easily could have slipped both his arms inside the waistband. His hair had gone from distinguished silver at the temples to old man's white. His face was no color at all. In the middle of her cheerful blue and white office, Leonard looked diminished and passé, a scene on a tiny fifties black-and-white TV.

"Hello." Lee stood behind her desk, making no move to shake hands or come around to greet him. This was not a conscious, lawyerly ploy. Her body refused to let her move and her mind was in no condition to countermand the order.

"Sorry to drop in on you like this," he began. He sounded nervous, but she was relieved that his voice was still the same, a slightly raspy Brooklyn baritone, rather pleasing, but with an accent that made it sound as if there had been some game in his neighborhood in which all residents tried to speak with Oxbridge diction—and only Leonard had not gotten that it was a big joke. "I suppose I should have called first."

"Please sit down," she said.

Carefully, he lowered himself into one of the chairs that faced her desk. His thumb caressed the arm, reflexively checking out the fabric, as if considering it as a possible lining for one of his coats. "I don't know how much Valerie's told you," he said.

"About what? Look, I'm not being coy. She's fourteen and a half, and she tends to be a little self-involved."

"The actor. Did she tell you I called her an 'actress' and got a big lecture?"

"She doesn't talk much about what she does when she's with you or her father. Except if you take her to the theater, you and—" Lee realized her father was waiting to see what euphemism she would come up with for family members, so she came up with none. "—Mom or Jazz and Robin. What is it that Val might have told me about?"

Leonard shook his head: I can't find the words. Lee leaned

479

forward. The swivel mechanism in her desk chair squealed. Maybe she wasn't having a stroke, but her head did not feel right. Healthy people do not feel pressure against their temporal bones. What could Val be keeping from her? Some relationship? Sexual? Could she be pregnant? She'd had her period for a year. But she had invited only two boys—old buddies from elementary school—to her bat mitzvah: two boys and twenty-three girls. Drugs? What else could it be? Had Val broken down and confessed to her grandfather that when Lee was working late, she sneaked bottles of wine spritzers up past Puella and was one of those secret teenage alcoholics? Had Lee been overestimating a child's ability to cope with a working mother, a retarded uncle, a Holy Roller housekeeper, a ten-year-old accordion prodigy, three dogs and two cats and a perpetually present black Republican?

"I don't know where to begin," Leonard said.

As this was what ninety percent of the clients sitting in that chair said, Lee at least knew what she had to do: ask something, anything, that would demand an answer. "How is Mom?"

"You do know!"

"No. What? Is something wrong?"

"Wrong? Metastasized stomach cancer."

Lee hugged herself, her arms enfolding her belly. "I'm so sorry."

"She's got two, three more months, the doctor says. Sloan-Kettering."

"She's in the hospital?"

"No. What can they do for her there? I have her home."

"Is she in pain?"

"No."

"Who's taking care of her?"

"I'm semiretired these days. I do what I can."

"Is there anything I can do?"

Leonard sat back and crossed his legs, too suave a gesture for talking about cancer. "Is there anything you can do?" he mused. "Let me give you a bit of background. I don't know if you read the financial pages, although you must. You're a lawyer."

"The financial pages?"

"Wait. Hear me out. The fur industry is, as they say, enjoying hard times." He gave a harsh laugh, the sort where no sound is emitted because the lips are too tightly clamped together. "*Our*

480

business is not doing well. Don't worry. I didn't come here for a loan. I came because I felt you ought to know about your mother."

"I can't believe Val didn't say anything," Lee said.

"Well . . ."

"Have you actually told her that her grandmother has cancer?"

"No," he admitted. "Not in so many words. She knows Sylvia's been under the weather. But you don't say 'cancer' to a fourteen-year-old."

"Yes you do."

"Well, we don't. Anyway, this is the thing: about the business. What I was trying to tell you. All those anti-fur people were marching up and down in front of the salon." He uncrossed his legs and leaned toward her. "For three years! *Screaming* at anyone who came in. They picked four or five targets, and we were one of them. Because of our clientele. The best and the brightest: That's who we've had right from the beginning. We hired security men, but that just kept them from throwing red paint. It didn't make the customers come in. They were afraid. Those animal people are psychos. You know about them? They throw paint on the garments!"

"I've heard." About a year earlier. Will had been over. As they usually did before he left, they turned on the TV for the news and the Johnny Carson monologue. The screen filled with protesters in front of a department store, screaming, cursing, hooting at fur-wearing women. Spontaneously, Will and Lee broke into applause.

"And it's not just the psychos. The real problem is, it's not the eighties anymore."

"You were doing all right before the eighties."

"But all that was nothing compared to the eighties. We couldn't get to the bank fast enough. And now . . . dead." He rubbed his hands together. They made a sandpaper sound. The backs of his hands were protuberant blue veins, large brown blotches. "We had to close Le Fourreur. Valerie didn't tell you?"

"No. I'm sorry to hear it."

"Last year we did no business at all. Nothing. And this year is going to be worse. Less than nothing. All the Furhavens—the low-end stores: Our profit margins are shaved to almost nothing, and we're not even making our rent. We've already closed the two in Jersey. What can I tell you? Everything is nothing."

"What about all the money you made in the eighties?"

"It was tied up. Real estate. We both had co-ops in the city. Me and Jazz. Jasper."

She almost smiled. "I know who you mean. I didn't know you had places in the city. Val's not a very good gossip."

"I'm surprised she hadn't said anything. She'd been to both places. They were beautiful. I was on Fifth, near the museum. Jazz was Park in the Sixties, one of the most exclusive buildings in the city. And I had the house in Palm Beach." He looked to a wall lined with framed photographs Will had taken. "Not the house you were in," he said to the photographs. "Another one. On the ocean. And Jazz had one close by, and one in Vermont. They're all great skiers, the whole bunch—"

"I don't mean to be rude, but I'd like to know why you're here."

"We sold them all, but you wouldn't believe it. These days everybody's trying to unload everything they bought in the eighties, when prices were sky-high. There's a glut on the market and everything, everything we sold we sold at a loss. Terrible. The art your mother bought. We practically gave it away. Robin's jewelry. Edwardian. It was auctioned at Sotheby's. They wouldn't have taken it if it wasn't quality stuff. Everything. We poured it into the business. We hired a new designer, someone very hot. I can't tell you what we spent on advertising and public relations. But in the end . . . nothing. It got so bad we had to let Greta go."

"I know she's not with you anymore."

"Val told you?"

"No. Greta comes to dinner every Thursday."

"She does? How is she?"

"She seems all right. She's been coming to dinner once a week for years—since Jazz switched sisters. It's the only way she could see me and Kent."

"For God's sake!" Lee could not tell if her father was angry at her remark about Jazz switching sisters or about his housekeeper's secret life. "Greta didn't tell you about closing the stores, or about us having to let her go?"

"No. We never talk about you. A few months ago, she told me

482

she retired. She never was a big talker. And she's very proud. She wouldn't say she was fired."

"Believe me, I felt bad. But she had a nest egg. They're a very frugal people." He shook his head wearily. "In my life, I never could be frugal. It's not my nature. But it wasn't bad being the other way, generous, because I knew I had to make the kind of life I wanted. It was an incentive. The better I wanted to live, the more I made." He shook his head. "Not anymore. I had to put the house up for sale. The house you grew up in. Do you know why? Because we need money to live! It's come to that. Every night I pray for a buyer. Jazz and Robin had to put their place up too. A showstopper. Right on the Sound. I wish you could see it."

Lee knew that when she repeated that line to Will she would laugh, but just then, she could not. "Why would you wish I could see it?"

"Sorry, I didn't mean to hurt you."

"Then or now?" Leonard pretended he had not heard her question. "You know, talking about then . . . Right after Jazz left me, I thought: It's understandable that he would want Robin. She's so helpless, so beautiful. She makes Jazz feel important. Useful. Manly. All I seemed to be able to do was diminish him. But now . . . I can see it more clearly. Once Jazz knew he had overreached, marrying me, there really was only one alternative: Robin."

"I don't understand," Leonard said warily.

"Sure you do. He couldn't make it as a lawyer and you gave him the perfect out: a thriving business. What a life he had with you! All he had to do was find some way to continue it without dragging me along. And he did. He found someone who hated what I had accomplished as much as he did, and together they were able to make their dreams come true: to bring me down and keep living high—off you. That's what happened."

"Then I guess this news is making you happy. You're probably thinking: This is justice. They got what they deserved. All of them." He waited, but Lee did not say: It doesn't make me happy, or You did not deserve to come to this. "I'll tell you why I'm here," Leonard said, just before the pause became unbearable. "Besides your mother. Do you want to hear?"

"Do you want to tell me?"

483

"Hart's Hill."

"What about it?"

"Fos and Ginger can't keep it up anymore."

"They couldn't keep it up twenty years ago."

"It's on the market now for next to nothing. Three mil. That's a *steal*."

"And?"

"We're hoping to keep it in the family." Lee studied the thin, gray man across from her. Had he lived with his own illusions so long that he now believed he and the Taylors were one? "I know this is a long shot, but hear me out. Hart's Hill means something. It has meaning for your daughter. It's her heritage. She's a Taylor."

"It may be part of her heritage. But the other part is a fourteen-year-old Jewish kid from Port Washington who gets ten bucks a week from me and baby-sits for the rest. Three million is a little steep for her."

"Lee," her father said, moving to the very edge of his chair, putting his dry hands on her desk. There was still a shadow of grace in his movement. For just an instant, she saw the man who could hold up a rat's skin and convince some rich matron it was better than mink. "Come on," he urged. "How about it?"

"How about what?"

"How about you? Who better? Think about it: You don't just have one Taylor, you have two living with you! Kent. He actually grew up there. And can you imagine how thrilled Valerie would be to move—"

"I don't have that kind of money."

"You don't need as much as you think. Jazz talked the whole thing over with Fos. He's willing to take back paper. He said he always liked you. Fos, I mean. And if it goes to a stranger . . . Don't you see? It would be out of the family."

"I don't care. It's not my family. My family lives with me in Port Washington."

Leonard pushed himself up using the edge of her desk, but he didn't get very far. Embarrassed, he pretended he had not tried to get up at all. "You're a lawyer. This is a good business proposition. The next real estate upswing, you could double your money."

"By the time the next upswing comes around, I'll be double my age." He braced his hands against the arms of the chair, but he did not try to stand. "Are you all right?" she asked. "Healthwise?"

"I'm fine." He pushed and, finally, with a grunt, managed to get up. "Don't close the door on this, Lee. For the sake of your child."

"For her sake and my sake, she's going to have to make her own way in the world." Leonard turned and moved to leave. Lee walked around her desk and held the door for him. "Does Mom need nurses?" He shrugged. "I'll be glad to help you with that."

"That you have the money for?"

"Yes, for that I do. My checkbook's at home. I'll have an envelope messengered to you tomorrow." Up close, just beside his mouth, she could see a small patch of white whiskers his razor had missed.

"You know what's interesting?" Leonard inquired.

"What?"

"From our room, lying in bed all day like she does: You look out the window and what's the only thing you can see? Hart's Hill."

The following day, Lee wrote a check. She took it herself to the house in which she grew up. When her father answered the door, she handed it to him, along with a list of nursing care agencies. It was four in the afternoon, and he had not yet shaved. The white whiskers near his mouth had grown, and they stuck out of his face like an on-off button. She told her father that her check would cover one week's worth of nursing care. After that, the agency could send the bills to her: simpler bookkeeping.

They both understood that Lee did not trust Leonard to spend thousands of dollars on a dying woman who was not in pain.

Lee told him she wanted to see her mother. He said he would go up and see if it was okay. She waited in the front hall and looked into the living room. She was not surprised that none of the furniture was familiar. Asian, she thought. Some country that had become stylish during the eighties. Sri Lanka, maybe, or Burma. Will would know. The fieldstone floors were bare. She wondered if that had been stylish or if they had sold the rugs. Leonard came down and said: You can go up. I guess I don't have to show you the way.

*　　*　　*

She was seven weeks away from dying, but Sylvia looked better than her husband did. Her frosted blonde and gray hair, pinned softly on top of her head, emphasized her fine-boned face and long, thin neck. She looked like Katharine Hepburn would have looked if Katharine Hepburn's forebears had come from a Galician shtetl. "Come in," she summoned Lee. Asia had been carried up to the second floor. The bed was a huge four-poster of white wood, every inch carved with flowers and—Lee looked closer—animal heads. It was the only piece of furniture in the room. For some reason Lee was not sure she comprehended, the bed stood at a forty-five-degree angle in the middle of the room. "Like it?" Sylvia asked.

"Yes. Beautiful." Lee stood at the foot. The bottom of each post tapered into the head of some big cat—panther, maybe, or jaguar, dangerously stupid, with a flat, broad skull and fashionably elongated snout.

"Turn-of-the-century. Ceylon." Lee realized her mother was watching her examine the room's bareness, its white-painted walls and white-stained wood floor. "You've heard the expression 'Less is more.'"

"Yes. Mies van der Rohe."

"I don't know anymore. I'm not sure he was right."

"I hear you're not well," Lee said. She had to force her eyes from the white-lacquered flowers onto her mother.

"You heard what it is?"

"Yes. I'm sorry."

Sylvia made a cynical sound, a sniff, a laugh. "How have you been?"

"Fine."

"I was positive you'd remarry."

"No." Lee knew that if her sister had been there in her shoes, she would have had the sense to perch on the edge of the bed and confide about each and every man she had dated, being fair about their assets—a firm chin, a thriving rheumatology practice, a powerful backstroke—laughing at their devastating liabilities. Why couldn't she do that? The woman was dying.

"Are you seeing anyone special?" Sylvia pushed herself higher up against a pile of white pillows. She looked interested, almost hopeful. The pillows were serious white: not a ribbon or a ruffle had been permitted. Her nightgown, too, was unadorned white, as if it had been made from one of the sheets, although Lee guessed it had been hand sewn by exploited child laborers. "I mean, seeing someone you're thinking of marrying?"

"No." She saw her mother expected at least something more, so she gave it to her. "I wish I could find someone. I tried not to be too exacting, but if a guy pees on the toilet seat—"

"Urinates."

"Or if he wears a gold ID bracelet there is no way I can marry him, much less love him."

Her mother smiled. "You can wipe off the seat, but the ID bracelet . . . Did you ever get over Jazz?" she asked quietly, as if afraid of being overheard.

"Yes. Do you want to know why?" Lee was surprised to find herself sitting on the edge of the bed, beside her mother. "Because there wasn't that much to get over. I missed his liveliness for a while. His energy. Jazz could make a party in a paper bag. And I missed the sex." Sylvia did not blanch, but she paled a bit. "I'll answer your unasked question," Lee went on. "Yes: He may have been carrying on with Robin for years, but right up to the end, he was getting two for the price of one."

"I always wondered," Sylvia said softly.

"Now you don't have to wonder. But getting back to the 'did-I-get-over-him' issue—"

"You really *are* a lawyer. Like my father. That's where you get it from. You can pick up right where you left off."

"Usually. I got over Jazz because my love for him was never that profound. He wasn't that profound. I guess that means I wasn't either. But beyond lack of depth, he wasn't interesting. He wasn't good."

"Good at what?"

"He wasn't a good person."

Sylvia studied her wedding ring. "Well . . . ," she said. It was a syllable pregnant with meaning. Pull it out of me, it seemed to say. It *wants* to come out. It may not surprise you. I might say: He's a good father. He had a good business head. Or: He's been a good husband to her. Not good. The best. Sensitive to her sensitivity like you would believe. But it may be precisely what you want to hear. He had a bad business head: If that fool had

487

had any foresight, we would still be mink marketers to Manhattan's elite. Or: He's not good. He's cheating on Robin. Has been for years. Well, why shouldn't Lee be midwife to all the unfinished business of her life? It wasn't a hard job. She understood that all she had to say was: Come on, Mom. Please? Not in a pushy way. By being cute. A little tease in the voice. And out it would come. Such a small effort, and she would be the daughter this dying woman had always wanted her to be. And the dying woman had so much she could tell.

"It took two or three years to get over Jazz," Lee said. "What I have never gotten over is the betrayal of my mother and father and sister."

"Oh."

"I'm sorry, but that's the truth."

"If you want to know the truth," Sylvia said, "I thought the whole thing was terrible. Tacky."

"No. 'Tacky' is for tasteless clothes. This was treacherous."

"Whatever. I cried over it. I wanted to say something. I don't mean to Robin. I *did* say something to her. I said: 'Don't you have any feelings? Don't you care about what people are going to say? Your sister's husband!' And I even wanted to say something to you."

"What?"

"I can't remember. It was too long ago. But your father said: 'Keep your mouth shut, Sylvia.' Actually, he said 'yap,' not 'mouth.' 'Keep your yap shut. There's nothing we can do. We can't take sides. We have two daughters. And Jazz is my business partner.'"

"So you listened to him."

"He's my husband." Sylvia closed her eyes. Her head wobbled until it found a place on a pillow. Her breathing was deep, untroubled. Lee thought she had fallen off to sleep. She got up from the bed. Sylvia opened her eyes. "What could I do?" she went on. "Go against my husband? Do you think he would have stood for that?"

"I don't know. We'll never know."

"I couldn't risk it. He could've walked out."

"I told Dad I'd take care of paying for nurses for you."

Sylvia perked up. This was clearly news to her. "Starting . . . ?"

"Starting now. For however long you need them."

"Thank you."

"You're welcome."

"They'll give me sponge baths."

"Yes. Whatever you want. They're going to be well paid, so let them treat you royally."

"Can you believe we've come to this? No money." Sylvia was not sad. She was offended, as if someone had pulled a cruel practical joke on her. "He canceled the gardeners. It's a good thing there hasn't been too much rain this spring."

"I'm glad I can help out."

"How come you're doing this? So you don't have a guilty conscience later?"

"I'm doing it"—Lee bent over and kissed her mother's cheek—"because it needs to be done. Okay?"

"Okay. I didn't mean that. About a guilty conscience. It just came out."

"Don't worry about it. If you need anything, call me. Or have Dad or your nurse call me."

"Lee."

"Yes?"

"I like your shoes."

Lee kissed her mother for the last time. What could she say? I hope it goes well? I love you? Good luck? Goodbye? Bon voyage? She said nothing. As she pulled back from Sylvia's cheek, she glanced past the foot of the bed, out the window. From her mother's eye level, she could see green lawn, the aqua pool, the trees, and just beyond, the poison-ivy-blanketed bluff at the end of the Whites' property, which rose toward the Taylors'. But her father had lied to her. You could not see Hart's Hill when you lay in that bed. It was much too high.

Lee White and Will Stewart did not stay long at the victory party in the catering hall on that first Tuesday in November. Being Holly Nuñez's first supporters and having made the most generous contributions the law would allow, they were now not only members of the inner circle but also on a hugging basis with her. So as "Happy Days Are Here Again" was played for the one hundred sixty-second time that night, they dutifully hugged Holly, congratulated her yet again, then allowed her to be swept away from them into a sea of red, white, and blue balloons by a wave of delirious Democrats.

Will walked Lee to her car in the parking lot of the Chateau Briand, a catering hall that featured linguine in clam sauce, shrimp teriyaki, fried wontons, and absolutely nothing that was remotely French. "Well?" he asked. "How does it feel to be a queenmaker?"

"She was wearing hair spray tonight. I smelled it when I hugged her."

"Not an impeachable offense." Lee searched through her handbag for her Jeep key. "Are you tired?" Will asked.

"I'm forty-five and premenopausal. How can I not be tired? The point is, I'm not overtired. What about you?"

"I'm not menopausal." She took out her key, but he leaned against the Jeep, right beside her, against the door.

"What's up?" she asked.

"What time is it?"

"A little before midnight. Is your watch broken? A hundred billion dollars for that fancy Swiss thing, and it's broken? You can't even call it a watch. 'Timepiece.'"

"It's not broken," Will said. "It's later than I thought."

Lee looked up at him. If the hard yellow light of the sodium-vapor lamp was unflattering to Will, she could only imagine how she looked at almost midnight. "Is this later than you thought business about the time? Or are you making a cosmic statement?"

"It's fairly cosmic."

"You're feeling old?"

"I'm ten years older than you, kid. Keep that in mind."

"But you don't show your age the way we do."

"Which 'you' is this?" Will asked. "Blacks or gays?"

"I was thinking of blacks, but now that you mention it . . ." He shifted his weight from one foot to another, then back again.

"What's with you?" Lee asked. "Is something wrong? You're acting strange. Nervous."

"Will you marry me?" Lee's head whipped around as if looking for someone to ask: Can you *believe* this? But they were alone. All the gladsome Democrats were still inside. She turned back to him. "I'm serious," Will said.

490

"I'm sorry. I just can't believe it." She hesitated, then added: "It's one thing to switch parties for an election. But to switch your sexual orientation?"

"Please! Do you think I'm harboring an illusion of some elaborate conversion ceremony to heterosexuality? A notch on my foreskin and a Master Mechanic wrench set? Come on. I asked you a question: Will you marry me? I deserve an answer." There was no wind, but it was a chilly night. She looked to see if he was shivering. No. If his hands were in his pockets. No. "There are no better friends in the world than we are," he added.

"I know," she said.

"Neither of us is really the mushy sort, but we do love each other." She nodded. "Lee, you can say 'yes.' It's not binding."

"Yes, of course we love each other. I said it. Are you happy?"

He moved from the car and stood in front of her. "Not yet."

"I don't think you're going to be."

"We speak to each other first thing in the morning, last thing at night." Lee had watched him trying cases so many times. Will was a great planner. He believed in rehearsals. But in court he would stop, think, talk, then stop again. So he didn't trip up. So he didn't look slick. His performances always worked. Judges, juries, court reporters: They all believed Will Stewart was thinking as he talked, and talking right to them. From the heart. This time, though, there were no hesitations. Will being Will, she knew he had thought out everything he was saying. But he had not rehearsed. This time, there was not a single prearranged stumble, not one practiced pause. He was allowing his heart to be as articulate as it could be. "We're a unit. There are no decisions— other than about sex—that we don't make in consultation with each other."

" 'Other than about sex'? That's one of the main reasons people get married, Will. For sex."

"What about the other reasons? For companionship. For fun. For love. For family. For a mutuality of interests. For security. For the social convenience. We have every single one of those reasons in our relationship. We've never had sex and we never will. But doesn't it mean something that every holiday we're together? Doesn't it mean something that when we win or lose a case, or we read about a new attachment for the KitchenAid, or we hear there's a new Sondheim show opening, we call each other? We're together five or six nights a week. I hold your wool when you wind it. You go to Mets games with me. Do you realize both of us got private lines in our office three or four years ago? How come? It wasn't to facilitate our sex lives. Those guys still have to go through our secretaries. It's because we both felt more natural making and getting—what is it?—seven, eight calls a day right to one another. 'Hi. It's me. I just got back from State Supreme in Suffolk County and I found wonderful bread-and-butter corn at a farm stand.'"

"So why can't we just continue the way we are?" she asked.

"Because it's later than either one of us thought. Because I don't want to be alone anymore. Because I hate it every time I have to leave. Every damn time. And so do you."

Will was facing her, so he did not see the doors open and a few celebrants emerge from the victory party and head toward their cars. "We would only hurt each other," Lee told him.

"How? I know all about Terry. You know I go to the city one or two nights a week. Would you be standing by the door with a rolling pin in your hand when I got home?"

Lee rested her head against the cold glass of the car's window. "What if one of us met the man of our dreams?" she asked. "An *available* man of our dreams."

"I've thought of that. Quite a bit, because I've wanted to have this discussion since right after the whole Torkelson business. When it was over and you were thanking me, do you remember what you said?"

"I guess so." She remembered nattering on and on, but could not think of exactly what statement he was alluding to.

"You said the reason you loved me for what I did wasn't that I was brilliant and got Mary out of jail—although that hadn't hurt. It was that I knew my place was at your side, even when the shit hit the fan. *Especially* when the shit hit the fan. So my answer is this: I truly do not believe I could betray you or you could betray me. I love you. I would be your husband. That means for better for worse, for—"

"I'm acquainted with the language."

"Lee, you were conned by a couple of pros. You got hurt.

Haven't you learned anything from that? Don't you know by now what's false and what's the real thing?"

"But it wouldn't be a true marriage."

"It wouldn't be a marriage with sex. And to the extent that it would provide a cover for me, that I could parade around as the Happy Hetero, it's pretense. But what's between you and me is real and true. And you know it." He held her face in his hands. "That doesn't mean I wouldn't have an affair with a dream man. That doesn't mean it wouldn't break my heart if he said goodbye. Not if. When. But this is the bottom line: I want to spend the rest of my life with you." He put down his hands. "I want a *home*. I've never had one. I was a black kid in a white world, a gay man in a straight world. When I'm in your house, with you, with all of them, I feel what I've never felt before. I belong here. This is my home. Now tell me your bottom line about me."

Her face still felt warm from his holding it. She wished he would put his hands back. "All right. My bottom line: I love being with you. There's nothing I do that isn't better with you along." She hesitated. "Except one thing." She waited for him to pat her head, amused. Or kiss her cheek. But he did not, so she stood on tiptoes and kissed his. "Don't take that as encouragement."

"I want you to ask: What's in it for me," Will told her. "Go ahead, ask."

"What's in it for me?"

"Family."

"I have a family. Do you feel you need one to pass or something all of a sudden?"

"*Need* one? No. People accept that I'm a bachelor. I don't have to say: 'This is my wife.' I'm not talking about the pretense of family. I'm talking about the real thing." He heard sounds and turned away from her. When he saw the people spilling out of the party, heard the car doors starting to slam, he turned back. "You know how important Val and Kent are in my life."

"And you in theirs."

"But they're adults. You're not the kind of woman who thrives on an empty nest. Everything I know about you—and I know a lot—tells me you would love to be a mother again." She knew he was waiting to see if she would deny his assertion. She could

493

not. Will continued: "And all my life, I've wanted a child of my own."

"To have—"

"We could go to the lab together, hold each other's hands."

"While you're whacking off into a test tube? No way!"

"If you don't want to get pregnant, or if it's too late for it to be a healthy proposition, we could adopt."

"You could adopt as a single parent."

"But I want the child to have a mother. And more, I want you to be my wife."

Headlights came on. "You just want to go out and buy a Dress Stewart receiving blanket."

"You guessed it. And have it embroidered with the Weissberg family crest. Well, Lee? What do you say?"

She was not able to say anything, for at that moment, Holly Nuñez, trailed by her press secretary and two campaign aides, was upon them. "Hi!" Holly chirped. "God, you're still here! Hope I didn't interrupt anything. Did I thank you enough? The two of you! *So* great. I thought you left ages ago. How come you're still hanging around? It is *cold* out. You're weren't standing here plotting my overthrow, were you?"

Will shook his head. "Not at all. We were planning your next campaign, Governor."

"Senator," Holly replied.

"I have no doubt we'll get to that," Lee told her. "But do you know what Will and I were planning just now?"

"What?"

"Our wedding."

As soon as they were finished with Holly's hugs and the press secretary's mazel tov and the campaign aides' Hey, fan-tastic! and waved goodbye, Lee put her hand into that of her future husband. "I have something to confess."

"What?"

"It never occurred to me that a black gay guy would turn out to be the love of my life."

"I always knew."

"You did?"

"Of course. Way back when, when I was this amazing stud

with muscles on my muscles and the best Afro north of Niger, I always knew I was going to wind up with a middle-aged female lawyer."

"Go ahead. Tell me," Lee said. "It was written on the stars."

"It was. But most people can't read that kind of writing until they're old enough for bifocals. It's the fine print."

And as it turned out, the way it often does with choices made with wide-open eyes and wise hearts, it was fine. Not what they had dreamed of when they dreamed, mind you. But very, very fine.

Epilogue

Lily White had the first word but she cannot have the last.

There is only this to add about the Torkelson case. On a Thursday in March 1996, a night when Lee White and Will Stewart, husband and wife, were hearing *Un ballo in maschera* at the Metropolitan Opera with a group of friends, Carolee Eckhart of Portland, Oregon, went to the police to report that her fiancé, Douglas Wallace, had been missing for forty-eight hours. Ms. Eckhart was fearful he might be hurt. Or worse. His ex-wife was an unbalanced woman, hateful, wanted to see him ruined. No, she had never seen the ex-wife, but she'd overheard her once when she left a message on Doug's answering machine. Terrible, vile, crazy.

Ted Sato, the detective who took down the information, was new to Missing Persons and quite an eager beaver. He fired question after question. Following nearly an hour of polite interrogation, he discovered that in addition to Mr. Wallace, seventy-five thousand dollars in bearer bonds that had been left to Ms. Eckhart by her grandfather were also missing.

It took Detective Sato only seven minutes on his computer to discover that Douglas Wallace's modus operandi matched that of Norman Torkelson, and another fifteen seconds to learn that, like Norman, Douglas was six feet five with blue eyes, and knew all the words to "Bright College Years," the Yale alma mater. Subsequently, Sato had a chat with Detective Sergeant Sam Franklin on Long Island, who predicted, accurately, that the Portland police would never find the bonds, that Douglas Wallace was long gone—and that Carolee should be thankful she was still alive. Some people never learn.

Some people do.